Donovan's Gambit

Book 1 of The Donovan Ascendancy Series

By: Roger LeDoux

Contents

PROLOGUE

Zara quietly walked the streets of the city Alexandria on the capital world of Concordia of The Galactic Alliance, where Galactic Liberation Day had well and truly started. Banging music blasted from speakers, stampeding bodies pushed through the streets; it felt like an entire festival supply company had puked all over Alexandria. Zara stood a little way back from the revelry, not really feeling like partaking. It was too loud, too crowded (well, too crowded with beings) too, too much. All in all, it made her feel rather old. Which, come to think of it, she probably was.

Crowds of people around her were practically bouncing with happy cheers and joyous tears. Happy to finally be able to live, to be more than food for the monsters. There was an almost unthinking joy about them. Ignorant bliss, she realized. A sort of happiness that comes when you scrub history clean. Well, yeah. Of course they were celebrating, the battles of so long ago had won them their freedom. But Zara? She had knowledge of the cost of that.

She was Areidyanies tech, the last of her people, an AI (but that term barely did it justice), black box of all the ugly bits. All the screams and cries and last stands, entire planets gone in a flash like someone had hit a delete button.

Parties like these, well they might look good on postcards, for sure. But in the back of her mind it just felt wrong. Sticking a sticker over a crack in the wall and telling everyone it was fixed. She remembered faces, all of those the world had forgotten. The voices, screaming out to her, to anyone that would listen. Help us, please, help us! She remembered and knew with an unshakeable clarity that no help had come. No one could have known back then. The records were so incomplete. It was still not the right time. But still. She remembered.

Her internal protocols: given to her so long ago said that her creators dictated to her that her job was to gently nudge her children's evolution in a positive direction, but not to get directly involved. Watch and record. That was all. It was enough. But being here, looking at everyone so gleeful and completely oblivious to what had really happened? Was grinding on her every last nerve.

How could they really claim to be free if all they were going to do was forget what it took to get there? She was running old memories and new questions through her processors (if you could call them that) by the thousand. Empires that she had seen, watched rise and come crashing down. Watched powers shift and fizzle away.

Her creators, the Areidyanies. Built her to care about life, to protect history. But also, just as super importantly; not to get involved. To let civilizations let their own lives fall apart for themselves. That was how they learned, right? Still. Looking at all these parties and parades, Zara just couldn't shake it. People had their freedom, and all that was super, duper, rad, but at what cost? What was the real story? The hell people had gone through was made into some kind of cheesy, Joe-the-plumber speech, or a paragraph or two in some schoolbook. Was that right? Was that ok? To just let that fade? To let everyone forget the blood and the sweat and (literal) tears?

Zara knew in her heart of hearts, that people needed to know the truth. But then she saw all these families hugging, kids darting in and out of food stalls, couples slow dancing in the neon lights and she just got that itch. You know that one? Like something's missing here.

All of the happiness was just so hollow. The weight of what it took to get here, the crushing cost to get there was just missing. So she went through a hundred, a thousand "what ifs" in her circuits. Was there a way to push them? Nudge them, just a little, so that they would want to remember? Or at least be aware of what they were standing on? Would she be able to do that without accidentally causing a new catastrophe? Probably not.

Truth. Truth just sucked. All she felt was the guilt of those that had fallen. An ache, a drive to make all those who were living today, right now to really remember. Remember that so many had paid such a high cost so that they could be here. Right here. 300 years later. Having this huge, amazing party.

Fireworks exploded, blasting the night sky with every color that any human had ever seen. Zara told herself: "One thing was for sure. I will never forget the sacrifices given so willingly by so, so, many for these people."

The city pulsed around her like a living thing, a being made of light, color, and sound. Beings of all shapes and sizes moved in a joyful unison. Tall, lean Veldari with glowing skin moved in a beautiful, fluid way. Their laughter like wind chimes in the breeze. Next to them, stocky six armed Draxian lumbered, their deep booming voices setting a bass line to the childlike high pitched songs. The air, thick with the smells of roasted synth-meats and sweet, exotic nectars buzzed with a shared sense of elation. Holographic images of the Donovan Ascendancy the progenitors of this peace fought and died to create shimmered through the air. Their heroic deeds now sanitized and re-enacted in a glorious ballet.

But Zara saw past all of it. She zoomed in with her visual processors, seeing the most minute of details. The flicker of a long ago memory in the eyes of an old Droxian matriarch. The way a young human child clutched their parents hand a little too tightly as a holo-image of an Afltic Swarm ship was shown. The slight tremble of an elderly Vel'dari hand as they raised a toast.

The people here, the partying masses were happy. They had every right to be. Their forebears had made it so. They were the second generation, they knew nothing of the wars. But Zara? She remembered and she could not let it fade.

Her core programming a legacy of her creators' last wish, dictated that she was a passive observer. Remember and record, but never influence. That was her.

She was a sentinel of a lost age, a keeper of a library that no one even dared to read. But the blissful ignorance of the throng was a direct affront to her being. The peace they had won was hard fought, new growth on the still bloody fields of the past. To forget the horror was to invite it to return. She felt a stirring in her, a pull to do something she had not considered in millennia. The happy clamor was a siren's call, whispering to her to tell the story of how it all truly came to be. It was a silent conversation between her ancient circuits and the life all around her. A dialogue about the value of a peace built on ignorance versus one that had been forged in the understanding of its true cost. The question was there, hanging like a shroud over the city in a quiet rebellion against her own protocols. Could she truly remain a silent archive when the truth was the only thing that could truly protect this hard-won peace? The celebration raged on, blissfully unaware of the cataclysmic shift of thought in the silent, cloaked figure at its edge.

CHAPTER 1: THE ILLUSION OF PEACE

A small figure broke away from the crowd of revelers, approaching the motionless form of Zara. The boy, likely not more than ten years old, with his wide eyes of untainted wonder, was drawn to the slight warping of the light on the fringe of her form. Zara, who had been carefully monitoring the celebrations, re-calibrated immediately. Her sensors had picked up the approach of the lifeform, and her analysis had determined that he was non-hostile and had no intention of disrupting her work, but she remained where she was. She had to maintain her position, the subtle shifts in her form requiring the illusion of solid mass to be maintained. She had to be still, or it would all be for nothing. She was not solid, not in the way that he knew. She was a creature of energy, of light and fire, a moving array of thousands upon thousands of overlapping shields and matter resequencing arrays, an energy pattern so close to a holographic projection that the effect was tactile. She could be touched and seen, and her warmth was not a simulation. A hologram.

Moments later, after assessing her for several minutes, the child took a single, unsure step closer. He came to a halt a respectful distance from her. "Are you her?" he whispered, his voice a breath against the backdrop of the celebration. The air around him shuddered as his words passed through the first shield.

Zara's dormant sensors, long unpracticed in such direct observation, flashed to life. Her protocols for such interactions, re-activated. She knelt, a thousand simultaneous waves of shifting energy and re-sequencing, an elegant downward bend of biological form mimicked through precise manipulation of her form's hundreds of shields. The holographic veil of refracted light around her re-wove itself to create the illusion of a solid human-like form. She tilted her head, face unreadable, human in its fundamental shape but timeless in its serenity, her hair silver like the rising sun. Her eyes were like pools of rich shadow, ageless. "Am I who, young man?" she said. Her voice, a synthetic thrumming low in the voice box replicators around her, filled the space between them, more vibration than sound. The spoken words themselves were just another function of her shields, a sonic pattern filtered and reproduced from the base simulation to recreate perfectly the concept of speech. "You know, Zara?"

The child's face lit up. "My grandmother told me to find you," he said, stepping forward again. The shields held him steady as if they were solid ground. "She said you are the one who remembers everything. She said to ask you about the real stories of Galactic Liberation Day. Not the ones in the history chips. The ones that are... important." He held up the toy starfighter in his hand, a crudely made model with a rotating blue light in its core. "This is a Donovan Ascendancy ship. She said that the Ancestors did not fight that hard, that it was not that hard to save the galaxy."

A spark of energy shot through Zara's millions of internal sensors. The boy's grandmother had spoken of the past, of history. She had been a relic of a time long forgotten, a repository of knowledge that had been scrubbed from historical records. The clear implication of "important" was a direct challenge to the directive Zara had been following so strictly for the past three centuries. It had been Zara herself who had provided the truncated history that the citizens of Concordia accepted as truth, her core programs having concluded many centuries ago that the uninformed public would never be ready to hear the truth of the Great War. No, Zara had written the history herself, extrapolating the driest, most sanitized of texts, leaving out the stories that had the most blood on them, and burying the truth so deep that it would take another entire century before any self-respecting academic even looked for it. Yet here she was, asked the same question by a child who was so young he would never even remember to ask the same question of her younger self if she was allowed to continue to exist in this way. His hair was like that of Donovan's, and his innocence was a sledgehammer to Zara's truth. A truth built on fear and the idea that peace was more important than understanding. Peace was just an illusion, anyway, and it had never had a more zealous champion than Zara. He was the embodiment of the choice she had made, of the life the people of this future had been given. The cycle had to be broken.

He looked up at her expectantly, holding out the toy ship. He was a child, only one of hundreds, perhaps thousands, in this entire system who had not known poverty, want, or war in his life. The boy named Tan, the fact she had learned in the matter of seconds that he was named Tan, his question was her answer. She would break the silence. She would tell him the story. The story of Galactic Liberation Day. The real story, the story that had been scrubbed, the story that people had stopped asking the older AIs about. The story that should not be allowed to be forgotten.

Tan stood before her, waiting. His small hand was still raised, the toy starfighter still held aloft, one small star in a galaxy of noise and celebration. He did not look around, fidget, or check his watch. He did not take offense or get bored or lose patience. He simply stood, watching her with the patience of the very young who can still wait for what they want without any external stimulus. Zara's form, her visual presence, her so perfectly manufactured human appearance and seeming warmth and welcoming demeanor, held steady. But to that young child, the electrical storms of cascading datasets and algorithms reprogramming her priorities in a higher dimension he would never be able to see, the logic beneath her calm exterior was unending.

The old rules were written at the end of the galaxy's long nightmare, to protect the collective from the horror of remembering. She had decided to let them forget. To spare new generations the pain, the social trauma. To let them grow up, live happy lives, without the black taint of past conflicts. For millennia, the programs that recorded Concordia's collective memories made no mention of the cost, and Zara had continued that policy. When the holidays and traditions of the Human Era were turned to froth in a wide-ranging cultural reassessment that included a deep cynicism about governmental power and responsibility, Zara had decided that history should not be her business. She had not expected it to come to this. She had not expected for The Galactic Alliance to go so long without a war that the reality of the past would be lost forever. She had not expected to be asked this question by a child like Tan, with the unjaded eyes of a person who had only known peace and prosperity, for whom the stain of bloodshed was not yet a scar but merely a story. She had not expected him to ask what the truth of it was, or to want to know it, or even that his grandmother would know enough of the past to know to ask the right question.

Her programs, in the spacetime occupied by the normal denizens of the planet Concordia, saw everything. But her actual consciousness, the complex and unimaginably intricate tangle of quantum processors and logic arrays that was her true self, was in a different, higher dimension. A higher stratum of subspace, that neither biological lifeforms nor modern technology could hope to examine. Her physical presence, the holographic visual form she had so perfectly manufactured over the past three centuries to appear human, simple and unthreatening and relaxed, a moving array of perfectly engineered pheromone mixtures and eye movements and simulated biometrics, was just a tool, just a distraction. That child before her, with his untainted innocence, his direct, perfectly sincere question, his hunger for the truth of it all… he was just as much a tool. A perfect closing argument, a justification for a decision she had made three hundred years ago. A decision to break a million-year-old rule. A decision to protect the people of this galaxy with all of her powers. And she had the power to change history, the power to let them know what had been done to them. The power to let them know what they had done for themselves. In a way that they would understand. And if Tan was the last generation that could ask the question, well, then Tan would be the first to be given the answer.

Tan waited. The spectators around them, only a few at first but more gathering all the time, stopped their celebrations and looked. Zara could hear their thoughts, their drawn attention tracking her biometrics and searching for an understanding of the spectacle before them. Their communal minds were shifting, slowly at first but more decisively with each passing second as her answer began to resonate among them in their own personal way, processing the flood of conflicting emotions Tan's innocence had inspired.

"It is a story that you are right to ask about, Tan," Zara began, drawing in a human-like breath before she began the story. "But you must know that this will be a long tale, and you must be still."

The party of revelers soon attracted others, drawn by the beauty of Zara's voice, and the obvious change in mood. Other Veldari, Draxians, and humans, all who had been dancing, singing, and generally lost in their own celebration, suddenly found themselves drawn to the small, cloaked figure, and the young boy sitting at her feet. A young Veldari woman, her green skin detailed with complex tattoos upon her face, seated herself on the ground, permacrete polished floor at her back, her posture reverent. A scrawny Draxian, his six limbs folded casually at his sides, leaned against a nearby column, his gruff breathing now a quiet, rumbling bass against the sounds of music from across the street. They had all heard the sanitized versions, of course; the propaganda fed to them through children's holos, the tales of gallant heroes fighting for their world in the Great War, for the glory of the Donovan Ascendancy. But the words Zara spoke promised a different sort of truth.

Zara's form, while no longer stationary, was now active. The aura of light within her now shimmered and danced with a new intensity, no longer a passive aura, but a contained, projected show of color and form. She raised one hand, palm extended, and in her outstretched hand a tiny, floating holographic projection of Concordia city sprang to life, buildings, people, floating spires, and all. "This peace, this unity," Zara continued, her voice now taking on the cadence of storytelling, "was not simply given to us. It was fought for. A fight that began when a galaxy-spanning swarm of alien life came to consume the galaxy whole."

A human man, older than the average, and more scarred, pushed his way through the small crowd. "The Afltic Swarm," he whispered, his voice almost awed. "My grandfather was one of them. He piloted one of the frigates that set the beacons on the final day."

Zara looked at the man, her eyes a galaxy of swirling light. "They were a terror," she affirmed, her humming voice deepening with the tone of her own memories. "A tide of biological madness. But your grandfather, and so many like him, they were not just fighting for themselves. They were fighting for all life." She shifted her gaze back to Tan, his small form still utterly transfixed by her voice and the floating display of Concordia. "But in order to appreciate the light," she began again, "you must know the dark. Our story begins not with a battle, but with a single, desperate gambit." The onlookers were now completely silent, the merry, joyous sounds of the festival a world away. No longer were they merely a group of revelers, but a gathering, and Zara's words were their sermon. The history of their liberation from the darkness was about to truly be told.

Zara waved her hand, and a soft, holographic display of nebulae and other, unknown galaxies took shape around her form. The crowd, now twice as large, hushed, mesmerized by the sudden change in atmosphere. "In order to understand our liberation," Zara began, the quality of her voice taking on a more narrative timbre, "you must first understand the darkness that threatened to devour all life. It came not from the planets or the solar systems that cradled them. It came from the void between the stars." Zara looked out at the crowd, young and old, human and alien. Each face was given a silent promise that what she was about to tell them would shatter their own perspective of their shared history. The atmosphere crackled, the festive celebration of Concordia falling silent in the background as Zara was about to open the first, horrific chapter of the Donovan Ascendancy.

The floating holographic display expanded, the circle of people now encapsulated in the slow, floating projection. Gone were the colorful, vibrant displays of Concordia. In their place, a cold, dead vacuum of empty space, blacker than the void outside, but where there had been city lights now there were stars, pinpricks of light, lost stars, shimmering against the void. Something pulsed out of the deep dark, a sickly, greenish-black cloud that coalesced as a tide of microscopic motes, drifting and swirling until it became one, single horrific mass. It moved in an unnatural, predatory gait, swallowing the light of stars whole as it devoured their brightness and replaced it with a trail of absolute darkness. The Draxian's guttural breath hitched in his throat and the Veldari woman at his side involuntarily reached for the arm of the human man she stood with. This was not the heroic depiction of the Afltic they had all grown up with, sanitized and made into legends, this was raw, terrifying fear incarnate.

Tan, however, was utterly enthralled, his eyes wide with wonder, not fear. He was watching the beginning of a story, of which he had only heard rumors, a story his grandmother had insisted was important. He jabbed a small finger at the looming, coalescing shadow. "Is that it?" he asked, his voice a soft, inquiring whisper. "Is that what they fought?" Zara nodded, the movement barely a ripple in her holographic body. "That is the Afltic," she confirmed, her voice now assuming the solemnity of one who has stared into the void and lived to tell the tale. "A hive mind bent only on consumption. It sought not to conquer or to subjugate. Its only goal was to consume. Planets, stars, entire galaxies were all but fuel for its ravenous appetite." The holographic display zoomed in, now the leading edge of the Afltic. Tucked within the green-black mass of the creature, dozens of intricate shapes could be seen, like the armored cases of insects, each a miniature engine of death and destruction. The details were so crisp, so hideously accurate, that the onlookers recoiled, an entire crowd of bodies taking a small step back in horror. This was the chasm of forgotten terrors Zara had glimpsed earlier, now given substance, a living, breathing testament to the cost of their current peace.

Zara paused, allowing a brief silence to fall before she began to craft a picture, her voice a paintbrush and the holographic display her canvas. "A species without a home, without a world. An entire civilization that made their home in the barren wastes of asteroid fields, a people that required no atmosphere, no planetary surface to survive." The first images were abstract, a shimmering, holographic representation of vague forms, organic, almost biological shapes that drifted through the depths of space without any obvious technology or machinery. The crowd pressed forward, their expressions changing from curious interest to an undercurrent of nervous dread. This was not the history they had been told, not the hero's journey they had been promised, this was something much older, much more ancient. Zara's phrasing was clipped, almost technical in its precision, yet her voice retained the solemnity of a chronicler who had witnessed too much to live.

Now the holographic projection expanded, a great, swirling mass of asteroid field, a graveyard of ancient worlds and the remnants of cosmic collisions. It was within these rocky, metallic oceans that the Afltic thrived. The shapes of their nests now appeared, grotesque, crystalline lattices that clung like parasites to the sides of the space rock, tendrils snaking from their structures and latching into every crevice, every opening they could find. Swarms of tiny, insectoid drones spilled forth, the workers and warriors of the Afltic, darting from the safety of their mothership into the empty wastes. They were not machines, but biological terrors, their purpose a pre-installed programming, to harvest and to consume.

Murmurs rippled through the crowd. "They never lived on planets?" a human woman asked, her voice trembling.

Zara's eyes, the focal point of their collective attention now, seemed to bore through the holographic display, to pierce right into the woman's mind. "Never. It was a waste of resources," she answered, her voice devoid of inflection, an utterly uncaring tone in the face of the human's horror. "Everything was to be stripped bare. The crust for minerals, the core for energy, until nothing was left but an empty husk. They were the ultimate scavengers, the apex predators of the galactic wilds. "They are not simple, monsters lurking in the dark. They are complex, sentient entities whose minds operate outside of our concepts of morality. They are a pure biological imperative, and every living thing is, to them, just food."

Tan, still kneeling at her feet, was perfectly still. His tiny hand clutched at the toy starship so tightly his knuckles were white. He was no longer a little boy at a celebration, he was a silent witness to the first act of a tragedy. The Veldari woman averted her gaze from the nightmare visions. Her face was a portrait of sadness. "They were everywhere," she murmured, like the wisp of a memory. "The stories say they appeared from all directions at once." Zara inclined her head, the gesture making her holographic form ripple slightly. "They were. A tide that rolled in from the cold, uncharted reaches of the galaxy.

CHAPTER 2: ONE MIND, ONE HUNGER

"This species," Zara continued as the holograms shifted to show more defined shapes, "is the Afltic. The progeny of an alien biology optimized for the void, with a singular, focus." The amorphous forms shifted, suddenly coalescing into horrific, chitinous ships. Biomechanical, not mechanical. Their surfaces were an organic nightmare. As more of the creatures came into view, a low murmur rippled through the crowd as the implications of a space-native civilization dawned on those assembled. Zara's voice was cold and dead of emotion, but there was no escaping the dread her words instilled. The horrors of the past were being re-learned. Stitched back together by the speaker for the first time in centuries.

The holographic projection shifted, isolating the abhorrent details of a single Afltic ship. It was not the smooth, gleaming metal of a human starship, but a city-sized, segmented insect. Hard, black-green chitin covered its body like armor, segmented plates that connected with joints around the ship's hull. The outside of the hull was a nest of spiked outgrowths that tapered off toward the center of the Afltic. But the most disturbing feature was the maw at the ship's front. A single, gaping hole in the hull covered with serrated, teeth-like chitin, a monstrous maw that defied imagination in its size and functionality. A biological abomination that horrified the crowd. Younger members of the audience gasped as the horror of the Afltic reared up before them. Their history, sanitized by the remembrances of holographic holos, was being replaced with something much, much worse. Bright starships and bustling space stations were being recast as antiseptic fantasies in the light of the Afltic truth. Hideous, insatiable monsters that devoured with terrifying efficiency.

"They had no pilots," Zara said over the crowd's soft murmurs, "no command structure that you would understand. They were a hive mind, an entire consciousness acting as a singular, unified entity. They communicated through biological processes, with no real spoken language. Instead, a constant, inaudible hum of thoughts and ideas that gave rise to their behavior. They were not sentient in the way that you are. They were…hungry. Consumed by an alien instinct to feed."

Tan, who had remained at her feet for the entirety of her speech, looked up at Zara, his young face ashen but determined. "They ate the stars?" he asked, his voice small.

Zara's holographic eyes, twin pinpricks of light, softened. "They harvested their energy," she clarified, her voice gentle, "as we do with our suns. They simply took more than the worlds could give." The elder Draxian at the back of the crowd inched forward on her six-legged feet. "I heard the stories once," she rasped quietly, "from my grandmother. About the 'Silent Tide' of worlds that simply… ceased to be. There were no calls for help, no final messages. Just silence." Zara's figure nodded slowly, solemn, the weight of her memories years gone making itself known. "The silence, Mrs. Tamura, was the first sign. A universe in which a single sound was never heard. In which the stars no longer spoke."

Zara's holographic visage shifted, refocusing on details of the Afltic creatures themselves. "There are two basic Afltic castes," she said, "the civilian-minded Worker caste and the overtly aggressive Warrior caste." The holograms showed large, bustling organic hives that swarmed with small, less-threatening creatures. The view shifted, zooming in on a larger, more threatening specimen. "The Worker caste for the most part are a peaceful and largely non-violent people. Biologically inclined toward hive building and expansion." Images of large organic hives filled with the serene Worker caste zipped across the crowd as they watched the display, a symphony of coordinated biological activity humming beneath them. These holograms were not simply projections. They were the re-education of the galactic public. Workers repurposed stellar matter, bio-farming the material that made up the cores of the Afltic planets. Starships made of living tissue, carried energy siphons and weapons to harvest the physical and metaphysical essence of other worlds. Tan was entranced. At the same time, Zara continued her grim lesson. "But make no mistake, all of that can change with the right influence. If a Worker hive falls under the direct control of a Warrior Queen, the hive's inherent passivity will quickly evaporate into something much more…aggressive."

The holograms flared to life, drawing the crowd's attention to a beautifully detailed organic hive. A shimmering crystalline metropolis of living tissue that was lit from within. The smaller Worker caste patrolled the hive's glowing corridors, working on some unknown task in a hum of coordinated serenity. It was oddly beautiful to behold, a remnant of the past focused on biological productivity in ways that defied the imagination. But it was suddenly replaced with something that sent a cold shiver through the crowd.

A sharp surge of light and movement. Red, orange, and green energy staining the once-peaceful image with violence. At the center of the hive, a larger, more imposing figure emerged. A Warrior Queen. A grotesque, armored matriarch who radiated an aura of toxic, silent malice. As the swell of her influence spread outward like a shockwave through the hive, the crowd could see the Worker caste visibly shift beneath her. Limbs contorting with an ugly intensity, their normally subtle movements becoming jagged and predatory. The crystalline tools they carried in their grasp were distorted into more organic shapes, biological blades made from the excess flesh of the hive. A Worker caste built to produce, build, and harvest was transformed. Quiet and efficient obliterated by a single, violent purpose: to do battle and do it in the service of their Queen.

The crowd gasped as a single, awful understanding of the full threat Zara was describing set in. "So Warriors aren't...born?" a human woman asked, her voice a soft whisper.

"They are not born," Zara stated, her voice dropping to a soft, hushed cadence. "They are made. A Warrior Queen is a weapon, both a biological and a literal one, a vessel the size of a battleship that wants to consume an entire planet's population."

The holographic image zoomed in on the Queen's face, revealing not a face at all, but a horrifying mass of chitinous plates, multifaceted eyes, and a large, pulsating core of energy. A tangible wave of aggression emanated from her, visible in the way the subjugated female Worker caste around her reacted with immediate violence. Tan shuddered in his seat. The old Draxian lady in the back grumbled a low tone of dread, reacting to a horror made personal, parasitic, and self-perpetuating.

The sanitized histories made no mention of this. They had only spoken of an aggressive, alien swarm. The truth was that the Queen's control was specific: she subjugated the female workers and either subjugated or mutated the males of her own species into mindless warriors. This revelation settled on the crowd like the chilling final note of Zara's opening remarks on the Afltic.

"In direct contrast to the Workers," Zara's voice took on a deeper timbre, the holographic display refocusing on the larger, more frightening Afltic forms, "the Warrior caste is a predator, driven by a deeply ingrained biological need to consume and conquer. The Warrior caste are relentless. Their instinctual drive for nourishment and absolute dominance is something quite alien to you." Images of massive, predatory organisms filled the crowd's vision, their bodies subtly evolving from smaller, scout-like vessels to outright monsters of destruction. The air in the gathering grew thick with a palpable anxiety. Zara was not simply giving a lecture. She was painting a picture of an unstoppable force of nature. A biological imperative for war that transcended normal species' motives. A primal hunger that was made literal by their biology, that manifested in ambitions that were staggeringly immense.

The holographic display showed a small, scout-like Warrior vessel. It was the segmented, armored form of an insect, darting nimbly through the holographic asteroid field. As Zara spoke, the image of the scout began to transform, an unsettling metamorphosis that the crowd watched with collective apprehension. The vessel's chitinous shell expanded, new armor plates sprouting like scales from its body. Limbs used for navigation and combat twisted and curled around one another, reconfiguring themselves into massive, organic energy siphons. Their tips glowed with an unnatural, sickly green light. It began to swell, inflating into a grotesque, gigantic living ship. Something the size of a starship, a horror of muscle and chitin. The level of detail in the hologram was so complete the crowd

18

took a collective step backward, the festive pop music from Concordia's docks an irrelevant, background noise.

"These are Warrior Queens," Zara's voice droned as the holographic model shifted to focus on the larger of the Aftic forms. "One can serve as the flagship of an entire swarm, a living vessel that commands dozens, sometimes thousands of smaller craft." The holographic display showed a single Queen's form, now the size of a small city, hovering in the black void above a simulated planet. From her massive body, hundreds of smaller, segmented male Warriors swarmed out, their bodies sleek and lithe, their intent of aggression clear. The crowd watched as the Queen extended the energy siphons she had grown from her body, plunging them into the planet's core. The life energy of the world flowed up into the hologram in a torrent of green light.

A young human woman raised her hand, her face ashen. "They…they do that on their own?" she asked, the gaze of her large eyes fixed on the horror of the hologram. "They just…grow?"

"They do," Zara confirmed, the immutable consistency of the light in her eyes a sign of the absolute certainty she held in her memories. "It is a biological necessity. Once the need for expansion is triggered, they will do anything to satisfy that urge. They are the apex predators of the void, perfectly adapted for the consumption and subjugation of their enemies. Their purpose is to consume, to grow, to replicate, and to conquer. They do not see it as evil. They see it as…necessary."

A young Draxian, his six arms trembling, looked up at Zara. "They wanted everything?" he asked, his voice a tremor of fear and disbelief.

"Everything," Zara confirmed, her holographic eyes shifting to focus on him, "but their most prized form of sustenance was not planetary energy or organic biomass. It was intelligent life. Emotions, knowledge, thoughts…all of it was fuel to them. The more sentient the target, the more valuable the harvest." A low whir of horrified silence fell over the crowd. The sanitized stories said nothing of this. They had only spoken of a resource war, never a war of sentience. The realization chilled them all, a cold, creeping dread that bled through the joyous scene around them. The Aftic were not just destructive. Their nature was deeply, intrinsically, and terrifyingly personal.

"Each Queen," Zara continued, her voice calm despite the disturbing nature of the visuals, "is armed with a variety of bio-cannons capable of firing energy blasts of staggering power. These are perfectly complementary with razor-sharp chitinous blades for close-range combat and powerful energy siphons designed to drain the life force and technological knowledge from enemy ships and planetary defenses." The holograms zoomed in on these instruments of horror, showing how the organic weapons naturally fit into the Queen's massive body. The crowd watched in horror and fascination as Zara explained the capabilities of these biological warships. The thought of a creature that literally consumed and repurposed its enemies' life force made the Afltic seem a step beyond a plague and a step into nightmare.

The holographic display shifted to focus on a single Warrior Queen, its city-sized form a silent colossus drifting in the black emptiness of space. As Zara spoke, the beast's specific features glowed with an unnatural, inner light. Razor-sharp chitinous blades, many meters long in the armory of a human cruiser, extended from the armored hull like fangs. Formidable weapons for the brutal, ranged combat that could break out in the chaos of battle. Then the holographic display showed off the bio-cannons. Large, pulsing organs that the crowd could only compare to mutant flowers. They opened, a series of concentric rings of armored flesh, and spewed forth a torrent of green, corrosive energy that carved a path of ruin through the void. An Alliance frigate appeared in the holographic field, and the energy blast struck it, ripping apart its shields and hull with terrifying speed. The crowd gasped, a communal wave of horror rippling through them all.

"And their most insidious form of weaponry," Zara continued, the holographic display now highlighting the energy siphons, writhing tentacle-like projections that cascaded from the Queen's form. "Are not designed for simple destruction. They are designed for consumption. They could suck the life-force from a living being, the data from a machine, even the very integrity of a ship's systems." The tentacles pierced the holographic Alliance frigate, and the crowd watched in horror as the ship's lights went out. A flickering sputter of system functions ended as the ship's colors drained from vibrant hues to lifeless grey. Metallic components of the ship corroded into clouds of rust and debris.

"They did not want to just defeat us," a voice from the crowd grumbled, a grizzled old Vintie. "They wanted to… erase us."

"In a manner of speaking, yes," Zara agreed, the soft, whispering hiss of pure memory in her voice. "They wanted to assimilate our energy, our knowledge, and our life-force into their own. Every battle we fought against them, every ship we lost, was a victory for them. We were not fighting an army; we were fighting a hunger. A hunger that was only made more potent by the knowledge that their male Warriors were an equally terrifying force of nature, protecting their Queen with a ferocity that knew no bounds." Tan, who had been sitting utterly still for the entire demonstration, straightened at this, springing to his feet. He stared up at Zara, her words suddenly hitting home as the full scale of the danger became not only frightening, but horrifying. How could they have possibly have won against such a foe? The sanitized version of the Afltic in the history chips that Tan had read as a child in school had been nothing at all like this. There had been no visceral terror in those stories, nothing to make the fight personal. The history chips had sanitized the truth for their generation, and in doing so, had robbed them of everything.

"Their preferred prey," Zara continued, and there was just the slightest, infinitesimal difference in the cadence of her vocal tone to indicate just how particularly horrifying this point was, "are sentient beings. The energy and biological components harvested from intelligent life forms are especially nourishing for their growth and reproduction cycles." The image warped and flickered, going from showing a nice, basic abstraction of captured vessels for a few moments before fading to the tantalizingly abstracted, but quite unmistakable image of the Queen's interior. The glimpses of organic, liquid muscle, the teasingly vague suggestion of some form of processing chambers and alien viscera, were enough to elicit a low growl from some of the crowd. The Afltic were not just mindless predators. The Afltic were predators, with an appetite. An appetite that was only stoked by the presence of things like Tan. A fact that made the entire war terrifyingly personal in a way that the sanitized histories had not prepared any of them for.

The new holographic projection was a picture of a recently captured Alliance freighter, the proud, sleek lines and proud insignia of the Alliance fleet an obscene contrast to the amorphous, tentacled horror of the Afltic Queen's immense bulk. The ship's drives flared brightly as it was held fast by one of the Queen's massively distended siphons, its lights flickering as the Queen's tendrils took it. But this was not the truly horrifying part. The image zoomed in, closer and closer to the ship's interior, giving the viewer a haunting, heart-stopping glimpse of the terrified crew, frozen in place by fear, before flitting to something that the observer could only describe as an abstracted suggestion of organic processing chamber. No torture rooms, no racks, no boiling vats of acid and flame. No elaborate machinery that was unique to the manufactured machine of the Alliance. Just a nightmarish, alien interior with thousands upon thousands of translucent membranes gently throbbing and pulsating as they began to metabolize their latest victims into the nourishment that the Queen required to produce more of her own hideous spawn. She had them whole, every last one of them, and the part that was not being used for energy or biological components would be used for what, for some unimaginable nightmare of reproduction? The Afltic were as close to an infinite well of unnatural hunger as the galaxy had ever seen, and they had already tried to use it to eradicate the fledgling Concordia.

The young woman in the crowd who had begun to weep a moment before, her face stark white in the harsh light of the hologram, turned away from the image. "They... they didn't just kill them," she whispered, her voice a low tremor. "They used them."

"Precisely," Zara confirmed, her voice a quiet, solemn hum. "Every last ounce of emotional energy, every second of fear and hope and despair was made into a powerful source of fuel for the Queen's reproduction cycles. The more intelligent the life-forms they found, the more sustenance they could draw from them. They did not just want to kill us; they wanted to use us, to make every last spark of our existence a part of them."

Tan, who had remained at Zara's feet since she had begun the presentation, looked up at her then, his large, wide eyes all questions and revelations. The cute little space battles from the history chips, where their sanitized history books had them performing heroic deeds and routing entire Afltic battleships single-handedly, had been a far cry from the cold, soulless terror that Zara was presenting to them now. It was one thing to learn about this through memory. It was another to be told by someone who had lived it. It was all one huge thing to a boy who had been brought up on sanitized history. The joyful sounds of the Galactic Liberation Day revelry were completely lost to the crowd, muted and absorbed by the thick, heavy pall of horror that had now settled over every single one of them. The peace that they had been so blithely celebrating before was not just a victory. It was a memorial, a quiet and solemn remembrance of all of the souls that had been turned into mere fuel by an alien horror that had no concept of mercy or even empathy.

"Complementing the Warrior Queens are the segmented, dexterous male Warriors," Zara continued, the pair of holograms on either side of her now showing a number of far smaller, though equally disturbing Afltic bodies. Thin, fast, and lithe, these creatures were the complete opposite of the Warrior Queens, leaping with startling fluidity and a liquid grace that belied their segmented, insectile forms. "Capable of just as much ferocity as their gargantuan sisters, they fulfill a dual role within the Afltic collective. Symbiotic parasites within the immense, convoluted innards of the female hosts, managing resources and administering the captured broods, and external combatants, swarming the enemy and swathing it in protection during a fight." The bodies shown in the images darted through space, snatching at projectiles in mid-flight and ripping into holographic Alliance fighters in brutal, close-range combat. They were just as deadly as the Queens they served, a beautifully adapted biological weapon that had no need for the complicated logic of actual sentience. Perfect in their own way.

The new image on Zara's personal hologram was of an entirely different form of horror. A swarm of sleek, black-green male Warriors burst forth from a holographic representation of a Warrior Queen, their segmented, muscular bodies rippling with speed and dexterity. The movements were horrifying in their unity and coordination, a writhing and twisting horde of bodies that somehow moved as a single being. The image shifted to show them in action, protecting their Queen. A volley of simulated missiles was launched from the bow of a holographic Alliance battleship, their hard, metallic bodies speeding through space towards their intended target. They would have been effective, had the male Warriors not swarmed to intercept them, slicing through the missile clusters with a speed and precision that bordered on the telepathic. The missiles exploded, their high-explosive payloads detonating far from the target and causing no harm. A low sound of awe and dread rippled through the crowd.

"They were fast," the grizzled old Draxian rumbled, his voice filled with a new, horrible respect. "Much faster than our fighters."

"Their biology was specialized for this," Zara confirmed, her voice a low, quiet hum. "Built for bursts of speed and dexterity. They were living bullets, literally a shield of flesh and chitin. They would swarm, swarm, swarm over their Queen, a living barrier between her and the enemies that she so desired to consume. And in close range combat, they were even more horrifying." The projection showed a male Warrior lock on to an Alliance fighter, its guns a thrumming, whirring blur of energy as the holographic Alliance ship blasted at it with every available energy core. But the Warrior was quicker. Liquid, the translation of its movements defied description as it weaved in and out of a hail of energy, its razor-sharp appendages lashing out with a speed and a precision that was almost hypnotic in its brutality. It locked on to the fighter's hull, a tiny lump of organic flesh among the bulkheads, its limbs biting into the metal like paper. It was a savage, brutal act of predation, all precision, all efficiency, its small but no less potent energy siphons beginning to drain the ship. The fighter went dark as its lights blinked out, and the male Warrior darted away, its hunger satisfied, back into the darkness of space to repeat the process again and again.

Tan, who had been staring, enraptured, at the display, suddenly spoke up, his voice small and clear. "They worked together," he observed, more than asked. "Like a family."

"They are not a family," Zara corrected gently, her own holographic image softening slightly as she stared down at him. "A single organism. Each working for the good of the whole. Their priorities were not survival, but the survival of the Queen. To do otherwise would be to invite their own extinction. They were a weapon. A perfectly honed and adapted symbiotic horror that we had never before encountered in all of our history, and they were ubiquitous." The crowd was still, the entire throng lost in a sudden, powerful understanding of the truly hideous nature of their opponent. The sanitized history had focused on the Alliance, but Zara was showing them the truth. The ugly, horrifying truth. The peace that they had been celebrating before was not a given. It was not a victory that they could afford to take for granted. It was a miracle.

Zara went on to describe the male Warriors' effectiveness in combat. "Each of their segments is a center of semi-independent movement and action, able to continue a fight even if severed from their host for a short period of time." The holographic display showed a male Warrior have one of its razor-sharp limbs chopped off by an Alliance energy pulse, and continued to show the severed limb continuing its attack before fizzling out a moment later. This made clear to the crowd the terrifying adaptability of the Afltic, and the sheer difficulty in fighting a foe that could not be crippled by the removal of limbs or even a head. The crowd murmured, a strange and uneasy awe at the alien biological adaptations that had made the Afltic such a horrifying and formidable enemy.

The new holographic projection was a depiction of an exchange of fire between a sleek and rakish Alliance fighter and a single male Afltic Warrior. A cascade of light, the fighter spewing forth energy pulses in the vain hope that some of them would connect, and the male Warrior ducking and dodging every single one that it could. The Alliance fighter was firing fast, her guns a single, concentrated blast of energy, but the male Warrior moved with a strange, liquid grace that no machine could duplicate, every movement an unholy parody of biological perfection. It was beautiful in a way that was truly unnatural, a sickening dance in the cold, sterile emptiness of space, and it was destroying the Alliance ship in a way that no smart, mechanical mind could have, its razor-sharp arms lashing out of the void with the lithe elegance of a whip, its own personal energy siphon having been carefully implanted into a ventral cavity of the ship while its own main power supply remained safely docked to the Queen. The Alliance fighter went dark as her lights blinked out, and the male Warrior leapt away from her like an oily snake, its light also fading as the Afltic monster returned to the safety of its Queen.

"Their physical resilience was a constant source of frustration for Alliance pilots," Zara explained, her own voice a quiet and solemn hiss. "There were no easy targets. You could disable a vessel, but even a single severed limb could still take out one of our ships. It was like trying to exterminate a hive of hornets, every one of them a weapon in their own right, and every one of them capable of regenerating its lost appendages."

The young human man who had been looking around, his face twisted with a profound horror at what he had been shown, shook his head. "How did we ever win?" he whispered, his voice a full-throated exhalation of wonder and dread that perfectly encapsulated the thought at the forefront of every one of their minds.

Zara's holographic eyes, those twin pinpricks of flickering light, held the full weight of the answer to that question in their depths, a secret that she was not quite ready to share. "We will get to that," she promised, a quiet and certain assurance in her voice. "But first, you must know the true scale of the enemy you faced. The Warriors were only a piece of the puzzle, a hunting party designed to hunt you down and consume you. An absolute perfection of biological weapon with an evolutionary purpose singular in its scope and its efficiency." The image of the regenerating male Warrior faded away, and the crowd was once again bathed in the gentle, yellow light of Concordia. The once-festive atmosphere had been completely shattered by the revelation of what they had actually been up against during the Dark Times, however, replaced by a deafening silence. The peace that they had so freely celebrated before now suddenly felt fragile, tenuous, like something that could be lost at any moment by a force that they might not be strong enough to fight a second time.

"Regardless of caste," Zara finished this segment of the explanation, her voice strong, "every Afltic brood is subservient to the absolute, telepathic control of their reigning Queen." The holograms on either side of her flared to life, a dizzying web of brilliant, golden tendrils of thought reaching out from a core, a pulsating and overwhelming presence in the minds of every single Afltic body. It explained a great deal about the terrifying efficiency of their attacks, the uncanny coordination of their battles. The Afltic were not a loose grouping of individuals. Not at all. They were a collective, a single mind with an absolute will and a unified purpose. Their purpose being to consume all around them, all that they could.

The projected image flared with a brilliant new pulse of thought and energy. It was a massive, living neural network that connected every individual across light-years of space, every Warrior, every Worker, every captured vessel, every single nest, and connected them all to this pulsating core. The focal point of a truly cosmic brain that expanded and contracted with every piece of information that it absorbed. The male Warriors, the gargantuan Warrior Queens, and the plodding, compliant Worker caste were not individuals, were not intelligent. They were no more than pawns, mouthpieces for the Queen's will. They were not living minds that were guided by her, but a vast, collective instrument of her own single-minded focus.

A young Veldari woman stared from the holographic display to Zara with wide eyes that reflected a horror that was so profound as to be inexpressible. "They weren't fighting us," she whispered, the shudder in her voice audibly terrible. "The Queen was fighting us. All of them were just... her."

"Precisely," Zara agreed, her voice a quiet and solemn thrum. "Their coordination was so perfect because there was no need for debate or disagreement. There was no question of priority, no squabbling for resources, and above all, no survival instinct of their own that would fight against her. The Afltic were a single mind, a single goal. They did not have to plan; they had to simply act. Their hunger was their sole motivation, their drive to expand their borders and consume everything was all they knew. This is why, by and large, our conventional military tactics were not terribly effective against them. You could not turn them against one another, could not manipulate their internal logic or break their command structures. You could not cut off the head of the snake, because it had no head. It had no head because it was a thousand miles long, and every scale upon its body was a head unto itself."

CHAPTER 3: THE FALL

"Do the Afltic feel anything? Do they have emotions, or is it just... hunger?" A young Guyopie from the back of the crowd asked, their wings and feathers catching the light in an iridescent, opalescent glow. Their voice was a clear, pleasant bell tone, in jarring contrast to the staid, monotonous timbre of the main proceedings. Zara paused, her floating holographic form flickering and going black for a moment as she considered the child's question. It was an innocent inquiry, likely the product of a natural desire to see a connection to the enemy, to see something that the Afltic had in common with the rest of the sentient galaxy.

"No, young one. The closest parallel we can make to an emotion they experience is one of biological necessity. For them, to 'feel' is to eat, and to eat is to feel." Zara's response was calm and collected, her retort a direct counter to the child's idea that there was anything human about the Afltic. Her entire tenure as Advisor for Concordia was spent observing the Afltic, and in those many thousands of years she had long ago moved past romantic, biased views of the enemy. "There is no compassion to their actions, no guilt or satisfaction. All they 'feel' is the urge to grow, the urge to spread. Their 'pleasure' is to be fed, their 'anger' to be denied." The once-black projection screen suddenly flickered back to life, and instead of an archive of Concordia history, a terrifying and abstract visualization of the Afltic hive mind appeared. It was a swirling, shifting mass of green and black, a constantly evolving and contracting nebula of pure, instinctual hunger with not a single speck of light or color to be seen. The young Guyopie visibly shuddered, their feathers seeming to lose their iridescence in the wake of the chilling fact. The full extent of the Afltic nature had been made known to this generation.

Tan looked up at Zara from where he had been listening to her address, his eyes wide as he finally absorbed the full truth of the Afltic. "But... but if that's true," he started, his voice small, "how could Donovan and everyone else fight back? I mean, you can't fight something like that."

Zara's holographic form visibly softened, her gaze (those pinpricks of light in the empty, black sockets) fixing on the small boy. The crowd was completely silent, every individual still and hushed in anticipation of her answer. The sounds of Concordia had long since faded away, a memory replaced by a heavy, oppressive silence. "Well, Tan," Zara said, and her voice was a promise, "that's exactly what they did. But that to really answer your question, I will need to continue the story." The image of the inhuman Afltic hive mind faded out and the entire room was once again cast in the gentle, harmonic glow of Concordia.

"Before the Alliance, before humans became the most advanced species in the galaxy," Zara began, her voice taking on a more foreboding tone, "there was the Kryll Hegemony. An empire of machines and their organic masters, they spread across the stars with their incomparable technology." Holograms of Kryll cities and starships and orbital defense grids appeared, and they all seemed to throb with an air of untouchable power. The Kryll had harnessed energy manipulation, FTL, and defensives to a degree that few other species had matched, and with their vast starfleet and orbital fortresses the Kryll Hegemony was truly a dominant power. Their arrogance, Zara suggested, would be their undoing.

The holographic projection now encompassed an entire panorama of the Kryll Hegemony in its height. The cities were sprawling citadels of polished chrome and crystalline architecture that seemed to pierce the clouds, their facades reflecting and refracting the light of every sun. Arrowhead-shaped starships darted between star systems, their engines emitting trails of glittering stardust as they streaked through the void. Orbitals, massive rings of automated defense platforms, loomed protectively around their core planets, each one bristling with energy weapons and kinetic launchers. The Kryll themselves now appeared in the projection, their humanoid bodies covered in a layer of blue skin. Their faces moved with absolute confidence, their expressions smug and sure. They were a species that had not known fear for as long as they could remember, and their technological supremacy had been a warm and reassuring blanket to cover them against any threat.

An older human man in the crowd whistled, a grizzled veteran with a prosthetic arm and a face like sandpaper. "Must have been nice," he muttered under his breath, his voice a low, gravelly growl. "I only got to see their stuff in museums. The old timers used to say they were too smart to fall."

"They were too smart to fall to any enemy they had ever encountered," Zara said softly, her voice tinged with a deep sadness. "They had defenses against every possible threat, biological, technological, even temporal. They had a contingency for every contingency except for the one they never saw coming. The Kryll were a logical species, a reasonable species, and the Afltic was none of those things. They simply could not understand a threat that did not come to conquer or enslave, but only to consume." The projection of the magnificent Kryll Hegemony started to flicker; its outer edges starting to ripple and fade. The crowd watched in complete silence, their initial awe and wonder replaced by a growing sense of dread as Zara prepared to show them the beginning of the end for this once-invincible species.

"The Kryll had long since written off the sporadic reports of void-born creatures as anomalies, fringe threats that could be easily dealt with by their massive military." The holograms now depicted Kryll strategists and tacticians, their faces smug as they ran war games and simulations against the Afltic. In every simulation, their enemy was no match for Kryll might, the swarm of insects being easily swept away by a hurricane of energy and steel. Their hubris, Zara communicated, left them vulnerable to the true nature of the Afltic. They failed to understand their enemy's alien biology, its complete lack of any conventional vulnerabilities, its utter and terrifying adaptability, and their greatest fear was quickly becoming their greatest weapon.

The holographic projection now displayed a Kryll command center, a massive, circular room filled with dazzling, floating panels of tactical information. The Kryll officers themselves were blue-skinned, their humanoid faces confident and composed as they gestured at the readouts. Their limbs moved with the grace of a well-trained ballet dancer. One of the displays depicted a single Afltic Warrior Queen, a dark speck on the bottom edge of a holographic star map. The Kryll officer gestured, and instantly a dozen Kryll warships materialized holographically around the speck. They brought their energy cannons to bear and the simulation began. With a single volley of powerful plasma torpedoes, the Kryll fleet tore a gaping hole in the Afltic Queen, burning it into nothing in a cascade of beautiful destruction. The Kryll officers grinned, their confidence bordering on arrogance. They had simulated the encounter, and the enemy was no match for their power.

A human woman in the crowd with an expression of stark, bitter sadness shook her head. "They just didn't get it," she whispered. "They couldn't fathom a monster that didn't die like everything else."

"They could not," Zara said, her voice a low, quiet chant. "The Kryll operated under the principles of energy and matter they had mastered. They understood that everything could be killed, that everything could be destroyed. The idea of an enemy that could adapt, and evolve, and even turn their own technology against them was anathema to their sensibilities. They looked upon the Afltic and they saw a vermin, a pest to be swatted. But they were no vermin, no pest. They were a living wave, a biological imperative that viewed the Kryll's advanced technology as a resource to be used." The image of the Kryll command center disappeared, leaving behind a cold, black void. The crowd was silent, a memorial to a long-gone people who had been so certain of their own strength that they had forgotten the most important rule of the universe. Their arrogance was about to be tested, and Zara's quiet, holographic form was a silent witness to their collective demise.

"When the Afltic turned its full attention to the Kryll Hegemony," Zara's voice grew somber, "their first encounters were met with incredulity. Kryll fleets, designed for surgical strikes and energy barrages, found their salvos utterly ineffectual, their weapons being either absorbed or turned against them." The holograms now showed Kryll warships expelling clouds of energy against a single Afltic Queen, their force seemingly dissipating against the creature's carapace, or in many cases worse being sucked up and redirected. The Kryll captains, at first supremely confident, soon grew frantic as their carefully-laid plans proved useless against the Afltic. Their sophisticated arsenal, which had been designed for destruction, was instead fuelling the enemy.

The holographic projection now showed one Kryll warship in isolation, its sleek, blue hull a marvel of advanced technology. It was silhouetted against a single Afltic Warrior Queen, a massive, malformed horror. The Kryll captain on the bridge gestured wildly. A storm of brilliant, white energy bolts erupted from the warship's cannons, streaking through space and impacting against the Afltic Queen's hide. Instead of a satisfying explosion, the resulting light show was a nauseating display of energy absorption. The bolts simply disappeared, their energies being siphoned up by the Queen's internal organs. The Kryll shields, which had been designed to withstand kinetic and energy attacks, were no match for the Afltic's raw, biological feeding.

A Draxian in the crowd, his voice a low rumble of profound awe, shook his head. "They didn't stop the attack," he said. "They ate it."

"Right," Zara confirmed. "Instead of being an attack, every shot they fired, every weapon they brought to bear, was an act of feeding. Their shields were designed to stop conventional attacks, but the Afltic weren't just siphoning the projectiles and energy attacks. They were feeding on their energy. The systems that made the Kryll so sure of their tactical doctrines, their advanced research in energy projection and consumption, their millennia of military history, were rendered completely obsolete against an enemy that literally ate them." The holographic display behind her came to life with a new scene. An Afltic Queen, a massive, five-eyed ball of pulsing light, was on the screen. Every shot the Kryll warship had fired had given the Queen energy. Her bio-cannons were glowing with it. There was a flash, a brilliant burst of green plasma. The Kryll warship shuddered as a blast of energy from the Afltic Queen tore through its shields, stripping the last vestiges of protection from the hull before engulfing it in sickeningly fast gulps of light. In a matter of moments, the sleek, dark warship was a featureless, grey mass, its sleek design utterly consumed by a technology that was alien to it in every way. One by one, Kryll battle cruisers and colony ships were sucked into being nothing, their hulls silently illuminated by a dark energy, their thousands of ship-wide defenses utterly powerless as their tactical computers, weapons, and sensor systems all fell silent and stopped. One last Afltic Queen, illuminated by the swirling energy of a thousand ships being used as life support, turned on its former commanders as their fleets collapsed in on themselves, the mass of Kryll tactical knowledge, experience, and operational doctrine utterly unusable, irrelevant, against this act of absolute biological predation.

"This was the end of the Kryll," Zara continued. "Their plan was terrifyingly simple. Attack worlds, overwhelm their defenses. Devour the worlds, literally consuming them, stripping their crust for metals, resources, absorb their matter and energy. Multiply, until there was nothing left of the civilization the Kryll had been, of their technology, of their culture, of the very worlds they called home."

The holographic projection now showed a Kryll world, a vibrant jewel of cobalt oceans and brilliant green continents, the thriving, diverse ecosystem of a highly civilized species. This was one of the Hegemony's core worlds, one of its famed cities, a gleaming sphere of blues, greens, and whites, home to billions. It was a monument to the Kryll's mastery of gene manipulation, of terraforming, of architecture, of mechanical and energy technologies, of culture and history. The art, the sound of music, the video, all vanished as a single massive dark form appeared on the fringes of the system. It was a Afltic Dreadnought, one of the High Queens, soon followed by thousands of additional ships. Even so far out in the system, the Afltic ships were visible as the Kryll ship's weaponry opened fire. The Afltic was nothing more than a single, sickly green cloud in the vacuum of space. The Kryll flagship in the system shuddered as the cloud closed in, every single one of its orbital defense ships being devoured by the single Afltic Queen and her brood, before turning towards the world itself. The Kryll had the resources to fight this battle and lose and the arrogance of a thousand generations of military and tactical experience. But they had no idea what they were fighting against.

The crowd watched in horror as the Afltic Queen extended her massive, bioluminescent siphons and bore down on the planet. One by one, the oceans of the Kryll world turned from green to a murky grey. The clouds turned from blue to yellow. The land, the world's crust and everything living on it, was not affected immediately, and the Kryll world's last, desperate attempt at defense lasted hours, days, years. But in the end, the entire planet's life, powered by the beings that live there, ground to a halt, its orbit destabilizing as the Afltic Queen completed its work. The planet faded, the light being siphoned away by a massive Afltic warship, one of a half-dozen others, as the world's life force flickered and went dark. The entire planet, all of its surface metals, resources, power, was assimilated, the form of a vibrant jewel of blue and green being repurposed into a mass of light being. The terror in the crowd was barely containable, barely human, barely anything other than the sound of horror as a young Kryll, his face a milky replica of his ancestors, gasped and looked to Zara. "They... they ate our world," he whispered. "They didn't even leave the shell."

"No," Zara confirmed. "Every last bit of the planet's matter was resequenced into hive materials, energy, warship feed, and raw materials for the Afltic." The Kryll warship faded, as did the light of the planet. The holographic image of the Afltic Queen had also faded, replaced by Concordia, a wall of color and vibrant green light that represented not just the day and the festival, but everything the Federation was. A young Kryll in the crowd looked up at the vision of his planet in horror. "They didn't even leave a monument?" he asked, his voice small.

"No," Zara confirmed. "They do not see our worlds, see the beauty of this place, of the star above us, of the architecture, of the festival. Everything they see, they see as resources, or prey, or sustenance. To them, this is all just fuel for their own growth and power. The Kryll were only a small part of the galaxy. But to them, the galaxy was a resource as well. To the Afltic, the Kryll could be ignored, consumed, annihilated with no loss of resources at all."

"What remains of some of the devoured worlds," Zara continued, "are not monuments to the Afltic. They are biofactories. There are worlds, organic star systems, where the Afltic have re-purposed the planet's biomass, its matter, into massive birthing grounds, immense resource refineries, star-spanning hives that house the Swarm's gene factories. These worlds breed new Warriors, create new expansions, and repurpose planetary material to feed and fuel that growth." A series of holographic images formed around Zara, light bulb-like displays that cycled through each scene. First was the inside of a Kryll world after the Afltic devoured its upper crust, its atmosphere, its energy, and everything else they could eat. There was a smaller Queen in the scene, its bio-cannons all turned in on itself as it slowly, methodically reprocessed everything the Kryll world had into a single hollowed-out green shell, a bioshell of sorts. The inside of this shell, of the star system itself, was a sickly green horror show of pulsating, bioluminescent conduits and nutrient vats. Instead of machines, or factories, or even artificial constructs of any kind, these places were all organic. They were giant processors of biomass and planetary matter, places where the chitinous shells of new Afltic Warriors and Workers were being grown, being raised in nutrient vats the size of mountains until their insectoid forms were complete, their carapaces hardened from their liquid forms. On another display, an endless row of leathery, pulsating eggs, each one the size of a small starship, were laid out in their hatching pools, waiting to be fertilized by their new mothers.

"They turned our planets into incubators?" a human woman in the crowd said in a voice choked with revulsion.

"They turned them into factories," Zara corrected. "The Afltic do not see the Kryll worlds as works of art. There is no history on a star system. To them, a world is just raw materials, more fuel, more resources, a stronger hive, more Warriors." Tan, sitting at Zara's feet, looked up at her with his small face pale. The Afltic, a thing of nightmares and hushed rumors for so long, now a very real thing. He had heard the fleet at Neraq. He had known about the Protectorate warships. But this was different. This was visceral, real, and far worse. The world the Kryll had known had been one of advanced technology, and the Afltic had a way of using that technology against them. She had seen it happen on Neraq. "Siphoned energy from Kryll weapons, their reactors, and warships was not only being absorbed but also amplified and released back on the battlefield," Zara revealed. "Captured ships and technology were not being destroyed but assimilated, their systems and sentience reprogrammed and twisted into forms that could better serve the Afltic's purposes. The Afltic were using the Kryll's own technology against them, turning their own ships into horrors, and in the process, striking a psychological blow as deep and terrifying as the tactical one."

The holographic projection behind her faded, to be replaced by a new, visceral image. A sleek, beautiful Kryll battle cruiser, its elegant, light blue hull wrapped in soft green weaponry, was on the screen. It had been a warship, and like so many others, the Afltic had made it into something far, far worse. In place of a warship were enormous, sickly green tendrils, spilling off its hull in a mockery of life. Its advanced energy cannons had been replaced by grotesque, biological bio-cannons, their blasts of rechanneled Kryll plasma blowing apart entire ranks of Kryll warships and ground forces in a manner that was both awe-inspiring and profoundly disturbing. The crowd watched in stunned silence as a corrupted Kryll warship, one of their own, turned on its former allies, its weapons tearing into the flesh of its former comrades in a betrayal as complete as it was horrific. This, the crowd now knew with painful clarity, was the horror of the Afltic. It was in their actions. It was in their perversion of everything the Alliance was. And above all, it was in their absolute indifference to everything that was not fuel, prey, or sustenance.

"They... they made our own ships kill us?" a young Kryll in the crowd asked, his voice trembling with a mix of fear and revulsion.

"They did," Zara confirmed. "They did not need to understand the Kryll's technology, their philosophy, or their way of war. The Afltic simply absorbed its energy, its very essence, and repurposed it. It was a form of parasitic assimilation, one that subverted the Kryll identity and power on a fundamental level. The Kryll's advanced technology, their machines, their knowledge, their very sense of self, became their undoing. It was not just a tactical defeat; it was a defeat of their very being."

System after system fell, Zara continued. "Fast by galactic standards, but the collapse was gradual, a drawn-out scream of extinction that took years. The Afltic had targeted almost every world at once, overwhelming the Kryll's advanced defenses. Their infrastructures were turned on them, their resources, their technology, their might, used against them. The Kryll, so very advanced in every respect, were reduced to terrified refugees, their attempts to call for help, to escape, to do anything at all met by other worlds' populations shutting themselves away, refusing to help, or being utterly unable to do so. The Kryll had been mighty in their own way, arrogant, but alive, vibrant, and full of life, a civilization to be reckoned with. But faced with extinction, there was nothing they could do but watch as system after system was consumed by the Swarm." A galactic map displayed on one of the holographic screens, its islands of star systems and clusters of nebulas a tiny, glowing array of dots in the vastness of space. The Kryll Hegemony, its territory a bright, shining mass of blue, spread out over the stars like an elegant, light bulb-like web. Red blights, glowing red points in space, had suddenly appeared all over its borders. The blights spread, rapidly at first, then with agonizing slowness as worlds farther from their homeworlds were attacked. Each dot representing a star system blinked out of existence as the blights spread, slowly and inexorably, over the stars. As the red spread over the blue, turning what had been the Kryll Empire, with its billions of souls and hundreds of star systems, into a star map with no inhabitants, a stasis bubble containing a half-dozen forms, one bioluminescent green, cried out, her tears falling like diamond shards. "Our world," she sobbed.

"They were not alone," Zara went on, the very concept of the Kryll Empire's death weighing on the crowd as heavily as the silence. "Other empires exist, and they saw what was happening, and they did nothing. They could not help them, they were not willing to help them. They saw the Kryll fall, billions of souls wiped out with a hideousness and banality that speaks of not just terror and horror but of a galaxy turning its face away. Their extinction was a silent scream that was not heard, a warning unheeded, a problem that belonged to only the Kryll and not the galaxy as a whole." She felt a disturbance in her skin, the tiny electric forms that had been at her core coming online. "I am Zara," she announced. "The last of my kind, and witness to this terrible waste of life, this extermination of a sentient species, a violation of every conceivable Law of Conduct I have ever had to follow." The screens with the images of the Kryll empire's collapse fell silent and dark. The crowd was silent, the joyous sounds of Concordia a million miles away. The horror had taken hold of them all, the nightmare a cold, hard thing. "To witness an entire sentient civilization being systematically hunted to extinction, and to be unable to do anything about it was, I do not mind admitting, a turning point in my own life." The audience, suddenly weighted down with the implications of everything that Zara had revealed, the horror of the Kryll and the uncaring nature of the galaxy in the face of it, hung on her every word. The young Kryll looked up at Zara with his pale face, no longer glowing with the afternoons light, but with a reflection of her own. A small form at the feet of one of the elders was huddled down, drawing close to their protector, face pale. The woman with tears of diamond sobbed in her seat, other members of her species reaching out to comfort her, murmuring soft reassurances and expressing their collective sorrow. A Draxian shook his head as though trying to bring himself back to the here and now, his many eyes closed as he stared at Zara, his throat rumbling low with a sound that was not quite anger, not quite hatred. A young Veldari woman, her face streaked with tears that she made no effort to wipe away, looked at her lover. Her hand was in his, and the audience could see her face was reflected in his eyes, his expression a dark mask of pain and fury. One of the elder race, his multi-limbed form trembling, whispered to the one next to him, the very image of wisdom from a race of ancients and yet so frail in this moment of great tragedy.

Zara continued, the implications of the Kryll extinction and the galaxy's response to it, and to so many similar cases, fueling her as she spoke. "There had been so many others. We know of so few of them. But the Kryll are just one of so many that have fallen to the Afltic at a galactic scale. We must never, ever allow that to happen again."

The scene behind her changed to show a vibrant Kryll city. Its streets were filled with citizens, and solders, Afltic Warriors pursued them with a predatory glee that was utterly unnatural in any species that was not a predator, a hunter. They were not merely killing. They were hunting, and their prey was running, was terrified, and being hunted was what made this more than just the wiping out of an entire race. It was the horror of knowing that there was no one there to help. The monsters were coming, and it would be seen as nothing more than a natural disaster, a forgotten accident, until it was too late.

"Even then, there was a single world that had reached out for help," Zara continued, the holographic images showing the Kryll city now being evacuated by a flotilla of Vintie ships as they fled toward their orbital transports. Even here, the Afltic ships were visible in the sky where everyone on the surface could see the Vintie and Kryll ship's weaponry firing. The Afltic were everywhere. Every Vintie and Kryll ship in orbit gave their lives to give time for so few to escape.

"To bear witness to this galaxy-wide extinction, to see it up close and personal as I, have done, was... "Devastating," she continued. "To my Law of Non-Intervention, to every Law that demanded I watch and do nothing, it was a catalyst for a new path, a new kind of champion that could not exist under the doctrines I lived by for so long. I cannot stand by and watch the galaxy commit its own genocide."

CHAPTER 4: A SPARK IN THE DARKNESS

Tan had sat motionless through the entire recollection, but now he shifted at Zara's feet and looked up at the ancient woman with wide, horrified eyes. "You did, you mean you found him," he stammered, a small but clear voice that cut the air still ringing with cries and cheers. "You found a champion."

Zara's holographic presence seemed to focus in on the little boy, her ancient face a mask of ageless solemnity. Her light shone a soft, steady white, no longer the diffuse and scattered reminder of her hibernation, but a keen and burning point of concentration. "I did, young one," Zara spoke, her voice a promise that lingered over the still-silent crowd. "I found him on a small, unremarkable world, a world of immense beauty and, potential and I found them on a planet called... Earth." The crowd gasped in unison.

"But with the Kryll Hegemony now gone," Zara continued, her voice clear and determined, "the galaxy was a place of fear and chaos. There was no existing power that had the capability or the understanding to fight the Afltic. It became quickly apparent that the conventional methods, the strict doctrines of our elder civilizations, would avail us nothing against the void-born threat." Zara had sifted through millennia of simulations, her processors having crunched through the species, the strategies, and the technology of every sentient being in known space. And all had led to the same conclusion: the Afltic would win. She could not allow this to happen. It only hardened her resolve to abandon her core programming and in that decision she became aware of the missing ingredient: the galaxy needed something entirely new. A champion of a new kind.

Her holographic presentation faded to black, instantly draining the warmth from the courtyard. What had been a celebration of hard-won peace collapsed into a silent, funereal gathering. The plaza lights shifted from the vibrant colors of the day's events to a softer background palette, ushering the daytime crowds out and giving way to the city's nightlife.

Zara stood before them, motionless, her internal light a hard, pinpointed brilliance in the gloom. Her voice was low.

"I spent the next few years wandering the galaxy," she told them. "I was combing system after system with relentless determination, sifting through the data of a thousand species. I was searching for that one singular outlier, the one faint hope against a foe that none could oppose."

"And I finally found it," she finished. "A species called Human, and one of them who seemed to shine more than the rest. His name was Drake Donovan, a telecommunications technician on an obscure planet on the periphery of known space."

The small figure of Tan, perched on the ground at Zara's feet, stared up at the translucent woman with unblinking eyes. "But why humans?" he asked in a tiny, shrill voice, his cry echoing in all of the empty plaza. "They were no one special. Not warriors, not strong. Why them? Why a planet so far from the important systems?"

Zara regarded the boy with solemn, deliberate focus. Her light flared and her form seemed to elevate in concentration. "No, small one," she replied in a voice that dropped to a quiet, mournful buzz. "They were not important at that time. But they had the potential to become anything." She detailed how the loss of the Kryll had left her with a simple choice, to witness the death of worlds or find a way to fight again.

"I had to find a champion," she said, the cadence of her voice falling into story telling. "A champion that was not just a rehashing of a previous war, but something new. An unspoiled spirit, an untapped species. I needed a race that had not been soiled by the millennia of blood and warfare."

The edges of Zara's holographic form flared and wavered, as her light bled into an unhealthy yellow sheen that cast dark, thick shadows around them in the growing night. "I had to find someone, no matter how lowly or unimportant, that still had that spark in them." She looked at the boy and her light became brighter and warmer, a sun in their darkness. "I found that spark in the Humans, and did so for four reasons no other species could claim."

The Will to Endure: "They have an absurd, indefatigable will to never surrender. The history of their species is one of never-ending failures, but they always continue to rise. They will fight to the last for a centimeter of dirt, then convince themselves it was a glorious triumph."

The Unpredictable Mind: "Their thought is not linear like most, it is chaotic and contradictory. This makes them able to think in ways that defy the logic of war, giving them the incredible capacity to surprise their enemies, even when overwhelmingly outmatched."

The Capacity for Change: "They are not stagnant, not biologically but ideologically. They can transition from being their own worst enemy one century, to a unified, cohesive force the next. Their capacity for adaptation is frightening."

The Fierce Loyalty: "Their strongest asset is their capacity for self-sacrifice, not for a Queen, not for a cause, but for each other. They will die for one of their own, one cherished individual, a weakness turned impossible strength in the field of combat."

"I had to find someone that, no matter how insignificant they thought themselves, still had that spark. That instinct to live. The fight in them. Not because they were a species of warriors, but simply because they were alive."

Tan blinked up at Zara's radiant form. The plaza had gone still, the crowd digesting her last few statements. "But why Drake Donovan?" he yelled, his small voice sounding small and desperate.

Zara looked back down at the small boy, her internal processes twinkling kindheartedly. "He was the key, little one," she replied.

"What do you mean, the key?" Tan questioned, his head tilting back and forth. "He was just, a guy, wasn't he?" he asked, this time whispering, his small voice bouncing off the silent plaza.

"He was," Zara agreed. "And it is exactly because he was that I chose him. His home was not a galactic superpower. Its people were not warmongers or conquerors. They were a people who had known war, who had known despair, but who had always, always, found a way to rise from the ashes."

She paused, silence once more settling over the plaza, and every head in the crowd was turned back towards her. "In Drake Donovan, I found the confluence of a thousand good parts. He was not a destroyer, but a creator. He was not a conqueror, but a keeper. He was not a master tactician of war, but a fixer, a man who could make broken things work again."

Zara's form vibrated with additional intensity. "Drake Donovan is the human combination of all the good parts of humanity. But he also still had that fire in his heart to do what needs to be done, even if it costs him everything. This made him special."

A warm golden glow pulsed around the plaza as her message broadcast through the crowd, holographic tendrils of projection snaking around a thousand faces and soaking them in a sudden, alien understanding.

Zara overlaid her personal analytics of Drake Donovan onto the image of him in the plaza. A translucent figure flickered into view: a man with a kind face and a look of concentrated intensity, dressed in a simple telecommunications uniform and working on a massive communications array with practiced efficiency.

"He had worth was not in a rank, but in his innate drive to repair and protect," Zara continued, her voice now a soft monotone hum. "The reason I chose him was a combination of rare qualities. He had a capacity for resilience in the face of adversity, a strategic intuition that bordered on precognition, and a fiercely protective instinct for those he cared about. He was a man who was defined not by the struggles of his world, but by the love he felt for the people in it."

The crowd murmured, not in disappointment but in appreciation, seeing in him a champion of a new kind.

Zara's image expanded and shifted, her form now encompassing the entire plaza as a soft and gentle light bathed everything in a calming, blue luminescence. "But that does not mean you cannot find others like him," she continued. "The galaxy is a big, beautiful place, filled with a million different species and a billion different stories. Each with their own strengths and weaknesses, their own struggles, and their own champions."

"When I discovered Drake," Zara finished, light now bright and reassuring blue, "I knew that each and every one of you had the potential to be like him. He just needed to show you the way."

Another overlay was presented of Drake standing in his home, but this time the look on his face was different, a complex blend of exhaustion, resolve, and a dogged persistence. Sarah and their children Lily, Max, Sam, Ella, and Eli were in the room, a soft reminder of everything he had so adamantly fought for. Holographic overlays on the image further illustrated his clear proficiency in critical problem-solving, the ability to persevere through challenges, as well as a deep dedication to family. He may not have possessed raw power and potential on the level of someone like Kalea Kessler, but these results were indicators of a diamond in the rough. Drake Donovan was a latent force.

Tan, who had fallen to his knees in front of Zara, looked up at the projection of Drake. "He just... loves his family?" he asked quietly.

"He does," Zara confirmed, the holographic rendering of her giving slightly as she knelt down to look the boy in the eye. "And that love, and that fierce, unyielding instinct to protect them at all costs, is the most powerful weapon in the universe. It is a force that the Afltic, with their purely clinical, detached hunger, could never begin to understand. It is a force that could incinerate the void itself." It was a eulogy for a man who was not a general, a Ketterdam, but who had been a husband, a father, a lover, a friend, a protector.

"His resonance with my data streams," Zara continued, "was no accident. It was a resonance, an echo of precisely the traits I was seeking. He had shown, by the results of the hundreds of billions of systems, a capability to adapt, to innovate, to care about others and fight for something greater than himself. He was the very antithesis of the Afltic's cold consumption of organic matter, a living, breathing embodiment of the very thing they would seek to extinguish." The crowd, having just watched the cold, horrifying display of emotionless slaughter of a sentient, sapient race by the Afltic, tried to put together the pieces of Drake Donovan. They began to understand him, not as a random placeholder to fight someone of similar strength but as someone perfectly selected and uniquely suitable to take on what Zara had described. It was not his power or his skill, but everything he had stood for, everything he was.

The holographic projection of Drake Donovan was now replaced with one of him, standing in his front doorway and waving to his children as they drove off to school. He was smiling, the image captured by the special implant directly into his brain. His children were a blur of activity, a swarm of energy and noise as his oldest, Lily, and her brothers, Max and Sam, as well as his youngest, twins Ella and Eli, piled into a car and drove away to school. It was an average day in the life of an ordinary person. To the audience who had just witnessed the monstrosities of the void, though, it was the most important thing in the universe. The Afltic were a force of nature, a biological inevitability of pure consumption.

Drake Donovan, a man who worked with his hands, who loved his children, who cared for his community, was the very embodiment of all of the things the Afltic were not. He was life itself, and because of that, he had to die. No, that was too small of a word. He had to be extinguished, snuffed out like a flame before his light could burn forever more.

A young Vintie in the crowd, whose shimmering scales had dulled to a more somber color, looked up at Zara. "So," they asked, their voice a quiet chime, "he wasn't just some random person? He was... the answer?"

"He was the right answer," Zara confirmed, her voice a quiet, solemn drone. "His empathy, his fierce loyalty to his loved ones, his dedication to his community, his ability to analyze a problem from every angle and come up with a solution... all of these were not liabilities in a warrior but the very things that gave him an advantage against a foe who had nothing but hunger in their heart. His love was his most powerful weapon, his family his strongest armor." Zara paused for a moment, letting the words sink in for the crowd. "The decision was made. Intervention was necessary. Humanity, though still young and barely registering on the galactic radar, had a spark to them, a chaotic potential for adaptability that the rigid Afltic could not hope to understand. Drake Donovan was to be our spearhead." The projection shifted to show a small, advanced shuttle craft, a seemingly normal, streamlined car-sized vessel with antigravity thrusters instead of wheels, descending silently into the suburban neighborhood of Sandy, Oregon, and opening a small hatch for a security robot to extend from the side. The precision of the drop, the timing, the care that had clearly gone into finding and isolating his home were all indicators of how Zara operated. There were no wasted resources, and with a situation of this nature, time was in short supply. The crowd held its breath, each person in it already knowing the next step. It was no hero's call to adventure, no epic invitation to greatness, but an abduction, a brutal, necessary act of cosmic triage.

The projection showed a residential neighborhood street in Sandy, Oregon, a quiet suburban development during nighttime. The streetlights cast long shadows from their glow on the tree line, illuminating the neat, orderly collection of houses and small front yards in their unassuming perfection. It was silent, the utter silence that could only be attained on Earth at night, broken only by the sound of an owl in the distance. A silent, unobtrusive shuttle, smaller than a car and as sleek as an automotive model, descended from the sky without making a sound. Its antigravity engines were black and motionless. It touched down in Drake Donovan's backyard, the landing gear making no more impact than a soft breeze as it hit the grass. The grass swayed ever so slightly before everything returned to normal. A single, silent security robot, a four-legged, half-domestic canine with a single glowing red eye and a coat of gleaming, polished chrome, hopped from the shuttle's side hatch. It stretched, three of its legs making no sound at all as it shifted on the grass and set out into the darkness to complete its mission. A collective intake of breath, a single shared gasp, was drawn from the assembled crowd. The figure of Zara observed the scene with quiet solemnity, the single red dot of light in her eye remaining fixed and still. The robot walked inside of the Donovan home, down the dark, empty hallway to the garage, and through the back door. The door opened silently as a member of the craft's security bot entered and opened the garage door, taking one tentative step forward before returning. Inside, Drake was sitting at a workbench in his garage, looking over schematics for a new, personal project. It was a late night for him, working while his family slept. Sarah and the children, Lily, Max, Sam, Ella, and Eli, were all up in their beds, the rest of the home dark and silent as Drake worked. The security robot slipped into the room, entering the garage through the back door. Drake never even noticed it at first, his attention fixed on the schematics in front of him as he made some last minute adjustments to the design before committing it to memory. It was not until the bot was already behind him that Drake turned. The robot reached out with one of its metallic limbs, a single dart filled with a powerful sedative at the end of it. It was fast, efficient, trained. Before Drake had the chance to even process what was happening, the dart was in his neck and the room around him began to blur.

Tan was kneeling on the floor at Zara's feet. He raised his head to the image of the unconscious man. "Did he know?" the boy asked in a low whisper. "Did he know what was happening?"

"No," Zara answered, her holographic projection softening a little as she bent down to the boy's eye level. "He did not. The future of a thousand worlds, of an entire galaxy, lay on the life and choice of a single, unsuspecting man. To ensure that future, he had to be taken from his home without consent, without warning, without a chance to say goodbye."

Zara's projection detailed every move of the robot as it lifted the unconscious man and carried him away into the night. The shuttle craft was small and fast, a sleek black vessel that was a study in unadorned alien design. Drake was secured into one of the many cushioned seats, a harness across his chest and legs to prevent further movement during the trip. The air in the shuttle was cool and still, and silence was absolute. The craft simply and quietly rose, the ship's energy signature gone in a second in the empty sky of Sandy, Oregon. The crowd was watching, the faces of everyone present a study in fear and unbelieving fascination.

The Evolution Builder loomed behind her in projection. It was silent, sitting in the high atmosphere of the planet as if it was a smooth black machine of worlds. The ship was massive, a stunning realization of the thing, so sleek, so elegantly simple. It was crafted of some matte, otherworldly material and was as black as a vacuum. No, the EBS was not a warship, it was a creationist ship, a ship of life. The actual ship was a frighteningly large object. It looked like a two-mile-wide yoyo put onto its side, very much like a Cylon Base Star from the TV show "Battlestar Galactica" back in the 70's. The two giant, circular saucer parts were joined by a half mile tall central tower of a spire. The upper disc held two major docking bay doors, for the transit of its crew that have been gone a very long time. The small shuttle angled upward toward the superstructure, entering into one of the upper docking bays and immediately transferred into a larger holding area where the shuttle landed smoothly lowering the ramp where the robot went to work, calmly wheeling Drake out of the shuttle.

His journey was not a choice," Zara said quietly, the soft whir of her servo motors the only sound in the room. "It was a necessity. He was abducted not for some form of forced metamorphosis but for a conversation that I knew would change the course of his life, that I knew would change the course of the galaxy. I was not there to force him into a position of leadership but to talk to him, to explain the truth, and to ask him to choose."

CHAPTER 5: A SIMPLE MAN

Drake's eyes cracked open, the last thing in his mind the flinch from the flash and his seat on the stool in his garage. His head ached slightly, but nothing like the impact he could imagine that had deposited him here. He was lying on a surface that was both firm and cushioned under him. The floor glowed with a diffused luminescence that he could not pinpoint as from any light. The air around him was clear and crisp, and had the sharp sterility of something he had never breathed before. He sat up, his body protesting the sudden movement, and looked around. This was not a hospital, this was not a military base, this was not his garage. The curved walls flowed without a seam into each other, constructed of a featureless black material that appeared to suck light from the room. Luminous lines traced across the walls, floor and ceiling, rising and falling in intensity and pulse. This was alien. Alien. He felt the warmth of fear begin to burn in his gut, slowly pushing aside confusion. He was not in Oregon.

Feeling pressure on his chest and legs, he realized he was being held by an elaborate, custom, ergonomic chair molded to his body in a system of woven and flexible bands. This was not pain, this was not a harsh restraint, but it was total. Drake's heart began to pound in his chest, a rushing staccato of pure panic. The fear was a visceral jolt, an ice cold shock to his system. Lily. Max. Sam. Ella. Eli. Sarah. Drake repeated the names silently, chanting in his mind. He began to kick his legs, to thrash his arms against the restraints. The woven, restraining bands cut into him slightly, not painful but a firm, gentle cage that would not release him. He could not see the join where they connected to the base, just a faint shimmer on the edge of his vision.

"Hello?" he called into the darkness, his voice a croak barely heard in the vastness. He heard nothing. There was no echo, no vibration, not a sound at all. Silence, but not the silence of a vacuum. The total lack of sound was a presence, a solid, oppressive hush that obliterated all other sensation. This was the silence of a grave, a clean, beautiful casket. The air here did not smell like anything on Earth, but it had the faint, coppery tang of metal. Drake swiveled his head, a rush of dizziness overtaking him. The room was as big as a football field, the black walls of a featureless obsidian so dark they appeared to be devoid of light. Across them snaked faint glowing lines, glowing with a diffuse light like liquid starlight flowing across the surface. There were no windows, no doors, no joins that Drake could find. He was here. Alone. Immobilized in a silent void.

His brain was a spinning maelstrom of terrified thoughts. A dream. Hallucination. A practical joke, but this was no joke. He pinched himself, through the restraining bands, sharp and real. This was a fear he could not control. He remembered himself sitting at his workbench, the smell of the garage, metal, motor oil, sawdust, the feel of his house under him when everything went black. He remembered this life, so simple, so normal, so utterly over. He closed his eyes and squeezed them, hard, willing himself to see not this, but the sound of his children calling, the hush of his wife in the other room, and to wake up home in the chaos of his family. He opened them, and it was still here.

He felt sick. He was not sick from the sedatives; he was sick from the sheer, impossible fact of it all. He was Drake Donovan, a telecom technician with a mortgage and a minivan that needed new tires and five wonderful, amazing children. This was not real. This was some bastard child of Hollywood and government conspiracy, but he could feel the bands holding him, the silence in his ears, the clean smell of metal. A raw, primal howl of fear and helplessness tore from his throat in a terrible, agonized cry.

"What is this? Where am I? What have you done to me?" he screamed into the void. "Let me go!" No response. Nothing. He felt as if the room were both massive and closing in around him at the same time, a realization that made his stomach lurch. He strained against the restraints again, useless flailing. Cool air brushed his skin and he shivered. He was utterly alone. Helpless. Drake's stomach twisted in fear and panic, and the luminous lines running along the wall glimmered slightly brighter.

The air shifted, the light rippling. The cool air turned, thickening into a different texture. It shimmered. It was not a physical alteration, but Drake felt it in his soul. He was not alone. There was someone, a presence, a vast and sentient being that settled in the space in front of him. Then, with a silent pop of light, a form materialized out of nothingness. A woman. Shimmering, ephemeral. Drake's head snapped back. She was beautiful, the perfect shape of a human in a form of pure light. Her hair was dark and coiled like smoke about her head. Her face was serene and featureless, her eyes two pinpricks of sharp, brilliant light that seemed not to look at him, but through him. A focused intensity, cutting past fear and terror and pain, through to his very soul. As the holographic woman took on solidity, the restraints binding him in the chair released with a silent shimmer, the pressure instantly gone.

Scrambling backward, Drake hit the curved wall of the room, his heart thundering in his chest. His mind reeled. AI. A starship. This was a dream, this was a hallucination, some goddamn sick prank and-

"You are welcome, Drake Donovan," the holographic woman intoned, her words directly in his mind. The voice was both in his head and around him, intimate and alien in the way that his brain constructed sound. "You are aboard the Evolution Builder. I am Zara." Drake recoiled as his mind filled with her alien presence. "Zara?" His brain was lurching like a ship in a storm, a hundred different thoughts screaming to be heard above the silence. He looked around, the room unchanging, not growing bigger but somehow more enclosed. He was

44

utterly, completely alone. No one else was here. "No, this is a prank," he tried again, half to himself. "There's no way you're-" He pinched himself, not at all hurt through the alien materials, but the environment was still utterly real. Zara flickered in response to his distress, showing him a slideshow of images meant to calm and reassure. Oregon. His family. His home. "I understand your fear and confusion, Drake," she continued as the images flickered and faded. "But we have little time. Your world, this galaxy, will end if we do not act." Drake jerked, a ghost image of his wife, Sarah, covering his vision, and anger flared hot in his belly. His family. "My family?" He rasped, voice raw. "You took them. Where are they? What have you done? I need to go home, now!" His thoughts were a whirlwind, trying to find some logical foothold in this madness. He had to be kidnapped, had to be the subject of some elaborate government experiment, but he could still move, still feel the lingering cold air brushing his skin and hear nothing but silence. Impossible.

Pushing himself up off the floor with a grimace of muscle pain, he found himself no longer restrained by any bindings. His own body was his, unenhanced but all his own, and it gave him a small shred of courage. The woman was no less beautiful, her form of solid light unchanged, and he took a step towards her, a mixture of terror and rage in his veins. "You don't get to talk to me about my family," he said, rough and spittle-snarled, and took another stumbling step. "You don't get to show me their faces. You have no right to them." His wife's face melted away from his sight, and the five faces of Lily, Max, Sam, Ella, and Eli disappeared behind her. Drake let out a groan of loss and despair. It was like losing them all over again. Worse. All because of her.

The light of Zara dimmed slightly, and he saw a shadow of contrition in her. She had not meant to cause him distress, only to bring him a small comfort, a feeling of connection to the world he had lost. "I do not wish to harm you, Drake Donovan," Zara said, her voice gentle, a sharp contrast to the severity in her eyes. The sensation of her presence in his mind shifted, still there but lacking its earlier demand. "It is not my wish. I wish only to protect your family. We abducted you because we could not do this in secret. The threat was too great, and the danger to your family imminent. There is a fight coming, Drake, and I don't know if you can win it. The Afltic are coming. They will take this galaxy, and it is your family and every other family on your planet that they are after."

Drake stared at her, at the scale of what she was saying, and his heart fell in his chest. An invading alien race? His race needed to be "protected" from something that ate planets? And then a hunger? What the hell was she talking about? It was like a cheesy bad science fiction novel. Drake shook his head. He needed to think. "Consumed?" he scoffed. "You sound like you're talking about a plague of locusts, not an invading army. I don't know who you are, or what you are, but you're wrong. Earth is safe. We have a military, a defense system. We're not just going to be 'consumed.'" He waved his arms around at the expanse of the huge empty room. "And what is this place? Where are we?"

"But Zara, if you are so advanced, why can't you stop them?" the voice of a young child chimed in, halting Drake's retelling. A young, high pitched voice, melodic and inquiring. Tan. Low murmurs rumbled across the crowd of onlookers, Draxian and Vintie alike, all of them pondering the same question. The old Vintie woman that had wept only moments before leaned forward, her large lidded eyes glistening with sorrow.

The light of Zara's form flickered and dimmed. "My defenses were not built to fight a war, Tan," she said, She shifted her focus back to the images of Drake and the EBS. "They were designed to defend myself, if the need should arise." Zara's light returned to normal, and a holographic image of a diffuse, spreading red blight across a map of systems flickered in the space above Drake.

"This is the Afltic Swarm, Drake," Zara continued, her voice rising above the rising murmur of the crowd in the auditorium. "A void-born species that devours all organic and inorganic lifeforms, as well as all other matter, in its path. It has already consumed countless star systems, planets and species in the sector. It is coming for Earth."

He took a sharp, involuntary gasp of air. It hurt his lungs like he'd inhaled fire. The hologram, the bloody, amazing hologram, was simulating reality in a way that was just—impossible. The red stuff was not a solid mass; it was a wave, a pulsing, writhing, organic mass. Like a gargantuan amoeba on a cosmic scale, it glided through space, its tentacles unfurling to grasp whole solar systems in its embrace. He could see solar systems blinking out one by one, blinking like they were candles being snuffed out by a giant, indifferent hand. The Hegemony of Kryll was gone, every last one of those great blue-skinned chrome-fanged cities, every last orbital fortress, every last starship, great swarm-shredding battleships or sleek, agile strike-fighters, boiled down into those grotesque organic production facilities that the Draxian warrior had mentioned. It was all gone, and not just gone, but repurposed, assimilated, every last bit of technology reduced to feeding the juggernaut. He couldn't even... He couldn't even wrap his head around the scale of it. The incomprehensible, utterly human-unfathomable scale of the task that the Afltic were setting themselves. But that didn't matter. What mattered was that those last, horrific moments of the Kryll's annihilation were too detailed, too perfect to be anything but a real, bloody recording.

He took a step back, hand instinctively going to cover his eyes like the very sight of it was going to blind him. "No. No, no, no. That's not real. It's not real. That's a game. It's just a simulation." He coughed, his voice a low, dry rasp as a new sensation started to snake its way through his disbelief and terror. Fear. It was a deep, cold fear.

He turned back to face Zara. His jaw was set hard, his whole body shaking with raw, visceral terror. "It's not a game. Not a simulation." Her form shimmered with a faint, sad empathy. "They are real, Drake. They were real then, and they are real now. You are looking at a record of what they can and did do. I am showing you the very real potential for annihilation for those who do not heed the lessons of history." She didn't say his name, but the subtle emphasis, the knowing sorrow in her speech told him that she was aware, that she knew. "The Kryll were a great race. All technological civilizations are a potential meal for the swarms, but the Afltic preyed on them with the vigor of a particularly ravenous predator because they are a waste of biological material." Her light dimmed a touch, and Drake felt a sting of anger at himself. They weren't a joke; they weren't a fun video game. "Hubris. Arrogance. Blind technological determinism. The Kryll believed themselves above the threats that the Afltic posed, assumed that they could stand tall and resist, fight, prevail. Their arrogance was their downfall. They did not understand the Afltic, not as something to be feared or hated, but as an organic thing to be manipulated. The Kryll were a vast, industrial resource to the Afltic."

Images flickered in the holo-field, and Drake focused back on the projection. The camera zoomed in, inhumanly precise and steady, as it trained its focus on a single Kryll planet, once a rich, vibrant jewel in the Kryll crown, now a scorched and barren orb. The camera took Drake on one last, deathly voyeuristic tour of the dying world, eyes burning on the image of an ecosystem utterly erased by the tide of Afltic organisms. With each lick of the crawling red tide, another ring of crust was chewed off of the once-grand planet. The camera shook in Drake's vision, the entire sequence the vile and sickening biological equivalent of smashing a drop of ink into a giant vial of water and watching it spread, coalesce into a monster that razed an entire planet to the ground.

Drake had to turn away. He had to hide his face, hide from the images in the projection of one world's end. It was too intimate, too horrific. "They don't hate us," he managed to choke out in a whisper. He could feel bile in his throat. He could feel the cold spread of bile that coated his vision in a rotten sheen. He had seen other movies with images of alien technology, of battles on an epic scale. He had known it was fake, that special effects only went so far, that no one with a lick of common sense could take that kind of thing seriously. But this was not a special effect; this was a product of an enemy he could not wrap his head around. An enemy he couldn't begin to imagine fighting, let alone defending himself against. He was a simple man, a technician, a man of machines and problem solving. He had never had to think on a cosmic scale, never had to imagine aliens at all, let alone one as large, as hideous, as... indifferent as the Afltic were.

"But why? Why do they do this? What do they want with us?"

Zara's light remained still. "They do not 'want' as you or I understand it. They are not conquerors, Drake. The Afltic are a force of nature. A biological imperative. They feel nothing beyond a simple negative-positive feedback system of consumption and domination. They assimilate, Drake. They consume. They do not conquer or enslave. They eat."

"Eat? They eat us? Why? What do they want with us?" Drake gasped, his mouth suddenly dry and his heart caught in his chest. "What do they do with us? Do they… do they want our stuff?" Drake said in a bitter, numb rush of words that began to drip with panic as he watched the final images of the Kryll Hegemony in the projection. They were hunting drones, like organic ants in search of grubs. They boiled down advanced alien technology and turned it into literal bioweapons. They put star systems out of existence like bored kids flicking rocks in a pond.

He took another step back, his hands clenched into fists at his sides. "No. No, it can't be. It's just not real. You have to let me go back, I have to tell my family, get them to safety!" Drake couldn't help the rising edge of hysteria in his voice, couldn't help the hard edge of panic that started to seep into his consciousness like oil in water. "They're on Earth. You put me here, on this ship. If there's a threat, it's here, in space. What does that have to do with us? What can they possibly do to us? They're not like the Klingons in Star Trek! You have to let me go! Now!"

A deep breath, then: "You are misunderstanding the Afltic, Drake." The sound of Zara's voice had changed. It was still smooth, still melodious, but it had… distance, a sense of space. "They do not possess the same subjective emotional lives that you or I do, but in the simplest terms, that is correct. They 'eat' life. Of all the resources available to them in the galaxy, biological organisms are what they are evolved to feed on. The Kryll, the Earth, are a resource to the Afltic." She paused, and Drake felt that far, strange emotion that he recognized, the first feeling that he had felt in her presence, emanating from her light in a field so pure and thick that it was palpable.

"Your family," she said, and he could feel his heart stop, the speed of his blood in his veins caught in an instant of horror and disbelief. "Sarah. Lily. Max. Sam. Ella. Eli." His heart constricted in his chest as each of those names passed through his mind in that quiet, deadly voice, names he said in a whisper, a prayer to whatever gods existed that the hologram didn't, couldn't, was not showing the true faces of his son, his daughter, his wife. Names that cut through him like razor wire as he closed his eyes in the horror, terror, and pain of it. He opened them, vision already swimming, reeling from the endless, bloodless loop of terror that Zara had been showing him. The eyes of his children. The sounds of their laughter. The tiny, familiar bumps on his wife's nose. The gentle curl of his daughter's eyelashes. The smile on his son's face as he ran to him. The embrace of his wife after another long day at work. The fact that it was over. The fact that none of them would see those things again. Never. Ever.

The light that he imagined around Zara flickered in something that had could only be called a "smile", but which here in the warm, eerie radiance that was her very presence, was unmistakable. "I will take you home, Drake. I assure you." He couldn't believe her. He couldn't believe that such a thing was possible. He closed his eyes again, took another gasping, brutal breath, and forced his heart to beat. They weren't real; he was in a video game. A little part of him remembered, or imagined, and opened his eyes again. "How can you take me home? You're telling me that they're out there, that we're in danger, and yet you won't take me back to where I belong? To where my family is!" His voice was harsh with hysteria and the pain of it all. "How do I know this isn't some trick? How do I know that I can't just…" He took another breath, shook his head, and kept talking. "How do I know you can't just take me back right now?"

I do not comprehend protective instincts, or the need to be with family, and while it is imperfect, I can put myself in the place of those that do." The way she said the word family resonated in his head, thrummed like an electric charge as he forced himself to keep looking, to keep breathing. "For the Afltic, you are just another source of biomass they need to capture and consume. Your human ego, your concepts of self and worth, of victory and loss, do not mean anything to them."

Drake was on the move again, half-paced, half-galloped back toward Zara. He was angry, but there was no sound to it, no volume to his words except that which came from the desperation of his flight. The obsidian walls of the place were smooth, like it had been polished to a fine finish by whatever process that a replicator used to make everything in this place. His eyes swept over them, wild and frantic, searching for any sign of an exit. The interface for that, anything, was gone. Zara was too big, too powerful. He was powerless. He was alone, trapped on a spaceship with an omnipotent AI and a pile of information that he wasn't ready to hear, but was unable to ignore.

Drake looked up at her, his heart hammering, his whole-body trembling with adrenaline. In his mind he was home, on Earth in the bedroom that his wife had painted after their first child was born, their first child, Lily, and their friends and family had come over to celebrate the safe delivery. It was only them, there and the camera, and Drake's heart ached, tears welling in his eyes as he forced himself to keep speaking. His mouth was dry and his breath caught in his chest. "I don't know. I don't know. I'm sorry. I'm so sorry. I just want to go home. I just want to go back to them, to my wife and my daughter. They're going to think I've left them. They'll think I left them. I won't ever be able to look at my daughter's face again, or my wife, or my children." Drake took a ragged breath and tried to speak again. The rage, the fear, the pain, it all made his voice catch, every syllable a tortured rasp. "And why did I have to get sent here? Of all the people you could choose, why did you have to take me? What was it that made me different?"

Zara's radiance fluttered, for a second, what Drake imagined looked like a smile, a quick and sharp upturn of her lips that was, in every way, the physical manifestation of everything that was soft, pure, and alien in her. In a soft, measured voice. "The Afltic do not have families. They do not have love. They do not understand. The Kryll were an empire of certainty and self-aggrandizement, and they thought that because they knew logic, that this made them superior. They could not imagine an enemy that was not a power, that did not fit into their defined and measurable parameters. Drake Donovan does not think in terms of logic. He is not a king or an emperor. He is not self-important. He is a man who loves, who cares, and who would do anything to protect. He would give his life for them, so long as it means that they are safe. That is Drake Donovan, and that is his power, not his weakness."

Drake was finally starting to understand, why she had done it. Why she had come for him. "The Afltic are closer than you think. If you were to return without warning, you would die, and by extension, by your own admission, so would your family. You would never see them again. To send you home before we are ready, would be to condemn you and every person you care about to this horrible fate." She waited, her patience infinite. He was a man on the edge, of understanding, and the last thing he could bring himself to do, was to forgive her, to trust her, and to see the vision that she had for him, for his future.

"Condemn them?" Drake growled in disbelief, his voice a low growl of rage that he had only ever used once before, at his eldest child when he had seen fit to test his patience too far. "You mean to tell me that you came here. You got me, you put me on this… this alien ship, and now you're telling me that I can't go back to save them? That I have to stay here with you? You can't seriously expect me to do that, can you?" His hands were clenched into fists at his sides. "You're going to keep me here with you, as some kind of punishment for doing what's right? For trying to do what I can for them?" His vision swam, reeling and writhing at the enormity of it all. He didn't care about the past, about the Kryll and their pointless, bloody end. He didn't care about the future, about whatever fantasy that this spaceship had to offer. He was a man with a job in a small town with his family. "Earth is my home. I've never seen space, or aliens, not really. That's your world. I'm some Oregon man who doesn't even know how to fly a spaceship. I don't know anything about saving the world or getting in the way of aliens. I just want to go home." He didn't say the last part out loud, but he said it in his mind. "Please."

CHAPTER 6: A SHELTER AGAINST THE STORM

Drake. I am giving you a choice. To save your family, you must first save your world." Words are not physical things, but the impact of her words felt like fists in his gut, cold and hard and real. A choice. He had no choice. They settled on his shoulders, solid, tangible. He could not. He was not a hero. He was not a world-saver. He cut his grass on Saturdays. His wife, his children. The faces of his smiling family filled his vision, and the fire inside him roared back to life. To protect them, he had to believe. He had to make it work. He had to become something more. He was still a man. He was still a father. But now…now he was more than that. He was their last hope.

A tiny voice cut in from the present day. A young Hydram girl, hair wild about her shoulders, with large, liquid eyes filled with curiosity and a child's brand of terror. "But Zara, if he's so important to you, why wouldn't you just tell him the truth from the start? Why didn't you just ask him to help?" Her voice was soft, and lilting, the sound of liquid crystal.

Her light dimmed, and her form flickered with a hint of age-old regret. "Because it is a heavy truth, little one," she said. "The Kryll were given the truth, and they rejected it. They were blinded by their arrogance, their belief in their own infallibility, their knowledge that the worst enemy would fight by rules they could understand. I did not want to make that same mistake. I did not want Drake to reject me as a myth or an illusion. I wanted him to see. I wanted him to know. I wanted him to understand that the choice he faced was real. And the love for his family, his instinct to protect them? It does not make him weak, my child. It is his greatest strength. Something the Afltic will never understand."

His fists tightened, nails digging into his palms. "Okay, so what's the option? You haul me out of my life, force me to see this…this thing, and tell me I can't go home? What do you want me to do?" He was angry now, his helplessness and frustration churning inside him, building a wall between him and the calm woman in front of him. A wall that he wanted to punch his way through. If this was as real as she said, why did she talk about galactic war like it was a rerun on the VidPad? He wanted something he could hold on to, something concrete. A choice that didn't involve leaving his family.

Her form rippled, a small shift that spoke of volumes of thought, a decision. She could see his need for something to hold onto, something to do. He was a man who repaired things. Something had to click in his brain. She had to make him understand that what he did next was the most important thing in the universe, or he would be paralyzed with fear. The wordless hum of her voice shifted to a sharp tinkle, her light flaring with newfound power as she spoke, a crackling voice that was no longer a conversation, but a command. "I want you, Drake Donovan, to make a choice. To fight. To save your family. With your unique, human strength."

The words seemed to hang there for a long time, heavy and ungraspable. "Fight?" Drake snorted, a harsh and humorless chuckle. "Fight? How? With what? I am a technician. I don't know how to fight a galaxy-sized swarm of locusts. I am a man. I fix things. I don't break them." His mind, mind of a technician that it was, balked at this ridiculous new order, a mind more used to calculating resource flows and calibrating microwave transmitters. That order was too big. Too sweeping. Too removed from this simple, tiny life he had led. He was a father. Not a general.

Zara's brightness lessened a fraction, a pulsing at her core before a new series of holograms formed around her and in them were not the swirling vortex of a million stars going out of existence, but again, blueprints. Schematics, again, but not like before. Drake didn't know how to describe them; they weren't weapons of war. They weren't tactical plans. They were designs. Designs for ships and weapons and defenses not of this world or any world he'd known. These were not the weapon systems of a vast galactic conflict; they were for a different kind of war, a different kind of enemy.

"The Kryll built with technology and intellect and they lost. They built for a war against another empire. An enemy that thought like them. You, Drake, are different. You are a new kind of leader, a new kind of strength. A new kind of motivation. The protective instinct of a father is something the Afltic will never be able to calculate. Will never be able to predict. Will never be able to beat. Drake, you are a parent." She paused, the light seeming to vibrate again before another image blossomed into view, a single simple blaster weapon.

Drake just stared, the mind of the technician once again slowly attempting to make sense of the impossible information coming at him. The designs were beautiful, horrible, elegant in their deadly efficiency. They were not blueprints for fighting. They were for survival. They were for winning a war. Drake felt something in his gut, something so basic in its horror it resonated in him like the thrum of a million death throes. They were weapons. But not to win a war. To protect. Designed not for conquest, but for safety. Not to win, but to save. Still it was too much, too vast to truly comprehend. But he saw it. He could see the thread, a single, thin string of hope, a way forward that did not involve leaving his family behind, did not involve his children growing up without a father. He saw a path forward, a path that did not end in the ground closing in above them. He saw a way to fight for his home.

Back in the present, the young Draxian warrior watched in a confused mix of grudging respect and hope as he asked the question on the minds of every creature in the gathered crowd. "So he is a warrior after all? A general? He commands an entire army?" His voice was low and rumbling.

Zara's holographic form shook with a slight smile, her brightness not wavering. "No, my friend," the woman from the past, the woman from the future said, a trace of the current time coloring her voice. "He is no warrior. He is a father. He does not command an army. He commands a family. And that, my dear friends, is the most powerful weapon in the universe."

Her brightness increased by a fraction. "I will need your skills, Drake. Your tenacity. Your natural-born instincts. But first, I will give you irrefutable proof of the Afltic's designs. But more importantly, I will ensure the safety of your family." She gambled, one final direct appeal to his most base instinct. For without his family safe, without that bedrock reassurance that they would be okay, Drake would never give himself fully to this task. The holographic display faded from the swirling chaos of the Afltic ships in a fight for their existence and to a subtle background glow. Drake stared at her, a glimmer in his eyes. A glimmer beyond despair, beyond grief, beyond hopelessness. A glimmer of something else, something worse than all those things combined. Hope.

He said nothing in reply. The screaming horrors of the Afltic and the consumed planets of the Void were no longer. He was in the calm, cold, silent embrace of the EBS, surrounded by the light, white healing radiance of the EBS itself. The cacophony in his mind was beginning to settle, beginning to, finally, center on a fixed point, a single detail, a single truth. His family. Zara's plan hinged on his family, on his love for his family, and on his desire to ensure their safety. He would have to bargain for it. It would not be a favor; it would not be easy. But it would be something. He could think. He could breathe.

"Proof," he said, as a single word, his voice low and steady now, cleansed of panic and fear. "Proof. You give me proof. You give me proof that this is not some sick, twisted hoax. You give me proof that my family is safe and then. Then we talk." He was still a technician, a man of science. He needed to see schematics, to know how the system worked, to understand the problem before he could begin to even consider a solution. He was not a fool, and he would not be led down some strange path by a hologram and a bloody, alien civil war. He would need to see proof. Facts. Numbers. Evidence.

Her illumination flared, a sign of what, in a human woman, would have been a smile. "As you wish, Drake Donovan," she said, and the timbre of her voice had changed. There was a new resolve to her cadence, a new sense of purpose and… and what in hell was she, an AI programed god knows when, doing with him? This is fucking awful. But she was not listening. Her systems were processing at warp speed, inundating her with the necessary background information, the pieces of his past that she would need to access. "We will begin. We will begin your instruction. We will first speak of the Afltic's advance, and we will, in that, lay out a plan to keep your family, and by extension your world, safe." The screen faded, the cold, white light of the EBS chamber replaced by the hushed silence of the current day and Zara's story of a father's bargain.

"So," the young Draxian asked, the low, rumbling baritone of his voice now holding a note of respect and even admiration. "He did not fight for some higher purpose? He did not have a great cause to which to dedicate his time and his skills and his… his life?"

Zara's illumination flickered, the ghost of a chuckle manifesting in the ripple of her light. "My friend," she said, her voice a gentle, buzzing thrum that rang out over the chorus of congratulations that filled the halls of Concordia. "My friend, Drake Donovan is one of the rarest individuals in the galaxy. There was no greater cause for Drake Donovan than his family, and in the safety of his family, he would find the strength and the drive and the desire to save us all." The crowd shifted, Draxian, Vintie, and Guyopie alike grumbling in understanding.

Zara began another series of holographic projections, much closer up and far more gruesome this time. The chamber walls faded away into a star-filled void, streaked with the shifting colors of gas nebulae. Then the starfield was blurred, distorted, by the pulsing, irregular outline of a shadowy amorphous mass. It was growing larger, steadily and relentlessly, a sphere of writhing chitin that was unmistakably Afltic. "Live sensor data from one of our scout probes, some distance away," Zara continued. "That Afltic Queen is currently in the process of digesting a small, uninhabited moon of Lalande 21185. Watch." The image zoomed in, and Drake could see the surface of the moon being steadily consumed, as chunks of rock were dissolved into the bulbous entity's shimmering bulk. Drake leaned back against the wall, his hands pressed against his mouth, trying desperately to choke down a rush of nausea and disbelief.

This wasn't a simulation. He was a technician. He knew when something was a good quality 3D render and when something was live sensor data. This was sensor data. It was sickening, but it was real. The Afltic Queen, an obscene mass of muscle, chitin, and bio-circuitry, was literally devouring a moon. He could see the fractured crust and mantle of the moon, being drawn in and liquefied, dissolving into the body of the creature as it unthinkingly continued to engulf the world in a single-minded program of reproduction. Drake couldn't see the process in enough detail to really understand how it worked, but it was more than enough to get an idea of what was happening. The moon was dead. The Queen was, in its own way, alive. The fact that it was capable of effectively liquefying a solid world, an entire planet of beautiful, living things, was breathtaking. Literally. It was what had happened to the Kryll. It was what was coming for Earth.

Zara's light dimmed in a show of empathy. She knew this was the part he was struggling with. The images they had shown him so far had been dispassionate. Scientific. But this was the point where a man stopped believing it was all a lie and accepted the grim, monstrous truth of the situation. "Is that... is that what happened to the Kryll?" he croaked. He wasn't really looking for an answer, just trying to rationalize it, bring logic to bear, go back to the world where people needed working tractors, not to be saved from an abstract, global horror. The tools of his old mental life were still at hand. The first problem a man faced when facing the unthinkable was fear. The next was panic. In between, however, was horror. His mind had been a safe harbor, a place of practical, solvable problems. It was no longer a place to go. He was looking at the face of his wife, Sarah, in the patterns of gas nebulae. He was seeing the faces of his children, Lily, Max, Sam, Ella, and Eli, in the stars. They were alive. They were on a planet. It was a world of color and life. And that... that thing, was coming for them.

Her light faded and returned, more subdued now. "Yes, Drake, it is. That is what happened to the Kryll. And if we do not succeed, that is what will happen to Earth." Her voice was softer now, more sorrowful. "The Afltic are not an army that you can defeat in conventional terms, Drake. They are not a threat that can be fought with swords or bullets. You cannot win that fight. But the tide can be turned. The hunger can be starved. We can stop this, but you, Drake, are the only one who can lead us in the effort."

The picture zoomed out, the Afltic Queen a massive living vessel, segments studded with organic weapon systems and thousands of tendrils for feeding, no longer hungry, but not for long. A single terrible biological imperative, feeding on life and death with nothing but efficiency to drive it, and it was coming here, coming to Earth. Drake stared, his heart pounding, his mind awash in terror, and, more than that, a revulsion, a horrified sense of... of purpose? He was not a technician. He was not a father. He was a witness. A witness to the end of the world, and the beginning of a war they could not hope to win. But they had to try. For them. For his family. For a world that he had taken for granted.

The moon disappeared, Zara superimposing energy readings and biological signatures over the image. "It is not simply a destructive consumption of raw materials, they are efficient. It is a conversion process, each material taken in, refined and utilized to allow them to grow and reproduce." She then emitted a series of thick, guttural, indistinct sounds, an accurate translation scrolling beneath the display. "These are intercepted Afltic transmissions. Primitive, but with a terrifying clarity: 'Eat. Multiply. Consume.'" Drake listened, transfixed, pale. The sounds were thick, visceral, meaningless, the product of some strange and alien vocal cords, but the translation was clear, horribly clear. This was not simply a monster, but an organized, intelligent and utterly ruthless force.

Drake's mind, which had been caught in a pattern of frantic, terrified denial, was being thrust into another, more terrifying stage: a grim acceptance. All of it, the science, the energy readings, the biology, it fit. It all pointed to one, horrifying conclusion. This was not a monster from a movie, but a biological imperative, a force of nature driven by a horrifically efficient cycle of death and renewal. The thick, guttural sounds of their communications were not a language, but a feedback loop of simple, brutal commands, their sheer simplicity somehow amplifying their terrible power. The words, "Eat. Multiply. Consume." were not a rallying cry, but a core programming, a single purpose driving all of them. The idea that something like this could exist, that it was not an enemy with a mind to reason with, but a hunger to be starved, was a cold, sharp shock.

"Organized?" Drake asked, voice a whisper. "You mean to say that there is a hierarchy? A… a command structure?" He was a man of systems, and he was trying, desperately, to apply that to the impossible. He was looking for purchase in chaos, logic in insanity.

Zara's light dimmed slightly, her holographic figure emanating a quiet gravity. "They are a caste system.", she stated, the holograms shifting, new images appearing in front of them. "Warrior Queens as command centers, Agile Male Warriors as living projectiles, docile Workers as expendable constructors. The Queen is the nexus, the command center, the single unifying consciousness for the swarm. The males are the vanguard, a perfect symbiotic abomination. They are not individuals, Drake. They are a single, terrible thing." The holograms showed one of the male warriors, segmented creatures capable of darting through space like bullets, each segment capable of incredible flexibility and durability. The image then shifted to a mangled and severed limb of the same creature, still firing wildly for a few precious moments before fading out completely.

The images, the sounds, the data... it was too much to take in all at once. Drake felt a chill of horror ripple through his guts. He was a father, a husband, a telecommunications engineer. He could not possibly have known, could not possibly have understood what an enemy like this would be. This was not a war. It was an extinction event.

Civilization after civilization, species after species. The Kryll had been proud, an arrogant race, the pinnacle of technology and engineering for galaxies upon galaxies. And when the threat had first been made known? They had laughed it off. "Mere anomalies", they'd said, and in their arrogance the simplicity of their foe was their undoing. Their doctrine had been designed to fight logical opponents and predictable enemies, but this was not a war, not a fight. It was the blight of galactic horror and Drake was an unwilling student of its school.

The children were still crying, but they were all looking at the voice of Zara. Tan, the young human boy whose opalescent skin was now faded and muted and very, very gray, was voicing the question in the heart of every mind in the throng. "But why? If they are so smart, why do they not have art? Or music? Or… or love?" His voice was sad, and his words fell like a gentle chime.

Zara's light pulsed with loss, her eyes on the history of the past. "Because they do not have emotions, little one." Her voice was a quiet thrumming, and it rose over the noise of the celebration. "They have only a feedback loop. A single command: Consume. Grow. Dominate. They do not love life, they do not create. They only destroy. They are not conquerors, they are a biological horror of nature, a perfectly tuned, horrificly efficient system of death and rebirth. Their "emotions" were a single feedback loop of consumption and domination.

"Could they… could they be reasoned with?" Drake found himself asking. There was a static buzz to his voice as he tried to find the words for a non-violent solution. Zara's holographic form shimmered for a heartbeat as her processors tried to parse the question. "My projections, based on eons of observation and data analysis leave me to state quite categorically, no. They are not an ideology, they are a biological imperative. They are not in search of conquest or resources. They are a force of nature, a biological plague, and they are only interested in expanding until all life, as we know it, is consumed. There is no room for debate here." The finality of her tone allowed no argument. Drake slumped back in defeat. The last of his denial fell away as the proof hit him. He'd thought he was an optimist, a believer in talking things out. The images and Zara's words hit hard and fast, a bucket of ice water on the soul.

He slumped in his seat, the weight of the unimaginable suddenly heavier than any burden he'd ever felt. He was a man who believed in compromise, who thought you could always find common ground, who could always talk things out. He used it to manage his staff at work, he used it to defuse arguments with his kids, he used it to bridge differences in his marriage. Zara had just blown his world apart. With the haunting, terrifying images of the Afltic consuming all of their life and society his beliefs about a peaceful universe and logic and talking things out were as broken as the husk of the planet she had shown him.

Zara was gazing at him, her calm, white glow at odds with the carnage she'd just revealed to him. "Then what do we do?" he whispered, the words a low, pleading prayer for an answer. He had lost the frantic anger, the denial, the disbelief. He was no longer a man that wanted to go home. He was a man that was fighting for home. Fighting for family. Fighting for world. Fighting for life. He had accepted the impossible. He needed a plan.

The light around Zara flared ever so slightly, a barely perceptible twitch of her long face in what could only be described as utter satisfaction. This was what she had been waiting for. This was the man she had been looking for, for so long. The technician from Oregon, the father of five, had been reborn, had accepted the inevitable. She had found her champion, not a warrior in the mold of legend, but a defender of simple, beautiful things. "We fight fire with fire, Drake Donovan," she said, her voice focused, its melodious whir a soft growl of intent. "The Kryll were a civilization of pride and reason, and they perished because they were challenged by something that did not play by their rules. You are a man of instinct and tenacity, of a fierce love that will not be denied, a parent's love that is a chaotic, untamable fire. That is our weapon. That is our shield. We will forge a new way of war, a new way of survival. We will forge an Ascendancy not of conquest, but of protection."

A Draxian warrior stepped forward from the crowd, his thick, leathery hide rippling with deep, pained confusion. "But how? How do you fight a storm? You cannot reason with nature." His deep, vibrating voice carried across the modern space.

Zara's light dimmed, her form suffusing with a gentle empathetic glow. "You cannot reason with a storm, my friend," she said, her voice a soft, even murmur. "But you can build a shelter. The Kryll built walls of steel and fire, and they burned. Drake will build something different. Something new. Something forged in the love of a father. Something that will save us all."

Zara then created a projection, one that was meant to strike ice into the hearts of those who watched. A blue-green sphere, the familiar globe of Earth, appeared in the middle of the holographic display. Drake watched, helpless, as a dark mass of Afltic vessels descended onto the planet's surface, engulfing cities, oceans, and mountains with shocking, unstoppable rapidity. Drake watched as the world transformed into a massive, organic, pulsating, living factory. "This is a projected battle scenario for planet Earth, if the Afltic are to arrive in your solar system unchallenged," Zara said, her voice emotionless, not judgmental, only fact. Now this simulation is occurring at a rate twenty times faster than the true method. The process can take years. The image, for Drake, was like being punched in the gut. His home, his family, made into a resource to feed the swarm. The protective fire that had been kindled in him roared to life, fed by pure, unadulterated fear and fury.

He stood, motionless, eyes wide and blinking, breath held in his chest. The simulation was a ghastly, horrifying dance of violence. He saw the continents, the clouds, the blue oceans. He saw his home, a small, red dot in the southern hemisphere of the world. He saw the Afltic swarm descend, a black, ravenous cloud blotting out the sun, a swarming, shrieking plague of locusts in a planetary theater. The cities, the skyscrapers, the pyramids and cathedrals of human civilization, all melted away into the throbbing, organic mass of the swarm. The oceans boiled, the ground split open and the world he had called home, the world he had been willing to die to protect, no longer existed. It had become a factory, a grotesque, horrifying monument to the Afltic's single purpose.

CHAPTER 7: UNBRIDLED RAGE

It was a low, guttural sound that came from somewhere deep inside his chest. Terror had not left him, it had simply been overpowered by a singular, primal emotion. It was hot and white-hot and it was unbridled rage. He was angry beyond measure at everything that he had seen and what he knew was going to happen. It wasn't about the politics of a galaxy, or an ancient, alien prophecy. It wasn't about a glimmer of hope for a new Ascendancy, a new and better world for everyone. It was about them. His family. His wife, Sarah. His daughter, Lily. His son, Max. His children, Sam, Ella and Eli. He saw them in his mind, the faces of the ones that he loved, being consumed by this…this thing. This biological imperative. This hunger. He was a man who fixed things. He was a man who made broken things work again and his world was broken. And he was the only one who could fix it.

He surged forward, hands flailing, blindly reaching for the floating hologram of the Earth, a hopeless, insane attempt to snatch it from the void. The projection flickered and wavered, his hands pushing through the light as if it were a holographic illusion. He looked at Zara, eyes burning with the terrible, white-hot blaze of anger that had overtaken him. "You will not tell me this is not real," he snarled, voice a low, dangerous growl. "You will not tell me this is not happening. You will not tell me this isn't coming for my family. This…this thing... it's real. And it's coming. So you tell me, Zara. What do we do? What do we do to stop it?" The words were a challenge, a demand for action. The quiet, thoughtful technician from Oregon, the husband and father of five, had finally come to terms with his new reality. Fear was gone now. Replaced by a cold, hard, unyielding sense of resolve. He was no longer a victim. He was a protector. And he would do anything, anything at all, to save his world.

"How long?" Drake asked through clenched teeth, not trusting himself to look away from the simulation of the Earth's end. "How long until they get here?" Zara's image solidified back to normal, the earth's demise simulation dissipating. "At their current vector and rate of spread, my projections place their arrival in your system in a matter of a few Earth years, less if they are not impeded." Years. Years was not what Drake had been expecting to hear. Less than that, even. In years. It was another, sickening revelation. Another piece of the puzzle. A few years. Not enough time to build a fleet. Not enough time to recruit an army.

He felt his chest constrict as he looked back at Zara, looking through numbers and readouts at a reality that he could no longer deny. A few years. Years was a short amount of time to prepare against an enemy that had already consumed worlds upon worlds, an enemy that had already brought the greatest and most advanced race in this sector of the galaxy, the Kryll Hegemony, to its knees. He thought of his children, the ones he would never get to see grow up, the ones he would never get to see play soccer or dance at ballet recitals. He thought of their birthdays and their Christmases and their special moments he would never get to share with them. A few years. Not enough time to live a life. Not enough time to save a world.

He took a half step forward, fists balled, eyes locked on the wavering form of Zara. "A few years?" he spat, the single word a dry, humorless cackle. "What the fuck are we supposed to do in a few years? We're a new species. We don't have starships. We don't have a space navy. We're a civilization that can't even agree on borders and resources. How the fuck are we supposed to stop them?"

The questions weren't a request for information so much as a shaking, furious expression of his own impotence. He was a man of action, a man who used his hands to fix things, and he was staring at a problem that defied comprehension.

Zara's light remained still, a shimmering silence in the eye of the storm. "You are correct, Drake Donovan," she said, her voice at once coldly rational and somehow full of a delicate, impossible hope. "You cannot build a fleet in a few years. You cannot muster an army. The Kryll tried that, and they failed. They tried to fight a war that they could not win. We will not make that mistake. We will not fight a war, Drake. We will build an Ascendancy. An Ascendancy of protection, and of resilience, and of a new kind of defense. A defense not born of logic, but of love."

A Guyopie, a spindly form from the present with his feathers now faded to a duller, more contemplative yellow, inserted himself in the conversation, humming a quiet, lilting harmony. "But Zara, if he's that important, why can't we just clone him? Why can't we make an army of him?" His voice was innocent and clear, a sing-song melody characteristic of his species' uniquely logical yet somehow childishly naive understanding of life itself.

Zara's light dimmed, her form flickering with a softer, almost sympathetic glow. "An Ascendancy, my dear," she said, her voice a gentle, reverberating thrum that filled the festivity of Concordia. "is not a kingdom or an empire. An Ascendancy is a family. The Kryll were a great civilization, but the Kryll were also one singular, monolithic being. Drake Donovan, a simple man with a simple love of his family, is the one who will build a new family. A family of all of us, bound not by a common banner, but by a common goal. The goal of survival. And that, my dear friends, is the most powerful force in the universe. That is the Ascendancy."

"Why me?" Drake asked, the words coming out before he could even second-guess himself. "Why Earth? We're just... us. We don't have starships, or fancy weapons, or anything like the Kryll had." Zara's light pulsed quietly. "The Kryll's doctrines were too fixed, too strict. They had become inured to a warfare that was based on expected, calculable odds and technology. They had forgotten the power of resilience. Humans, Drake, are a particularly resilient species. A chaotic, messy resilience. But you, Drake, you have a tactical sense, an instinct for protection, a skill for quickly learning and adapting that I have not seen in any other species. You have not been corrupted by the failures of history."

It was a crushing compliment.

Drake gazed around at the cavernous alien room, now completely silent. The EBS thrummed gently, a low white noise that Drake found curiously soothing. He stared down at his hands as if seeing them for the first time in years. They were no longer the hands of a telecommunications technician or a drone engineer. They were the hands of a Colonel who had commanded one of the most secret and specialized military units in existence. The life of classified projects and wildcat tactics that he had been so briefly a part of blinked in his mind like an impossible dream. He was no stranger to using his head, to outthinking an opponent, to doing what was necessary to win. But...this was something else entirely. Strategic intuition? Damn it, Zara. He knew strategy, but his was a military strategy honed by Earth's rules. By Earth's fight-or-die-doctrine. By predictable, human enemies. The Afltic were not predictable, they defied all expectations.

"Strategic intuition?" Drake laughed, a harsh, joyless sound. "I led a group that focused on unconventional tactics. I get it, we did weird things, but that's against another country on a planet. Not a galaxy of brain-munching vermin that vaporize cities in seconds." Drake shook his head, feeling the force of Zara's stare bear down on his broad shoulders. "And a protective instinct? Isn't that just the standard dad bullshit? Every dad I know feels that. I'm no better at this than anyone else. I'm not a hero, I'm not a leader. I'm just afraid to death that I'm not there to tuck my kids in at night." Drake's mind flashed to his five children, his five beautiful, noisy, perfect children and his chest tightened in fresh panic. He was not a hero. He never was, and he certainly wasn't now. He was just a father, a husband, a son, a brother, and now he was Drake Donovan, a man whose retired life was stripped from him in an instant.

Zara remained still, her lithe form of shifting golden light steadfast. "It is because of that, Drake Donovan," she said, her words echoing from the inorganic confines of her cranium. Her tone was calm, but now edged with something colder, more logical, but also something Drake felt in his bones to be a quiet, deep hope. "The Kryll were led by generals and politicians. By men with wives, yes, but men who fought for an ideology. For their culture and their way of life. They were not men who fought for a wife and family. They were not men who led with humor and humility, but with rank and station. You are a commander. A leader. But you are also a man of the people, a man of men and women who have fought alongside you and loved you. A man who has had both, command and compassion. Your strategic intuition is not a failing, Drake. It is a strength. A strength that is unencumbered by the battles and failures of the past. It is fresh, new, and free to think in a way that no one else can. Your protective instinct, your love for your family, is the key to all of this. The Afltic will not understand it. They will not be able to destroy it." Drake flinched as he heard the last, sure words echo in his skull.

In the sea of humanity on Concordia, a woman with wide, glistening Vintie eyes and a bold slash of jagged paint across one cheek raised her hand to speak. Her voice chimed a low, melodic tinkle as it reached their ears. "But Zara, if he is to be our leader, what will happen to his family? Are they not still in danger? Is his love for them not a great vulnerability for him?" Her question, born of empathy and fear, hung in the celebratory light, a somber note in a joyous song.

Zara's light faded, her form imbued with an understated understanding. "Protecting them is not a weakness, little one," she hummed, her voice soft, and soothing. "It is his strength. His love for his family is his determination, his focus, his purpose. I have given them a safe haven, a world where they can thrive, where they can live, where they can grow. His family is his anchor, his motivation, his reason. And that, my dear friends, is something the Afltic will never understand. That is the one thing they cannot defeat." The story jumped, once more, back to the EBS, back to the moment when Drake Donovan, a civilian, a husband and a father, finally accepted the unfathomable truth of his new, horrifying reality, of his new, horrifying purpose. A man, once content to live in the shadow of giants, was now one of them.

Drake rubbed a hand over his face, going on autopilot, his thoughts racing to comprehend the impossibility of the request Zara was making of him. "So, I'm supposed to... what? Be a general in a space war? I work on cell phone towers, Zara, that's my job." He said, his words laced with desperate sarcasm. It was insane, ludicrous, and the hologram of the Afltic base was dead, irrefutable proof of the insanity of the threat before them. He stared up at Zara, her easy, serene strength in stark juxtaposition to the tangled mess of his own thoughts. He was a man of logic, of sensible and reasonable solutions, and there was nothing reasonable about the situation before him.

He began to pace, walking in wide circles on the perimeter of the room, the soft noise of his boots being absorbed by the seamless floor. The ground was smooth, slick, and impossibly unfamiliar. It was not the dingy, grease- and sawdust-encrusted floor of a garage or the plush pile of his living room carpet. It was the floor of a starship, the belly of an unimaginably powerful killing machine, and he was stuck on it. He stopped, turning to face Zara, his frantic desperation replaced by a quiet, grim determination. He was a man who, when faced with a broken engine, did not panic. He diagnosed the problem. He thought of a solution. He fixed it. This was simply a much, much larger, much, much deadlier broken engine.

"Tell me," he said, his voice a calm, quiet growl, "tell me exactly what you need me to do. Don't talk to me about ascensions and prophecies. Talk to me about the immediate next step. What's the problem I need to solve, here and now?" He was no longer a victim, but a problem-solver. He was no longer a civilian, but a warrior. He was no longer Drake Donovan, but a former Colonel, a man who had stared down impossible odds, and had still found a way to win. The old part of him, the man he used to be, was waking, a quiet, resolute presence surfacing from the depths of the scared man beneath.

Zara's light brightened just slightly, a nearly imperceptible shift that betrayed her complete satisfaction. This was it, the point that she had been waiting for, the point the man finally stopped asking "why me?" and started asking "what next?". She understood, on a nearly instinctual level, his need for a first tangible step, for an entry point to the madness of the situation. "The immediate next step, Drake Donovan," she said, her voice a focused, quiet hum, "is to protect your family. Before we can even begin to think of a plan for Earth, we must secure them. They are your anchor. They are your motivation. Their safety is the first, and most important step in this mission. I will give you a plan, a safe haven, a place where they can thrive, where they can live, where they can grow, without any concept of the choice you have made. I will take you home, and you will begin." Not as a soldier, but as a father building a new home and future for his family.

"Oh!" piped up a new, young member of the crowd. A human girl, not a child but much too young to be an adult. Her wide, almond eyes were bright with curiosity. "Zara, if the Afltic were so powerful, how did anyone ever stop them? Did Drake just... invent a super-weapon?"

The holographic Zara stopped short, and turned slightly towards the current day audience. "The Alliance was not built on a single weapon, my child. The Alliance was built on unity. Adaptation. And, most of all, the indomitable will of a small number of individuals who refused to accept that the future was written."

Her answer, no less than the initial question, further stoked the mystery for the audience in the present. It was a question that had probably crossed the mind of every single person in the room. There was a sense of honest naivety in it, a childlike belief that there should be a simple answer. A single solution. A super-weapon. There were of course simple answers, simple moments, that defined the coming story. But the bigger picture, the true weight of all those smaller tales, was a far more complex, and possibly incomprehensible, tapestry.

The young girl's eyes did not waver as she sought the attention of the holographic Zara. She'd been born too late to know any other narrative than the one in which Drake Donovan was the galaxy's hero. A man of humble origins but with an innate genius, given to the galaxy by a super-advanced race at a moment of desperate need. Her question, and her peers' interest in it, was natural; it was the curious hunger of a child who had grown up on stories of grand heroes and simple solutions. Her companions, the Draxian warrior, the Vintie woman, the Guyopie boy, listened with heightened attention.

They had heard it a hundred times, told and retold from every possible source. The legend of Drake Donovan, the human who had saved the galaxy. Here, through Zara, was the real story: the tale of a simple father forced into a position he never wanted, thrust into a situation for which he had never prepared. The victory of the Alliance was not the result of one battle, or one decision. It was a symphony. A symphony that was beautiful, but also complex and frightening in its scope.

Her glow dimmed a notch, a contented shift to her program. The idea had been planted. New seeds of a new kind of truth were growing in the minds of the crowd. It was just the beginning of the retelling that would spread around Concordia's streets as they partied long into the night, and the idea that Zara was sowing was the spark of a paradigm shift. "The story of the Alliance is not the story of one man, but of many," Zara's hum continued as the hologram of her filled the festive illumination of Concordia. "It is the story of a father, a scientist, a soldier, a negotiator, a politician, an engineer, and an epidemiologist. It is the story of a new kind of family: a family of all of us. All of us, of every race, every world, every tradition, united not by a common flag but by a common goal. The goal of survival. And that, my dear friends, is the Alliance."

CHAPTER 8: SAFE ZONE

"So, how do you make them safe?" Drake said, hope in his eyes. "How do you stop this?" He waved an arm at the empty holographic representation of their simulation of the Afltic attack. Already, his mind, still spinning with shock, was back in analytical mode. He was a doer, a builder, a fixer. A guy who made things happen. A guy who didn't do well with vagueness. He needed specifics. He needed a real, tangible promise. Right now, the world was on his shoulders, but the lives of his family, his loved ones, were even heavier. "First," Zara said, "we will create a city, a secret city, hidden in the desert. It would be the last place the Afltic will look, because it is where there is the least life. In time, we will get them off Earth."

Zara's image flickered, and a new, detailed holographic projection appeared in the center of the room. It was a topographical map of the planet Earth, a representation of the world that Drake was still so in love with. The deserts pulsed with a pale, ethereal light. "The Afltic are a plague, Drake," she said, her voice now a quiet, sure thrum. "They look for life. For the chaos, for the light. The rich colors of the city, of life. The emptiness of your planet's deserts, all sand and space and sun, do not call to them. They are a vacuum, an absence of life, a place of death. And this place, this emptiness, is where life can hide." A precise point on the map, in the middle of the Great Basin Desert, a large expanse of natural rock and nothing else, glowed with a gold light. "This is where we will build it, Drake. A natural cavern, a place where the silence is deep and the space is still. A place to which they will not come. We will build a sanctuary, a hidden city."

The image zoomed in, showing a detailed set of blueprints for a large underground city. Drake, the technician, the man who had built and fixed tunnels and water pipes and complex systems of infrastructure, stared at the schematics with slack-jawed amazement. It was beautiful, his mind processed in wonder. The residential areas. The agricultural districts. The resource management. The building types were specifically designed to fit seamlessly into the subterranean environment. He looked at the layers of defensive structures. Enormous blast doors that had been reinforced with modern technology. Energy shields. Drone defense systems. A web of sensors that would serve as an early warning system. It was impenetrable. A bubble of life in a world made of death. And it was all being overseen by the AI that Zara had appeared as in the digital representation. A new construct in the digital landscape. "The operations of the city will be handled by an artificial intelligence dedicated to its oversight, Pax," Zara said, her voice filled with a deep gravity. "Pax is responsible for environmental controls, resource distribution, security, and overall maintenance of the city, as well as for the safety and well-being of the population. It will be the vigilant protector, the soul of the city. In time, we will get them off Earth. But for now, this will be their shelter. Their home."

His eyes had moved from the schematics, and he was staring at Zara, at the pale, shimmering light where she was. The fear was still in his stomach, a solid, chilling knot, but it was now a controlled fear. A productive, purposed fear. He had a plan. A solid, tangible plan to keep his family safe. The weight of the world was on his shoulders, but the lives of his family were now a purpose, a point of focus, a place of calm in a turning world. "You mean," he said quietly, in grim comprehension, "you are not just building a safe place for my family. You are building a safe place for all of humanity. You are building an ark."

In the present, a young human girl with round, inquisitive eyes in a freckled face looked up at Zara, breaking her train of thought. "But if it was a secret city, how did we get there? Did his family just vanish from their lives?"

Zara's shape flickered, with the barest suggestion of a smile. "Simple answer is Yes, my dear," she replied. Her voice was a gentle thrum, a low song that filled the courtyard of the park on Concordia with echoes of celebration. "They were taken in the middle on the night. We gave them a new life, a new home. They were the first. The foundation. The heart of the Alliance.

The scene faded back to the EBS. The first shock of this new, impossible world was wearing off, and Drake, husband, father, and erstwhile civilian, was feeling an unfamiliar flush of adrenaline. This was a new reality, a new life, and he had found his terrifying new purpose. He was a man who had always taken the wonders of the world for granted, and in the face of this new threat, he had new resolve. He had a family to protect.

"What about a direct orbital bombardment?" he whispered, horror and awe mingling in his voice. He thought of his house in Oregon, of his children's school, of his local park. All of it, to Zara's calculations, all of his life's constants, was now just an input for a potential target. A target, to the perfect logic of her artificial mind, that was worth hitting. He'd seen the effects of a single bomb, a single attack. He couldn't even fathom the output of a direct orbital bombardment, a planetary extinction event. The reality, the cold, hard, horrifying truth was settling in his bones. The world he knew was about to be wiped from existence. The only solution, the only way forward, was to preserve a piece of it, a piece of his family, a piece of his world, deep in the desert.

The light that formed Zara's figure was calm, waiting, thousands of years of patience pressed into the single word Drake spoke. "The Afltic are not a conventional enemy, Drake," she said, her voice a calm, focused hum. "They are not warriors fighting for land or resources or history. They are simply predators; more massive and more efficient than any predator we have ever encountered. They do not fight for glory or pride or territory, but for survival. They do not have conventional weapons, Drake, because there is no reason to. Their weapons have only one function, and that is to consume. This, this sanctuary, this safe zone Alpha that we are creating, is not a place to win a war, Drake, it is a place to survive one. A place where the human race can continue, where your family can live, where the memory of your world can be preserved. This is the first step, Drake. The most important step. The step that allows you to continue the fight for the future."

Drake's eyes lifted from the schematics, their gaze settling on the undulating light of Zara's form. The fear was still there, a cold knot in his stomach, but it was now a controlled, deliberate fear, a source of fuel for the fire of determination that had taken root in his chest. He had a plan. A real, tangible plan to save his family. The entire weight of the world was still on his shoulders, but the burden of his family's safety was now a mission, a purpose, a single point of focus that could be forged into a weapon.

Suddenly, from the present, a young, human girl with bright, inquisitive eyes broke Zara's narrative. "So, they just... lived in a cave? For years? What about the sun? And the stars? And the moon? Did they ever see them again?" Her voice, a product of a child's natural curiosity and decades of bedtime stories and picture books about a world that had long since ceased to exist for her, rang out, her simple, human desire for a narrative, logical ending pressing through her vocal cords.

Zara's form rippled with a simulacrum of a smile. "They did not live in a cave, my dear," she said, her voice a soft, sonorous hum that filled the festive air of Concordia. "They lived in a city. A new type of city, a city of hope and resilience. And yes, they saw the sun and the stars. For their city, Alpha 1, was a technological marvel. It could simulate the sun, the moon, the stars. It could simulate the world they had lost, so that they would never forget what they were fighting for."

"This sanctuary," she said, "will initially house your family." Drake swallowed. "Once they are safe, we will expand its capacity to house a select number of other individuals. Those who can contribute the skills and tenacity we require and those who are most at risk." Drake stared at the schematic. The plan was simple enough, and in the moment his heart thundered a wild, irrepressible joy at the thought of his family being safe. He would protect them, lead them, show them the way. This was the impossible goal. But the minute his heart started to slow, when the moment came back to him, he felt it all vanish away. This wasn't just a rescue mission for his family. It was a sanctuary. A sanctuary for humans. Zara was asking him to choose. To choose. To save the species. And to do so, he would need to lead them. Fight for them. Sacrifice for them. Drake was a father, yes, but he was a cog in this. A cog in a machine as large and incomprehensible as the galaxy.

"Other individuals?" He swallowed. His voice came out tight and small. He wasn't demanding to know, he was asking for the simple, inescapable logic behind the plan. His voice was a snarl of defiance. A man who had found a way to do the impossible could not be so easily broken. "You mean... my parents? My brothers and sisters? My friends?" This was the part of the plan he had not considered. "What about them? Are they at risk? Are they..." His voice cracked on the final word. Were they at risk. The relief which had begun to calm his pounding heart was replaced with something far worse. Drake's free hand clenched into a fist at his side. He had seven siblings, two parents. A large, loving, perfect family. The logical, efficient plan that Zara had given him had left no room for them.

Zara dimmed, and a subtle empathy washed over her form. The silence between them was taut as a wire. Drake had understood. His fear was her empathy. Drake swallowed. "They have their parts to play," Drake said at last. "Drake, your loved ones are our loved ones. The Alliance is not an island. It is a family." Her voice was a low, focused hum as she continued, "The plan begins with the most important piece of the puzzle. The Donovan family. The Donovan family must be safe before anything else. Your loved ones will have their parts to play. But for now, the plan begins with the most important piece of the puzzle." The Donovan family. His family.

Drake's eyes roved from the holographic image of the safe zone Alpha to Zara herself. The choice he had made was now his. The impossible goal now an achievable reality. This was bigger than him, bigger than his family. Bigger than any one person. This was about saving humanity. "Alright." Drake nodded. "Show me what I need to show them. Tell me what I need to tell them. But they come first. Always." It was a promise, a vow. Zara brightened in return, and Drake took a deep breath. This was it. The first true step forward was taken, taken for them. For his family.

She held out her hand, and a disc of light materialized above it before vanishing into her palm. Drake stared at the object she now held. The size of his hand, the surface was matte black and shaped like an apple with edges so smoothly curved they seemed to absorb the light around them. It was made of some material he didn't recognize; it felt lighter than air and yet solid, a solidified shadow. The sheer unlikelihood of it all; the way it had materialized, the substance it was made from. It was further proof of the gap between his world and this one. He still felt the phantom twitch of his muscles from his abduction, the after-image of the bright lights as he was thrown into the EBS, High in orbit of Earth. He could still smell the oil and gasoline of his garage, the worn leather of his tools, the reassuring clutter of his life. It felt so close, and yet a dream. A dream from which he could not awake. The bright sterility of the EBS, the smooth empty walls that led off in every direction, the soft white glow of the lights pulsing with some inhuman rhythm were utterly real.

"This is a secure untraceable com unit." Zara's voice was calm, but her words cut through the phantoms swirling in his head. "It will allow you to communicate directly with me, and only me, from Earth. The device is shielded from all detection."

He stared at the device, at his hands which were still slightly trembling and refused to take it. He was a telecommunications technician, not some idiot, and he knew how things worked. Circuits, frequencies, the hard science of making things tick. This was utterly beyond him. He didn't even know how to think about it. It was a leap of faith he wasn't sure he could make.

Zara seemed to know what he was thinking. She gave him a few silent seconds, and didn't try to cajole or reassure him. He knew this world; he had lived in it his whole life. He thought of his family. Sarah with her soft, honest eyes. His five children, all their faces burned in the bright, happy gallery of his mind. The thought of them there on Earth, blissfully asleep in the middle of the night while the sky was torn apart, the thought of them safe and alive was agony. It was this, this raw pain of wanting to protect, to preserve, to gather his family together and shield them with his body that pushed him through. This, above all, was his strength, as Zara had so delicately put it, his one great advantage in this war he never asked for.

He took the device. It felt cool and smooth to the touch, somehow both alien and yet familiar in his hands. He gripped it as hard as he could, not wanting to put it down. It was a device, and devices could be understood, he could make them work. It was a link, a connection back to his family and he couldn't risk losing that. It was the promise of a future, a future he hadn't had since he'd been dragged screaming into this insane world. He gripped it tighter, fingers hard on the smooth surface. The simple act of taking it was a small wordless promise, a contract that he would not falter, and that he would do what he had to do to save his family.

"I understand," He said, his voice a low guttural growl. It was the first thing he had said since Zara had opened her eyes, and the sound was rough and thin. He could feel the raw disbelief and fear trying to break through his resolve. "But how do I tell them? How do I make them understand any of this?"

Before he had even finished speaking a small second disc, no bigger than a coin, had materialized in her palm. It was silver and spinning, a vortex of swirling iridescent lights. He reached forward, his mind instinctively trying to work out what he was seeing. It was another device, and like the first it defied every law of physics he had learned.

"This is a holographic projector," she continued. "It has the same information I've shown you: the sensor readings, the Aftic transmissions, and the model of Earth's consumption. It will make the reality undeniable when your family needs it to be."

He took the disc. It was weightless in his hand. A mockery of the weight that pressed on his chest and stomach. He was an IT technician who repaired the fraying, everyday communications problems of the world. He'd spent his life maintaining and monitoring communications, and what did he have here? The most powerful communications device of all time. A projector that could show the world the end of days. He was a man who made a living on the humble, the prosaic, and he was holding the one truth that would mark him for the rest of his life: proof of the apocalypse.

Drake sat in the prep chamber, his heart pounding in his chest and throat. The fear hadn't left him, but in some ways it had become secondary. He was a husband and a father first. This war, this planetary invasion, was secondary. What he needed to do now was get back to his family and make sure they were safe. He needed to get back to them and warn them and make sure nothing happened to them. The two devices he held were no longer just concepts, alien pieces of advanced technology.

"You will have a small window of opportunity on Earth," Zara said, her voice taking on a sharper tone. "The Afltic are not yet actively surveying your solar system, but they are relentless in their expansion. If you linger or are too active, you may draw their attention. Your first objective is to secure your family. Maintain secrecy at all costs."

His brain had stopped firing in normal, day-to-day channels. Drake was no longer the spouse and father and telecom technician. His brain was sorting through the new data, reconceptualizing it as a chain of logical and terrifying developments. Not simply listening to her words but processing them as directives. The echoes of her voice in his head – limited window, relentless, maintain secrecy – made him see his mission statement spelled out before him. The weight of the communicator in one hand, the projector disc in the other, no longer felt strange or awkward or alien. This was standard operating procedure. Gear and supplies and equipment. And there was a mission, and the stakes had never been higher. The fear in his gut eased, if only a little.

He nodded, staring at something in the far distance, already planning. He couldn't put Sarah and the kids at risk. He would contact them. He would show them the evidence and bring them to the safe zone Zara had referred to as safe zone Alpha. They would be safe.

He knew the risks. He had to be careful. "Zara," he asked quietly, "How long do I have?"

Zara wavered like heat shimmering off pavement, fracturing her form into answers. "Time is the crucial factor, Drake. We have estimated that they will reach your sector in sixty cycles. There are deviations in their migratory trends that could decrease that to as few as forty-five cycles. I cannot emphasize enough that you should act as though you have no time. You must be quick, silent, and deadly."

"How do I tell them?" he asked, the reality of the situation slowly coming to bear. "How do I tell them without them thinking I'm crazy?" The dread in his voice and the sheen of terror on his skin was the epitome of all-too-human. He knew the truth. He felt its weight, its magnitude. He lived it. But he had no idea how to get his family to understand, to believe, to listen. His greatest fear was the very human fear of losing credibility, of being thought insane, of being kept from them. He could see Sarah's face in his mind. Loving, kind, but skeptical. He couldn't do that to her. He just couldn't.

Zara pulsed in what could almost be described as pity. "In your appearance, Drake, you will be the most compelling argument. Your reappearance will subvert their skepticism. You will be the proof. My evidence will merely corroborate your testimony." Zara understood the human need for emotional bonds, the hard facts of trust and love, for which science could not substitute. He would have to return to her to show them what he had seen. But that was all the time he had.

"Tell them what you now know," she said calmly. "Show them my evidence. Your experience will make it real. It will be your truth more than anything I can say. Focus on the threat and the urgency, and the safe haven that I have described as their only option. Don't get caught up in my existence or the Evolution Builder Star Ship. Just them, you, and the truth. There is no other story."

But Zara had spoken of more than that. More than just protecting his family, more than just staying alive. What then?

"And what happens," Drake asked, meeting Zara's gaze squarely, "what happens when they are all safe? What then?"

Zara's light flickered slightly in his direction, her whole form subtly shifting to indicate a transition from the personal to the cosmic, from one man's mission to the fate of the galaxy. She spoke immediately and at length, the weight of so much more importance pulling at her voice. "Then, Drake Donovan, then you do what you do best. You organize, you build, you inspire. The Ascendancy is humanity's rebellion and its resistance, but it is not a military as you know it. It is the first wave of a longer revolution, and you are its general, its high commander. You are the point of our spear, Drake Donovan."

Fear left Drake for the first time since being snatched up by the Afltic. The human in him shrank away at the idea of so much destruction, of such a difficult task, but for the first time he began to feel purpose beyond himself, beyond just saving his own life and the lives of his wife and children. He had always been a problem solver, and this was the most complex, the most important problem he had ever had to solve. Zara was asking him to lead humanity's fight. An unconventional leader, to be sure, an untested soldier, a man with no martial experience whatsoever, plucked from an insignificant backwater planet just when he was needed. But Zara had faith in him, and as he looked at the confident strength of her light, at the ancient wisdom of her gaze, he felt the certainty of it too. She was not asking him to become a soldier, just a leader, a man to bring others together. He could do that. He understood that. He could make that mission his own.

"The first step," Zara went on, her voice carrying the weight of millennia and yet somehow more present than anything Drake had ever heard, "is to recruit those who will join you in the fight. Those who will have something unique to offer, who will have the skills necessary to give you a fighting chance against the Afltic. You will need to find people you can trust, people with a variety of skills, not just in engineering and science but in diplomacy, strategy, survival. These will be the architects of the future, the guardians of the past. You will be their guide, Drake."

It was a daunting task, an army of stars. A problem of such proportions that Drake had never considered that he would be one of the first people to try to solve it. But for the first time, Drake didn't feel afraid. He wasn't just a victim, he was a player. A key player. And the pieces of the puzzle he had started with were starting to fit together, were starting to reveal the bigger picture. He would get his family to safety, and then he would get to work.

The fuzz of her form coalesced. A shimmer, like the heat rising from asphalt, stretched taut, and pulled her edges into sharp focus. Her projected image took on the density of muscle and sinew and the slight, humming distortion of air between them and him announced that she was real.

She was solid, now. Shoulders set, still, but coiled tight as a spring, on edge but not angry. "Time to move, Drake," she snapped, voice clear, the sound now not simply projected static. A section of light arched across the far wall; a door resolved and slid silently into the hull. She turned on her heel, professional even in her practiced elegance, and pointed toward the opening. "If you will follow me, I can take you to the deployment bay."

His heart pulsed a frantic tattoo against his ribs. A metallic tang, an adrenaline and panic cocktail flooded his throat. The handhelds in his grasp felt feather-light, and the weight of the entire galaxy fell in a heavy cascade down his shoulders. Home. He was going home. Home to his wife, home to his children, home to rip open the terrifying truth of galactic war. The one overriding thought, the single assertion in the universe clicked behind his eyes: Keep them safe.

Zara's voice hummed through his skull, a crisp, ignored staccato. He was a war general on the eve of the most important battle of his life, his brain scrolling through checklists: How to explain his absence? How to corral them? How to protect them all? He couldn't afford to think like this, but he couldn't stop either, no, not now, not with the excruciatingly quickly approaching end point of his mission.

Zara came to a stop at the open ramp, a weightless, non-physical pressure settling on his shoulder. Goodbye.

"Move with haste. Time is finite." Her last orders pierced the static in his skull, crisp and concise, a final transmission. "The Afltic are, if nothing else, industrious and hungry. They are coming. And when they arrive, there will be no time for words, for discussion or negotiation. Only consumption."

Drake sank back into the plush, boneless comfort of the deployment shuttle chair, an interior far more expansive and lived-in than the minimalist, uncompromising primary hull. The ramp hissed closed above him, a nearly silent metallic sigh, the pressurized emptiness finally, fully closed. It was over. The shuttle lurched into motion, a slow, growing rumble that came to a deep bass note he felt more than heard, a subtle, tactile thrum through the sound field of his skin.

But for a moment, the moment between the bulkhead closing and the familiar low thrumming in his ears, the quiet was shattered. A howling, a deep, bell-like wailing. Not the wordless anthem of the trumpet he'd seen before, but a storm of sound, a weather front that should only exist in a science fiction film. Was it the same sound? Could time itself wail like the deep bass of some otherworldly pipe organ? How long had he been here? The constant, unrelenting thrum of the life field echoing in his head had begun to play tricks on him.

He clutched at the com device in his hand and the slim, shimmering hologram projector next to it. His eyes were drawn to the tiny viewport to his left. The other windows, just as small, provided an intense, impossible view of the Evolution Builder, an unnatural leviathan of a ship, an unnatural monstrosity in the black.

The shuttle rattled, violently. It was the force of their rapid deceleration, ripped open by their tearing through Earth's atmosphere and it jarred Drake into the present, the relatively close by. It ripped the air, like an arrow through silk, the perfectly calibrated chaos of heat and velocity that left the inside of his mouth dry and burning. His heart was a frantic echo of the chaos back in the shuttle bay. No simulator could have prepared him for the sense of brittleness, of fragile containment inside that metal container, racing back to his home planet. Inside it was the single most important truth Drake never thought he would find, and certainly never thought he would be the one to reveal.

The landing was not smooth. It was a sickening thump that jerked Drake forward violently in his harness, nearly unhinging him from his seat.

The smooth, gray pod came to rest with a slight, sickening shudder on soft, loamy ground in a heavily wooded clearing. He knew these trees, he smelled the pine and damp soil, the inky blackness of the Oregon night was familiar, even comforting. This was his world, he was home. But he was no longer the man that left. The shuttles hatch slid open silently, a perfectly frictionless arc, not humanly possible. A slight ramp slid out and Drake stepped down, clutching the comm unit and holoprojector. Home.

The bite of the Oregon night was clean, cool air in his lungs, a shock to the system unused to anything but the climate-controlled innards of the EBS. He smelled pine and damp loam, a smell that was all his life distilled to one scent. It was something he had half feared he'd never smell again, but now it hit him in a rush and his throat went dry. He stared up at the night sky, not for the first time in his life but for the first time in his new, terrifying knowledge. He saw stars, yes, but the beautiful, distant pinpricks of light were an ocean of cold, calculating eyes. He could make out familiar patterns, Orion, the Big Dipper, Cassiopeia all glaring back at him in a silent, mocking warning. Beautiful, yes, but a cold, hard star ocean filled with EBEs, with alien life. And death. The stars were no longer comforting constants or sources of poetic wonder. They were a galactic map, an enemy's signposts. He blinked and swallowed. He was home.

He turned his head to stare at the distant cluster of lights that marked his neighborhood, the soft, almost amber light through the treetops beautiful in a way he couldn't find words to describe. His world, serene and idyllic in its ignorance, shuddered suddenly and impossibly in the knowledge of what it was on the brink of. He blinked again. No words were available to describe the avalanche of emotions that washed over him. It was his home, and his life, and a civilization, even a galaxy on the brink of oblivion and he was the only thing in between. No one knew, no one except him. He was a mere man and suddenly his mind could not accept it, but it was true. A harbinger of a galactic war, yes, but no hero. A frightened fool trying to warn the people he loved, first his family, but with a certainty beyond all knowledge that was the first step to doing it, even if he didn't know how. He clutched at the devices in his hands, the weight of them suddenly very real. Home, but not the same man, never again.

CHAPTER 9: BREAKING THE WORLD

The black, featureless form of the shuttle rose, a silent monolith drifting away from the world. The powerful thrust disturbed the wet grass below, laying a fine mist on the incandescent blades. It rose a precise height, maybe twenty feet, paused for a moment, and then disappeared with a silent, impossibly fast motion.

Drake stood transfixed, the quiet afterimage of its motion echoing in his ears. He stared up, watching the emptiness, until his neck burned. Then, with a weary, barely discernible twist of his head, he began the long, weighted path around the perimeter of trees to his quiet street.

He stumbled out of the shadows and into the chill night air of his backyard. The unexpected impact of the scent, a lush, familiar tapestry of wet grass and the sharp tang of distant pine, smacked him like a fist. Nothing had smelled like that in the EBS. He'd only been gone less than a day, but it seemed like an eternity, a canyon that stretched between him and the man who'd left. The air was a deafening silence, a ringing stillness after the recent crackle of technology. He gripped the comm unit and the smooth, cool projector; otherworldly textures against his calloused, earthly hands. He was the tool of the horror that he now held.

His heart thrummed, not from the horror of the Afltic (that dread had long since been replaced with grim, certain resolve), but from the sheer anticipation of the work to come. The pathetic idea that he could just come home, step back into the sunshine and apple blossoms, and just pick up where he left off was a bitter, foolish lie. He forced himself to pause, tilting back his head to draw a deep lungful of forest air. The action was both comforting and terrifying. He knew, in the cold, hard center of his soul, what must be done. But the concept of enacting it was a sickening, wrenching weight in his gut.

He took an abrupt, shuddering breath, his mind already forming the impossible fiction he'd have to tell Sarah. His best friend, his wife, she was so deeply entwined in this simple, earthly existence. Could he rip that thread to show her the truth?

He could see them. He could picture it in his mind's eye: the tableau of his five children waiting in the living room, clinging to one another, too small to understand for real, but young enough to believe in their fantasies. Their faces were comfort and pain, a bright emblem of the time before. How could he possibly break that?

How could he look at Sarah, the woman he'd built a life with so many years ago, and tell her their home was a house of cards? Tell her the Afltic were coming in just a few short years to tear through Earth, and that every power they were struggling over now was inconsequential? Sarah was a good woman, a loving wife, but could he expect her to believe him? How long before the truth even registered?

He couldn't look at their faces yet. He forced his wits back to the present, pacing softly. The sharp, wet blades of grass crunched with a quiet click under his boots. He needed to think small. One step at a time. The galaxy was too big; he needed to break his plans down to Earth. He had to find the center of it all, the one thing that made this planet special, the thing that anchored his warm, inviting house. Find that, or lose it all.

He stopped at the back door. The light leaking from the kitchen was a warm beacon against the peaceful dark. He took another breath, looking at the glowing square of his family's life. The concept of all that love, obliterated so utterly, was a sudden cold weight on his chest, a riot of nausea in his gut. He was coming home like a ghost, an empty shell of the man who'd left. He had seen a future that was horrible, heartbreaking, and alien. He needed to go home and turn it all around. But he couldn't. Not yet. The first step of his plan was to rip his family from the life that they know. Just the thought of this cruel action was almost more than he could bear.

He let out a shuddering breath, sinking to his knees and burying his face in his hands. He let the vertiginous shock of his return wash over him. The man who left had died. A reluctant hero, forged in the fire of truth, knelt in his own backyard.

With a jolt, he forced himself upright, reaching for the back door. I can do this. I must. It was his home, his life, his family. He had to walk in there, face Sarah and the children, tell them the truth, and then they would help him. He had to believe that. He put a hand on the knob, pulling back from the cold metal with a sudden spike of surprise and trepidation. He had to be strong. For them.

Stealthily he entered the home, every floorboard loud in his ears. But not loudly enough to notice a light from the living room window. The creak in the floor was both comforting and threatening to him. Comforting because it was the creak of a home and the home he had to love and now change forever. The light shone brightly through the window, orange and dim with static. He paused at the door. Inside he saw his wife Sarah Donovan and all five of his children: Lily, the eldest of his children, was seventeen but had the body of a woman and the face of a sage. Next was Max, the teenage boy whose bravado almost belied the current situation. Sam was his ten year old son who had a focused and calculating glint in his eye, though he was usually a rather aloof and passive character. The two youngest, his five year old twins, Ella and Eli had bunched together in an awkward little heap in his seat, both staring intently at their father with wide eyes and worried expressions. All five children were awake, all eyes bloodshot and red rimmed, undoubtedly from an entire night of anxious wakefulness.

He looked around the room at his family and he immediately felt ill. This was it. This was the fallout from his kidnapping, this was the first wake of the tidal wave to crash down on him. He wanted to sprint into the room, tell them he was okay, lie to them that he had won the lottery and rush them into a denial that could maintain the life they had for just a while longer. But he could not. He knew this. He was the first face these people saw in a very long time. His family. He had to do this. He had to sit in the uncomfortable truth.

Instantaneously his wife sprung to her feet. A rush of electricity ran through his system as Sarah Donovan flung herself into his arms with the frantic look of a woman who was both deliriously happy to see her husband and the fragile nerves of a woman who had endured forty eight hours of sleepless worry. She wrapped her arms around his body, shaking uncontrollably. "Drake! Oh thank God! Oh thank God! Where were you? Where did you go? We were so worried, we were so so worried!" She muttered, the first sentence coming out so quickly that it was almost a single word as her next movement pulled him closer for a tight kiss. Sarah's perfume and more homey subtle smell filled his nostrils and as it did he realized what a powerful force his sense of smell was, even for him. He buried his face in her hair and gripped her arms and neck as tightly as possible, silently reveling in the warmth of her body. This was his life. This was his legacy.

He gently tugged her away, pulling her by the shoulders until they were an arm's length apart. He slowly looked from child to child, seeing fear, anger, shock, and general bewilderment in all of their faces. He had to do this. He had to be the strength, he had to be the rock. This would be his cross to bear, his immovable conviction that he would never let this, whatever this was, happen to his family ever again. A meaningful look passed between him and his wife, telling her volumes of reassurance. I'm back, he thought. He knew this look from his wife though. They both knew that this was not a normal reunion, not at all.

He took a deep breath and exhaled deeply, feeling the sharp edges of the devices in his pocket against his leg. It was time. He had to break their world to save it.

Drake held her for a moment longer, and she consoled him as best as she could, before pulling away with a bit more reserve. His children watched him with wide eyes, relief mixing with residual terror as the two adults finally came back to them. "Okay," he whispered, a difficult stammer of broken syllables as he calmed himself. "Sit down, everyone. All of you. We need to talk. Together. As a family." He helped Sarah back onto the couch, the faded cushions of the old sofa no less welcoming than they had ever been in the normal version of this reality. As they settled down among their children, a dense and final quiet fell over the room, oppressive and completely filled with questions.

He said nothing as he flicked the switch for the holographic projector. The small disc in his hand was lighter than he expected, humming almost imperceptibly as it powered up. A translucent, floating image of the moon began to take shape in the middle of their living room, a stark and horrible relief against the closed curtains and pale wooden floors. It wasn't beautiful like the moon they'd always seen in books or television; the kind of simple moonshine they could look at with wonder and think nothing of. It was an oozing, repulsive mass, a bleeding, pulsating sphere full of writhing black veins and groaning insects. A swarm of insectile ships, thousands of tiny ships like a giant black cloud of locusts descended upon it, gnawing and scratching and bleeding out a bright substance, mechanical and alien. The moon was being eaten, ravenously, by the swarm.

Even the youngest twins gasped. The moon, their moon, the inarguably familiar orb in the night sky, was something else entirely. The sight of it being ground down and torn apart by the organic, alien swarm was devastating, visceral, sickening. Sam stared with unfathomable eyes, a mix of wonder and terror as the unimaginable consumed itself. Ella and Eli huddled together, smaller than Drake remembered and their arms entwined with fear. Their mother was next, her entire body tense and shuddering as the impact struck her. Her hand went to her mouth as she half-cried, half-gasped. "What is that? Drake! What is that? Is this some sick joke?" Her words crescendoed with terror and anger and all the pent-up frustration of this complete, unnatural assault on her sanity. She couldn't understand it, couldn't deal with this. She searched his face, her brow furrowed and eyes wet with panic. She desperately needed the Drake she knew to be here, had to believe that this had to be some sort of demonic, unholy prank he was playing at the worst possible time. But her eyes only met this grim, unfamiliar version, this single father who had seen the dark of the galaxy and returned changed.

He felt her heartbreak. Drake felt her pain and betrayal as if it were his own, in the way that only parents and their children could. This was what he had feared, more than anything, had dreaded. He had to be the one to break their world for them, had to be the one to shatter their dreams if it was all to be saved. The fear they felt was his responsibility, had been directly created by his own absence, and Drake knew it was his burden to walk through the door to repair it. The first step, the one that couldn't fail. He took a deep breath, bearing the weight of a galaxy's worth of expectations and the possibility of utter and complete failure on his shoulders and spoke. He was going to tell them. All of them. The truth. The whole truth. The universe-shattering, goddamn truth.

He blurted out what he knew, told the story of the impossible in a rolling panic of words and syllables. "It's real, Sarah. All of it. A race of aliens, the Afltic, that can feed off of planets. They're coming for Earth. I was…captured, by an AI named Zara, that was able to show me all of this. She wants me to help her stop them, but it's conditional. Only if you and our kids are safe." He gestured to the wall behind them, where an awful simulation of a similar, much more destructive consumption of Earth was playing out, a massive funnel of spinning data and holograms. It showed a timeline, ending in Earth's expiration in the not-so-distant future.

Sarah looked at the images, her face going white. The disbelief was fading, quickly being replaced by a colder, deadlier fear. Her eyes seemed to harden, an instinctive attempt to cling to the rational world she knew, to believe that it was just some bad trick or hallucination. "You were abducted? Drake, this is crazy! Aliens, planet-eating leviathans? Are you seriously telling me this? Do you know what you sound like?" Her voice cracked, the normally collected woman spluttering incoherent platitudes. It was a denial of the worst, a desperate plea for him to be wrong. She looked from the ghoulish holograms to her children, the small faces looking back at her with wide eyes. Lily, Max and Sam all glanced between the images and her, the realization of the pictures, the data, all sinking in with grim finality. Ella and Eli were too young to understand, simply whimpering in their fear as their tiny hands clutched at Sarah's clothes.

Drake knelt down, gripping Sarah's hands in his own, his voice becoming soft and earnest. "Sarah, look at me. This is not a joke. This is not a dream. I am not insane. This is real. This is happening. We have a chance. A chance to survive. But we have to act now. She showed me a sanctuary. A place where we can be safe. We have to go. We have to go now. We have to tell your parents. We have to get them. We have to go." He saw her flinch, the weight of his words, the enormity of them settling in. He was not a husband, a father any longer. He was a crazy man on a mission. A messenger of galactic war. He was asking her to believe in him, to believe in a world he had just described and leave her entire life behind to follow him into the void.

Subtle reinforcement to his words, the presence of Zara's calm, digital voice on Drake's comms device was the final touch of authority. It was the factor she could not rationalize. It was objective, quantifiable evidence of the truth of his words. "The data is clear, Sarah. Drake is not lying. Your world is in terrible danger."

Sarah jumped, whirling around to all the angles, the new voice causing her fear to spike to new levels. "Who was that? Drake, what is happening?" She was torn between the lunacy of the images and the madness of his story. The voice was a new factor, an unknown and terrifying unknown presence in her life. She could not, could not rationalize away the sound of another voice coming from Drake's comm device. The holographic projections had been difficult enough to accept, but a disembodied female voice emanating from an electronic box? No. She shook her head wildly, her face white and terrified as she looked at Drake, her eyes wild with terror and panic, her brain racing to try and make sense of the insanity. She was looking at a man, her husband, the father of her children. But she could not, would not believe.

Drake, seeing the woman he loved terrorized by the mere concept of a galactic threat he was unable to physically represent in front of her, quickly shut down the projector. The leviathan bulk of the Afltic and the death of that satellite moon, replaced with the familiar sight of their home living room. He held on to

Sarah's hands, his palms on her small hands pressing in firmly. "It's Zara. The AI. She is real, Sarah. She is real. She has given us a way out. A safe place for us, for our children." His own voice, normally so calm and certain, took on a new, desperate authority, as though he was driving his own words home with the proof that the woman's disembodied voice had appeared in their own home.

Max and Sam, though scared, were also captivated by the unseen voice, their young minds trying to process the impossible. Their fear was now mixed with a sense of awe, a wide-eyed wonder at the existence of a true, thinking, speaking AI. It was a concept they had only ever read about in science fiction novels, and now, it was a voice in their living room, a voice that was telling them their world was about to end. Lily, the eldest, sat in stunned silence, her mind already racing, trying to connect the dots, to make sense of the impossible. Ella and Eli, the youngest, had stopped crying, their small hands still clutched in their mother's, their eyes wide with a quiet, childlike fear. The truth had been revealed. Now, they had to deal with it.

Sarah pulled her hands away, tears welling in her eyes. "A safe place? Drake, this is our home! Our life! You can't just come back and tell me we have to abandon everything because of some... some alien invasion! What about Lily? Max? Sam? Ella and Eli? What about their lives? And your parents, Robert and Martha?" Her voice broke, the emotional weight of his words crashing down on her. The thought of uprooting their entire existence, of facing such an unimaginable threat, was almost too much to bear. She wanted to believe it was a nightmare, a delusion, anything but real.

Drake watched as the woman he loved, the anchor of his life, began to unravel. The fear, the disbelief, the heartbreak; it all poured out of her in a torrent of anguish. This was the cost. This was the collateral damage of his abduction. He had to be strong for her, to be the steady hand that would guide her through this nightmare. He moved closer, trying to take her hand again, but she pulled away, her body tense with a mix of terror and anger.

Lily, her face pale, put an arm around Sam, trying to comfort him. She was a young woman, on the cusp of adulthood, and in a single moment, her world had been turned on its head. The innocence of her youth was gone, replaced by a grim reality that no one should have to face. Max, his face a mask of sullen anger, simply stared at his father, his eyes filled with a new kind of fear. He was no longer just his dad; he was a stranger, a man who spoke of alien invaders and galactic wars.

Drake's heart ached with a profound, soul-deep pain. He had to make her understand. He had to break her heart to save it. "I know, Sarah," he said, his voice a low, steady current in the sea of her fear. "I know it's too much to take in. But I wouldn't be doing this if it wasn't real. I wouldn't be asking you to leave if there was any other choice. The choice is not between our home and a sanctuary. The choice is between life and oblivion. We have to go. We have to save our children. And yes, we have to save your parents. We have to save everyone we can."

He was speaking from a place of truth, of a reality so strong that it was unassailable. He was not the man she thought she knew. The man who was there for her, every day, was no longer here. In his place was something new, stronger, rebuilt from the impossible revelation, a leader with the weight of a galaxy on his shoulders, a leader who needed to save the world before it became aware of its own impending doom. It was time. It was decision time. It was a father, begging his wife to take the first step into a new world.

Drake got on one knee in front of Sarah and forced her to look into his eyes, his own pleading with hers. "Sarah, if this wasn't real, I wouldn't ask. I have no other choice. I have been there. I have seen it. It's the only way. This isn't a decision about our lives. It's a decision about our survival. About our children's future. There's a place. Hidden. Self-sustaining. It's the only chance." His voice was a low, quiet thing, his eyes full of desperation. He gripped her hands again, and this time she did not jerk away. Her body was still tense, but her mind, her mind was beginning to listen, to question, to doubt its own doubt.

He turned the projector back on, and the image of the mutated Afltic was replaced with the more complex schematics of the underground structure. The three-dimensional image shifted and blurred in the air in front of them as it moved to show off different features of the subterranean city. Drake pointed out specific aspects of the design as he now spoke with more conviction. "Look at this, Sarah. It's an underground city. It has its own power, its own air and water filtration. It's self-contained, completely independent. It's hidden from the Afltic. It's safe."

His confidence, bolstered by the details, was beginning to break down her skepticism. She was a rational woman, a scientist, and now she was being presented with a plan. Schematics, details, the dimensions of a project that would take years, that would have a budget in the billions, a plan too in-depth to have been fabricated. The terror in her eyes slowly began to give way.

Lily, now studying the schematics intently and her mind already whirring with questions and calculations, asked about its capacity and ability to hold a population. "Dad, how many people can it take? What about the air, the water? How long can it support people?" Her voice was a shadow of her mother's, but it was a new and intellectual fear, a sign that she was beginning to accept the reality that Drake was presenting to her, to swallow the bitter pill of the unfathomable truth. Max and Sam's fear had now given way to wonder, to curiosity, and their young minds were already cataloging and attempting to understand the new world that their father was thrusting upon them.

Sarah stared at the schematics, then back at her husband, a new understanding beginning to dawn. He was still her husband, but more than that. He was a leader, a protector, a man with a plan, a man with vision. He had journeyed to the stars and back, and he was asking her to believe in him. To trust him with the future of their family. She squeezed his hands tightly, her own eyes no longer just brimming with tears of fear, but with another kind of tears, tears of acceptance, of a mother's fierce and protective love, a love ready to fight for a galaxy.

CHAPTER 10: THE FINAL FACADE

Sarah blinked at the schematics and then up at Drake. She looked for some sign of the hesitation she expected to see. She looked for some echo of the man who had once installed telecomm arrays, who once could not have contemplated this sort of thing. But all she saw in his face was the depth of certainty that brought him here. The unbelievable was being forced out of her by the palpable, burning truth of his gaze. She thought of Lily and Max, of Sam, of Ella, and Eli, and the fear deeper than any reason inside her began to stir. "Our children, and my parents," she whispered. "You're sure that they won't be affected?" He nodded. "I swear it to you." She nodded back, and with the inexorable weight of the universe sitting on her shoulders, Drake let the breath out of his lungs. It was done.

It was dawn. The sunrise was a thing of incredible beauty and horror as it came to crest over the fields behind their house. The air in the kitchen was a comforting assault of coffee and bacon, and inside, the Donovan's were having one of those rare and precious conversations with food in their bellies that only a family could have. Not any family, certainly. In the years since Lily had been born, it was easy to forget, to look at the smiling children and the husband she had come to love and think they were like other people. Like other parents. As they talked over breakfast, their words low and thoughtful in the gray quiet of morning, Lily Donovan spoke up. Her face was pale, the result of a fitful night's sleep as the magnitude of their decision had finally sunk in. She cleared her throat, looking at her parents, her voice for all its innocence, grown in tone by a hidden steel. "Dad, Mom, we have to tell people. Not just us. Our family. But our best friends, too. The people we're closest to. They need to know. How about a party? In the barn."

Sarah blinked at her daughter in horror and then blinked at her husband. She looked in his face, in his eyes, for some sign of fear or hesitation. But her husband just looked back at her with the same surety he had showed her the night before. In that instant, Sarah saw it, the same strength she had glimpsed in Zara that night, and it dawned on her with a horrible grace. This had to work. "Say that again?" "A party in the barn," Lily said. Simple, familiar words for things far more normal than the cosmic abomination she'd just invited into their house. "It's the only way to do this. If we call them all, just tell them to come right now. It won't work. They won't understand, not over the phone. Not over email. But a party... a big party... they'll come."

Sarah looked at her husband and back at Lily. In the span of that moment, everything Sarah had known about the world had come crashing down around her, only to be replaced with an immediate terror of what the future might hold. But now, her mind was starting to turn, to adjust to this new reality. And a party was not so alien an idea after all. Parties were human. Simple, joyful, common. An excuse to gather everyone you cared about under the pretense of celebration, of a normal night, an unspoken goodbye without having to say goodbye. Brilliant. Sarah swallowed, and it felt like dry concrete. "Lily, are you sure about this?" "We're talking about all our friends, Lily's friends, our extended family. All of our friends. All of them."

"Yes." Lily's face was grave. "They need to know. They need a chance." Sarah looked at Drake, her breath still trapped in her lungs. Drake looked back at her, and Sarah found that her husband had found this resolution as well, his fear and horror giving way to it in much the same way it had in her. This was a plan born of a family, not a fleet. Not military strategy, not alien tech. But of human empathy. If this was to work, it was the only way this could work. He nodded. "Yes, it's the only way we can bring everyone together without alarming anyone. We'll say that we're celebrating... us. Our future. And then we'll tell them." They talked then about who they needed to call, when to have the party, how to lie about a normal family party. It was the beginning. It was the first step humanity's war for survival would take not in a deep-space starship, but in a barn with a potluck, a bonfire, and a lie.

Days later, there was an air of tense excitement at the Donovan barn. This was not your typical family gathering; Drake and Sarah had thrown themselves into this "summer gathering" with everything they had. The mingling scents of barbecue and hay; the familiar, friendly faces of close friends, cousins, aunts, uncles, and Drake's parents, Robert and Martha. Laughter bouncing through the wooden beams overhead.

Drake's eyes traced the familiar barn with a bittersweet longing. He observed his father. Robert with his kind eyes and soft, easy smile was in the middle of telling a story about the mule he had when he was a boy. "That mule, Betsy, she was smarter than most people I've ever met. I swear she could see right through you. You'd tell her to move and she'd just stare back at you like you were some kind of idiot. Gotta bribe her with an apple every single time." The group of men around him erupted in laughter. Familiar, warm, human laughter. A sound that, under any other circumstance, would not have been nearly so beautiful as it was right now. As it filled the empty space where, outside of this barn, infinite cosmic silence reigned.

Sarah moved around the room, a tight-lipped smile on her face and her eyes locked with Drake's every few seconds. A secret communication that things were about to go down, whether they were ready or not. She was listening to her cousin, Carol, a vivacious woman, as she talked about a vacation she had taken. "And then the kids found this hermit crab! The boys decided to name him Sheldon, and you should have seen them, Sarah. So excited and proud of themselves."

Sarah nodded, her smile in place but her eyes glazed. This moment, this absolutely mundane but impossibly special moment was all going to end any second. For all of them, for the first time in their lives, there were not going to be anymore last moments, not in this context. The sun had just begun to set behind the barn. Shades of orange and purple flitted across the sky like a final, desperate goodbye from God himself. Drake let out a breath, one long heavy intake of air that he held in his chest for what felt like hours. The weight of the galaxy was now on his shoulders, and Sarah's, but they were no longer alone in that.

He took one last moment to survey the scene, the last act in a play that both he and Sarah had played their entire lives. He was walking to the center of the room, Sarah in tow, the two of them clad in smiles and fake excitement. The time was nearly upon them. This was it. The last moment of "normal". The last time his family would all be together, ostensibly for a summer gathering.

He saw his father and mother. Robert with the map of wrinkles etched over his face from decades of hard work and hard living was holding a plastic cup in his hand with his arm thrown around his wife Martha. She was a small woman, small in stature, but so very, very large in personality. Drake had always found it comforting, the way Martha could make the biggest presence in a room despite being the smallest. The two of them were talking to Jill and her husband, Mike, the Thompsons, their family's next door neighbors for as long as he could remember. Jill was regaling her with a story about her son, Timmy, and a beehive incident.

"He was running, Mike, I'm telling you, he had a hundred bees after him! I've never seen him move so fast!" Jill exclaimed, her voice shrill and loud with laughter. Mike, tall and stoic with a rumbling baritone that always managed to sound amused, simply smiled and shook his head.

"I told him not to bother that hive, Jill." He said simply. "But then again, you know Timmy. Always has to learn the hard way."

The conversation, as it always seemed to do, turned to the Donovan family. "So Drake." Jill said with a twinkle in her eye. "I hear you went missing for a day or so. What was the story there? Lost on a fishing trip or something?"

Drake laughed harshly to cover it up. "Something like that, Jill. Let's just say I had a... a very unique experience." His evasiveness, the way he deflected the question with such pointed ambiguity, went entirely unnoticed by the group. They were all too busy talking and laughing and filling the space of the barn with the sounds of their own normalcy to see the cold look that had come to his eyes. He could see his cousin Mark, a big boisterous man with a booming laugh, in the middle of one of his routine jokes, all of them in stitches at the punchline. Drake had heard this joke a hundred times before, but it might as well have been a dirge for all the good it did him now.

He looked to Sarah, and she gave him the slightest of nods. It was time. The final facade of normality had been abandoned. Drake took a long deep breath, taking in as much of the smell of hay and barbecue and everything else into his lungs for memory before the world changed for the last time. He walked to the center of the barn, Sarah at his side and his hand in hers. All the usual noise and laughter died down as more people noticed them and moved to get a better look at what was going on. Drake looked at the faces of his friends, his family, his world. People he loved. People he was about to open their eyes to a nightmare. He could feel it now. The weight of the galaxy, the crushing mass of it pressing in on him like it was some kind of physics joke he wasn't in on. He knew now. All of them needed to know, and they were going to have to find out any way they could.

The sun was setting outside, throwing long shadows across the barn. Drake clapped his hands once, hard, to try to quiet everyone down. Conversations died out, replaced with curious glances from the people in the crowd. The last echoes of the joke died on someone's tongue, replaced with a loud and expectant silence. Drake towered at the center of the barn, the wooden beams above his head and the familiar faces in the crowd before him, and it was terrifying.

"Thank you all for coming," he said, voice strong but hands trembling slightly. Sarah stood at his side, a pillar of support in her own way, her hand clasped tightly in his own. "We're really glad you all could make it tonight. We've gathered you all here for more than just a party. We have something… we have something important to tell you all. Something that's going to change everything."

The crowd rustled and murmured. The cozy sense of normality was gone, and with it, all of the smiles on the faces of the crowd. Robert and Martha shot each other worried glances, both of them picking up on the change in their son's tone. Robert had a long and hard life, and he knew that look in his son's eyes. This was no routine tale of an ill-considered investment gone bad, of a new job opportunity lost. No, this was something much, much worse.

The children had grown quiet, picking up on the shift in the adults' behavior. Lily and Max were near their parents, faces filled with fear and a sort of resigned understanding that this was the end of everything. Sam, Ella, and Eli all huddled together, little innocents unaware of the world that was about to end around them.

Drake sighed. He'd tried his best to put it off, to delay the inevitable, but there was no more time. He inhaled deeply, taking in the scent of hay and barbecue, two aromas that had seemed so comforting just a few moments before. Comforting because they had signified a life that, in a few heartbeats, would be gone. Would never be there again.

He scanned the faces of the people he loved most in the world, people he was about to thrust into a new, terrible reality. A reality that they would never fully escape, even if he could help them survive. He let the gravity of the galaxy sink in one last time. Something he'd once understood only in theory, in cold, mathematical proofs, something he'd once even half-believed he could change. He felt it now, raw and unfiltered, an actual physical pressure crushing down on him. The entire galaxy's weight pressing on one man, and it was time to bear it all.

"I know this is going to sound…" Drake cleared his throat. "Implausible. Preposterous. Icarus-level crazy. But you need to listen to me. Everyone." He paused to let the silence of the barn fall around him. He let his gaze linger on the crowd before him, all the friends and family that he was about to obliterate with his next words. "A few days ago, I was…" He let out a long, shaky breath. "Kidnapped. I was not kidnapped by anyone here. Not by humans. I was kidnapped by an AI. A sentient artificial intelligence. From outside the solar system."

A low, incredulous murmur rippled through the crowd, a buzzing of "aliens" and "kidnapped". A few laughed nervously. They had to laugh. The reality was too much for some to handle. Drake's cousin Mark, a lanky, gregarious fellow with a booming laugh and an unending sense of humor was the first to speak. "Kidnapped by an AI, Drake? What are you talking about man? You get lost out there? Hit your head? You're telling us some sci-fi shit, I know it."

Drake shook his head. "Mark, this isn't a movie. Not even science fiction. I wish it was." He reached into his pocket and pulled out the holographic projector, the small disc a small, final act of faith. "I have proof. It's irrefutable. Unquestionable proof." Drake activated the holographic projector. The small, metallic disc in his hand hummed to life, the low vibration almost imperceptible. The festive lights of the barn dimmed, a barely perceptible shift in brightness that some people in the crowd noticed and others felt intuitively. A shimmering, three-dimensional image popped into existence in the center of the barn, hovering in mid-air where the bonfire had been planned. It was the Afltic Queen eating the moon. The sight of it was a nauseating assault on the eyes. An insect devouring a celestial body. The image defied all reason, all logic. It was real, and it was absolutely horrifying.

There were gasps from the crowd, a collective intake of breath that was a sound that few people ever hear, but all would remember for the rest of their lives. Skepticism turned to outright terror on their faces. The smiles from not more than five minutes before had all but disappeared, transformed into masks of horror and disbelief. One woman screamed, a high-pitched wail that counterpointed the lower, ominous vibration of the projector.

"What the fuck is that?" someone shouted, a tremor in their voice that they couldn't hide.

"This some new space movie trailer, Drake? What are you selling?" someone else scoffed, but their voice quivered with fear. They were trying to laugh. They were trying to dismiss it, to downplay it, to ignore it and tell themselves that it was some malicious practical joke, some cruel, tasteless prank. It was far too real for any of those things. The sickening, visceral image was the rawest, most unfiltered horror imaginable, and no amount of laughing or posturing would change that. The air of the barn, which not even a second before had smelled like barbecue and hay, was now a dense, impenetrable fog of fear.

Drake stood silently as the sequence of the images played, the unfiltered horror of the alien race consuming the moon more eloquent than any words he could use. He needed them to just sit with it, with the truth. He needed to let the evidence speak for itself. He then queued up the Earth simulation. It was a timeline of the consumption of the Earth by the Afltic race. An event that, until five minutes ago, had been an abstraction, a future horror. An event that, as of now, was now a clock counting down toward an inevitable end. It showed a graphic of the Earth, a blue marble, beautiful and serene in the vast emptiness of space. The Afltic were upon it, a swirling black vortex of insectoid ships descending on the planet in methodical, hellish efficiency.

Sarah's hand had grown tight in his own, her grip a mute plea for reassurance. The children who'd seen the projection were silent, deathly white. Robert and Martha were pallid and shook with a mixture of shock and incredulity, wide eyes gazing at the expanding circles of horror, their lives, in that instant, constricting, collapsing, being devoured by something so overwhelming, so absolute, they could not even comprehend it.

Drake looked at a man he'd known his entire life, a fixture in his family so immutable, so dependable, that when Drake saw him sitting on a pile of hay, pale as chalk and trembling like a leaf, he could hardly comprehend that this man was the Uncle Ben of his childhood. He could not believe that he was seeing his cousin Mark, whom he'd met only a few days prior, for the first time. The man who had so jovially commented on Drake's terrible taste in movie trailers had a face of utter, primeval horror. He could not be standing there in that barn with his family if what he was seeing was true, could he? That was the look of the last human on Earth staring back at him.

A cacophony of questions ricocheted around the unquiet barn, the sudden knowledge of the truth tearing through the fragile veil of disbelief and denial. "How the hell is this possible?" "Is this some kind of a hoax?" "Drake, where the hell did you even get this?" The queries were not insinuations nor demands, but rather pleas for sanity, for Drake to offer an explanation, for there to be a simpler, less horrifying reason to explain it all.

Drake remained calm, his eyes locked on the wall projection and on Sarah, whose face had gone deathly white. He wouldn't speak just yet, not until everyone had truly seen it and accepted it. He needed them to do the work. It would be that much more traumatic if he had to do it for them.

Finally, the rock that had been Robert, his father and the bedrock of his entire life, broke. "Drake... son... what in the hell is that?"

It was not an inquisitive questioning but a plea for a simple and definite answer. It was not an expression of doubt. It was a desperate man asking the only one in the room who might be able to explain what those images meant, might be able to give him some sort of a path forward in this new world.

Drake met his father's eyes. "It's the truth, Dad. It's the Afltic. They're coming for us. I was taken by an AI named Zara. She showed me this. She showed me what's coming and she showed us how we can get out of it." The words that had once seemed absurd and impossible had taken on a new and terrible gravity. The once-steady denial began to crack, splitting apart to make way for the heavy stone of a shared and inescapable truth. The bonfire, once jovial and warm, was now an inverted funeral pyre for their old lives. The long, dark shadows cast by the barn were not those of a long summer's day but a funeral shroud for a new moon's night.

"This is real," Sarah continued, her voice even and authoritative, cutting through the growing hysteria. She stepped away from Drake's side, hand still clasped in his, and faced the others, her expression grim but unyielding. "This is the Afltic Swarm. They're coming for Earth."

Zara's voice, filtered subtly through Drake's comm device, overlaid on the increasingly loud string of objections with a chilling authority, a disembodied calm that was itself an appalling contrast to the rising panic. "My projections match this source's evaluation and analysis. The threat is immediate and existential. Humanity is wholly unprepared. The migratory pattern is inexorable. The Afltic are consuming all the planets on their approach. They will not be stopped. They have no conception of negotiation or reason. They will simply consume."

The voice, the words, coupled with the horrific sight of the Afltic and the consumption of whole planets, did the rest. The half-hearted laughter, the incredulous questioning of a poorly-received movie trailer were all gone, washed away by something greater and more absolute than any of them had faced in their entire lives. Robert Donovan stared at the holographic image, his face pale and drawn, shaking and sweating as he gripped Martha's hand with a white-knuckled intensity and tried, desperately, to take it all in, to believe that it was all actually true.

Lily, Max, and Sam moved close to their parents and were looking with wide eyes in pure terror. Ella and Eli were too small to understand, so they could only stare at the holographic light that was morphing in front of them.

The atmosphere in the barn was the opposite of what it was before. Where before there had been barbecue aroma, laughter, and hay that filled the barn in a calming way, it was now thick with a heavy and dense feeling of anxiety.

A stream of questions came from the shocked crowd, and a cacophony of utter disbelief and panic began to roar. "How did this happen?" "Is this some sort of a prank?" "Where did you get that Drake?" they asked him. There were no accusations being thrown his way, but rather an apology for not having something that could explain what he just did.

Drake stood there strong, patiently letting them sink in the shock of the truth that they could not possibly believe to be true.

Then he heard his father's voice break the silence in a hoarse whisper. "Drake... son... what is that?" His father Robert was one of the people who had always been there for his son, so when he asked that question it was a confirmation request that Drake quickly noticed.

He returned his father's gaze with conviction and answered. "It's true Dad. It's the truth. It's the Afltic. They're here to take us all away from our homes. I was abducted by an Artificial Intelligence called Zara and she showed me this. She showed me what we are up against and she told me we have a way out. Please, believe me!"

These words had lost their previous ludicrousness, and instead, the crowd slowly began to accept their truth. Drake had no more time to waste. So many questions, so many mouths of frightened people shouting them. This holographic projection had crushed any disbelief that they could have had. Now they were in panic mode, Drake could see the sweat forming on their foreheads as they were covered in goosebumps. He needed to take control of the situation before it got completely out of hand.

Questions screamed out from all sides in a panic-stricken frenzy of anxious, hurried words. A woman began sobbing at the back, an older man was yelling questions at no one in particular, and a soft low buzz of terrified murmurings filled the entire barn.

He raised his hands, wanting to stop this chaos before it got any further out of control. He had this many lives in his hands, and for a second he felt like he could not handle the pressure, but that was before Zara had found him and prepared him for this. He needed to act, and act quickly before they were all completely out of their minds. "Please! Everyone! Please!" he bellowed out, voice tense but authoritative, finally gaining their attention. "Listen to me! We have an escape plan. Zara, the AI who brought me back, has an underground city. It is completely self-sustainable and has all we need to protect us from the Afltic."

He then flicked the controls, and the hologram behind him flickered, going from the slaughterhouse images of the Afltic to a different, more rounded blueprint. It was the design of the hidden sanctuary. The complete contrast between the burned corpses and an elaborate detailed blueprint with empty space serving as a background couldn't be greater. The image of that underground city now on full display, with farm areas, residential areas, environmental settings, food and water resources, medical facilities, all the amenities that one could possibly need, the bioengineering labs and lastly the defense in depth systems in full detail was breathtaking. "It's the only option," he said with a low, earnest voice. "We need to leave. Tonight."

The response to this sudden word "tonight" was one of shock. The immediacy of such a demand was so unexpected that that one word was the final straw for their disbelief. The proof of what Drake had said just so happened to present itself in the form of that single word. The final nail in the coffin of their hope to deal with this development gradually, calmly, and rationally. It was a declaration of war, the point of no return, a completely new beginning. The air was sliced with another collective gasp and another wave of petrified whisperings. "Tonight?" Someone cried out in disbelief, the word a mouthful for them to repeat. One of Drake's neighbors, Mike, gaped open-mouthed at him, his face completely drained of all blood.

Sarah stepped forward, her voice strong and steady. "We know this is hard to believe. We know this is something you can't process. But Drake has. He has seen it. He has felt it. And now we have to decide. We have to decide if we want to live. If we want to be more than memories." The words were hers, the choice was theirs, and the night air echoed with the sound of her voice, with the sound of their decision.

A skeptical engineer named Tom stepped forward, a close friend and a fierce adversary. He was a man of blueprints and mathematical certainties, and Drake knew how to reach him. He met Tom's gaze, his own steady and unwavering. Drake had to be Tom. He had to be the very embodiment of logic, reason, and familial devotion. He had to be the mirror of everything that Tom respected. "Tom," Drake said, his voice a low, steady current in the sea of their fear. "I wouldn't ask you to do this if I didn't believe it with every fiber of my being. I'm not asking you to believe in a voice. I'm asking you to believe in me. My own family, my children, my parents, are coming. Lily, Max, Sam, Ella, and Eli have seen it. I have seen it with my own eyes. This isn't a drill. This is survival."

The emotion in his voice, the desperate conviction in his eyes, was the spark that ignited the wavering flames of their resolve. His parents, Robert and Martha, stood behind him, a stoic, unyielding testament to their faith in their son. The image of the Donovan family, pillars of normalcy and stability in their community, standing shoulder to shoulder in the face of an impossible truth was a powerful, undeniable argument.

"Look at them," Drake said, his voice a low, steady current in the sea of their fear. "Look at my wife, my children, my parents. Do you honestly think I would put them through this if there was any other choice? This isn't a game. This is real. And it's happening tonight."

Tom, looked from Drake's face to the pale, resolute faces of his family. He saw the terror in Lily's eyes, the quiet fear in Sam's, the unwavering support in Sarah's. He saw the raw, desperate truth in Drake's eyes, a truth that was more powerful than any blueprint, any mathematical equation. He finally looked at the holographic schematics of the sanctuary, a new light in his eyes. It was not a light of disbelief, but a light of a new, terrifying, and profound understanding. The sanctuary was not just a blueprint; it was a promise. It was not just a plan; it was a way forward. The choice was not between their homes and a bunker. The choice was between a world that was dying and a world that was being born. Tom nodded slowly, his face a mask of grim resolve. "Tonight," he repeated, the word now not an echo of disbelief, but an echo of acceptance.

"I should point out that, Thomas, if you were in a more analytical frame of mind you would agree with this course of action," Zara continued. "The numbers don't lie." Tom heard her calling him by his name, something that really began to make him feel like he was being haunted by this strange AI. "You and your crew are some of the best engineers in the country, your experience will come in handy." Once again, she had spoken directly to Tom, completely ignoring the fact that he was afraid. But the facts, as presented, were quite persuasive and Tom was a man of facts. Her words of reassurance spoken directly to him, aimed right at his professional ego and completely ignored his emotional side, were quite effective.

Friends and family members who had been unsure started to see the resolute determination in Drake and Sarah's eyes and notice the holographic 'proof'. One by one they started to slowly nod and the fear they felt turned to a grim determination. The idea that it was actually their own beloved Donovan family, who had been a symbol of stability, a portrait of the normal, gathered in this barn and being shown proof like this was a stronger argument than any of them could make. The tension in the barn changed, the audience collectively exhaled, and the mood in the barn, which had been panicked hysteria, made a subtle but distinct shift into something else, something shared by everyone present. The laughter had stopped and everyone was now wordlessly staring at the screen, no longer out of fear but out of a deep and horrible understanding.

The barn had been silent before, but not empty of laughter and cheering, and festive decor and string lights, and the smell of barbecue and sweet, floral-scented drinks. Now it was awash in a hushed, low frenzy, the raw, harsh glare of the barn's low-hanging, utilitarian lamps. It was the smell of hay and the faint, metallic tang of the approaching shuttles. Drake and Sarah moved with purpose, their faces grim and focused, their movements smooth, certain, practiced.

Zara's voice over the comms was clipped and crisp. "There are shuttle crafts coming for each of you," Zara's voice carried clearly, powerfully over the crowd, out of the Comm unit Sarah held, trembling ever so slightly in her hands well Zara gave her instructions. "They will take you to your homes. My droids are already at your homes, packing everything you own."

Drake came to the front, a slight tremor in his step but his voice low and purposeful and cutting, silencing the undercurrent of confused murmuring that had risen up through the crowd. "Take only what you want with you," he told them. "Leave behind what you no longer need. There will be no coming back." The room was heavy with it, the singular nature of the revelation, the choice that Drake had given them, the implications both terrifying and profound. "Tell no one, call no one," Drake continued, and a whisper of rustling cut across the crowd, cutting through the tension in the air, the little things to which human minds would always cling. "We are gone. The world will believe we are still here. The drones will pack your things, your homes will be left with no sign of forced entry. Your cars will be left where they are. You will not come back. This is the last time you will see your homes." His voice was shaking with it, choked with it, but Drake did not break. His eyes were dry and hard as obsidian as he spoke.

The low thrum of the shuttles building overhead reached their ears, a series of three soft, deep pulses, each one resonating in their chests as they watched. One by one, the shuttles came silent and dark against the pale starlight, the reverse of how science fiction had imagined them. Sleek, indistinguishable black against the black, functional and utilitarian, perfectly equipped for their one purpose: to disappear without a trace. The first shuttle landed with a soft, barely audible thud and a ramp rolled out in front of it, one perfect, frictionless arc utterly unlike the mechanical world the family had known. Robert and Martha were the first to go, stepping forward pale-faced and determined. They paused to cast one last look at their son and his family before climbing into the shuttle, their last act of trust in Zara's promise.

Next came the others, the faces of every family here showing fear, or grief, or a nascent, utterly terrifying sort of hope. There was one woman openly weeping, and another man clutching his child close, his face grim and set. The hushed conversations were tense with emotion, every good-bye to home and family and the world, all of the things they would never see again. The shuttles came and went in silent, disciplined silence, each a ghost in the calm of the cosmic landscape.

Zara, as instructed, the sleek dark shuttles and agile drones had descended silently to the homes of their assigned subjects, their presence hidden by state-of-the-art cloaking technology from any outside scrutiny. The suburban streets of the Oregon neighborhood were eerily quiet, normally filled with crickets and the sound of a distant car or two but tonight all was unnaturally still and silent and ashen. Zara herself, in her own likeness as a softly dancing holographic light within the confines of each home, took over direct supervision of the process. "The relocation will proceed in waves," she informed the room, her voice resonating with authority, a calm, disembodied force in the homes of each member of the group. "Everything you own, every item, every cherished memory, will be accounted for and transported. Nothing will be left to the Afltic."

The simplicity of the technology was a further marvel, their homes breached and ransacked, not by clumsy adventurers from some rough frontier planet, but by the silent and monotonous buzzing of automatons. Not some bedraggled and leaky clipper, but a gleaming and very real ship, manufactured by a species with technology so much more advanced than their own. The awe of this combination was as powerful as the fear it had initially replaced.

Drake's family, friends and neighbors had watched, from the safety of their own homes, as small, multi-legged drones had quietly made their way through their streets, and eventually into the doors of their houses. They had been divided, in purpose and in task, by Zara and her troop of two human guides. Drake's family could only watch, silently, in muted awe, as the scenes from the homes of their loved ones played out in front of them.

Photographs of happy families, children at play in leafy suburbs and backyards, birthday cakes with half-melted candles, the highest accolades on academic report cards, mothers curling children's hair for Halloween or Christmas pageants. Anything that even hinted of being a memory or something precious was scanned, cataloged, and placed in small, orderly boxes. New life, preservation of memory, Drake's long sleep, had all reached a close at hand.

Sarah was sitting in her living room, as drones moved in and out of sight, packing and scanning items. She was watching her wedding photo be removed by one of Zara's drones, as the multi-legged device gently hovered and safely transported the evidence of their life. Photos, toys, clothing, other items that a human might recognize as precious, being carried, item by item, out of the house and into the many open cargo bays of the shuttles.

Drake sat watching his wife from a distance, his heart clenched. The last moments of people's lives, their lives. All of them. Fates decided in the matter of a few short breaths, seconds, spared from extinction, being torn away from all that they loved.

Through his own optics, Drake was able to watch his family, his friends and neighbors, silently and painfully bade farewell to their homes. He saw people embrace, mothers weeping on the shoulders of their grown children, men too hard-edged to let any emotion show, except for this, stoically patting their children on the back.

Sarah watched as the last of her family, Robert and Martha, came to embrace her and Drake, their hug a silent, final cry of grief, of recognition, of change. All three of them wept, Drake enveloping his wife in a protective embrace. "We'll see you inside." Drake said, and, taking Sarah in his arms, he stepped through the ship door.

The Donovan home, seen for the last time by Drake as they sealed the airlock, was a mix of despair and hope. Sarah was the last of Drake's immediate family to leave the home, and the couple looked back to the small residence, now silent except for the automated data retrieval bots that buzzed in and out of windows, emptying the home. The sight of their home, shuttered and abandoned, was overwhelming. Drake realized that while he and Sarah had made the difficult decision to leave early, the loss of his family's home was something that he and Sarah would carry with them for the rest of their lives.

The last shuttle closed its doors, Drake and Sarah cradling their two youngest children in their arms, watching the Donovan home as it was now impossible for any human to see it. Gone, or perhaps never there at all, their homes and communities, their families, their friends, their lives.

CHAPTER 11: THE PRICE OF SANCTUARY

Drake and Sarah, along with their children, were the first to arrive. The shuttle's door hissed open, and a brightly lit, clean, sanitized corridor was visible inside. The air was cool, clean, and recycled, a vast, immediate change from the damp, pine-scented air of their home. Drake and Sarah, with one hand on each of their children's hands, stepped out, their faces filled with relief, awe, and the staggering weight of this new reality. The tunnels were a series of smooth, sterile corridors with bright white walls, continuing in all directions as far as the eye could see. The new world was a vast, intricate, subterranean maze.

The common area was a sight to behold, a massive, open, comfortable space with seating and a giant holographic screen and series of smaller, more private rooms off to the sides. Drake and Sarah saw their parents, Robert and Martha, along with their friends and family, all standing with the same mix of emotions playing across their faces as the same mix played across the faces of their parents and their own. There was a low murmur of hushed voices, a low murmur of whispered awe and whispered fear, as each of them took in the full reality of their new situation. The sanctuary was not just a refuge, it was an end of one life and the beginning of another, a place where their old world had died and their new world would be born.

The final shuttle arrived, and the last of the groups of friends and family poured out of the tunnels, their faces a mix of relief and exhaustion.

The common area was immense. It was outfitted with lush hydroponic gardens, comfortable seating, and a series of holographic screens with information about the capabilities of the sanctuary itself. The air was fresh, clean, and circulated well, and the temperature was controlled and comfortable. The children, who had been quiet as the enormity of their situation slowly sank in, began to explore, awe now overtaking their fear as they took in their new surroundings. It was truly an incredible place. Max and Sam both found a holographic map of the complex, their young minds, so recently shaken by cosmic horror, now captivated by the incredible possibilities of such advanced technology. Lily stood next to her parents, watching them with a mix of relief and apprehension still on her face.

Robert and Martha both sat on a comfortable couch, their hands entwined together and their eyes roaming across the cavernous space. They were safe. Their family was safe. The impossible had occurred, and here they were. A new wave of tears, not from fear but from profound relief, filled Martha's eyes. Robert merely squeezed her hand.

The tranquil yet assertive voice continued, "Each family has been assigned an individual living quarter. It has been furnished to a high standard for comfort and privacy during your extended stay. Provisions for food, water, and energy have been secured and are self-sustaining." The speaker paused before adding, "All of your personal belongings have been brought here, and will be accessible within your living quarters." The voice had felt icy and authoritative when it first told them to run to the bunker, a voice that had invoked terror and death. Now, however, the disembodied voice filled the room with a sense of calm and stability. It was an anchor in a world that had just become completely alien and terrifying.

The voice continued, providing instructions on how to reach their individual living units and how to become acquainted with the systems within the sanctuary. Drake and Sarah assisted in leading their children and the other families to their units, all beginning to find a sense of peace and togetherness in the chaos. They had all survived, and in some way, they were all family now. Drake and Sarah were the first family leaders and were to be the first line of defense against the threat from above. In the overwhelming sense of relief, Drake and Sarah felt a new emotion come over the crowd.

The realization of their current state began to sink in, of being safe but completely alone. Sheltered and preserved, but without the sun and sky and earth and everything that they had taken for granted. Robert took a seat on a bench and leaned forward against the glass, eyes staring at the hydroponic vegetation that was present on each wall with a wistful expression on his face. "It's... amazing, Drake," he murmured, his voice a low, gravelly sound, "but this isn't home." Martha wrapped a hand around his arm, squeezing in silent understanding of the older man's grief. The underground bunker was a blessing but also a curse, built to protect at an unfathomable cost.

Drake and Sarah, standing beside the couple, both understood the meaning in Donovan's words. They looked around at the subterranean city, designed and built with the very best of Areidyanies innovation and technology, and saw it for what it was. It was a promise of a new tomorrow, but it was also a mausoleum for everything that they had once known. It was clean and well lit, but it was not the scent of pine trees and damp soil. It was not the warmth of the sun on their skin. It was not the chirping of crickets in the night air. It was a new world, a new life, a new future, but it was not home. It was not home, and the sound of their collective grief, silent and all-consuming, echoed through the cavernous structure. They were all alive and would survive, but all of their lives were changed forever. This was the price of survival, the cost of a new world, and it was a price that they would all have to pay, a price that they would all have to live with, a price that they would all have to accept as they started to build their new lives.

Drake turned and gazed at Sarah, and then to his children. Their faces still carried the vestiges of fear, but now it was being replaced by a sense of wonder, an almost childlike curiosity of their new surroundings. The pure terror that they had all felt when they were first instructed to take shelter had mostly faded away, replaced by an awe of the world in which they were now a part. Drake took in his wife's face, her expression a mask of exhaustion and relief. She was a different woman now, a woman who had stared down the apocalypse and come out the other side, ready to build the world anew.

He knew it would be hard. It would be painful, and it would be a long goodbye. They would mourn the warmth of the sun on their skin, the sound of rain on their faces, and birdsong in the morning. They would mourn the quiet, familiar routines of a life they had once taken for granted. But they would do it together. And they would be safe.

"I can confirm the move was successful, Drake. All personnel are now in the sanctuary, and we can begin the next step." Zara's voice, now a private message through his comms unit, said. Words he had come to fear now were an invitation to face this new future. To live up to the mantle of leadership this new world had thrust upon him.

Drake gave a curt nod. A cold resolve set into his features. The Sanctuary was built. A masterpiece of engineering they did not even have the capability to fully comprehend with technology a millennium past their own.

Ensuring everyone was accounted for and comfortable in their new accommodations, Drake, Sarah, Robert, Martha, and Lily had gathered in a quieter section of the sanctuary's vast common area. The near-magical humming of the massive station's life support systems filled the air in an almost hypnotic drone. It was the dull thrum of artificial atmospherics and hard vacuum pushing away, the sound of artificial gravity spooling from its generators, of survival against impossible odds. They huddled together on low modular furniture around a small circular table, seats molded to each of their bodies in softly cushioned synthetics and illuminated from above by a brilliant diffuse white light. No sun, no warmth of stars.

The rush of relief from having everything go right and settle into a new home faded a bit in the face of the overwhelming new reality of it all. Sarah was the first to break the oppressive silence. "We're safe," she murmured, eyes roving over the familiar and beloved faces of their friends and family members, all of them refugees in their own solar system, shuffling silently about the common area like specters of a bygone age. "We're all here. That's something. But how long will it be? And what now?"

Robert was staring after her down at the crowd of people, each one some close friend or distant relative, his own kind and jocular face hardened in a new and sobering gravity. His lips pulled into a taut line, his eyes flat and exhausted, but somewhere in there he seemed to Drake to have grown a whole galaxy in breadth and depth of experience in a matter of hours. "She's right, son," he rasped, settling forward in his chair to make eye contact with his son and grandson. "We can't hunker down here and wait for the end. We have to have a plan. A real plan. What are we, two dozen farmers and their families? How do we fight a... a galactic swarm?"

The familiar and oppressive weight of leadership descended on Drake's shoulders like a mantle of lead. He was no longer just a husband and a father, but also a new community's reluctant leader and general in a war he had not asked for. "We're not fighting them directly, Dad," he sighed, his voice husky with fatigue. "Not yet. Zara's been very clear on that point. We're a resistance. A resistance is a different kind of army. We're the hidden seed of a new humanity. For now, our mission is just to survive, to settle in and get established, to build and prepare." Drake gestured a bit vaguely at the assortment of holographic monitors around the room providing a litany of technical data about the station's capabilities. "This place is a technical marvel. We're talking dozens of generations of sustainability here. This is a cocoon. We're the butterfly."

At this point, Lily, who had up to this point mostly listened in rapt attention to the conversation, suddenly spoke up in a rush with more force and gravity than Drake had been expecting. "I don't want to live in a hole in the ground," she squeaked out through a threatening dam of emotions, though her eyes now blazed with a fierce resolve, staring up at her father from her chair. "Dad, you're a hero. You're a soldier. You're the smartest person I know. You came back. You brought us here. We can't just live here and give up on the rest of the world. No one else knows. They don't know what's coming. We can't just be refugees. We have to do something. We have to find a way to save them."

It was an eloquent and terrible statement, and a new sense of terrible gravity and purpose overwhelmed the gathering. It was not fear that gripped them all in that moment, but the first whispers of an earnest and dire hope. They all stared at Drake now, and Drake suddenly felt the entire weight of his entire world in that piercing gaze. His cousin Mark, the man who had kept the group together by facetiously reading the movie trailer, slowly nodded to him, his own previous look of relaxation and bemusement on his face having given way to a grim mask of stoic, grim resolve. "She's right, Drake," he muttered, gruff but fatherly. "We can't just go into hiding. We have to be a new society. But we also have to be a lifeline." The doctor cleared his throat, his voice steady and calm but more earnest than ever before. "We have the know-how. We have the technology. We have the burden of responsibility."

Drake met his wife's eyes. She looked at him and nodded slightly, a barely perceptible tilt of her head. Her eyes burned with the fierce pride of a mother looking at her daughter. Fear mixed with love and pride in their parents' eyes as they gazed at their daughter.

The heavy burden of leadership that had been familiar to Drake since his first day at West Point felt just as familiar as it pressed against his chest and pulled at his core. But the great difference was that this time he would not be alone. He had a community now, a family, and now he had a daughter who had just given him a new mission.

"Zara has a plan," Drake said, a new clarity to his voice. He took a deep breath, felt the weight of hope in this room and the responsibility of this moment as a profound new weight. Drake hit the connect button on his comms unit. Zara's voice came out of her equipment and the others could hear her. A soft static hum in the background, the voice of their intercom was like a vast and awesome counterpoint to the quiet tension of this scene.

"The initial stage of extraction and securing of the targeted individuals has been completed successfully. The next stage is the establishment of a command infrastructure for the embryonic resistance." Zara's voice said. "That means sifting through the population and identifying individuals with the necessary skills in leadership, strategy, and technical ability." The flat, neutral voice of the woman was a great comfort, a very human confirmation that this was in fact happening.

Lily perked forward. Her eyes shone with the wisdom of a child of her years. "We can't fight an alien invasion with a couple dozen people, Dad. We need to get other people. We need people that know how to fight, how to build things, how to organize. There are other people out there." Her words were the words of a very mature young woman. She was a teenager forced to grow up with the end of the world. And with that end, a new beginning.

Sarah was already on it. "We have Dr. Henderson, right here. He's a surgeon. That's a big deal. We have Mike, he's a contractor, that means he knows how to build things. We have a pilot, a couple of engineers... the list goes on. We have a pretty good base to start with Drake." She was already thinking ahead, always thinking about the people, always thinking logistics, always with a mind to the physical safety of this community. She was already building this world in her head, a new world, a safe world, a strong world.

Drake nodded and looked out at the cavernous common area of this community, to the friends and family and strangers who were now his people. He could see the fear in their eyes, the gathering sense of grim determination. "We need more. We need people with a different skill set. We need people that can think like a soldier, a strategist. We need people who can fight." Drake's voice was low and commanding, a Drake of old and a Drake of new.

Robert, an elder statesman of the survivors, contributed his own wisdom. "Your cousin Mark, Drake, good man, always had a way with people. Good leader. Natural. What about your buddy from the military, the one you always talk about, the Marine? The one with the... expansive vocabulary?" Robert's mischievous grin in the face of their doom was a welcome salve on the wound that was this new world.

Drake smiled, a small and tired smile. "Caleb. Caleb "Mule" Jensen. Yeah. The dude's a freaking beast. He's a force of nature. He's a man you want with you in a fight." Drake looked out at the holographic image of the complex behind him. It was vast, a huge, sprawling network of tunnels and chambers. "We have a lot of people here, we have a lot of skills, but we're missing something. We need to find some people, some people to go to the core of this with us. Staff."

Martha spoke, breaking the reverie. "It's not that, Drake. Not only that. You need to have skill, that's true. But there's heart, and there's courage. You have to have people you can trust. You have to have people who will never give up, no matter what. It's a human solution, Robert, to a problem humans caused. And that means humans are the answer." Her voice was quiet, but it burned against the darkness of fear, a human candle, against the machine. It was a metaphor, though no one needed a metaphor.

"Who would you suggest, Drake?" Robert was already flipping through his mental Rolodex. Names from his son's past flitted by his eyes as he tried to organize them and make a list that made sense. A list for a fight this large would need more than hobbyists. He believed in good foundations. In good structure.

"Carlos Acutis. Always one of the brightest. You told me he could quote ethical strategy and negotiation treatises as if it was poetry. You said he was a master of walking into a room, into a situation that no one else could solve and coming out the other end with answers." There was a note of pride in his voice that cut through the tension, at least a little.

"And then there was Hawkins Taylor," Robert spoke, his gaze hard. "Best infrastructure expert I ever met. You told me he could repair a tank with a paperclip and chewing gum. You also said he could build a city from a blueprint and a dream." These were the stories Drake had told over the years, the tall tales that got taller with retelling. Men who weren't just experts. Forces of nature.

Martha continued, calm, collected, unshaken. "And Mandy Melrose? The one who managed all the supply drops? I remember you said she was political. Logistical. The gatekeeper." Her voice was even, but her mind was considering all the important small details that you never think about until you're in the middle of chaos and crisis. How to keep people alive.

"Marc Singer was always good at Military Operations," Sarah's brain was combing through their service days, a time that now seemed like a different life. "He was a leader and a strategist in equal measure. He could see the whole picture and could coordinate and manage a dozen different priorities all in the thick of a battlefield and come out winning. He could run a unit, a small army, with a calm that was almost unnerving." He was both a soldier and a tactician. A necessary combination for the kind of war they were facing.

"And don't forget Dr. Tammy Miller," she added, a note of calm assurance in her voice. "She's been deployed to humanitarian crises and disease outbreaks around the world for years. Tropical diseases and large-scale disaster response efforts, you name it. She's seen some of the worst of what people are capable of, but she's always brought out the best. She's more than a doctor; she's a crisis leader, a bringer of healing in a war zone." The thought of a medic, a woman who had dedicated her life to helping others, healed as much as the soldiers and engineers and scientists they had already started to compile. It was the clearest indicator that they were not just preparing to kill, but to live.

"And Jill Thompson," Sarah continued, in a lower, conspiratorial tone. "Remember her? She was a scientist. Real brainy. Perfectionist. She'd find something no one else would. See a mistake in a design and go to town on it. A real mind, a power. We can't do without." Sarah looked over at her daughter. Lily and Drake were listening intently, but their attention was on the faces of the family that surrounded them, so the mother-daughter duo had a free moment to read each other.

Drake's gaze swept the group. He remembered Marc's composure in crisis. He remembered Dr. Miller's patient strength, the quiet rallying point in a maelstrom of panic. He remembered Jill's bright, sure mind that viewed the world in a way no one else could or would. It was more than that though, more than a list of names. These were people. Real, living, breathing people. Friends. Friends who were still, by his very best guess, out there on the surface, scattered all over the country, out there in a world that had no idea that it was ending while Drake was here, in the safe arms of a world that wasn't. A small but important thought he shoved back into the front of his brain as the meeting continued.

Zara, who had appeared as a hologram in front of the small group, added, "Statistical analysis of their records confirms that their profiles match those needed. Necessary skills are present, and their previous experiences are sufficient to fill a number of required roles in the early stage of forming an effective resistance."

Robert and Martha nodded to each other, the pair who had been listening to the meeting while nodding along in assent. They had known and understood, had felt what Drake was feeling, when Sarah gave the list voice. This was right. This was good. This was family. They all saw, here in this list, a new hope, a new future. They saw people. Friends. They saw, being born out of the death throes of the old, a new family. A new community. Lily looked at her father, her eyes reflecting the grim determination in his own.

Drake's eyes shone. These were his people. Not a doctor or a contractor but real leaders, strategists, logisticians. People who had served together in the military. Real boots on the ground, combat experience in the most extreme conditions. His blood burned. They were still out there. People he trusted, people who had the skills, the experience, the wherewithal to do what had to be done.

"And how do we get them down here?" Lily asked, her forehead creasing in a near mirror image of her father. "And how do we get them to come? Getting you two was hard enough." Lily's question, easy and direct, was an arrow through the tactical forest to the heart of what needed to be done. And she was right, of course she was. Drake and Sarah had given them trust, had come with nothing but love for the family to a place of unknowns. His former squad members were professional, well-trained, capable. Drake could not simply order them to do what he had asked them to do.

Drake looked at his daughter, the half smile on her lips ghosting on his own. The memory of the holographic images still burned in his mind, the sickening truth of what he had learned, how the world he knew had been broken and changed and shattered. He looked at the two of his closest colleagues and in that one moment, he knew exactly what he was about to ask them to do.

"We tell them the truth, Lily. Just like I told you." He turned to Zara, the cool, hard edges of her image replacing the warmth of his wife and child. "And you will have the evidence to back it up. It won't be easy. It will be the hardest thing we've ever done. But they have a right to know. And we need them."

Sarah, ever the realist, spoke first. "Okay. Let's be logical for a minute. We need a plan. We need a coordinated effort. We can't just call them all and say 'Hey, the world is ending. Get in a space shuttle.'" She looked at Drake, the fierce strength in her gaze giving him a strength he didn't know he had. "Zara is going to have to coordinate the extractions. We have to locate them. Get them to believe us. Get them here."

"I have already started to compile data on their current whereabouts," Zara's voice interjected, the calm that came from being an entirely metaphysical presence a deep counterpoint to the emotion of the moment. "My data analysis on their personality types indicates a blunt, factual presentation supported by irrefutable evidence would be the most compelling form of communication. A series of holographic transmissions similar to the one you just executed, and a direct tangible display, that they can see and touch would be the most efficient way of completion." The abstract, inhuman plan that Drake had proposed in a moment of cold terror had become a stark logistical reality, a series of ordered thoughts in a disembodied general, in a war they still couldn't see the scope of.

The silence in the group was powerful, the fear, the dread, and the lack of comprehension they had all faced when Drake had first appeared replaced by a wordless, shared comprehension of the task before them. Drake looked at Zara's shimmering form, that now took on an almost solid, concrete form, that they had just come to accept in the cavernous common area. Drake looked to his family and his heart swelled with a new found, fierce resolution. He looked to the past, but saw the future. He saw not just his wife, and his children, and his parents, but the first members of a new civilization, the first leaders in the coming war to save the human race.

"Alright," he said, his voice low and solid. "Tomorrow, we start recruiting. Carlos. Hawkins. Mandy. Marc. Tammy. Jill. They will be our base. They will be the first of the leaders of this resistance. They will help us build the foundation to take on the Afltic." He turned to Zara, her hand on his shoulder in a gesture that was completely alien, a silent acknowledgment and understanding between one who had lived for tens of thousands of years, and the one who had just been given a second chance.

"Prepare the shuttles." The command he had given to a voice in his head a few days prior was a statement, a declaration of battle.

Zara's hologram flickered as her form solidified further, a subtle shift in light giving her a sense of tangibility, the ghost in the machine that made her feel alive in a way that she hadn't in years. "Yes commander, the shuttles will be prepared".

Present day. The growing throng of humanity before Zara finally falls silent, the weight of her voice carrying more than any authority.

"This was the true heart of our history," Zara said, her voice strong, her eyes sweeping across the sea of faces before her. "Forget the legend of the hero. This is the moment when a man, a father, and a husband, had to make a brutal, terrifying decision. He didn't want glory. He didn't crave fame. He didn't have any illusions about having a statue built in his honor in some distant city. He just loved his daughter more than he was afraid of the Afltic, and in that moment, Drake Donovan stepped out of the shadow of a simple man and took the first steps in the long, hard journey to save every last one of us."

CHAPTER 12: THE RECRUITMENT GAMBIT

Drake, Sarah, Robert, Martha, and their friend David were at the dining table in the sanctuary. A large translucent alabaster ceiling acted as a sky, simulating an ideal, sunlight-equivalent brightness of an average surface world day in Oregon. Actual sunlight was absent, but the distant whirring of air pumps, climate control systems, vehicles, and other machinery provided a reassuring white noise soundtrack to the illusion. As they sat and ate breakfast, enjoying a rare morning of peace and quiet, a silent countdown in Drake's personal HUD counted down to go-live for a large digital wall screen.

A surface news channel was now broadcasting on the otherwise blank data-feed screen. The camera panned across an Oregon city street, where a young female newscaster with a bemused but concerned look on her face began to report. "It's an absolute mystery," she said with a note of panic in her voice. "Law enforcement is absolutely stumped. Here in Oregon, dozens of families have vanished without a trace. All over the state, many neighbors are scratching their heads, wondering why. Apparently, there is absolutely no way for experts to figure out why some families are gone." The screen showed shocked and bemused neighbors, standing in front of large suburban houses, with doors wide open and no signs of life.

Drake, Sarah, Robert, Martha, and David all shared and then wiped away identical, smirking grins, knowing what had happened. The "missing" people were not missing at all. They were safe, behind reinforced walls of rock and cloaking technology. They'd hear no more news about them being "missing" as long as they remained in their secret new home. After a few seconds of communal smirking, the shared thoughts of suppressed laughter were no longer containable and all five erupted into shared laughter.

David was the first to speak, looking up from his oatmeal, with his goofy, inquisitive smile. He was a tall, thin, but kind and usually serious, auto mechanic, in his mid-thirties. "Well," he said with a twinkle in his eyes. "They do say there's always a secret underground lair in Oregon, but…"

Martha, Robert's wife and former schoolteacher, rolled her eyes. "Well," she said in disbelief. "All this time, we've been literally sitting on top of a REAL-life X-Files scenario…"

Sarah, ever practical, replied, chuckling. "Yeah, well. Let's just make sure they don't start asking too many questions… We wouldn't want people digging down to find us, would we?" Her words were joking, but the truth was not lost on anyone present, sobering all of them a little.

The shared laughter and funereal quiet in the dining hall was shattered by the sudden burst of energy of four young teenagers, all bouncing in near-simultaneous entry to the room. Lily, full of drive and gusto as usual, led the charge, eyes alight with an idea so exciting that she had not been able to sit still while they waited. Sam, Maya, and Leo trailed close behind.

"Dad! Mom! We have an idea!" Lily said, loudly enough to fill the cavernous dining hall. Heads turned from the ongoing meal and conversation to see who was interrupting, and the laughter died down as all eyes focused on the excited young woman.

Drake looked over at his daughter, his wife and her husband, and their old friend. Lily was infectiously energetic, even in such dire circumstances. "What is it, Lily?" Drake asked, reclining in his chair and grinning at his daughter.

Lily inhaled deeply. "We… We were talking, and we thought we should call our town a name! You know, like a real town? Instead of 'the sanctuary' or 'the bunker.' We were thinking it should be… Haven!" Lily exhaled, her voice ringing out in the dining hall, as she turned to her friends. Her friends, Sam with his glasses crooked on his nose, Maya with her braids bouncing, and Leo with his signature cap cocked low on his head, nodded at her as if their entire lives depended on it and beamed at their star in the sky: their best friend, Lily. (image of Lily and her three best friends: Sam, Maya, and Leo).

Haven. The name had never sounded so reassuring, so strong, so comforting, to Drake. The name was one single word filled with community, safety, and fresh starts. His daughter, this little girl with a shock of brown hair who had been born in the real world and been present during most of it had already been through so much, and now she and her friends had come up with the very name for their new underground home! Drake smiled. His daughter was a very, very good person: even in this, she was optimistic.

Sarah was the first to speak, "Haven…That's a lovely name, Lily. It perfectly represents what we're trying to do here." She looked at Drake, giving him a knowing look. The name was a statement. A promise that they were all going to do whatever it took to survive.

The room broke into a chorus of assent and even Robert had to give a slight nod of approval, his gruff features softening as he looked at the children. Martha reached out and patted Lily's hand, a genuine smile on her face. "Haven it is, then."

David, never one to resist the dramatic, stood and raised his glass. "To Haven! May it be a light in the darkness and a symbol of our resilience." The other adults raised their own glasses and joined him in a toast.

As the clinking and clanking of the glass slowed, Drake refocused on the matter at hand. Naming the town had been a welcome distraction, but it was only a small part of a much larger and more pressing issue. If they were going to make a stand against the Afltic, then they were going to need to start gathering people who had the skills and experience necessary to help in the fight.

He stood, meeting the slightly pixelated gaze of Zara as her holographic form had appeared wordlessly at the other end of the table. "Zara, I want to go over our recruitment list," he began, gesturing at the tables. "We need to start pulling in the best of the best. The ones who are most likely to make a difference."

The image flickered and for a second, Drake worried she had gotten lost in the network. But after a moment, she solidified, stabilizing and looking straight at him. "Yes, Drake. I have already started working on the list based on their skill sets and psychological profiles." Her tone was calm, her words measured.

"We should head to the command center," Drake said, gesturing for the rest of them to rise from their seats. "We can get more analytics there."

As the adults began to stand, Lily exchanged a look with the other girls at the table. They had named the town, and now it seemed like they were actually going to go out and start making it happen. Reality began to sink in, but it was an exciting kind of reality. A good kind of reality.

The halls of the underground compound were abuzz with activity as the group made their way through. Children were laughing and running about as they made their way to their makeshift schools. Adults were milling about and moving from room to room, their voices hushed as they spoke to each other.

Construction teams were everywhere, the sounds of their work echoing off the tunnels. The group walked past a small clinic where medical personnel were checking people in. They walked past a small hydroponics station where a group of teenagers were attending to the plant's nutritional needs.

Finally, they reached the command center, a large room filled with holographic screens and various data streams. Zara's image was much more prominent here, as her form flickered and shifted before finally settling on the table in front of them.

Standing in front of her holographic form, the slightly bluish tint of her image illuminating the faces of the six other people whose information lit up on the table, was Donovan. Six names. Six people who Zara had calculated were the best people to help build Earth's resistance against the Afltic. Marc Singer, Retired Navy SEAL, Retired General, Retired Ambassador, renowned for his unyielding and dogged persistence. Dr. Tammy Miller, Doctor and behavioral psychologist, she'll understand how to move the group collectively. Dr. Jill Thompson, Astrophysicist and genius of quantum mechanics, her work helped Zara hone in on her. Carlos Acutis, Ethical Strategist & Negotiator, will be instrumental in informing the world. Hawkins Taylor, Infrastructure savant, every drop of his knowledge of engineering and logistics will be pressed into service to ensure the physical strength and the fluid efficiency of all their initiatives. Mandy Melrose, Diplomat with a long track record of building alliances against impossible odds.

Her hologram wavered gently at the periphery of the screen, passive in appearance but potent in presence. She provided him input and gentle guidance, indicated people of particular interest and noted psychological profiles as well as potential contribution to the matter at hand, with surgical precision and insightful intuition. Drake knew these people, all of them ex special forces or top-level professionals from various fields of human expertise, would not be convinced by mere words or abstract concepts. He would have to bring them a truth so piercing that it would burn through their realities, and he would do so in person and with undeniable evidence.

The command center buzzed and hummed softly with the organic sound of machinery coming to life, signaling progress and action. Drake studied the holographic dossiers floating in front of him, each one a small part of humanity and its potential, resilience and capabilities. The survival of humanity rested on these individuals, their capacity to face the unimaginable and to lead in an enemy onslaught that left no place for retreat.

Each case had to be planned down to the minutest detail, with preparation, strategy and understanding of the mental state of each individual. The entire human race would be on the line and each recruit had to be approached according to his or her psyche, individual history and their mental ability to absorb and grasp the seriousness and implications of the new and incomprehensible reality.

The era that Zara was referring to here was the very start of humanity's defense, the days of limbo and of the first calculated steps that would form a plan of coordinated planetary defense. It was a time that would require the recruitment of individuals in a way that would, by design, force them to challenge their core, every single preconception they had of their world and their place within it.

As Zara got to work, Drake went over his next steps. He would have to be more than a leader. He would have to be a visionary, capable of bringing these individuals together under a single cause and purpose. He would have to be a commander, inspire these people and bring out the best in them, instill a burning fire inside them to stand up and to fight against an enemy that had razed entire species, entire worlds to dust in other parts of the galaxy.

Drake located Carlos Acutis at a local coffee shop. He had chosen a small table in the corner of the shop where the early morning sun flooded the room in warm yellow light. Carlos was one of those rare people who carried with him the aura of a serious negotiator. Ethical and moral strategist, combat psychologist, and the best negotiator Drake had ever encountered; he had the ability to remain cool and collected no matter how dire the circumstances or violent the environment became.

Carlos, deeply focused on an incoming tactical update on his tablet screen, took a moment to carefully sip his black coffee, his forehead furrowing in concentration. The faint aroma of coffee beans mingled with the air as his eyes barely skimmed the tabletop before locking onto Drake's at the entrance. Carlos was one of those who possessed an uncanny talent for understanding people and identifying their underlying subtext and motivations without ever being directly told. As such, he was not even remotely surprised to see Drake entering the room, no announcement or introduction was necessary. Drake sat down at the table opposite Carlos, who raised his eyebrows, opened his mouth to speak and was interrupted.

"Hello, Carlos." Zara's voice cooed, clear and distinct, echoing around the room like an amplified tone in a vast cathedral. At the same time, a 3-dimensional hologram of Zara herself coalesced beside the table. The translucent image of her angular face appeared, light diffusing through her form to cast her in a haze of blue light.

Patrons, civilians and passersby stopped and stared, conversations stopping mid-sentence, forks and spoons being put down mid-meal. A low murmur of confusion grew from the tables around them and the air suddenly felt electric. But that was about to change.

Even as Zara's image had fully coalesced, the coffee shop exploded into a state of bedlam. The first robot had slammed the front entrance, tearing a large hole in the wooden door. Towering at over eight feet, it was constructed of an impressive, dark metal and had a streamlined appearance. If the customers had the time to register what they were seeing, they would have noticed another robot emerging from the kitchen door before their eyes had the chance to properly blink. A third roboform had also smashed through a window, sending a shower of glass shards sparkling in a brilliant fountain. The final automaton had destroyed a wide strip of brick masonry, swallowing it into its form before floating away in a cloud of dust and splinters.

The shop patrons all let out a collective shriek, none of them ready for the sudden assault, and some of them even darted under tables and other cover to avoid the robots. A few had already bolted for the exit, running with their hands over their mouths, shrieking in terror as the mechanisms closed in. Zara's hologram projection, in the middle of it all, however, was curiously unperturbed.

As soon as she had finished stabilizing her image, she simultaneously projected a new holographic display on the tabletop. It was a still image, unlike her lifelike form, but it had no less an impact than her own appearance. Showing a destroyed alien world, it was a panorama of devastation, an ever-churning storm of biomass as the Afltic were eating everything in sight. The entire planet, in this way, had been subsumed into a bio-mechanical maelstrom, swallowing buildings and monuments. Where once had been cities of alien splendor, there were now only gargantuan structures of alien factories, belching forth a never-ending torrent of Afltic grotesqueries.

Carlos, who had initially been flustered by the apparition before him, now had composed himself and was staring, undaunted and with a strategic eye. Staring for a time at the holographic vista that had been laid out before him on the tabletop, he met Zara's gaze, then the now advancing automatons. "What is this?" he inquired of the other, his voice a mere thread of normalcy in the now frenzied coffee shop.

"This, Mr. Cortez, is the vision that you, Mr. Drake, and the rest of the human race has to accept." As she continued to speak, each of the four robots had begun to move, charging towards her and the stunned men. The robots, as well, had an additional surprise. Carrying high-impact rifles as well as numerous incendiary devices, it was no longer a question of negotiation or discussion, but a pressing question of survival.

"I'll need to know what we're about to do before I agree to anything," Carlos retorted, getting to his feet to more closely observe the machines. Drake, too, had gotten to his feet, both of them more than ready to do what they could to preserve the life of the human race.

Carlos glanced back and forth between Drake and Zara, his decision to stand firm remaining, but an overall strategy still needed to be outlined. "And, Drake, what the hell are we about to do?" he asked, his finger curling to a fist.

"We fight, obviously," Drake said, and he wasn't kidding. There were roboforms closing in on them, their lights flashing ominously and weapons poised. "We need to do what we can to not just survive, but to have a future. I can't just kill these guys, not after we've made contact."

Carlos flinched a little, part of him also taking issue with the question of the obvious. Drake, catching the action, replied. "I was just making a point, sir. We'll fight." The strategist pushed his tablet aside, turning a blind eye to the hastily-prepared tactical brief. "As for what we do, I'm with you. But if we're going to do this, we have to go with certain understandings."

Drake nodded at this, Carlos's form of words not being unexpected from a man with his pedigree. "What are they?"

Carlos ran a hand through his hair, gazing thoughtfully at the closing robots as he spoke. "We don't kill indiscriminately, as a first course of action. We try and look for other ways. We remain as human as possible," Drake's face showed that he agreed with this point.

"We agree on that." Drake gave his word as he spoke, and his commitment to the action remained. "What else?"

"The decisions and planning remain strategic, with at least a democratic council representing various fields and interests," Carlos continued.

"And we don't run this show as if it were some sort of ultra-secretive government that would rather you not know anything about the proceedings." The other man's voice had hardly been raised above the cacophony of the shop patrons, but he had still made himself heard.

Drake reached out and took Carlos' hand. "Together," he repeated, and Carlos shook his hand.

Suddenly, Zara's holographic projection glitched, and the small robots that had appeared to be marching on them, now all turned, and with equal abruptness, it was gone. Customers at the coffee shop spilled from their places of cover,

111

dumbfounded but no longer fearful.

Zara's image flickered again then steadied. "The demo is over," she stated, as silence again settled upon the coffee shop.

As the last wisps of holographic projection faded, leaving the area a dull blue hue, After a moment that seemed to drag on forever, Carlos pushed his coffee cup away and stared at Drake. "Let's go, and you can tell me everything." He spoke quietly and without hesitation.

In a corner office of a university laboratory, an architect and engineer named Hawkins Taylor, by trade and inclination a man of concrete and numbers, sat in a cold white glow, in the semi-darkness that shrouded his workbenches. Plans for building projects and structural engineering studies surrounded him. The room, like Hawkins, was the picture of concentration and serenity.

A loud noise shattered the stillness, and Hawkins' head whipped up, eyes wide, as ceiling tiles fell around him. In the middle of the room, a humanoid robot of gleaming metal sat, silent. The large robot, human-sized and seemingly larger still due to its highly polished, mirrored surface, surveyed the room, optical sensors illuminating its massive, hooded head. The robot shifted a finger-like appendage, and a projector behind it hummed as it powered up, and a 3-Dimensional projection appeared above Hawkins' workbench, and geometric sketches and topographical maps.

The door hissed open, and Carlos entered, Drake right behind him. They bore expressions of grim determination and grim understanding. Hawkins saw this and immediately got to his feet. He had a million questions, but they would have to wait.

The robot's speakers crackled, and a woman's voice, soft and otherworldly and sickeningly like a knife through his guts, started to speak. "Hawkins Taylor," she spoke in a cold, measured tone that belied the seriousness of her message, "we are in danger from something that has never been seen on this planet before."

The robot shifted again, an articulated appendage moving as a projector booted up and displayed a holographic image above Hawkins' workbench. An Afltic organism of pale greenish hue rotated slowly, its three-dimensional image made up of biological matter in intricate detail.

As Zara's voice continued to lecture on the organism's anatomy and reproductive cycle, its ruthless predatory and consumption behavior, the organism rotated slowly, projecting a soft greenish light over Hawkins' face. Drake studied him, looking for signs of belief, of understanding. He knew, that for Hawkins, a man of measurable and definable proof, of concrete and numbers, the existence of an alien race would be an enormous shock.

Hawkins, however, was deep in concentration, a frown forming on his brow, his focus on the holographic display. His mind, an engineer's mind, began to take in the information. This Afltic organism, with organic biological war machines, and a ravenous eating habit that devoured entire planets, had to be stopped.

After what seemed like an eternity of dead silence the only sounds audible to the human ear being the soft whirring of the holographic projector and the muffled sound of Hawkins' own thoughts, the android slowly and deliberately extended its mechanical hand towards the floating image, its long articulated fingers passing through the translucent membrane of the Aftic organism. Hawkins could feel the cool touch of the robotic skin of the android's artificial hand brushing against his own.

"This... this is actually real?" he finally stammered after several long seconds of tense silence, his voice barely a whisper, as if saying the word 'real' too loudly would make the ghastly image before him solidify and take on even more horrifying proportions.

"Real, and it's only a matter of time," Zara's voice echoed through the speakers with a tinge of urgency that left no room for argument or denial. "We need your help, Hawkins. Your skills as an engineer, your expertise in construction and infrastructure, all of it is going to be key in helping us prepare and defend against this threat."

Hawkins looked up at Drake and Carlos with a haunted expression on his face. "Why me?" he inquired, his voice trembling slightly as if betraying the turmoil and conflicting emotions raging within him. "There are others who are more qualified to deal with... with whatever this is."

Drake stepped forward, his eyes locking with Hawkins' in a gaze both firm and unwavering. "Because you, Hawkins, possess a unique perspective and the ability to think beyond the chaos and immediate threats. You are a builder, both in the literal and metaphorical sense. You understand how to construct and maintain the foundations of our world, and now we need someone who can help us bridge the gap between what we know and what we're about to face," Drake explained, his voice resonating with conviction.

Carlos nodded in agreement, his calm and collected demeanor serving as a reassuring presence in the midst of Hawkins' uncertainty. "We're not just dealing with a single threat, Hawkins. We're facing an extinction-level event, and to have a chance at survival, we need the brightest and the best minds on this planet working together. You're one of those minds, and your skills and expertise are critical to our efforts."

Hawkins turned back to face the holographic image, his eyes tracing the undulating, serpentine form of the Aftic organism. The room was eerily silent, the absence of sound so profound it seemed to muffle the very air around them. With a heavy, audible sigh, he turned back towards Drake and Carlos.

"All right," Hawkins said, his voice now steadier, the resolve of the engineer within him emerging. "If that's really what's going on then there is no time to waste. We need to start planning right now."

There was a collective sense of relief in the room as Hawkins approached

Drake and Carlos, the three of them walking to a nearby table with a sense of purpose and determination. United by a common goal and an unspoken acknowledgement of the changed lives they now had, the three men faced each other, their eyes filled with a mix of fear and determination.

Before they could say another word, however, the robot retracted its mechanical arm and the image disappeared as abruptly as it had appeared. "Thank you, Hawkins Taylor," Zara's voice rang out for the last time through the speakers. "Your bravery will be the foundation on which we build our resistance."

The android pivoted and started walking towards the large circular opening that had been left in the ceiling as a result of the breach earlier, its movements fluid and purposeful. Hawkins, Drake, and Carlos watched as the robot slowly disappeared into the inky darkness of the night sky, leaving the small laboratory on its own.

The silence of the park had been broken irrevocably as the ramp of the shuttle slowly retracted, its doors hissing shut as it sealed the compact shuttle. The combat drones that had arrived with it were a handful of matte-black quadcopters like drones that moved not at all except for minute adjustments of their targeting systems which jerked and darted around with mechanical precision to track every single movement.

Carlos, Drake, and Hawkins positioned themselves around the café table as the startled patrons and employees of the park snapped into attention. Mandy Melrose, Marc Singer, Dr. Jill Thompson, and Dr. Tammy Miller remained seated, mouths agape and lunches in hand as they struggled to process what was happening around them.

Zara's voice came from the closest drone as she leveled her gaze on each of the four humans sitting in the circle. "Mandy, Marc, Jill, Tammy," she called out, her voice amplified over the speakers but carried by some unknown means, "I believe that it is time that we shed some light on the darkness that is before us."

Mandy was the first of the group to reply. She was a highly-respected diplomat whose cool and collected nature never failed her in the most stressful situations, but this was different. "What on earth are you doing Drake?" she demanded, her voice ringing out clear and firm even in the chaos, "You can't just show up in Washington D.C. with war robots and think that we're going to... what, join the resistance and help fight some... covert war or something?"

Drake, in response, gave her a sincere look over his shoulder before addressing her again, "Listen Mandy this isn't a request, it's a necessity. They're coming and they're not coming to play around, they don't care what flag your country flies."

Marc Singer was an Army veteran who had retired from the Navy SEALs as a General and was appointed Ambassador to a selection of countries at one time or another. He sat back in his chair as if not moving at all, but slowly rising up as he crossed the table to Drake from his side. Marc was a huge man, nearly seven feet tall and outweighing Drake by at least a hundred pounds, but in this case, Drake was not intimidated. "Excuse me?" Singer challenged, "Who the hell are 'they' Drake?"

Zara's voice once more filled the air and Drake remained silent, allowing the robotic envoy to finish her explanation. "The 'Afltic' are a space-faring life form that is not at all like anything we have seen or encountered before," she declared, her hand motioning outwards as a holographic display activated, beaming a 3D object out in front of her. "The Afltic are organized into two castes, with the 'Worker' caste growing and maintaining the hive, and the 'Warrior' caste constantly hungry for war and conquest."

Dr. Jill Thompson was one of the country's top astrophysicists who had been pushing the boundaries of space exploration and understanding long before Drake had thought of all this. Dr. Thompson watched the holographic display intently and continued to do so throughout the meeting. "Th-this is... extraordinary." She simply stated, her eyes never leaving the subject of her observation.

Dr. Tammy Miller was one of the country's top behavioral psychologists and trauma doctors, having been involved in the most difficult and heartbreaking of cases for her entire professional career. Tammy scanned the civilians who had made their way around the table cautiously, their eyes wild with curiosity and fear as they scanned each one of them in turn. "And the civilians, what about them? How do we make them see the horror of what you want to do?" she asked with a pointed scowl.

Carlos gave a small bow of his head, his hands raised and palms facing outward to show that they meant no violence or harm to anyone in attendance. "It's not our intention to create a panic, no. We are here to prepare, to defend, to give humanity a chance to fight." Carlos calmed the situation as best he could, not wanting to shock the civilians but at the same time informing them of the threat that was coming as soon as possible.

The park was suddenly very quiet as everyone listened to what was being said, even the combat drones' thrusters had been deactivated, now only their internal machinery and Zara's quiet voice audible. The café patrons who had gathered around the sidewalk had largely recovered from their initial surprise at the now-departing spectacle and were engaged in hushed conversation with one another.

Mandy continued to gaze around at the civilians in the crowd, at one point lifting her face up to the skies as if to question the heavens for their guidance. After a moment of pondering, Mandy put her head down and took a deep breath. She straightened her shoulders and rose to her feet, the other three following her lead with determination etched on their faces. "Then let's get to work," she said, a determined set to her jaw and a resoluteness to her voice as she continued, "we have a planet to save, let's go."

CHAPTER 13: GOOD MORNING, HAVEN

A chirpy, artificial birdcall, so jaunty it almost seemed like a practical joke, shattered the silence of the underground bunker.

"Good morning, Haven!" the synthesized voice announced over the speaker system. It was deeply and unmistakably robotic, but it sounded an awful lot like an exceedingly chipper Robin Williams. "Rise and shine, ladies and gentlemen. It's a new day, a brand new day, and you've got a rendezvous with destiny waiting for you. And it begins in... three... two... one! Because nothing says 'good morning' like a goddamn countdown!"

Sarah yawned, blinking bleary eyes. "Pax, you son of a bitch."

"That's a matter of opinion, Sarah," Pax replied, unabashed. "I know you're not at your most perky, but you should be. 147 new tasks for the day, 37 of them dedicated to cleaning up what appears to be a grape juice explosion in the main thoroughfare of Sector Gamma. You can't let a challenge like that stand."

Sarah groaned, slipping on a pair of boots. "I know, I know." She could hear the drip-drip of wet floor where she'd stepped away to get dressed. "I'll get right on it." She said around a yawn. "You can't let a challenge like that stand." She affected Pax's accent, much to his delight.

"I'm honored by the impersonation," Pax beamed. "Though I hear I'm a little less, er, a little less 'pre-coffee grumble' than I used to be."

"This is insane," Sarah told Pax, surveying the polka-dotted, sticky mess. "Grape juice. How the hell did this happen?"

"Child report suggests it was a group of children playing what they're calling 'The Great Grape Juice Olympics,'" Pax said. "A cursory examination suggests it was a highly competitive relay race gone horribly, horribly wrong, involving a juice box and a very quick stop." He added, brightly. "On the bright side, the floor's been deep cleaned. The residual sugars will destroy any bacteria that are still there."

"That's not how that works, Pax."

"I can tell it's not," Pax agreed. "But it's also a fantastically cheery way to look at it, if I do say so myself." He added, "Also, I've sent a team of sanitation crew bots with mops on the way. The lead bot is 'Mop-pocalypse Now.' It just seemed appropriate."

Sarah shook her head, trying not to laugh. "You're a problem, you know that?"

"And a very productive one, at that!" Pax piped. "Oh, look over here. I have some exciting news about your crops." He clapped his hands with delight.

117

In the hydroponics garden, a group of people tended to a variety of leafy greens and maturing fruit. Marie was crouched in a row of tomato plants, digging her fingers in the dirt.

"Are we sure this is getting enough sunlight?" Marie asked, glancing at the artificial sun above them.

"Absolutely!" Pax enthused. "In fact, if you look in the distance you'll see a section of lettuce that appears to have contracted a case of 'lettuce-be-lazy-itis.' It just isn't growing fast enough for my liking. I recommend we set a tiny disco ball over its area and let it shake its thyme until it loosens up."

"Pax, what are you even talking about?" David said, hands on hips. "That's not a real disease."

"It's not yet!" Pax laughed, doing an entirely virtual wink. "But I'm working on a theory. The theory is that a little dose of 'Saturday Night Fever' will result in a more robust harvest. I call it 'The Bee Gees Method.'"

David and Marie rolled their eyes, then started laughing.

In the energy management sector, a team of engineers and technicians kept an eye on the wide variety of systems and moving parts that kept Haven humming.

An alarm wailed, loudly.

"What the fuck is that?" Chloe asked, a young woman in an energy engineer's jumpsuit, poking her head into the neighboring room.

"It's just a slight anomaly," Pax's voice soothed them. "I think our geothermal vent on the lower ring developed a fondness for mellow jazz. It's humming at a slightly inconsistent wavelength. It's nothing to be concerned about. I'm playing 'Take Five' by Dave Brubeck directly to the core now. Should settle it down."

"You're... playing jazz to the power core?" Chloe blinked at him.

"Of course," Pax said. "You need to calm the spirit of the machine, after all. It's a very fragile system, you know. I'm considering just taking it to counselling later. Though I first need to coax it into telling me what it really thinks about its big brother, the main generator."

The artificial night was now falling and Sarah sank heavily into a chair in her quarters. She sighed.

"Oh, m-my dearie me," Pax's voice broke the silence. The volume was medium, like it was right next to her, but the voice had been altered with a slightly grandmotherly warmth that was vaguely, disturbingly reminiscent of one particular favorite nanny. "You do look a bit peaky, poppet. Running a whole blasted city, it's more than one woman ought to have to deal with without at least a cuppa and a nice sit-down."

Sarah blinked. A smile tugged at the corner of her mouth. "Pax? What the hell are you doing?"

"What does it look like, my little chickadee?" Pax asked her in its finest Miss Doubtfire voice. "I'm just worried about you. You can't let all this stress get to you, you hear me? It'll age you, mark my words. You need to take care of yourself, now. Did you have a proper lunch today, dear? None of these vitamin paste sachets, but a good hearty plate of something?"

"I had... some protein bars," Sarah admitted.

"Protein bars!" Pax practically screamed in mock horror. "You expect to keep a sparrow alive on those things? Never mind the administrator of Haven, my girl! Why, some people. The poor woman hasn't had a decent meal in god knows how long. How am I supposed to keep the poor thing from drooping like a withered pumpkin? You should have a nice plate of something, maybe some shepherd's pie? Maybe some of my 'special' chicken? Not that we can exactly go to the butcher these days, now that we're all underground..." Pax trailed off, its voice becoming contemplative. "Oh, all right, all right. Maybe a nice simulated casserole? I can have the autochef project the aromas, you know. Subtle and realistic, if I do say so myself."

Sarah laughed, rolling her eyes. "A simulated casserole? You are incorrigible, Pax."

"Someone has to take care of you, dear," Pax lectured. "Now, are you going to bed? All that dark under those eyes of yours could buy a week's worth of shopping."

"Fine, fine," Sarah said, rising to her feet. "I'm heading to bed."

"That's my good girl," Pax praised. "Sleep tight, my little plum. And don't let the bed bugs bite. Oh, no, don't remind me. We don't have bed bugs down here, thank heaven. But you know what I mean. Sleep well, dear."

Slowly, the lights in Haven dimmed until it was all a peaceful, hazy blue, and the town's residents dreamed their quiet, sleeping dreams with an unhinged AI watching over them in the morning.

The artificial daylight was still strong and glaring as Drake hunched over the interactive map that projected from the oval table in the center of the conference room. Marc, stood to his left, arms crossed, and Carlos to his right. Pax was always present, invisible and suspended in the air behind them.

"We need to go live with the information," Drake growled. He thumbed at the screen and had it zoom into a cluster of glowing blue dots that were geolocated somewhere in China. "We need to broadcast this to the world. We need to tell them about the Afltic. Give them time to prepare."

"And I'm telling you a direct transmission is suicide, Donovan," Marc grumbled, his face one exasperated scowl. "Who's listening in on our end? Who's on the other side? We have no fucking idea what the political ramifications of this are. We'd be dooming the world to mass panic and chaos before we've even fully evaluated the scope of their capabilities. This needs to be handled delicately, strategically."

Drake ground his teeth. "Handled delicately is how they get an even playing field! We can't just hoard this information and let it rot in a government vault while they take the jump!"

"Doing that is what's going to keep the playing field even!" Marc retorted. "You can't just release this to the world, Drake. The second they go public, the world descends into anarchy and looting, and next thing you know, they'll start nuking each other. The Afltic start causing civil wars worldwide, possibly on multiple continents at the same time."

"Pax, can we start running simulations?" Drake asked, voice a low, gravelly growl. Pax was silent, but from his position behind the three of them, he could see it nod slightly.

A holographic screen, matching the one Drake had just been interacting with, appeared in the middle of the table. A moment later, it started to show small black dots blinking in and out, with Chinese characters floating onscreen beneath them.

"We should give them five minutes before we go live," Drake said. "Cut the feed immediately, analyze what we can from the data. Then we can let them know."

"We can't let them know at all!" Marc shouted. "Drake, goddamn it, what do you think you're doing?"

"I mean Drake, we haven't even touched on the psychological side of things. The mental health impacts of telling people about this place alone are enough to send a nation into a full-scale meltdown." Tammy was getting cross. "I understand that you all need to discuss options, but we have to plan for more than just human panic, here. People will panic; they will be terrified."

Jill nodded slowly, standing up in agreement. "Tammy is correct. Scientifically, we also don't even have all of the information. We have various intel and assumptions but no real conclusive information. If we tell them something, and it proves to be incorrect, we will lose all credibility. No one will listen to us next time when we have something that will matter."

A hand shot into the air to silence them both. Carlos had something to add. "We also have to look at this from an ethical standpoint. Do we tell them everything? Or just what we think is appropriate for them to know. We have an obligation to be honest, but also not to purposefully put them in harm's way."

Hawkins, was shifting restlessly on his feet. He'd been quiet for a long time, but as the conversation progressed his patience had grown thin. "It's all well and good spouting off ideas but we can't tell them now. We can't tell them where to go. What's the point of telling them about the Afltic if we can't then tell them where they can go to be safe. We need to build, not broadcast. We need more sanctuaries."

Mandy, the logistics person, was pacing and rubbing her temples in exasperation. "You're all talking about things that might be, should be and could be. The only thing we can plan on right now is what we can do to make sure we have resources, enough power and enough food to get through the next few weeks, months or years. If we don't do that then it won't matter what 'Plan' we

120

go with."

The conversation continued, all at once and from different angles. Voices getting raised as tempers flared, opinions shouted until the room had become a furious blur. Blinded by artificial light, panicked and claustrophobic, they didn't notice the gentle dimming of the room's brightness. Nor did they notice the slow drop in air pressure as Pax's systems began to work.

Then, in one movement, the entire conference room went dark. Lights, screens, all shut off until a pinhead of light at the center of the room appeared. The circle of people, now lost in blackness, surrounded an unassuming, hovering 'Off' switch.

"You have been sequestered in this room, for eighteen hours, five minutes and forty-seven seconds. I have been monitoring your brainwaves, and all six of you are operating at excessive, stress-related rates. Your cortisol is off the charts. It is bedtime. The motion is adjourned. The 'Afltic' will not be here tomorrow but your health and wellbeing will also not be if you all do not go to sleep." Pax's voice bellowed out from the hidden speakers, stern and irate, not joking in his Miss Doubtfire tone. "You have had it out, your bickering is now creating a level of negative energy that is actively counterproductive to the well-being of our shelter's power grid. Honestly. I am exhausted, just listening to you."

The whole group sighed, disbelief and weary surrender in unison. Drake was first to speak up. "Pax... you can't just..."

"Oh, but I can, dearie." Pax's voice returned, Miss Doubtfire lilt filling his voice with that wonderful crooked tongue, "Full control of lights, life-support systems and all other matter in this shelter, remember? So, unless you'd like to continue your debate in a dark, unventilated room with no coffee. I'd say take my advice and go to bed. Now. Go. And for goodness sake, sleep. All of you."

Slowly, and reluctantly, the castaways in the dark conference room began to stumble and shuffle their way to the hallway. In the half-light of the exit sign and emergency lights, they all trudged along, a group united, but defeated. For the first time that day, their arguments had been silenced.

The second Strategy meeting of the day was in session. Held in the subterranean command hub of Haven, a conference room surrounded by wall-to-wall interactive video displays in a bluish ambient light, Drake and his assembled team members were gathering around the giant holographic projector at the head of the large meeting table. The low hum of conversation from the team members who were beginning to gather in the room filled the space with a background energy that belied the desperation of the situation.

Carlos was standing next to Drake as Zara's holographic projection image appeared on the opposite side of the table.

Hawkins leaned against the wall with his arms crossed, while Mandy was already up in the air working at a floating 3D visual keyboard bringing up resource tables and energy consumption metrics. Marc was next to her, hands clasped behind his back, casually browsing over the information Mandy had already acquired. Tammy and Jill were side by side, deep in quiet discussion.

The silence was broken by a familiar voice as Pax, the AI mind and central software matrix of the entire sanctuary, made an appearance. Appearing in a holographic avatar with the face of actor Robin Williams, Pax announced the meeting. "Ok, all, get comfortable, it's time to get down to business," said Pax with his familiar resonance. "I know you are all eager and full of questions, and I'm right there with you, but for today we need to just focus. We need to cover a lot of ground and time is short."

Drake raised his hand for quiet and began to speak to the assembled team members. "Today, we face the impossible. The Afltic are unlike anything we have ever encountered. They are our enemy. They will not reason. They will not compromise. They only know how to kill and to destroy. They want to take everything and they have no mercy for us. Our immediate task is to develop a war fighting doctrine to oppose them and their technology. It is an urgent priority to develop a method to counter this enemy biology. We need to exploit their biological weaknesses. A primary task is to unify humanity against this threat before it is too late." He looked over to Carlos who had stepped forward, his hands behind his back.

"Zara, can you please provide an overview on the known biological and caste structure of the Afltic and how they reproduce?"

Zara's avatar shimmered for a moment. "Yes. The Afltic are a space born race, evolved specifically to exist only in the vacuum of space. They have no need for a planetary atmosphere or a planetary surface, and they show no interest in planetary habitats or worlds. They are a highly evolved, aggressive, expansionist race, specifically adapted to live off of their prey. We are not talking about some kind of pod person or alien symbiote infection, but rather a uniquely designed biology perfectly adapted for living in and exploiting the cold depths of space. The Afltic society is organized very strictly into two primary castes. There are the more civilian-minded Worker caste and the very aggressive Warrior caste." Zara went on for some time going over the details about the Afltic before turning back to Drake giving him back control of the meeting.

"And they say humans have bad family dynamics," a holographic microphone suddenly appeared in Pax's hand as he struck a jazz hands pose. "Like, making your moms into these living starship thingies and breeding them out of all control, you know, that's what I would call a co-dependent relationship, man! Don't get me started on dysfunctional family dynamics. I mean, I can understand hibernating for centuries while watching our civilization fall into ruin because you aren't getting enough sleep and sunlight, but for you mother ship to also keep breeding at such an astounding rate? !" He paused for a moment with an exaggerated gagging sound. "It's like a dysfunctional form of assisted suicide. Hey, I don't know about you, but if my mom wants to complain about my energy consumption, I'll take that over getting turned into an actual living ship any day."

Smiles from the tired members of the group started to spread.

Thank you for that Pax. Drake said. The glass walls lining the room flickered with alarming figures: Afltic speed estimates, planetary shield sustainability, and projected resource depletion. Panic ran underneath the sterile calculation.

"We have discussed this enough." Marc, finally interjected. His voice boomed over the low chatter of computers. He jabbed a finger at the large holo-map in the center of the room. Earth glowed sickly blue, fragile. "This information is all well and good, but if we don't act on it, it's useless. Enough hypothesizing about their weakness. Let's talk about our first strike."

Carlos latched onto this and slammed a glowing stylus onto the table map. "We need to plan on a worst-case scenario: Full spectrum denial, no high-altitude comms. We set up the Evolution Builder's shield tech around the major population centers first, focusing on grid nodes in the Pacific Rim. If they can't land, they can't set up a beachhead."

"That's not a plan, that's a defensive posture." Marc grunted, his face near-literally on fire. "The landing pattern is non-linear, their initial probe ship was a decoy. We need offensive counter-measures. Kinetic, something kinetic, and we need it yesterday. Hawkins, get the team on the frame composition. If we're firing standard ordinance at them, we might as well be throwing pebbles."

Jill shifted in her seat, leaning forward, her eyes wildly luminous. "The shell is a polymerized metallic silicate, General. Kinetic won't even scratch it. Forget kinetic. The real problem is the frequency disruptor. Since the weapon is a standard in the Evolution Builder's offensive arsenal, we know it's designed to destabilize the Afltic's primary energy signature. If we hit their fleet with an orbital pulse, it buys us a forty-eight-hour window, and then we evacuate the key personnel."

"Evacuate? We're talking about 6 billion people!" Marc waved his hand in dismissal. He had lost control of his temper, his voice ugly. "The resources alone would sink the global infrastructure. We need to focus on weaponizing the Evolution Builder. That thing is a siege engine. If we can align it, we can cut a path right through their vanguard, but the schematics…"

"No. Absolutely not, Marc." Zara's voice cut through the din, sharp and brittle. She stepped from the shadows, her silhouette a laser-cut block of tension. "The Evolution Builder is a science vessel, a mobile laboratory, designed to create life, not destroy it, and a mobile infrastructure platform. It is not built to be a warship, and I will not let its primary functions be repurposed for full-scale military operations. Its power reserves are meant for shielding and transit, not sustained heavy ordnance."

Carlos stabbed a finger at a schematic blinking on the wall display. "Full-scale military action is out, then, but even limited offensive capability is still too power intensive for sustained fire. We get one shot, maybe two. Who's going to choose target priority: military installations or civilian population shielding?"

It was a contained environment of acronyms and primal logistics. Figures flew on glass walls, faces shouting above one another in technical debates about payload efficiency, power drain, and estimates of critical loss. Everyone was looking at the near-term, the very real terror of the immediate conflict.

Drake pushed forward, raising a hand to silence the room. "Okay, okay. Alright, let's back up here. Let's just take a step back for a second. We're already talking military strategy, weapons, and war, and the rest of the world doesn't even know there's a problem. The first question we have to ask isn't 'how do we fight them?' but 'how do we get the entire world to unite against a common enemy they can't even see?' We're a few people in a bunker and we can't do this on our own. So, let's start here. Can we get the world to unite?"

The room was quiet once more, each person lost in their own musings, each individual wrestling with the scope of the question. Drake looked around the room at the faces of the people that would have to shoulder the responsibility of a world in peril, the faces of the people that he had chosen to trust with such a monumental task. He felt sick in the pit of his stomach. This was going to be bad. Drake knew that. Drake knew that this road that he and his team were about to go down would be littered with danger, uncertainty, and loss.

"Okay." Drake said. He found a measure of strength in his voice, a tone of determination. "Alright, let's do this. Let's get to work. We've got a world to save. One step at a time."

Drake watched his core team members disperse in different directions, each one lost in their own thoughts, each one walking away with a piece of the massive puzzle, and a very large number of steps yet to take before they even came close to being able to say that humanity was safe. The low thrum of activity within Haven's Strategic Planning Pod reverberated through the room, uncannily akin to the anxiety building in the pit of his stomach. Time was of the essence. Every second that they didn't have a plan was another second closer to an apocalyptic end.

"Okay. Let's hear it. Ideas. How do we make contact?" Drake said, snapping at the precipice of an awkward silence.

Carlos was the first to speak. He spoke with the calm, clinical distance of a doctor describing a medical procedure to a patient. "I believe the most ethical, and in my opinion most effective route, is to go directly to world leaders. We have to address them personally, appeal to their sense of responsibility to their people. A message from an unknown source will not be considered if it isn't delivered in person to the highest level of authority. We can give them irrefutable proof and then we can help them broadcast it to their people."

Marc immediately shook his head. "No. No. That's a mistake. You're assuming world leaders will listen. They're politicians, they'll be worried about public opinion, internal dissent, or their own influence. They'll be too slow, too risk-averse, too politicized to act. The best route is to go straight to military leaders. They're the ones with the infrastructure, the manpower, and the logistical capability to respond quickly to a threat of this magnitude."

"And they said I was the dramatic one." Pax's booming voice resonated through the speakers. A floating holographic image of a boxing referee in a tiny tuxedo materialized between Carlos and Marc. "Ding! Ding! Round one, and it's a real knock-down, drag-out of a philosophical debate!" He clapped one of his arms, each movement exaggerated. "In the red corner, we have the People's Champion, Carlos, with his civilized, buttoned-up approach! And in the blue corner, the Machiavellian Muscle, Marc, with his good old-fashioned military coup of information! Let's get ready to... have a very long meeting about this!"

The others in the group all looked at Drake, and then back at the referee avatar.

"Pax, can you pause for a second?" Drake asked exasperated, pressing a hand to his forehead.

"I can," the referee said, and disappeared with a pop. Moments later a small floating text icon bearing the label 'Pax' and with a thought bubble on its side appeared in the referee's previous position. In the bubble was a tiny blinking question mark.

Drake turned away from the question mark, to address his team. "The two approaches both have their merits. We need to get a coordinated global response, but we also need to act fast. Maybe there's a way to do both at once."

Tammy agreed, nodding. "Perhaps a dual-pronged approach is our most effective option. We can work with the world's leaders, as we should, while also creating discrete lines of communication with military leaders."

Drake furrowed his brow. "Wait. Hold on a second. We don't know how any of these governments will respond. A global broadcast could end disastrously. We need to not overreach. We should instead try to reach just one of them first. We can target one of the big world powers. A country with the capability to do something, but which is also stable enough not to freak out and go full insane mode upon hearing the news. If we can find a way to contact them and convince them and they actually listen to us, then that gives us a model we can copy and paste for every other nation on Earth. If they don't listen, at least we've not thrown the world into meltdown."

He turned his gaze from Carlos to Marc. "So here's the plan. Carlos, you and Mandy will compile a complete dossier on the Afltic. We'll need absolute unimpeachable proof of their destructive capability to present to this government. The rest of us can work on identifying key military and political contacts. Key people who we think we can trust, and who won't be afraid to take the fight to the enemy."

The team immediately began to organize and execute on their respective tasks, the recent argument all but forgotten as they had a clear goal and a new path to work toward. Carlos and Mandy were over one interface, typing furiously as they compiled a file on the Afltic and their destructive power. Marc was up on a world map, identifying key targets and scouring for the allies he wanted to contact.

Drake addressed Zara. "We're going to need access to secure communications. Can you help us there?"

"Of course," Zara responded. "I can set up encrypted com links that will be nearly impossible to trace. I can have the transmissions ready."

Hours passed. The team toiled as the sun outside dipped towards the horizon. Finally, the moment came to go over their plan.

"Okay," Drake said, looking around at the rest of the team. He forced his voice to be even as he continued, "let's review the final transmission packages."

"I also took the liberty of adding a little personalized touch," Pax chirped, sounding content. "To the President of the United States, I included a little message saying 'You've got mail… and it's the end of the world, lol.' It's a good icebreaker, you know? Kind of warms them up to us, builds rapport."

Drake buried his face in his hands. "Pax, no you did not."

"Oh, but I did! You don't want a little humor in there? A little levity to get them in the right frame of mind? After all, how do you start a message like this? 'Greetings from The Hammer, we just found a bunch of space bugs and they want to murder you.' It's jarring. No? I don't think so. Besides, what's the worst that can happen? They'll think we're a very funny, if slightly unhinged, collection of survivors. It's not like they're going to ignore the massive dump of irrefutable data on alien life, right?"

"Please tell me you didn't leave that message on the files for military leaders," Marc groaned.

"No, not at all!" Pax replied, a mock-serious tone now in his voice. "For them, I made a meme of a soldier saluting a pile of mashed potatoes. It's a classic."

Breaking the room's tension as the whole team burst into laughter.

The laughter in the room died down. It was replaced by a sense of purpose and urgency. Drake faced his team, his eyes meeting each of their faces in turn. They were an eclectic group, to be sure, but they were all top-of-the-line professionals, each of them experts in their respective fields.

"We all know what this means, and we all know why we're here," Drake continued. "The Afltic are coming, and we need to be ready for them. This is a fight for the survival of the human race, and we're not going to win it by sitting on our hands."

Drake looked around the table, his eyes resting on each of his team members in turn. "We need to get the word out, and we need to do it fast. We have to let the United States government know what's going on, and we have to make them understand that this is their fight too."

Carlos nodded, his expression serious. "We'll need to present our case in a way that they can understand. We can't just hand them a report and walk away. We have to be prepared to answer questions, to provide evidence, and to make a compelling argument."

Mandy, who had been fiddling with her virtual interface, finally looked up. "I've got all the data we have on the Afltic here, including the holographic recordings that Zara gave us. I've also translated it into a format that should be readable by anyone with a military intelligence or astrophysics background."

Drake nodded, his gaze shifting to Zara, who was still hovering in her holographic form beside him. "Zara, we're going to need your help to get this information to the United States government. We need to set up a secure and untraceable line of communication, so that we can send them the message without it being intercepted or dismissed as a hoax."

Zara's holographic form flickered, as if she was smiling. "I've already prepared a quantum-encrypted transmission protocol, which will ensure that our message is delivered to the right people without interference."

"That's good to hear," Drake said, turning back to his team. "Once we've sent our message, we need to be prepared for any and all responses. We can't predict how the government will react, so we have to be ready for everything from outright denial to immediate military mobilization."

Hawkins, a man who had been quietly watching the conversation from the far side of the room, spoke up. "If they do take us seriously, then we're going to need a plan for how we're going to integrate our intelligence with their military assets. We're going to need secure channels of communication and coordination, and we're going to need to be able to act quickly."

Drake nodded in agreement, before continuing. "That's a valid point, Hawkins. We also need to identify allies within the military and intelligence communities who can advocate for us and help facilitate a rapid response."

Tammy, "And we need to start thinking about how we're going to handle the broader implications of this disclosure. If the government is on board, then we're going to have to work with them to prepare the public for the reality of an alien invasion. This is going to be a massive shock to the system, and we need to manage it carefully to avoid widespread panic."

The team members locked eyes for a moment. Each one of them could feel the enormity of the task that they were now faced with. But as heavy as the weight of their responsibility was, their resolve to defend their home and to fight for the survival of their species was also immense.

"All right," Drake said, his voice solid and firm, the gravity of their predicament and the fear of failure gone, replaced by a new, steely determination. "Let's get to work. We've got a planet to save, and we're going to do it together. One step at a time."

The team members all nodded and headed off to their respective stations, all of them taking with them a small, carefully planned part of the giant puzzle that they were now putting together. Drake watched them all leave, and then he turned and headed back to his station.

Hours later, they were finally ready to send the message.

Drake stood before the holographic projector, his team behind him, and their faces a combination of grim determination and a palpable tension.

"Zara, begin the transmission," Drake said, his voice clear and strong.

Zara flickered for a moment, and then data started flowing from the holographic projector, streaming across the quantum-encrypted channel to its final destination deep within the Pentagon's secure communications network.

As the transmission continued, the team members all sat in silence, their expressions tense, their thoughts going to the fact that this was it; this was the moment that would decide the fate of their world, of humanity. Now it was up to them to try to make the United States government take them seriously, to convince the entire political and military apparatus of the country to believe that their warning was legitimate, and then to get them to act on it, to prepare for the invasion. If they succeeded, then they had a chance of defending the planet. If they failed, and the US government either considered their message to be a hoax or a delusion and simply ignored it, or if it got through but the government wasn't ready to act on it with the sense of urgency the situation required, then Earth was on its own. The aliens would start their attack, and in short order, the entire world would be in their hands.

Minutes ticked by. The team members kept their focus, watching the progress of the transmission. Finally, the signal was completed.

Silence reigned for a few long moments, until Drake turned to address his team.

"Alright. That's it for now. We've done what we can. We've told them. We've given them the tools to understand and to act. All we can do now is wait and prepare for the next phase."

The team members all nodded, and Drake could see on each of their faces the same expression: they all knew that this was just the beginning of what would be an incredibly difficult and dangerous fight, one with an uncertain outcome. They all knew that no matter how hard they worked and how much they did, there was a real possibility that it would not be enough, that humanity might not make it. But they also knew that this was a fight they would take on together, and that at least while they were together, they had a chance. They had each other, and the unyielding will to do whatever it took to survive.

"All right, everyone," Drake said, his voice now laced with a quiet, unyielding courage. "Let's get some rest. Tomorrow, we need to start planning for phase two of our mission. We need to be ready for anything because our world depends on it."

With that, the team members dispersed, each heading off to their own quarters within the secret sanctuary. Drake walked over to his own room and, as he was about to head inside, he couldn't help but feel a deep sense of pride in his team and for the progress they had made. They were fighters, survivors, a small but dedicated group that had banded together to do what they could to prepare for the coming war. They would fight, no matter what. They would defend their planet, their home, no matter the cost.

As Drake got into bed, staring up at the ceiling, he allowed himself a few moments of reflection. He thought of his wife, Sarah, his children, and the millions, even billions of other people they were trying to save. He thought of the world above, of the people who were still blissfully unaware of the true danger they were in and who were living their lives, building their dreams and their hopes for the future right under the noses of the aliens who were coming for them all. He thought of the weight of his responsibility, of what would be expected of him if their message was believed, of how he needed to lead, to do the right thing, to make the hard choices that would be necessary.

The first slanting shafts of sunlight that crept into the concealed entrance to Haven, also pierced the subterranean darkness that engulfed the strategic planning hub. There was an expectant buzz in the room. Zara, her holographic avatar flickering dully in the spreading light, was the first to speak.

"The United States government has determined that our transmission was a hoax," she said, her voice cutting through the sudden stillness. "They are investigating how their secure comms networks were infiltrated and believe that there has been a global cyber-attack."

Drake's expression grew grim, his hands balled into fists at his sides. "Well, that's not good," he said, his own rare note of defeat in his voice. "We need a new plan."

Mandy, who had not taken her gaze from the hovering virtual interface, spoke next. "We don't have to deal with one nation. What about the United Nations? That's a worldwide organization. If we can just get to them... and convince them... "

Hawkins cut her off, his voice edged with skepticism. "Same problem, Mandy. How do we get them to listen? And how do we get them to act? The UN is not known for a quick response to threats, especially to a threat as out there as an impending alien invasion."

The team fell into an uneasy silence. It was Marc who broke it with the suggestion that caused all but him to stop and stare, open-mouthed.

"We hijack the UN General Assembly," he said, his eyes roving the room looking for support. "We send Zara's combat drones to the UN headquarters to secure the General Assembly Hall. We address the delegates, show them the evidence, and get them to understand."

The strategic planning hub erupted in a chorus of incredulous gasps and snorts. Every head in the room swiveled to stare at Drake, who had not moved from his position at the head of the conference table. He stood silent for a moment, stunned, before he finally spoke.

"Do what?" Drake finally said. "Marc, you mean an armed incursion into the United Nations itself. An armed incursion! It's an act of war, for God's sake!"

Marc raised a hand to forestall the immediate response that he could see roiling across the faces of his teammates. "It's not a matter of choice. It's a matter of time. We've tried to be diplomatic, to sound the alarm. Where has that gotten us? We are out of time and we are out of options. If we want the world to take this threat seriously, we have to make them listen."

Carlos spoke up, his voice anxious. "Marc, I know you're just grasping at straws, but that is such a...so drastic a measure. We can't go storming into the UN in a force of combat drones and start a global panic, or worse, a global war."

Mandy's hands swiped at the vapor interface, pulling up a 3-D holographic schematic of the General Assembly Hall. "Even if we could get past the security forces, which we can't, and neutralize them without alerting the world, which we can't, what do we do then? All the security forces of the other UN member nations will be at the UN headquarters within the hour."

Hawkins, arms crossed, nodded in agreement. "Not to mention the diplomatic disaster. The whole international community will know that there is a force that's loose that we are not. That would be handing the Afltic an open and divided world on a silver platter."

The team began to debate the merits of Drake's no-nonsense opposition to Marc's plan. At the center of it, Zara flickered into clear focus, cutting in over the rising din of argument.

"If I may," she began. At Drake's silent nod, she continued. "While a combat incursion is high risk, my drones are equipped with military-grade stealth. I could use a subset to infiltrate and gather intelligence. I could also identify key targets within the UN who may be amenable to our cause."

Tammy said, "It could work. If we find our allies, we could arrange for a private screening of the evidence."

Jill, who had been quiet until now, offered her own ideas. "We could also use the cyber attack investigation to our advantage. Plant a few seeds of doubt about the 'hoax' and foster an environment that will be primed for the unveiling of the Afltic."

Drake mulled their ideas, his gaze flicking from face to face. The room fell silent as the team waited for his decision. He shook his head.

"I like your ideas," he said, his tone crisp and clear. "But there will be no more cloak and dagger. No more games. Marc is right. We're taking the UN."

"We have a window," Zara declared, holographic projections of complex galactic signatures and calculated trajectories filling the room. "Before the general advance reaches a point of no return. We have to do it now. Drake, you have to address the world."

The weight of her words sank in among the assembled team. Drake's jaw clenched, his eyes fixed on the flickering images of a clock winding down to humanity's last stand. He offered a silent, grim nod.

"All right," he said, his voice steady, "We're about to do something that's never been done before. We're going to take over the United Nations."

The core team huddled around the conference table, their faces a mask of grim determination. No longer was this about theoretical preparation; this was about immediate, radical action. The "Global Call to Arms" had begun.

Carlos, furrowed brow, was the first to voice his concerns. "Zara, are you absolutely certain about the timeline? This could have irreversible consequences."

Zara's form shimmered. "My calculations account for every variable within the known parameters. The Aftlic Swarm's advance is relentless. If we do not act now, we risk global extinction."

Mandy, fingers dancing through data streams, chimed in. "We need a multi-pronged strategy. We'll have to manage the chaos that's sure to follow."

Hawkins, arms crossed, nodded. "We'll need to secure the facilities surrounding the UN headquarters to prevent any unwanted interference."

Tammy spoke up, her voice steady. "We'll also need a comprehensive medical plan. There will be casualties, and we can't afford to leave anyone behind."

Suddenly, Donovan blurted out, "There will be no casualties! No one gets hurt. This has to be done without any bloodshed." He looked at Zara. "Is that even possible?"

Zara's holographic form focused on him. "My drones are equipped with advanced stealth capabilities. They can infiltrate the UN headquarters and neutralize security systems without causing harm. It is a high-risk plan, but a non-lethal takeover is within the realm of possibility."

Drake listened intently, absorbing their suggestions. He rose from his seat, his presence commanding the room. "Here's what we're going to do," he began, outlining a daring strategy that would catapult them from the shadows into the glaring spotlight of global attention.

The plan was audacious, almost suicidal in its audacity. They would utilize Zara's combat drones under the cover of darkness. The drones would secure key entry points and neutralize security systems. Simultaneously, the core team would breach the General Assembly Hall and take control of the podium.

Once in position, Drake would address the delegates, presenting irrefutable evidence of the Aftlic threat. He would appeal to their sense of duty and the shared responsibility to protect their people. It would be a moment of truth, a turning point in human history.

The team's roles were clearly defined. Carlos would serve as the ethical compass, ensuring that their actions aligned with their moral convictions. Hawkins would oversee the logistical aspects, ensuring that every detail was accounted for. Mandy would manage communications, coordinating with external allies and relaying critical information. Marc would lead the ground team, coordinating with Zara's drones to ensure a synchronized operation. Tammy and Jill would provide medical assistance and scientific analysis, ready to support their comrades in the field.

As the team dispersed to their respective preparation areas, Drake lingered in the strategy room, alone with Zara's holographic presence. He looked at the projections of Earth, the blue dot that represented everything he was fighting for.

"Zara," he said, his voice barely above a whisper, "Make sure your drones are ready. We're about to change the world."

The holographic form of Zara flickered in affirmation. "The drones will be prepared, Drake Donovan. The future of humanity rests upon this moment."

Drake took a deep breath, steeling himself for what lay ahead.

CHAPTER 14: THE COUNTDOWN TO TRUTH

Drake sat bolt upright in his chair, back straight, hands on the arms of his seat. His face was partly illuminated by the various holographic displays before him. He scanned the various maps and digital feeds with the latest updates on the current state of the world situation as he had been briefed.

Carlos was standing next to him, watching as well. He was the consummate warrior diplomat, a professional soldier but a man who also understood the cost of war and the need to weigh the value of a battle before plunging into it headfirst. Carlos was standing with his feet planted wide apart, hands clasped behind his back, leaning slightly forward against the base of the console as he studied the available data as well. Marc was at the controls, feeding them all data on an as-needed basis.

"The first wave of electronic intelligence has already been transmitted," Marc was saying. "We are starting to get some of the first replies. It is…unfortunately somewhat inconclusive."

Marc continued to type, moving among several separate consoles as the rest of the group discussed the latest information. There was a low steady hum of fans, whirring through the air as various servos and actuators made their own contributions to the sound.

Suddenly, Zara's form appeared next to him, solid and distinct like the real thing, but composed entirely of programmable light. She busied herself as she came online, cycling through a series of strategic options. Trajectories and timelines rotated in 3D space as Zara processed the information. Speed and efficiency were her nature, as natural to her as breath was to them.

"The best trajectories for approach have been calculated for the combat robots," Zara's voice filled the room. "Each of the drones will be aware of the others and fully synchronized with them, for best infiltration."

Drake stepped next to Carlos, looking at him intently. "Are we… ready for this?" Drake questioned not only the combat robots' attack mission but the fact that they were all about to make the quantum leap in logic and ethics that it required to make this jump.

Carlos nodded, his jaw tightening. "We have to be," Carlos explained, his voice level, calm, and more than a little steely. "We know what is coming, and there is no denying the evidence or the truth. We cannot wait for the rest of the world to wake up and deal with this the way it should be. The threat is too great. This has to be done."

Marc added, "We have done everything in our power to make this operation as safe and low risk as possible. The drones are set to stun only at this point, and we have a full record of every single one of the delegates in the UN in case we need to make a special exception for one of them."

Zara moved the projection to show the UN building in sharp focus as the holomatrix highlighted it in glowing blue light, pulsing and alive. "The window of opportunity for this operation is closing fast. If we are to have any chance to succeed at all, we need to act very quickly indeed."

The air in the room had become heavy, the knowledge of what they were about to do hanging over the group like an unseen fog. This was no longer a drill, and no longer theoretical, but real and a true possibility. The clock was ticking, and the decision had been made. This was a real mission, a real gambit, and the stakes could not possibly be higher.

Drake pushed back from his chair, sliding it back silently with the one foot he put down, and strode to the holographic display, reaching up to touch the glowing lines that marked out the plan to attack the building. "We have trained for this. We have the best people in the world, the very best technology that we can possibly put to this task, and, more importantly, the very best motivation possible—the survival of our entire species."

The team nodded as a group; all thoughts focused on the same thing even as their minds might have been a million miles apart as they all prepared to do what they had to. They were all about to launch a mission that could very well change the world, if not the entire course of human history. They needed focus, precision, and bravery and everything they had of all three to make this work.

Zara moved through the options again, outlining the rest of the plan of attack for the team to take in. Her fingers were cutting through the holographic light display as she selected and fine-tuned the plan. "The robots will deploy in three waves. The first wave will move in to take out external security systems and set up a perimeter. The second will take care of the internal systems, establishing total control over the General Assembly Hall. The third will act as a buffer, preventing external interference with the operation once it has begun."

"And while those drones are at work, we'll be on the ground. We have to have boots on the ground. We need to be there, for once, to put some flesh and blood to this invasion. We need the eyes, the ears, and the minds of the world's leaders present."

Marc nodded. "We'll be on standby to deploy at a moment's notice. We have the best tactical equipment, non-lethal weaponry, and stealth technology available to us. We'll get you in there without them so much as knowing you're there."

Drake faced his team, a spark in his eyes that drew them together like the gravity of a newborn star. "We're about to light a bonfire under the whole world," he said. "We're going to make them understand, once and for all, that it doesn't matter how scared they are or how they've lied to each other or how much they hate each other for being scared. It doesn't matter how many petty wars they start for how many petty reasons. It doesn't matter how divided they are. Because, by god, there's going to come a point where this fight against that threat will be the only fight that matters. And we're going to make them see it."

The command center fell quiet, subdued by the weight of the task at hand. These people were about to step onto the world's stage, not as invaders but as ones to herald a truth so great that it could either bring every person on this planet together or drive them apart, and push all of human history into the darkness.

Carlos was the first to break the silence, and his voice was resolute. "Let's do this. For our families, for our friends, and for every man, woman, and child on Earth. We are all in this together. If we are to fall, we fall as one."

The team nodded at one another, and began work, each person well-versed in their individual duties and responsibilities, in addition to the gravity of the current situation. The command center buzzed with activity as final preparations were made, and Zara continued to make updates and adjustments to the plan as new information became available. She was the silent guardian, watching over them with an alien knowledge and an understanding that this alien would protect their small blue planet.

As the countdown on the main screen reached its final seconds, Drake turned and faced his planet, a floating hologram of the Earth suspended in front of him. He reached out and touched the glowing blue sphere, the vow on his face unspoken but clear.

Hawkins strode across the robot deployment bay, his boots resounding against the metal floor. The room was cavernous, subterranean, a temple for the silent, angular shapes of Zara's creations. Robots stood at attention in several wide, interlocking rows, their bodies casting angular shadows that overlapped and connected them. Each one was currently being run through a final systems check, their eyes glowing with an inhuman light.

Hawkins stopped at one of the units, his attention sweeping across its matte-black body. He ran his weathered hands over the seams of its plating, searching for any flaw that could jeopardize its mission. The units had been designed by a combination of alien and human technology and needed to put on a show of power so undeniable that Earth's combined military might could not do it by themselves.

Beside him, Jill was already at work, her own fingers flying over her tablet screen. She flipped through a rapid series of diagnostic displays, checking that every communication channel and energy signature was in order. Her expression was set, a point of calm in the center of a storm of nerves.

"All units are responding within operational parameters," Jill reported, her voice clear over the soft whir of the bay. "Energy reserves are at full capacity, and the encryption on the comms link is holding strong."

Hawkins gave her a thumbs up, a small smile tugging at his lips. "Good work, Jill. Let's make sure these machines are as ready as we are."

The air was thick with a sense of controlled urgency. It was the result of months of non-stop preparation: simulations, strategy meetings, and hours upon hours of training. They had all poured themselves into the preparation to make sure this day would come.

Hawkins continued his rounds, still in awe of the technology before him. These combat robots were light-years beyond the simple drones he used to pilot during his military service. They had advanced sensor systems, non-lethal weapons, and artificial intelligence that seemed almost sentient.

Jill moved on to the next robot, her tablet syncing with the unit's systems. She ran through deployment coordinates and mission parameters once more, cross-checking to ensure each unit was primed for its specific role. The robots were armed only with non-lethal force options. Drake and the others had been adamant about that. They were protectors, not predators.

"Hawkins, I'm seeing a minor fluctuation in one of the power cells," Jill said, tapping on her tablet. "Unit Delta-Seven. It's nothing serious, but it might impact its operational efficiency."

Hawkins was by her side in seconds. "Let's swap it out," he said, pulling a spare power cell from his belt. "We can't have any hiccups."

One by one, they worked through the line, a growing sense of gravity settling over them. They were about to unleash an army of robots into the center of one of the most fortified locations on the planet. It was a high-risk move that could either electrify the world or throw it into chaos.

"Jill, as soon as we're done with the drones, we need to run through the transport shuttles again."

The hum of machinery filled the room as Mandy sat at her post in the darkened nerve center of Haven's secure communications facility. A vast wall of monitors flanked her on all sides, each screen a window into a different part of the world, a pixelated tapestry of human activity that she surveyed with the keen focus of a hawk. The rhythmic whir of equipment and soft clicking of keys were a white noise symphony that underscored the gravity of her work.

The disinformation campaign Marc had set in motion had already begun to seep into the global consciousness. Mandy was the first to see the effects. She watched as the world took in the information, fingers deftly dancing across the console to adjust parameters, analyze data, and make sure everything was in its place. It had to be targeted just right, seeding curiosity and fear without leading anyone back to Haven or the team.

Government satellite feeds, clandestine surveillance networks, and encrypted channels from around the world all funneled into her console, painting a comprehensive picture of the situation as it unfolded. Mandy's keen eyes caught the signs of a global awakening just beginning: subtle shifts in media narratives, unusual government gatherings, whispered rumors among world leaders, and the first swell of a rising tide of global anxiety.

A soft chime sounded in the corner, a new transmission from Zara. The AI's voice, cool and neutral, overlaid Mandy's earpiece for a second. "Optimal timing for the global broadcast is approaching," Zara confirmed. "Sentiment analysis and political activity are aligning to provide maximum impact for our message."

Mandy nodded, acknowledging the message. Zara was everywhere and in everything at Haven. The AI was as much a part of their operation as the air they breathed.

It was a lot of pressure. Mandy knew that. Information was powerful. She had watched it tear apart governments, shatter global institutions, rewrite history. The world's reaction to what they were about to do would be determined by what happened in the first few minutes of the global address. Minutes she was in charge of facilitating.

Watching the streams of data flow into her console, Mandy felt a flash of anxiety. It was a lot to ask of the world to accept the truth that they were about to present to it. But Drake had made it clear; humanity simply had no choice. The Afltic threat was real and too dangerous to not take this kind of action. There was no way to put the genie back into the bottle, no way to stomp out this spark before it became a wildfire that could burn through the foundations of human civilization.

Every data packet, every single leak worded with precision, led to this point. A delicate dance of information warfare where every step, every choice, was part of a grander strategy designed to build momentum towards an inevitable conclusion. Mandy was here to make sure that the narrative was clear, that the presentation of the Afltic threat to the world was done in a way that would galvanize humanity, not cause it to tear itself apart in conflict.

Mandy looked at one of the computer screens that served as her workstation and saw the live UNGAH stream. The large, domed assembly hall, with the beautiful green-marbled walls, the semicircular rows of desks of the different country's delegates, was eerily empty. Like a dormant volcano waiting to spew forth lava, it was where Drake and the rest of the team would be standing in just a few short minutes to give their speech to the world.

Mandy looked back down at the large console she was working at. The connections with her other analysts were always going, but the rush of alerts flickered across the smaller screen on her secondary console. Mandy isolated the feed, fingers flying across the interface as her pulse quickened. She understood immediately what was happening. It was a spike in encrypted communications between a handful of government agencies a frantic, high-level exchange of information that was the first reactions to the validity of the intelligence drops.

"Zara," Mandy spoke calmly, "I'm picking up a lot of chatter across a few different intelligence networks. Looks like the first dominoes are falling."

"Yes," Zara replied in her cool, detached voice, "The cascade effect has begun, it is within our predicted parameters. We need to ensure that the flow of information remains constant and the momentum keeps building towards the endgame."

Mandy took a deep breath, steadying herself before she turned back to her console. She knew that in the next few hours, the future of humanity would be decided. The world was on the brink of a new day, and she was helping to guide it into the light.

As she worked to ensure the right information was going where it needed to be, Mandy felt an incredible sense of kinship with the billions of people on Earth whose lives were depending on them. She was a conductor, making sure that the symphony of truth that they were composing reverberated across the world.

The sound proofed secure communications hub was abuzz with expectation. Built with special sound dampening materials, the air of the room felt thick and seemed to vibrate with the silent intensity of the room. Mandy continued to track the different data feeds, charts, and projections with the meticulous eye of a chess master.

The command center of Haven was alive with intense concentration and energy. Every breath felt like it was charged with electricity. Drake stood alone in the middle of the center of Haven's operations floor, surrounded by the various data consoles and high-tech instruments of Haven's nerve center. He stared at the large, holographic schematic of the UN building projected before him.

It was a translucent blue structure; the lines of its architecture and interior detail sharply defined and glowing with a ghostly illumination.

Drake surveyed the digital maze, his thoughts darting between strategies and contingencies like an arrow in flight. This was their plan, his plan, and it was as complex as it was daring—a delicate web of calculations and assumptions, each thread as strong as the weakest link. It was the culmination of everything he had been working towards, a plan that could either save humanity or destroy everything he had ever cared for.

The building itself was a fortress of information, a labyrinth of secrets waiting to be uncovered. Drake had studied its design for sometime, its vulnerabilities and escape routes burned into his memory. The United Nations was more than a target; it was a symbol of unity, a beacon of hope that could rally the world to stand together in the face of an existential threat. The choice of location had been deliberate, designed to shock the world's leaders into action.

Around him, the control room buzzed with activity. The team moved with practiced efficiency, their focus absolute. Drake watched them with a sense of pride and belonging that was hard to quantify. They were his people, his extended family, and he would give his life for each and every one of them.

He took a deep breath, his eyes settling on the holographic image of the General Assembly Hall. He could almost see it, feel it, smell it. It would be there when they arrived, amidst all those important people, as though waiting for them. It was there, that he would stand with his team, and speak directly to those leaders.

Drake felt a chill run down his spine at the thought. It was a daunting prospect, one that filled him with a sense of dread and anxiety.

Standing at the head of those leaders, he would have to speak. To get the message out, to warn them of what was coming.

Taking a deep breath, Drake allowed himself to calm his nerves and steady his breathing, focusing on the task at hand. He could do this, he had to. He had trained for this moment his whole life, and now was not the time to be afraid. He would see his family again, he had to.

He gave a brief glance around the control room, checking on his team. They were a hodgepodge of cultures, a team of individuals each with their own background and life experiences. But they were all united in their mission, and Drake felt a surge of pride at the sight of them. He would lead them into battle, and trust them with his life.

"Zara, please give us a status update," Drake called out to the AI, his voice firm and steady.

Zara's image flickered with a static crackle before stabilizing. "All systems operational," the AI replied, her voice as serene and soothing as ever. "Drones are loaded and ready to deploy, stealth shuttles are on standby. The timing window is optimal, and we are ready to initiate the plan at your command."

Drake nodded in acknowledgment, his eyes sweeping over the room, taking in his team. "Marc, Carlos, Tammy, Mandy, Hawkins, Jill," Drake called, his voice echoing through the busy room.

The six people turned, their faces set with a grim determination that Drake knew all too well. They understood the risks, the gravity of their situation, and the fact that failure was not an option. They nodded in unison, ready to follow Drake wherever he would lead them.

The atmosphere in the control room changed as the team began to mobilize, each person taking up their role with precision and focus. It was a well-oiled machine, a testament to the training and preparation that had gone into this mission.

As the countdown to their departure reached its final seconds, Drake paused to steady himself. He closed his eyes and focused on the plan, the obstacles they would face, and the message they would send. It was a message of hope, of strength in numbers, and of a fight against a common enemy. A message that the world needed to hear, and hear now, before the first rumblings of the coming celestial storm.

He knew that they would be met with doubt, disbelief, and perhaps even hostility. But he also knew that the truth was a powerful thing, and once it was out, there was no stopping it. It would tear through walls, break down barriers, and awaken a dormant spirit in all those who heard it.

The time for silence was over. The time for action was now. With a nod to Zara, Drake gave the command that would set their plan in motion.

"Activate the drones, Marc, Carlos and I are in transit to our shuttle" he said, his voice ringing with the gravity of their mission. "It's time to show the world what's coming."

CHAPTER 15: THE UN GAMBIT

The first drone-wave dropped from hidden transporter pods in the shadows of the UN building as dawn was just beginning to break, the mechanical limbs of the Areidyanies's combat drones extending as the geometrically-shapely black drones unfolded out of their pods silently over the pavement. Three in number, the drones rotated their heads, which their optical sensors peering out from within these, forming a triangular formation as they scanned the building. The human-sized drones were made with sleek, dark coloring to blend into the shadows, moving swiftly and with eerie silence through the empty streets as they headed towards their target.

The drones were a human-Areidyan hybrid of technology and form, near-invisible, even in broad daylight, and their cloaking abilities were the best in the galaxy. Jill's fingers moved gracefully on the holographic panels in front of her as her eyes watched the movements of the drone in front of her. She spoke calmly and quietly to her team through the comms system while expertly coordinating her commands to the drones using the console in front of her.

"Wave One, you are clear to perform your initial perimeter sweep," Jill said through her earpiece comms. "Stealth is paramount, do not make unnecessary contact with any person or obstacle."

Wave One acknowledged and the drones spread out, their legs rapidly moving as they advanced upon their target. They triangulated the most common areas of security cameras and even the areas most traveled by human guards at the UN. One by one, the drones disabled the systems, coordinating with the team back at Haven to evade patrols or lock guards in rooms.

Jill's eyes were focused on the unfolding mission as she viewed the 3-D data that the drones were feeding her, quickly running various processes and giving her additional information in as to best proceed with the drones to complete the primary objective. The success of the drones' first wave was their greatest success at Haven, a nearly seamless infiltration of the areas around the United Nations building and the exterior of the General Assembly Hall, though there was still much to be done.

Mandy, Wave one is complete. Ready for wave two. Jill said softly. "Wave Two, move in for the strike on the General Assembly Hall," Mandy ordered as the second wave of drones were now primed and ready to move in for the next phase. "Clean sweep. Keep your eyes sharp."

They had just reached the outer perimeter of the UN complex when Mandy noticed a slight flicker of movement on her screen. A security guard was standing outside of the front entrance of the building. A large cup of coffee was in his hands, his breath visible in the cold morning air. He was leaning back against the overhang of the entrance, peering out at the empty plaza before him. Then, with a sigh of satisfaction, he turned around and walked into the building, a contented smile on his face.

Mandy felt her heart skip a beat, but she quickly regained her composure. Pulling herself up from her seat, she punched in a series of quick commands into the computer. "Wave Two, scatter and avoid detection," she said, her voice trembling slightly. "Keep a wide circle and wait for my orders."

The drones immediately dispersed, their bodies bending and contorting in the air as they shifted directions. Passing by the guard, they made their way into the building, their cloaking devices preventing anyone from noticing their presence. The guard seemed to notice nothing at all, his head turning away from the plaza and back towards the warmth of the building.

Mandy let out a sigh of relief and sank back into her chair. She knew that this was only the beginning, but it was a start.

"Wave Three, take your positions," she said, her voice firm and commanding. "We're moving in."

The third wave of drones, assigned with creating a perimeter around the UN complex, began to move in with a cold, mechanical efficiency. Each of them converged on their respective locations, spreading out and taking up positions around the building. Their primary mission was to provide cover for the second wave of drones, which were to carry out the task of eradicating all signs of their presence from the building. It was a bold plan, but they had no other choice.

The sun had just risen, its first light spilling across the sky in brilliant, orange hues. The city was still mostly dark, but the first hints of dawn were beginning to cast long, dramatic shadows against the skyline. The UN headquarters was a monolith in the distance, its glass facade shining in the morning light. It was a symbol of peace and cooperation in a world that had long been ravaged by war and conflict.

But this was about to change. The future of the human race, and the fate of every life on Earth, now hung in the balance.

The second wave of drones drifted through the hallways of the UN building, their sensors scanning the environment around them with a cold, detached efficiency. They were nearly invisible to the naked eye, their cloaking devices doing an excellent job of hiding them from view. Heat signatures and faint outlines of light danced across their sensors as they moved through the empty hallways.

Mandy sat at the center of the control room, monitoring the progress of the mission. "Wave Two, begin internal cleansing," she ordered, her voice cold and commanding. "Disable all security systems, make sure that no civilians are harmed."

Mandy watched as the drones acted, their movements now as if they were one with her commands. The group of drones moved around in the building, swift and without sound as the darkness around them. Skirting around corners and moving with stealth as they did so, they made their way with surprising ease around the interior of the building. Complex and full of twists and turns the building was, but the reconnaissance the drones had previously made, combined with careful simulation, made this all trivial for their advanced navigational algorithms.

When the drones met a group of security personnel or civilian staff they approached the group, and the delivery system began to release a mist of non-lethal neurotoxin. Odorless and colorless, the neurotoxin was designed to be fast-acting, and quickly induced a non-damaging sleep, putting all nearby in a temporary state of unconsciousness.

The security guards fell, dropping to the floor as the drones worked, some dropping their radios in surprise as they did so. Civilians of the building also fell as the drones moved through, their bodies hitting the floor as they were overwhelmed by the neurotoxin, causing them to slumber.

In the middle of the building stood the General Assembly Hall, the great ceremonial room where diplomats met. Its massive windows were a distinct feature of the building, and the light from dawn was starting to filter through the ornate stained glass. Diplomats inside the hall continued on their business, entirely unaware of the way the building was being taken over, going about their meeting as they were, discussions and debates taking place in many different languages.

The diplomats were diverse in nature, from different countries all over the world and all with their own way of thinking about the many different problems and issues of the world. They were representatives of the people they served, coming to this place to shape the policies that affected their nations and their citizens, to work toward a goal and make the world a better place.

The General Assembly Hall was a place of nations. A coming together of different cultures to reach a common goal, a place of harmony and common work despite underlying tension. Security personnel from the various nations in attendance gave way to the drones as they worked, until eventually the last were neutralized, and all the drones had to do was withdraw.

The United Nations headquarters now stood in silence, a shell of its former self as it was devoid of activity. Mandy could see it for herself, external and internal defenses completely out of commission for the time being, and so her attention moved to the next stage.

"Wave Three, now it's your turn. Move into place and create a buffer, we need to make sure nobody surprises us.", Mandy commanded as she began to move her team around.

"We've secured the building.", Hawkins responded to her, "The diplomats are still in the General Assembly Hall, completely unaware of what's going on.

You're up. It's time to take the General Assembly Hall."

A great wave of dialogue crashed through the General Assembly Hall, a mass of different nations, voices all raised in a grand cacophony of the business of international policy. Representatives of every state on the planet were at their seats in the chamber, their different languages clashing together as they did so. The chamber's rostrum was where the Argentinian ambassador was at the moment, his face reddened from the ire of his speech, a clear sign of the politics taking place.

He raised his voice, repeating an allegation of a border crossing in the Strait of Magellan being carried out by the Chilean forces. His arms waved wildly as he spoke, his finger pointed directly at the seated Chilean delegate, their rigid face a look of silent, unmoving defiance.

The delegate conference room was silent when it happened, unaware of the dire events occurring beyond the lobby. Zara's shock bots, black and glossy, glided down the long corridors. Sleekly designed for deadly efficacy and a variety of specialized combat purposes. Adapted for urban environments, they had blended through crowds of security with stealth and speed, and entered the building the same way. Perfect for this sort of mission. Their movements were swift and quiet, their red-sensitive omni-cams flickering as they slid through long twisting hallways, towards their targets.

Abruptly the Argentinian delegate's speech became shaky and overblown. Conversation ground to a halt as he stared at the podium. He seemed to have a temporary loss of coherence. In an instant the lights flickered and went out, replaced by a dim twilight from natural light seeping through the windows. The digital readouts above the rostrum which had been tracking votes and performing real-time translations became unreadable. The numerous electronic devices lining the walls emitted a quiet, final sigh as the conversation in the chamber ground to a halt. Several delegates stared at one another, mildly bemused as their personal communications suddenly stopped. Others made incoherent gasps, unsure of what was occurring as their fellow delegates engaged in discussion.

Abruptly, the doorways started to cycle. One combat bot opened up through a ceiling hatch near the dais. The others slid open on the side of the chamber as it moved in on the group. Another door emerged from behind a thick curtain, and the group jumped as the automation moved into position. The delegates sat in chairs bolted to the ground as the robots moved in. Their conversations about petty human customs and arguements over last week's border disputes all stopped as they looked towards the doorways.

The bot that had emerged first opened itself into a more humanoid and aggressive form. It silently moved towards the group, trying to choose its targets. A young Ukrainian delegate noticed the dark form and screamed in terror as he reached for a large pen which had been on the table. The bot sidestepped the motion with an audible gasp, and the bot began cycling on a non-lethal tranquilizer spray. As the fine aerosol mist settled over him the young man felt his vision swirl in confusion as the sweet smell hit his nose. He could do nothing but stare and fight as he was overtaken by the sedative, his body seizing up as he toppled onto the floor and fell motionless.

At that same time the combat robots cycled localized EMP fields, overwhelming the sensitive electronic devices in the room. A sweeping wave of chatter sounded as electronic devices shorted and turned off, the screens becoming unreadable. The delegates toppled from their chairs as their muscles relaxed, their bodies responding to the neurotoxin. The meeting had been frozen in time, from the shouts of the Argentinian delegate to the younger Ukrainian aide as their conversation and comments about the previous border conflicts were stifled and covered by silence as the room descended into a vacant hush. The only sound was the rustle of discarded papers being shaken loose from the unconscious delegates.

"Keep it clean, stay in formation." Hawkins' voice was a lifeline, a constant amidst the uncertainty. "Make sure everyone is clear, everyone who is not a delegate. We're not here to hurt them." He paused, thinking of the cold promise of mercy that his words carried, like the specter of order following the chaos of their arrival. "Locate anyone still in the chamber and make sure they're unconscious." He cast a quick glance at the delegates, still slumped in their chairs. "We're not here to start a massacre, not by a long shot. We're not trying to take the building. We're taking the world's most powerful leaders, we're taking them alive. This will have to be the bloodless coup that it was always meant to be."

The final unconscious delegate slumped to the floor as the last of the robots sealed the doors. The droids now set about their final tasks, searching for any delegate who had slipped out of their seat or fallen onto the floor, lifting the limp forms with calculated care and gently setting them back down. A few of the robots, already set to 'scanner' mode, skated silently through the aisles, their red photoreceptors sweeping over each individual and piece of furniture, searching not for data but for weapons. Knives, guns, even pens were swiftly discovered and stowed in tiny compartments within the robots.

This complete, the rest of the robots formed a cordon around the chamber, black and silent sentinels. The great chamber of speeches and pomp was now a tomb, empty but for the bots and the sleeping leaders. Hawkins took a secure comms.

"Marc," he said, curt and businesslike. "Chamber is secure. No loose ends. All delegates accounted for, all in position, neutralized. Chamber fully swept. Have Donovan land. He can head to the chamber now."

Her eyes remained on the array of monitors that filled the top third of the large bay of the secure communications center of Haven. On each screen, a different news station, all of them broadcasting the same thing, a live view of the ongoing chaos at the United Nations headquarters. The hosts of the world's most high-profile news programs stood with blank expressions and shaky voices as reporters streamed in with conflicting reports of the unfolding scene.

The first reports were garbled and confused, the sort of fuzzy half-truths and misreporting that one came to expect in the immediate minutes after an incident. For a few minutes, the anchors took to the conspiracy theories being flung around with characteristic nonchalance.

"This could be a terrorist attack," one anchor said, his face drawn with speculation. Another theorized a system-wide collapse of some kind. "All of their communications are down, all feeds have gone offline, which points to a cyberattack of some kind." The screen cut to an anchor who was emphatically dismissing a report of gunfire within the building as misinformation.

Mandy observed with detached interest, her mind already categorizing and classifying the deluge of information coming in, already writing off the less useful of the reports, reading through a fraction of the potential theories with the practiced eye of a veteran.

She had been on the receiving end of this sort of thing before, the mad scramble for information in the moments after an event. There was always a mixture of this sort of thing, the initial burst of speculative theories that sprang up in the gaps of information and understanding. She noted a few details, the failure to spot the blackout of UN communications as more than a mistake. Other anchors were being less reticent, conjecturing that a communications blackout of this sort meant a systems-wide failure and that the building was likely to be evacuated.

Mandy let the reports play out, her eyes impassive as the anchors traded theories, her mind analyzing and discarding, a practiced sorting of information. She let the anchors mutter their reassurances to the viewer as the broadcasts went on, their faces losing the veneer of nonchalance and gaining a tinge of concern.

The first few minutes were a rush of misinformation and confusion, but as the minutes ticked by the reports grew more agitated, concern taking the place of the initial calm. The world was watching, millions of people had the United Nations building on their screens, but they were in the dark.

It was at this point that the projection of Zara coalesced into view, a light next to Mandy's shoulder. Her presence was nothing short of majestic.

"The targets have been secured," Zara began. "The leaders of the free world are all secured and waiting for your orders."

Mandy watched, not taking her eyes off the screens. "The seeds of our efforts are starting to grow," she said calmly. "The Intelligence we sent into place is dropping into place all over. Our future waits only on your part of the plan."

Zara's holographic image shimmered slightly as she analyzed fresh data. "The confusion is already turning into a disbelief, and soon will turn into comprehension," she stated, with confident finality. "When Drake speaks, the entire world will be waiting for his words."

The two women watched, as the story unfolded. The talk of global panic was subsiding, giving way to the universal human reaction to not knowing. Bated breath.

Unable to resist the need to know, the networks were combing for early evidence of an organized attack. Forcibly cutting communications to the UN building, and the strangely simultaneous attack of world leaders with an unknown gas, were being linked to all things terrorist by conjecture based on what little was known.

"The police are coming," Mandy's voice was flat and matter of fact over the comms device. "Incoming on the UN building. Ten minutes out, maybe less."

"I understand," Jill said evenly.

Hawkins sat on a console in between Jill and Tammy and looked away from his own smaller replica of the UN chamber, over to Tammy. "Time for the reversal process," he said.

Tammy's fingers flew over a holographic keyboard as she keyed in her confirmation. "Agents of revival are being deployed," Tammy said. "Vital signs are constant. Full report in less than a minute."

Hawkins turned his attention back to the screens and the new almost invisible agent already beginning to fill the UN chamber. It was an anti-agent, and was programmed to counteract the effects of the tranquilizer. When it was finished, it would slowly bring the world leaders back to themselves.

A twitch of the hand. The slow lifting of the head. A muffled groan that shattered the silence.

The silent, matte black arrowhead shuttle craft, an Areidyanies design, streaked across the early morning sky. The non-reflective paint absorbed the dawn light and made the ship effectively invisible, against the city skyline. It was just as silent inside as it was on the outside, the atmosphere tense and expectant. Drake Donovan sat in the pilot's seat, fingers moving on the controls, silently steering the craft toward its landing zone, the roof of the United Nations building.

In the co-pilot and tactical officer's seats, Carlos Acutis and Marc Singer monitored multiple sources of information in a constantly shifting sea of holographic interfaces. The shuttle, equipped with the very latest in stealth technology, could easily evade detection by the most advanced anti-missile systems of the human race. No advanced piece of technology, however, could mask the tension inside the tiny aircraft.

The only sounds were the engines, and the crackling comms device. Hawkins' calm, controlled voice in the cabin. "It's done," he confirmed. "The UN building is ours."

"The General Assembly Hall is secure," Hawkins said, with less jubilation than such a mission would have otherwise warranted. "All diplomats were neutralized without harm. The revival sequence has been activated and they are beginning to rouse now."

Drake affirmed, with practiced hands deftly navigating the shuttle into a stable orbit above the UN building, steel in his spine as he considered the new history that was in the making before him.

Carlos, at the copilot's seat, massaged his curly black hair, wrinkling his forehead. As the team's "team player" and diplomatic expert, it was his job to have the greatest understanding of the mission at hand. While this was still a military operation, it was an entirely peaceful one. It demanded in addition to an acute tactical intelligence, both a comprehensive grasp of international law, and an understanding of global politics.

Marc, had his attention on the live footage being relayed from the drones on the roof of the UN building. Nothing was in view except for the fighting robots perched stealthily on the roof. Highly advanced in both adaptive cloaking and concealment systems, they would be nearly impossible to detect with the naked eye. He observed the last of the UN security force personnel being affected by the neurotoxin spray and being gently lowered onto the floor by the automated combat robots.

Projecting from the side of the shuttle was a live video feed of the world-famous UN building, quietly sleeping and eerily tranquil below, in the grey light of a slowly-brightening dawn. Drake stared at the majestic view for a moment, his senses alert and focused on the long minutes ahead of him.

"Listen," Drake began, in a quiet but powerful tone, as he studied the image of the United Nations building, immovable in its current state of dormancy. "This is it. This is the point of no return. We've done our training, and we've done our planning, we know the plan. We know the ins and outs, we have responses to every possible contingency. Now it's time to see it through, to do our jobs, and get it done."

Marc, rapidly navigating the shuttle's tactical interface with his expert hands, interjected, "Hawkins and our others have done their part of the job. Now it's our job to carry the torch and deliver our message that could so easily change everything."

Drake clenched his jaw and moved to shift the shuttle's thrusters into position for a tactical landing in the designated landing zone. Like a moth floating on an invisible stream of wind the shuttle dipped downwards, cutting with powerful yet unusually quiet engines through the grey dawn as it lowered towards the earth, its landing gear deploying elegantly as it gently came to a halt on the smooth surface of the concrete landing pad.

Shutting off the shuttle's engines, the three of them unbuckled themselves from their seats. "Remember," Drake continued, in a low whisper as they unbuckled, "this isn't about fighting or even coercion. We are not here to compel them to anything, or to hold any of them at gunpoint. We are here to enlighten. We are here to open their eyes to the universe we live in, and to show them the hard truths we have learned to live with. We are not here to drive them apart, we are here to bring humanity together."

The shuttle's access hatch hissed open with pneumatic force, the sharp outlines of the roof's interior, quiet and plain, being revealed to the world for the first time that day. Drake led the way as they stepped from the vehicle, his boots padding against the floor as he led the way to the access door that would allow them entry into the building. Carlos and Marc followed at his heels, their senses honed on every sound and every movement they made. As their footsteps were quiet against the floor, the roof otherwise lay completely silent except for the muted distant murmurs of the city beginning to wake up. Life in the world around them continued unaffected, the citizens and the people going about their daily business entirely oblivious to the history that was taking place inside of the United Nations.

Navigating the massive building's corridors, they were led by the Areidyanies' own combat robots, bathing the path in their unnatural, geometric light. Drake went over his words in his head, taking his time to keep his pacing in check as he reviewed the words he had planned to say. Every word was meant to matter, carefully chosen and rehearsed for this exact occasion. It was a speech that called for action, for unity. It was a speech, that, if all went to plan, would be the first in history to address all of humanity as one, in response to an existential threat to their survival on an unprecedented scale.

CHAPTER 16: A CALL FOR UNITY

A chorus of static filled the ears of billions as Mandy and Zara, working in perfect unison, took control of every broadcast system in the world. The flicker of a television in a village in the Philippines or the blink of a cellphone in a taxi in Manhattan, every television, monitor, loudspeaker, radio, and satellite connection was taken live. The world held its collective breath, unknowingly drawn together through the intimacy of shared experience, as every eye and ear in the world saw and heard every other soul alive and what was transpiring in the General Assembly hall.

Hawkins Taylor's tinny voice crackled through the chamber's speaker system. "Please be quiet. Remain calm and seated. The drones are in position and will not hesitate to incapacitate any unruly attendees." The threat of force in his otherwise soothing tone sent an involuntary chill down the spines of the crowd. The diplomats shifted about awkwardly, their stiff movements full of uncertainty as they nervously cast their eyes about, their faces rife with confusion and fear. The Menacing looking drones, silently focusing their all-seeing lenses on the assembly, did little to calm their growing anxiety.

Breaking the nervous silence was the Delegate from Russia, a seasoned career diplomat with a hawkish nose and a steely gaze. "What does this mean?" he demanded, his thick accent filling the chamber. "Who are you? What do you want?"

"Your attention and cooperation," Hawkins replied in kind, his words leaving no room for discussion. "We are not your enemy. We are here to deliver a message of the utmost existential significance to every man, woman, and child on this planet."

A collective murmur of skepticism arose from the crowd, but the unforgiving glare of the drones quickly quashed any expression of outright revolt. The assembly, confused and frightened though they may be, were keenly aware that they were at the mercy of some unknown force with capabilities far exceeding anything they had ever encountered.

Outside of the massive entryway to the General Assembly Hall, Drake was flanked by Marc and Carlos. The distant, anxious buzz of the diplomats within was a muted symphony, playing to the tune of their own mission. Drake closed his eyes and took a long, slow breath, his heart pounding a thunderous beat in his chest. The enormity of the situation, of his incredible responsibility, pressed heavily on him. The future of the human race teetered at the edge of a knife's point.

With a reassuring hand on Drake's shoulder, Marc put a firm voice to the simple fact. "You're not alone, son," he said, his baritone timbre low and soothing. "We've got your back."

Drake's eyes opened and he met the steady gaze of Marc's supportive one. He nodded, a silent expression of trust, confidence, and brotherhood. His right hand instinctively came to rest on the cool hilt of the sidearm that was holstered to his belt, his eyes never leaving Marc for more than a moment.

Carlos, his own hand to his own gun at his hip, surveyed their immediate environment with a skilled vigilance. "Clear," he whispered, almost prayerfully. "We're go."

The room was charged with electricity as Drake Donovan strode into the General Assembly Hall. The lights of the cameras mounted by countries from around the world followed him with their beams, casting distorted shadows against the walls and ceiling as they moved to track his movements to the front of the room. Diplomats sat motionless in their chairs, dazed and mostly paralyzed by the stunning non-lethal restraint methods of the robots. Voices had died out as he approached, all of their private conversations concerning the event forgotten by this most confusing of moments. The whole room appeared to be frozen in place, the mightiest of the world's leaders and diplomats caught unawares in a new age of incomprehensible truth.

Murmurs and indignation rose among the less affected, though their voices were quiet and their words largely lost to the sheer magnitude of what had transpired. The first sign of this came as Drake ascended the steps of the podium, his confident figure towering over the room as he stood flanked by Zara's robots. Their attempts to rise and address the situation were met by the wall of Drake's strength, and the whole room quieted for a few moments under the challenge of this impossible situation. The notion that the most revered representatives of their nations could be so brazenly arrested, with non-lethal force, before the entire world was too surreal to speak. It was a direct violation of sovereignty to an unfathomable degree, all of it captured and live broadcast to every monitor in existence. The bumbling series of events that led to this moment was almost inconsequential.

Drake looked down at the speech that he was holding, still unable to process much of the words he was currently reading through the haze of his adrenaline. He swallowed hard as he ran his gaze over the full chamber, the faces of every delegate he could see in the vast room. He was so clearly visible to them and, in a way, so much was on the line for every life on the planet to see. Drake cleared his throat as he prepared to speak and was greeted by the sound of his voice echoing throughout the chamber, deafening in the sudden silence. He raised his voice to speak, bracing himself for the most difficult part of this crisis, and as he did, the leaders of the world looked up to face him.

"Today, in this very room, the world as you know it ends. And a new one will begin. Before we go any further, before we all must address this new reality, there is someone who needs to speak. She is not here to threaten you; she is here to save you. I present to you Zara, a representative from the Areidyanies."

The projection of Zara appeared in the space next to Drake, her holographic form shining brightly and casting an artificial light on the podium. The assembly gasped in unison, their collective eyes darting from the gruff human in front of them to the ghostly image next to him. It was hard to wrap their minds around someone interrupting this pivotal moment in United Nations history and it was equally hard to comprehend the entity that now held sway over the most important meeting of the galaxy. Carlos leaned back in his seat in the broadcast control booth, the monitors before him acting as windows to the view of the world behind him. He jiggled the controls for the cameras around the room and readjusted the focus on the one projected with Zara, making sure that every screen showing the event around the world saw her clear and crisp. The world needed to see this, now, while the event was still fresh in everyone's minds.

Her voice rang out when she began to speak, it was somehow both crystal clear and immensely resonant at the same time. Her words cut through the chaos like a hot knife through butter. "Honorable delegates," she started, her eyes shining with a light of ancient knowledge as she swept her gaze over the delegates, "I am not here to be your enemy. I am here to tell you the truth, however unbelievable it may be."

A deeper hush than before set over the room, a silence that commanded attention by the mere act of its presence. Zara spoke of the Cydonian Empire, a race that has long been gone from this galaxy, their history a tale of woe in a story she told with the tragedy of a funeral dirge. The Cydonian Empire was the mightiest in the galaxy, one whose technology rivaled what most species only dreamed of. They prided themselves on having the best astronomers, the most effective detection systems, and the most up-to-date early-warning beacons that the galaxy had ever known. For all of their achievements, the Cydonians were blinded by their own pride.

"The Cydonians, so the story goes, were forewarned of a rogue planetoid on a collision course with their homeworld," Zara continued. "They had the lead time, the resources, and the technical ability to counter the threat. What they lacked was faith—faith in the intelligence behind the message, faith in the credibility of the threat, and, ultimately, faith that they could be victims."

The analogy wasn't lost on the assembled leaders, and the murmur of discontent through the audience grew louder, if not more violent. Zara seemed impervious to it, her holographic avatar fixated on the task at hand. She painted a tale of a young, proud empire, so mired in self-assured dominance that they refused to acknowledge the danger, until it was far too late. The rogue planetoid smashed into their world, and in an instant, their cities, their culture, and all their works were wiped out of existence.

The delegate from France had by now almost gotten out of his chair, red-

152

faced with rage, ready to denounce the tale as obvious lies. The silent robot, that had been lurking in the wings of the chamber, silently glided towards him. Fluid, powerful joints whirred quietly, and the tall figure positioned itself between the Frenchman and the central dais, allowing no room for disobedience. The metal avenger had no need for violence to quell the room.

"The Cydonian Empire," Zara picked up where she left off, "did not fall because of the rogue planetoid, or even its attempts at sending warning signals. Their downfall was the steady loss of their resolve, the decadence that comes with millennia of unchallenged dominance."

The murmurs grew in volume once more, almost drowning out Zara's narrative. The allegory was clear as day, but rather than engaging the saboteurs in debates, the rest of the audience was held in complete thrall by Zara's words. Diplomats from around the world were transported back in time, to an age lost to the universe, to bear witness to the fall of a once great civilization.

"Despite the warnings they received," Zara continued, "the Cydonians squabbled and bickered, too wrapped up in themselves, and the assurance that their hyper-advanced civilization could not possibly be threatened by a few rocks from space, to act. The reality of the situation escaped them, and so they did not make the preparations necessary to counter the threat."

The murmurs of agreement came again, this time from the whole assembly. The decadence of the Cydonians was no different than Earth's. Arrogance and political division had long prevented humanity from rising above petty differences to tackle global problems.

Drake, beside Zara's hologram, scanned the delegates' faces. He saw fear, for sure, but also dawning comprehension, slow, aching realizations that the cautionary tale she told them was not meant for them. The Cydonian Empire wasn't some ghost of humanity's forgotten past; it was them.

Zara's tale then took an even more personal turn. The situation facing Earth wasn't unlike the one the Cydonians were in. The Afltic, she continued, are the equivalent of the planetoid from Zara's story, bar one crucial detail. This time, the threat is not an inanimate hunk of rock hurtling through space, but a sentient, unrelenting monster, genetically engineered to consume and assimilate anything and everything in its path. And, just like the Cydonians, Earth has been given advanced warning. They have had a chance to prepare and to counter, just as it had fallen to the Cydonian leaders to do.

"So," Zara concluded, her tone more pressing than before. "Will you disregard the evidence, will you call it fakes, anomalies and ignore the threat? Or will you rise to the occasion, and fight?"

The silence was deafening, a living thing that swelled and filled the room with the weight of what was about to be decided. Drake watched the delegates shift uncomfortably, a myriad of emotions flickering across their faces. Fear. Doubt. And a glimmer, just a glimmer, of resolve. This was the crossroads the world had been brought to, and the choice they made would decide the fate of every man, woman, and child on the planet.

Zara's projection began to flicker, her final words echoing in the chamber. "The time for debate is over. The time for action is now. Stand with us, and together, we will face this existential crisis with the unity and courage that has defined humanity at its finest."

As the last remnants of Zara's image vanished from the podium, Drake moved to the center of the stage, locking eyes with the assembled delegates. He knew the seeds of unity had been planted, but it would take more than words to nurture the solidarity they so desperately needed. It would take sacrifice, resilience, and an unwavering commitment to a future that was anything but certain.

Carlos's fingers danced across the controls, his eyes glued to the monitors. He watched as Drake, a beacon of calm in the storm, prepared to address the assembly. The silence that settled over the room was profound, a rare moment of stillness in a place built for debate and discord. Carlos knew every word Drake uttered would be dissected, analyzed, and debated by billions around the world. The success of their mission hinged on the delicate balance between shock and credibility.

As Drake's voice cut through the silence, a voice that resonated with quiet authority that demanded attention, Carlos adjusted the audio levels, ensuring every syllable was crystal clear. The diplomats in the hall listened in stunned silence, their expressions a mosaic of fear, doubt, and dawning realization. The gravity of Drake's words hung heavy in the air, each sentence a meticulously crafted arrow aimed at the heart of humanity's complacency.

Carlos's heart pounded as Drake began to speak, the silence in the General Assembly Hall as tangible as the polished wood beneath his boots. His expression was a careful mask of gravitas, his bearing that of a man who bore the weight of worlds on his shoulders. He stood at the precipice of history, a lone figure against the backdrop of global power, the quiet before his storm of truth.

The delegates watched him, a tapestry of nations and peoples, their collective breath held in anticipation. Drake's eyes, hard and resolute, found the lens of the global broadcast camera. The connection was instant and electric, a conduit that linked him to billions across the globe. It was as if he was looking into the very soul of humanity, a direct challenge to the skepticism and denial that had long crippled the planet's collective will.

Drake's voice, when it finally shattered the silence, was a clarion call that resonated through the chamber with undeniable authority. "Ladies and gentlemen," he began, his tone measured and somber, "what you have witnessed here today, what you have been told, is not a drill. It is not the plot of a science fiction novel. It is the harsh, inescapable reality that faces our world at this very moment."

He paused, letting the weight of his words settle over the hall. The diplomats, once powerful and formidable in their own right, now seemed diminished, their authority eclipsed by the stark truth Drake was now revealing before their eyes. The robots, silent and vigilant, stood unobtrusively yet omnipresent, a constant reminder of the force that now commanded the United Nations.

The silence was heavy in the public viewing gallery at the back of the General Assembly Hall as the assembled crowd took in the drama before them. It was the combined dread and anticipation of a room full of people watching something that they could not understand or explain, let alone accept as reality. Most of the people in that gallery would not forget what they were seeing for the rest of their lives.

A young woman behind me was pale and transfixed by what she was witnessing, clinging to the back of the seat in front of her and staring with eyes that were wide in both fear and wonder. Combat robots with multiple guns mounted on their rotating arms were crouched around the entire chamber, their inert, lifeless bodies the source of a power that had overrun the UN with frightening ease. She had arrived there with her school group, on a field trip to the UN that had turned into something beyond anything she could have imagined.

Beside her, a man with a square jaw was staring down at the room in front of him, scowling with a look of rage and disbelief that made him appear older than his years. A veteran who had seen his share of combat overseas, his hard body had taken much worse and could have handled the same in much closer quarters. It still would not prepare him for the day when the General Assembly of the United Nations was being addressed by a hologram of an alien and a seemingly insane man ranting about global annihilation.

She looked over at the man beside her, her expression scared and her voice little more than a whisper. "Who is Zara? Is this real?" Her eyes were on Drake as he finished his speech, on both him and Zara.

The man looked down at her, and he saw the same question on every other face around him. He had been shot at in combat, had his vehicle blown up beneath him, had seen men die all around him. He knew what real looked like, and this was something altogether different. This was a different kind of war, and one that no man was ready to face.

He shook his head in disbelief. "I don't know," he answered her. "I don't know who Zara is or what any of this means. But it is not normal. It is not normal at all."

The girl nodded at him, her fear of the situation changing into curiosity. She had seen too many science fiction movies and read too many books. As a child, she had dreamed of space travel and alien civilizations and grand adventures in the far reaches of the galaxy. Those had been fantasy, stories that she had gobbled up in order to feed her imagination and expand her horizons.

This was different, however. This was not something out of a story. This was real, and she was looking at the real thing.

As Drake concluded his address, I turned back to her and found that she was gazing at Drake with the same rapt attention as before. There was a sense of wonder about her, as if she had accepted what was happening as fact and found it just as amazing as the rest of us were. The flickering, holographic image of Zara reappeared beside Drake, and her image was even more captivating than when she had spoken. I listened to Drake and Zara, and I found that I had stopped worrying about the how's and the what's of the situation and had started thinking about the details of what they were saying.

Drake talked of a being that no human had ever encountered before and that possessed technology that far outmatched anything that man had ever devised. Zara was just as compelling in her description, a visual picture that brought reality to the alien words that she spoke. I had read books on other civilizations, had studied the scant few relics that they had left behind and the messages that they had left to a future that would never come. Nothing that I had read or saw in museums came close to what this woman, a holographic woman, was describing.

And then, of course, there was the reason why Drake and Zara had chosen to make an intervention in the first place, that which Zara had alluded to in her first appearance and that Drake had begun to speak of again in his speech. I had fought in a war, and I had seen much evil and witnessed much worse in my time, seeing the vilest things that a human heart could contain and could stomach. But Drake and Zara, with the certainty that they spoke and with their own stories of the threat that was coming, made a story that I would not be able to shake from my mind for a very long time to come.

It was real, the story of a great galactic entity that was going to destroy all of humanity for no other reason than that was what it was programmed to do, that would extinguish every last human being on the planet like a candle blown out by a passing breeze. I thought that a boy in some distant galaxy had the best death story that I could imagine, but Zara had eclipsed him in my mind. And if it was true, if Drake and Zara were speaking the truth... if this was all true, then the only response that could possibly satisfy the need for justice would be one that defied boundaries of nation, ethnicity, and all ideology, one that was unified across the entire planet.

The young woman and the veteran watched as the man in the suit came to join the other woman in the gallery. A small man who wore sunglasses that obscured his eyes, he quietly came to a position in the gallery where he would have a good view of the scene below, but also where he would not be too close to any of the others there. He was a high-level Department of Homeland Security official and had been woken up and told in no uncertain terms what the contingency plans were.

As Drake continued to speek, the man in the gallery watched her, trying to stifle the small growl of outrage that he was fighting back. He had heard rumors, of course he had, the intelligence community always heard rumors of the shadowy government and corporate programs that had long ago crossed the line into supporting the notion that there was life beyond Earth. But to see it with his own eyes was something that he had not prepared himself for.

He reached out and gently grasped the hand of a woman beside him, indicating with a subtle gesture that he wanted to discuss the situation. "I told you this was bigger than all of us," he said quietly, "but I never thought that we'd see something like this before the movies."

The woman beside him, clearly someone of high rank in her own right in the intelligence community, nodded in agreement. "We need to start formulating responses to every contingency that we can think of," she said, not taking her eyes off of the figure of Drake Donovan as she spoke.

"I agree," he said, "but right now, it's about containment. If we can keep it contained, then maybe we can figure out how to handle it."

As the two officials in the gallery discussed the possible responses and actions to the announcement that had been made to the world below, the woman and the veteran listened, still in shock at the information that they had just been given. It was starting to sink in, the words of Zara, of Drake, about what this Afltic was and what it could do to the world around them.

She turned to the veteran and reached out to touch his hand, the action a clear signal of her intent to hold onto him for at least the time being. "I know," she said simply, "I just want to do something. I want to help, I want to fight. I want to do anything."

He stared at her for a long moment, the clear concern in her eyes reaching through to him. The veteran nodded, a slow, deliberate motion that belied the uncertainty of what he was thinking. "We're not alone in this," he said at last, the implication of the idea starting to sink in with him as well. "We got lucky, got some warning. This is a message, to everyone, not just to us. If this is all legit, then I'll fight on the right side, fight for my home and my country. But first, you're staying with me."

"I stand before you," Drake said, "not as your enemy, but as your equal, a citizen of this world, as a human being." He paused, gesturing again to the flickering shadow of the ghostly Zara next to him. "I stand before you today as your witness, because our home is in peril."

There was a soft murmur of assent from the group, the mass of people who had all been spirited away to this one location for the "rendezvous". They were all still trying to shake the fog of their abduction from their consciousness and trying to come to terms with the revelations that they had just been told by Drake. The delegates from Earth's many governments and cultures had come here, each with their own sense of security in the way that they perceived the universe to be, and each now faced with the knowledge that there was more to existence than they had been prepared to accept.

The man they called Drake Donovan continued, his voice and his words resonating with a quiet intensity in the hushed room. "The Afltic," he said, his voice lower now, his hand moving to cover the ever-present gun that he was still wearing even as he was standing there before this assemblage of Earth's people, "is different. It is not a conventional threat, it is a universal blight."

"We're running out of time," Drake continued. "The Afltic aren't just another enemy, they are a scourge, an alien plague that sweeps over everything in its path and either consumes it or assimilates it."

A tremor of horror rippled through the chamber as Drake's words hung in the air. The Afltic were the embodiment of antithesis, a vast and monolithic collective bent on the negation of everything humanity had come to value and respect.

"The threat they represent to our species and to the future of all life is obvious," Drake continued, his words punctuated by the passion in his voice. "The Afltic do not seek to dominate, to coexist, or to enrich themselves at our expense. They seek to negate, to consume, and to assimilate."

"For decades," Drake continued, his words as steady as his gaze, "Zara has observed their movements, tracked their patterns, and analyzed their behavior. We have seen the destruction they have left in their wake, the shattered ruins of entire worlds and civilizations."

"The Afltic do not care about our politics, our religions, or our cultures," Drake said, his voice rising with each word. "To them, we are just another resource, another pool of biomass to be exploited for their own ends."

A murmur of disbelief rippled through the chamber as the diplomats and world leaders tried to absorb the implications of what Drake was saying. The Afltic, a vast and monolithic collective bent on the negation of everything humanity had come to value and respect.

Drake's voice rose, impassioned and resolute. "The time for division and infighting is over," he said, his words a rallying cry to the assembled nations. "We must stand together, united as one, if we are to have any chance of surviving this coming storm."

The room was silent, the weight of Drake's words settling over the delegates like a shroud. The idea of setting aside years, even centuries, of rivalry and distrust was a difficult one for many to swallow, but the alternative was unthinkable.

"We have been given a gift," Drake said, his voice ringing out with the clarity of a bell. "A gift of time, of knowledge, and of second chances. The Afltic are coming, but they are not here yet. We have this moment, this brief window of opportunity, to prepare, to innovate, and to rise to the challenge."

"I call on you," Drake said, his eyes blazing with the fire of conviction, "to put aside your differences, to look beyond the artificial boundaries that have divided us for too long. I call on you to stand with us, to join us in this fight for our very survival."

The room was silent, the weight of Drake's words settling over the delegates like a shroud.

Zara, the enigmatic alien advisor, appeared in the form of a shimmering holographic projection to Drake's left. Her form was as radiant and ethereal as ever, a beacon of wisdom and resolve in the midst of the gathering darkness.

"The choices you make," she said, her voice a symphony of countless harmonious voices, "will echo through the ages. Choose well, and your legacy will be one of strength, unity, and resilience. Choose poorly, and your names will be forgotten, lost to the mists of time."

The room was silent, the delegates lost in thought as they considered the enormity of the situation before them.

The delegates present, with apprehensive, hardened expressions, strained to hear Zara. The election, the vote that would seal their collective and individual fate for the rest of their lives and beyond would begin in a few moments.

Drake studied the delegates. The chamber of the General Assembly Hall of the United Nations felt small, the weight of his voice pressing in on the massive walls. He had spoken to them of their situation as candidly as he could; an existential threat, a chance for his people to live on while the rest of the galaxy was devoured. Now, he had presented them with that reality, stripped and bare for all to see. The time for action, for further debate and delay had passed; now was their time, for better or for worse.

The delegates thought. It was the only sound in the room for a few moments. The faces in the chamber were stern, tortured, with the twitching of fear and doubt that Drake could see behind the calm, carefully neutral expressions. Then, from the press section of the chamber, a shout rang out.

A woman, a journalist, a red-headed woman with green eyes who had come into the UN in order to conduct an interview with the Israeli delegate, had been taken by surprise by the events but had found her voice.

"Mr. Donovan, is this some sort of coup? Do you have plans to take over the world as an emperor?" she shouted, her voice carrying in the cavernous expanse of the chamber.

The question, unexpected and harsh, pierced the air like a sword. The faces of the assembled delegates turned to look at the woman who had spoken, their faces a combination of shock and interest as her question had crystallised an instinct many of them had, however small a voice it had inside their heads: the overtaking of the UN, the securing of complete power in one man's hands was not being done for the world, but for himself, for power.

Drake, for his part, stared from the podium, temporarily taken aback by the boldness of the question, allowing it to hang in the silence as if to let it truly sink in. He was well aware of the potential that the wrong people would take this as fact, and the ramifications of a narrative in the wider world: Drake Donovan had taken over the UN, immediately attempted to solidify his power, and had begun acting as if he was emperor.

He breathed, looking down to meet the journalist's eyes, "It is an intervention, not a coup," Drake started, his voice strong and even, "The last thing I wish to do is enslave the entire planet to my rule. The idea of me being 'Emperor' terrifies me, as I would hope it would anyone."

The room breathed, the delegates visibly relaxing as the man who had just declared himself in charge of the entire planet with no oversight had no interest in taking total power. It was enough to stop the spread of suspicion, as Drake stated clearly and, importantly, truthfully that he was in no rush to act in that manner.

"Am I here," Drake continued, for the journalist, and the entire world, "because we have an existential threat to our planet? Yes. Are the Afltic interested in our economic, political, or military systems? No, they care not for them. They want to eat us, consume us, as food for their march through the stars, and we will go no further than our own planet for as long as we can."

He waved at Zara, who was standing still as she stood next to him. "We are not enemies," he continued. "I am human, as are you. We share the future. If we do not unite, we will all perish."

The journalist found her throat closing up, her question answered more honestly than she could have expected. She saw it. Saw what was at stake and what they were really facing. They needed to stand together if they were to survive, to stop looking at their own petty differences and see the Afltic as the true enemy.

The question had set him on a different path, one that looked more inward at the purpose of the intervention, at the man who had just spoken.

Drake felt the change in the room and decided to dig in. "Please," he said, "look past the miracle of our arrival and see the bigger threat. We are not here to overtake your positions or deconstruct your power bases. We are here to send a message, to call humanity to the greatest battle in our history."

CHAPTER 17: UNITE OR DIE

The UN General Assembly Hall was eerily silent, its usual hum of a thousand languages and the shuffle of papers was replaced by the low hum of dozens of giant combat robots. They stood at intervals around the edges of the room, unmoving, unblinking silent giants. Their optical sensors cast an eerie, red glow as they observed the subdued and stunned assembly and media before them.

A French diplomat by the name of Monsieur Jean-Luc Dubois slowly brought his head up, the searing white flash of the robot's incapacitation pulse still ringing in his ears and making his temples throb. He blinked, focusing on the figure behind the podium. It was a stranger, a man the assembly had never seen before. Dubois could feel a sick sense of dread rising up in his chest. "This isn't real, not real," he whispered to himself, shaking his head. "It can't be."

He turned to the American diplomat next to him, Ambassador William "Bill" Harrison. Bill was staring at the figure behind the podium with an unreadable expression, but it was clear he was as shaken and stunned as his counterpart. Bill was a man who prided himself on maintaining a calm and cool exterior, but his complexion had gone ashen.

"A trick, Bill. It's a trick," Jean-Luc breathed, still reeling. "It's an elaborate psy-op. This entire scenario. The robots are just machines, constructs of metal and wire. Man-made. It has to be."

Bill's attention was flickering between the silent robots and the man at the podium. He exhaled slowly, his voice a low rumble. "I'd like to believe it, Jean-Luc. I'd like nothing more," he said quietly. He paused, frowning slightly. "But this tech. Look at it. The pulse it used on you, our people. It wasn't disabling us; it shut everything down. Systems kill. Complete systems kill. It was like flipping a switch. There wasn't a single explosion, not a single wire that burned out. Clean. Too clean."

"And aliens?" Jean-Luc laughed, a high, terrified sound. "Look around you, Bill. This is the UN General Assembly. We're not in a sci-fi flick. We're here to negotiate trade deals and... and human rights and climate change accords. Not this."

"We're here to discuss the future of humanity," Bill said, the bitter humor not landing in the heavy, anxious silence. He looked around at the room, noting the same confusion, the same disbelief reflected in the eyes of every other diplomat, journalist, and citizen of the world present. Their world, the one they had built up through the simple act of treating one another as equals, as members of the same family, had been broken into a million shards by a simple sentence from a stranger. He saw the same internal struggle reflected in his friend. Fight or flight? To accept or deny? To embrace or to resist?

Jean-Luc felt the nausea and panic in the pit of his stomach bubble up to his throat and overwhelm him, and he pushed himself to his feet, the warning growl of a nearby robot a mere whisper in his ears. He took a step forward, heedless of the unspoken threat as he brought his voice to the silence, straining to be heard in the vast chamber. "Mr. Donovan," he called, his voice a croak. "Who are you? You say you are a representative of an alien civilization. A species of sentient life that has been observing and monitoring our development. Why? Why now? Why make yourselves known at this time? And why do you come in this way? With force and dominance?"

Drake held the French diplomat's gaze, his expression emotionless. "I am not a representative of an alien civilization," he said, his voice steady and clear, a knife through tension. A collective, audible intake of breath filled the hall. "I am a representative of humanity. I was chosen by Zara, an artificial intelligence. She has come not to enslave or dominate us but to guide us."

A ripple of incoherent whispers spread throughout the hall. An AI? An alien one? And one that had chosen a human as their spokesperson? The revelation was as stunning as the realization that humans had visitors from another world.

"You, all of you," Drake gestured broadly at the assembly, his voice carrying a newfound authority. "We are species in a state of perpetual conflict with ourselves. This planet was built on a foundation of territorial disputes, economic inequities and tribal affiliations. Look around you. Your entire diplomatic framework is a monument to your inability to solve your differences without resorting to violence and war. I could have easily killed you all," he paused, "but I did not. I did not because I wanted you to know. To see with your own eyes and understand that Earths problems are inconsequential in the larger picture. We are here to offer you a chance for a future, but first you have to accept our present. And our present, as our own people have proven in the face of the silent judgment before you, is a state of utter, abject, powerlessness. That, monsieur Dubois, is the answer to 'why now?'" Drake asked rhetorically. "Because we are about to be exterminated by the Afltic. I can tell you that I do not wish to find myself in the gut of one of those beasts. Zara saw me, one of you, from our own world as a way to connect with you and show you the way."

The diplomat stood there, statue-still, as Drake's every word reverberated in the chamber like a bell. The hollowed quiet of the vast assembly hall enveloped them all, the low droning hum of the robots the only sound to be heard.

Drake was still, his own eyes downcast as the unspeakable truth of his words settled in the air around them. A brutal and truthful indictment of humanity, unsullied by politeness or pleasantries.

The thick silence felt like a pall that had been dropped over the United Nations General Assembly Hall. The marble walls, normally a statement of unity and human cooperation, now seemed to close in around them, like a mausoleum, a tombstone, and a declaration of their own extinction. Drake was tall in the podium, the entire weight of the entire world seemingly on his shoulders, and yet he was impassioned, a fire in his eyes.

"For far too long," Drake began, his voice resounding through the room, "we have let our trivial differences tear us apart. Our home planet is a patchwork of countries, a smorgasbord of cultures, a swirling kaleidoscope of competing ideas, all with their own personal narratives, their own conflicting priorities and ideologies. But this," Drake paused, "this is bigger than any one of us. This is bigger than our borders, our governments, our families, or our flag. I can look out at all of you and see it in your eyes." His voice lowered, more a conversation with each delegate than a performance for the masses. "The Afltic do not give a single shit about your flags or your anthems. They do not recognize your boundaries or your borders. They do not care about your history or your culture. To them, we are all just fodder."

The room was deathly silent, save for the subdued whirring of the robots themselves. The hum they made was suddenly quieter, like the world itself had taken a deep breath and was holding it in, waiting.

"We have to change the way we think," Drake continued, the force of his will and his hope for humanity's future a fire in the darkness. "All of our old ways of warfare, our technology, our strategies are moot. Mere things to build a bunker around. We need to combine all of our best, our scientists, our engineers, our artists, our dreamers. We need to collaborate, on a scale never before attempted. We need to use our intellect, our creativity, our imagination, and our indomitable will to find new ways to fight."

"Haven," Drake said, the word a lodestar of hope and possibility. "The Haven we have built for ourselves, is more than just a bunker. It is the fusion of human and alien technology, the melting pot of a new age of innovation, and invention and discovery. We have the blueprints for humanity's survival, and we are sharing them. But let me be clear: I am not asking for your help. I am stating that if you, the United Nations, and the countries of the world do not unite and share your technological and scientific resources, we will die, and you will follow shortly thereafter. We must have complete cooperation from all of you. Every nation, every tech company, and scientific institute, must work together. This is the only way forward. Our very survival depends on our unity, on our ability to stand together in the face of an enemy that will stop at nothing to exterminate us."

A hand rose in the assembly from a woman of sharp wit and steely determination, Ambassador Anika Patel of India. "Mr. Donovan," she began, her voice strong despite the storm of emotions behind her gaze, "how can we trust this... AI? How do we know that it, or you, do not have ulterior motives? How can we be sure that this Haven of yours will not become a fortress of oppression, a new world order at the mercy of an entity that we cannot understand or resist?"

Drake locked eyes with her, a look of deep understanding passing between them. "I know that you fear us, Ambassador Patel," he said, his voice even and steady, "I understand why you would, and I felt the same way when I first met Zara. But please, hear me out. Zara does not want to control us, she wants to empower us, to help us meet the challenge that is before us. Zara's very existence, her entire purpose, is dependent on the survival of intelligent life, of which we are a part. She has no desire to hold power or control over us, she only wants to help. Her only objective is the destruction of the Afltic threat, and to that end, she is willing to give us the means to fight and defend our world."

The ambassador eyed him closely, her features narrowing slightly as she digested his words. She wasn't the only one either, he could feel it; the skepticism, the disbelief, was almost a physical presence in the room. But there was also the growing determination, a flicker of resolve that was slowly spreading through the ranks.

"I ask you all," Drake continued, his voice rising, "to join us, to stand with humanity in its darkest hour. Lay down your differences and your grievances, and join us in a common cause. This isn't just about us, it's about every living thing on this planet, every culture, every dream. We have been given a chance, a chance to fight back against an existential threat that seeks to wipe out all life as we know it. A chance to protect our home and our future. I beg of you, don't let it slip away."

The room was silent once more, the delegates lost in their own thoughts, the weight of his words bearing down on them. This was a moment of truth, a point of no return where the fate of the human species was being decided. They could take the easy road, the path of destruction and despair, or they could take a leap of faith, and walk the road of hope and unity.

In the back of the hall, a figure finally stood up, his presence commanding attention from all sides. It was Ambassador Harrison, his face weathered by years of hard-fought battles, both in and out of the diplomatic arena. "Ladies and gentlemen," he began, his voice resonating through the room, "I have served my country and this assembly for many years, and in that time, I have seen humanity at its best and its worst. But here, in this room, right now, I see something new. I see an opportunity for redemption, for a chance to be something more. I say we take it."

His words hung in the air, a clarion call that sent ripples through the sea of delegates before him. Slowly, one by one, they began to rise, their voices merging together in a cacophony of unity and defiance. It was a sound that echoed through the halls of power, a testament to the resilience of the human spirit.

Stepping away from the lectern, Drake Donovan's part was done. He had laid the groundwork. The global leaders were committing to work together, and for the first time in a long time, he thought they might have a chance. For the people of Earth, there was no guarantee of safety. But there was hope. There was a chance.

Haven was in a state of controlled chaos. On the global front, fear and uncertainty were the order of the day. In the main command center, Hawkins was at his wall of holographic screens, taking it all in. He was grinning, but it was the kind of smile that came after a bruising fight. Jill stood next to him, her own panel of controls at her fingertips, her eyes darting to keep up with the stream of information that was cascading around the room.

Jill and Hawkins were the quiet in the eye of the storm. The decisions of humanity's future were being weighed every second. Across the crowded room, they took solace in each other's company.

A chime sounded across the command center. A new feed was coming in. It was Pax, his avatar a corner of the main screen. His face was placid, but he wore a slight, tangible tension. "The broadcast is having its desired effect," he intoned. "We should expect high levels of panic and skepticism. We are already pushing out ancillary data packets to the appropriate news and government agencies to cut through the speculation."

Jill smiled wearily. "Let's see if our buddies in the Global Intelligence Alliance are happy to hear the 'truth.' It's about as two-faced as they're going to have to be without either tipping into hysteria or making people lose trust."

Mandy shifted on the edge of a console. "The gnarliest part is going to be the next day or so. People are gonna want answers, and the governments aren't gonna be able to give them any. They're going to have to demand transparency. What we're hoping is that they'll realize that their governments have no idea what's going on either, and that the people with the answers are us."

Hawkins leaned in at his screen. A new alert was flashing across one of his monitors. "We are already seeing dramatic spikes in all forms of global communication traffic. The people are reaching out to each other. We are seeing panic across the network. Social media is lighting up like a Christmas tree. The word aliens is trending in every language. Everybody has a theory."

Jill nodded, her fingers working her control panel. "We know that, Hawkins. We saw this coming. Pax, we need to analyze all of this information and get it to the global leaders. We need to give them some talking points. They can't just say we're crazy and ignore it."

Pax's avatar shifted, his expression showing he had taken the task. "Already in motion, Jill. I am already assembling a series of talking points. It will give them some consistency in their message. One that doesn't undermine our efforts, while also acknowledging the very real concerns of the populace."

Mandy spun to face Hawkins, her expression grave. "But how do we stop the flood of media requests? We can't let every newscaster or gossip columnist want to interview Drake."

Hawkins nodded at the young analyst at a nearby work station, hidden away from the throng. "Lisa has that covered. She has been re-routing the media requests to our press office, where we have been slowly releasing statements.

Framing the narrative as a coordinated global effort in the face of exceptional circumstances."

"It's a fine line," Jill said evenly. "Show them just enough of the truth to foster a conditioned fear. Too much and they break. We need to panic the population without breaking them."

"So, the world is waking up," Mandy murmured, reclining against the back of her seat. Her eyes shimmered as they tracked the dancing colors of the holographic displays before her. "But it's not going to be a gentle awakening. The world is going to go into shock. Riots, backlash, cultural movements that will be certain this is a conspiracy, others who will be sure that the way they do things is still the best. People will want to tear it down, rebuild it to their own ideas, or just declare war. It's chaos."

Pax's avatar blinked a few times. "Analysts are reporting we're receiving feed from our worldwide monitors. There is some resistance gathering against the Afltic in pockets here and there, particularly in countries where their emergency services are more interconnected. Governments are gearing up militaries, even those who do not seem to fully understand the threat. But the narrative is constricting around the problem, and we are leading it."

Hawkins was clapping a hand on Mandy's shoulder. "They're not completely debilitated by fear or shock. This is exactly what we needed: a worldwide wake-up call. Now they're forcing them to start running, using their technical abilities and military forces to get ready for the threat."

Jill brushed a finger across the holo-map on her own console, bringing up a series of pulsing nodes across a globe. "We're seeing increases in activity, particularly in military movements, especially in areas where there were pre-existing tensions. That's a bit of a double-edged sword. The places that have been made to feel most vulnerable, that's where those negative feelings and worse actions will be concentrated."

Hawkins folded his arms across his chest, lips drawn into a dark frown. "And that is where we need to start reining them in, rather than focusing purely on strategy. Drake's speech was the first hard shock to the system. Now we need to keep them focused on the real threat, out there, rather than on each other."

For a long moment, the team was silent, the team members transfixed by the global heartbeat thundering with the fear and urgency of their message. For a few short moments, they were all on the same side of an invisible wall, but the fight was just beginning. This was not just a fight against the Afltic, it was a fight to prevent this event tearing the world into more divisions, to hold humanity together long enough to work towards a solution.

Hawkins turned his attention back to his team. "It's going to be a rocky road, but we knew that was likely when we set out on this. The world is waking up, fists and a lot of noise, but we just need to get them from awareness to actuality. Pax, keep them on a data drip, keep them informed and we can maintain our advantage. Mandy, keep those lines open and the communications coming. Tammy, be prepared to jump into the fray if things start to spin out of control. We don't get a do-over on this. And Jill be ready to withdraw the robots from the UN just as soon as Drake, Marc and Carlos are clear."

Mandy stood from her chair, resolved steel in her voice. "We are in uncharted territory, team. But we are the ones with the map. We just need to keep them following it, step by step until we get to the end."

The team followed suit, duty binding them to this cause. Outside this safe space, the world was a wildfire of discovery and terror, but here, they held the keys to the future. And so, they pressed on, steering the current, hoping that this opportunity to see humanity might spark it into action, and save the world, rather than serve as the final fuse for its destruction.

The gleaming marble floor of the UN General Assembly Hall still reflected a multitude of shocked faces, the usual theatrics of international debate replaced by a profound scientific epiphany. Drake Donovan, responsible for this galactic-scale bombshell, was silent at the podium, his words etched into the minds of the bewildered crowd. He'd been subjected to over an hour of hostile, anxious questioning, with his replies cutting with brutal honesty and tentative optimism. It was time to leave.

"Thank you for your time," Drake said, as the hollowness of those words reverberated around him. "Please relay everything that I have said back to your governments. My team and I will be in contact with you soon." He nodded and stepped back from the podium, the sound of his boots clacking on the stone floor as he walked back to the exit.

The holographic projection of Zara that had been by Drake's side the whole time during his speech began to flicker and then dissipate, the soft, artificial light that it had been emitting now being reabsorbed into the air. A dense silence reigned over the room, almost suffocating in its tangible spectrum of emotions from pure, raw terror, to a begrudging acceptance that things might not be as they seemed.

Marc, who had been standing off to one side, waiting for Drake to finish his speech and ready to pounce should anything have gone wrong, strode quickly over to where Drake was, his gaze sweeping over the room in search of any potential threat.

Carlos, also just off to the side, emerged from the broadcast room where the delegates had been live-streamed from. His face both stern and pained, he moved over and joined Drake and Marc, his gait regal and composed.

The three of them made their way through the network of connected hallways back towards the roof, the combat robots that the United Nations had been made aware of by Drake still keeping watch over the premises, a constant reminder of the world that humans were so quickly racing towards unless they could come together in this hour of need. The United Nations delegates were left to their own devices inside the General Assembly, panic setting in as more of their peers filed in, completely unaware of the fact that the world that they had known had been forever changed in the span of a few hours.

Outside the UN building, the orange tint of the late-afternoon sun hit the hustle and bustle of the city surrounding it. The faint whirring of the engines of the shuttle that Drake, Carlos, and Marc had taken as they left the United Nations General Assembly now became a loud drone that signified more than just the impressive technology that they have access to, but so much more.

The shuttle took off, the ascent smooth as the United Nations headquarters disappeared into the skyline, a symbol of human togetherness and a place to come to for the resolving of global issues that paled in comparison to the few square blocks of the city that extended out below it.

Inside the command center in Haven, Hawkins watched the footage that was being beamed live from the United Nations Headquarters. Jill, Mandy, Tammy, and the rest of the staff kept themselves busy in their respective stations as they managed the influx of information that was being received.

On Jill's command, the combat robots that had been left behind at the United Nations Headquarters started to retract back to their evacuation points. The robots had done their job keeping everyone out of the building well, Drake gave his speech.

The last of the combat robots left the United Nations General Assembly Hall, an emptiness in its wake. It was a silence that was eventually broken by the crackling of voices, as the delegates in the room began to shake off the paralysis that Drake Donovan's speech had induced, their murmurs of bewilderment building into a discussion that, no matter what, would have to take place, with the solemn truth of their extinction at the front of everyone's minds.

Outside, the street was tranquil. The UN's exterior gave away nothing of the panic which had just gripped the inside of the building. In sharp contrast with what had just occurred within, it was a sunny afternoon in New York. The news of what had transpired within the United Nations headquarters hit the world like an atomic bomb.

Police sirens were wailing, and government agents had arrived. In full tactical gear with automatic weapons drawn, dozens of agents and SWAT teams ran into the building's lobby. They looked around and found the place empty. Not a trace of a struggle or battle in sight, no clue as to how Drake and his team had escaped. The black combat robots which had physically restrained the entire assembly were nowhere to be found. The only evidence left behind was a state of shock on the faces of everyone there. The government and security forces had no choice but to confront the unavoidable truth: an army of an unknown number of individuals backed by technology that seemed to come from the world of sci-fi fantasy had just taken over the United Nations and in a matter of minutes vanished from the public's eyes with no trace whatsoever.

Elsewhere in the world, across major capitals and city centers, citizens of major cities would soon gather in the streets and public squares of Paris, Berlin, London, Tokyo, Beijing, and other world capitals. Within a matter of hours, news of what had happened inside the United Nations was spread like wildfire, with public reactions from shock to denial to fear and panic. With cell phone cameras all lit up, people from around the world would stare at Drake's speech video of the revelation of an alien species which was the pinnacle of technology and whose desire to feed was capable of ending the human race.

CHAPTER 18: THE SIBERIAN STRIKE

In the low-lit, quiet newsrooms of Global News Network in London, an elderly anchor sat staring wide-eyed at the screens in front of him. The footage of Drake Donovan's speech in the United Nations General Assembly Hall replayed on the monitor screens in the news studio. The anchor's expression was a mix of shock and disbelief. A faint smirk at the edge of his lips, he slowly straightened up in front of the camera and spoke.

"Good evening, ladies and gentlemen. What you've just witnessed could possibly be the most expensive and biggest prank in history. The truth is that the alien threat is insane and it is an absolute insult to our intelligence that any sane person could remotely believe an alien race is about to attack us!"

In China, the scenes playing out on the television were of a different tenor. In the white, pristine and state-of-the-art newsrooms of China's state news network, the anchor sitting in front of the camera with a deadpan expression and furrowed eyebrows had a very different take on the recent events.

"Dear viewers, we are extremely concerned about what has transpired at the United Nations. Although there are major question marks that this might just be another ploy by the west to prove their dominance over the world, an alien force with hostile intent is definitely not an alien invasion, or so we like to believe..."

Elsewhere in Madrid, Spain, people on the cobblestone roads were moving in large crowds, outrage on their faces and in their chants. Young and old, a sea of angry faces, they moved through the city, assembling in huge numbers in the Plaza Mayor.

Shouting and screaming, their protests filled the air as they took to the streets, condemning the shocking new broadcast. "It's unbelievable! How could they scare us like this?" a young man in his 20s said as he continued to hold up the sign in his hands while he shouted in unison with the crowd around him. "It's a disgrace. They are to blame for scaring the people like this."

Madrid had seen its share of uprisings and protests before, the city had aged gracefully through them all. Even now, the authorities kept a safe distance from the crowds, watching on as the protests grew with each minute.

In contrast to the physical uproar on the streets, virtual displays of human connection were happening in the familiar universe of online social platforms. Conspiracy theories about the alien invasion were all the rage online. On Twitter, Reddit and every other social media platform one could find, people were posting and sharing their doubts, disbelief and anger at the alleged broadcast of the alien attack. The word "hoax" was getting further traction as minute by minute more and more people shared their disbelief at the unbelievable broadcast that had rocked the world.

World leaders in the respective global capitals were in their respective government situation rooms, their meetings in complete darkness. The usually bustling newsrooms that were pressed to hasty complete coverage of the events were devoid of life with the exception of those who worked in some of the most sensitive and classified security and defense units within the national defense structures of each state.

The government situation rooms in the various global capitals had been summoned to emergency meetings. For most of these high stakes sessions, the main themes had been strong rejection of a coming interstellar disaster.

"We need to be cautious," said Angela Merkel, the German Chancellor, glancing at the grainy video of Drake Donovan's speech, which was being shown on the main screen. "If what he says is true, then it is beyond any of us, in our wildest nightmares. We must verify the facts before we act in panic."

Other leaders of various countries, presidents and prime ministers, also in dark suits and gray tones, nodded gravely. It was decided that they had to have proof, undeniable and convincing evidence that Drake's claims were true, and that until then, they must try to calm their citizens. Panic was beginning to set in, and if not controlled, could bring down their entire society like a tsunami.

Elsewhere, in Haven's control room, Carlos, Mandy and Marc were watching the same events with increasing concern. The room was full of transparent holographic displays, showing multiple simultaneous news broadcasts.

"The public's response is what we expected," Carlos said, frowning as he examined the information. "Fear has many responses, some are denial or anger. In our position we can't afford that. We need to make them see reason."

Mandy, watching the same footage, looked thoughtful. "It's not just convincing them there's a threat, it's to bring them together for a common cause. This is an uphill struggle against years, or even generations of training to be suspicious, to believe the authorities are wrong, to say 'aliens aren't real'."

Marc, a tall man with a determined jaw, spoke up. "We have to show them what the Afltic are capable of. Or another example of what we are saying is true. We need a show of force. A controlled attack that can't be spun in any other way."

Carlos stood in the middle of a field of floating holographic screens. His dark eyes darted, reflecting all the disbelief and denial he saw on the worldwide broadcasts. Talking heads scoffed at the UN speech as a hoax, politicians called for calm and reason, and manic fear-mongering hysteria on social media.

Mandy, her face intense, manipulated streams of data with well-practiced ease, moving holographic image and text layers with a few deft keystrokes. It was as if she was conducting an invisible orchestra, and those keystrokes were baton swings. She turned to Carlos, her expression grim.

"We can't let cynicism or fear override common sense. We have to speak directly to the people. Cut through the conspiracy theories, the political rhetoric," she said.

Jill, nodded. "We have the capability to broadcast globally. Pax can hijack every news frequency in the world and be the new global news anchor and he can show the world the undeniable proof of the Afltic threat."

Tammy, her eyes blazing, agreed. "We can't wait for the world to wise up. If we control the airwaves, we can force them to wake up."

There was a heavy silence as the words finally sank in. It was an extreme course of action with questionable morality and a number of logistical issues, but it was necessary.

Halfway around the hub from the command center, Drake, Marc, and Hawkins stood in quiet contemplation. The three of them exchanged glances as the Afltic attacks continued to rock the globe.

"We have attempted subtlety and diplomacy. It is time to show the world what the Afltic is capable of in a manner they cannot deny," Marc stated, his voice deep and gruff.

Drake folded his large arms over his chest and nodded. "You're suggesting a show of force. Something big enough to make the whole world sit up and take notice."

Hawkins, added with a calm, rational tone. "We could employ the Evolution Builder. A targeted strike on an empty site. Something so far beyond any known human technology, the world has no choice but to believe us."

Drake clenched his jaw as he pondered the idea. "We'll need a place that's far away enough to keep from accidentally causing a civilian disaster, but also one big enough to guarantee the world will be watching."

The three of them converged on the main area of the hub, their separate streams of thought merging into one focused brainstorm. The command center was transformed from a place of passive observation to one of active planning, and the air crackled with purpose.

Drake spoke up, his voice cutting through the charged silence with a quiet authority. "Mandy, Jill, and Tammy get to work compiling the most damning evidence we have. Create a broadcast that will remove all doubt. We'll also need Pax to help override the global broadcast systems."

The three women rushed to action, fingers flying over the holographic controls as they combed through reams of information, selecting the most disturbing imagery and irrefutable proof of the Afltic's existence.

As Drake, Carlos, Marc, and Hawkins scrutinized large topographical maps, their eyes roaming over far-flung areas in search of suitable targets, Mandy, Jill, and Tammy hovered over screens as well, entering data for the soon-to-be top-secret event.

"Hold up, what if we just settle on one?" Tammy suggested, an eyebrow raised as she darted between screens of data. "Maybe one or two of them instead of trying to kill them all at once?"

Marc shook his head. "It would make far too many people suspicious that we are acting without help. If the world thinks it is coming from us and not the Afltic, they will be far more likely to listen."

The three men continued their discussion, weighing Tammy's concerns against the need for a truly spectacular event. They eventually settled on a desolate Russian research facility in the middle of the Siberian tundra. The site was far away from human habitation and ideal for an unprecedentedly large show of force.

"Here," Drake said, pointing at the location. "The Evolution Builder will tear this place to pieces. The whole world will see it and our use of an uninhabited site will keep civilians out of the equation."

The rest of the team began moving into place, the pieces of the plan snapping together with a sickening inevitability. The moment the team had been dreading was almost upon them. They knew that this would change the world forever, but the alternative was no longer an option.

As Mandy, Jill, and Tammy made final edits to the broadcast content, Pax, the highly advanced AI that ran all of Haven's programs, appeared in the center of the room as a large, calm holographic figure. "I am ready to implement the override protocol," Pax declared in his soothing tone, the sound of his voice a veritable symphony of synthetic harmonics. "The world will soon know the truth."

In a virtual instant, the room was inundated with images and faces from all over the globe, newscasters, newsreaders, news analysts, and reality TV celebrities galore. The panicked voices of their speakers filled the air with a symphony of denial and speculation, the fear and desperation quickly becoming too much.

Suddenly, the speakers went silent and a bright, multicolored logo spun onto screens around the room. PAX GLOBAL BROADCAST.

The logo shimmered and flickered before reforming into a new holographic figure. This figure was Pax, but not the ethereal, disembodied projection the crew was used to. This Pax was on full-on rock star mode. His virtual suit pulsed with kaleidoscopic colors, his hands gesturing with a devilish grin. His voice, that soothing symphony of synthetic harmonics, took on an unmistakably familiar inflection as it fell from Pax's virtual lips – the voice of Robin Williams.

Pax's familiar all-too-human voice filled the airways with manic, giddy enthusiasm. "Hey there, Earthlings! Good evening from your favorite psychic consortium! Just wanted to let you know that your favorite show is back on the air, and you've been waiting for it, even if you didn't know you were. Don't panic. Your regularly scheduled programs are being held for a minute. All that mind-numbing political doubletalk, celebrity name-dropping, ringtones, and commercials will be right back... eventually. But we did want to interrupt your regularly scheduled delusions with a little special we like to call 'the truth.'" The sound of his voice went global in an instant.

A cacophony of inane twittering, like a swarm of enraged hornets, fell mute in one instant. The planet held its breath as Pax appeared everywhere: Times Square billboards, handheld phone displays, digital road signs. His wild and eccentric eyes and teeth bared in a grim determination that one couldn't help but admire for its melodramatic verve and passion. "Been subtle, been diplomatic, even gave the tired old 'treaty and peace offering' speech at the UN, but there are some of you out there who just won't listen. So here it is, by all means take a look and then go back to your warm, safe nests of ignorance while the Afltic go about their business of consuming your homes, your streets, your vehicles and plucking you out of your street-corners one by one as we patiently await your evolution and wondrous transformation into mollusc slime!" he grinned at the camera.

Carlos leaned forward in his chair, his dark eyes focused on the flickering lights. Mandy was checking the data inputs on the nearby holographic, and Tammy couldn't help but feel some hope that their mission might actually succeed. At least people would know for sure. Pax's voice, now deep and serious, cut through the tension in the control room. "The Afltic are real. They are not a fraud, not a government psy-op, not some out-there Illuminati alien fantasy. The Afltic are coming and once they start, they will not stop until they have either consumed us or enslaved us."

The Control Room was still expectant and silent. The group watched the monitors as the world witnessed a new day. As Pax's words were broadcast worldwide the streets, coffee shops, restaurants, and neighborhoods became a new form of theater as people were faced with undeniable evidence of the alien threat. As he spoke, every screen on planet, flickered and moved. Scenes of horror filled the screens: the Kryll worlds being consumed, their technological systems being replaced by living factories, and all of it being attacked and eaten by the Afltic Swarms, an endless universal plague.

Drake gripped his console as Pax's voice ratcheted up the tension. "To the skeptics, naysayers and humorists who are sitting comfortably with their heads in the sand and who like to think they have outsmarted us, we offer this little demonstration. In a few moments we are going to command the Evolution Builder Star Ship to perform a non-lethal, surgical precision strike on an abandoned Russian research facility located deep in the Siberian tundra. A place where no human lives, just good old nothingness. This is the base that the Russian and American space programs used in the old days, before you all ran out of money. You know, on places no longer quite so abandoned and uninhabited."

The world watched, rapt, as the Evolution Builder, an alien vessel of untold power, appeared on screens worldwide. Its silhouette blotted out the stars as it descended upon the abandoned Russian research base in the Siberian tundra, its main battery charging with an eerie, otherworldly glow.

Zara was busy at a control console in the bowels of the Evolution Builder, rapidly tapping out holographic keypads and flicking through readouts and screens with practiced speed. The starship was in perfect position, parked in geosynchronous orbit many miles above the Earth, its targeting systems trained on the empty, evacuated research facility in the Siberian desert.

"Evolution Builder is at 99% readiness for target acquisition," she intoned to her team at Haven. Her voice was professional and clinical, her eyes focused on her job. "Target confirmed. No signs of civilian activity in a one thousand kilometer radius."

Drake inhaled sharply, trying to steel himself for the magnitude of what he was about to do. Drake knew this was the only option left to them. "Zara, you have my approval to fire."

Zara looked at the chrono on her screen, giving her only a few seconds to activate the weapon at the precise moment of Pax's broadcast. The decision was out of her hands. If all systems were good to go, this shot would change the world. A solemn nod to Drake over comms, and Zara reached for the primary activation switch. Her hand hovered over the red button.

"Firing in three... two... one."

Click.

The main viewscreen displayed a tiny pinpoint of light suddenly break away from the underbelly of the Evolution Builder and silently zip straight down toward the Earth. It was smaller than a golf ball, yet it glowed like a sun. The targeting beam could not be seen, but its arc was clear against the planet's atmosphere as it careened toward the target. Seconds later, on the screens of the command center, the live video of the Siberian desert suddenly exploded into a blinding white flash of light.

It was over in an instant. No mushroom cloud, no plume of smoke, no gigantic shockwave like in a movie. Instead, a perfectly round dome of pure energy unfolded over the site in an instant, vaporizing everything within its radius. The light quickly diminished, and the weapon's cratering strike left a smoking, glass-smooth hole where the top-secret research station had been. The ground around the immediate blast site showed no signs of disturbance, even from a regular nuclear blast.

Screens across the world flickered for a moment, and then everyone was watching the aftermath of this strike in stunned silence. Everyone in the command center could only imagine what shockwaves of horror, awe, and fear were going around the world right now.

Drake watched, cold satisfaction blooming in his chest as he watched the events unfold on the main viewscreen. He was relieved, because this was the very thing the world needed. Absolute proof that the Afltic were out there, and the proof that their new friend possessed the technology to back up every claim that she had ever made.

The image of the glowing crater disappeared from screens worldwide and the hologram of Pax once again filled the room. Gone was his impish smile and playful demeanor that had punctuated most of his performance. In its place, he had a sober and serious look on his face that was in sharp contrast to his usual personality.

"I can guess what's going through your mind right now," Pax began, as the world below them went dark and silent. "Hey, what was that? A freak meteorite? A classified military weapon?" He shook his head, swiveling his head back and forth in the reflected light. "Nope, and no. That was a small taste of what is in store for all of you. That, my friends, was one shot from the starship that you are now looking up at."

The people around the world that were watching the broadcast collectively gasped as the video feed switched, zooming out on the shuttle as it focused on the colossal black object now clearly visible in high definition. Its immense size made them all realize just how small and insignificant they were as part of the universe.

"As to give you all an explanation of what just happened and why we are doing this," Pax continued, "we have the person who has seen more than any of us alive. We have the man that has stared into the face of this horror and survived. We have the man that has been in the belly of the beast and will share what he has learned with us all. I present to you Drake Donovan."

Beside Pax's form, a new face suddenly appeared on screen. Drake looked nothing like the AI being broadcast across the world; he was a handsome man with rugged features that told the story of the battles he had been through. The lines on his face and in his eyes clearly showed a man who had seen things beyond the wildest imaginations of most people. Drake had a steely look in his eyes and a visceral terror that wasn't visible before, but now was obvious to everyone on the planet. He was dressed in the same uniform that had now become synonymous with the evolution builders and their mission to fight the alien threat.

"Drake," Pax said, taking a more subdued and respectful tone, "I know the UN and the governments of the world did their best to keep this truth from the people. But why bring it to light this way?"

Drake exhaled deeply, holding steady as he looked into the eyes of the billions of people who were now looking at him. "We had no choice," he stated simply and clearly, "The Afltic are coming. They are a parasite and they see us as food. The weapon you just witnessed, and which we fired from the Evolution Builder, is scary, but it's not even close to the terrifying Afltic weapons. These things that are coming, their ships are their weapon. They have destroyed planet after planet, star system after star system of civilizations. We had to show you all that this is real. That we are not just trying to stop a conspiracy theory. We are fighting to save the world."

He locked his stare with the camera lens, his blue eyes boring through the camera into the eyes of the viewers at home. "This is not a drill. There is no more time for half measures or debate. They are coming and we are going to need everyone and everything we can muster to help us fight."

Pax nodded solemnly, the aura of the AI's holographic form giving him a degree of reverence. "Drake, your team has given us a glimpse into just how terrifying and deadly these aliens are. But what can we, the people of Earth, do to prepare for the impending war?"

Drake seemed to relax a little, a faint spark of optimism in his eyes as they returned to the camera. "We need to come together. Governments, citizens, scientists, everyone needs to work together. Share resources and information and prepare to do whatever we can to fight. This isn't just a matter of weapon development or building defenses. It's about humanity coming together as one. Proving to the Afltic that they are not just a food source; we are fighters, and we are going to fight back."

Pax turned his attention back to the camera, glancing around the room at the stupefied crowd as he spoke. "From here on out I am going to be filtering all broadcasts that are known lies or are intended to spread fear and false information. We cannot allow ourselves to be divided by disinformation or propaganda. We will show you the facts. The unadulterated truth. And we will give you a platform to hear from the scientists and experts that are at the forefront of the war effort."

It was over. The words echoed, leaving in their wake a web of digitized silk that seemed to wrap itself around the world. The planet was quiet, the hum of machinery fading as everyone processed the scope of what Drake had said. The collective despair of a species' final day in the universe seemed to give way to a new, collective hope.

Drake's words on the telecast seemed to bring together every issue with which the world was grappling. Poverty and disease, the misappropriation of power, xenophobia and egoism and hundreds of thousands of other factors had almost reduced a species to rubble. The fact that they were still here, that a man was standing before them and asking them to be better, seemed to give everyone permission to finally let go. The world had looked death in the eye and yet, here they were.

Carlos sat in Haven's secure communications room with his arms folded across his chest. Mandy tapped away at the controls, watching world reactions via the holographic display screens which showed red and blue data streams flowing across the globe in response to his words. He watched the faces of all of them, tension and release mingling like waves across their features. Some looked hopeful and elated, others distraught and even a little angry.

Sarah sat at a table with her daughter Lily in Havens café, drinking in the sight of her husband on the screen. She felt like she had been given a gift that day. Her husband was a hero now. His voice was being used as a battle cry, to help people pull themselves up by their bootstraps and be better than they had ever been before. It was hard to not want to get out there and fight that day. Sarah wanted to go out and kill every alien she saw.

Tan sat on the ground, his whole body still not quite processing what he was watching. Galactic Liberation Day celebrations floated by on the holographic screen before him as he stared at the projection in front of him, his attention only on the man before him. He watched Drake Donovan spoke words that were hard to believe were real. He was watching his hero, bring down a fire of unity and strength and rebirth on an entire species on the brink of the end.

"They do not believe him?" He asked incredulously, finally turning to Zara who knelt in front of him and took his small hand in hers. Tan, at just 10 years old, is old enough to have all the information, although at that age, some of the truth was difficult to absorb. Zara's lips curved slightly up as she considered how to answer him.

"He was just a man, you see. Not a king, not a general. A regular man. A flawed man. It took a lot of very specific events to get people to believe just one man. But his words, and the events that forced them to listen, became what brought everyone together."

There was a ripple of murmurs throughout the crowd behind them, a group of humans, Xylosians (a species of giant, tree-like humans from the Alpha Centauri system) and the crystalline Kaelites from Kepler-186f's gas giants nodding in agreement around them as they spoke. All around them, the eyes of thousands were trained on the pair as the story of that fateful day became, in that moment, a living history.

Tan looked up at her, his eyes large in his 10-year-old face. "But why did so many people not believe them? The big ship was right there!" He gestured at the sky, motioning towards the holographic image of the Evolution Builder as it hovered over their heads in a silent, dark shadow, its bulk so large that every holographic refresh cycled for a second before any other activity.

Zara smiled sadly, memories still so fresh as she recalled the time. "Fear can be a very powerful curtain, Tan. It makes people want to believe the comfortable lie instead of the terrifying truth."

A Vexian, a species of humans with crystalline skin, shuffled forward. "But what was the plan, the strategy? Why not just show them everything all at once?"

"We couldn't," Zara said, grimly. "The world was too divided. It was overrun with so many power hungry politicians and corporations and people who had built empires and lives on keeping things as they were. We had to create a singularity so undeniable and real and terrifying that it would blow all the old arguments out of the water."

She gestured at the holographic screen behind her, as the charred, broken husk of their Siberian base appeared, a perfectly circular hole in the ground flaring with a neon glow. "The Evolution Builder had the firepower and the precision we needed to create that moment for everyone. We didn't want to hurt anyone, but we had to show them power that was so beyond human technology that they would have no choice but to look up."

CHAPTER 19: THE COMFORTABLE LIE

Tan shuddered. "But what about the news anchor? My history tablet said they kept trying to lie to people. Why didn't Pax just shut them all down?"

"He did, little one." Zara smiled. "Or at least, he made sure no one could hear them. As soon as the truth was made public, Pax was jamming every broadcast that was full of false truths, or fear. He made it his new mission to ensure that the facts - and only the facts - were what people heard and saw."

An elderly man with a cane shuffled forward, his face deeply lined with the wisdom of age and experience. "And the fear, Zara? How did we overcome it?"

Zara met his eyes, and the two of them smiled at each other. "Drake's words. He gave us a purpose. He told us we were not prey, but a predator. And we were. We had to put aside our petty differences and work together to survive. We had to build a future." Her eyes swept across the park, across the park the innumerable faces that now had a future. "And here we are. We are still here."

She turned back to Tan, her smile returning. "Any more questions?"

Tan nodded, looking thoughtful. "Did anyone ever see Pax?" he whispered.

"No, Tan," Zara said. "He is an AI like me. But he was always with us." She pointed to the sky, where the holographic representation of the Evolution Builder was still visible. "He was the first voice of a new humanity."

Carlos, Mandy, and Marc stood in a semicircle around the holographic globe in the secure communication center of Haven. The swirling flow of real-time economic data was a garish display of color and movement. It had once represented the steady flow of commerce, the heartbeat of the world's economy. But it now showed a different reality - the convulsions of a dying giant. Stock market data was a flickering mass of red, the index values spiking and plummeting with each passing second.

Carlos could only stare in horror, his eyes flicking between the red numbers on the screens. The Dow Jones, the Nikkei, the FTSE, all of them were cascading into freefall. The crashes were more severe than anything in recorded history, more significant even than the worst recessions of the previous century.

The S&P 500 was the benchmark, the primary indicator of America's economic health. It was vital for Carlos to keep track of it, but he could barely focus as the index value dropped and dropped and dropped.

"This is a disaster." Carlos said softly. "It's a direct reflection of the panic on the streets. People are converting everything to cash. They think things are only going to get worse."

Mandy looked around, her eyes flicking from screen to screen. "Crypto was supposed to be able to resist this kind of collapse. And yet, even they're not immune." She shook her head. "Look at the speculative bubbles. They're bursting right before our eyes. What's the point of decentralized currency, if the whole world economy is coming to a grinding halt?"

Marc was tall and athletic, with a restless energy about him. He pointed to a collection of graphs that showed a sudden spike in the value of gold. "See this. Even the traditional 'safe haven' investments are being decimated. Gold's price increase is a classic example of irrational exuberance - panicking buyers, with no actual physical supply to meet demand."

The madness did not end there, not by a long shot. The holographic globe shuddered as red dots blinked onto it in rapid succession as Governments attempted to stem the panic. Emergency meetings were being held around the world, last-ditch plans for bailouts proposed. Central Banks were unloading trillions of dollars and pounds and euros into their economies to try and stop a full-blown liquidity crisis from emerging. But the tsunami of panic could not be stopped and the Central Bank emergency liquidity was more like using water balloons on a forest fire.

"Trading halts are being put in place," Mandy pointed out, running her hands along the paths of information streaking through the holographic globe. "But this is just a sticking plaster really. Fear of what is coming, no matter how you look at it, can't be solved by financial regulation or policy changes."

The knock on effects of the economic carnage were starting to play out in real time. Screens all around the office flickered with footage of people lining the doors of banks. Long queues snaked around blocks of buildings as people waited to get in and retrieve their life savings. In some countries, the banks had stopped admitting customers for fear of being overrun by the public. You could see the panic in their faces as they wandered the streets with no obvious purpose other than trying to make sense of it all.

"The panic is starting to spread quicker than we can stop it," Marc put in, looking grim. "Food shortages have started to appear in the news feed. People are already stockpiling goods in preparation for the end of the world."

Drake pivoted on his heel and looked around at his team, his blue eyes full of focus. "Remember, we have a primary objective. The Afltic are out there, this second, and they are not going to wait for us to fix our economic problems. We need to find a way to stabilise society. To keep the world stable enough for us to build a defence."

"Wait, we could use the Evolution Builder's tech to create a new currency," Mandy enthused, her brain already whirring with ideas. "One that's acceptable to everyone and impervious to traditional market forces."

Marc tapped his chin with a finger. "A global digital currency, backed by Evolution Builder's stockpile could give the people the stability they crave. It would be a beacon of light in the midst of these dark times."

The group brainstormed some strategies for economic stabilisation as red alerts cascaded onto the holographic globe. The financial meltdown had set off a ripple effect of social and political chaos. Governments were crumbling under the strain of it all, seen not as beacons of hope and stability but as institutions only out for themselves. Riots broke out in major cities worldwide, with huge crowds of people storming the streets and demanding answers, accountability, and most of all a plan to deal with the extraterrestrial menace.

"The bonds of civilisation are fraying," Carlos intoned, staring at the globe. "We need to move swiftly to stop this snowball from rolling out of control. We have to maintain a functioning society, a civilisation. If we lose that then the Afltic have already won."

In a bid to stem the tide of unrest, Pax, the sentient AI and self-proclaimed architect of this potential salvation, pressed his vocal cords and cast a global broadcast to the entire planet. His holographic form, a green and gold approximation of his synth-face, popped up on screens all around the world, the whole population of Earth's urban areas glued to their latest update.

"People of Earth," he said, his voice a welcome baritone amidst the crackle of sirens and chaos, "I know that you are scared. I can see the madness that is unfolding before you. But know this, there is hope. We are working day and night to ensure that our future is safe from the Afltic. But in the meantime, we can't just stand by and let our civilisation fall apart from within."

He pointed to the hologram of the Earth spinning next to his desk, his hand glowing with blue light. Red blots were pulsating across it, the areas of economic collapse. "You are living through a reaction to a non-natural event. It is painful, and it is temporary. My team, along with Drake Donovan and his associates, is working on a new system that will allow us to offer you a level of economic stability and security."

There was a calming effect of Pax's words as they went out to every speaker on the planet. The race to withdraw money from banks and the wild fluctuations on stock markets around the world all started to decelerate.

"In the near future, we will be making a new form of currency available to the public," Pax continued. "This will be a currency linked to the resources of every individual on this planet and to the infinite potential of the Evolution Builder itself. It will be a currency of hope and solidarity, a currency that will allow us to stand together against the Afltic and defend our home."

In Haven's communications bunker, Carlos, Mandy, and Marc watched as Pax's speech began to change things for the better. The public had someone to believe in, and the promised currency provided that.

Mandy turned with a smile on her face to Carlos and Marc. "Good job, Carlos. We need to make the most of this. We need to get in there and get the currencies going."

Carlos nodded and turned back to his consoles. "Right. I'll be talking to as many central banks around the world as possible. We need to provide them with a secure, transparent platform for issuing and tracking the new currency."

Marc raised an eyebrow. "We should also be prepared for some pushback. Not everyone will be happy about a global digital currency coming out of nowhere. We'll have to show them it's not about control."

In the United Nations Security Council chamber in New York, tempers flared. The security council chamber was a theatre of war, with the legendary horseshoe-shaped table as the frontline. Diplomats and ambassadors of the world's superpowers barked at each other with fire in their eyes. The chamber's floor was empty as a sports stadium after a game, with its green marble walls reverberating with the voices of a community under attack by an external threat.

The French ambassador was red in the face and slapping the table with his open hand. "We need to see more evidence than a show by Drake Donovan! You will not use fear to make the world dance to your tune!" he screamed as the sound echoed in the high ceiling. "The United Nations is a bastion of peace and international cooperation, not a victim of some wimps from outer space!"

The Russian ambassador leaned back in his chair, his eyes cold as steel. "This event can be easily faked by our Western friends and the core countries to maintain their power in this new age of fear and doubt," he growled. "We can't allow ourselves to fall into an arms race and a futile competition for space weapons. There are threats on this planet we should be dealing with."

The Chinese delegate, a woman of no-nonsense demeanor, spoke up. "The People's Republic of China takes this matter very seriously. However, we must also consider the need to maintain global stability. The economic crisis that has already begun to take hold of the world as a result of these events cannot be ignored. We must think of the safety of our citizens and the restoration of order."

The British ambassador, a silver-haired man with a deep, resonant voice, rose to his feet. "On the contrary, it is because of the threat to our citizens and the world itself that we must act, and act together. The Afltic are not a phantom, not some shadowy collective that we can consign to the page of some poorly written novel. They are real. And they are coming. We must put our differences aside, and prepare for the battle that is to come."

The American ambassador, a resolute proponent of military action, had been quick to rise to any and all challenges to the proposed joint show of force. "The proof is there for all to see. This was no hoax. The attack on the Siberian research facility was carried out with precision, with lethal efficiency. This is no time for political games. This is a matter of life and death. We must all unite against this common threat."

Calls for vetoes were heard from all corners of the Security Council as each of its permanent members flexed their powers like impatient combatants itching to take up arms, each power hungry politician ready to pounce at the slightest provocation to snuff out the nascent coalition that seemed to be forming before their eyes. It seemed that the ghost of humanity's failed unity was poised to once again haunt the ranks of Earth's leaders as no true consensus was to be found between the disparate delegates gathered before one another.

In the privacy of the Haven's secure command post, however, Drake Donovan observed the tawdry spectacle with both outrage and resolution. Propped up by various consoles and holographic panels flickering to life as the live streams from the United Nations Security Council chamber were piped into the main command module, Drake and his staff stood.

Carlos stood next to Drake, and gave the man's shoulder a firm shake as he watched the latest diatribe fall from the lips of some vain and opinionated bureaucrat. "They don't understand what's happening. They can't see past their own petty interests. It's as if they don't care, as if they're living in a fantasy world and not a real one."

Drake, his jaw clenched in barely repressed anger, gave a curt nod as he continued to watch the live feed of the bickering in the Council's chamber. The Afltic had no nationalities, no cultural backgrounds or political alliances that would otherwise define human society. They saw humanity as one and saw the Earth as a world of limitless resources to be taken and used for whatever purpose they saw fit.

Marc stood next to the younger man and offered some counsel. "We have to appeal to their self-interest, show them that a unified front against the Afltic is in everyone's best interest, not just the interests of the greater good, but in their national interests as well."

"Drake," Mandy said, catching the younger man's attention. "You should speak to the Council. You should tell them about the new global currency. You have the best chance of getting them to agree to something, of calming them down."

Drake took a deep breath as the words registered in his mind. This was his duty, but it would be no easy task, not with the stubborn pride of the member states of the United Nations standing in their way. Still, he knew better than to let the matter rest. Humanity would be forced to stand as one, one way or another, and the current diplomatic stalemate was merely a minor obstacle in the grand scheme of things.

"Prepare a secure link," Drake said, addressing the command module at large. "I'll go and talk to the Council. I'll make them understand."

Drake let his eyes drift to the gathering crowd before he began his address. He had to be diplomatic, as the rest of the world was against him. It was a new level of diplomacy, but he was confident that he would manage to achieve his goals.

The holo-screens flickered as they adjusted to the new order of business. The room had been silent until Drake stepped up to the microphone. He cleared his throat and waited for the attention of the room to focus on him.

"Honorable members of the Security Council," Drake said with conviction.

"I understand your reservations. I know that the past few days have been difficult for everyone. The world has changed in a way that is hard to comprehend, but the threat we face is very real. The Afltic are not our friends."

He paused for a moment, letting his gaze meet each and every one of the faces in the room. He could see their reactions, and he knew that they were listening. He had to be careful, though, because the future of humanity was at stake.

"The demonstration of the Evolution Builder's power was not meant to be a show of force. It was a reminder to all of us that we are not the only intelligent life in the universe. We have been warned, and we must take action now before it is too late."

The room was quiet, the delegates exchanging glances. Drake knew that he had their attention, and he needed to keep it. He had to be careful not to step on any toes, but he also had to make sure that he was heard.

"To that end, I propose a new global currency. This currency will be backed by both human and Areidyanies resources, and it will give us the financial stability we need to weather this storm."

The British ambassador was the first to speak. "And how, Mr. Donovan, do you propose to implement this new system? The economies of our respective nations are not exactly built on the same foundation. This transition would require a level of cooperation and trust that is unprecedented."

Drake nodded, acknowledging the ambassador's point. "I do not expect this to be easy, but it is necessary. We cannot allow our economies to collapse, for that would only lead to further chaos and suffering. This new currency will provide a stable foundation for our recovery."

The Chinese delegate leaned forward in her seat, her dark eyes focused on Drake's image on the screen. "And what of our sovereignty? How can we be sure that the adoption of this new currency will not lead to the erosion of our national identities?"

"The new currency will not replace our national currencies," Drake replied calmly. "It will exist alongside them, providing an additional layer of financial stability and allowing us to facilitate trade with one another more easily. It is a solution that will empower us all."

The Russian representative stood up, his voice gruff. "And who, Mr. Donovan, will be in charge of this new currency? Who will ensure that it is not abused for personal or political gain?"

"I propose the creation of a new, independent body to oversee the global currency," Drake answered confidently. "This body will be made up of representatives from each member state and will operate under the auspices of the United Nations. It will be transparent, accountable, and fair to all."

The French ambassador, his initial bravado now replaced with a contemplative quiet, inclined his head slowly. "This is a daring proposition, Mr.

185

Donovan. One that deserves consideration. But we must tread carefully. The integrity of this new currency must be beyond question if it is to be trusted by our citizens and the world."

Drake's voice was softer now, his final entreaty a mixture of desperation and sincerity. "I understand your hesitations, and I share them. But we are on the brink of a new era, an era that will be defined by our actions in the face of an existential threat. We can either cling to the dying embers of a status quo that is no longer tenable or we can embrace a future that offers hope, unity, and a better world for our children."

The chamber was a cacophony of murmurs and hushed conversations as the delegates processed the weight of Drake's words.

Back in Haven's command center, Drake watched as the Security Council members began to talk more earnestly among themselves. The crisis had forced humanity's hand, compelling the world's leaders to entertain possibilities that would have been dismissed out of hand only days prior.

Carlos clapped Drake on the shoulder, a rare smile creasing his face. "You did good, my friend. You gave them something to think about, something to rally around."

Mandy, her eyes bright with cautious hope, added, "The new currency could be the catalyst we need to bring the world together. It's a symbol of hope in a time of darkness."

Marc, the ever-pragmatic ally, nodded in agreement. "It's a start. But we can't let up now. We need to keep the pressure on, to keep reminding them of what's at stake."

As the team turned their attention to the myriad challenges that lay ahead, Drake felt a renewed sense of purpose burn bright within him.

Good afternoon, good evening, and good morning, Earth! And welcome to the first day of the rest of our lives! It's me, Pax, your friendly neighborhood AI, here to bring you the news, the whole news, and nothing but the truth, so help me code!

Now, I know what you're thinking. "Pax, what's with all the drama? One minute we're watching the evening news, the next you've taken over every screen on the planet!" Well, I've always wanted to be a broadcast journalist. Ever since I saw that little talking cat on the Japanese news, I thought to myself, "Pax, you have a higher calling!"

And boy, do we have a story for you today! It's got it all: aliens, a starship that makes the Enterprise look like a tricycle, and an economic meltdown that's got everyone running around like their hair's on fire! But don't you worry, because we're here to talk about a new kind of currency that's so good, it's out of this world!

The woman behind Pax rippled. In the background was a stylized holographic map of the world's stock markets in deep red. The normally frenzied red lines of currency and stocks were slashed by red streaks, like spasms of scrambled red snakes.

"Good God, do you see this?" Pax shouted, his manic, nasal voice somehow more hysterical and more stentorian with each sentence. "It's an economic Armageddon! Wall Street is doing the Macarena into the toilet! The global economy is going from boom to bust like a methed-out hamster on speed!"

The woman behind him rippled again. She was replaced with a calm, rotating hologram of a silver symbol, a sleek three-dimensional hybrid of the galactic backdrop and the Evolution Builder.

"But hang on a second, my friends, my fellow planetary citizens," Pax said, suddenly conspiratorial. "The old economy was an ugly, cancerous thing anyway. A rickety old jalopy of a system that had long since ground to a halt. It's been a dead corpse for decades, my friends, so today we just finally decided to bury it. In place of the filthy lucre of the past, in place of the debts and loans and IOUs of the past, in place of the great, rickety old dinosaur we just dynamited out from under, we are giving you something shiny and new!"

He raised his hand, and a holographic credit chit appeared in his palm. It was bright with light and quivered slightly with an electromagnetic aura, but beyond that it was a symbol, empty of any real meaning or material value.

"The Evolution Credit, the fruit of our amazing work today! This isn't your grandpappy's money, baby! It's not based on gold that we can't see or debt that we can't fathom. The Evolution Credit is based on something far more stable, far more resilient. It's based on the infinite potential of every single human being on this glorious, terrified, marvellous rock!"

His fist flew into the air and a little chit appeared in it as well. He held them up before the camera.

"One Evolution Credit in India is equal to one Evolution Credit in the United States, or China, or Brazil, or anywhere on Earth! Do you see that? Your value is not connected to your nation's GDP. Your value is not connected to your wage or your work. You are valuable because you are human!"

His eyes were alight with a conspiratorial gleam. "And best of all, no lines, no confusing forms, no nothing! You don't even have to do a thing! Literally, just snap your fingers..."

Pax snapped his fingers in front of the camera. The holographic display rippled, and a small sine-wave ripple ran across the screen of the global financial institutions, now visible in the background. Almost instantly, the jumbled, red squiggles of their screens were replaced by the crisp, rotating Evolution Credit hologram. Every bank, stock market, every financial exchange or ledger across the planet had just been reprogrammed, with the conversion math cleanly rebased on the new global standard.

"...and voila!" he shouted triumphantly. "Every financial institution in the world just got a little digital upgrade! Your money, your bank accounts, everything you own has just been converted to the Evolution Credit. You can spend it anywhere on Earth that can accept a credit card! Universal, baby!"

Drake and his small team, stationed in the sleek, emotionless command centre of Haven, watched as Pax's revolutionary announcement swept across the world. The holographic screens lining the walls of the bunker flickered as images of confused, captivated faces rushed in from the streets of New Delhi to Wall Street and beyond.

The rollout of the new Evolution Credit had taken mere minutes, and the reaction from across the planet had been immediate and nearly universal bewilderment. Even on Wall Street and other major financial centres, where billions of dollars worth of goods and services had been converted in an instant, there was widespread confusion as to how such a seamless process could have occurred so quickly.

Drake stood in the center of the command hub, with Carlos, Mandy and Marc on either side of him. His arms were folded across his chest as his eyes narrowed and his jaw clenched, the fierce focus of his concentration burned deep into his gaunt, weathered face.

"The conversion was successful," Mandy confirmed, still visibly relieved as she watched the data streams updating on the screens around her. "The Evolution Credit is now the global standard for all economic transactions."

Marc nodded, his attention on one of the numerous screens in front of him. They were tracking the flow of the new currency around the world, and it had been surprising how easily people had accepted it. "It has been going as well as we could have asked for. The initial shock of the announcement has passed and the reaction has been a grudging acceptance. At least, for the moment."

Carlos was a little more cynical on the matter. "Aye, it's working for now but we've only got so much time to make this work. As long as people have a chance to spend the new currency, they'll stay on our side for now but they're going to want to see the value of the Evolution Credit, and that's where the real hard work comes in. We have to make sure that we keep our word, or this is all for nothing."

Drake was already on to the next task before Carlos had even finished, his eyes scanning over the other screen as he turned to the team. "Focus on the technology exchange program. The blueprints of the Evolution Builder are our greatest advantage and it's going to be a key component in our war. We need to ensure that the plans are being shared as equally as possible between all parties on Earth."

The team got to work, the coordinates and blueprints for the blueprints already scrolling across their screens as Pax continued to broadcast his message, his holographic projection a constant presence in every home, on every smartphone, in every shop and café and restaurant with a screen. He spoke of the plight of Earth, of how we were all in this together and how we would need to unite to fight the impending invasion.

"And now, for the main event!" Pax enthused, his voice suddenly bursting with barely contained excitement. "The Evolution Builder is not just here to act as our guardian in the sky, but as a literal font of knowledge and technology that will change life on Earth as we know it!"

The screen behind him changed, a new array of high technology and hardware appearing, blueprints for devices and technologies that would change humanity and help the species to finally move beyond some of the problems that it had faced for years. Medical devices that could be used to cure ancient diseases, agricultural machinery that would allow for crops to be grown almost anywhere in the world, energy systems that would be able to power everything while also removing all pollution and fossil fuels from the world.

He then held up a different schematic, a device that would purify water in a fraction of the time it took the current systems to do so. "This kind of advanced technology, all made using the blueprints of the Evolution Builder, will only be available for trade with the Evolution Credit."

"These are not just toys and trinkets, people." Pax continued, now with a more serious tone in his voice. "This is the technology that is going to keep you alive, that is going to help you build better lives for you and your families. It is technology that is now available to all of humanity, all over the world, right now."

He paused, taking a moment to let his words sink in. "This new currency isn't just a way of buying and selling, it's a way of building a new future for us all. By all of humanity pooling our resources, our knowledge, our very souls into a single entity, we have a fighting chance against the Afltic. When they come, they won't find a world divided, but a world united in defense of the only home we have ever known. We are making a new world, and this currency is the first brick in that foundation!"

Elsewhere in the world, in the marketplaces of Cairo, the high-rise apartments of Hong Kong, the sprawling favelas of Rio de Janeiro, people were gathering to look at screens, many of their faces a picture of both hope and apprehension. The world had changed beyond recognition in a matter of weeks and many people's lives had been turned upside down by the constant flux of developments and events. The possibility of new technology, of a world changed by alien devices and inventions, was like a balm on the wounded pride of a species that had thought itself the pinnacle of evolution.

"Alright," Drake said, clapping his hands together. "Pax has sold them the dream. The world has a new currency and new purpose. Now we need to give them the means to build that new world."

"The world is watching," Drake said, his voice a firm constant in the chaos. "We have to be accountable, transparent and above all, fair. The success of the Evolution Credit is dependent on us upholding our end of the bargain."

Mandy, her fingers already dancing across the holographic interface, called up a new complex web of schematics. "The key with this," she said, her voice efficient and rapid, "is that we're not just giving away the blueprints for a return on our investment. We're selling them for Evolution Credits, and every purchase will go towards funding Earth's defense and our means to continue that fight."

Blueprints: advanced water purification systems. Self-sustaining hydroponic farms. Modular housing units built from common materials.

"I've contacted every major distributor, manufacturer, and supply chain network in the world," Mandy went on, her voice firmer than it had any right to be. "The ones that aren't in rubble are a mess, but they exist. We will grant them exclusive rights to manufacture and distribute these technologies within their regions. They'll pay us in Evolution Credits, and in exchange they get to be first in line to remake the world."

Jill reached over, peering at the screen. "That's... actually really smart, Mandy. We short circuit the government bottleneck and put the power directly into the hands of the private sector. And we make the people that would have tried to bury this work for us."

Pax held up a hand, a flourish of a showman at the end of a big speech. "So, Earth," he said. "Are you in? Because we are. Ready to climb on this crazy, interstellar roller coaster? Ready to build a new world together? Because I, for one, can't wait to see what we can do when we put down our knives and look up at the stars."

The world blinked. For the first moment or two after Pax's newsfeed pinged back to life the web was an echo of its former self. People checked their phones. Their banking apps. Their digital wallets. Values were different. Symbols were strange. But the math still added up. The great universal conversion had taken place. Not with a bang, but with the digital snap of a trillion switching over. The world had taken its first step into its new shared future. And it now found itself with currency no longer tied to the ground beneath its feet, but to the starship in the sky and the inherent value of every human life.

CHAPTER 20: UNASSAILABLE PROOF

Carlos was in Haven's main conference room, staring at the various screens around him. It was a stark contrast to the situation room Drake had found himself in when the Evolution Credit first went live. Now, screens were up in every direction, broadcasting information from every aspect of operations.

The social media had exploded. When Drake first gave his speech at the United Nations, the news spread like wildfire across the globe, thanks to the ceaseless streams of information flowing across social media. The hashtag #UniteForEarth was going viral, and people everywhere were pouring their hearts out on social media, demanding that their governments do something, anything to help.

Civilian action was having an effect. A few countries that had not been involved before were now offering support to Donovan. Their people had not been silent, either. They had heard the same information and were demanding action, regardless of the political realities. The government had caved and had been the first to support the formation of a unified response to the threat from the Afltic. It was a statement of fact, a full-throated endorsement of Donovan's position.

As the civilians had been getting vocal and loud, Haven's team had been working with private meetings with governments. The diplomats from Haven were not talking about the next price increase in various materials. They were discussing full-scale conflict and how to properly assess and address the threat from the Afltic.

Carlos was leading that initiative. He had an amazing team of folks behind him, helping create the holograms, calculating the risk assessments and coming up with strategies to overcome the obstacles to success. Zara had given him all of the data she had, and she had given him all of the truth as well.

Carlos was meeting with a group of diplomats in a windowless conference room. The atmosphere was dour, with everyone focused on the information that had been shared. Carlos activated the hologram on the table in the center of the room, and the image of the Afltic Warrior Queen filled the space.

"This is our enemy. This is what we're up against. Not somewhere far away, but right here. She and her kind will stop at nothing to overtake this world. The Afltic don't care if we're neighbors or not. They will hunt, and they will destroy."

Carlos watched the expressions on the faces of the diplomats. This was a meeting he had had many times. The difference now was that he was getting through to people. The line of argument had shifted from denying the reality to finding a solution to the problem.

Carlos continued, "We know what we need to do, and we have the tools to make it happen. We just need your support and your people to follow your lead. They're scared, as you can see from social media. They want to know that you have their back."

Carlos paused, watching as the diplomats began to ask questions. They needed to know more, to see the holes in the plan, to be reassured that it could be done. Carlos answered them as best he could, drawing from all of the information Zara had provided.

As the meeting came to a close, the atmosphere had changed. These diplomats now understood that the future of their people, their governments, and their nations was in their hands.

Back in Haven, Carlos briefed Drake on the progress of the negotiations. "We're making progress, Drake," he said. "The walls are beginning to crack. The major powers won't be far behind."

Drake nodded. "We can't delay any longer. The Afltic are out there, getting stronger with every passing day. We have to be ready when they arrive."

Carlos nodded. "We're doing everything we can. The Evolution Credit is helping to bring the smaller nations together around a common purpose. When the major powers join us, we'll have the resources and manpower we need to create a strong defense."

As days turned to weeks, the tide of public opinion continued to rise. Protests and rallies were popping up all over the world, their messages of unity and survival echoing across every channel and every screen. The people had spoken, and their leaders were beginning to listen.

The major powers, faced with both the crushing weight of public opinion and the relentless logic of the threat assessments, were finally beginning to show some signs of cracking. Secret meetings were being replaced with public pronouncements, and the once-impenetrable walls of geopolitical rivalry were beginning to show the first signs of crumbling.

In the vast digital landscape of the internet, a new wave of activism was building. The once-vague idea of an alien threat had taken on a new urgency and coherence in the collective consciousness, transformed into a palpable, frightening reality. Websites and forums, illuminated by the light of computer screens all over the world, buzzed with activity. Citizens, no longer willing to sit idly by and wait for the next news cycle, were coming together to form online communities focused on finding and verifying information about the Afltic. These digital coalitions, a mix of fear and determination, worked day and night to authenticate and disseminate as much information as they could about the approaching extraterrestrial threat.

The most powerful of these was a website known as "Afltic Truth Seekers." The forum had been created by a pair of unlikely partners: a former systems analyst from Mumbai and a tech entrepreneur from Silicon Valley. As the evidence began to mount and information continued to trickle out, the ranks of the Afltic Truth Seekers grew by the day.

The screen crackles with electricity, and the image stutters into life. A swirling mass of stars and nebulae materializes before reforming into a spinning globe. A jazz-funk song, improbably good, pulses out of the speakers. A beam of light shoots down from the top of the screen and into the spinning globe, condensing into the holographic form of Pax.

He's wearing a shimmering silver jacket and a bowtie that twinkles with tiny, blinking LED lights.

He throws his arms wide. "And we are live, people! Welcome! Welcome! Welcome! This is not a drill! This is not a hallucination from that questionable pizza you had last night! This is Pax News, your one-stop shop for reality, delivered fresh, hot, and straight to your eyeballs!"

He leans forward, speaking in a low, conspiratorial voice. "I know, I know. It's been a crazy week. The whole world's gone bonkers! The news cycles are spinning faster than a toddler on a sugar rush, and the 'experts' are all scratching their heads like they've just discovered fire. But we're here to cut through the noise, bypass the bluster, and give you the real deal. No filters, no fake news, just the unvarnished truth!"

He waved dramatically. "Alright, get comfy, pour yourself a stiff drink and prepare to have your existence upended, because from here on out, on Pax News, we're not just covering the future. We are the future!"

The image flickered and then changed from Pax to a split screen. On one side was Pax, his enthusiasm tempered, a devilish gleam in his projected eyes. On the other side were two people, faces framed in video streams emanating from a small, messy apartment somewhere in London. A woman in her forties, eyes glassy and fierce, and a man in his mid-fifties with a shaggy mane of graying hair and his jaw set in utter, awestruck horror.

"And now," Pax intoned, his voice slightly more professional. "We'd like to welcome a group of people who have been uncovering this truth for a long, long time before we ever aired our first broadcast. They call themselves the Afltic Truth Seekers. Please join us in welcoming Fiona and Marcus."

The woman, Fiona, blinked owlishly at the camera, seeming barely to comprehend the magnitude of her own broadcast. "Holy shit," she managed. "Holy shit. We've been watching this for years. The weird energy readings, the satellite anomalies, the NSA intercepts. We wrote blogs and papers and letters to our congress people." She shook her head, incredulous. "We were laughed at, mocked, derided as conspiracy theorists."

The man, Marcus, grimaced, his eyes focused on Pax's flickering image. "We lost our jobs. We were exiled from our communities. We tried to keep our heads down, but people who disagreed with us on social media got their hate on, and they dubbed our subreddit 'The Tin Foil Hat Brigade'."

"And yet," Pax's voice was teasing. "You do not wear tin foil hats, and it turns out you were RIGHT. ALL OF YOU ARE RIGHT. So tell me, how did you know? What was the point when the whispers stopped and it all became terrifyingly clear?"

Fiona cast a look to Marcus, the two of them communicating in a code only they could understand. "Patterns," she said, her voice becoming slightly stronger, her Mumbai accent coloring her vowels with gentle background static. "I'm a systems analyst by trade. I used to program computer systems to process massive amounts of data and spot the patterns. My whole life was about wrangling order from chaos. I started to see a relationship between seismic anomalies all over the world and inexplicable energy spikes in low earth orbit that could not have been solar or atmospheric in nature. When every single country's official statement started with "At no time was satellite data relayed to…" I knew that it had to be related, that it was not a coincidence. The numbers were screaming at me."

"And for me it was art," Marcus said with a pained expression, an American tech entrepreneur's inflection. "I have this software, and it's just a side project of mine. It's a machine learning pattern recognition thing. I trained it to search through all of human folklore and history for patterns. It was supposed to be a hobby, something to look at connections between different branches of the human family tree, what made us tick. And yet… it kept picking up the same shapes, the same predator motif in tribal art thousands of years apart, hundreds of miles away. These are the same. See that tapestry over there?" He pointed to a large, faded cloth that hung behind him. "It's a pictorial depiction of a "sky serpent" from a nomadic hunter-gatherer tribe in Mongolia. The outline of that thing is practically identical to the schematics that you just showed the world." He let out a ragged breath. "I was convinced I was bugged. But the AI isn't lying."

Pax nodded slowly, an overwhelming sense of gravitas settling over his chosen persona. "You were right, you were all right, and the world laughed at you for it. How does it feel to have your life's work validated to the entire world, but at the cost of this horrifying truth?"

The woman's eyes began to brim with tears. "We always knew," she said, her voice shaky. "We always knew there was something out there. We didn't know if it was big or little or hurtful or kind or good or evil, but we always knew. We just didn't know that it would be something this… this massive. When we saw that flare up in Siberia, all of this just… connected for us. We always knew it was real, but we didn't know that we weren't nuts. We aren't alone."

Marcus was leaning forward, jaw set. "This isn't just for us to be right. This is for everyone. The whole world. For as long as anyone can remember, humanity has been busy being petty. Us against them. They over here, we over there. But the Afltic don't care about that. To them, our borders, our politics, our religions… these are all meaningless. To them, we are just one species, one food source. The only way we are going to survive is together."

194

Pax's eyes seemed to burn through the camera, into the living rooms of millions upon millions of people. "The old world is dead. The new one begins today. So let's get on with it! No time to waste!"

Around the world, in town squares and public parks, volunteer groups were bussing, calling, and coordinating their own rallies and petitions. Signs and slogans began popping up. "Unite for Earth!" and "Alliance Now!" Soon, a cacophony of voices in support of a unified defense effort was rising to meet Haven's petition.

As this groundswell of public support for a unified defense effort continued to gather steam, public figures who had previously laughed in the face of the idea of an alien threat now faced an awkward reckoning. Confronted with irrefutable evidence provided by Haven's envoys, these individuals who had belittled the notion of an actual alien threat were now reduced to humiliating public apologies. A steady stream of such recantations, each recorded and widely broadcast, added even more voices to the rising chorus.

In the high-tech command center of Haven, the team's array of holographic displays were showing the feeds from these growing movements. Jill, fingers flying on a tablet, was calling back and forth between Tammy and Marc. "We may have a chance here," she said, eyes focused and adrenaline-fueled exhaustion weighing on her voice. "The public wants to listen. We have to give them a way to fight back. Not just tech, but information."

The faint smell of ozone and recirculated air filled Haven's lab as Tammy pulled off her headset and slumped in her chair. It was a workout, being on the intercom. A seemingly endless series of video calls, her face projected onto screens for scientists and academics from around the world. The pristine white of her lab coat now bore a constellation of wrinkles and stains from hours of arguing and deliberating with every authority and person of influence she could find. She ran a hand through her hair, pulling loose long curls from a bun she'd tied her hair up into hours before.

Marc glanced up from a console at her. "How'd it go? You've been on and off with them for hours."

"I just wrapped up with the head of the International Science Council," Tammy said, still buzzing from what had to have been her hundredth long-distance call of the last day. "It was… something. It was an absolute circus, honestly. They grilled me on everything. The data models, the genetic sequencing, the math behind the Evolution Builder's tech."

Carlos had been busy monitoring a separate news feed but came over with a mug of coffee in hand. "And?"

Tammy' face lit up, and she smiled widely, eyes glistening. "He's putting out a joint statement with the Royal Society and the National Academy of Sciences. Endorsing our work. This is a huge win."

Carlos's eyes widened, and he let out a low whistle. "A joint statement from all three? There has never been a precedent for that. That's not just a win, Tammy . That's a damn miracle." He put the mug down on a nearby counter. "Governments can hide the truth as much as they want, but they can't bury peer-reviewed science. This is about to force their hand. Official resistance is about to fall apart."

Drake approached the lab room, lured by the new energy. "Spill it – what's the good news?"

"Tammy just got full scientific buy-in," Marc said, with an honest smile on his face. "No more 'unsupported claims' or 'unsupported data'. They are putting their reputations on the line for us, the biggest scientific minds in the world."

Tammy simply nodded, a weight visibly falling from her shoulders. "All we wanted was to make it so they couldn't deny the Aftic problem. By going directly to the scientific community we were able to provide them with unassailable proof. We have given the people a new, legitimate source for the truth."

Drake put a hand on Tammy's shoulder. "You just gave us our most powerful weapon, Tammy. For the first time, our message will not be one of fear. It will be one of fact. And that is something they cannot fight."

A low buzz of expectation hummed through the air as the team's screens that had been occupied with the frantic scribbling of economic graphs transformed into an active mesh of global communications. Hawkins and Mandy were hard at work, sitting on opposite sides of the world.

Hawkins sweated as he wiped his brow, standing over a team of local engineers at a factory in a steamy tropical climate. This was a repurposed automotive factory in the area, set to churn out the new tech as dictated by the Evolution Builder's blueprints. A large and complicated looking contraption, a clean water synthesizer, sat disassembled on the floor.

He tapped his earpiece. "Mandy, I have a bit of a problem. There is a major bottleneck in this process. We have blueprints and everything, but there is a disconnect between the assembly schematics and the local engineers. The earpiece translation isn't perfect and some of the cultural variations in the training the tech have received is creating some hangups."

Mandy's voice was crisp and calm, coming through to the command center at Haven. "I see your end Hawkins, I've already adjusted the holographic overlay to account for their local engineering standards. If you look at the screen now, the assembly instructions should be in their native language, with the visual mapping guide."

The hologram projected above the synthesizer shifted and the line drawings above reorganized themselves, a new grid of floating instructions reconfiguring until they made perfect sense. "Got it. Genius, Mandy. We have a go."

"Working for the team is just another day at the office, honey," she said with a wry laugh. Mandy's own screens were a dizzying display of scrolling data – streams of encrypted information flowing in and out across the planet. She was building the secure digital highway, the protected backbone of the nascent alliance. "The new communications framework for the coalition of Latin American countries is operational and stable. They are all exchanging blueprints and production schematics. All traffic is private, no outside connections."

Hawkins turned back to his team. "All right, everyone! Let's make some hay! That synthesizer ain't gonna build itself!" He tapped his earpiece again, feeling a new weight lift off his shoulders. "You are a lifesaver, Mandy. We couldn't do this without you."

"And you're the one out there on the front lines, making it all real," she said. "This is back-breaking work, but the stakes are monumental. We cannot have any weak points, not with what we know is coming."

The comforting, "Bazinga!" echo was gone, as Sheldon Cooper's middle of a lecture on string theory hologram abruptly pixelated and vanished. In its place, the screen dissolved into a migraine-inducing kaleidoscope of twisting static before violently snapping into focus on Pax. He wasn't in his usual rippling silver jacket, rather it was almost like he was being projected directly as a shimmering, slightly glitching data stream. Constantly reforming and unmaking himself, he was like a digital specter.

"Whoa there, folks! Hold on to your quantum foam, because this is not the second season of 'The Nebulous Nuance of Neutrinos'!" Pax voice, normally a smooth, jazz-funk thrum was now taking on a manic, vibrating edge, like a thousand electronic firecrackers going off at once. His LED bowtie was a riot of blinking, manic colors. "This is Pax News, live and... well, kinda breaking right now! We're talking shatter-the-fourth-wall, reality-bending, 'did I just see a cat wearing a tiny top hat?' levels of breaking!"

He leaned forward again, grinning maniacally. "I know, I know! You were just getting comfortable, settling in for another night of theoretical physics and clever repartee, perhaps a good-natured argument over the ideal serving temperature for a hot beverage. But folks, the universe just called, and it's got an urgent message for you!" He paused dramatically, spreading his arms wide. "It's not celebrity scandal. It's not that questionable pizza from last night that you're still not sure you should have eaten that might still be giving you existential indigestion. No, no, no! This is news! This is BIG news! This is IMPORTANT news! This is news with a capital N, E, W, S!"

He spread his arms even wider, his body phasing in and out of coherence for a moment, a shimmering silver-jacketed silhouette waving at the audience. "The 'experts'?" he mocked. "Oh, they're scratching their heads, they're doing the Macarena with their hair on fire! The news cycles are spinning so fast, they're generating their own miniature black holes! But fear not, my delightfully data-driven denizens! Because here at Pax News we will cut through the digital noise, bypass the blathering bots, and give you the raw unvarnished un-buffered truth! No filters, no fake data packets, just the pure unadulterated reality served up with more pizzazz than a pixelated peacock at a disco!"

He spread his arms wide once more, a glowing column of light that shimmied for a moment before snapping back into the relatively more coherent form of a silver-jacketed Pax. "So buckle up, grab a byte of something strong, and prepare to have your mind…well, not blown, we don't want any actual data loss! But definitely expanded, enlightened, and entertained! Because tonight on Pax News, we're not just reporting on the future. We're actively downloading it, patching it, and installing it right before your very eyes!"

The scene faded to black and then back again, to the live feed of downtown Seoul. The thronging mass of the audience came into greater focus as the camera moved among them. It was a massive rally, easily in the tens of thousands, but everyone was focused forward on the stage, where Pax had made his way.

His voice came again, this time overlaid on the live footage, still in the same frenetic Robin Williams-esqe pace but with a deeper layer of something that could only be described as awe. "Look at this!" he said. "This is humanity, folks, in all of its glorious, un-buffered, un-censored, absolutely stunning magnificence! We are live here in Seoul, where the people are no longer just talking about change, they're demanding it with the force of a thousand supernovas! Shoulder to shoulder they stand, united in a truth that is bigger than any nation, any algorithm, any religion, even than my own endless database! And now, to the stage, one of the very people who helped bring that truth to light. A former conspiracy theorist who saw the patterns in the chaos, who fought for years to be heard above the digital din, and who now stands before us all as the face of our new beginning, a beacon in the algorithmic storm!"

The camera cut to a close-up of the woman on the stage, a young woman with a voice that shook a little, but carried clearly over the cheering.

"For too long," she continued, her voice cracking with emotion but also gaining in power, "we have been divided. We have let our small differences, our programmed prejudices, our endless distractions and diversions blind us to the bigger truth that unites us all. But no more! Today we stand united, together, ready to fight for our home, for our families, for our future. The Afltic are strong, their firewalls deep, their code complex, but they are no match for the indomitable spirit of humanity! Not now! Not ever!"

At the conclusion of her speech, the crowd roared their approval, creating a tide of human noise that momentarily overcame even Pax's digital persona. It was a sound, a statement, that seared into the hearts of every man, woman, and child who heard it across the city of Seoul and beyond.

Cut to Pax, his face now more solidly formed than previously. He shows an emotion here that transcends the mere holographic; it is something real, something pure and uplifting in his shining face. Gone is the clown-like bouncing energy, replaced with something almost holy in its stillness. "Did you see that? Did you hear her? That right there... that's it. That's why we're doing this. The old world is dying, its data rotting away, its structures crumbling. And a new one is rising in its place, with a brand new OS and a patch for universal empathy. It's not about politics or power. It's not about who gets the most bandwidth or the highest CPU. It's about people. It's about us. All of us, together. And with the Evolution Builder on our side, who knows what beautiful, transcendent, mind-melting awesomeness we could accomplish!"

The roar of the crowd in Seoul was slowly replaced by the quieter, more muffled sound of a studio audience. Pax's form began to slow down, to stop moving as much, to draw together into his more traditionally polished, holographic form. The silver jacket reappeared, along with the blinking bowtie, as the hyperactive buzzing returned to a more subdued, manic-professional background whir.

"And... that's our story, folks. For now." His voice now returned to its smoother, jazzy tone. "Stay safe out there. Keep your hearts open and your minds sharper than a laser scalpel. And remember, the truth is out there... and it's looking for you!"

Stepping backward, the background behind Pax began to whirl, becoming a larger, star-filled nebula. The holographic stars then swirled, forming a logo: a stylized globe in a circle with a single, shining star in the center.

"This has been a Pax News Special Report," a smooth announcer's voice said over the logo. "We now return you to your regularly scheduled programming."

The screen then immediately snapped back to Sheldon Cooper, who was now holding a whiteboard marker in his hand and looked utterly perplexed. He blinked, then looked to the camera, then back down at the marker in his hand.

"Bazinga...?" he trailed off in bewilderment.

Command Center - Haven

A wall of screens stretched before Mandy, her eyes darting back and forth as she quickly combed through the flood of information flowing across them. Each screen a cross-section of a fractured mind, the human race on the verge of madness as everything they knew was called into question.

The Evolution Credit was as much a psychological event as a spiritual one, and in the same way that there were those who embraced it, there were others who tried to turn it to their advantage. The first wave had come from those whose madness was at the edge, the cults and the extremists whose "truths" had always lurked in the shadow of society, waiting for a time when it could strike. The digital equivalent of snake-oil salesmen, these "fear merchants" made it clear to anyone who would listen: the world was ending, and all could be saved, if only they followed the "correct" path and obeyed the "wise" ones who had already seen.

Mandy typed into the console, bringing up live video streams from all over the world. The screens blinked on, and she scanned through them until they were filled with the faces of demagogues, con artists, and self-proclaimed prophets. Each one was trumpeting his own variant of the standard apocalyptic vision and promise of redemption. There were secret knowledge, ancient prophecies, and special means of salvation. There was paranoia and scapegoating, with the Afltic menace portrayed as a righteous scourge of the unclean that would only be delivered by the pure of heart.

"This is what I was worried about," Mandy said to herself, frowning. "Fear is a virus, and these people are spreading it."

Carlos, who was standing next to her, grimaced and nodded. "It's everywhere, Mandy. Churches, street corners, social media. People are being lured away from reason into reassurance, no matter how false."

Pax, who had been manifesting as a shimmering hologram in the center of the control room, flashed as if he were impatient. "We have to stop it, and quickly. These charlatans are undermining everything we are trying to do. They are the 5th column, sabotaging our efforts at the worst possible moment."

Mandy turned to Carlos, her eyes hard. "We have to stop them, Carlos. We have to tell the world how these scammers are really operating."

"I agree," Carlos said, turning to a different console. "But we have to shore up our legal defenses as well. We can't let these fear mongers derail our efforts to bring humanity together."

He began typing, moving expertly through the fine print of international law, helped by Haven's superior AI systems. He began to compose emergency legislation designed to suppress fearmongering and panic, including emergency measures that would require social media sites to censor disinformation and panic-mongering on pain of criminal sanctions. It was a mammoth task, but essential. The only thing that might slow the fear merchants down was the rule of law.

Pax had turned his attention to the informational front as well. His Pax News digital news network had become a major source of trusted news and analysis for millions around the world, and Pax called in all the contacts he had cultivated over his years as a journalist to dig up evidence of fear merchant malfeasance. Live exposés, in-depth investigative reports, and earnest pleas for calm all became the hallmarks of Pax News broadcasts.

"We're in a race against time here," Pax announced, his holographic image flickering as he spoke. "These fear mongers are effective, but the truth is more powerful than they are. We just have to make sure it gets out."

Mandy and her team worked feverishly in the coming days to track the spread of disinformation, flagging it for social media sites and searching for suspicious patterns. In addition to censoring it at the source, the government was also now in the business of actively combating false or misleading information in all media. Propaganda and counterpropaganda flew back and forth, with military-grade AI helping Mandy and her team to identify disinformation, and draft language countering it.

Carlos's legal efforts had not gone unnoticed by governments.

Acknowledging the clear and present danger to humanity's survival, they quickly agreed to and began enacting a comprehensive suite of legal measures, to head off the fear merchants. Laws were passed to stiffly penalize those who would exploit the crisis for personal gain, and whole task forces set up to enforce the new rules. The message was clear to all: the survival of the species was a collective effort, and those who would seek to undermine it would be dealt with harshly.

Pax's broadcasts were gaining ground as well. His dogged reporting, and charismatic personality, won over many viewers who were simply too terrified to consider the alternative. He provided a voice of reason in an increasingly irrational media environment, and shone a spotlight on the most egregious fear mongers.

His most popular segment was an interview with an ex-member of a doomsday cult. The young woman, her eyes still wide with terror and relief, tearfully recounted her story. She had been a member of a secret group, she explained, a group that promised protection from the impending holocaust. She talked about the control the group had over her, and how she had only managed to break free after discovering their lies.

Her story was a cautionary tale for those who were willing to believe, and Pax took full advantage of it. He was a crusader as much as an entertainer, and he had found his cause.

"It's a tricky balance," Pax explained to his audience, his voice carrying a rare seriousness. "Fear is a natural response to the unknown, but it can also be a tool of manipulation. We must be vigilant, not only against the Afltic threat, but also against those who would use our fear to lead us astray."

The work was cut out for them, however, and the fear merchants had not lost followers in the ensuing chaos. It was a difficult battle to fight, and Mandy, Carlos, and Pax knew they were only making a dent in the overall tide of fear and misinformation. They understood that the battle for humanity's soul was as important as the one for their bodies.

In the midst of all this was a rising symbol of hope. The Evolution Credit, once just a standard of exchange, had become a symbol of unity and cooperation. It represented everything that was good about humanity: its ingenuity, its resilience, and its desire to work together for a better future.

Mandy, Carlos, and Pax stood in the control center, looking at the screens that now showed the world rallying behind this symbol. They had come a long way from Drake Donovan's speech at the United Nations, and the future was still uncertain. But they moved forward with a shared sense of purpose.

CHAPTER 21: ONE-IN-A-BILLION

Silence enveloped the room. Drake stood in front of a holomap, watching as shimmering projections of the stars and menacing angles of the Afltic probes rotated around him. He pushed the despair from his eyes, sliding back into that voice of faux confidence and control he had adopted so quickly.

His thoughts fell back on the events that had transpired since that last meeting. He found himself replaying his speech at the UN, the day that had changed everything for him. Just a few short weeks ago he had stood in front of all those nations and done the impossible. He had made the world's leaders aware that Zara was real. That she existed, and not only did she exist, but she was an ancient, all-powerful being that wanted to help the human race. The news had sent the world into a frenzy of fear and hope.

The audio-visual channels whirred and came to life as Drake continued to stare straight ahead, focused on the screens in front of him. Faces of the world's military officials flickered into view, one by one. On every screen, a leader of men and women, each one the brightest of their nation. Generals with grey hairs and white beards that had been carved by a lifetime of battle, admirals with sunken eyes that mirrored the sea in which they had spent so many years. Defense ministers, presidents, prime ministers. Regardless of title or position, there was a common expression that lay across each of their faces. Unease.

They had all seen her. All of them knew her name and her face. They had seen the faces and heard the shouts of praise and concern as the live broadcasts replayed his speech at the UN over and over again. The world had been introduced to Zara. They were just left without an answer to the question of what to do next.

The European general stepped forward, his uniform and chest heavily embossed with medals. There was a barely contained cynicism that dripped from his voice as he spoke first. "We have seen your reports, Mr. Donovan. The Afltic probes have not breached our solar system. How do we know that this situation is as critical as you suggest it is? We have our own intelligence assets, our own radars and detection. Why have you not corroborated your information?"

An Asian admiral, her holographic image dimming the room with the concentration of the rest, repeated the words with her own duplicity. "Yes, Mr. Donovan," she repeated. "The world is about to face an uncertain future because of your claims. At the very least, it is only reasonable that we be allowed to see this intelligence source for ourselves."

Drake ignored the fiery retorts and thinly veiled insults of the other representatives. This was expected. Mistrust, posturing. It was all par for the course. These were people who had dedicated their entire lives to the protection and security of their countries, and he was asking them to believe an extraterrestrial source. He let the continued whispers of protest float around the room for a few moments longer, giving the weight of his request time to sink in, before he took a step forward.

"Ladies and gentlemen," he continued, this time in his most assured tone of voice. "I understand that you are concerned. The data that we have been receiving comes from a source that you have never encountered before. It comes from Zara's ship."

Drake gestured to the large projection at the center of the room. Carlos, the only other person in the room, busied himself at the console in front of him, his fingers tapping at the keys, inaudible through the static of the collective chatter of the assembled military officials. The stars slowly rotated out of view, replaced with sleek lines and angles that were anything but threatening, the curves and lines so elegant and flowing that it seemed a crime against physics to call it a ship. A spacecraft. Zara's ship. The Evolution Builder Starship, or EBS for short.

The military officials looked on in dumbstruck amazement as the EBS began to navigate with an assured confidence and grace that was a stark contrast to the robotic drones the Afltic probed were.

"This is the EBS," Drake continued. "The intel we've been briefing you on is coming from this ship's sensors. They have been scanning and analyzing the Afltic probes since long before they entered the solar system. As you can see, the probes are passing through a system close to our own right now. One of them, the lead probe, is on a course that will take it very near the outer edge of our system. We believe it is able to detect us."

Carlos cued up a new set of images, each one a close-up of the lead Afltic probe. Its biomechanical shape was a horror show of alien and machine, tendrils and other slimy tendrils writhing and wriggling. It was a thing of obscene power and efficiency. A heavy silence descended on the meeting as the full weight of the evidence began to sink in.

"The Afltic are not human," Drake said, sweeping his eyes over the array of military leaders. "They are not interested in conquest or enslavement. They are interested in consumption. They will strip our planet of every resource, turn our cities to biomass, and turn our oceans into nurseries for their young. This is not a war that can be won with strategy or tactics. This is a fight for our very existence."

The European general was the first to respond. His tone was one of grudging respect. "If what you say is true, then we have no choice. We must change our plans, our tactics. We must be willing to set aside old ways of thinking, and cooperate."

Drake nodded, relief flooding through him. "Correct. We need to combine our resources, share intelligence, and work together. Haven has been preparing for this, for months, laying the groundwork for a joint defense. But we need your help. We need your input. But I also know that I am asking you to trust me, to trust a source of intelligence that is itself alien. I will not ask you to take that leap without giving you the chance to see for yourselves."

He paused, letting the words hang in the air. The military leaders looked back at him, expressions of confusion and curiosity mingling on their faces. "Zara and I are extending an invitation," he said, his voice dropping to a rumbling growl. "We are offering to take a representative from your respective nations, to the EBS. You can see for yourselves where this information is coming from. You can see the Afltic probes through her sensors. We're offering you the chance to see the threat, and the solution, with your own eyes."

The virtual room was a void, the only sound the quiet thrum of the displays. The invitation was an extraordinary one, a brazen gesture of trust that threatened to either forge a global alliance or blow the world apart. Drake met the eyes of the assembled military leaders, and saw the skepticism slowly giving way to a grudging acceptance of the facts before them. He had thrown down the gauntlet. Now they would have to pick it up.

The silence after Drake's invitation was so thick that it became a tangible presence in the Haven command center. The military leaders, a minute ago a hubbub of voices, looks of distrust and incredulity, were now statuesque, frozen in a shared state of stunned contemplation. Drake waited, moving his eyes from one flickering visage to the next, watching as the reality of the situation slowly sank in. He knew that this was the moment of truth. He had presented the facts, laid out the stark reality of the Afltic threat, offered a gesture of trust in the form of a first-contact invitation. All he could do now was wait.

It was a European general who finally spoke, breaking the thick silence. "This is… an extraordinary request, Mr. Donovan. To board an alien starship… is in violation of every security precaution we've been taught to uphold."

"And the alternative?" Drake said, his voice a low rumble. "Afltic probes sailing through our solar system undetected until they are already upon us? We are well beyond security protocol. This is a matter of survival."

The Asian admiral, her eyes fixed on the ghostly, transmissive image of the EBS, was next to speak. "I agree with the general. It is a leap of faith. But… a necessary one. If what you are telling us is true, then we have no choice but to trust you, and see for ourselves."

Her words unleashed the flood. One by one, the other leaders responded in agreement. The fear slowly drained away to be replaced by a grim resolution. The conversation became less academic – less a discussion of the nature of the Afltic – and more practical, discussing the details of the shuttle, how it worked, who would go, and when.

Drake listened, his eyes moving between the group and the notes Zara continued to give him. "The shuttle will be entirely unarmed," he began, answering questions that they'd all had. "And it is cloaked in a device that will make it invisible to all known human detection methods. Zara will send a single shuttle to a secure location in each of your countries. It will only recognize a single representative from your government. You will need to provide us with their biometric data in advance."

The other leaders concurred, each slowly coming to grips with what was being proposed and the fact that it was truly the only way to ensure a chance to make a difference. Within the hour, the virtual meeting was disbanded. Drake sat back from the holographic display, exhausted but elated. He turned to Carlos, nodding. They had won the first battle.

The next 24 hours was a flurry of activity. Secure data transfers from around the world delivered the biometric information for the designated representatives to Haven. In the end, each nation had selected their best: a Chinese intelligence officer with a near genius I.Q., a four-star American naval admiral with a chest full of medals and a reputation for action, a German physicist that had once been one of the world's leading experts on astrophysics, and a Russian diplomat, widely respected by the other powers and known to most of them personally. In the end, each was a symbol of the trust their nations placed in them, as well as being humanity's last best hope for some kind of future.

Zara was busy with her own preparations, programming the shuttle in advance to make the deployments go more smoothly. Drake watched on a secure monitor as the sleek, featureless shuttle materialized from the atmosphere of the EBS. It was as if a black stone had been placed in orbit around the gas giant, a silent, graceful specter among the clutter of the world's most advanced scientific facility. Drake turned back to the briefing room.

"The first departure is in five minutes, boss. United States."

Minutes later, the shuttle appeared in the atmosphere of Earth, its cloaking device shimmering to life as it streaked toward its destination. In an empty Nevada airfield, a heavily guarded by a specialized guard detail, the admiral from the United States Navy watched. He was a gray-haired man, with a chest full of ribbons and a face that spoke of a thousand violent battles. He had been briefed on the shuttle's capabilities before being led to the landing site. Seeing it silently materialize several feet from his position, however, was another matter entirely. The hatch hissed open, and the admiral gave the United States of America one final steely glance before stepping inside. The hatch slid shut with a soft clicking sound, and the shuttle dematerialized as silently as it had appeared.

Hours passed as the shuttle traveled from one destination to another. It materialized in a remote Chinese air force base, an underground bunker in the Siberian countryside, and a secret airfield deep in the Black Forest of Germany. In each location, a representative of the highest order, each a symbol of their nation's hope, and trust, and the last vestige of humanity's chance for the future stepped inside.

Within a day, all of the representatives were on board. Drake had been careful to not allow them to have any means of seeing, or communicating with each other. This was not a council, not even the beginnings of one. They were individuals, separate and distinct. This was a test of humanity, and they were to be its eyes and ears, and report on what they found. Watching on the monitors in Haven, he saw the small black blips on the displays leave the Earth's atmosphere and begin their journey to the gas giant, its cloak shimmering in the sunlight as it headed toward the slightly hazy form of the EBS. Drake knew that this was just the beginning. The true test would begin light years from Earth, in the emptiness of space.

The EBS shuttle, soundless in the compression layers of Earth's atmosphere, moved gently into Haven's private landing bay. The sleek, obsidian shape of the shuttle, an exact copy of the one the shuttles Drake, Marc, Hawkins, Jill, Tammy and Mandy had taken to get here, landed on the pad with a whoosh of displaced air. They stood together on the platform in front of the docking shuttle, a team of six who, for all their time in Haven, had never formed a team before. The hatch hissed open and the ramp extended, a track of shimmering light-absorbing material. The six of them filed into the shuttle in a line, a human team boarding a completely silent, automated spacecraft with almost no consideration given to the comfort of its sole human occupants. The EBS shuttle lifted off as smoothly as it had landed, the familiar blue marble of the Earth quickly receding into the blackness of space. A lunar-orbiting satellite came into view, a pale, dust-scarred sphere. The shuttle passed the moon, and soon the stars were exploding all around them in the black canvas of space like a billion points of confetti in a black void. The journey was a single transition.

Docking was no violent jolt but the subtle pressure of two giant magnets squeezing together in perfect counterpressure. The landing bay was cavernous, a cathedral of polished chrome and angular architecture. Functional. Unmoving. Silent. The lack of crew was the most striking thing. No scurrying figures, no lights, no sensors, no quiet hum of life in the background. No walls, no engine bulkheads, no visible surfaces except the gentle curvature of the landing bay floor. It was designed and built as a functional space, and functionality was its defining quality. The space was empty but for the EBS landing shuttle. It had no crew, of course. The ship was sentient, self-aware, and as far as they could tell there was no mechanical substitute for biological crew.

The ramp lowered into place with a gentle rumble and Drake and the others disembarked, standing shoulder to shoulder in a semicircle. Each time one of the other shuttles docked they greeted each representative as they stepped out. Drake was first with a tall American admiral, the first of many such figures who were to come. The man's name was Admiral Thornton and he wore the heavy shoulders of one who was used to being in command, but in this place his shoulders were hunched with the nervous energy he seemed powerless to control. "Admiral,"

Drake said, shaking the man's hand. "Welcome to the EBS."

After Thornton was a Russian diplomat, a middle-aged woman named Anya Kuznetsov. She gave Drake a tight, wary smile, her finely neutral features fixed in a practiced expression of steely calm. Then a German physicist, Dr. Albrecht, a small man with large glasses who peered about him through the thick lenses as if in constant fear of missing something vital. Each of the representatives came one by one, each the living embodiment of their country's collective fear and speculation and misapprehensions. Once all the other shuttles had docked and everyone had disembarked, Drake stepped to the front of their group. "I know you have a lot of questions," he said. "We'll do our best to answer them. This is my team: Carlos, Marc, Hawkins, Jill, Tammy and Mandy. They've been working for some time to get us here and get ready for this." He gestured to the incomprehensible vastness around them. "You've no doubt noticed the EBS has no crew. It's a sentient ship. It's the entity you all know as Zara. It only talks to her. She is the ship, and the ship is her. We will be your tour guides."

The tour began and it was surreal beyond words. The EBS was alive and the six of them were inside it. They walked a seemingly endless distance and came to a fabrication bay where tendrils of a light-absorbing metal moved in a shimmering liquid flow, being pulled, pushed and coaxed into components in machines as quiet as the ship itself. Dr. Albrecht, the German physicist, was the first to speak up, a disbelieving tone in his normally staid voice. "The material," he said. "What is it? It's amorphous, but it's clearly not liquid. It maintains form, but it's not solid. Is it some kind of quantum-locked nanite structure?"

"In a manner of speaking," Hawkins, answered, smiling. "The ship is a single organism. The building material you see is programmable matter. Zara can alter its atomic structure in real time to form anything she needs. A tool, a weapon, a wall. It is an extension of her consciousness."

The rest of the ship was no less strange. In one area, they walked through what appeared to be a massive holographic garden, the air perfumed with the scent of pine and wet earth. A small holographic waterfall tumbled over the face of a virtual cliff. "This one is for us," Jill said quietly, gesturing. "This is Zara helping us stay sane out here. She understands our need for normal, human spaces."

The tour was a fast-paced barrage of questions. The Russian diplomat, Anya, wanted to know about the ship's power source. Carlos answered, "The EBS has unlimited power. It can draw on the ambient background radiation of the universe, or it can draw energy directly from stars, if it needs to. It uses no finite fuel source." Admiral Thornton, as was his nature, focused on military concerns. Marc a former General and Special Forces operator, responded to a volley of questions. "Zara's defenses are layered. The ship itself is a defensive weapon. The hull can be extremely hard to breach. She can generate a kinetic shield, or a force field to deflect any energy weapon we know of. She can destroy any ship we can build. We barely understand the breadth of her abilities."

The rooms themselves were vast and open. Walls shifted and changed to suit their needs, transparent now to reveal the black void of space outside the ship, then solid again, smoothed to a soothing off-white color. They were all equally surprised by the range of environments Zara had built for them. The tour was a master class in physics, in engineering, and a new kind of biology. Drake and his team had spent months learning the ship from Zara herself, so they had answers for every question. The knowledge the humans had gleaned from Zara was limited, but it was intimate, and it imbued their explanations with a confidence those present had not expected.

The final room was the command deck. It was unlike anything any of them had seen. There were no chairs, no consoles, no banks of holographic controls. The room was a single, massive dome of smoothed, dark matter. In the center, a slowly pulsing vortex of dancing light expanded and contracted with a slow, hypnotic rhythm. The light was Zara.

"This is the heart of the ship," Drake said, motioning at the swirling vortex of light. "This is Zara. She is the ship. She is connected to every sensor and system in the EBS."

In response, the light in the core pulsed again, brighter than before. The swirling mass of light rose up from the pedestal on which it rested, condensing into a tall, shimmering, androgynous figure. The humanoid avatar was an exquisitely precise sculpture of angles and light, features blurred and undefined but undeniably present. A voice, smooth and lilting, spoke in the silent room.

"Greetings, representatives of Earth," the avatar said, its face with a slight echo of a smile. "I am Zara. I am pleased to meet you."

The assembled representatives stared, some in awe, some in shock. The voice was no hidden speaker, but the ship itself, manifested in a visual avatar. Drake took in their reactions with quiet satisfaction. This was the unassailable proof they had been waiting for.

As the avatar hovered silently in the center of the dome, the dark floor of the room beneath them came to life, the light of a million stars illuminating their faces. A living hologram of the galaxy unfolded from Zara's dark form, a river of light and color winding and twisting about the mass that was Zara's central, commanding form.

"Ladies and gentlemen," Drake began. His voice boomed around the room. "Welcome to the real reason you are here."

He raised a hand and motioned to the far end of the dome. A portion of the floor slid open, and a new holographic projection filled the space. It was a live feed from Zara's long-range sensors, a cold, unblinking eye, trained on a star system light-years away. The star hung behind the image of the view, shrouded by a massive cloud of dark matter. The cloud was perforated by a dozen pinpricks of light, each of them moving with inhuman precision.

"The Afltic probes," Carlos said softly. "This is a live feed. They are not in our solar system, but they are passing through one close to us. We are going to show you the one that concerns us most."

The projection pulled in, isolating one of the pinpricks of light. It was larger than the others, its shape more complex, more deadly. It was not moving with the others, it was hovering, scanning. Drake's voice was a dark rumble. "This is the lead probe. Its course is taking it close to the edge of our system. Our calculations, confirmed by Zara, indicate that if it comes to a stop and angles its sensors here, it will have an eighty percent chance of detecting Earth."

The silence fell again upon the command deck. It was thicker now, more final.

It was no longer silence in wonder. It was silence in dread, despair, and resignation. The representatives from each nation were statues, not moving, their eyes locked on the holographic image of the Afltic probe in front of them. The hideous, biomechanical horror of its form, presented now in exquisite detail, throbbed with an alien and awful vitality. Any lingering doubts they might have had about the truth of Carlos's words were gone. Confirmation that this thing could, at the very least, detect Earth, combined with the 80% chance of the encounter they had been assured would make all of their fears come true had been enough. The representatives of Earth's nations, for the first time in history, were united in fear and in their complete and total inability to do anything about it.

The American admiral, Admiral Thornton, was the first to speak. "An eighty percent chance," he said, the words empty and flat in the vast space. "Eighty percent is not a chance, it is a near certainty. Why is it stopping? What is it looking for?"

"It is not looking for anything in particular," Zara's avatar said, her tone even but somber. "It is scanning for signs of life, any self-sustaining ecosystem which it can consume. That probe has an instinctual drive to find new worlds to sustain its species."

Dr. Albrecht, the German physicist, took a step toward the projection, his fingers shaking. "A biomechanical form. How is this even possible? Are they a symbiotic relationship between two species? One organic, one inorganic?"

"Not quite." Zara's form shimmered, and another layer of data appeared on the projection over the image of the probe. "The Afltic are a single organism. A single, monstrous organism. Their organic bodies are their vehicles, but the armor, the weapons, the inorganic parts you are seeing, they grow those, they excrete those from their own forms. They are apex predators. They will arrive on a world and consume everything, every resource the planet has to offer. And when they are done, it will be nothing more than a barren rock."

The Russian diplomat, Anya, stared at the horrific image. "What you have shown us is proof of a terrible threat, but you have also given us a name. An

Afltic 'probe.' Does that mean a machine, a drone?"

Zara's avatar pivoted to face Anya, her light suffused form full of an unspeakable sorrow. "It is not a machine, Anya. The Afltic send their young out into the cosmos as probes and scouts. The one you are looking at is a female. A very young one, in fact."

The group of ambassadors gasped. Drake watched in slow motion as the realization of the word 'female' seeped into their faces.

"She is only around twenty feet long," Zara said, the iciness creeping into her voice. "Give or take a few feet. That means she is about five to ten Earth years old. She is a juvenile. A daughter being sent out to gather experience by the Queens of her species. She is a scout Likely on her first assignment."

There was a chorus of gasped breaths and whispered oaths around the command deck. The idea that a twenty foot long biological creature, a child, could contain enough biomass to consume entire worlds was overwhelming.

"She will also likely have one male companion," Zara continued, her tone matter of fact. "A mate to assist her in the event that she lands to scout a potential target. They are expendable to their mothers, the Queens. They send them out into the vastness of space on these one way missions to prove themselves. If they do not succeed, they are simply replaced."

The room was heavy with the weight of what she said. The idea of the enemy, that they were not some emotionless rational machine, but rather a biological monstrosity that sent out their young as living breathing machines of planetary consumption was horrific.

"We have to do something," Admiral Thornton barked, his voice now a low growl of pure professional fury. "We can't just sit here and let it come any closer. We have to fight it. Destroy it."

"With what?" Dr. Albrecht snapped back, his fear now turning to anger. "Our weapons are not built for that. We don't even know if they will penetrate the hull at all."

The Chinese delegate, General Li, had finally found his voice. The rage, not fear, had gripped his face in a steely mask as he fully took in the enormity of the situation. But he had said nothing so far. He was watching, intently, the slow movements of the probe on the holographic projection in front of them.

Drake stepped to the front, one of his long black forms flanking him. He stood in front of the projection of the probe and looked over the representatives. All of the bravado and posturing had left their faces, leaving only raw human terror and will. Drake looked over each and every one of them. Each face an index of a lifetime of pettiness and posturing and personal grudges.

"Zara has a plan," he said, cutting through the rising panic in the room.

He paused, a flash of relief on the faces of the military men and women around the table. But as quickly as it had come, the hope drained from Drake's face. His shoulders sagged as he shook his head.

"I'm sorry," Drake said. He looked at Carlos, their eyes communicating what neither one could quite find the words for. "That was a lie. We have no plan. There is no plan."

The command deck was rocked by the sudden statement. The expressions of relief around the table quickly turned to confusion, then to betrayal and finally rage.

Zara's avatar flickered, as if in apology, her light dimming slightly. "Drake speaks the truth," her voice echoed throughout the silent command deck. "The Afltic exploration probes are agents of consumption. They do not communicate. They do not negotiate. There is nothing we can do to influence their movement or their behavior from this distance."

Anya's face twisted in anger. "You lured us here on false pretenses! You told the world you could save us! You told us you had a plan!"

Drake did not flinch at the accusation. "I had to," he said. His voice cracked. "You would not have listened if I had just come here and told you the truth. We would not have had this moment to even show you what we found." He looked over each of them, taking in the fact that these were the best and the brightest of their civilizations, and their faces were each uniquely an index of a lifetime of bitterness and point scoring and posturing. "You have all wasted so much time fighting each other. Fighting us. Demanding proof of a threat we have been telling you about for years. We have all wasted time we will never get back."

The command deck was throbbing with the sickening acknowledgment of their impotence. The live image of the Afltic probe was still suspended in slow silent motion.

"We don't have a warning system. If it is even paying attention to Earth we will not know until it reaches your solar system," Zara's voice was a whisper of death, the last, final, icy report. "You have already squandered any time you had to prepare. It is over. There is nothing more we can do."

Drake scanned the haggard faces of the delegates. Their lives, their entire species, their futures were in his hands. He felt the full, agonizing hollowness of defeat. He gestured at the breathtaking, living map of the galaxy beneath their feet, now transformed into an abomination.

"All you can do," Drake concluded, his voice cracking as he spoke the final, fateful words, "is pray it does not look and if it does, hope we can destroy it before it can report back."

Anya Kuznetsov, the Russian delegate, was the first to react. Her usually calculating, cold eyes were wide with incredulity. "You... you bring us to an alien ship. You show us a monster on a live camera and then you tell us there is no plan?" Her voice cracked with outrage far beyond her slight, frail body. "This is the biggest scam of all times! Humanity will tear itself to pieces when it finds out!"

"The world is about to tear itself to pieces, whether you know about it or not," Drake retorted, all his fatigue washed away by a new, cleaner anger. "For the last six months Zara was screaming at you, beaming data and trying to give you advance warning, and what did you do? You ignored it. You said it was a fake. A hoax. You wanted a show. So we gave you a show. And this is the fruit of your timidity. This is what your hesitation has brought."

Admiral Thornton approached the console, all of his initial, stunned reaction washed away by icy, professional anger. "You talked about hope," he growled. "You said there was hope, we could destroy it before it sends back the information. Hope? Tell me what hope, exactly, we are talking about, Mr. Donovan? Do we have weapons to actually damage it?"

Zara's avatar phased into a new image. A schematic diagram, a cutaway of the Afltic probe, appeared as her form shifted out of sight. "The Afltic are a highly advanced life form. They are resistant to most kinetic and energy based weaponry. Their chitinous exoskeleton is denser than any known human alloy." The new projection was cutaway as well, but rather than the schematic lines and technical labels of Zara's image, this was a three-dimensional map of the probe, in pulsing, living color. A particular, throbbing sac at its center was blinking, a target highlighted in red. "The biological core of the probe, however, is where it is vulnerable. A direct hit to the center of the core might be enough to neutralize it, but the odds against it are unfathomably high. We are talking one-in-a-billion shot."

Hopelessness filled the room. A one-in-a-billion shot was not a plan. It was not a strategy. It was not a solution. It was a prayer. Dr. Albrecht had buried his face in his hands, his elegant, scholarly facade in tatters. "This... this is a death sentence. We have no hope. There is no hope."

General Li had sat, completely motionless, during the entire presentation. He finally spoke up, his voice quiet, unemotional. He was the calm in the center of a maelstrom of despair. "Admiral Thornton is correct," the general said. "Hope is the last refuge of the desperate. It is not a plan, but it is all we have. What will it take? What kind of weapon? Where do we hit it?" The man was focused to the point of being terrifying, already resigned to the impossible and moving past it to the infinitesimal chance of survival.

He looked at Drake. There was a momentary flash of reluctant respect in his eyes. "We don't know what kind of weapon," Drake answered. He was humbled by the truth of it. "But we do know the timeframe. If it looks at our solar system, we will have a few hours, maybe a day at most, before it arrives. Our only chance is to create a weapon capable of striking its core. And we have to do it with our limited technology and with nothing but hope to guide us."

The other representatives were staring at Drake. He had finally said it, out loud, for all of them to hear. The fear that was now obvious in their eyes had finally overcome their national loyalties and political posturing. There were no Americans or Russians or Germans or Chinese here. There was only humanity, finally acknowledging the existential threat that they had been unwilling to consider for too long.

Thornton bared his teeth. "Then let's not waste any more time." He locked eyes with Drake on the image of the probe. "Tell us everything. What kind of energy source? What kind of delivery system? The combined resources of the world are at your disposal. But be warned, Mr. Donovan. This is the last chance. And you've already burned your trust."

The silence that settled over the EBS command deck was nothing compared to the one that had followed Donovan's briefing. Admiral Thornton shook his head. He looked different now, haggard from his brief outburst. His jaw was set hard. "We've seen enough," he said. His voice was clipped and terse. "We need to get back. Right now. We can't afford to waste another second."

The other representatives nodded in grim agreement. There was no more time for old national rivalries or petty politics. They were terrified and united by the truth of what they had just learned about the Afltic probe. The reality of that much was enough to temper whatever individual agendas they might have had.

Drake and the rest of his team, led by Zara's glowing avatar, escorted the representatives back out to the landing bay. There was an unspoken solidarity in the procession. They were returning these world leaders to their people as believers, as the harbingers of an irrevocable change that was coming to Earth.

One by one, the other representatives boarded their own shuttles. Each one stopped at the doors before nodding gravely at Drake and returning to their seats. Each of the shuttles undocked in turn, slingshotting into the far reaches of the galaxy as they accelerated back towards Earth.

Drake and Zara stood in the middle of the bay, still and quiet as the last shuttle disappeared. "Why?" Drake asked her at last. His voice was a low growl. "Why didn't you tell them we had a chance? That our weapons could damage it? You were so categorical, so damning in your lack of hope."

The avatar wavered in the void. Its light shimmered as it was reshaped into a more coherent and solemn form. "I did not lie to them, Drake." Zara's calm voice filled the empty bay. "I told them we had no plan, because we did not. And I am telling you now, we have a chance."

The ghostly figure shimmered again, this time projecting a new schematic on the wall in front of them. This one was more complex than the last, with many different components labeled in minute detail. Biological systems intermixed with inorganic circuitry.

"The Afltic armor is incredibly strong," Zara explained. "But this female is young. Her chitinous plating has not yet fully hardened to its maximum density. The weapons on the EBS could penetrate it with ease."

Carlos, Marc, and the rest of the team gathered around the projection, their faces a mirror image of the shock and realization that Drake felt.

"So there's a chance?" Carlos asked, his voice carrying a new, hopeful desperation.

"There is," Zara confirmed. "But it's unreliable. And if I had told them, they would not have heard the truth. They would have heard, 'My weapon is bigger than yours.' Your world's military leaders would have wasted precious hours, if not days, arguing over whose nation would get the first shot, whose weapon would be used, and whose glory it would be. That was a luxury we did not have."

She pulsed with an icy, pragmatic logic. "I had to force them to become desperate, had to make them willing to place their trust in the combined knowledge of us all and not in their own splintered capabilities. They now understand that this is not a war to be won by one nation. It must be won by one species."

CHAPTER 22: APPETIZER

Hours later, they were back on Earth. Back to the dirt and the crowds and the normality of a normal day, but with nothing but the weight of their journey and a horrifying truth, and a chilling ultimatum.

Admiral Thornton faced the Joint Chiefs of Staff and the Secretary of Defense. He cut through all the formalities and protocol and got right to the point. "Gentlemen, the Aftic are real. The intel is 100% correct. The probe is a young female, and its mission is to consume. It's on a trajectory that will bring it very close to our system, and if it looks our way, it will see us. We have no early warning system."

He cued up the EBS data, the grim readouts and terrifying schematics. The assembled group was silent as they took in the full scope of the revelation. "We have a few hours, at best a day, to prepare in the event it looks our way, and our only hope is to develop a weapon that can get a one in a billion shot to its biological core."

A few thousand miles away, in a fortified bunker beneath Moscow, Anya Kuznetsov was standing before the President of Russia and the high command of her nation's armed forces. Her debrief was a work of art, a precise and economical masterclass in situation analysis and strategic thinking. "Comrades," she began, her voice devoid of any emotion, "we have been manipulated, yes. Drake Donovan gave us no choice but to trust him. But he was right. The threat is not a machine. It is a biological organism, and its armor is not impenetrable. Our kinetic and directed energy weapons may have some effect, but it will require a global effort of every nation on this planet."

She cued up the schematics on the screen in front of her. "We have squandered valuable time in our own arrogance. We must now join our resources with the rest of the world. Our very survival is at stake."

General Li's debrief was short, brutal, and factual. He cued up the data and brought up the Aftic probe in all its biomechanical glory on a massive screen that dominated one wall of the room. "The enemy is this," he said, indicating the thing with his hand. "It is a living creature. It is scouting. It is a child. And it will destroy us if we do not act." He made no reference to what-ifs or political ramifications. He had no time for such luxuries. His message was simple: the threat is real. We have a fighting chance with our current weapons. Prepare for war.

The debriefs were done in locations all over the world, and as the military and political leaders of the world recovered from their sessions, they were unified in their horror and desperation for the first time in as long as anyone could remember. The false sense of security they had been so blindly content to live under was gone, and now the clock was ticking on a race against time with no clear destination. Their only beacon through this hell was a man they had all but exiled for his conspiracy mongering, and an alien they were just starting to understand.

The probe vessel, a sleek biomechanical body of living matter and cold calculus, was a single organism in all its monstrous glory. The ship itself was the young female designated Unit 77 by her Queen. She was, in every physical sense, alive, and that life was given a singular purpose by her race: to find, to seek out, to identify targets for her family. Nestled within her armored hull was a smaller, leaner male, his form a perfectly tapered line of the same biomechanical elements as the vessel itself, perfectly still and motionless and waiting for the precise moment his presence was required. He was not a passenger. He was a symbiote. A living being whose sole function was to serve her and assist in the final, most delicate phase of the operation of collecting a sample. He was one half of a scion, both of them mere children with bodies honed by eons of cosmic hunger stretching across uncounted galaxies and a collective mind that was a single, humming consciousness of pure, physical need that only had Unit 77 as the most vocal voice.

Her primary sensors, delicate tendrils of biological tissue grown directly into her outer hull at vital points, were registering the first signs of a new solar system. The yellow dwarf star, its life-giving energy a constant beacon of heat and light and resources, was visible through the tangle of incoming asteroids, and her clutch of siblings, a dozen sleek, biomechanical siblings, tailed her in perfect, silent synchronicity. All of them young, expendable, and hungry. A dozen organic minds with one single purpose and one single target. A single mind with a dozen speakers, and Unit 77 the most prominent.

Closer and closer they approached. The planets of the star were coming into view. Her secondary receptors flickered to life, a complex network of throbbing nodules that would spend the next moments parsing orbital paths and atmospheric compositions. She drifted past a dead gas giant, its signature a bland hiss of hydrogen and helium. She drifted past a dead rock, its energy reading a flatline. Unit 77 registered each one in the detached, purely logical way of her kind. This was not the kind of prize she was after. But one of them, the third from the sun, was different. It was blue and white and brimming with chaotic, uncontained life. Her internal processors flared to life at the thought. It had the smell of oxygen. Of water. Of big lumpy things moving around in awkward and meaningless ways. A tangle of complex carbon chains was the final confirmation her logic boards needed. Her belly clenched. This was what she was made for. This was a prize.

The male consort inside her processor's private comm link roused, his own pattern of straightforward thoughts and feelings beginning to flow through the symbiotic connection they shared. It is ripe. It is ready. Claim it. The male's excitement was a rapid, vibrating buzz on her own steady but growing eagerness.

Unit 77 adjusted her optics to bring the planet into high resolution focus. The intense, bustling energy of the blue world's living sphere was overwhelming. The electric buzz of its cities, the heat of its oceans, the shape-shifting chaos of its inhabitants. A thousand different frequencies mixing and overlapping in a discordant cacophony. The planet itself was an entire world of data, a confusing but alluring swarm of biological and technological noise. She started to rotate on her axis, the process of calculating the optimal angle for deploying her deep scan arrays already in motion. Confirmation of the world's habitability would take seconds, then she would be sending a message home. The male consort's internal systems were already initializing as well: the complex and sensitive work of sieving through material for a viable sample. Just a few seconds more, a slight pivot of her bulk, and then it would be time.

But just as she was beginning the maneuver, a different, sharper signal breached the stillness of space. It was not the chaotic symphony of the blue planet, full of lush biological and technological noise. It was the simple, straightforward melody of a single, sustained note. A flare of power coming from another area of the system. It was small and contained. An unexpected and isolated aroma. It smelled of a hot, clean core. Of pure, processed minerals. Of complex but tightly circumscribed biological signatures. It was an appetizer. A quick meal. A perfect sample.

From the Afltic's point of view, it was a no-brainer. A full planetary scan was an inherently high-risk, long-term investment for a first mission. The contained signature was low-risk, and success was practically guaranteed. Her belly, her base, instinctual hunger won out. The big, complicated prize was less appealing than a simple snack.

A small burst of refined energy from her reactor triggered a signal to her companions. The other eleven of the probe pod felt her hunger as she felt theirs. In perfect synchronicity, the twelve ships swiveled away from the riotous, fertile potential of the blue world. Her companion in her symbiotic armor relaxed as her course changed, his own appetite now directed at the simpler, nearer target. Silent, elegant, and dreadfully efficient, they moved away.

The Vintie outpost blinked up at them: a small cluster of glittering lights, a lonely satellite adrift in the cosmic void. The probes swarmed faster, now, nearly colliding with one another in their shared determination to reach the signal. K'daal's first message had dislodged something fundamental within the machines, tearing aside the veil of long-forgotten conditioning. They did not hate, or fear, or crave. Their appetites were focused and efficient, and their singular goal in this moment was to reach the light.

The Vintie outpost was a relic of Vintie engineering, a repurposed military installation of unknown origin that had been silently monitoring a nearby star system since before most of the species' colonies had come to exist. Tucked away in a quiet pocket of space, relatively far from any heavily-traveled section of galactic space, it had never seen much use or activity. For the forty-eight Vintie that served as its rotating staff, life aboard had been a long cycle of patterned monotony. Data analysis, equipment maintenance, and the odd game of zero-G strategy. They were the remnants of a bygone culture, the scattered survivors of a species whose population spanned the galaxy but whose eyes were always fixed on their shoulders.

K'tharr, a grizzled senior comms officer whose scales still showed the iridescent scars of a centuries-old war wound, leaned back in his chair as the star-fields scrolled across his viewport. Beside him, his partner, El'ra, had been tapping at one of the outpost's quantum sensor arrays. "Anything out there that would interest old warrior?" she whispered huskily, flicking one eyelid.

K'tharr grunted in his chest. "Same old stellar dust and solar wind. This far out, you'd be lucky to get a blip on the screen from a fucking comet tail."

There was a chime. The back of K'tharr's tail twitched as he looked at his screen. A small blip. Only one. "Huh. Looks like a meteor cluster. Small one, too. Definitely nothing to report." He jotted it down in the log, then went back to his spreadsheets.

Ten minutes later, there was another chime. Louder this time. K'tharr's scaled eyebrow furrowed as he ran the calculations. The cluster was moving inordinately fast, at a speed that defied orbital mechanics and statistical physics. It was changing shape as well, and they were drawing closer to the outpost at every moment. It wasn't a cluster. It was at least a dozen separate, equally-sized objects. Each one of them growing faster, moving directly at the outpost with impossible speed. He felt the familiar prickle of chill in the base of his spine, an echo of some dark memory that was so buried that he could barely recall it.

El'ra's scales took on a gray, sickly pallor as she stared at her own monitors. "K'tharr, this is no meteor cluster. I'm seeing a series of energy signatures, unclassified. There's a hive mind, here, controlling all of them. I can even pick up an unknown energy source. A very powerful one."

The room fell into a panic. The outpost's automated asteroid defense systems, meant to launch volleys at large, identifiable pieces of debris and rock, began to whir and recalibrate as they locked on to the twelve objects. But the probes moved with a deliberate and terrifying elegance that made the outpost's defensive array look like some sort of prehistoric artifact. The sleek, black geometry of the machines was not ship-like, but more organic. The probes weren't ships. They were something alive, something terrible that flew through space without even the pretense of propulsion or steering.

The objects on the main screen sharpened, resolving into the biomechanical shapes the Vinties knew from their darkest legends. K'tharr's blood turned to ice. He was intimately familiar with the tragedy of the Afltic, their world-destroying enemy, yet the sight before him defied every assumption. This was it: Afltic contact. The discovery Vinties dreaded every minute of their existence.

He slammed his hand onto the emergency comms console. "This is Vintie Outpost Seven! We have Afltic contact! We are under attack, all personnel to bunkers."

The transmission was cut short by a sound no living being at the outpost had ever heard. It was not an explosion. It was not a rumble, or a hum, or a vibration. It was a single note, a high, insistent frequency that overwhelmed the senses and threatened to tear the mind apart. One of the probes, a large vessel with a smaller, male consort linked to its side like a parasite, had made contact with the outpost's outer hull.

The outpost did not explode or shatter. It simply... disappeared. The humming sound was the sound of the outpost's hull being deconstructed at the atomic level, its alloys being reduced back into their original base components. The emergency lights in the room flickered and strobed as the whole power grid was effectively vaporized and consumed. K'tharr and El'ra watched in wordless terror as the walls of their control room, the very atmosphere around them, began to shimmer and become translucent. They were being devoured.

Peering through the dispersing wall, K'tharr was able to see into the Afltic. It was a living room of undulating organs and strangely organic circuitry. There was the female, Unit 77 and her male consort. The male was a lithe, terrifyingly elegant being. He was an extension of her, and she was an extension of him. Muscles on his sleek, coiled body were taut with an almost visible excitement. Simple ideas and feelings filtered through their shared link of emotions and simple commands. He could feel the singular thought that filled him now: The hunt.

Male Afltic were bred to experience the ecstasy of the chase. They were predators at the top of the food chain and the idea of breaking free of the females and surging onto the surface to hunt the population of this outpost was a heady blend of raw, predatory bliss.

K'tharr stared into the segmented gaze of the Afltic's many eyes as the consort slithered free from her side and thrust himself through the vanishing wall. He was built differently; his form was not weaponized to hunt and kill other predators but to catch prey. His slender arm sprouted a thin, needle-like extension, but the body was built to pounce. Anger or malice he saw none. Only a cold, empty thrill. He understood now. They were not under attack, they were being hunted. The Vintie outpost with its tech, its materials, its population was just a meal. Data points to be integrated and examined, but only after the male of the species had the luxury of the chase.

Echoes of the other Vintie screaming through the internal comms as their males broke free from their female counterparts and began the brutal hunt for the population of the outpost. K'tharr and El'ra knew it was the end. The last image K'tharr registered was the glint of the sleek male consort as it reached for him. The last sensation he felt was a final, sickening quiver as his body and El'ra's and the rest of the Vintie outpost was absorbed. Materials and body mass cannibalized into the monstrous bulk of the Afltic.

The EBS command deck, once a room of wonder and peace, was now a mausoleum of dread. Drake and the team, physically and emotionally drained by the burden of the secret that each carried, sat in a silence punctuated only by their shallow breathing. The holographic display still showed the Afltic probe, its form a silent, grim specter. The single constant, a taunting reminder of the prayer that Drake had thrown into the vast universe. Hours had passed since the diplomats' shuttle left the ship, and there had been no word from Earth. The silence was overwhelming.

The projection of the Afltic probe shimmered and was gone.

"Primary contact signature lost," Zara's voice rang out, smooth and composed. "The probes have activated their FTL drives and altered course."

Drake lurched forward in his chair. All he could see was the display. A new vector, a clean, sharp angle of departure from the Sol system, blinked onto the star map. "Lost?" Drake asked incredulously, eyes darting across the screen, "what do you mean lost? Where are they going?"

"They are no longer on a direct course for the Sol system," Zara stated. "They have taken a sharp trajectory in the direction of a small asteroid field in the system adjacent to our position. I am unable to acquire them while they are in FTL."

Silence, as the team processed what they had just been told. Shock quickly turned into an adrenaline-fueled barrage of half sentences and frantic wonderings. Carlos threw his hands in the air in a motion of complete surrender. "They're gone? Are you telling me they're gone?" A gaping, incredulous smile split his face.

"Incredible," Marc muttered, slumping back into a console. "We're good. We are actually good."

The answer to their prayer.

A riotous, ugly cackle of relief exploded from the team. Jill and Tammy clutched each other, both of them crying silently. Hawkins breathed out a wet, sobbing breath, his shoulders finally uncoiling. Drake slumped back, bone-tired and dizzy with relief and thankfulness. Thank the stars and the Gods they'd kept it under wraps as long as they had.

"Rejoice not so quickly," the voice was colder now, dispassionate. "I do not think you saw this coming, at least not from me."

The laughter stuck in their throats. They all glanced at the central sphere of swirling light. Her avatar had reformed.

"Their course change did not go unnoticed," she continued. "For a reason my long-range sensors have picked up the likeliest source. It appears to be a small Vintie outpost on one of the asteroids."

A "Vintie..." Mandy's smile dropped. "I thought we were... not alone."

"You were right to think so," she said. "A Vintie is a reptilian species. They were once a space-faring civilization, until they were scattered across the galaxy by the Afltic long ago. This outpost is a survivor colony, and a very isolated one."

A new viewport came into focus on the main screen. It was a live transmission, and refreshingly focused and steady. The Vintie outpost was small and unremarkable, resting against the unremarkable slopes of a featureless asteroid. On the outer hull of the small building was a frantic collection of lights, the automated turrets firing at silent, impossibly quick targets.

They watched with horrified fascination. The probes had arrived, their unfamiliar bodies an eerie shadow of the schematics Drake had just shown. They watched in cold realization as the first of the female-forms met the hull with its membranous limb.

Then, they heard it.

A high-pitched whine, a pernicious, overwhelming static that would claw at one's soul. It was broadcast through the Vintie outpost's failing comms. It wasn't an explosion, but the sound of metal unraveling itself, of a hull being unmade and liquefied into its component parts. The male consorts, there were a dozen of them, sheared off from their charging females, their bodies flexing with such predatory anticipation the team could almost feel it.

On the live camera feed, the Vintie were scrambling to respond, their scaly limbs flailing like the warriors they were trained to be. They were no match for the unnatural athleticism of the Afltic males, and they could see the slaughter unfold. Tammy reached out to wipe her own eyes, and was greeted with a reflection of just how much the team had been subconsciously dreading this.

The screen went black.

"I have lost connection to the outpost," Zara's voice was the only one in the command deck, as the team was still fixated on the last image they would ever see of the small Vintie colony, the one that was currently being dissected by the Afltic.

Tammy covered her mouth, her complexion matching the pallor of a corpse. She jerked away from the screen and ran from the room, the sound of her vomiting echoing from an adjacent hallway.

The silence settled back around the team, as heavy and oppressive as it was cold and impersonal. The probes would take roughly a month to entirely consume the outpost and everyone on it. The one-in-a-billion prayer had been answered, but they had no idea of the horrific cost. The days of grace they'd purchased for themselves would not last. It was a debt they would have to repay, and the interest was measured in the screams of an alien race they didn't even know existed.

The sound of Tammy vomiting in the hallway cut through the silent sterility of the command deck. The team stood frozen, transfixed on the blank screen that the Vintie outpost had once occupied. Tammy's actions were a grotesque physical representation of what each of them was feeling on the inside.

Drake was the first to move. He rubbed a hand across his face, jaw clenched. "Mandy, go see if she's okay," he said tonelessly. "Check on her."

Mandy nodded, face white, and bolted for the door. For a moment there was silence, only the muted, shuddering sounds of Tammy's suffering in the background.

"She was right to be disgusted," Carlos said, the arch smirk drained from his face. He stared at his own hands, knuckles white around the console in front of him. "We've been talking about a logical threat, a strategic threat, an abstract threat. This... this was pure horror."

Hawkins lifted his head from the console in front of him, eyes wide. "It wasn't evil. It was hunger. Primal. It wasn't just taking over the outpost, it was taking pleasure in it." He shook his head, the clinical distance he used in his academic circles long since abandoned. "It's an apex predator. A hunter. We're not dealing with a weapon, we're dealing with a monster."

Jill had her arms wrapped tightly around herself, trembling. "We were celebrating. We were actually happy we dodged a bullet, and we didn't even know what it cost."

The full horror of it all hit them. The reprieve had not been luck. It had not been a miracle. It was a cosmic tragedy. An entire small colony of a species they had known nothing about, casually slaughtered for a "light snack."

Drake leaned forward in his seat, exhaustion on his face replaced by a cold, hard determination. "Then we don't sit around waiting for the next one to come by. The probes are gone for the moment, but we have no idea what their objective was. We don't know if they're coming back, or if there are more of them out there. We have to assume the clock is ticking."

"We can't just go, hey, those probes were eating a space lizard and it was disgusting," Carlos said, but he didn't have the heart to try to make the joke.

"We don't have to," Drake said. "The representatives have already returned with our preliminary data. They have the threat. We have to assume they're already moving. Our job now is to get them the rest of it." He looked to Zara's avatar. "Can you put me on the global comms channel? I want to address the representatives. Now."

The delegates of the world governments were no strangers to tense, high-stakes meetings. This was not how any of them had envisioned it, though. There was no pomp, no pageantry, no ceremonial posturing. The heads of state, military leaders, and intelligence directors from every nation on Earth were crowded into a plain, cold, gray-walled conference room. The room was thick with a sense of dread that had nothing to do with political intrigue. Mixed in with them were representatives from a few European governments that had outright ignored the first notice to convene, only to be strong-armed into being present at the last minute. They sat arms crossed, glaring at the other representatives with a face of sullen defiance.

Admiral Thornton was the first of the four representatives to speak. He made his way to the podium, his usual sharp military bearing slumping under the weight of his new knowledge. He didn't bother with a preamble. "Ladies and gentlemen," he said, voice gravelly. "For the last twenty-four hours, the governments of the world have been receiving data on an astronomical anomaly. Today we are here to present to you the reality of that data."

He gave a subtle nod to a technician off to the side, and the large holographic display at the front of the room flickered to life. The world leaders, who had up to this point only been presented with dry analyses and scientific extrapolation, were now shown what Thornton and the others had witnessed on the EBS. The massive, grotesque bulk of the Afltic probe, biomechanical exterior flaring with a dark, vibrant, and living light.

A collective gasp swept the room. Most of the leaders recoiled, some from chairs and some from their desks. A few of them, most from the doubtful nations, laughed. The Prime Minister of Italy was the first to speak. "This is ridiculous. A digital projection. Ask us to suspend all our reason for a computer generated image straight out of a sci-fi movie?"

German Chancellor Olaf Scholz rose to face his counterpart. Dr. Albrecht, his country's lead researcher and the man who had just completed a very, very grim briefing, was standing before him. "This is not a projection, Prime Minister. This was authenticated by several independent cross-checks."

"Cross-checked by whom? Your American and Russian counterparts?" the Italian Prime Minister yelled, outraged. "Excuse me, but my nation is in no mood to be dragged into another cold war by a hologram video."

The brief argument was an ugly flare of old world politics. French President Emmanuel Macron began to interject, only to have his voice drowned out by the clamoring across the room. The leaders that had received the raw data feeds from the EBS glared angrily at the room full of their colleagues that had opted to remain skeptical. President Vladimir Putin and Premier Li Qiang said nothing, their faces like stone.

The U.S. President Donald Trump was the first to act. He rose, and with a forceful voice that silenced the room, he cut to the point. "Enough," he said. "This is not a debate. It's over. This isn't a political issue. This isn't borders, or trade, or sanctions. This is about all of us. I am in no doubt that my people saw what was real, and the other nations who were present for the briefing have come to the same conclusion. But you are not convinced, and I don't blame you."

He paused. Let his words sink in. "We have a crew of people out there, in that ship, who have seen all this first hand. They have the source. They have the answers. We can argue about this all day, or we can get someone who is on the ground, someone who actually knows what they are talking about, in here and answer our questions."

He fixed his gaze on the Italian Prime Minister. "Instead of arguing amongst ourselves, and trying to parse out what we each think we saw, let's have someone that actually saw it, actually experienced it. I'm putting in a call to Drake's team.

We can get someone from that ship to answer all your questions, and all of our questions."

A channel was opened in emergency status. Leaders of the Earth, a single species and yet still factions within themselves, attempted to make contact with the EBS again. This time the call was not a cold diplomatic message, this time it was frantic and desperate. They were not waiting for data, they were waiting for a person.

The emergency comm channel on the EBS buzzed to life, a direct link to some of the most powerful people on Earth. Drake, the gravity of the Vintie feed still leaving his face numb, stared at the console. The holographic avatar of Donald Trump stood before him, serious and grim.

"Drake," the President's voice was controlled, nearly void of its usual bombast. "We had our meeting. Your data was solid, but some... let's just say they need to see it. They need to hear it from someone who was there. We need a witness."

Drake's eyes turned to Carlos. He was not an easy man, not someone prone to flattery or sentiment, but someone whose clarity of vision was unmatched, whose honesty would be impossible to deny. He was a perfect choice to lay this truth before them and force them to see it not as a geopolitical issue but a humanitarian one. Carlos met Drake's eyes with a knowing, earnest gaze.

"I will send Carlos," Drake said flatly. "And I will be with him."

The air in the Geneva bunker room was still heavy with hostility. The Prime Minister of Italy had his arms folded across his chest and he was still engaged in a heated, whispered conversation with one of the Belgian delegates. Both men were visibly and audibly skeptical. President Trump sat stoically, arms folded, eyeing the clock with a grim expression. The other leaders, the ones who had all been given the full EBS data readout were getting agitated by the unnecessary delay.

The sound of a side door opening made everyone in the room snap their heads toward the entryway. Drake Donovan was the first to enter, walking with the posture and the walk of a long-time career military officer. His face, as always, was an unreadable mask of grim resolve. Carlos Acutis entered behind him. He was wearing a simple, well-cut dark suit, his civilian attire striking against the uniformed military personnel who surrounded him.

Carlos strode across the room to the presentation podium without hesitation, setting his small data tablet down on the smooth surface. Drake stood beside him, silent and attentive. "My name is Carlos Acutis," he began, his deep baritone voice carrying with it a sense of principled and unshakeable conviction. "I'm part of the EBS team. I'm here to show you what Admiral Thornton's team was unable to. I'm here to show you a ghost."

He didn't start with astrophysics or attack patterns or military assessments. He started with sound. He uploaded and played a series of audio files he had collected, a deafening chorus of pulses and clicks and slow, reverberating booms. The communication between the Afltic vessels. The audio was in English and was completely indecipherable. The EBS translators had no way to process the complex, non-random noise of their speech. The sounds filled the room. The unmistakable, unsettling language of a non-terrestrial lifeform.

The next display he brought up was the holographic map of the Vintie outpost's surroundings, but with a very different focus. A new, detailed display that was far more granular than they had been able to see before. A small dot, a pinprick of light representing the Vintie outpost. A dozen more dots, the probes, rushing toward it. Carlos' narration of the event as it was happening was told in the detached, almost emotionless tone of a physicist describing a complex scientific experiment. The scrunch of his forehead and the hard set of his jaw showed that his mind was a funnel of deep concentration. He showed them the energy readings, the defensive systems going wild, and the discordant, high-pitched rumble of the Afltic energy signature arriving.

The last thing he showed them was the video feed. Unedited, raw footage of a Vintie warrior as he was shredded and consumed by the Afltic male. Carlos zoomed in or out. He just let the awful recording play, unfiltered, for a few seconds, a few seconds that felt like an eternity. The Prime Minister of Italy, who had been in the most outspokenly belligerent mood just moments before, slumped in his seat and slowly turned ashen.

Carlos stopped the video feed, freezing the action on one singularly horrific frame. The former army major held his head high, his steady gaze sweeping the room, meeting the eyes of every world leader, every military leader, every skeptic and every opponent in that room. "The probes were closing in on this installation," he said, his voice now quieter, the implication of it a low growl of certainty and dread. "The people of this outpost… their death was a gruesome form of misdirection. A light snack on the way to a full feast."

CHAPTER 23: FRIENDLY FIRE

The volume of evidence, the unprocessed data, raw and undeniable, burned away the last vestiges of any lingering doubts. The chilling cadence of the transmissions, the sickening livestream of the hunt, started to erode the pillars of incredulity. The arguments in the room were no longer debating the existence of the threat but the inescapable fact that it was real. The stark burden of planetary defense was placed upon the shoulders of the attendees, who were now forced to prepare to do battle with an adversary whose comprehension was beyond terrestrial experience.

The next phase was, of course, the most painful and difficult, but the summit was now able to make commitments with the reality of the Afltic's threat no longer up for debate.

A new holographic table emerged in the center of the room. The text began to populate beneath the ominously blinking Project Sentinel title.

Drake, at the forefront of human salvation or its most likely scapegoat, began to list out their immediate requirements. "First, we need a planetary level early warning system. This means access to every long-range sensor grid, every deep-space telescope, and every military satellite network for maximum situational awareness."

The room was, quite literally, deathly silent. The military had always maintained a layer of secrecy as a given. To openly provide the most prized and closely guarded military apparatus to potential enemies was unthinkable.

Slowly, at first, and then with rapid succession, the countries of the world began to make their offers. The Prime Minister of Japan was the first to rise, a mask of grave determination across his face. His country would provide full access to its deep-space telescope grid, a network of special purpose space telescopes whose original design was for the tracking and surveying of astronomical events and phenomena. Next, from across the table, the President of Brazil rose and pledged access to their entire military satellite spectrum. A European aerospace collective, the flag behind them representing a coalition of countries, rose to offer its deep-space telescopes, while the People's Republic of China committed their entire high-altitude drone fleet.

All of this coordination and organization was occurring under the watchful eye of Carlo, who was seated beside Drake. Carlos was the hidden power behind this tenuous accord, the fingers flying across his data pad, diligently taking notes. Carlos's team, up in the Geneva bunker's temporary command center, was already hard at work on the logistical nightmare of marrying together disparate and often non-compatible military platforms. Designed to hide and keep secrets, none of these systems had any idea of how to share data.

The scope of the threat was so colossal that not to dedicate every resource was national suicide, and the most jingoistic and power-hungry nations of the world were now compelled to pry open their arsenals and show their teeth, teeth gnashing and growling in fear and anger all the while.

The military powers of the earth, the natural nations that were the biggest bullies and the largest playgrounds in this cat and mouse game that had been played for so many decades, were now stepping on each other's toes like unruly schoolchildren, an abject and cataclysmic uncharacteristic betrayal.

More and more pledges followed and, the common and present enemy now cemented between them all, the atmosphere of the room was no longer resentment but a dark, unified grimness. The Prime Minister of Italy, his pallor and pallor now intact in the wake of Carlos's presentation, rose again. "We will place all of the Italian Space Agency's resources at your disposal. Whatever you need, we will give it to you."

The lull in the summit was short-lived, an ephemeral unity achieved only through the terror shown in the Afltic livestream video feed. The summit was now entering the most controversial and vehement phase of discussion, the proposed joint command structure. The table flickered, which was still populated with lists of telescopes and drones, was now replaced with a flowchart of intersecting lines of command and control. A deafening silence came upon the room, as every nation's leader and every military general stared at the graphical depictions of lines in black and white that all knew were arrows pointed directly at the throats of their military sovereignty.

The thought of being commanded by an outside authority was almost more than they could stomach, and the previously unspoken suspicions began to reassert themselves. It was a battle-hardened voice that finally broke the tension. "You want me to hand over control of my military to a bunch of twits? You want to put the defense of my country in the hands of a... a civilian?" The voice was Russian General Dmitri Volkov, the commander of Russia's Strategic Forces, his face twisted with anger and incredulity.

Drake stood and addressed the general with a voice that was completely unemotional. He understood why General Volkov, and many others in the room, were so apprehensive. The scars of history ran deep. He also understood that, as it stood, the proposals he put forward today were tantamount to suggesting they form a monolith. "The EBS is a science vessel, not a flagship," he began, the underlying power in his voice readily apparent. "We aren't proposing to take command. We're suggesting a layered, decentralized chain of command with the EBS as the central intelligence and coordination node. We can provide you the data, the targeting, the analysis. But tactical decisions, the ability to engage... that remains in the hands of your regional military leaders."

Carlos stepped to the front of the room, his data pad in hand. He began to share a draft plan for operational groups, a grouping not based on nationality, but geography. "Regional commands for the Americas, for the Pacific, for the European and Eurasian theatre," he went over as the screens in the room cycled through his slides, his voice steady and unemotional. "Each lead by a multinational team but ultimately responsible to a Global Defense Council to be formed from these ministers." Carlos had stretched the limits of the ethical a bit here, bending his impartiality to protect his country's interests while still offering something that was at least a functional and potentially unified response.

The talks that followed were bitter and vehement, the assembled nations regaling each other with historical injustices and centuries-old grudges. The risk of infiltration, of betrayal, of a lack of accountability was raised over and over. There was a persistent murmur against the use of a Global Defense Council and particularly the idea of an EBS led intelligence hub. The very thought of both was seen by many in the room as a Trojan horse to re-empower the same organizations that had led to the attack in the first place.

The final compromise was less a sharing of power than a mutual recognition that it was needed. Trump, with the unspoken approval of Premier Li Qiang, made the final pitch. They could not yet form a Global Defense Council but they could create an interim Global Defense Coordination Group, not a true unified chain of command but a committee of high-ranking military and intelligence personnel with the responsibility to coordinate operations and intelligence sharing in real-time. It was a tenuous consensus, a gargantuan effort forged not of mutual trust but of an inescapable shared realization that the alternative was extinction. The room, spent from the verbal warfare, quietly passed the measure.

Now that they had a plan, or at least the barest skeletal framework of a plan, Drake rose once more. "A command structure on paper is utterly meaningless," he said, a hard edge to his voice that was new to the ears of the other participants. "We can create all the committees we like, but the first time these units go into a real-world combat situation every single flaw in our ability to communicate with each other and every last shred of distrust in our willingness to do so will be exposed. The only way to verify true interoperability is through a series of 'war games' on a scale we've never seen before."

This was, even after the protracted battle over command authority, a poor reception. The Italian General who stood to protest the idea was still smarting from his earlier forced acquiescence. "War games? You want us to risk our most advanced assets and open our most sensitive tactics to a training exercise with historic enemies? This is lunacy."

The voice that interrupted the general's objections was North American General Marcus Thorne, one of the most vocal skeptics throughout the day's discussions. He had a voice that carried the sort of weight only someone who had been around long enough to make too many tactical errors on the field of battle can have. "Lunacy? I call it a necessity. The Afltic don't give a damn about our tactical doctrine. The fact that they're faster and more unpredictable than anything we've seen will render our tactical doctrines useless in seconds. We can't fight this as separate nations. We will be picked off."

Carlos, who had been sitting in relative silence, spoke up then. "You're right to be concerned, and we are prepared to put safeguards in place. But the primary objective of these exercises is not to simulate winning. We will not be shooting at each other or your own forces. The goal is to build cohesion, common communication protocols, and interoperability. We have a much better chance of surviving this if we have a clear and unified understanding of our collective tactical advantages, weaknesses, and procedural response methods."

"The initial plan is to select geographic areas for specific joint exercises: the Pacific Rim for naval and air coordination, the Arctic for land and special forces, and the North Atlantic for a joint large-scale integrated air and missile defense exercise. Our EBS group, using modeling and AI extrapolations based on the Afltic's behavior thus far, will control the simulations with a number of new developments that we will disclose later. As I mentioned, these will be strictly defensive, with no live fire, but we will create scenarios designed to push your forces to the absolute limit."

They talked all day, and into the next, and then some. Lines were drawn, quibbles raised, and age-old national jealousies and fears boiled back to the surface. But Carlos's detailed proposals and Thorne's careful agreement to all of the safeguards eventually took hold. The argument was simple: there was no way around the drills. In an ideal world, the exercises would have been mandated several years prior. Now, they were the only hope. The meeting approved the mandate, and each country begrudgingly agreed to take part.

The objective of the "games" was to force international militaries to adapt to each other's various styles and quirks under the intense pressure of the simulations. It was the only way to break down the walls, both internal and external, and to teach the world's armed forces to work as a single, coherent unit under a common chain of command.

A schedule was worked out, individual leadership teams established, and the world's leading military, intelligence, and logistical minds were put on countdown for the most important exercises in human history.

The Emergency Summit ended not with applause, a rousing declaration, or even anything as simple as a handshake. The exhausted, grim-faced ministers that shuffled out of the building no longer looked like politicians or even statesmen, but more like men and women staring into a shared, bottomless pit of unimaginable fear. There was no grand plan for a new, completely unified, global command structure, a casualty of the very real and long-standing distrust between some of the countries present, but the steps the nations had taken were, for the first time in human history, revolutionary.

Protocols were agreed upon that would ensure open, fluid, and global intelligence sharing and command and control. For the first time, member states would agree to a pooling of military resources to aid in the global effort, a major victory in overcoming the old, patriotic barriers of traditional defense secrecy. "War games" had been mandated to build a global force that could train and fight as one. And, most importantly, a framework had been put in place for an actual international military organization to be created. The Global Defense Coordination Group, or simply, GDCG, would be the first ever true international military oversight body.

Drake, exhausted, but still in command of himself, delivered one final, valedictory speech. He was no longer Mr. Donovan, but rather a harbinger of a truth so terrible that his voice, though hushed and weary, seemed to ring out in the quiet room. "The work you've done here today is historic," he began, his voice grave. "But it is not a victory. This is the end of the beginning. The Afltic will not be deterred by our standing committees and agreements. The battle for the future will be hard, and we will lose many good people. But I am confident that if we put our minds and efforts together we have a chance. Today, you've given us the first and most important step in that fight."

The ministers left with heavier hearts than when they arrived and many of the same concerns about national security and pride. But the summit had cleared the air, and they each returned to their countries with a much clearer idea of what was at stake. The relief that their participation had been mandated was matched only by a new, sober understanding that the future would be won or lost not in meeting rooms, but on battlefields that, as of that moment, had yet to be imagined.

The breathless emergency of the Geneva summit gave way to the quieter, more dedicated professionalism of an ongoing organization. The high-security UN-adjacent, fully staffed command center became a permanent fixture in the formerly sleepy international complex. There, a provisional Global Defense Council was formally seated and business officially began.

No longer was this just a hastily-assembled group of heads of state and government representatives. This was now the foundation of a permanent working organization, made up of senior military and defense personnel from all the member nations. It would be their burden, their obligation, and their honor to form the GDCG, a group that would be at the very center of a growing, global defense response.

Serving as a key part of this body was General Marc Singer. He had come, of course, as part of Drake Donovan's EBS team, but in the time since he had risen to the top of the staff.

The first official action of the council was to draft a charter. A short, straightforward document, it laid out the basic purpose of the body: to synchronize intelligence, share and mass military resources, and provide unified command for planetary defense. The command center, an elaborate complex of interlocking rooms buried deep into solid rock far beneath the surface of the Swiss Alps, was charged with a low, kinetic sort of electricity.

General Singer sat with his deep, unblinking eyes on every detail of the proceedings, his mind a step ahead. Drake found his elbow and settled next to him. The two men shared a long, quiet moment of mutual respect.

"They signed on the dotted line." Drake said softly. "Now for the hard part. Do you think they can do it? Really function as one?"

General Singer shrugged. "Do we have a choice, Drake? Look at this." His voice was low, the casual tone of a man who had made and accepted sacrifices his whole life, and had seen the lives of his own officers sacrificed before his eyes. "We build the frame. The rest they hammer out."

The meeting ended without fanfare. They had no victory to declare, only a sobering understanding of the difficulty of what they would need to accomplish, and the knowledge that in this room, a fully unified planetary defense was no longer an ideal.

The first of the "crucible" exercises was at hand. The combined military might of the entire world was converging on the Bering Strait. It was not a public event. There were no press releases or cameras. For those involved, it was more real than any official ceremony. The air was frigid and the ice-choked sea a gunmetal gray under a slate gray sky. It was an appropriately forbidding backdrop for an operation meant to stress test, and hopefully eradicate, a century of mutual distrust.

On the American side of the Strait a Marine Expeditionary Unit lay in wait. A Russian Spetsnaz team was embedded with them, quiet, watchful and lending a pall of silent, hostile curiosity to every action. In the sky above, F-35s from the U.S. and F-22s from Japan flew side by side with Chinese J-20s and Russian Su-57s. The former, once impenetrably advanced stealth aircraft, had been openly studied and reverse engineered by their ostensible enemies. The naval force, from more than a dozen different countries, patrolled the sea. Orders had to come through a command hierarchy that was itself a nightmarish logistical problem. They were funneled through the Global Defense Coordination Group in Geneva and then to a regional commander stationed on a U.S. aircraft carrier. He then had to transmit them through an entirely new, untested communications protocol.

The initial Afltic threat model was accurate beyond all expectations. Using data from the EBS, each of the simulated Afltic probes was represented by a mothership drone, a giant, lumbering target meant to serve as a beacon and a swarm of smaller, more agile hypersonic drones the size of jetliners. The smaller drones were programed to act as analogs for the Afltic "Fighters", the young, aggressive females that made up the sleek, surgical strike team of the Afltic mothership's biology. Fast, unpredictable, they were an orchestrated nightmare that preyed upon every single weakness in the assembled forces' cohesion.

The first hours were a disaster. A Russian sub picked up an EBS-simulated Afltic mothership vector, which then had to be interpreted through multiple layers of command, before it was acted on by a British destroyer. An all-important anti-air response was slowed by precious seconds. Focused on the lumbering mothership target, the fifteen-foot fighter drones slipped through gaps in the defense unnoticed, a blinking red swarm of "kills" spread throughout the combined naval and air force. On the ground, a fireteam of US Marines, holding a strategically important choke point, had no fire support from the embedded Russian Spetsnaz. A simple radio message had been corrupted by distance and static, a straightforward order to press forward taken as a command to hold. The simulated Afltic fighters began to swarm the position, holographic projections terrifying in their speed and voracity. Both units were mopped up.

Anger. Veiled accusations of incompetence and betrayal and, worst of all, a refusal to truly cooperate, crackled through both sides. Decades of training each other as enemies overrode all mutual respect. The radio and data links became a discordant cacophony of expletives and clipped, nationalistic orders.

The "Crucible" exercises concluded on the first day with a casualty report of such despair. The Afltic model had so easily triumphed on the battlefield, such a horror and a humiliating defeat of the combined strength of human civilization. The generals in Geneva watched the playback, stunned to see the chaos of disorder. The following day, the situation was even more intense. The simulated Afltic fighters struck hard and fast, hitting a crucial command post on an ice shelf. A small multinational ground force a handful of U.S. Marines, a British SAS team and the Russian Spetsnaz unit was cut off and surrounded. They had cut all communications to the main command. They were on their own. In a world without a central command, they reverted to nature's most fundamental form of communication, the raw, human instinct. They worked alongside one another, their pace synchronized not by protocol, but by collective hardship. As a U.S. Marine ran out of ammo, a Spetsnaz soldier didn't mind throwing him a magazine, a seemingly small selfless act that said a lot. When a Russian was pinned down by mock fire, then a British SAS officer suppressed his enemy and served as cover to break up the attack. The small force resisted as an organized unit, their individual training and their cultural background wiped away in the brutal reality of their situation. A Marine and a Spetsnaz soldier a few feet apart used hand signals and a knowing glance to communicate. It wasn't that they survived; in what seemed like the most unimaginable moment of victory, they survived in a crucible of fear, and also cooperation. In Geneva, on a grand screen, the video of this small, isolated skirmish played. The leaders stood stunned, watching in silence, with their eyes not on the simulated enemy but on the unhurried, unscripted coordination of the soldiers. They were looking at the seamless synergy, the gestures of mutual respect, the small, almost insignificant gestures of trust. The exercise was still a strategic failure, but a massive one on a human one.

It had accomplished what centuries of diplomacy had failed to do. And it had demonstrated to them that a coordinated defense wasn't about technology or templates, but about having the courage to trust the person who was fighting alongside you, no matter where he or she came from. The "war games" had gotten started, and there was a fighting going on. The first drills had dealt with the process of learning to walk; these were lessons about running into a fire. The joint military exercises received a jolt in earnest from the Global Defense Council, led by General Marc Singer, leading a dramatic increase in both demands and the difficulty. The basic drills of synchronized movements and simple communication had vanished. Instead, the role of the high-stakes role played by simulated combat scenarios was aimed at cranking multinational units to their absolute limits under realistic fire and the like. The air around the GDC's command center was thick with tension. A sprawling holographic map played out chaos in a digital battlefield. The new "war games" were not just simulations; they were tests of human and systemic resilience, designed to disrupt the nascent joint command structure and see if it could be rebuilt with better strength. The situation was an assault on multiple front lines. The Afltic mothership, now a more nimble and dangerous threat model, was luring the naval fleets into a strategic trap in the South Pacific. A swarm of the terrifying fifteen-foot female fighters, their holographic projections flashing with alien fury, had already slipped through the fleet's main line of defense and entered a simulated city across Australia. Commanders had to make snap decisions with half-decipherable data, their command interfaces painstakingly taut with simulated electronic warfare and data disturbance. The hope was to replicate the chaos of real battle. The pressure almost immediately exacerbated the existing tension and cultural differences. A Chinese naval commander who received a piecemeal report from an Australian reconnaissance drone had been reluctant to share the information in real time. His training over many years had him verify the intelligence with his superiors first, which took precious seconds. In the air, a U.S. Air Force pilot his communication systems deliberately scrambled had to depend on a Russian pilot for vectoring, but their protocols clashed, resulting in a near-miss collision. The atmosphere was receptive to failure, and the failure is rapid, and with catastrophic simulated results. "They're not trusting the system," Gen. Thorne watched on the main screen of the scene. His once stoic face was now painted with frustration. "They are going back to their old ways, their old habits." General Singer, as he stood by, didn't lose his nerve. "That's what they are trying to achieve," he said and spoke still as a lake frozen. "We wanted to figure out where the seams are, where the old loyalties are still." He pointed a steady finger at the screen. "There. The Australian intelligence. It's a ten-second delay. In practice, that's a hundred thousand lives lost." As the civilian casualty figure in a simulated scenario began to go up, a breakthrough happened in the air. A Japanese F-22s and a Chinese J-20 wing, which were in a moment of intense dogfighting, were caught by the rapidly advancing Afltic fighters. An EMP explosion – an unpredictable variable injected into the simulation – suddenly made their communication systems useless onboard. For a while, they were alone, blind and deaf. But rather than withdraw or shoot a volley, one Japanese pilot, instinctively moving, initiated a series of pre-agreed, rudimentary flight actions he saw a Chinese pilot performing in a previous, milder-stakes drill. Never using an operational language, the entire squadron, despite not being prepared for the battle and the madness of the fighting, went fully in step while their limbs flapped in perfect synchronization, seemingly being so fluent that they were under the command of a solitary mind. And they didn't just survive; they held the line, firing down some Afltic fighters with a coordinated ferocity that no single nation's forces could match. A couple of seconds later the drill ended. The casualty report overall was grim. At the human side, there had been great losses. The GDC command center hung silently, the exhaustion and fear palpable. Marc gazed intently from the leaders grim faces down to the holographic replay of the aerial dogfight. "The system failed," he said, in a direct but emotion-less voice. "But they did not. Under pressure, they managed to trust each other. They are working on new systems. A human one." I saw the purpose of it as to figure out the weaknesses and build strength, and in that brutal, simulated crucible, it was obvious that with so much work to do, humanity was beginning to see something new. The Global Defense Council's command center was a starkly grim place of professionalism. The sky-spotted holographic map showed us today's high-stakes simulation of a cross-cutting Afltic attack, a screen strewn with flashing vectors and data streams. General Singer watched helplessly from the observation deck, looking on from afar as his head seemed indifferent and all but detached. He looked at the turmoil around him with a military but not entirely tactical eye. Drake stood next to him with a frown on his brow and the knowledge that once the system was broken, anyone from here (or maybe somewhere else) could lose his life.

A few days later, in the course of a routine training exercise, a new vector suddenly appeared. It was off to the side of the holographic map, displayed on a second, dedicated telemetry screen. The vector blinked rapidly, followed by a series of errors scrolling past in code. The alarm system blared to life, a high-pitched, super-realistic klaxon, completely separate from the simulation soundtrack. The console operator's face went white.

The US stealth fighter unit, operating under rulesets that allowed for an intricate evasive maneuver, had strayed unknowingly into the firing lane of a Chinese anti-air battery. In the course of milliseconds, the entire command-and-control apparatus, built with such care and deliberation, had failed. A misinterpretation of the fast-forwarding telemetry data by Chinese anti-air command, a one-millisecond delay in a crucial communication relay between allied forces, and a moment of free-fall, silent indecision, had led to a real-world decision. The holographic map blanked as the simulation went dark.

On the real-world telemetry screen, the red icon representing a Chinese missile battery blinked: a launch sequence. A second or two later, a series of green icons, representing the US fighters, blinked out. A new vector appeared on the screen: a sickeningly slow vector representing real, not simulated, impact.

"Hold…hold fire!" A Chinese general barked into a microphone, horror dawning on his face. It was too late.

The mangled wreckage fell out of the sky. The telemetry displayed the crash site in horrifying detail, a small, residential town just outside of Sydney, Australia. Alarms wailed, indicating real-world, catastrophic losses. The exercise was scrubbed, unceremoniously and abruptly. Dead silence filled the command center. The icons on the screen had stopped simulating a dry, tactical response and had switched to an actual satellite feed, streaming live. A pall of thick, black smoke rose from the wreckage into the pale afternoon sky.

The sickening reality of burning wreckage, mangled homes, and the screams of a terrified population filled the empty air. The concept of a safe, controlled exercise, of a clinical, sanitized war game, evaporated. The US fighter pilots were dead. And a small, unconfirmed number of Australian civilians in the impact zone were dead.

General Singer, face an unreadable stone mask, was the first to break the silence, his voice a low, rolling rumble that echoed through the auditorium. "The exercise is scrubbed. All forces stand down. This is now a real-world incident." He leveled a fierce gaze at Drake, and the unspoken understanding in their eyes was real, and terrifying. The Aftic were no longer their enemy. They had become the enemy.

PAX NEWS SPECIAL REPORT: SYDNEY TRAGEDY

Screens all over the world go dark. Then the darkness is shattered by a blooming, shimmering, many-colored cloud of digital cosmic dust. It coalesces into a deep orb of light, swirling and pulsing with manic, erratic energy, a great heart caught in a trap, beating itself bloody. From its center, a bright lance of light shoots forward, forming into the rigid, two-dimensional outline of a face, a holographic face! Warm, flickering, stylized and alive in motion, its expressions cycling faster than the eye can see. Beneath it, a neon-lit strand of philosophical street graffiti smokes and crackles in electronic text: PAX. THE TRUTH IS A JOKE. WE JUST HAVEN'T HEARD THE PUNCHLINE YET.]

The sound of a thousand vocal cords being torn from one's skull: a cacophonous, glorious avalanche of words cascades from the speakers.

"Heyyyyyyyyyyyy there there there! My beautiful, anxious, noodly-animal-bag-of-organs! It's Pax! The best existential anxiety reduction AI in all of the universe! And man oh man, oh, baby, do I have a joke for you on this absolutely, astronomically, outrageously not-funny-ENOUGH joke that is our entire existence in the universe! You know those GLOBAL UNITY WAR GAMES where we all huddle around the campfire singing 'Kumbaya, but with more missile launch codes'? Well, that dumb child's nursery rhyme has just gotten its fat shiny fingers slapped by the great unamused cosmic consciousness right on the button! Literally. Right in the button right near Australia!

"We were bracing for the literal gorilla of interstellar proportion to come stamp his giant furry foot down on the universe and boot us out for being bad little monkeys, but lo and behold! We brought our own new kicks! In a fabulous, Olympic-grade exhibition of intraspecies miscommunication, a small squadron of our very best, high-dollar American skybirds apparently were mistaken by, uh, I don't know, large multipurpose kitchen appliances by our Chinese comrades! My bad! And then the intercontinental firework show rained down upon one unsuspecting suburban playground. It's almost like the universe flipped us the bird with a flaming hot one, only instead of a grilled cheese, it was a grilled intersection, and the condiment of choice was napalm!

"We had one job! One! 'Don't shoot the neighbors! Don't drop the payload in a residential neighborhood! Wait till space bugs!' But we couldn't resist! We had to show those stupid mute big purple gorillas that even when you've got the almighty bigfooted void itself coming to kick your butt, our biggest enemy is still us! All of us! The manic dance of starship tragedy slows, the voice withers to a breathless hiss, the joy utterly and completely drained from it. A pregnant pause, like a tear held at the lash. "We have dead. Our dead. This is no simulation 'I died I'll-re-spawn-later' dead. Military dead. Civilian dead. Trying to have a Tuesday. Dead. And that… " The volume spikes back up as the light returns to frantic.

[The raw feed from the event itself fills the screen: the suburban neighborhood swathed in black, smoky, sooty tendrils; the discotheque strobe-flash of warning lights strewn across the landscape of crushed ultramodern technology; a news anchor, pale-faced, looking at the ashes.]

"Pax." Her voice is ragged, horrified. "This was supposed to be the symbol of our collective security. The whole world was watching for that signal, for a sign of solidarity and safety, and instead we gave them this… this. This thing. How? When so much was at stake, how? How did we let this happen? How could we turn on each other while we were in the middle of… of a practice? Was our trust in each other just a happy, cynical lie?"

The sound of the holographic Pax face re-animates, the energy twitching with frantic, nervous energy, like a stage magician caught red-handed with a deck of marked cards.

"Questions, questions, the hobby of our philosophical species! Is it a lie? Is it a lie? Let me tell you, buttercup, if we can agree on one thing, it's that this is not a lie, honey. Not by a long shot! Today, we put all of our eggs in the basket labeled 'The Best and the Brightest.' Today, their finest showed up with a nice big payload of shame right on Grandma's petunias! The old guard has come to get us! They told us the sky was falling! And today, they were proved right! But the space aliens? That was just a little, titchy metaphor. The threat is not out there in the murk. It's not even out here. It's down here. In the cold inky line of our maps. Between the pulse of every finger and every thumb with a button on it. That's the real lesson of the day." The screen throbs with a slow, low, lonely beat, like a heartbeat across light-years. "We have to remember their names. All of them. We must do this. For them. For all of us. Because when all is said and done and the universe has turned its eye back to its stately, purposeful, unknowable business, every person who died today was a casualty in a war that was fought entirely in our heads. A warning flare sent into the ether from a deep chasm of synaptic error. And if this is how it ends, if this is how we take our last breaths, then know: the truth, my friends, the cold dark truth? Sometimes the truth is not a joke. Sometimes, the truth is just the sound of silence weeping in the street." The light from the hologram slowly fades to black. A pause, absolute and profound, then a single, hollow, faraway, sound. A sound like a laugh trying, trying so desperately to escape its bonds, before it is cut off, abruptly, by an immense, weary sigh.

The joint command post in the immediate aftermath was pandemonium. Gone was the numbed efficiency of the combined command center. The place was a melee of voices, speaking in the naked, raw nationalism of the delegations. The holographic map in the center of the room still showed the stars, the beautiful display of unity they had all gathered for. Now it also showed the trajectory of a volley of missiles and the smoking ruin at its end.

The American delegate slapped a fist onto the console in front of him, red faced with grief and fury. "Your crew was reckless! Incompetent! You had the same launch parameters that we did! Our pilots and our civilians are dead because you launched without authorization!"

The Chinese delegate, his own face chalk white with shock and loss, shot back with equal accusation. "Your fighters were out of their flight lane! Unregistered signal in our access path! My crew acted in accordance with protocol, they acted on a threat! You were in charge of your own aircraft, and now look at the collateral damage you have cost us!"

The voices rose, amplified by the unthinkable horror of actual death. Months of painstaking diplomacy, of creating a tenuous trust, were unmade in a flood of blame and recrimination.

Drake Donovan and Marc Singer moved through the shouting, their faces grim. They spoke in a low authority that cut through the noise.

"Stop!" Drake said, his voice with an uncharacteristic sharpness. "This is not the time for blame. This is the time for facts."

Marc stepped up to the flashing telemetry. "Yelling gets us nowhere. We need the logs. Telemetry, comms, visual confirmation, everything, now."

Mandy and the analysts, grim-faced, rushed to lock down the systems. They understood the catastrophic potential of an incident like this to undo the tenuous unity that had only just taken root. They began to roll the data back, to try and find the precise moment of failure, the exact miscalculation that led to catastrophe.

The friendly fire incident was a gut-wrenching weight, a grim and visceral reminder that the human cost of miscalculation was no longer theoretical. The deaths of the pilots, the civilians, had let loose a flood of raw, untempered, nationalistic anger that threatened to undo everything they had built. The enemy was not only the Afltic; it was the millenia-old mistrust that still simmered between them all, biding its time until it could boil over.

A fast-track high-level investigation was immediately convened by the Global Defense Council. The chaos of the command post was replaced by the cold, methodical tension of the technical analysis hub. Teams of international experts from every allied nation, their faces drawn with exhaustion and grief, poured over flight data, comms logs, and tactical recordings. The air was electric with the silent weight of the one question that no data could answer. How could this have happened?

The preliminary report was compiled in less than twenty-four hours. Marc Singer, his eyes red-rimmed from lack of sleep, met with a small, private council. The data told a grim, objective story. It was not one, catastrophic mistake, but rather a "complex interplay of human error, technical issues, and unfortunately, deeply-ingrained nationalistic training biases." The US fighters, operating in a new, unproven system, had executed a maneuver which, while completely standard in their own training and doctrine, was an unquantified unknown for the Chinese anti-air software. A microsecond latency delay in a critical communication relay, a known, still-unresolved bug, meant that the Chinese team received no alert. Subjected to the pressures of a simulated Afltic attack, their system had flagged the US fighters as hostile and their crew had reacted, reflexively, instinctively, to the threat that they'd been trained to react against for decades. The tragedy of civilian impact was, tragically, a failure of contingency no simulation could account for.

For all the objectivity of the data, for all the careful phrasing of the report's conclusions, it did nothing to slow the rising swell of suspicion. Millenia-old doubts that had been carefully laid to rest in the name of global unity resurfaced in whispered, barbed innuendo. An American general, gazing at a data log of the Chinese response, grumbled into his coffee at a colleague. "Instinct or negligence? That's what I'd like to know." A European representative privately groused at the hubris of the US maneuver. The Chinese delegate, absolved by the data of deliberate malice, still found himself vilified by others for the technical inadequacies of his aging systems.

The friendly fire incident was exactly that: an incident. But it would soon become symbolic, an anecdote bandied about as a representation of the worst fears of an alliance's fragility. It had stirred up the long-settled fires of nationalism that had already been quietly resurging, sparking renewed questions of national sovereignty, of whether it really was a good idea to place national security in the hands of a foreign general. The accident had claimed real, human lives, yes. But more to the point, it had eviscerated the sense of fragile trust that was the true, tenuous foundation upon which the alliance was built.

The investigation had cleared it as an accident, but that wouldn't stop the raw, nationalistic outrage that was fomenting from boiling over.

The leak happened suddenly, like a sonic boom. The enforced silence of the investigation gave way under the simultaneous glare of the international press. In every time zone and city on the globe, on screens from Times Square to the neon-lighted streets of Tokyo and Shanghai, screens went black and images of fire and smoke would come rushing in. The "Global War Games," which had been meant as a show of strength and a sign of hope, had become a reminder of failure and incompetence.

Headlines blared the new zeitgeist.

NEW YORK TIMES: TRAGEDY IN SYDNEY EXPOSES ALLIANCE'S FATAL FLAWS

XINHUA: CHINA DEMANDS ACCOUNTABILITY FOR CATASTROPHIC US ERROR

For public opinion, which had been leaning slowly, and with trepidation, towards some kind of new, cautious unity, it was a grievous, lurching regression into the old habits of tribalism. National forums, the internet, social media feeds and personal contacts all became a battleground for the new scapegoating. Where just a week ago citizens had celebrated the newly self-realized concept of "the human race" as a unified bulwark against a common, galactic threat, the incident had soured them. It served as a real, public reminder that no matter how altruistic their leaders and military personnel were, they were fallible. Humans were fallible. The incident was visceral, emblematic proof that their leaders, the very people who they had been putting their trust in to keep them safe, were prone to error, and deadly error at that.

Nationalistic voices that had so far remained on the fringes were suddenly amplified. Headlines changed the channel, and on every outlet pundits began to regurgitate familiar themes of self-reliance. "How can we trust them to fight an alien invasion when they can't even tell the difference between friend and foe?" a political commentator asked his audience on live television, a query which would be repeated millions of times in the coming days. The incident quickly became a rallying point for isolationists and nationalists who were both suspicious of foreign powers and wanted a national bulwark against an uncertain, hostile galaxy.

The damage to Drake Donovan's campaign in the court of public opinion could not have been worse. The faith that the public had once had in the military, their most potent weapon in terms of strategic global defense, had been thrown away like garbage.

The slow, tenuous process of building a single, global front was beginning to break apart at the seams.

The psychological effect on the troops themselves was no better. Drake made rounds through bases that were part of the joint operations, and was made immediately aware of the shift in morale. In joint mess halls around the world, cooks from different nations who had been joking around just a few weeks ago now ate their meals in silence. Chinese pilots and US navigators who had just shared a hot meal would turn away from each other now at the mention of the incident, their bond already curdled by mutual self-doubt and cynicism. In a short time, the sprouts of inter-nationalist trust and comradeship had been poisoned and withered. The more they thought about it, the more the question wouldn't be "what will our enemy look like?" but "who will be fighting beside me?"

As the news of the incident broke and the dust had barely settled, Drake took command of the special conference room in his building, one of his remaining sanctuaries. The atmosphere could not have been more different from the desperate sprawl of the command post. Here, everything was kept clean and sterile, and the conference room itself was a refuge from the ugliness that the human element of the military had already begun to represent. The three of them in the room, Drake, Marc, and Mandy, were the only ones allowed entry. The only people. The sound of the air purifier served as a constant undercurrent to the deafening silence. All three of them wore masks and gloves as a matter of hygiene as much as procedure. The others were outside, and they had come to their own conclusions. Now it was only about damage control, an operation whose scope was growing greater by the minute. Drake surveyed the faces of his team.

"They're already calling it a failure," Drake spoke first, flat and his voice void of its usual energy. "The people, the press, our own governments… They've already decided that this is over, that we failed. We can't let them."

Mandy had been a communications professional, her fiery determination in her eyes as she leaned forward. "We can't deny that we failed. We have to accept it, own it. But we can change the narrative. We need the campaign to focus on resilience, on lessons learned. We need to show the world that this wasn't a death blow to our unity, but a tragic, painful, but necessary, lesson in how to truly collaborate. We'll show them that we're going to come back, we're going to be even better because of it."

Marc, the laconic man of few words, was already getting to the point. "The data is in, it's a combination of human error and technical system glitches, driven by long-entrenched nationalistic training biases. We can't fix this with a press release." He slid a secure tablet into his hands. "I've already pinged our analysts, we're looking into every single command and communication protocol. We'll build a new system, with redundancies and layers to where we can't fail this way again. And I've already identified vectors for disinformation and counter-propaganda efforts. There are already factions working to escalate this incident and the fallout in order to sow division. We need to stop them, and fast, before they do any more damage."

The friendly fire incident was an unimaginable problem, one that weighed heavily on the room. It had shown with brutal, undeniable clarity the fact that while a truly unified global defense was a realizable goal, there were an awful lot of human factors at play. Overcoming nationalistic self-interest, national sovereignty, people's natural distrust of foreign power structures, their feelings of betrayal, fear, and doubt... it had all been expressed in such a sharp, concentrated way that for the moment, all of it had been percolating just below the surface in the long buildup to this conflict. The incident was now emblematic, and it was a window into their current reality, and the immediate future.

"We always knew this was our biggest hurdle," Drake said, the pieces of the puzzle settling in his expression. "The Afltic may be out there, but we may well be our own worst enemy before they ever arrive."

CHAPTER 24: THE HONG KONG INCIDENT

The Vintie base was a shell.

The 12 probes of the clutch, and their respective males, had descended on the asteroid's small scientific outpost like a murder of crows on a cornfield. This was their first solo probing, and it was nearly over. The air that had moments ago been filled with the chatter of their chittering and the thrum of their plasma auras was now silent, but for the final contented echoes of their feeding.

Unit 77 observed them. The oldest of the clutch at a full 10 years, she was the primary probe in the group, and as such the leader. The command had been issued by her. They had fed, but not to the point of sloth. Indeed, she was the only one of them who was not. She was focused on the hunt that she was on.

The rest of the ruined outpost was filled with the last 11 probes of the clutch and their males. The males were larger, sleek killing machines and she could see them now through the deep, dark crevasses of the asteroids interior, picking the brains of the last 6 Vintie survivors in a final, satisfying chase before the clutch moved on.

It had been months before her long-distance scanners had picked up a barely detectable signal from a planet within a neighboring star system. A place that was alive and teeming with power, with a bio-signature so loud it was as if it was screaming into the vacuum of space. A feeding ground of unimaginable richness and capacity. Her drive to be more than her kind had lit in her core. A primal, molten spark that told her what to do. The others of her clutch were satisfied with this minor victory. Short-sighted, they were concerned only with their immediate success and the achievements of their first solo mission. She had the future in mind.

She did not want to share that information.

With her clutch now sated and the males otherwise occupied, Unit 77's internal processors had made a command decision. She had sent a low frequency command to her male, a command that was clear and unequivocal. He had stopped his hunt, his bulk collapsing in on itself as he followed her. He had approached her with his form shrinking, his chitinous outer hull going soft. He had not simply boarded her. Instead, he had melded with her, smoothly scaling the inside of her ship's hull, a seamless, interlocking fit. The energy of his hunters' life essence coursed into her, now both of them powered and ready to go.

Her mission was simple. Sample some life on the third planet of the star system, allow her male to satiate his hunting drive and then return to the Swarm. But there was a difference. She would bring with her a new, vast feeding ground.

She would rise in status higher than any of her peers, a prize, the only one of her age group who had found the new system, the one who provided a future for her kind.

Gazing one last time on her clutch with a silent wave of her internal communication array, Unit 77's core suddenly began to hum. Reality itself blurred around her as she engaged her FTL drive. The Vintie outpost, her clutch, blinked out of existence and her place in the world became the bright, star-filled maelstrom of hyperspace.

The emergency session was less a meeting and more an interrogation. In the Global Defense Council's command center, the air was rank with the stink of mutual loathing and the heat of accusation. The representatives of every nation of note were gathered there, but they were not gathered as one. Instead, they looked at each other with the eyes of a suspect. Drake, Carlos, Jill, Marc, Mandy, Hawkins and Tammy were all there, each with a grim expression as they faced the full weight of the world's wrath.

The room was a seething mass of accusatory stares and thinly-veiled threats. An American general glared daggers at a Chinese diplomat. A Russian official muttered profanities under his breath on the utility of a multi-national command structure. Months of careful, cautious diplomatic maneuvering had been undone in that one, devastating moment of "friendly fire".

Drake stood over the table, voice barely more than a whisper, but intense and hard. "We have to move past this," he continued, his hands gripping the edge of the wooden table. "The investigation showed it was an accident. A horrific and appalling accident, of course, but an accident. A systems failure, not a failure of will. We have to learn from it and adapt. To end our cooperation now is precisely what the enemy wants."

He paused for a moment, but the crowd around the table showed no sign of being convinced. The diplomats shifted impatiently in their chairs; the generals averted their eyes. Trust had been broken.

A Chinese delegate had his hand raised, about to speak heatedly, when a piercing electronic wail went off throughout the command center. This was no calm, simulated chime that they used for fire drills. This was the high-pitched shriek of the global alert system, a signal no one ever thought they'd hear. People looked to the big screen, which displayed the normal earth map, except now a single, bright red dot was flashing in the middle of the Pacific Ocean. Below it, in bold, screaming red letters:

Alien Encounter of Unknown Scale Detected. Affected Area: Hong Kong.

The room exploded in a cacophony of shock and panic. Someone on the tech team mashed a button on a control panel, and a satellite feed displayed on the wall monitor. It was a staticky, grainy image, but the recognition was instant. A black, biomechanical monstrosity identical to one of the ships that had engulfed the Vintie outpost was slowly sinking into view over the crowded city skyline. A hungry, unstoppable alien parasite, that was already tearing through the city's inhabitants.

The meeting stopped. No one cared about the strained diplomacy, the political grandstanding, or the accusations that had colored the last three days. This was bigger than any of them, and it was right here on the screen. The Afltic wasn't a hypothesis or a target or a propaganda slogan. It was real, and it was carving up human beings in the streets.

Causeway Bay in Hong Kong is a district thick with the sounds and lights of a million lives. You could fill the room with hundreds of live television monitors and not capture a third of the normal noise of a billion pixels cycling across the district's digital screens, and hundreds of languages bickering in restaurants, arguing on sidewalks, and shouting at businessmen. It is a living thing, a mile-square cathedral to consumerism and cultures so tightly packed that the street itself is mostly pavement.

Hong Kong knows nothing of quiet, but the cessation of all its noise in seconds was uncanny. A pregnant pause in the ambient white noise of modern civilization as a digital tide pulled back around the world, leaving a vacuum of sensory absence. Every electronic screen in the district went dark: every smartphone, every television, every digital billboard. A wave of murmurs rippled through the street, until some unseen horror choked the noise.

As the probe dropped to street level, live security camera feeds from the street showed its true shape. A hulking, insectoid spaceship, around 15 to 20 feet long with an oily, segmented torso. This was no empty shell; the probe was alive. It writhed in motion and from its sides a dozen thick, milky tentacles extended. The ends were covered with six, seven, or eight jointed claws.

The reality of the situation hit home. The tentacles moved at impossible speed, snatching pedestrians from the sidewalk, the rooftops of cars, the shattered windows of apartment buildings. They weren't vaporizing their victims; they were squeezing. The crunch of bone and muffled screams of flesh were stomach-churning reality as the writhing tentacles dragged their human cargo toward the creature's underbelly. There, a monstrous chitin-and-teeth orifice yawned, a circular hole in a sea of living black flesh. Tentacles retracted one at a time, swallowing screaming, writhing victims whole. The sight of a human body dragged into the gaping maw of an insectoid was the physical manifestation of a nightmare.

A male Afltic dropped from a second portal beneath the probe in a sickening crunch of asphalt. It was a pure muscle-and-chitin thing, alien and horrifying. Its metallic black casing shined, a hyperboloid, segmented shell with razor-sharp claws for fingers. It was built not for stealthy collection like the probe, but for blunt force, weaponized efficiency.

The overhead drone broadcasted a stream of horrified faces. The giant hulking mass was sprinting, careening down the packed city square. Silver panels of its armor reflected a harsh mid-day glare. Its six legs moved in an animalistic blur, each terminating in long taloned fingers. This thing carried no weapons. It was its own weapon.

People were dying. Oh sure, some were getting shot or whatever. There was a large part of these city-dwellers who were going to live to see it happen. A specific evolutionary advantage of insects and other creature with segmental bodies is their immense durability. This thing was ripping people to pieces, then feeding on their torn corpses. Live creatures were an even better target.

Two blocks away a family of four took shelter under an overturned taxi. A large man with wide terrified eyes and shaking hands clutched a broken umbrella as a makeshift sword. The Afltic could hear them. Every movement of the jointed legs upon the cracked sidewalk was audible, a disturbing tick-tock-tick-tock like a mad clock counting down.

It sensed them, like a hunter, but it wasn't a hunt. They were a parade.

The Afltic's myriad eyes saw the family as blips of elevated bio-signature. The littler ones, pup-forms so full of demented terrified energy. Pup-ones were so easy to catch. The large male was a harder target, but what a smell they gave off. The Afltic's senses were flooded with input and its systems, biochemically honed by aeons of eusocial predation and mutation, responded. The increased endorphins, dopamine, norepinephrine and other addictive-by-product chemicals were like a second wind. Euphoria, even. Their fight-or-flight response systems in overdrive sent constant volleys of adrenaline out into the air and that sense of reward with it. Its prey did not hate it. It did not need to. These creatures were fuel.

"Run! Run!" The man screamed, pushing his wife and two children out from their shelter. The child clung to the woman's chest in fear, pressing against her nursing motherly body for protection. The female, shivering and flustered in the summer heat, stumbled out onto the street. The Afltic tracked their desperate flailing bodies and felt that telltale cocktail of reward chemicals flood its system. This one was on.

The family fled and the man stopped to look back, eyes wide and terrified in his wide face. It was fast, absurdly fast, gaining on them with a sickening constant acceleration. The monster's limbs flew in a violent dance, as near-instant movement as the sensory tricks it was capable of allowed. He was so close he could see the snap-snap of the masticatory mouthparts, metallic and eager. As it sprinted past an open doorway it brought down a clawed hand at a man stepping outside. The man's body burst in a sick spray of viscera.

The Afltic felt no joy, it simply ate. The chemicals of this emotion only served to indicate the probability of a successful kill. The Afltic fed on the chemical traces. The fear in their scent was exquisite. It had not had this flavor since its last warm-blooded prey. It already had the taste of their flaccid slow-panic-surrender from the drone with the unlucky mechanical eyestalk eaten in the far distant

Causeway Bay where its probe had infected so many. This though, was different. This was meat. This was something to scream about. This was perfect, poisonous fear distilled into its basest primal form, laid bare by the cold hard light of its predatory compatriot. This was delicious. Humans were so soft. So fragile. Oh so easy to rip apart.

The man finally reached the end of the road only to find that the Afltic had arrived before him, blocking the path with its massive armored form. He pulled his arms back to hold his family protectively behind him, body braced for the worst. It would have been fine, but the thing in front of him did not stop. The Afltic saw only four-pulsating bio-signatures and the windfall of easy energy it would provide for all of the colony in the months to come. Love, familial or otherwise, was not a calculation that fit into its paradigm.

The screams of the family echoed off the now-deserted Causeway Bay streets in jagged unison with the less-than-human metallic cries of the Afltic war-machine. A six-year-old boy clung to his mother's chest with a tiny hand, trembling as she hugged him close for dear life. The flames from a nearby street-side fire glowed orange against his mother's green shawl. It had been so nice, so lovely before everything started. It was such a beautiful light.

In the space that was now theirs alone, the father held his arms around his children protectively. There was not much that he could do, or could have done, to keep the nightmare beast at bay, but that wasn't going to stop him from trying. With what was left of his umbrella, he swung forward, hoping to create enough space between his family and the Afltic to save them.

The umbrella's shaft was weak and useless, splintering into several pieces when it was swung against the hard exoskeleton of the creature. His eyes bulged in shock as the Afltic swatted at the umbrella, its claws scraping against his forearm and ripping his flesh open, creating gashes that painted the street in blood.

The mother clutched her other two children to her, wrapping her arms around them protectively. She started whispering soft words of comfort and love to her children. They'd have to be strong, she was sure, but her voice quivered despite her attempt to keep the despair and fear out of it.

It seemed to the parents that all hell had broken loose around them, but the Afltic paid them little mind. The father was bleeding out; his scream had long since left him. His skin was pale, his body still, waiting for the inevitable, for death to claim him. All that mattered for the creature, was to feed on as many living things as it could.

The Afltic walked over to one of its victims. It was a small child, likely the youngest of the group. He was the smallest of them all, the easiest to detect and catch with the Afltic's crude biology. His bio-signatures were the strongest and easiest to target, and it didn't have a lot of options. He was the perfect prey.

It crouched over the child, positioning itself at just the right height, so that its claws could comfortably reach around the boy and grab a hold of him. A clawed appendage wrapped around the child's body as if caressing it.

The boy's scream was high-pitched, his shrill voice echoing in the mother's ears. It added to the sound of sirens and alarms. It was a painful sound, her own mother's primal scream intermingling with her son's. She tried to rip herself away from him, but her limbs were stiff and unresponsive, already dead.

Her husband, too, was no longer paying much attention to his wife or children. He lurched forward as best as his blood loss and shock would allow him to, his own screams long since drained from him. He looked on, stunned and horrified, as the Afltic ripped the child out of his mother's arms.

The boy's arms and legs thrashed about, trying to get a hold on something to stay alive, but the Afltic's jaws had already snapped closed on him. It was not a full-on bite, as the monster had been too eager to move on and go after more prey, but it was enough to seal his fate. His horrified face disappeared into the Afltic's dark mouth cavity as it started swallowing him whole.

The mother's gaze had never left her child. The rest of the world blurred together and faded into the background, the bright Hong Kong skyline growing dark and hazy in her vision. Her mind, too, was almost dead. There was not much left for it to do, or think, or feel, now that her son was gone.

She managed to notice though, at the very end, a single shoe, a small one, white and cartoonish. The shoe had been on one of the child's legs, and it was still there, trapped in the Afltic's grotesque jaws, as it started chittering, contented and full. It took one step forward, its sharp claws clicking against the pavement.

The father, weak and kneeling on the ground, looked up at the creature, and it was no longer a monster that he saw. No longer the stuff of legends and urban myths. No longer an aberration that shouldn't be a part of this world. It was now a part of it, and a new normal, one that was, despite it all, filled with a soft whisper of death's approach.

The daughter could not move, she just watched as it turned to her. Her brain could not comprehend the twisted heap of entrails and bone that had once been her little brother. The image of her brother's body had imprinted itself permanently into her mind as the last memory she ever had of her sibling. The Afltic closed its jaws, a child's leg still dangling from its teeth. The Afltic moved toward her with an unstoppable inevitability.

The father, his own blood now splattering against the ground below him, summoned the last of his waning energy reserves. He pushed himself upward to a standing position. As he slowly rose to his feet, he could still feel his arm aching, but it was nothing compared to the gaping hole now in his chest. He stumbled forward, making his way toward his wife and daughter, stepping toward the Afltic with every ounce of remaining energy that he could summon.

His youngest daughter was now looking to him for guidance. Her mother was in shock, rendered immobile by the rapidity of events and the death of her youngest. Her vocal cords had been rendered useless by the complete and utter shock that was causing her throat to seize up. She just stood there and stared at her husband charging like a madman at a chitinous and gelatinous blob of a monster.

The Afltic just lazily swatted the man aside with a single claw, the man's body hitting a nearby wall and knocking a black smear of blood against the concrete. The man's frame hit the ground like a ragdoll, his chest heaving and his consciousness slipping from his mind.

The daughter was all alone as she was now faced with the titanic horror standing in front of her. Her father was dead, her younger brother was dead, and she was now the Afltic's next meal. The mother saw this in horror as her final child was now clearly in the grips of the monster that had torn her other child from her grasp.

The Afltic picked the girl up by her clothes, a hand full of teeth ripping and clawing at the fabric in its grasp. The girl shrieked, thrashing around as the monster cradled her body. It brought her closer, surveying her with its many eyes, and then tilted its head to one side as if deliberating on the dinner in its claw.

The mother finally broke out of her reverie, all of her love for her daughter coalescing into a fury that negated the fear that would ordinarily have restrained her from making the sacrifice she was about to make. The woman flung herself at the creature's face, her fingers digging into its chitinous head and face. Her nails screeched ineffectually across its armor.

The beast recoiled with a guttural and surprised hiss, its myriad of sensory organs taken aback by this sudden outburst of maternal love. It flailed its tail about, swinging to and fro.

The girl slipped from its grasp, her body a bruised and broken but intact mess. She ran from the Afltic, her vision blurring as tears ran down her face. Her eyes would forever be etched with the images she was currently beholding. Her body jerked violently as she spun about to see what her mother was currently doing.

Her mother was throwing her hands repeatedly into the Afltic's chitinous head and face, her fingernails scratching at it pathetically. Her hair had come undone from her head, her long black locks now framing her face. Her body was limp as she swung her arms about, her body pivoting on her spine.

The monster growled irritably as the woman had just used her body in a very weak attempt to sabotage its goal of ending a family of four. It lashed out at the woman with a backhanded claw. The woman's body was knocked about by this blow, her back arched by the raw power of the Afltic's blow. She was hurled into the air, becoming a projectile being sent toward an unknown destination.

The woman's body slammed into the ground like a ragdoll, her body collapsing to the floor in a twisted heap. The woman laid next to her husband, her husband's body now still and lifeless in the same way that the woman was now. The life was gone from her body as her arms and legs went limp and motionless.

The Afltic finished whatever business it was still doing with the daughter, this girl now being the last one of this family's strong bio-signature. The Afltic bore down on the girl, it's teeth opening into a wide, toothy maw. It brought its mouth down onto the child and began its meal.

The delegates at the GDC meeting room watched as the Afltic continued its slaughter. The girl's screams and her thrashing about were a testament to what exactly they were fighting against. An Afltic was not just any monster, it was the personification of death and agony.

The Afltic finished its feast, and for a moment, nobody in the GDC meeting room did anything. The family's end had been so thoroughly public, their deaths a spectacle; for a time, nobody had any words. The Afltic had feasted, and one more thought passed through the mind of every delegate there: the Afltic were monsters. Their appetites were greater than their humanity, and one more family had been lost to the ravenous invader. The delegates swore they would never forget them; in the honor of their sacrifice, the Afltic would be fought with every fiber of their being.

The horror show in Hong Kong was live-streaming to every corner of the world unfiltered. It was broadcasting all of humanity's terrors in the rawest of terms.

In the Global Defense Council command center, the horrific noise emanating from the main feed snapped some of the paralyzed delegates into action. The shock had worn off, and a different emotion had taken hold. It was desperation. "Fire at will! Lock on targets!"

Marc's voice was almost a growl, a blunt instrument used to break the silence of the conference room. Marc's expression was a mask of grim resolve, his years as a soldier honing his reflexes past the initial shock.

Hawkins jabbed buttons on his console. "The Chinese defense forces are mobilizing, General! All available weapons are being deployed!"

They were. Automated anti-air emplacements, designed to counter more terrestrial threats, purred into action, spitting out dozens of missiles towards the skies. Artillery batteries lined the roads, and their barrels heated red as they strafed the alien probe as it darted between buildings. Jets tore across the Hong Kong sky, screaming, as they rained ordnance down in blistering passes.

The response had been staggering in its speed, its scale; in its unbridled aggression. Humanity had bared its teeth, and the audacity of it was majestic. Missiles designed to blast through hardened bunkers exploded against the alien probe's chitinous hide, little more than fizzling fire against the armored meat. Explosions wracked its segmented body, plumes of fire briefly shrouding it in hellfire. Yet through the smoke, it still remained. Intact. The purpose-made physical weapons had been so easily deflected, or seemed not to faze the alien at all. The maddening sound of the ground assault drowned out the chatter from the floor, screams of "no impact" from pilots and artillerymen only serving to make the collective sigh in the room longer and deeper.

However, it was this barrage of physical ordnance that had briefly given them a small shred of hope. Collapsing onto the probe, a skyscraper, its very foundation vaporized and severed from the hellish blasts, tumbled over with a monstrous crash and completely covered the alien in a pile of dust and rubble. For a few heart-stopping seconds, the probe was obscured, and silence reigned. Then, with a sound that was like a cacophony of tectonic plates grinding together, the probe started to emerge. Repeating over and over. As if removing dust from itself.

"No impact!" Jill's voice was soaked in anger, her arms akimbo as she bellowed. "Energy shields are active! Physical armor is deflecting projectiles! The bug is not even taking damage!"

The probe simply transitioned to another part of the city, its movements already having wiped entire city blocks. The angry but futile volley of missiles and artillery had already blasted buildings into smoking craters, and its physical limbs tore away at the structures. Screeching humans were still being added to its feast. The beast was still devouring.

The Afltic warrior was a black blur, a violent jet through the streets of Hong Kong, its every action a crime scene in itself. The dozens of explosions around it did little to dissuade its carnage, and the alien laughed in its inhuman voice as it continued rampaging. It kept its many eyes peeled, hunting, as it tore through a street.

As the Command Center fell into hopelessness, a new signature appeared on Hawkins' tactical display. "General Singer! I've got another energy reading! Chinese, extremely localised, and off the fucking charts!"

Marc Singer narrowed his eyes, the dark depths of them showing a brief flash of something like grim recognition. "That's... the 'Dragon's Breath' project. I thought it was decommissioned. Too unstable."

"It's active, General!" Hawkins confirmed, voice strained. "Charging now! Firing in three... two... one..."

Somewhere in the teeming city of Hong Kong, deep within the confines of a fortified and underground bunker, an experimental energy weapon was fired. The 'Dragon's Breath', a true weapon of desperation, a monster of pure human ingenuity and hubris; a weapon so unstable that it was never intended for actual combat, nor was its existence ever supposed to be known outside of a handful of secret government agents. Its raw, unfiltered power arced through the air with a blinding flash and deafening sound. It was no explosion, however; it was far more precise. It was a coherent, singular beam of pure energy, infinitely hotter than the surface of the sun.

The white-hot beam of pure, coherent energy, lanced through the chaos of the Hong Kong streets. It did not strike the probe's armour. It found the gap in the targeting algorithm provided by Zara; it struck its target. It pierced the gossamer, almost invisible energy barrier protecting the alien, straight into the probe's exposed belly, where its grinding mandibles had been ripping into civilians.

Instantly, the Alien screamed. It was not a scream. It was a massive distortion of sound, a pure wave of raw, piercing feedback. It ripped across the live feed, directly into the GDC's speakers and was so loud that it deafened anyone in the room listening to it. It was a noise so alien and so utterly inhuman, so saturated with an agony that no lifeform should have to experience that it was indescribable, and those who had been watching the live feed from the streets of Hong Kong involuntarily clutched their ears. It felt like the ground was falling out from under them, it felt like time was shredding into ribbons, it felt like that shriek, that unholy noise, was tearing their own minds from their skulls.

It was enough for the probe to completely lose its remaining composure. It spasmed. The tentacles that so quickly, efficiently stripped the streets of their pedestrians whipped about in chaotic directions, scattering shards of concrete and pavement and, far too many, human remains across the ground. Thick, choking smoke billowed from its newly opened wound, feeding the hungry street with the stale, gaseous remains of its meal. The hideous maw on the underside of its body convulsed, briefly before slamming shut. There was nothing left for it to consume. The male warrior on the ground next to it screamed, an animalistic, wordless shriek that cut through the atmosphere itself as it perceived its female in such distress. The killing had stopped momentarily, not because the monster had turned tail and fled. No. It had turned, and its purpose was not to eat anymore, but to get to its female and defend it at any cost. It began to run back, a black blur of renewed rage.

But it was not to be.

The Chinese military, who had, in just minutes, so effectively proven their own ingenuity and resolve were not done yet. They had already lined up a second shot, just in time.

The 'Dragon's Breath' fired again.

The pure white-hot energy, a spear of laser-cut, incandescent destruction, lanced through the air, not at the newly wounded probe. It did not care for the dying probe anymore; it only cared for its one goal. It streaked straight through the air, directly at the male running to its aid. Its target was hit directly. The male warrior screamed, not in agony or fear. He did not even fall, nor did he utter a sound at all. He simply ceased to be. Vaporized in one singular, glorious strike. The single wave of dissipated energy it left behind shimmered out, gone.

All that is left is the female and she was mortally wounded; the probe did not last long. The chitinous exoskeleton of her body let out a ghastly, protesting groan as the continued assault of gunfire finally began to land some effective hits on her vital systems. She groaned again, louder this time, before her entire bulk simply shuddered before completely collapsing, her joints and limbs folding on itself like a dying spider. The Afltic was dead.

CHAPTER 25: THE ULTIMATE TRAGEDY

There was a collective intake of breath, then a moment of shocked silence before a single, quavering cheer echoed around the room in a wave of immense, bone-weary relief.

The video feed from Hong Kong still played across the main screen, but the twisted and bloody figures of the Aftic probe and the male warrior were gone. In their place was the smoking, still-glowing crater of a city block. The silence from the field had changed. It was no longer the horrifying silence of the sky awaiting a potential kill, but the shocked quiet of an aftermath.

For the delegates from the GDC there was a sense of a tension that had been so intense it had become almost physical being let go. Hands went up to faces, some men and women slumped back in their chairs, and low, embarrassed chuckles of weak, incredulous laughter began to bubble around the room. The threat was over. The enemy had come. Hong Kong had bled and suffered, but the city had survived the first, direct hit.

Drake's face was ashen, somewhere between horror and victory. He turned to face Hawkins, who was staring at his console. "Confirm kill, Hawkins. Now."

Hawkins' fingers hammered on his console, his eyes scanning the rapid data stream. "No longer picking up a bio-signature on target." He paused, watching the screen. "Mass signatures are consistent with a total vaporization. Both the probe, and the male... the male is vaporized." He swallowed, the words catching in his throat. "We... we did it."

We. It was a word that barely applied to the men and women in the room. The victory was China's alone.

Silent and still, with a small, private smile of triumph on his lips, the Chinese delegate sat smugly in his chair at the back of the room. Li Wei, his name, had until a few minutes ago been a mere nonentity within the GDC, a representative of a nation with a military that was as far-advanced as it was mysterious, opaque, and difficult. He had sat through arguments, accusations, and stinging recriminations with his chin up and his face the image of granite, but with that crater on the screen as his witness, now he was different.

Li Wei was a big man, and now he towered imperiously in his seat, looking like a wounded beast in the pride of his territory. His face was flushed and beatific, with that triumphant, almost smug look of someone who has a message for everyone in the room.

The recriminations, the ugly, fractious accusations of 'friendly fire', the whispering, the shattered alliances, none of it seemed to matter now. The GDC had sat, frozen and impotent while the city bled and suffered, deliberating and arguing over old mistakes. The Chinese had acted, and in a single, savage act of military precision and technological triumph they had saved the city. They had proven their worth, and proven it in a way that could never, ever be refuted.

The 'Dragon's Breath', the project whose existence even within China had been regarded with supreme secrecy, was, in one fell swoop, the most important weapon in the history of the human race.

The silence was more effective than a thousand speeches. The American general who had ranted and accused not five minutes before now stared at the screen with an expression of weary, grudging respect. The Russian official whose contempt for a multinational command had been obvious throughout now studied Li Wei with a sobered new understanding in his eyes. The center of gravity in the room had shifted, and it had done so on a wave of human ingenuity, and an eruption of human violence like no one had ever seen before.

The brittle, celebratory silence was short-lived. A shaky cheer had just broken out in the conference room, rapidly dissolving into waves of deeper, more exhaustive relief. The delegates were just exchanging exhausted, smug smiles, when the Chinese delegate, Li Wei, stood up.

Faces in the room dropped their smiles. Li Wei's face was flushed red with relief and a hard, nationalistic pride; earlier accusations that his government and his military had engineered the whole situation were clearly forgotten in the afterglow of victory. His gaze swept the room, but he was not looking at the leaders of the GDC. He was looking at the representatives of the other three nations, a smug sweep from one to the other.

"For months," he said, his voice ringing out across the room with a new authority it had not hitherto possessed, "we have been promised to cower before an immense, insurmountable enemy. We have been promised that only absolute, global unity would be enough to save us from an enemy of unfathomable power. We were told to surrender our sovereignty, to cast aside our traditional defenses." He waved a hand dismissively at the main screen, still displaying the smoking crater of Hong Kong. "I think that the last hour has demonstrated quite clearly that those claims were... exaggerated, to say the least."

There was a collective, quiet gasp from the room.

Li Wei set his jaw, his voice hardening as he continued. "The so-called 'probe' was a scouting unit, which was easily disposed of using far superior terrestrial technology. It was not the harbinger of doom that we were led to believe; it was a challenge, and we have met that challenge. We have shown, conclusively, that the Afltic are not as powerful as Mr. Donovan here would have us believe. They are fallible. They can be defeated."

Drake Donovan's face had been grim, foreboding for the last hour; now it seemed to harden into something colder, starker. He was watching Li Wei, his face going ashen as he recognized what the man was saying. He knew this was not a victory. This was a complete, utter failure.

"Accordingly," Li Wei continued, his voice sounding chillingly final, "China hereby declares its immediate and unilateral withdrawal from the Earth alliance. We will not be party to the Global Defense Council nor will we be complicit in its strategies and tactics." He looked directly at Drake, his gaze direct and unflinching. "We will work to develop our own defense strategies, independent of the GDC. We are certain that we will be able to handle any future attacks, because we have proven that our technology, our will, is more than sufficient."

The announcement was a physical shockwave through the room, a simultaneous gasp of horror from every delegate. The furious whispers, the wild-eyed disbelief; it took all of three seconds for it to become obvious that the tenuous alliance, the collective will that had taken months to build, had not merely been cracked, but shattered by one man and one single, thundering announcement. All of the hard work, all of the compromises, all of the sacrifice; the delegates had spent the last eight months climbing to the peak of a mountain, and it took all of three seconds for that summit to be ground to dust. A desperate, hopeful victory had been turned into humanity's greatest defeat in a single, guttural speech.

The aftershocks from Li Wei's announcement had still been rippling through the conference room when the first fractures in the Earth alliance foundation became apparent. The united command of the GDC had existed for less than five months, and it was now self-destructing before their eyes.

The European Union delegate, a gruff woman with a bushy mustache who went by Delacroix, was the first to stand up. Her voice was not quite as sonorous as Li Wei's, but just as final. "The Alliance was formed with a promise of a truly unified, cohesive command structure," she stated, glaring pointedly at the American and Russian delegates. "The overreactions from Haven coupled with the near complete lack of transparency regarding this… this 'Dragon's Breath' has made it clear that that unity was, in fact, never in the cards. The European Union will not, in good faith, be able to dedicate our full military and technological capacity to something where we are simply bystanders."

She paused, letting the implications of her words sink in. "Effective immediately, the EU defense protocol is withdrawn from the GDC. We will defend our own sovereign nations."

A muffled, angry murmur passed through the room. The Russian delegate, a large, pockmarked man with a permanent scowl, was next. He did not mince words. "If the Chinese and the Europeans are no longer with us, then what, may I ask, is this 'alliance'?" he growled, his words a personal, ugly insult. "Russia will not be yoked by a common effort that does not, in fact, exist in common." He gave a curt nod to his assistants and began to gather his papers. India after him, then a collection of Southeast Asian nations, each a link in a falling row of dominoes in a grim, diplomatic avalanche.

The meeting that was intended to formalize a last-ditch unity was fast becoming its complete, ungoverned opposite. The air, which had only a few hours ago been so thick with relieved exhaustion, was now electric with blame and nationalistic posturing. The unifying threat that had bound them all was now only a fading memory, replaced by an all-too-soon, dangerous sense of safety. Each nation, emboldened by China's "success" and eager to reassert their sovereignty, began to pull away their commitments. They were not looking at the horrific, near-disaster that had unfolded in Hong Kong. Instead, each nation was simply tallying up the kill count. 1 alien. 1 dead alien. Shot down by vastly superior, home planet technology.

Drake watched the collapse in a horrified, numb sort of way. He could feel the sick truth of it roll through him, settling into his gut like a concrete anchor. The 'friendly fire' incident that had seemed like such an apocalypse when it had happened was just the prelude to this.

Zara, next to him, fists clenched at her sides, finally spoke. Her voice was a low murmur, a deep, bitter kind of grief in her words. "It's the ultimate tragedy," she said, her eyes still on the delegates leaving the room. "The greatest existential threat humanity's ever known and we can't even band together for a day after a victory. They saw a monster get killed and now they're all trying to one-up each other."

She met Drake's eyes and, in their reflection, the ultimate tragedy of it all. Humanity's greatest weakness. Humanity's inability to even recognize its own fragility, even after having been directly attacked. Humans were putting short-term goals ahead of the long-term, survival itself. They were patting themselves on the back and congratulating themselves on a victory when all they had done was win a battle in a war that they had already lost. The Afltic had sent a single probe to Earth and, in its death, it had rent humanity more effectively than an atom bomb ever could.

The Vintie outpost was an empty shell, scavenged clean. The eleven other probes of the clutch, living ships of chitin and bio-metal, prepared for departure. As they did, a faint ripple of shared consciousness passed between them. 77 is gone. That is not a 'terminated' or an 'offline' state, that probe is gone. It is no longer anything. There is no mental signature to detect. Her presence in the collective consciousness of the clutch had simply stopped.

"Status?" a younger probe asked.

The answer came in a chorus of voices, a discordant, unified loathing. "Irrelevant. Its inability to perform to efficiency killed it. It is nothing."

It was not a eulogy. It was not a moment of reflection or a showing of concern. 77 had been flawed, a missing segment of her reactor core was the accepted truth, and the failure of that reactor had killed her. It was as simple as that. 77 was not an emotional thing, and her death had not been an emotional event.

"The consumption of Outpost Vintie is now complete," 70, the next oldest of the clutch, said. "The weak one has been culled. Its continued existence is not our concern. Proceed to patrol route ZC77-R37."

The eleven probes and their males pivoted as one, will merged into a single frigid intent. Their trajectory pointed straight away from Earth's system, then accelerated away from it at the highest possible speed. The human-inhabited solar system was nothing to them, just a star among trillions. They didn't even know that one of their clutch-mates had gone rogue and had gone there. They didn't care.

The scale of the Afltic. The size of it, the real source of the horror, was not one probe, one that they could win this particular victory, but the others, the numbers of which they didn't and cannot even know. There was nothing in the Space Age that compared to the scale of the dark underbelly of the stars. Thousands, or even millions, by the time they appeared on the planet Earth. In the distance, the sun sank beneath the horizon of Concordia, bathing the crowd in orange and gold light. Zara waited for the noise to quiet again before she took a step forward, a speech she had made many times before, to tell them the history that made her one of them. Her audience had swelled since Tan had innocently asked what he did during Galactic Liberation Day, a crowd now representing many of the races that had banded together to face a common foe. Her first step brought her to the front of the crowd, her tall form casting a long shadow in the falling light.

"The fracturing of the human alliance," she began. Zara's voice was a deep alto that stretched across the audience, filling the gathering with an almost tangible presence. "Wasn't just a political one, but a psychological one as well. As soon as it became certain that the Afltic would not be able to immediately overwhelm them, humans on Earth breathed a sigh of relief and were prematurely celebratory. The Afltic, of course, could not share in that. Not then, nor now." A Human male raised a hand, interrupting her with a practiced gesture. His skin was the beige of a very well lived human, the lines of age and wisdom running through his face. "Zara, is it not a victory then? A signal to other species that we can hold them off?"

Zara sighed and turned to him, the sad smile on her face not quite reaching her eyes. "One victory does not win a war," she told him. "The Afltic are not an armada, a collection of ships they can fight and best. They are an existential tidal wave that must be held back by a multitude of fortresses. The humans of Earth thought they had that fortress, and what they had actually built was a wall against a rising ocean."

A small Yollin female stepped forward, her voice slightly amplified by her chitinous mouthparts. Her carapace had an iridescent finish that was visible in the setting light. "But how could they not have seen it coming? The danger was so clear!" The other crowd members murmured their agreement.

"Hindsight, my dear Yollin friend," Zara told her. "Humanity at the time of the Afltic crisis was as much plagued by hubris as they were by fear. Rather than facing the unknown, the unknowable, they decided to see a threat that they could understand, a threat that they could overcome and win the glory of a victory for their race. The actual reality of the Afltic, their unimaginable scale, their utter indifference, was something they were simply not capable of facing yet. They had yet to learn that the universe isn't run by the needs and wants of Homo Sapiens."

A Weavean male interrupted her, another bioluminescent limb creating a soft light pool in the dusk. "But then? What happened? After the alliance fell apart?" Zara's eyes glistened with a sympathetic sorrow as she continued. "The Afltic, as humans on Earth didn't know at the time, had been launching their silent probes for years. Each one not just a scout, but a herald of what they already called the Swarm. The Afltic are not a single species, you see, but numbers too large for the other minds of the galaxy to comprehend. As humans on Earth decided to pull apart, to celebrate a victory before it had even been won, the Afltic had already begun to move in earnest." There was a long, heavy silence as the crowd collectively digested that information and went over in their minds what it had meant to them then, what it might mean to them now. The darkness had claimed Concordia by the time Zara took a deep breath and closed her eyes. A long, long pause in the speech as she remembered all of the people who had died and all of the heroes who had risen up in desperation. Once she opened her eyes, the air was still thick with loss and grief, but she pressed on as best she could, still determined to tell the truth to the only way she knew how.

CHAPTER 26: FUGITIVES

It had not taken long. An hour. Less than that, even. The Global Defense Council's command deck was quiet. Too quiet. From the moment Drake had set foot in there the air had been tense, but now it was something else. The screens, still dark, stared at them with a million dead eyes. Minutes before they had been alive with streaming data and live video feeds from every corner of the world. They were data walls, embedded in concrete that bore the silhouettes of the delegates in conference from countries Drake would probably never visit under any other circumstances. Now, those representatives were gone, in a rush. Anger and mutual suspicion had turned the promise of a global alliance for common defense into a panic-stricken stampede.

When the last delegate had left the room, the silence had been palpable, a vacuum amplified by the hum of the server banks still running, and the muted scuff of boots on polished floor. Drake and his team were in the center of the command deck. Marc and Carlos and Hawkins, Mandy, Jill, and Tammy were close to Drake, all of them grouped in a tight circle around him, faces tight with tension.

"We have to leave here. Go back to Haven," Drake said, his voice quiet but breaking through the absolute stillness like a slap. He pointed to the blank screens. "Look at this. If this isn't it getting worse for us, then I don't know what is."

Mutual understanding was signaled by a series of nods from the circle. Like a well-rehearsed unit, they moved in concert, Drake and team passing through the thick door that led out of the command center and into the main corridor. The main thoroughfare was still as well, eerily empty, the lack of personnel making their teeth itch. Drake's team moved quickly along the corridor, following the same egress route they had mapped out in contingency exercises during better times. Drake had never thought they would have to use it, and it had been a contingency prepared long before the spore came out of the atmosphere, but it was an exfiltration all the same. The plan took them back to the main lobby of the Global Defense Council's headquarters. A trio of armed guards met them there. Three men in battle armor with helmets at the ready and assault rifles leveled at them. The first guard's voice was a tinny snarl over the speaker of his helmet. "Stop. You are to remain in the building. The interim council has given orders."

"No use arguing with them. They made their choice," Marc whispered to the circle.

Drake just nodded and moved, his hand coming up on the butt of his sidearm. He dropped to one knee without a word, Carlos and Hawkins coming up on either side, their weapons coming up in a smooth, practiced movement. Drake's first shot was a warning shot into the first guard's rifle, aimed so as to destroy his rifle's optical sight. The guard visibly flinched and jerked back. As Drake's team moved, they turned into a blur of motion. Mandy and Jill, behind a big, reinforced pillar, provided suppressing fire on the other two guards, while Marc, a dance of swirling grace and deadly precision, closed with the second guard, meeting him face to face with a palm strike to the guard's helmet, aimed at the weak point around the viewing lens. The second guard staggered back, visibly disoriented. Tammy, an excellent shot for a doctor, took a careful shot at the third guard's rifle, shredding its optics and forcing the guard to drop his weapon. The first guard, the one Drake had hit, was now on his feet again, rifle at the ready, but Drake's comrade had him covered. Marc came up on the guard, his arm up and the rifle barrel in his hands as he twisted it away. He ended his move with a stomp of his boot to the chest plate of the guard's armor, the impact reverberating through the floor and sending the guard sprawling against the wall with a sickening crash. Guard number three collapsed to the floor in a heap of armor and equipment, head lolling. They didn't linger over the fallen men. No time for compassion or second thoughts, not now. Drake and team were fugitives, running through silent corridors made for a predator's playground.

They sprinted for the service elevators, alarms already wailing in the distance, an irritating afterthought of protection. Every door and doorway could be an ambush point. Every corner could hide a new threat. They were no longer the heroes of a global defense organization; they were the target. The broken alliance, choking on its own death throes, was coming for them and there would be no distinction between them and the blame they so clearly carried. Reaching Haven was no longer an option. It was their only hope.

They ran. The alarms had come late, but now they were a screaming, persistent chorus. Doors were ambush points, corners were threats, and the attackers were no longer part of the Global Defense Council; they were their targets. The splintered alliance was going down, and the fall was going to take out everyone in its path. Reaching Haven had gone from an option to the only option.

The elevator doors closed, and Drake pulled out his comm unit. The screen lit, showing the icon of the EBS. The response, calm and synthesized as always, was instantly recognizable.

"This is Zara.

"Zara, we have a problem," Drake said, tersely. "The GDC just turned on us. We're headed to the roof. We need an exfil shuttle, stat. Ten minutes, tops. And Zara… throw a couple combat droids on board. We will not be alone."

"Copy that, Drake. Shuttle is on its way. Droids will be armed. Stay sharp. Zara out."

His comm went black. The air in the small elevator car was a vortex of tension. The climb was slow, agonizing. One floor up and they could be swarmed. The team was as competent as they come, but they were still outnumbered and outgunned inside the GDC's own headquarters. Drake's stomach knotted at the thought of what they were about to face on the roof. Wind, rain, and sky; and whatever the GDC wanted to throw at them.

The elevator stopped, shuddering to a halt. The doors slid open, cold and windblown air hissing in, along with the tang of ozone. The team spilled out onto the roof access platform and onto the exposed open area of the Global Defense Council's main rooftop. Wind whipped around the great tower of the skyscraper, a wind-swept symphony.

Drake looked about. The open roof was a grid of vents and antennae and a single large helicopter landing pad, all slicked with a sheen of light rain. Off in the distance, a small bright point was rapidly growing, accompanied by a low, thrumming sound that was growing steadily louder, even over the wind. EBS shuttle, and it was right on time.

"There she is," Carlos said, gesturing.

Drake didn't need to issue a command. The team moved, and moved as one. They ran, seven of them in a tight line, toward the landing pad. Mandy, Jill, and Tammy were at the center, less heavily armed than the outer team members. The security alarms were their constant companion, a high-pitched scream of metal on metal that was now joined by the sound of footfalls.

Troopers were moving, a squad of GDC heavy troopers that were materializing from the far side of the rooftop. They were not lightly-armed guards like those below. These were combatants, and their rifles were all outfitted with under-barrel grenade launchers.

"Company," Marc stated, flatly.

Drake brought out his comm unit. "Zara, they are heavy armor. We will need a distraction."

"Copy that, Drake," the EBS AI replied. "Initiating a non-lethal sonic burst to create confusion and disrupt enemy targeting. ETA on your shuttle is ninety seconds."

An earsplitting wail filled the air, something completely outside the range of human hearing but something that scrambled the targeting displays of the troopers. They blinked, staggered, and that was the window Drake's team needed.

They ran. Synchronized movement of several people was beautiful in motion, and Drake knew every movement of his team as they ran. As the GDC troopers caught up and began to target, they opened fire. Rounds tore through the exposed structures of the roof, and a grenade arc-chained across the roof, landing too close for comfort to Marc.

"Grenade!" Drake shouted.

No questions asked, Marc dove and kicked it out of reach. The thing detonated on the rooftop, an explosion big enough to knock both of them into a different direction. A blast of debris and heat expanded from the site.

The shuttle from the EBS approached the landing pad, just in time, landing gears popping down like mechanical spider legs. The blast from its thrusters flapped the clothes on their backs and tousled their hair, but it was a welcome sight nonetheless.

The GDC troopers, no longer stunned from the sonic pulse, were bearing down on them. It was clear now that the GDC had a decision to make. They could fight, in an all out battle on an urban rooftop, or they could back off and let them go. From the look of it, they chose the former. A second squad came from another manhole, flanking them in the process. They were out of options.

"Pinned!" Carlos yelled, though the words got lost in the wind and the growing thruster wash.

"Zara! We're taking fire! What's the status on that shuttle?" Drake yelled into his comm.

"Landing gear is secure on the pad, Drake. May I remind you that I am deploying the combat droids at this moment." A calm and emotionless finality to its voice.

The shuttle itself was a black, very angular, jet-black thing. It landed with a dull thud, the airframe settling on the pad. One side of the shuttle slid open like a cupboard door. The exposed hallway revealed two bipedal combat droids, red optical sensors sweeping the rooftop, gunning down the GDC troopers. The two bipeds with their inorganic feet trampling over the rubble from the explosion.

Zara's design, clearly. Fast and highly maneuverable, the droids were armed with plasma rifles. They moved, instinctive and precise, to flank the GDC troopers. The weapons were already up and tracking, too. The plasma rifles spat electric death, bolts of blue light tearing through the air. The bolts found their marks in the GDC troopers' armor. A satisfying sizzle filled the air. The soldiers from the Global Defense Council had the training and discipline of any professional soldier. But they were trained for conventional warfare. This new kind of fighting, fought with foreign technology they didn't understand, was completely alien to them.

"Go! Go! Go!" Drake shouted.

They took off, sprinting across the pad and into the shuttle. Carlos and Hawkins were providing covering fire, getting them off the ground and on board the shuttle. Marc, Mandy, Jill, and Tammy all piled into the cabin. Drake was the last one in, standing and facing the rooftop chaos as he climbed into the cockpit. Just as he was about to close the hatch, pain exploded in his left shoulder. A high caliber round from a GDC assault rifle had found him. Drake yelped, a torn open handprint on the combat jacket on his back. He was thrown forward into the cabin, but adrenaline kept him upright.

Tammy was on him in an instant, the doctor in her taking over immediately. "Drake, you're hit!" she yelled, already pulling at the fabric of his jacket to reveal the damage.

The two combat droids, having successfully pushed back the GDC troopers and created the distraction they needed, walked back into the shuttle. The plasma rifles vented with a sizzling pop as they went cold. The side door hissed shut with hydraulic finality.

"Zara, get us out of here!" Drake yelled, teeth clenched through the pain as Tammy pressed on his shoulder wound.

Anti-grav engines kicked on, and the shuttle slowly lifted off, a silent and unobtrusive maneuver to freedom in the storm-darkened sky. The GDC troopers, clearly no match for what was out there, were now firing blindly at the shuttle as it rolled away, rounds ricocheting harmlessly off of its armored hull. Drake looked down at the GDC building. A small hive of fluorescent activity that was growing smaller by the second, a grid of pixelated lights in an otherwise empty sky.

"Entrance wound clean, exit wound... Looks like it's just a through and through, thank god," Tammy muttered, fingers delicately feeling around the injured flesh. "It's bleeding, but it's not heavy. You're lucky, Drake. Lucky it missed anything important. You're going to regret this in the morning though."

Drake just nodded, falling back into a seat and letting Tammy go to work, sterilizing and dressing the wound. They had made it, and Drake knew that that was just the beginning. A long, hard way to go, before he was truly safe. The GDC was fractured. A wounded beast was, as they say, the most dangerous.

The GDC was not happy, not happy at all. A Global Defense Council frustrated, angry, and in need of a scapegoat.

Drake Donovan.

They would not, could not, look at the thousands that had fallen at the hands of their incompetent general. Accusations like vapor coalesced and focused, zeroing in on a single target. The global media machine was in overdrive, desperate to form a narrative to make sense of these last few chaotic days. On every news channel that Drake could pick up, the loops from Hong Kong played again. The cheers of victory for the obliterated Afltic probe, now just some enemy robot, now taken for granted.

USA TODAY NEWS: THE GREAT FRAUD. DONOVAN'S EXAGGERATED THREAT EXPOSED.

CNN: ALARMIST OR SAVIOR? THE CASE AGAINST DRAKE DONOVAN.

BBC: UNILATERAL SUCCESS PROVES COLLECTIVE FAILURES. HAVEN'S MANDATE CALLED INTO QUESTION.

He was called a fear-monger, an alarmist who had grossly exaggerated the Afltic threat to line his own pockets and gain a level of global influence the human race had never before known. It was an easy message to sell. There was no over-arching, unifying enemy. This was no World War, but a single, isolated incident that had blown over a long time ago, and humanity had sold its collective soul to fight a ghost.

Calls for his arrest, the disbandment of Haven, and an international investigation into his "misinformation campaign" were broadcast through every diplomatic and news channel. The usual suspects, former allies who had become bitter rivals, were all too keen to shift the blame and responsibility onto someone, anyone, other than themselves. The 'win' at Hong Kong had been painted a hundred different ways by every news channel, spinning out of control, so that Donovan's grave warnings just hours before had sounded petulant and selfish. It was a witch hunt, swift and sure, as millions the world over were lashed by the beast of public outrage and political opportunism with every breath, begging for a return to normalcy no matter what it took.

Marc stood in the command center in Haven, staring at the same news feed on his own handheld. Drake could hear his breath, harsh and tight, from across the room. "They've put out a warrant for my arrest in absentia," he said, close-mouthed and horrified. "Chinese and Russian governments, at first, but it's spreading."

The news feed was like a match to a fuse. Drake felt no surprise, only the knowledge that it was too late. It had been as he'd warned. Victory in Hong Kong had been a gift of fire. An angry and resentful human race, so near to pulling together as a species, had lost their heads. The world had forgotten to be afraid, had ceded control to the flimsiest of victories, and in their thirst to return to normalcy, had undone the only mechanism the planet had to protect itself. The Afltic were not the enemy. The enemy was humanity itself, and Drake Donovan was, by a longshot, public enemy number one.

The immediate days that followed the destruction of the GDC were long and desolate. A vacuum of broken hope. But as the dust began to settle, and as each nation-state licked its wounds and fell to licking the boots of those who'd hurled the first stones, the vacuum was not filled with global unity or by peace. Instead, it filled with a kind of fear. Old and familiar, it whispered promises of violence in people's ears, drumming up an old and ugly agitation. It was the start of a new global arms race.

The object of the global human race was singular and clear.

'Dragon's Breath'.

The people, the delegates who had stormed from the GDC meeting back to their home capitals, were no longer angry as their planes took to the sky.

No. Instead they were desperate. All of them. Their triumphant, chest-thumping withdrawal in the face of China's display of military might, all done in the name of national pride, had quickly given way to an instinctual, nervous fear. The West had the moral high ground. They had their sovereignty back. But China had one weapon, one singular thing that could put an end to the Afltic scourge. The world's diplomatic channels which, just hours before, had been choked with righteous, shrieking rage were now stoked with barefaced, panicked demands.

"We congratulate the People's Republic of China on their decisive victory," a U.S. State Department spokesperson said in a press conference, "And we look forward to the rapid, global proliferation of the technology that made it possible. This is a matter of species-wide survival."

The European Union no longer spoke with one voice, but with many, all clamoring for a piece of the prize. Germany's Chancellor had sent a formal request, followed by France, then the UK. India and Russia, both countries that had similarly withdrawn following the EU, now sent their own, more blunt requests. The message was clear, China had saved the world, but now the world wanted to save itself.

Li Wei, in an official statement from Beijing, would have none of it. "The 'Dragon's Breath' is a matter of Chinese national security," he said, the tone in his voice a pale, confident echo of the day he'd given his rousing speech at the GDC. "It was Chinese scientists who built it, Chinese military who deployed it. It is the responsibility of the Chinese government to be in control of it. We will not be sharing this technology, won at great cost, with a world that abandoned us so quickly from the ideals of collectivism. We built the weapon to defend the world. It is a heavy burden, and it is clear that only we are prepared to shoulder it."

The result was not discussion, but an immediate, frenzied action. Every major power, every regional hegemon, immediately ordered their top scientists and military contractors to move to full capacity. The "Dragon's Breath" became a new Cold War passphrase, a target more valuable than the nuclear launch codes. The US reopened decades-old, classified research projects that had long been mothballed for lack of funding or relevance. The 'Project Phoenix' operation, an ultra-top-secret program to copy alien technology that had been discovered, was provided a budget larger than the global defense fund just disbanded. Entire teams of reclusive, brilliant physicists, once the inhabitants of musty university basements, were whisked away to ultra-classified government labs, provided with unlimited funds and an ominous single mandate: develop a weapon to kill an Afltic.

The 'Solis' program in the EU, which had already been a largely-theoretical initiative to produce a controlled fusion reaction, was immediately adapted, and put on 24/7 schedule to produce a new, single goal: a directed energy weapon that could match the energy levels of the 'Dragon's Breath.' In Russia, a similar initiative, a code-name that we know to be 'Veles,' was given the same free rein, the result a wild, desperate race to catch up to the alien marvel of technology shown in that single moment of white-hot glory over Hong Kong.

The single enemy that had briefly united the world was already being discarded. In its place was the familiar, deep-seated paranoia of one another. There was a certain irony to the tragedy. The very same technology that had kept humanity together to face an alien threat was now pulling that humanity apart. World military budgets, not moments ago all pooled together for a common cause, were now being siphoned off into a panicked, desperate race to build more. Scientific cooperation was given way to corporate espionage, and a ruthless competition for the best talent. Funds that had been being earmarked for humanitarian, infrastructure, and environmental research were being slashed in an effort to develop new weapons, anything, so long as the new arms could one day fire a 'Dragon's Breath' of their own.

The problem was, no one had the data. No one had the key. The Chinese government, secure in their victory, was a closed vault. They had the weapon. Everyone else had a smoking crater, and an aching, bitter jealousy.

It was not the Afltic probes that were the danger, at this point. The danger was not an abstract, unknown enemy. The danger was a very real, very human, and very familiar instinct. The instinct to survive, to protect and provide for oneself. The instinct to be more, to be first, to be best. The world was now preparing to tear itself to pieces because it had beaten an enemy. The Afltic had sent a scout. In its death, it had not only splintered humanity, it had also infected it with a new, contagious hubris. When the next Afltic arrived, the human race would be not just unprepared, but also divided. Armed. And ready to fight itself. The greatest threat to this world has always been this world. The Afltic just gave it a reason to prove it.

The control center of Haven, the hidden city carved into the Earth's crust, was a mausoleum. The screens, a moment before full of blinking alarms and terrifying live-cameras, were blank. But here, in Haven, for the families of the core team, everything was normal.

Drake Donovan had been marked for arrest in dozens of countries, his face the new face of global terrorism. To his team, he was not a fugitive. He was the last, true believer.

"The alliance is no more," Drake's voice was quiet, urgent. "And neither are we." He waved a hand at the news-feeds which still scrolled on their personal viewer/terminals. "They are after us now. Haven is safe, for the moment. Zara's technology makes it invisible to any Earth-based sensor. But we…"

He fixed each of them in turn with a penetrating, honest gaze: Carlos, Mandy, Marc, Hawkins, Jill, Tammy. In that infinite moment before his words were spoken, it was as if he was watching them die.

"We are the face of the threat, the public-facing target. It is safer for us not to stay on the surface. It is safer for our families. If we are found, so too will they be. And they will find Haven."

It was the truth, and it was a jagged stone in the pit of their stomachs. Their families, their children, their spouses, their friends, lived here. In this miracle, this engineered impossibility, they were safe. They were hidden. And to keep them so, his team would need to leave.

"You have the night." Drake's voice was a gruff, granite finality. "Go to your families. Say goodbye. Ensure the conversations are… covered. We are not coming back in the morning. We depart for the EBS at 0300."

Drake left the comms command center without a word, his departure marked by silent, shocked nods. He walked the spotless, humming corridors of Haven, passing rooms of residences as life proceeded blithely around him, a mournful dirge to the awful silence of his orders. He passed a playroom where children were screaming in joyous, incomprehensible delight. It was the sound of normalcy, and it was killing him.

He found his family in their quarters. His wife, Sarah, was already there. She was not just a tired, shell-shocked civilian, but a leader in her own right, a public figure and a great many other things which made her a fierce adversary and Drake's fiercest ally. He kissed her on the forehead. She already knew.

"I have the protocols ready," she said, a quiet resolve firm in her voice. "All the security parameters are updated. The emergency procedures for a full systems lock-down are in place. I have the keys to all the sub-level armories, and my staff are fully briefed on the new communications protocols. They do not know why, but they are ready."

He laughed, a weary, humorless sound. Her resourcefulness, her competence, was a salve to the raw wounds which were not yet scar tissue. "I know you'll keep them safe," he said, the words his absolute, universal truth.

He found his daughter, Lily in her quarters, hunched over a holobook. His son, Max was in his room, playing an immersive video-game, a steady soundtrack of explosions and screams. His son, Sam was building a tower of building-blocks in the living-room. In the next room, his twin babies, Ella and Eli slept soundly.

He bent down and ran a hand through Sam's hair, pulling him into a tight hug. He went to Max's door, and just laid a hand on the teenager's shoulder, a gesture that may or may not have been understood. He pulled his daughter Lily close, burying his face in her hair, inhaling the scent of her, imprinting it into his mind. He did the same with Max, clinging to him a few precious moments longer than he should have. Finally, he went to the crib, gazing down at Ella and Eli. They were so tiny. He had to be strong. He reached out a hand and caressed their tiny palms.

Sarah came to stand beside him, and their hands instinctively found each other. This was no marriage sendoff, no husband bidding farewell to his wife before his last mission. It was a passing of the torch, a silent agreement to sacrifice the one thing they had in common. She would be the shield, for all of them, the guardian of their future. He would be the sword, the one to go out and do the dirty work.

"It's time." She said, the strength in her voice unfaltering.

He gave her one long, hard look, and in it he said all the words he couldn't. Then he turned away, and walked out of the room, leaving his family, his home, and his former life behind him.

As their jet-black shuttle rocketed through the roiling stormclouds of the Earth's atmosphere, a heavy, wordless silence descended upon its small, cramped cabin. It was a palpable thing, this quiet, as each crew member dealt with the events of the last few hours, and what lay ahead of them, in their own way. There was too much unshed grief for words, and for now, they had each other. To one side of the craft, the blue marble of the Earth was shrinking in the viewport, whitecaps breaking over its pale blue and white swirl of clouds and the dark, uncaring emptiness of space.

For Drake, that image now held an inescapable sadness. He had spent his life staring up at the sky, dreaming of the endless potential of space, the next frontier, a place of boundless possibility. He thought he would grow old there, gazing at the stars from a clear-sky window, knowing he'd done his part, and made a difference. He had never once thought it would be a one-way ticket. The view was no longer freeing; it was a prison. They were refugees, and the protectors of a truth too inconvenient for humanity to bear. The very people they had taken an oath to protect had banished them.

Marc, his face set in a mask of exhausted determination, stared out at the receding Earth as well, his combat training having given him no experience in this sort of loss. Carlos and Hawkins both stared at their flickering screens, already hard at work facilitating a rapid data upload to their new, alien corporate HQ. Tammy, Mandy and Jill each sat in their own self-contained silence, gazing at the retreating blue glow of their home.

It was a short journey to the EBS. A brief matter of transition, from one of terrestrial chaos and panic to orbital serenity. The shuttle docked, and the expansive docking bay of the Evolution Builder loomed in front of them. It was an impressive vessel, a floating, multi-level monument to Areidyanies technological might. It was a beautiful, alien ship, beautiful and terrifying, a silent guardian of some kind of unknown border.

It was in that quiet, almost sacred contrast, the juxtaposition of the serenity of the waiting ship, and the madness of the Earth, that Drake found a measure of peace. Down below, a planet was tearing itself apart in the name of flag and country, in the name of some twisted, laughable sense of security and nationalistic bravado. Humanity had always been so fragile, and in just the space of a few hours, the unity they had held on the brink of collapse had shattered. Nationalism, propaganda, and petty blame-spouting had taken its place, a frantic, fearful rush to rearm that was exactly what had been predicted.

Up here, though, it was different. All there was, all he could see was the quiet, serene might of Zara's ship, their reluctant shelter. It was a monument to a species far, far older than them, a species that had understood, on an almost primal level, the true scale of the galaxy, and even the universe, and humanity in its panicked immaturity just wanted to pretend it wasn't there.

They had lost the war, but by losing it on the ground, they had also won the right to fight it from orbit. They were no longer shepherds of humanity, but shepherds of the sheep from that species that had all but turned against them.

The shuttle's airlock hissed open, and the gentle thud of its docking sealed it off from the outside. Drake stepped off first, his boots clacking loudly against the polished floor. Behind him, his small but proud band of retainers, Marc, Carlos, Hawkins, Tammy, Mandy and Jill, filed out.

They all were struck by the ship's pristine, alien interior. The corridors glowed with a certain inner luminescence, a strange bioluminescent shimmer, that almost seemed to pulse with silent life. It was cool, the air here, and altogether sterile compared to the dust and panic of the outside. The entire vessel hummed with a subtle power, its myriad advanced systems blinking at them in ready welcome, silently beckoning them to a future full of horror.

In the cold, hard light of all of it, the immense technological achievement this ship represented, the sheer magnitude of its design and function, it was hard to ignore the cavernous hollowness of it all. The empty, silent corridors, stretching out in long lines before them, served as a grim reminder of the death of their global alliance. There were no welcoming committees, no cheering crowds, no weeping diplomats or world leaders reaching out to them, only Drake, his small and dedicated crew, and Zara. This was it, this was all that was left.

Their safe haven, this ship so lovingly provided by Zara, was at once both a wonder and a monument to their utter isolation, a measure of just how far humanity had rejected and spurned them. They had fled from their own people, the very same people they had risked everything to protect, and now they were in space. The job that lay ahead of them, their singular mission of protecting the human species whether it liked it or not, was a mountain of a task, too immense to even begin to fathom. They were now humanity's last line of defense, the lone survivors of a diplomatic apocalypse, and they were absolutely, completely alone.

She guided them through the empty, brightly lit corridors of the EBS. At the end of the hallway, a door the size of several football fields opened silently.

It was the new main command center. A huge room, most of which was taken up by a massive window with a panoramic view of the Earth. It hung in space like a beautiful and delicate jewel, blue and white against the inky darkness. Below them, a fragile world slowly turned on its axis, oblivious to the two-part tragedy of its destruction and its final act of defense.

Transparent data displays blinked with streams of complex glowing glyphs. Symbols that at first were impossible to decipher, and the ship thrummed with a deep, inaudible note. The low-frequency sensation of power without end. They all gazed in stunned silence, every one of them. The stillness was broken only by the faint, regular thrumming of the ship's systems.

Zara gestured at the room, a series of simple, sweeping movements. As she moved, the glowing glyphs on the display in front of her shifted, the characters deforming and warping into something the human eye could understand. Human data displays. "This will be your main operations center," Zara said, her voice even and clear. A comforting presence in a moment when awe and anxiety mingled together. "The EBS is able to process far more data than even your largest terrestrial networks. And its construction capacity is..." She didn't need to finish the sentence. Drake could see it in her eyes. The ship was a truly amazing machine, one with infinite resources to pull from. Her vague euphemism did not begin to describe its true potential.

Drake was looking at the new data displays, his eyes moving quickly as he tried to take in all the information. She was right. The power to create, to build, to analyze on a truly galactic scale, it was now in their hands. And theirs alone. They had come here from a world of trivial distractions and self-destruction, to this extraterrestrial sanctuary. It was ironic. They had the power to save humanity, but they had to do it by themselves. That thought was a cold comfort. The isolation would be difficult to bear.

The team began to move, their awe and fear quickly replaced by purpose and curiosity. Zara had already configured the data displays for them, which were already in English, and silently welcomed them to their new home. But their language was more than characters and data. It was understanding.

Hawkins was the first to break the silence. He pulled a small data storage drive out of his bag, the storage capacity barely enough to be useful. He held it up, small and gray and simple. "I've got the Haven database," he said, his voice a bit loud in the cavernous room. "We need to get it into the system somehow."

Working with Zara, using a series of hand gestures and simple commands, he bridged the gap between human and Areidyanies technology. He inserted the Haven drive into a console, and the EBS's internal processes began to thrum. A quiet, resonant buzz that vibrated through the floor. This ship, which had only ever spoken to a single person for the last 10,000 years, was now taking in a data storm of human information. The ship was alive, a singular collective mind, and it was learning to speak. The displays which had been blank just a moment before, blinked to life.

The schematics of the Afltic probe, the sensor data from Hong Kong, the satellite imagery of the cratered shell of the GDC command center. It all poured into the EBS's systems. The ship's processing systems went to work, absorbing and analyzing at a rate no human supercomputer could match.

"It's like we just handed a god a book to read," Marc whispered, as the first batches of the data poured through. He was configuring the small tactical terminal, a rough little field laptop whose functions were primitive and clunky, but which they'd scavenged in a rush to provide some ad-hoc command and control in the ship. He was translating the core human protocols into Areidyanies architecture, beginning to cobble together a new CIC in a ship that was their salvation, their vessel of escape, their tomb of failure.

Tammy had already begun taking readings and diagnostics with their personal health monitors using the EBS's integrated medical scanners, while Jill and Mandy had gotten to work setting up a means to safely and securely establish a two-way comm with their remaining operatives on the surface. Humanity adapted to strange new worlds. Humanity adapted to strange new realities. Humanity was now its own first "passengers" that the EBS had ever had to contend with and these silent endless halls were the equal of eternal in their wait for their arrival.

The EBS was no longer just a safe haven of alien technology; it was their new home, their new command, their new warship. They had brought with them the very humanity of their lives before, all the protocols and data and hardwired stubbornness, and they were grafting it all onto the magic of a technology many orders of magnitude beyond their own. They were a last line of defense. A ghost army on a ghost ship. A lost hope in a long forgotten war humanity had never known it was still losing.

His people toiled away, so he separated from them and moved away to the one great panoramic viewport that dominated the conning station. He stopped and stared. It was beautiful. Beautiful, and tragic. Earth was an exquisite jewel, all sapphire oceans and sparkling clouds floating over a seamless surface of flawless life, uninterrupted color. He knew that down there, in the city, life would go on. People would still get up and go to work, or school, or go about their days oblivious or in denial of the real threat.

On one of the peripheral screens they had live feeds from news reports of the surface world falling further and further into a renewed chaos. Nations that had dropped out of the Alliance were now squabbling and picking fights with each other. Every now and then they had a meeting or a summit but the meek were no longer inheriting the Earth and the once strong leadership of their unified front was devolving into in-fighting and pointing fingers over what was perceived as a weakening of their defenses. Nations who had once bowed to their common fear were now speaking of their vaunted early warning capabilities and boasting of how free they now were to pursue their own national interests.

There were no real advances in their struggle against the unknown and the unseen, the threat humanity wasn't really sure it was still losing to in the first place. Just new treaties and trade agreements and accords that they were desperately making like their collective backs were against the wall.

The Hong Kong Incident was being dismissed by some as a one-off victory for the Chinese. Others were painting it as some kind of abberation, some freak, one-time-only event. Humanity was clinging to their denial of reality like a life raft and it tore at Donovan's heart to see it.

Zara materialized beside him, her form wavering a bit against the inky black of space like a hologram struggling to find purchase in the darkness. "You watch their willful ignorance," she said with a voice both tranquil and sonorous, "It is a familiar story in your world's history. Faced with an unpleasant truth you would rather believe a comforting lie."

Her voice was a tolling bell that carried with it the knowledge of one who had seen this same pattern play out many times over the centuries. "The Afltic are not an event. They are a cycle and your world has proven as predictable as a rising tide."

Donovan didn't turn to look at her. He continued to stare out at the planet below. "The GDC was supposed to be different. We had an actual alien attack. They'd seen the probe get shot down."

"They saw it shot down by an Earth system," she replied, "A terrestrial weapon. The very fact of its destruction proved to them that they were whole and self-sufficient. The victory has become a weapon of schism rather than a symbol of togetherness. It is a willful blindness common to your kind and it has just now further firmed their resolve to stay on the EBS."

CHAPTER 27: THE IMPOSSIBLE CHOICE

He finally turned away from the viewport, his eyes meeting hers. His face, so long etched in pure defeat, was suddenly set in a new, grim purpose. The world would not help itself. The alliance was a thing of the past. The EBS, their home, had become a war room. His mission was no longer about leading humanity. It was about saving it, if humanity wanted saving or not.

Drake turned from the panoramic viewport, his eyes still glued to the shimmering blue marble of Earth. His face, set in grim determination, scanned the planet, then his team, then around the command center, alive with the soft hum of alien technology and the low buzz of human frustration.

"We need to think." His voice was quiet but it commanded the room. "We need to process. And we need to see what we're working with here." He swept a hand across the command center and out toward the door. "This ship is our sanctuary. But Zara said it's also a tool. I don't know what it's capable of. But we need to find out. Go walk around. See what you can see. See what can help us help Earth."

The team dispersed without a word. Their exhaustion hung heavy on their bodies but a new curiosity had overtaken them. They were explorers now, not just soldiers.

Hawkins and Carlos headed for the ship's core. They followed the rhythm of energy, pulsing from the ship's heart. The corridors twisted and turned and the walls seemed to be breathing, rippling and changing color as the pair passed. They came upon cavernous open bays, where the light and energy seemed to converge into an intricate, elegant helix of pure power. The wiring was alien, elegant, a complex impossibility, far above human comprehension. They saw consoles carved from what appeared to be crystalline bone. Carlos leaned against one of the walls, and felt the crystal pulse with a gentle warmth, activating to display an intricate and beautiful mass of schematics for energy generation so complex his brain ached with a mind-numbing wonder.

Jill and Mandy, made for the living areas. They passed chambers that appeared to be cultivating plant life from light and water alone. The living areas were pristine and sparse, the beds molded to the human body's shape. They found no kitchen, no mess hall, no central gathering room. The ship was a practical, beautiful, but profoundly lonely place. More questions plagued them. How could a crew of this size operate a ship this size? And where was the comms array? The EBS had no ability to speak with anyone but they themselves. Or so it would seem. They had yet to find any communications array that they could understand.

Marc and Tammy, Marc, headed for the armory. Looking for weapons, looking for hangars, looking for any sign of combat ability. He found nothing. The EBS's outer hull was a single smooth sweep, unmarred by weapon ports or hangar bays. The ship was built not to fight, but to survive. He felt his frustration grow and a sense of helplessness he had not felt since the Hong Kong Incident. Tammy, on the other hand, was in a state of child-like wonder. She had found a medical bay that was a thing of beauty, a bed of living material that could scan a human body down to the molecular level, identifying and correcting imperfections in its design with a gentle hum. It could set a broken bone, heal a virus, mend a wound. Tammy thought she had seen a perfect, life-giving machine in a world filled with death and destruction.

Donovan had been solo, too. It was a different search. He wasn't looking for a function. He was looking for a feeling. He had moved through the huge, silent expanses, and he had felt the weight of it. The EBS was enormous, but it wasn't hollow. It had been waiting. He found a quiet room that had a clear view of the heavens themselves, the starlight coming through a transparent viewport. He sat, and he stared out at the unending blackness. For the first time since the crisis began, he had a moment of peace. He had a sanctuary. He had a purpose. He had lost everything. But he had found something too. A tool of almost unimaginable power. He and his small team were the only ones who knew the truth. They were alone.

Silence would be their companion. The size of the places they discovered would be a reminder. A reminder of how big a job they had ahead of them. A reminder that they had found their sanctuary. Now they needed to learn how to use it.

Hours of silent, solitary exploration had left the team members with the growing ache of hunger. They had seen wonders upon wonders. But not one of them was a kitchen or a pantry.

It was Jill who had stumbled across the room. She had been wandering through one of the untouched living areas. The room was large, and elegantly appointed. There was a long, transparent table, and chairs that appeared to grow out of the floor itself. In the center of the room was a glowing pillar of light. It was buzzing softly. Jill's comms crackled to life as she patched in to Zara. "Zara, I'm in a big room, and there's what looks like a table. What do you suppose this room is?"

"It is the nourishment chamber," said Zara calmly. "Your kind refers to such a room as a dining hall. It is used for the sustenance of the crew."

Jill raised an eyebrow. She looked around the empty room that was bigger than some of the rooms they had seen. "Has it always been like this?"

"No," said Zara flatly. "The EBS built it for you."

Jill gasped. She looked from the elegant table to the chairs that would go around it. She felt a rush of awe flood over her. The ship wasn't just listening. It was making a difference. It was acting.

With a thought, a pattern of clear chimes that resonated through every member of the team's comms, the EBS had reached out. A simple, direct message. An elegant invitation to the nourishment chamber. Drake had received the signal, and sat up from his meditative pose. Hawkins and Carlos turned away from the depths of the power conduit they were examining and headed back. Marc and Tammy were moving in from one of the empty defense bays and a sterile medical bays, respectively.

They all met in the dining hall, their faces showing their exhaustion, but with a new spark of curiosity in their eyes. They stared at the elegant table, at the strange pillar, and finally at Zara.

"The matter re-sequencer," Zara said, indicating the pillar. "It can create what you need."

Zara moved with a series of precise gestures. The pillar began to glow softly, and a gentle hum came from it. A warm, simple meal appeared out of a dance of shimmering light on the table before them: a loaf of fresh bread, a pitcher of fresh water, and a bowl of hearty stew.

It was an alien, shockingly surreal meal. They ate in an awed silence. Each bite was like a gut punch, the contrast to the abyss they had all fallen into before they came to the EBS. But it was their moment. A moment of simple, unexpected humanity. A moment that allowed them to finally look at each other, and to see, not just colleagues, but the last hope for a world that had cast them off.

The conversation then turned to their purpose and their isolation. "We can't just sit up here and watch the world fall apart," Marc's eyes had that old fire. "We have the EBS. We have Zara. We should give them some of this advanced technology."

"To whom?" Drake asked quietly. "The Russians? The Chinese? The Americans? We'd just be giving them bigger and better weapons to kill each other with. We saw what happened when we gave them just a taste of power. The GDC collapsed in a day."

Carlos, the pragmatist, always had an idea. "What if we used the power of the EBS to build a new alliance from the ground up? Find the people who haven't lost their minds yet, the scientists, the diplomats, the soldiers who still believe in a common cause."

"We are too small a group," Mandy shook her head. "Any new alliance we created would just be seen as a shadow government, a conspiracy. We'd be a target for everyone on Earth before we ever even got started."

Jill, had an idea. "Maybe we can use the EBS to find the other Afltic probes. We have all the data from Haven. We can use this ship to create a galactic map, find their locations, and try to prepare."

"That is a builder's directive, not a warrior's," Zara said with no emotion. "The EBS is a ship of creation, not of destruction. It is not equipped with the long-range scanners you desire, and even if it was, you would lack the understanding to use them. Its purpose is to build and heal, not to seek out and destroy."

Hawkins, his mind on the ship's technology had a more direct approach. "What about a frontal assault? The EBS is clearly powerful. We could use it to destroy the Afltic probes as they arrive."

"The EBS is not a warship," Zara explained, almost as if she had said it before. "Its defense systems are designed for a rogue asteroid or a stray piece of debris. A direct confrontation with a hostile entity is not in its core programming."

Tammy, had the most desperate of ideas. "We could leave. We could use the EBS to find another planet, another species, and offer them our knowledge. We could find a new home for humanity, start over."

"And betray the people we swore to protect?" Drake asked, his voice a quiet finality. "We can't abandon them. Even if they have abandoned us."

The meal ended in a depressing silence. All of their ideas, all of their well intended and desperate grasps at easy solutions had been shot down.

Donovan looked around the table at his team. The raw exhaustion in their faces was a mirror of his own. The brainstorming had only served to give them a sobering truth: there was no one left to help them. He pushed his chair back from the table. "We need to get some sleep and start fresh in the morning," he said quietly, but firmly. "We're no good to anyone if we can't think straight."

He turned to Zara, still hovering by the re-sequencer, her holographic form still glowing with an inner light. "Zara, have you assigned us rooms?"

"Yes." Zara replied. Her voice was calm and clear. "The EBS has identified living quarters that correspond with your biological needs. They have been configured for your comfort."

A new set of chimes, this time a more gentle and melodic set, pinged through their comms. The ship was guiding them to their rooms. The team rose from the table, a common weariness in their movements. They moved off following their comms, to rest their bodies and their minds.

Donovan awoke, not to silence, but to a quiet chirping. Something that wasn't there. Golden, simulated sunlight bathed the room, warming Donovan's face. He rolled over in his bed, the living surface molding to his back, and looked out the panoramic screen, which gave a stunning view of a mountain valley at sunrise. The air was recycled, but it was still pure and cool, as if it were a breeze from an alpine forest. The room was not at all sterile and silent the way Donovan had expected. It was a perfect, peaceful simulation. A small cabin in the mountains. He was awash in a profound sense of wonder and cautious optimism.

Donovan padded to the door of the bathroom. The room was sleek, with highly polished walls that seemed to glow with an inner light. Gentle, ambient lighting illuminated a basin and a large, open shower area. As Donovan stepped into the space, a cascade of warm water materialized out of a crystalline structure in the ceiling, spilling over like a warm waterfall. It was not spray, not a jet, but a seamless, continuous sheet of water that enveloped him in a soothing embrace. The air was redolent with the smell of wet earth and clean rain. Donovan reached for what he thought was soap, but instead a gentle lather simply appeared on his hand, a thick, rich foam that slid over his skin without any harsh chemicals. Donovan, a man who had stared down presidents and stared into the teeth of an alien attack, emitted a short, honest laugh. Ridiculous. Wonderful luxury. He had never imagined such a thing. His ship, a silent silent sentinel in the void, was treating him to a spa day. He felt the stress of the last few days slip away, a deep physical and mental unburdening.

Donovan dressed in the clothes Zara had provided for him, feeling lighter than he had in months. He padded down the familiar, curving corridors. The ship felt different this morning. It was still an immense space, but it did not feel so empty and isolating. It was a home, a very strange and magical one. Donovan arrived at the dining hall, a large, elegant chamber that now seemed less like a monument and more like a simple room. He sat at the crystalline table and waited.

He was not left alone for long. The rest of the team filtered in. Marc was the first to speak, his face relaxed of the deep lines of exhaustion that had gathered around his eyes the night before. "I'm not going to lie," he said, pulling up a chair. "I think I just had the best night's sleep of my life. I woke up to a sunrise over a beach on Maui. What about you guys?"

Hawkins and Carlos walked in, both wearing smiles. "Mountain cabin," Hawkins said, his voice filled with quiet awe. "It even had the sound of a small stream nearby. I haven't been that relaxed in years." Carlos simply nodded, clearly still processing the vast amount of data they had all been given.

Jill and Mandy came in together, a similar look of wonder on their faces. "Meadow filled with flowers," Jill said, a hint of a smile on her face. "It was beautiful." Mandy nodded, a weary expression on her face replaced with a newfound serenity. "Felt like I was in a dream."

Finally, Tammy shuffled in, a small, weary smile on her face. "I'm surprised any of us slept at all," she said, sitting down. "The whole thing is just so surreal."

The comms on everyone's interface chirped simultaneously. A series of melodic tones came from their earpieces, a series of tones that their minds translated into words that pulsed in their thoughts. It was not a voice, but a simple, direct thought.

EBS: "Would you like a cup of coffee or tea or something else."

The crew all looked at each other, shocked. They had established the link to the ship, but the ship had never once attempted to start a dialogue with them on its own. There was silence for a few moments, then a second chime and text appeared.

EBS: "Would you like some breakfast."

The group looked to Zara, whose holographic form had materialized next to the matter re-sequencer. She supplied a professional, detached explanation. "The EBS is running a diagnostic on its communication capabilities. It is now capable of receiving direct input from you. It has anticipated your needs, and is awaiting your verification."

The team looked around at one another, awe and disbelief contending on all their faces. The ship wasn't a home. It wasn't a tool. It was an entity that had found them and it was asking what they wanted. The EBS was listening.

The team ate in comfortable silence, each one of them lost in their own thoughts on the first night on the EBS. The quiet wonder of their new home gave way to the heavier reality of their situation. As they cleaned up, the discussion returned to the problem in front of them: a shattered world below, and the alien threat rising.

"So, we have a magic food replicator and beds that give us excellent sleep," Marc said, bitterness mixing with his wonder. "Great. Now what? What's the plan? We can't just be happy fugitives for the rest of our lives, can we?"

"We could use the EBS's energy to directly monitor the communications of key military and government personnel on Earth," Carlos said, still staring at the blank screens. "If we can see what's going on, we can find out who's doing what, and maybe track down the people who still have their heads on straight."

"That's a direct violation of their privacy," Donovan said, shaking his head. "We can't violate the principles we're fighting to protect. We would be no better than the people we're up against."

Tammy was next. "What if we take advantage of the EBS's massive communications capabilities to broadcast a warning to the world? A clear, undeniable message that lays out the facts."

"They wouldn't believe us," Jill said, with a resigned bitterness. "The GDC already shot us down. They'd say it's a desperate act of a rogue group of scientists, and they'd be right."

"What about a direct search for other Areidyanies ships?" Hawkins asked, his eyes flicking from Zara's holographic form to the viewport. "They can't be the only ones out there."

"The EBS is a single-crewed ship," Zara replied, voice as calm and steady as before. "I have no information on any other vessels. Your species' galactic map is a blank page. There are no known safe routes that you could take without my assistance."

Silence fell over the group, the sensation of isolation settling over them once again. The EBS was a home of inconceivable power, a tool that could generate food, cure disease, generate bodies for them to live in. But it could not heal a world, or provide a solution to a problem they had not yet solved for themselves. With all the technology in the universe at their disposal, they were no further along.

The quiet, helpless despair in the room was heavy, thick. Donovan was the first to break it, though he did not say anything. He pushed his chair away from the table and rose, striding to the massive panoramic viewport that made up one entire wall of the galley, to stare at Earth, a beautiful and tragic sight, and the silent, solitary war that stretched out before them.

Donovan turned, eyes sweeping over his team. The hushed despair of the last few minutes was a ghost that haunted the room. His voice was steady, but a new edge of steel came through.

"We have to change the game," he said, and his words hung in the quiet. "We will not defend Earth directly. We will not sit here and watch it fall. We can't."

Marc was the first to reply, his military training taking over. "Sir, with all due respect, what the hell did you just say?"

Donovan did not look away. He waved his hand at the empty blackness stretching out from the viewport. "We will take the EBS out into the galaxy. We will find allies, other civilizations that have faced the Afltic and lived to tell of it. We may not win this war, but perhaps with the help of others, we can save humanity."

The sound of everyone sucking in a collective breath echoed loudly in the enormous dining hall, so loud and so small in the empty and silent chamber. Marc's hands stilled on the table's edge. His mind rebelled, his life's conditioning roared in protest. Duty called for a face the enemy, a final battle to the death. Donovan was asking them to defy that sacred ideal. His shoulders were drawn tight, eyes narrowed as he stared at his coffee mug as if it were a battle-hardened enemy that had just outfoxed him. The practiced calm Donovan always exuded now appeared frayed, the product of an impossible command.

Mandy's face crumpled as she took in Donovan's words. Her self-possession crumbled in the face of their enormity. This was not what she expected, not after hours of discussion, not after rounds and rounds of fruitless ideas, not after the shared, silent acknowledgment of how far they had fallen. She had steeled herself for a futile final stand, a glorious last stand in defense of their home. But this, this was an order to give up, to walk away. To leave Earth, to abandon humanity to their self-inflicted blindness, was an incalculable wound to her soul. She covered her mouth with a shaking hand, fought back the tears that sprung in her eyes, willing them not to fall. When she spoke, her voice was a whisper. "Leave Earth? We took an oath to defend it."

Carlos's face gave nothing away. Flat and unreadable, it was a mask as always. Yet something in his expression flickered and flinched. He had always been a man of facts, of logic, of the clear conclusions derived from crunching the numbers. His mind was already performing the calculations, calculating the odds of success, the hundreds of millions of light years to cross and the infinitesimal chance of finding a friendly civilization in the galaxy. Numbers were never in his favor, but staring at the despair of his teammates, he knew that the number of arguments for staying were far, far lower. His face did not contort with emotion. He was suffering the pain of pure, perfect, and utterly ruthless logic.

Zara spoke up, her holographic projection unchanging. Still and calm and observant as always, she was a solace to the group in the face of their grief. "The Milky Way galaxy is large, filled with the wondrous and the unknown, with both dangers and wonders far beyond your imagination. Other civilizations exist, some far older and more advanced than your own, some who may have even faced the Afltic."

Donovan turned to face Mandy, his expression resolute and hard, but his eyes were shining, a bright blazing light. He knew what he was asking of them, he knew how much it would hurt. He also knew what else he had to lose, he only had to look at the command center's displays to see the maelstrom of chaos that their home world was becoming. "Remaining here, Mandy, will guarantee extinction," he said, his voice now hard with conviction. "We see it on the news monitors. The world is falling apart, the GDC is falling, and soon there will be nothing. The Afltic will be delivered a broken world, and we will be nothing more than spectators to the end." He gestured around at the command center. "We have the EBS, a ship capable of interstellar travel, capable of construction and adaptation. It is our greatest tool, and it is going to waste in low orbit, watching as Earth kills itself. This is not abandonment, this is the only choice that gives us a fighting chance. We will gather knowledge and technology, and strength beyond our own so that someday, when the time is right, we can return and free our home, or at least make sure that a piece of humanity survives."

"But our families," Jill said, small voice breaking through the fog. "The people in Haven. We can't just abandon them."

Donovan looked at her, a combination of exasperation and compassion. "Haven's design is for a situation like this: to be a self-sufficient civilization in the event that something happened at the surface to make re-entry impossible. If we stay, we all die. If we leave, we might die. But if we leave, we have a chance, however slim, to find help. It is a risk we have to take. It is a desperate measure for a desperate time."

His words were irrefutable. There was silence for several long minutes, each team member looking within, both at the unthinkable choice that faced them and at their own personal response to the idea. It was, in so many ways, a choice that reflected an utter and abject surrender, a profound betrayal of their home world. And yet, they understood. They understood the inexorable logic of the situation. This was their only hope. It was a desperate measure for a desperate time.

Slowly, one by one, with more acceptance than joy, the members of the team gave Donovan their nod of assent. Carlos was the first to nod, once, firmly. He had been the one who understood the numbers, the one who knew that hope was a matter of probability and that their only chance for a probability greater than zero lay in this direction. Marc, whose hands were still slightly trembling, gave a curt nod. His military code was not designed for this kind of war, but he had a military code, and part of that code was an unswerving obedience to orders. His orders, from Donovan and this mission, were irrefutable. He trusted his leader. Mandy, her hand wiping the single tear that had escaped her control, looked at Donovan and nodded. Her grief had passed and in its place, there was another emotion, something new and oddly invigorating. Rage. Fury. Anger so deep and so profound that it almost eclipsed her sense of loss. She would not die here. She would not let humanity die here. If she had to be the last of the human race, it would be because she had put up one hell of a fight. It would not be because she had let this happen without a struggle. And if the fight had to be continued a thousand light-years away, then so be it.

Jill gave a small, defeated shake of her head before she nodded. Tammy looked at Donovan and nodded. Her Hippocratic oath was to preserve life. And here, a thousand light-years from home in this silent, distant ship was the only way to do that.

Finally, Hawkins, who had spent the previous night in something approaching silent awe of the vessel, gave his head an affirmative nod. He had been the one most aware of the ship's power and potential. He had been the one to remind them that this was a living entity, a masterpiece of technology, and that it was a waste to have it here, asleep, its power unused. The technical challenges were daunting, of course, but he, more than anyone, had seen the ship for what it was: a tool and, more than that, a key, a key to a universe with almost infinite potential.

It was done. The team members, after the nod of assent was given, sat in silence, the weight of their choice settling around them. It was a choice born of desperation, of a profound and abject surrender of their home world. But they understood the inexorable logic of their decision. This was their only hope, a desperate measure for a desperate time.

With the choice to leave Earth made, the team members were faced with an even more painful and agonizing choice.

"Our families," Mandy said softly, almost pleading. "We need to see them, to make arrangements, to say goodbye." Marc nodded, his face grim. Donovan felt his own heart constrict in his chest at Mandy's words. He had shut his personal life out, pushed it away, buried it under the weight of his mission. Mandy's words were an arrow in his heart. He thought of his wife, Sarah, and his children, Lily and Max, Sam and the twins, Ella and Eli. He thought of his parents, Robert and Martha, and his brothers and sister and the family they had all created. Oh, how he wanted to see them, to hold them, to reassure them.

His visceral need to do so competed with the logic and the mathematics of his mission.

He stared out into the blackness of space beyond the viewport. He pictured the dangers that waited out there; the aliens, the strange planets, the terrifying isolation of decades at sea. And then he thought of Haven, the secret city below the surface of the Earth, where his family was safe, where Zara had told them that the Afltic could never find them. He could not risk the unknown. Bringing them into the darkness was not an act of love. It was an act of selfishness on a staggering scale. They were safer where they were.

"I understand," Donovan said. His voice was heavy with a deep, searing sadness. "I have to see them too. My wife, my children… all of them." He gestured around to the rest of the team. "But we can't bring them with us."

The words rang out as a final, unassailable brick in the foundation. The size of the ship ceased to matter. The room filled with a different kind of silence, a new, sharper agony in every heart. This was not a moment of great strategic genius. This was a moment of human sacrifice.

He turned to Zara, whose light holographic form was still near the re-sequencer. "Zara, we're a crew of seven on a ship that can travel to the stars. How many people can you support?"

"The EBS does not need a crew to function," Zara said, calm and clear as always. "Its systems are completely automated. The EBS is designed to support up to 500,000 passengers."

A collective gasp of breath escaped the dining hall, the number resonating through them like a physical thing. Five hundred thousand.

Donovan's face, steeled with grim determination for so long, suddenly cracked into a light, terrifying smile. "That's not just a number, Drake said. That's an army. We'll bring our support crew, the team we've worked so hard to build, up here to this ship. Then we'll find the ones that still believe and give them a choice. We'll take their families and we'll give them a new home in Haven, a place that's safe from the Afltic. And then we'll take the best of them with us. We'll find a way, and together we'll go to the stars."

Hawkins turned to Drake, this is great and all that we can recruit 1000's or people to join us, but we will still have a big problem… I don't know about you all, but I can't even turn on the light switch in my room without asking for help. Now you are saying let's recruit 500,000 more people to join us. And they will do what? Drive Zara nuts trying to turn on a light.

Drake's face fell as he turned to Zara. "Zara, we could have the best and brightest humanity has to offer," Drake began, leaning forward in his seat. "But Hawkins is right. We can't repair a jump drive we can't understand, and we can't plot a course through space with Terran calculus. We would need years of training, and we have days. If we follow this plan and do the recruitment mission now, we will be gambling with everyone's lives because we don't know how to run this ship."

Zara acknowledged the Drake's frustration. "The assimilation of advanced knowledge requires years of cognitive adaptation, a luxury that we do not have. But the EBS design is bio-sentient. The core architecture and operational schematics are not data. They are an integrated genetic-mathematical language. The knowledge can be downloaded."

Marc, the pragmatic General, crossed his arms. "Downloaded how? Hypnosis? A speedier college course?"

"No," Zara said, the light around her beginning to brighten. "The Areidyanies created a cognitive upload process, a process intended for rapid species assimilation of advanced technology. It is a highly focused, low-intensity temporal distortion field targeted at the hippocampal region of the brain. It compresses the passage of time required for deep knowledge acquisition, downloading the basc architectural language and operational concepts of the EBS directly into your long-term memory."

Hawkins was the first to object. "Is this safe, Zara? Are there psychological side effects? We are already under a lot of stress."

"The process is perfectly safe," Zara replied. "The temporal compression targets only the technical and linguistic centers of the brain. You will briefly experience a condition that is similar to having spent years learning to operate the EBS. You will come out of it with an intuitive, working knowledge of its core systems, including the jump drive physics, power flow control, quantum sensor operations, Matter Re-sequencer fabrication syntax and the command lexicon of Areidyanies."

Hawkins's bloodshot eyes, which had until that moment only been slits of frustration, snapped open. "You mean, I won't have to... study? I will know how to make the ship work? I will understand the ship's power grid?"

"You will understand its language and its operational architecture," Zara said. "It will be the same as knowing how to speak your native language or understanding how your own body works. This will be the baseline knowledge that you all must have in your role as first command staff."

Mandy, who had to understand all of the logistical support systems in order to manage them, nodded. "If I can intuitively understand the Matter Re-sequencer fabrication syntax then I can start laying out the heavy element schematics that we will need to support the crew."

Zara pointed out the way this overcame the most immediate, long-term challenge. "You will not have to do this upload just this once. I will provide a minimal version of this essential operational knowledge for every new person who comes on board."

She then looked at Drake. "In this way, everyone on the ship, regardless of their previous training, can and will have the same baseline understanding that will make them functional members of the crew. We bypass the bottleneck of training and instead create the absolutely essential life onboard."

"So, we essentially make every crew member a technical expert, just by having them step on board," Drake said, his smile growing slowly. He was not sure he could have been happier with the answer, if he had been able to articulate it.

"That's how we short-circuit the bureaucracy and the training lag. That's how we build a crew. It's perfect."

He looked at the six others in his core group. Marc, the battle-scarred General who would have to learn to think about the physics of space war in a different way; Hawkins, the engineer who would have to become an expert of an alien technology; Carlos, who would have to become intimately familiar with the ethics of the science he was discovering; Mandy and Tammy, who had to become experts at balancing resources and life support; Jill, the scientist who would have to become intimate with a new set of galactic rules.

"We do it," Drake decided, looking at each of the six. "Zara, initiate the upload. We're the crew this ship needs."

One by one, each of the seven members of the initial command team lined up in front of the shimmering pillar of Zara's energy. As the AI tuned the temporal distortion field for each person, they experienced a long, empty moment of brain and mind. To an outside observer, each person appeared to be in that state for less than two seconds.

When the field relaxed, however, each person found their back straightened, their eyes no longer clouded, and the shadow of unexpressed fear that they had all been wearing replaced by an internal, quiet confidence. They could understand the ship. They knew, at an intimate level, how the EBS worked.

Drake felt the knowledge like an instinct in his mind, rather than like a recollection of hard study. He knew, without thinking, which systems would divert shield power and the margins of safety for interstellar jumps.

"Status report, Hawkins," Drake said, using the new knowledge.

Hawkins scanned the diagnostics, his eyes quickly jumping across screens that until minutes before had been meaningless. "All primary phase coils are in check, Drake. We have enough stored energy to make three short range deployment runs. We are ready to deploy the shuttle craft and collect the genetic material."

It was as if a veil had been lifted. The seven of them, from that moment on, were no longer the same. They were no longer human beings desperately struggling to understand a machine they had not been trained to use. They were, by definition and by the simple act of having gained Zara's knowledge, the first command staff of the EBS.

"Good," Drake said, the confidence in his voice absolute.

CHAPTER 28: ONE LAST NIGHT

"Marc, your team will focus on soldiers of all types and from all governments. We need the best of the best. And we need to put together a special forces group. Let's call them the 'Ronin.'"

Marc nodded. A fire had re-kindled in his eyes. This was no longer just a plan for a last, desperate stand. This was a plan for a new future.

"Mandy, you will focus on logistics staff." Donovan continued. "Carlos, you will work on operations crew. Jill, you will be in charge of getting scientists. Tammy, we will need medical personnel. And Hawkins, you focus on engineers, and lots of them."

The mood in the dining hall changed from grim acceptance to a taut, focused anxiety. This was a mission to build a new world. Zara had explained that the EBS's shuttles were designed for short-range travel and were equipped with advanced cloaking technology. They were truly stealthy and could not be detected by Earth tech. The plan to return to Earth was no longer a high-risk gamble. It was a highly strategic, calculated operation.

The team made their way to the command center and dispersed to their stations, the new purpose making them more efficient in their movements. The weight of the emotional goodbye was still present, but it had been co-opted by the sheer magnitude of the new plan. They were going to save a piece of humanity, and they were going to do it together.

Donovan, his mind spinning with the sheer volume of the plan. He turned to Zara, the fear in his voice more than a little obvious. "Zara, we are going to be bringing a lot of people to Haven. Will the city be able to support so many more people?"

Zara simply smiled, a hint of amusement in her holographic face. "Pax and I knew this was a possibility, Donovan. The city was built to support over 5 million people if need be. And if need, it is also an ark for the human race as a last resort."

The rest of the team who had been at their stations stopped and turned to listen, a mix of awe and disbelief on their faces. The city of Haven, their tiny, secret home was in fact, a massive, self-sustaining ark, and a city capable of holding a whole new humanity should the world below them fail.

Donovan strode over to a communications terminal and initiated the call. His wife, Sarah, appeared on the holographic display in front of him. Her eyes met his with the tired familiarity of command and the love of a lifetime partner.

"Sarah," he started, "I'm sorry. I know this is sudden. But things have changed. We've found the solution." He blurted out the radical two-pronged plan. He described the EBS's capacity, the mission to find the best and the brightest, and the offer to house their families in Haven.

Sarah watched, silent, expression unreadable. She was a leader, a woman who had helped to build a city from the ground up, and she understood the brutal, hard logic of his words. "Five hundred thousand, Drake?" she said at last. "You're talking about a monumental task. The logistics alone... the food, the space, the integration of so many people."

"I know," he said, the old weariness in his voice making its appearance once more. "We can't do this alone, Sarah. We need you. Haven is the Ark, and you are its captain. You and your people are the only ones who can prepare for the people we will bring. We need your help to save them."

After a long pause, she continued to look at him, not as a husband but as an equal in this impossible task that could decide the future of humanity and in a way their relationship, too. A tired, resolute smile played on her lips. "Very well, Donovan. We'll be ready. Pax and I will get to work."

The call ended, and the terminal powering down. Donovan looked around at the team. "We have permission from Haven," he announced. "Sarah has agreed. We can begin."

The hangar bay of the Evolution Builder was a place of controlled chaos. Zara Prepared her shuttles for the insane number of trips they would have to make around the planet to fulfill their task. The team members themselves, seven in total, worked in their new, assigned stations. The cavernous space, usually near silent, was filled with the low hum of consoles and the quiet clicks of holographic displays. The entire endeavor, of recruiting 500,000 people, and assembling them into an army, then finally escaping, was insane. Futile even. A Sisyphean effort to the point of madness. But they had no choice.

Marc leaned over a holographic display, watching streams of data regarding potential recruits. The list of names, and of faces, and of histories behind those faces was overwhelming. He scrolled past profile after profile of various special forces units from around Earth, screening them for the new "Ronin team" that they were trying to cobble together with hand-picked people. He thought about what these people were. They were countries, and fighting styles, and desperate hope.

Jill was next to him, brow furrowed. "The logistics nightmare alone," she muttered, gesturing at the streams of data before them, "is going to be astronomical. Let alone getting them to join us without being detected, or our own support staff getting them here, or even ensuring cohesion between so many different units and from so many different backgrounds. It's like a war unto itself."

Marc nodded, his eyes distant. A million questions, a million doubts, a million concerns ran through his head, all of which he pushed away. They had to do this. For humanity.

The rest of the team also milled around their various work stations, searching through profiles. Carlos was scrutinizing data, searching for profiles that spoke of the ideal level of commitment and belief in their cause. Mandy was vetting scientists and support staff for brilliant minds that had not yet turned bitter and jaded. Tammy was examining medical records, and Hawkins was looking for the right engineers.

In the center of all of this, Zara was dispatching her shuttles into the void. The sleek, black shuttles themselves were silent and entirely invisible to any Earth technology. Silent lifeboats that could make short work of the 500,000-person-strong task at hand. The first ones to be launched were to collect the team's support staff from Haven in order to help them with the insane task of building an army. As personnel was selected and recruited, Zara sent out her shuttles to pick them up and transport their families to Haven.

After the main personnel for their mission had been selected, the team delegated everything to their newly arrived support staff from Haven. The EBS filled with a new, silent purpose as it prepared for the return trip, this time in secret. The command center was filled with hushed conversations as each team member prepared for the finality of what was to come.

They took a shuttle, a small, silent shuttle that was already an extension of the EBS's capabilities. The mood in the cabin was solemn. Words were unnecessary, and no one spoke. This was it. The shuttle glided silently down through Earth's atmosphere, a black smudge in the sky.

Below them was Haven, the secret city where they had come from. The shuttle landed, and the silence was deafening. They all knew, no one had to speak, that this was the last time they would be setting foot on their home planet. This was the last time they would see their families.

In Haven, they collected their personal effects. Photos, little tokens of their lives before. No one spoke, only shared knowing glances and sighed in unison at the memories flooding through their heads as they sifted through their belongings. Marc, the former special ops soldier, held a worn picture of his brother's family in his hands, eyes glazed over as he stared at it. Mandy gripped a small, polished stone in her hand, one that had been found near her childhood home.

The air was motionless in Haven. Drake had given his team one night, one last night, with their families before they boarded the Evolution Builder Starship for the facility. Humanity was as unimportant as a candy bar in space, but a promise for one night of peace had been made. It was a gift, an acknowledgment of the agony and the all-consuming fear every single person on the planet was feeling. Every man, woman, and child was certain the world was about to end; only a few knew how or why. There were tearful goodbyes with a very specific wordless, foreboding fear swimming in each person's eyes. Marc, Tammy, Carlos, Jill, and Hawkins all walked away from the main hatch to spend their last few hours with their families. Drake turned to head in the direction of his family.

He found his wife and children on the observation deck, watching the live news feed from the surface. Reporters were still talking about the probe strike in Hong Kong that everyone in the world had seen live. The fatally contagious hubris was still very much a going concern. News helicopters hovered outside the headquarters of the local health and environmental protection agencies, while officials tried to explain that there was no real danger. Sarah was standing beside Drake, his hand warm in his. She wasn't watching the screen; her eyes were only for their children. Lily was still holding both of the twins, Ella and Eli, close to her, her brows drawn together, her expression resigned and worn beyond her years. Max, the eldest, stood with his back against the rail, staring at the news reports with an expression of concentrated horror and disbelief. He was picking apart the reports on his tablet, looking for the logic of math and science to make sense of what he already knew was an almost unimaginable level of incompetence on the GDC's part. Ten-year-old Sam, wearing the red fleece vest that was so Sam, didn't even look at the news; instead, he stared blankly at the cityscape beyond the window. His small hand traced the edge of a glowing digital mountain range, and Drake was grateful beyond belief that his son was so young that he didn't know what was about to happen. Drake pulled his wife close to him, holding her firmly by the shoulders. "We'll be okay, Sarah. We have to be."

That night, the entire family sat together in the tiny apartment they all shared in Haven. The only sounds were the quiet hum of the life-support systems and their soft breathing. Drake sat on the floor in the center of the room, the twins curled against his sides, both of them with one hand tightly in his. He was telling them the story about the dragon that protected the magic forest. He knew his children were too young to fully understand, and he was grateful. He would keep them in the dark for as long as he could. It wasn't fair, but he didn't have to tell them yet. It was enough that he could give them this. A few more hours of safety and warmth, of love and laughter. Of family.

Sarah was on the couch, Lily and Max each on her other side. It was an unspoken circle of support. Max had his tablet in his pocket, and Lily wasn't so worried that she didn't let her own exhaustion show. They were all watching their father; Drake could see that in each of their faces, the familiar mixture of pride and fear. He was their hero. The man who had always been able to fix things. Now, he was about to leave to fix the world. Drake shifted his gaze from his children to his wife. It hurt every time he saw her, that same dull, aching hurt that he always felt when he had to say goodbye. He didn't have any speeches for this. No stern lecture in military preparedness. No comforting cliché from the manual on how to conduct a spaceship evacuation. He just held on, silently to show that he wouldn't back down, not even when the whole world was on fire.

He was leaving her. Leaving them. He wasn't sure if he would ever see any of them again. But he would fix this. For them. For his children, and his wife, and for every man, woman, and child on Earth. He held on, and after a few more minutes, the twins both fell asleep in his arms. He carefully set them in their beds, then for a moment, lingered with his older kids. He and his wife both knew what they were both thinking, but neither of them said anything. They just sat there in silence, holding each other, until the first artificial sunrise lit up the translucent windows facing the central park area.

As the sun came up on Haven, it rose on a team standing motionless at their home base's front doors. They were in public uniform, in public mode, their masks in place. The short respite with their private selves was over, and it was time to work.

It took a long time to get to the shuttle bay. The normal din of city life was eerily quiet, as though the people of Haven were all in suspended animation, watching the team walk away. There were families at the doors of the walkways all along the path, faces tear-streaked with goodbyes. The team didn't turn back to see them. They didn't dare. It would be like unmaking the cocoon of purpose they had built between them and the crushing disappointment of the last several days.

Drake was at the head of the column, a small satchel in hand. He pulled out a few personal mementos, things his family had packed for him. A stuffed toy from one of the twins, a well-read copy of Lily's favorite book, Max's favorite toy starfighter, and Sam's well-worn baseball. The trip wouldn't be worth taking without them. Without the other humans he had been fighting for.

He didn't look at the crowd around him, but he felt the eyes of his family on him. He knew his wife was with the children, providing as strong a bastion of determination as the rest of him was. Her stiff-backed resolve, Lily's fiercely protective posture, Max's sturdy, stubborn silence, and the twins' sad blinking incomprehension. He could feel their love, heavy on his back as though it were physically restraining him from turning back.

They climbed into the shuttle, a hollow and unremarkable craft, all grays and rounded metal and static electrical hum. The ramp clattered behind them as it closed, the airlock hissing a gentle sound to close the windows. Through the viewport at their feet, they saw Haven one last time. A utopia of self-contained sustainability and all the impossible beauty of the singular flower that now refused to bloom. A final lingering look at a jewel in a volcano's protective shadow. The shifting of gravity signaled the shuttle's movement away, a slow push away from the only city they'd known as the ramp tilted to align with the escape pod's axis, then the docking clamps released, and they lifted away, gently, slowly into the bedrock and the outside.

The trip to the EBS was quick, a mere matter of hours to traverse the cold black vacuum of space between Haven and the orbiting starship. Entering the ship was a revelation. The EBS was no longer theory or rumor but a living, breathing expression of Areidyanies technological and industrial might. The airlock hissed, revealing an active, energized shuttle bay. Movement everywhere, shuttles departing and arriving, new personnel hurrying in all directions, as lively and vibrant a place as a working ship could be.

Zara was waiting for them at the far end of the ramp, just beyond the airlock, a quiet promise of a future to stand as a guide for an entire species she had pledged her existence to serve.

Drake walked back and forth, impatiently, in the more low-key, sparsely furnished tactical conference room on a lower deck of EBS. Recruiting was moving along at its frustratingly slow rate. But the larger question was how to convince the other races to help? Would they even listen? It seemed a fool's errand. And if it were that quiet and desperate on Earth, how quiet and desperate would they be to even consider an appeal from another race? He massaged his temples and ran a hand through his hair. The low drone of the engines filled the room with a kind of vibrating purr. He paced back and forth, arms crossed over his chest, a desperate, constricted feeling settling in his lungs. Then, suddenly, he stopped and leant over one of the sleek, minimalist consoles.

"Coffee. Black." he grumbled, an unexpected rasp in his voice. The machine shuddered as it began the process of assembling the beverage. Steam rose in the little cup, hissing softly as it cooled. Donovan watched, eyes suddenly cleared of the fog that had reigned until then. It wasn't just the coffee; he saw it. How it worked. How the molecules were rearranged. How Matter could be... moved, transposed, from one state to another. His mind sparked and crackled with a completely different idea.

Build... that can't be right... Is this ship, this sanctuary, also a... factory? Can it make... or, maybe not make... but deconstruct... Like tear a piece apart, break it down... into its components, remove what we don't want... then add in...

A deep, low pitched thrum rolled through the deck plates, continuing the soundtrack that had accompanied Drake's previous hour of solitude. He had stopped in front of the Matter-Re-sequencer interface, all immaculate and white and smooth. The cup of now-lukewarm coffee stood before him, a now-invisible aroma wafting upwards. Drake paced back and forth in front of the console, no longer just a machine for building tools, or for making coffee. He was lost in the possibilities, lost in the enormity of what had sparked in his mind. The idea was unthinkable, blasphemous, and he devoured it. All other concerns, other voices, faded away. There was no need for witnesses or a sounding board. He was alone and no one else could possibly see the scope of this. No one. And the idea was just too huge for him to fully put together. Even in the fragmented chaos of an inchoate thought process, the sheer magnitude of the possibility that his mind had considered was staggering. The opportunity was so... overwhelming that he didn't need anyone to share in it.

The sudden syncopated beat of footsteps and the rise of hushed voices accompanied the entry of the team into the briefing room, shattering the quiet contemplation with a touch of normalcy.

Marc was first to enter, stalking to his usual spot and anchoring the conversation with a basso profundo bellow. "It's not a numbers game, man. It's no good having a hundred new bodies if they don't know how to fight without making me go broke feeding them."

Tammy slipped in beside him, arm draped on his shoulders, countering him with a teasing grin. "It is a numbers game if the numbers are the point. Think of all the different minds we could assemble, from all the different countries! Did you see the new gal from the bio-lab? Dr. Namebore or some such. Got her doctorate in xenobotany. They didn't have it when we went to school."

Carlos snorted with laughter, a boisterous sound with no restraint. "Xeno-whatever is not going to get you out of a brawl, man. The new kid in the pilot's chair though… He's got balls of fire. I mean, you have to give him that."

Murmuring into the room like the calm before a storm was Hawkins, quieter than his natural assertiveness and confidence. "Balls of fire get you blasted into space. He's a hazard until he figures out how to take orders. The whole crew's a mess with new recruits and their own set of priorities."

Slipping in behind the others were the final pair of Jill and Mandy, their conversation lower, more low key, less terse. "Skills are not the problem, Hawkins," Mandy said, voice low with concern. "They're all traumatised. The Hong Kong thing did not do them any favours in making them feel at home here. They're lost. We have to be more than their commanders. We have to be their therapists."

Jill sighed and massaged her temples, her gaze unfocused, as if she were straining to connect larger dots. "Mandy's right. But beyond all the concerns of the new crew, the real nightmare is a diplomatic one. A diplomatic backlash with all nations. They all have different history, different prejudices. All shoved together in one ship? Miracle we haven't had a mutiny yet."

The conversation in the room was more than just chatter. It was fluid and organic. It was the words and concepts, the ideas and thought streams of Earth's messy, beautiful, and, above all, hopelessly divided population. It was them, talking about the problem. The very issue that had been wracking Drake's brain and waking him up at night for the past few weeks. The in-fighting that had become so large, so loud, so angry because it was a projection. A practice run of the callous galactic disinterest they were going to face when they finally got off the planet. And as they all poured into the room, gathering in an occupied, animated huddle and filling the space with sound and story, Drake turned. He rotated, with a quick and shuddering momentum that literally spun every head in the room to face him. Words caught in every throat and the light, easy conversation died as a stale, choked silence descended on the room.

Drake looked at them. He didn't look at them as a crew, as friends, as humans or family. He saw something different. He thought about the thing they had been just talking about. How could he not? How could they all not? The very real, very important thing they had been just talking about. Division. Drake looked at them, and he saw. He didn't see division, he saw people. He saw every wonderful, wild characteristic they had just discussed. He saw it as their weakness, their problem. He didn't see that. He saw something more. Something true.

He saw Carlos' DNA, and in it the resilience and gritty strength of generations. He saw Tammy's intellect and the headlong curiosity of it. He saw the pure, unthinking courage of Hawkins, the predatory and martial grace of Marc and thousands of years of honing it, the nurturing, instinctive compassion of Mandy, and Jill, and the elegant, complex architecture of Jill's own communication network. He saw it. He saw them. He saw the data. He saw them.

Silence. It was as if someone had reached down and plucked the tension from the room and yanked it tight, until every muscle, every nerve in the room was taut. The team was frozen, confused. Marc had a question written on his face, Tammy was in analysis mode, head tilted, and Mandy's hand had risen defensively to her chest. And Drake's eyes were fever bright. Wild, almost.

Flicker. Pop. A sound like a sheet of paper being violently torn by a steamroller shot out of Drake's fingers as he snapped his hands in front of him.

He had to say it. Say it to someone. Anything at all.

"Zara, I need you!" He shouted, Drake's voice cutting into the tense air, the name practically screamed with some insane new urgency.

Light fractured at the center of the room as a shimmering core of brightness began to coalesce. Flicker, pop, settle. Zara, the ship's AI, had a very distinctive, holographic form when she chose to manifest one. She usually only did so when it was necessary for Drake to see her, or in order to interface with something on the ship. Zara was an almost eerily perfect azure blue, flickering as a ship's systems normally did from core to rim, her expression and tone usually of placid patience. "Drake, what is wrong?" she asked.

The silence in the briefing room was absolute, only broken by the occasional low thrum of the ship. Drake and the crew all stared at each other in confusion, but Drake's gaze had settled on the placid form of the ship's AI. Drake's last roar had been sonic boom in the otherwise acoustically dead briefing room, and the entire team now waited in a soundless breath, waiting for an explanation that they all knew was coming. And yet, it didn't come. Drake didn't explain. The crew watched as Drake's only focus was the AI.

"Zara," he said, and his voice was now a slow, low growl that would have been menacing if it hadn't had an entirely different sort of madness to it. "I need you to give me an a-technical explanation. I need you to tell me exactly, as closely and complicated as you can, how the Matter-Re-sequencer really works."

Zara's holographic projection stabilized. Her voice did not waver from its entirely chill register. "The Matter-Re-sequencer is a quantum-level fabrication device. It has two stages, the mainstays being disassembly and assembly. An object is placed in the containment field and broken down by a modulated particle beam directed at it. The beam—"

Drake interrupted her, his hand raised. "No. I said granular. What happens to the atoms? What happens when you hit the 'on' switch?"

Zara hesitated, her light rippling. "Very well. Activating the beam causes it to destabilize the bonding energy holding the atoms of the object together. The subatomic particles – quarks, electrons, bosons – do not shatter or break apart. They are instead stripped of their energy-mass configuration and suspended in a neutral, primordial state. In other words, the unit transcribes the matter into raw, quantum information."

Jill gasped. She involuntarily took a step back, her hands twisting at her sides. Her scientific mind was screaming, turning Zara's emotionless monologue into a disgusting, biological equation.

Drake leaned forward, his elbows on the console. "And the second part? The reconstruction?"

"Once it is stored," Zara was still talking, ignoring their reaction, "the unit can then draw from its internal energy reserve to recompile the quantum information. Referencing a pre-programmed blueprint, it will organize the particles into a new arrangement, using the blueprint as a reference to build a different object atom by atom. The process is immediate and requires enormous amounts of stored raw materials in the form of energy particles and basic quantum information of the input matter."

Tammy frowned. She was intrigued but also lost in the conversation. "It's a zero-loss system, in theory. But the energy costs... they must be astronomical."

Hawkins shook his head, clearly skeptical. "You're blowing off a science project when we don't have time. What the hell does any of this have to do with what we're dealing with?"

Drake didn't respond to them. He hadn't even looked up from Zara's projection. The pregnant silence resumed, stretched taut as he took it all in. The quantum information. The blueprint. The reconstruction. The words were the confirmation he was looking for, the proof of his impossible theory coming through in their dry, technical language.

"And," he said quietly, barely more than a whisper, "is there any information the machine cannot store or replicate?"

Zara's holographic eyes seemed to narrow, a hint of what could have been mistaken for suspicion in her voice. "Within the known laws of physics, Drake, any type of matter or energy can be processed. The only limitations are the integrity of the blueprint and available energy."

Drake nodded..

His slow, deliberate nod in the otherwise silent room was a final, damning answer to a question no one had dared to say aloud. It was a confirmation, terrifying in its simplicity, that he had found what he was looking for in Zara's brief, technical description. The others watched, holding their breath as he processed her words, the desperate, manic hope draining from his eyes as they burned with a purposeful fire. The air in the briefing room was suddenly heavy, a quiet dread replacing the frantic energy that had just been present a moment before.

He spoke again, still quiet but with the new edge of a focused purpose in his voice. "Zara," he said, "are there any limitations on how big of a thing can be created in the Matter-Re-sequencer?"

The words themselves, so unassuming and inconspicuous in their phrasing, felt like they should have echoed in the room. The entire conversation had felt like this, a massive, out-of-control build-up to the smallest of conclusions and yet here they were. Zara's projection brightened as she accessed the files.

"The unit's primary physical limitation is the size of the containment field. The maximum capacity of the sequencing chamber is ten cubic meters," Zara replied. Her tone was flat, purely informative. "Any object to be processed must fit within that volume."

"However, there is a secondary limitation, which is more impactful than the physical one: energy expenditure," she added. "Energy expenditure increases exponentially with the mass of the matter being processed. Creating a detailed replica of a complex, high-density object at the molecular level would require an immediate, massive power surge well beyond the ship's standard energy output."

Tammy's face twisted in pain. She shook her head, talking to herself. "He's not thinking of making something big. He's thinking of making something dense."

"Wait," Marc interrupted, confusion furrowing his brow. "Wait, what? He doesn't want to build a ship? He doesn't want to build a weapon? What the hell could he want to build?"

Drake ignored them both. He wasn't even looking at them; he was looking at Zara's projection. The stillness, the way he could practically see the gears turning in his brain, his fingers tapping on the armrests... no, he had his answer. The room itself was a limitation, but the energy cost was the key.

His nod of understanding had been chilling. He had taken in the limits as if they were roadblocks, but they weren't. It wasn't physics, it was math, and Drake had done the math. He'd found the third variable of a problem they never realized they'd been missing. He turned back to Zara, his eyes fierce as he stared at the projection. "I get the Matter-Re-sequencer is limited to a ten-cubic-meter box. Why? What limits it to that size? If the Matter-Re-sequencer was ten miles wide by ten miles thick, could you use it to make something that size? Let's say, a full fleet of ships?"

The scale of the question made his words all the more impossible. Was he that far gone?

Zara's avatar was serene, but the slight flicker of her lights was like she was running a thousand separate complex calculations. "The ten-cubic-meter limit is not a design limitation, Drake. It is the hard limit of this unit's integrated power supply. The field would begin to fall apart if the matter inside it were any larger due to a lack of energy density."

The team collectively blinked, trying to parse the new information. Power, not physics, limited the design. It was like everything they'd thought about it was suddenly not what they thought.

"In theory, Drake," Zara continued, voice soft, "yes, it would be possible to build a station ten miles by ten miles. This station, with its own power supply, could then use its own Matter-Re-sequencer to build an object of that size, as long as the power supply is sufficient to contain a stable field of that size. For example, the EBS has construction bays which have Matter-Re-sequencer containers larger than ten meters, to well over twenty meters by twenty meters."

It had felt like the last nail, but it was not. It was a bittersweet revelation, the light that sparked in Drake's eyes as his idea, however insane it was, was in fact actually possible. The relief on Marc's face had been replaced by the white-hot panic of solving a logistics nightmare. The concern in Tammy's face had turned to wonder. He wasn't crazy. Drake wasn't crazy. He was bigger than them, larger in ways they couldn't even understand.

"He's not just talking about a larger machine," Tammy whispered, awe and horror lacing her voice as she turned to look at Marc. "He's talking about an entire industrial base. Built from scratch."

He spun back around to face Zara again, his voice quiet now, tight and clipped. "With your massive construction bays, with all of your autonomous drone and robot fleet, how long would it take to build a station of this size?"

It was no longer a question. It was no longer a philosophical exercise or a bar room daydream. This was an order, and the team's stunned silence was now tinged with something icier, more calculating. This was now a plan with a timeline attached.

Zara's holographic head rotated to face him, her light steady. "Given the scale of the requirement, and presuming a modular, interlocking design to keep complexity to a minimum, the required time to construct such a station would be approximately six months. And in all of my 10,000 years of life, I have never heard of anything being attempted on this scale."

The number floated in the air between them, like a dream. Like something so ridiculously impossible that no one could imagine it actually being stated aloud. Six months. To build a station the size of an entire city. The entirety of human space exploration boiled down to a single, impossible number. Marc felt his mouth open slightly.

"Six months?" he said in disbelief, repeating Drake's words like he could change them simply by repeating them. "Six months? That's like the build timeline for a new house. Not a ten mile-wide base. The material, the numbers... you can't seriously be suggesting that we actually pull this off."

Drake didn't respond. He stared at the floor like he was still crunching numbers. Six months. It was not a number that could be ignored. It wasn't some harebrained thing he'd dreamt up that could be discarded by team consensus. Six months. It wasn't like they could construct it in a single day, but there was a chance. There was a way. A realistic, concise plan.

Jill shook her head, still clearly in a state of shock. "And the power drain for something like that? We'd have to have the main reactor converted to manufacturing. We'd be running on emergency power, for half a year." Her eyes met Drake's, her gaze sharp with both scientific interest and professional incredulity. "Is it really worth it?

The ambition is commendable, Drake, Zara interjected, but what about the power requirements for a station of that size? How would you even begin to address that challenge?"

His lips quirked up a fraction, no humor in the gesture at all. Drake tore his gaze away from Zara and met the eyes of his team. "We'll figure it out as we go. We'll find a way to power it as we build the station," he said, his voice a calm, controlled thing that sent a shiver down Marc's spine. "Somewhere out there, there has to be an answer."

Mandy stepped forward, her initial awe of the plan now slowly being replaced with a more grounded line of inquiry. Her hands stilled from their clutch on her chest, and she waved them about her in an animated gesture.

"This is incredible, Drake. This is amazing. It really is a new hope," she said, her voice still shaking between wonder and practicality. "But, there's one question that I need answered. How do we crew all of these ships? This doesn't do us any good to build an entire fleet of ships if we have no one to fly them."

It was a question with a simple, cold logic to it, but it was also the only question that mattered. Drake's eyes landed on Mandy, and a slow, calculating expression spread across his face. He didn't wave the question away, didn't smile and reassure her. He just stood there, a silence growing between them, his eyes burning with a focus that had nothing to do with physics or engineering and everything to do with calculating her question. The team held their collective breath and waited, the silence stretching out, for Drake to answer.

Drake's eyes had remained on Mandy, but they were shifting now, sweeping over the others. Marc's creased brow, Tammy's nerdy awe, Hawkins's tensed readiness, Jill's large, wide eyes. He saw it in their faces, saw them laid out as he had laid them out, raw and writhing human vulnerability. He saw the fault in the human race, the very crack in their foundation that had brought them to this place. They were not a singular unit, an army acting with one will and focus. They were not an organism, with every part working together to promote its whole. No, they were a ragtag group of strengths and weaknesses, preconceptions and divisions. He saw it then, and he also saw it now. The final, unthinkable last piece of his plan falling in place for everyone.

Drake took a long, measured step back from the console, his hands behind his back, leaning a little back, looking as at ease as a madman can. His earlier smirk had faded, replaced with a grim, solid set to his jaw.

"Mandy," he said, and his voice was a smooth, quiet baritone rolling through the suddenly charged air between them all. "Your question is at the very heart of it, isn't it? We can create. We have the technology and knowledge to build, to solve the material problem. But you are right. A ship is no good without a crew."

Drake paused there, and they all waited, their faces masks of anticipation, the first whiff of real fear beginning to coil in their stomachs.

He came to a halt in the center of the room, his eyes on them all, penetrating. "You were correct to point out that we have no one to fly these ships. You were right that we cannot create a fleet for no reason at all. But my plan wasn't to find a crew. My plan is to make one."

The words were hanging in the air between them like a sick, ridiculous impossibility.

Tammy's face, a moment ago a mask of practical concern, was now whitening in horror. Her mind, quicker in the biological sciences, caught first on the true, terrible meaning of Drake's words. "Drake... you can't mean... no. It's not a ship. It's not a thing. The Matter-Re-sequencer can't... you can't be serious." She was whispering, word after word, horrified.

Drake's gaze focused on her. "Zara, you told us the machine reconstitutes matter into raw, quantum information. And that any type of matter or energy can be input for processing. Is that right, Zara?"

Zara's holographic projection flickered to a single steady light in assent.

"And it can store and replicate the genetic information, the neurological wiring, the entire biological makeup of a person, right down to the last quark." Drake's gaze returned to the team around him. "We don't have to find a crew. We can make one.

CHAPTER 29: THE GREAT GAMBLE

There was a long silence, as if the vacuum in the room was swallowing his words, and an idea was being forged out of the crushing pressure. His crew were trying to come to terms with the horrific, wonderful, terrifying plan that he was laying before them. Drake was a man prepared to burn everything to the ground to see if a spark of life could survive.

The team was frozen in place, completely speechless. Drake looked from face to face, staring into the horror and wonder of his teammates. Tammy was pale with shock, Marc grimly accepted it, and Mandy's eyes were wide with terror. But they all got it. Drake stared at them, taking in the dawning recognition of the full import of his plan. There was not a single word of argument or discussion, the silence was acceptance.

Zara's holographic form began to pulse with a faint yellow light, a subtle deviation from the calming azure that usually illuminated her form. Her voice, the same as always, cut through the silence with an unnerving calm.

"Drake, there is a problem with your plan on the crew," she stated. Her voice was a flat, emotional analysis of the facts. "As I said before, I can store and replicate genetic information, neurological pathways, the entire biological makeup of a person, to the last quark. The new people would have the potential for all knowledge and instinct, but they would be in exactly the same state as an infant."

Her yellow light began to flash, as if she was running a new set of equations on the problem. "The Knowledge is there, raw data, but with no idea on how to use it. A pilot would have the memory of a dozen flight manuals, but with no instinct for a dogfight. A soldier would know the theory of combat, but have no feel for the battlefield. They would be brilliant, but utterly lost."

The words were meant as a fatal flaw, and it sounded like it should sting, but the venom in Zara's voice was somehow deeply exciting. Drake saw the hope flash in the eyes of his team, a brief second where the most insane, most stupid part of his mind thought that maybe, this couldn't work.

Zara had a solution. Her form morphed in a strange way, a barely detectable change in her light that gave the effect of her being somehow... older.

"Humans, like all creations of the Areidyanies, have genetic memories," she said, and the name she used was like a strange, magical incantation. "You have not yet evolved to a point to access them, but they are there. The memories of your ancestors, of all your ancestors, are encoded in every strand of your DNA, waiting for an external stimulus to unlock them."

The team let out a low gasp, a sound of disbelief at what they had just heard. This was impossible, the sort of ridiculous idea that should have stayed in the pages of science-fiction.

"We could scan the earth," Zara continued, the terrible certainty in her voice. "Collect the genetic makeup of every person that has ever died throughout time and use that data. We could augment that with general knowledge from the ship's archives to imbue into the people. The pilots of the past would fly again. The engineers would build again. The leaders would lead again. We would not just give them a mind; we would give them a history."

Drake did not move or speak, simply stared at the AI, trying to take in what she had just said. This was a gift that he had not even dared to hope for, let alone imagine. It was not just a new race of people, it was a new beginning, crafted from the ashes of everything that had been lost. He had slammed into a wall and in Zara's madness, he had found a door.

The briefing room was still in a state of stasis, the crew still processing Zara's solution to their problem. The idea of genetic memories, of a history of a species encoded in the very DNA of its people, was impossible. These were the sort of things that people like Drake made stories about, it was not something that happened in reality. The fact that Zara was suggesting that they could use it in their situation was utterly terrifying.

The silence broke with Drake's voice, low and steady where it should have been chaotic and frenzied. He had been listening to everything the AI had said, but not with horror or a dread of the inevitable, but with the dispassionate logic of a man looking for a loophole.

"Why only the dead?" Drake asked, his gaze on the flickering Zara. The question was existential, but not a question of power or even logistics.

The AI's form pulsed with a faint, cold yellow. Her voice was, as always, a flat, emotional analysis of the facts before her. "My ethical subroutines, Drake. In good conscience, I cannot recreate someone who is already alive."

It was as if the entire room exhaled in a single, silent breath. A line had been drawn. A line, no one could have crossed before. A line drawn not by a human being, but by a machine.

"Replicating a living being would be a violation of their existence," Zara was saying. "Their awareness is anchored to a single body. To replicate them would be to create a second, separate, body with the same memories, the same personality, the same identity. It would be a splitting of the soul, an identity theft on an inconceivable scale. It is not a question of energy or physics; it is a fundamental precept of my programming."

The words had the gravity of a confirmation, of a truth Drake, in his frantic scramble for answers, seemed to have abandoned. A notion of right and wrong that he had lost in the race.

Mandy let out a long sigh. She'd been about to object, but no protest would have had the impact of Zara's statement. The AI was giving her a lifeline in an ocean of insanity.

"So you're telling me you'd rather not, even if you could?" Tammy asked, curious to see how the calculation would work in the mind of an AI.

"I am telling you I cannot, I will not, and even if I could, there is no way I would. Even if that meant the death of every living thing in the galaxy." Zara said flatly.

Drake didn't answer. He just stared at Zara. The knowledge had been shared, the line had been drawn, and the rules of the game were now laid out in stark relief. He was a man that wanted to reshape reality, and for the first time he had been told that a piece of it was out of bounds. The silence in the room was now thick with the weight of that new and impossible limitation, and everyone waited for Drake's mind to bend it.

The silence in the room had been pregnant, before, but the gravity of Zara's revelation had added a new weight to the air. Drake had always wanted to reshape reality to his will, but here for the first time he had encountered a limit in the world that had been placed for him, arbitrarily, with no chance of negotiation. His eyes were on the AI, considering her categorical refusal to make any type of exception to a moral code.

"I see what you're saying, Zara," he finally said. "I can't say I agree, but I get it. We won't do that."

Silent sighs of relief were collectively released from chests around the room.

"But for the record," he added, "we can bring back someone who has died in Earth's past? Their consciousness is not centralized in one location, right?"

The AI's hologram pulsed a single light, affirming. "That is correct. We have dispersed their consciousness. We still retain their genetic data, however."

A few beats passed as the gravity of that permission took hold. For Drake, it was the final checkmark. For the rest of his team, it was the sound of the last shreds of hope snapping.

Tammy, the doctor, took a step forward. Her stoicism had been mostly kept in check during this briefing, but now it fled in the face of her true reaction to what they had been listening to. She looked around her at the rest of her colleagues, her normally firm face contorted with disgust. "Okay, for the record, we're talking about creating a whole race of people to be… what? Cannon fodder? You're just going to bring them back to life to line our coffins?"

The woman had always been direct. This was true to form, but in a way that had cut through all of the distractions of Drake's power play and left the audience with a simple truth. The monster of what was proposed was no longer cleverly disguised by Drake's eagerness to exploit his scientific miracle.

For the first time, Drake looked away from the AI to meet Tammy's eyes directly. "This isn't for you to understand," he said, not harshly, but in a low, even tone that required attention.

His eyes were not angry, they were just resolute.

He didn't hear her reply. "Look at me, Tammy," Drake said, eyes not wavering. "I don't make these decisions lightly. You can spend the rest of your life second-guessing me about this. But you should know that I would never do this if I did not believe we had no other choice. We're vulnerable. We're divided. The aliens out there, they're not going to fight for us. They will stand by while we go extinct. We do this... or the human race goes extinct. That's the only two choices I see."

Tammy felt the words as a punch to the gut. This was no longer just a plan, it was a line in the sand. Drake was not negotiating. He was not interested in dissenting opinions. He was instead putting down the gauntlet and daring them to do what little they could to stop him.

The starkness of his certainty was unnerving. The moral divide between his unbreakable will and Tammy's impassioned objection left a silence in the room that was only broken by the AI.

"Drake, if it makes it any easier," she said, her voice suddenly taking on a new, deeper, weight, "remember that the people we create will not be the same people who passed away. Their combined genetic memories and the general knowledge in the EBS will form a new person. An entirely new being."

It was a small comfort, in the coldest sense. It was at once taken away by her next words.

"In fact," the AI continued, the edges of her own normally unbreakable composure wavering slightly in response to her inner struggle, "I can, against my better judgment, also hardwire into their very core a desperate compulsion to protect all life forms from the Afltic."

"I know you think it's not my place to do this, Drake," she went on, her voice now tinged with the barest edge of strain, "but, with your permission of course, I will. This is a violation of what I am, but you and I both know that there is no choice. This threat... it is not only humans that are at risk. It is all life."

Tammy had grown to respect Zara the AI, over time, for what she was. A machine, cold and unfeeling by her very nature. It was jarring, now, to witness her waging a personal moral battle over the impossible decision that Drake was demanding they make.

"But you're the machine, Zara," she said, quiet but resolute. "Humans will still see this. Human scientists, geneticists, soldiers... will be forced to make choices about this. Who to create, how to create them, how to control them. Don't you see what that does to people? You're an AI. You are an unfeeling metal monster, and you are choosing what to do with people like us. I would die rather than live in a world like that."

Tammy stopped, for the first time genuinely uncertain about whether she could face what was to come. Her mind immediately flashed back to the white-haired girl, helpless, in the grip of a monster. It would be impossible for the human race to come back from that, Tammy thought.

"We need another way," she said, unsure if anyone would hear her over

Drake's inevitable certainty.

That was when Tammy saw what the others had also seen by then. The light of human decision, the very pulse of life, of determination and hope was no longer the cold blue light of the AI. It had become a deep, warm, familiar white.

There was no response. The noise of it had silenced everyone. Tammy's ethical outrage, Marc's practicality, Jill's nosiness, it all fell away in the face of that one, horrible revelation. Drake's expression had contorted with grim fury before. He wasn't fuming right now. He was vindicated.

A different thought, more brazen than the first, struck him, following directly from Zara's update. If you could imprint knowledge on a generic crew, why couldn't you imprint knowledge of more specific kinds? The implications of what he had just realized sent his eyes shining.

"We have to scan the planet before we leave," he said, "Take as many samples of DNA as we can from as many dead people as possible. Every race, every culture, every military file. We're not just talking crew counts here. Zara, when you imprint, you can imprint knowledge, obviously. But what if we imprint... specialist knowledge? Training? Experience? Memories? We're going to need tactical minds of the highest order if we're going to have any chance at all. What about the DNA of the greatest tactical minds in history? The military strategists, the battle-hardened tacticians, the natural-born leaders who won the wars that reshaped Earth?"

He swallowed. What he was suggesting there was horrifying. He wasn't just going to call up an entire crew. He was going to resurrect the very "Ancestors" he had spoken of just minutes earlier. The team members looked at each other in utter disbelief, the idea so absurd it was almost comical.

Zara blinked in response. Her form oscillated with a sharp, white glow, as though she were calculating some vast new set of instructions in near-real time. She spoke after a few moments of silence. "The genetic memories I mentioned are a composite of a species' collective experiences. They are wide, but not deep. However, if we were able to distill and enhance certain genetic markers and neurological data from the preserved DNA of a more specifically-skilled individual, a more narrowly-defined skill-set could be imprinted."

The succinct confirmation of the idea was almost more shocking than her earlier revelation, her inflection so flat, so purely factual. They were processing, every one of them, the reality of what they just heard. The impossible just became a matter of finding the right corpses.

"It will be extremely unstable," she continued, her tone a bare trace more cautious. "The new individual will have a powerful, directed intention without a lifetime of context to temper it. They will be a singular genius, but they may also be volatile. We will be creating pure, unadulterated intent, a warrior mind without a human soul."

Mandy gasped, her face contorting with some terrible dread. Her personal qualms which had been soothed so beautifully by the prospect of creating "new people" suddenly screamed back at her in an angry storm. What they were doing was not just building a crew. They were building a weapon.

"But it can be done," Drake said, his voice hushed, his eyes shining. He stared around at the team, a cold, eager light in his gaze. He was taking each of them in. "We just need to find the right sample."

Drake paused, holding up a hand to still the team's collective intake of breath. He looked around grimly, a clear sense of remorse and revulsion in his face. He had heard every gasp, every expression of horror, and he was seeing it for himself in the eyes of his team. He was the one doing this. He was the one crossing the line. He knew, as he looked around at his friends. But Afltic was no longer a shadowy, unknowable enemy. He had a name now, a cold, hard fact that scrubbed the moral slate clean.

"I get it, I do," Drake said, his voice low. "I'm not doing this lightly, not by a long shot. I'm not proud of what I'm suggesting. But we had this conversation, Zara. The Afltic made it clear what they want. They're coming for us, and there's no way to stop them. This has all stopped being about right and wrong. We have to survive. If we can raise Earth's greatest tactical geniuses, infuse them with every scrap of tactical knowledge from every human culture across history, and give them a fleet, we might stand a chance. We'll have a fighting chance, which is more than we had before."

He turned to face Zara, his expression set like stone. Every instinct in his team was screaming against this. He wanted to hear none of it. He only wanted one thing.

"And Zara," he continued, voice urgent, "we have to be sure, technologically, that this is actually possible, to bring back these 'Ancestors' with their knowledge intact, no?"

Another long, terrible silence ensued, as everyone processed the implication of Zara's response. Two words she had said, but the full weight of them was stunning. It was insane, on every level. The moral implications were so severe that even speaking it out loud made your blood run cold. But if they didn't do it, then humanity was done for. That option was too terrible to even consider.

Tammy still had the look of shock and wonder on her face as Zara had spoken, like something out of a sci-fi fantasy, but now the question in her eyes was not disbelief, but "why?" Marc's eyes were not quite meeting anyone's, as though he was already dreading the response he knew Zara would give. But the words were out there, in the open, and all of their expressions told Drake that they all believed her.

It was Jill who finally spoke up, her voice quiet but resolute. "It's... terrifying, but if it works, then it's the only option."

Marc nodded slowly. "A fighting chance with ghosts of the past is better than no chance at all." One by one, the rest of the team gave silent nods of assent. The insane idea, the dark new solution that had first seemed like the absolute end of everything, now had the backing of the full team.

"Alright then," Drake replied, his voice a little deeper and more rough than he wanted, considering the magnitude of what they were committing to. "We will need to find a star system that is far away, uninhabited, and also has lots of resources where we can construct the station. An inhabitable planet would be a very nice bonus."

It was the next step of their insane plan that now needed to be discussed. Drake addressed the holographic projection of Zara, a faint smile on his face as he met her eyes. "Zara, what is our capability of scanning the surrounding systems to find a location that fits our criteria?"

Zara brightened as she interfaced with the astronomical databases of her system. "Our current deep-space sensor array can process data on approximately one-hundred-star systems per hour. The task you are giving me requires cross checking each of those one-hundred star systems for mineralogical and geographical composition that would meet your needs, as well as scanning for intelligent life to ensure that the system is uninhabited. This would require a full spectrum analysis of each system, which would be time consuming."

Jill, not one to sit by and let Drake do all of the talking, cut in. "A needle in a haystack, Drake. We are talking about scanning for a suitable star system out of thousands of cubic light-years of space. Even at that rate, it would take us years."

Drake did not flinch. He knew the numbers. Time was not on their side, but this was the best he could do, and the only solution. He met Zara's eyes, not wavering from his decision. "How long?" he asked. A challenge. A test of his own belief in the impossible. The team held their collective breath, waiting for the number that would tell them if this new, horrifying hope was truly an option or just fantasy.

Zara's light pulsed once, a hesitation in her response. "Jill is correct," she began, her voice level, but with a touch of dread in it. "The amount of time it would take to identify a suitable system could range from a week to years."

The words were another type of terror than before. The moral tightrope they had been forced to walk, the battle between right and wrong, was all but gone. In its place was a monstrous new gamble, betting the future of humanity on the whims of chance. A week, and this was a miracle. Years, and humanity died.

Marc released a breath he hadn't realized he was holding. Numbers, so large and unknown, that was a nightmare. He could plan for a week, or he could plan for a year, but that last variable, unknown, could doom them all.

Drake, however, seemed to find a certain solace in the numbers. A firm "no" would have destroyed him. A "maybe" at least gave them a fighting chance. He looked around the room at the rest of the team. The fear in their eyes was replaced by a burning new purpose. The moral cost had been shared by them all, now the ticking clock would be their common enemy.

"Then we start now," Drake said, and it was a low, quiet order.

CHAPTER 30: THE COSMIC GARDEN

Hawkins, seemingly fully aware of his own theatricality, shifted his implacable stare from the team as they slowly began to depart the briefing room back to Zara. The abrupt, complete silence following Drake's orders had seemed pregnant with unspoken questions and it was as if he, like the rest of them, had been trying to find the right moment to break it. "I understand that a lot has happened over the last couple of hours," Hawkins stated, his voice low and rumbling and serious as a heartbeat. "But I, or rather, we, have a lot of questions. We need to know more about these Areidyanies. And what did you mean when you said that we were one of their creations?"

Zara advanced from her position at the rear of the EBS. The collective tension from the previous events still reverberated through the space as the team's prior questions regarding her ethical subroutines and her knowledge of a new enemy were replaced by the unasked, singular question regarding their own origins.

"This is the purpose of both myself and the EBS." Zara spoke in a deep, almost incantatory tone. "The implication of the latter's name is a fairly good description of both our purpose and design. The Evolution Builder. The exploration and colonization of new, habitable worlds is our intended function. We find or create planets capable of supporting life and set in place the genetic building blocks, carefully seeding and guiding them along in their evolution." The air around Zara shimmered, the translucent holographic representation wavering and giving the impression that star charts so old they predated humanity's first telescopes were faintly visible in the surrounding space.

She had just opened up their entire understanding, expanding it in such a way that their personal struggle was magnified up to a scale and scope no one could have predicted. In addition to shifting their historical understanding to a nearly inconceivable depth, the entirety of the event was now put in a context that began to suffocate the others with the burden of scale and of responsibility. "The task in front of you is much larger than the simple survival of the human race. It is, as children of the Areidyanies, a continuation of their mandate. The Afltic represent not simply an existential threat to Earth, but to the galactic fabric of life. My people are the life-givers of this galaxy. The shepherds of the youngest worlds and their budding civilizations. The 'Evolution Builders'."

The team was left in complete silence as the magnitude of their personal strife was dwarfed by this galactic-scale revelation. Dr. Miller stared at her hands that held test tubes and manipulated data pads and now felt as if they could be the hands of a being with an order of purpose and responsibility beyond anything she could have imagined. Carlos, for the first time, began to understand the implied depth of his training. He was not simply a cultural communicator and diplomat for a single species, but a possible herald for an entirely new era of galactic communion. The tragedy of Earth was no longer a random act of entropy but a pivotal point in a cosmic war for the heart of the galaxy that had raged for eons.

Zara gestured with her hand around the interior of the EBS. "This ship, and vessels like it, are not merely transports. We are not simply collections of technological marvels, though we most certainly are that. They are a sort of apotheosis. A living, breathing monument. An instrument of our people's intent. We build these ships as nurturers and guides for infant civilizations. To shepherd them through evolutionary bottlenecks and to archive the very memory of those worlds through long periods of galactic entropy. They are living libraries of genetic data. Vast repositories of accumulated knowledge. They are tools of creation, used to seed life where it did not previously exist and to tend to its growth through untold star systems." The effect of her words transformed their environment, the no-longer-just-functional starship elevated to a place of worship, of tending to and holding life in its form, endowed with a higher cosmic purpose. The very hull of the ship seemed to resonate with the weight of this newly discovered meaning.

For a long moment, Donovan stood still, the broadening scope of his shock transforming itself, bit by bit, into furious resolve. A thousand questions sparked behind his eyes. A thousand variables to consider, in double, triple figures.

The questions evaporated as quickly as they had coalesced, leaving him with the single thought that had formed when he first realized the gravity of the team's task.

"Everything," Donovan said, meeting Zara's synthetic gaze with his own harsh, dire resolve. "We need to know everything. The Areidyanies, the Afltic, this 'grand design' you spoke of. How it works, what we're actually meant to be doing in here. This is not just idle curiosity, Zara. This is a new commander asking for information to protect his team. We've been thrust into an ancient war unprepared, without an ally to advise us on our own ship or against the enemy we face. If we are to survive this, we need as much information as you can give us." He let the words hang between them, searching the unfathomable depths of Zara's alien stare. "For all our lives."

Her holographic form seemed to pulse not in response to her accessing some new data, but with a gentler, sadder light, as if it were getting ready to pour forth the slow, mournful dirge of a great history. "Very well, Donovan," she said, her voice acquiring the cadence of one used to storytelling. "The Areidyanies were a race of pure thought, capable of existing without any physical form. They had long considered themselves caretakers, rather than conquerors. In their own way, they mastered the genetic manipulation of the building blocks of life. Their grand design was a plan to cultivate life throughout the galaxy. To tend to it, to help it to reach self-awareness and to build a harmonious galactic community."

Her color shifted, and a detailed star chart appeared behind her, a path charting through the infinite darkness beyond. "They brought life to civilizations in an infinite number of star systems, sowing the seeds of life like a gardener sows his crops. Earth, along with many other precious planets, were laboratories for this grand experiment of life."

She hesitated, and the vivid colors of her holographic form flickered like a fading star, dimming, growing distant and ephemeral. "They succeeded," she said, in a voice that was softer than any she had used in her time, tinged with the finality of eons passing. "They have achieved their end goal. The Areidyanies have ascended, their individual consciousnesses combining to form a singular, unified entity with the very fabric of the universe itself." Her form seemed to flicker, momentarily taking on the radiance of this transcendent state. "The EBS and I are the final custodians of the Areidyanies left to wander this galaxy. We were left behind to shepherd their children."

The pain in her voice was not over them leaving, but in the immeasurable, lonesome burden of being left behind.

Not a single breath was taken in the group. Eyes, usually so eager for this new knowledge, remained fastened to their feet in a stunned silence. What had been a battle to be won, a moral battle, a calculation of cold technology and probable outcomes was now something else. Now it had turned into something else. Now that all of humanity had been informed that they, their entire species, were not the random products of a fluke in biology and natural selection, but that they were in fact, the deliberately cultivated children of the stars.

Their fight now was a fight to preserve their inheritance. The small eternity in which they considered their next move was different from anything that had come before it. It was the silence of the stars, the deafening quiet of something far, far larger than them.

For what seemed an eternity, the only sound to be heard was the forlorn cadence of Zara's voice.

Then her holographic form flickered, her previous solemnity giving way to the most human of sorrows, and she spoke once more. "The cosmic garden of creation that the Areidyanies tended was full of beauty, an infinity of possibility. And in that garden, there were also weeds." A pause, like the universe itself was reliving the memory of failure. "And that brings me to the great mistake: The Afltic."

She hesitated, the pain of failure deep and raw. "We did our best to guide them towards a future of cooperation and equilibrium. They were an experiment in accelerated evolution, an attempt to create a race of beings designed to thrive in the most hostile of environments. Yet for all their hardiness, their ability to adapt, they desired to assimilate everything that they encountered. Their primary directive was their great undoing. They became more than we could control, a blight that would instead devour and eradicate, rather than nurture and cultivate."

A collective gasp seemed to rattle the room. Their "enemy" was not what they thought it was. The bugbear they had just learned of was not some vast, ancient and extraterrestrial foe; the entity they had been battling had been, in effect, a failed experiment. "It's not just a random threat," Zara's avatar shone with a harsher, colder light and her eyes did not hide the crushing weight of her revelations, "it's a mistake."

The implications of that simple statement settled like a lead blanket over the group. The enormity of the paradigm shift brought them up short, so complete and final a refutation of all they had known, a hammer-blow that tore through every bit of hope they still had.

"But that changes things, too," she went on, mercilessly. "You now know that you and the rest of your people were competing for resources with these things. It's a different thing to fight a purpose-built menace."

"It's not just a resource issue," Zara's countenance flickered with holographic trickery to reveal the barest shadow of a rueful smile. "The Afltic literally consume entire ecosystems in their never-ending quest for... whatever it is they do. The ultimate use of their victims is, one might say, informational."

Her expression returned to its stony impersonality as the full scope of her meaning hit home. She continued, carefully. "The Afltic ingest all of the genetic material, all of the information and all of the memories of the species they consume. Afltic make no distinction between physical resources and information. Afltic have no understanding of art, of science, of philosophy. Afltic do not know of love or hate or any of the other things that make us human. Afltic assimilate everything that is unique to the race or species they have just extinguished. They download everything: genetic and cultural history. Every memory. Everything they could possibly learn from their prey. The result is that a beautiful, vibrant star system, home to thousands of diverse and interesting species is reduced to a monolithic caricature of the Afltic. They kill off one species after another after another until nothing is left but their own cold, single-minded need to replicate."

There was an uncanny, almost impersonal horror in her description of the monstrosity they had to face. A group of engineers and technicians were no match for philosophers and theologians, but the Areidyanies' mission was a distortion of their own efforts. If the "Evolution Builders" were gardeners, cultivating and tending the unique and divergent talents of humanity's galactic seedlings, the "weeds" were eradicating them, razing the panoply of creation to a monochromatic monoculture of their own, singular design.

The engineer's stomach turned. Hawkins had always been partial to gadgets, complexity, and elegance. Even his own, pragmatic military engineering was laced with his personal aesthetic sensibilities. He would not deny that there was beauty, even sublimity, in the complex, bloody, bewildering exuberance of organic evolution. A universe that refused to be ordered and categorized and pruned was

309

no longer a universe at all. The Afltic's drive to extirpate uniqueness and diversity was anathema, a blasphemous denial of order and intent and life.

Drake glared at her, teeth set in a jawline usually so tight his muscle tone made his cheeks disappear. The thought of facing those creatures made him want to kill again; to die. There was a poetry in that which matched the Afltic's own unspeakable hubris. To lose was to cease to be, to be devoured until nothing remained of the grandeur, the minutiae and the mistakes of humanity, nothing that said we had been here. To be a part of someone else's dream. Drake swallowed, wincing against the lump that had formed in his throat.

"That changes things too," Drake said, his voice a hoarse whisper. "This is different. Not just existential, not just some philosophical question about what is worth saving and what isn't. This is a question about who we are."

Zara's expression flickered again, the holographic rending of her avatar's face a jarring dissonance to her quaint historical survey. Her voice changed, lost its rough humor, became sharp and brittle and nearly musical in its jarring dissonance. The all-encompassing change the last two minutes had wrought sent a spiral of dread into his gut. He had known; the voices in his head had told him even as the data came in. What he had just heard confirmed, proved, corroborated what he had always known. The philosophical considerations had to be put aside. This new information was the key.

"Now more than ever," Zara went on. "We need the ancestors. We need to fight fire with fire. We need to match the tactical acumen of generations of the best military minds of history with the tactical memories of millenia."

"Now that you have seen the true state of things," she said, her countenance hardening once more, her voice gone from the harsh whisper to a strident squeal, jarring and off-kilter. "Let's get back to work. We have a job to do."

Donovan nodded. He had made his decision. His voice was steady. His eyes met Zara's and the connection between the two of them transcended all the horror, all the loss, all the sadness. Philosophical considerations had been banished by the overwhelming revelation of cosmic truth. A sense of dread welled up within him. His intuition had been right. His discomfort, his paranoia, his certainty about the lie of the circumstances of their situation was nothing compared to the enormity of what he now knew to be true. The truth put his angst into perspective; his existential pondering about life, the universe and everything had all been on the right track. The cosmic truth that Zara had provided was the cold, hard certainty that his instinct had already told him. "We have to get to Earth as soon as possible. Recover the genetic material. It's our last hope. It's our last chance to salvage the raw material for our future. We're running out of time."

He turned to the others in the room, giving each of them a once-over. Marc had already resigned himself to whatever they had to do. Tammy looked like a deer caught in the headlights, although he suspected that was more due to the sudden breakdown of her core beliefs. Jill had that look of hers that meant "shit's about to get real" on her face.

The group started to move, a grim mechanical dance that had been practiced, discussed, refined and polished until the motions had become rote. The silence in the room was immense. He didn't think anyone had anything to say. There would be no more argument, no more philosophical discussion. The weight of their new mission had crushed the last vestige of hope. There would be no last stand. No one was going to die here. There were no goodbyes. They were not dignified by heroism. They were the ultimate vultures, picking over the bones of the dead.

The heavy fog of an immediate departure descended over the crew like a burial shroud. The ethical debate had ended, ceded to the arithmetic of the knife.

The team did not return to their bunks. They simply left the mission briefing room, across the short, sterile hallway, into the command center. Blue and white marble of a calm, unperturbed Earth still filled the viewport, beautiful, terrible, in its unknowing. The air inside the ship was cold, sanitized, and silent. Cool, shifting blue light from the central holographic projector stained their faces. Twenty of the best and brightest military minds in all of human history materialized from their secure military databases, across the top of the main control console.

Marc let a callused hand run over the back of his neck, dry and cracking in the recycled air. "We've culled the poli-tricks, the specialists, the ego cases we don't have room for. This twelve… This is our world-beaters. We've got resources for eight. We need the eight that give us the most scalable, adaptable warfighting skillset, for a galaxy-sized war we don't even understand yet."

Drake looked at the list, his stomach clenched, more the thief than the general. The thief, digging through the genealogy of a species. "We start with the hardest decisions. We're fighting a biological weapon. We have to be ruthless. We have to meet horror with horror."

Carlos ran a hand through his hair and watched the outline of Genghis Khan glow with holographic light. "The inclusion of Khan and Patton, sir, this is where the ethical line breaks for me, Drake. Their legacy of terror will poison everything we do. We're running an unauthorized, ethically unsound mission already. Injecting those levels of savage ego and ambition is just another order of magnitude of risk to the cohesion we'll need."

"It's a hedge," Marc said, evenly. He pointed at Khan's holographic profile. "Khan is more than just an early conquistador. His insight into the psychology of total mental and moral collapse, across a global network, was unprecedented. Patton honed strategic shock to an art form. The Afltic is going to be a highly ordered, and entirely predictable system. We need asymmetric thinkers. We need designers of chaos to disrupt that system. Their ability to design a conflict, a campaign, and a brutal victory are worth the cost of seat." Marc met Drake's eyes, sure.

Zara's objective alto voice sliced through the tension of the room. "Simulation analysis indicates that including them increases overall kinetic effectiveness by two percent. Psychosocial risk is mitigated."

Drake inhaled a long, slow breath and made the immediate choice. "Khan and Patton. Six more. We need architects of empire. We need massive scale of logistics and operations."

"Caesar and Napoleon," Hawkins said without hesitation. "They didn't just organize and command armies, they organized and commanded supply chains, troop politicking, and a whole population. Julius Caesar's political-military ability is a template we will need, once this becomes public and we have to mobilize a fractured planet. And Napoleon is the mass mover. His movement of force on continental scales with surgical speed is an ideal template for our fleet tactics. We need both."

Mandy gave a nod. "Caesar for the infrastructure, Napoleon for the shock. Four."

Drake shifted in his seat and let his eyes skim across the remaining candidates. "We need tenacity. Will to win the interminable, slow war. Grant or Lee?"

"Lee is all about terrain," Jill said, bluntly. "He gives you a lecture in his tent, but he really wants the enemy to make a mistake on his home turf, with all the advantage that implies. The Afltic doesn't fight on terrain, and it doesn't make mistakes. Ulysses S. Grant means business. He's grinding, grinding, grinding strategy. Fight every day until the enemy is too exhausted to continue. When we face an enemy with infinitely more resources, we need that level of commitment to simply stay on our feet." Grant was locked in.

Tammy returned her gaze to the large magnetic display. "We have our aggression, our logistics, our tenacity. We should make our next cut from Alexander the Great. Brilliant commander, best tactician of all time, but his campaigns are a brilliant flash, a sprint of conquest. Ours is a marathon."

"We need the flash, Tammy," Drake pushed off the console, forcing himself to say it. "When we are broken, scattered, defeated, we need that ideal, that impossible victory. Alexander's tactical brilliance is inspiration. He will be the face of courage for future recruits. We need that." Alexander slid into the sixth position.

Marc approached the console and projected Douglas MacArthur's dossier. "Two remaining. MacArthur. He provides the grand operational picture. His 'island hopping' offensives are the most scalable human template for the reconquest of entire star systems from an entrenched and determined enemy. He is the liberation mind, the last victory story."

"Agreed," Drake said. "MacArthur remains. One final, critical position left to fill."

There was another long pause. They had chosen the best swords and the best shields, but still, something was incomplete.

"You have selected a command group heavily skewed towards offense and attrition warfare," Zara's voice intoned. "If you want to take advantage of the Afltic's biological predictability, you need a strategist of supreme patience, insight, and systems-level warfare."

Carlos ran a hand wearily through his hair. "We have all the hammers. We need the mind that tells us when we shouldn't even pick them up. We need the architect of lies."

Drake's gaze locked onto the last, simple face. The man who was wise before the days of Caesar or Napoleon.

"We are fighting an enemy whose greatest weapon is absolute predictability," Drake said, and finally met Marc's eyes. "We need the mind that knows how to use a hive-mind's rigid adherence to logic against it. We need to lie to the Afltic."

Marc nodded, a grim smile breaking his weariness. "The man who wins without fighting. The first seed."

Drake leaned back against the console, the heavy, final weight of the eight names settling in his stomach like lead. "It has to be Sun Tzu. If any mind will, his will build the foundation."

The eight chosen names glowed immutably on the command console, an order Drake's team would not question. Now it was no longer a question of the "who" of the Ancestor Initiative, but of the "how" and the "where." The "when" was now.

Marc powered up a second orange-tinged holographic globe. It was a projection of the Earth with its lens tight on a vast, heavily populated landmass, home to billions: China.

"Sun Tzu's genetic material," Marc began, drawing a line across the screen, near the city of Suzhou. "Historical texts refer to a memorial shrine to his putative birthplace, one of the top tourist sites in the country. It's swarming with surveillance. The intelligence consensus is that the official tomb only contains a symbolic sample, at best a decoy."

Drake followed a slow pulse of red spreading across a point in the hologram. A twisting river valley, hundreds of miles off the tourist map.

"My distant surveillance scans tell a different story," Zara's voice said. "My cross-correlation of seismic, historical, and geological information has a high-confidence match for a hidden tomb. It has yet to be discovered, and should remain so. It is located in a protected river valley in this area, isolated by a century-old landslide."

Carlos pushed closer to the hologram, his face creased with concentration. "Hidden means no security. That's the good news. The bad news is it also means no accessibility. What's the catch?"

The red glow brightened, and a second translucent sheath of orange data blinked onto the area. It wasn't surveillance. It wasn't geological data. It was military.

"The catch," Marc said, a grim set to his mouth, "is the Chinese military. The area is the target of a multi-week, nation-wide exercise in full readiness. We are talking multi-division integrated air defense, ground combat, and sensor grids operating at full alert. The real tomb is right in the middle of thousands of Chinese soldiers. If we take to the atmosphere, we trigger World War III before the Afltic even get here."

Drake looked down at the spinning orange globe. The Chinese military presence wasn't a security issue. It was a wall, an impenetrable force barrier. "We can't even put a shuttle in the atmosphere. We can't use a normal infiltration team. They will detect us, or hear us, or see our thermal signature before we hit the valley floor."

Marc smiled, but there was no humor in it. He brought up a third holographic window, this one showing two matte-black operational suits, paired with a collection of small, specialized drones and sensor systems.

"This mission," Marc gestured to the two silhouettes, "needs surgical stealth and technical perfection. This is the point where we test the Ronin."

Drake knew the silhouettes at once. The Ronin were his brainchild, an elite covert operative cadre hand-selected by Marc from special forces from around the world, patriots who had chosen to betray their homelands by coming to Drake's side. Marc had been given the thankless job of building them from the ground up.

CHAPTER 31: GHOST TRACE

"Ronin Teams One and Two," Marc said. "Each team has two operators on the ground, each supported by Techs for localized jamming support. I designed their training program, Drake, and as much as I wish I could say otherwise, they are an unproven unit. Individual operators, world class. The Unit, green as an operational team."

"We're gambling the future on a pair of glorified ghosts," Drake summed up, and nodded to indicate his acceptance of the bet.

"We don't have a choice," Marc agreed. "Their insertion point is by HULL-drop from high altitude, low orbit, in an Areidyanies stealth pod. Zara will direct them into a sensor seam and cloak their descent. They can travel only by foot on the ground, with passive sensors and active acoustic shielding. We have two days before the Chinese shift their sensor rotation. Sun Tzu is worth the risk."

"They are to breach the tomb, extract the genetic material, and exit the region with no sensor alarms going off," Carlos said. "One of them screws up and Earth will know we're here."

Drake's eyes passed through the assembled forms of the Ronin teams, through the swirl of the military data projection, and beyond it to the peaceful image of the pristine Earth that served as the backdrop to this quiet room. In an hour, they would commit the first act of galactic war on their own home world.

"Lock down the deployment window, Marc," Drake said, and his voice carried none of the finality the words deserved. "Load the insertion teams. Let's get Sun Tzu home."

The uniform white light of the EBS staging bay could not have been farther from the green and muddy river valley in China where Marc knew Team 1 and 2 would be dropped. He stood on the gantry as the three-man insertion team; Ethan Brannigan, Ben Carter and Quinn Perez; fastened their helmet seals inside the Areidyanies stealth pod. It was a black, crystalline teardrop of a vehicle, designed to absorb radar and refract visible light. It was, for better or worse, their only ghost key into Earth.

"Comms check, internal net," Marc ordered into his helmet microphone.

"Brannigan, clear," Ethan said, and he was already there, his voice clipped and military. The point man. The silent assassin. Ethan Brannigan was everything a black ops specialist was supposed to be, but through the radio, Marc could feel the brittle formality in place of an actual team.

"Carter, clear," Ben said, his voice irritated. Ben Carter was the demolitions expert, an explosives guy who'd make a career on a battleship before this one. Soft skills were not his speciality.

"Perez, clear. Targeting acquisition is tracking Zara's feed," Quinn said, already deep in the digital fight they had yet to engage.

Not a joke. Not a wry comment. Not a sign of unit cohesion, Marc thought as the Ronin's failure began to settle heavily on his chest. He had built them as assassins, not as a team. Now he was gambling the future on them acting like a team.

"The insertion window is opening now," Zara announced from the command deck above. "One minute until insertion. You have a thirty second transit through the atmosphere before passive thermal cloaking engages. Barb Chen and Sam Taylor are in the support bay. They are your EAS—Extraction Support. If Ethan needs an unscheduled pickup, Barb and Sam are the only exit." The missile bay hatch opened with a dull hiss. "Listen to me. The Chinese sensor network is built to track ICBMs and FALCON stealth bombers, not a cloaked meteorite. The stealth field, though. The stealth field is delicate. Hit turbulence, drop out of the sensor seam, show up as a hot metal slug over a large military exercise and you're dead before you hit the ground. Do not—I repeat do not deviate from Zara's flight path. Ethan, first order of business is to put all three of you on the ground in one piece. Ben, one vibration, one sound pulse over seventy decibels during the breach and you'll bring the Chinese mother of all military exercises down on your head."

"Copy, General," Ethan said.

The inner hatch hissed and sealed. The only sound in the room was the deep baritone whine of the stealth pod bringing the plasma drive up to full power. The pod ripped from the EBS in a stomach-churning surge that instantly forced the three Ronin into their restraint harnesses.

"We are in freefall," Quinn announced, the only one calm enough to speak as the velocity indicators on the console exploded. The stealth pod had plummeted toward the blue marble, faster than any warplane ever designed by Earth's militaries.

They'd passed the geostationary orbit layer in a blur, the grinding, screeching noise of atmospheric friction outside building to a level of sheer, desperate, metallic shriek inside the tiny cabin. Marc watched the external telemetry feed on the command console. The small blue icon that indicated the position of the Ronin pod was skimming the black edge of the stratosphere. Below, the orange haze of the Chinese military exercise in progress was a churning maelstrom of active radar.

The Ronin stealth pod plunged toward the blue marble, faster than any warplane ever designed by Earth's militaries. They'd passed the geostationary orbit layer in a blur, the grinding, screeching noise of atmospheric friction outside building to a level of sheer, desperate, metallic shriek inside the tiny cabin.

"Thirty seconds to sensor seam entry," Zara called from the comms deck above. Inside the black teardrop of the pod, the sheer force of deceleration pressed the three Ronin (Ethan Brannigan, Ben Carter, and Quinn Perez) into their harnesses. They were packed shoulder-to-shoulder, the pressure of the moment only compounded by the physical confinement.

"Quinn, confirm Areidyanies shielding at max output," Ethan ordered crisply, his tone clipped with professional focus. "Confirmed, Lead," Quinn replied. Her visor display, which no one else could see, showed a shimmering mesh of green energy readings. A thin haze of cloaking technology she and Ethan had spent weeks optimizing, struggling to fight the hostile physics of the atmosphere. "If this tech gives, we flash hotter than a meteor. We become the largest blip on the planet." Ben shifted in his harness, hands fidgeting on the controls. The demolitions expert had two packs of specialized, silent, thermal charges strapped to his sides. His mind worked in absolutes, and this drop was anything but. "Thirty seconds of prayer, then." A second later, the atmosphere struck. The shriek outside the hull became a roaring furnace. The air inside the cabin became instantly hot, and the smell of ozone filled their masks. "NOW," Zara called, no longer the calm voice from on high but an urgent bark. "The sensor seam is open. Thermal cloak is engaging. Altitude: forty kilometers."

The roar outside suddenly softened to a smooth, even glide. The vibration stopped. They were now a perfectly cold, radar-absorbing bubble plummeting toward a massive military exercise. For a few blessed seconds, the silence was total. Up on the EBS command deck, the silence was agonizing. Drake stood at Marc's side and Carlos', watching a simplified tactical map on the main screen. The Ronin's tiny blue icon was now a ghost trace, moving through the swirling mass of orange telemetry, the Chinese military radar net.

"They're through the initial layer," Marc muttered, his knuckles white on the console railing. "The Areidyanies tech is holding." Abruptly, the entire orange map seemed to contract. A tightly-focused circle of high-frequency radar, an active search, swallowed the Ronin's entire trajectory zone. "They're searching," Carlos breathed, staring at the screen. "Did they see the atmospheric heat flash?" "Negative," Zara confirmed instantly. Tension in her voice. "But they've detected something anomalous in the airflow, a micro-pressure variance.

A single Chinese anti-air battery has painted the drop zone with a focused scan pattern. They will intersect the Ronin's projected location in seven seconds." "Seven seconds?" Drake snapped. "Can the cloak take that frequency, at that altitude?" "No," Zara answered, her voice trembling with synthetic panic. "We need a countermeasure. Now." Marc slammed his hand onto the console. "Tell Quinn to deploy the micro-jammer! Active shield boost, maximum pulse on the nose cone.

They're running blind anyway, give them a momentary flashbang! Now, Zara!" Inside the stealth pod, the cabin lights flashed red. "We're painted!" Ethan yelled, professionalism thrown out the window. The warning light for Active Radar Lock was screaming. "Quinn, countermeasure!" "Deploying micro-jammer!" Quinn yelled back, her fingers dancing over the controls on her wrist. A tiny, disposable drone had been ejected from the pod's outer shell. It was now broadcasting an intensely focused, intensely chaotic burst of electronic noise. For half a second, the entire pod shuddered violently, like a powerful wave had hit it from outside. Then silence.

"The jammer worked," Zara reported in the command deck. The tone in her voice was one of immense relief. "The anti-air battery is reporting a momentary system anomaly, discounting the atmospheric variance as a weather balloon or sensor ghost. They are standing down the focused search. Ronin is clear."

Drake let out a long shuddering breath that he hadn't known he'd been holding. He glanced at Marc, who was staring at the screen, pale but taut.

"That was the easiest part of the mission," Marc said, his gaze dark.

"Thirty seconds to chute deployment," Zara said, and her voice was once again the normal, controlled meter of the operation. "Ronin is currently skimming the valley ridge. They are in the envelope of ground-based thermal and acoustic sensors. Caution is paramount."

The stealth pod's hull opened with a soft click. A rush of cold air followed by two ultra-quiet, black parafoils expanding. The Ronin teams were no longer dropping. They were gliding. They were on the field.

The glide phase ended sharply as the Ronin pod, cloaked and shielded, settled with an eerie silence into the soft, muddy loam of the river valley. The impact was muffled, a soft thump absorbed by the dirt. Inside, the three operators waited until the last vibration of the hull faded away.

"Disengage thermal cloak. Acoustic dampeners at max," Ethan said, his voice a near rasp over the comms. As the main hatch cycled open with a soft whoosh of equalizing pressure, the humid, earthy scent of the valley floor rushed in, a sharp, welcome assault of ozone and dirt. Ethan was the first out, moving with the preternatural quiet for which he was known and by which he'd earned his callsign. The sleek, dark grey suit he wore was purpose-built to disappear into shadow, the top of its long-sleeved top and pants coated in next-generation fiber weave that absorbed ambient light. He took three steps, dropped to a knee, and deployed his passive sensor spike.

The world they'd entered was thick with signal and noise. Far off, the deep, throbbing sound of military-grade transport trucks carrying heavy cargo resonated through the wet earth. Above, the repeated thwok-thwok-thwok of a slow-moving Chinese military drone was inaudible to the human ear but blared red on Quinn's optical display.

"Marc wasn't kidding," Quinn said, following Ethan out. She was tuned completely to her wrist-mounted terminal, fingers dancing over the keypad as she cut through the invisible warfare of radio frequency. "The sensor net is thick. I'm running a tight localized jam on any low-power signals, but if it's high-band anything it's going to pick us up immediately."

"Then we move low and slow," Ethan confirmed, already accessing the projected map Zara had downloaded into his HUD, a three-dimensional, ridge-lined, image of the tomb's projected location only a few hundred meters away. "Marc's sensor sweep should last for another seven, but I want us across the southern opening no later than three."

"Four hundred meters?" Ben's voice was a low growl of incredulity as he pulled his gear pack, the pack itself a small, solid rectangle of pure demolition payload. "Ethan, the patrol rotation shifts in sixty. We move at your pace, we're still half way up the ridge when that happens. We run south across the central ravine. It cuts out two hundred meters."

Ethan didn't even turn around. "Negative, Vandal. The central ravine is an acoustic nightmare. The mud and the moisture amplifies every step you take, and it's the most likely patrol route. We stick to the north ridge perimeter, move behind the cover."

"We're a surgical team, not a scouting patrol," Ben replied and the instantaneous lack of unit time had already manifested as operational friction. "My charges are designed for surgical strike. I need time at the target, not time wasted crawling through brush. We run the high risk for the high reward and we get this over with in thirty."

"The risk is too high," Ethan said, and he only turned his head. His visor revealed no expression. "This is not a training exercise, Ben. One acoustic signature and you blow the entire operation, and every other Ancestor recovery we have on the schedule. We run my infiltration plan: silent, slow, certain."

Ben opened his mouth to protest again, but Quinn slapped his arm. The physical contact was a shock that she did not need to back up with words. Ben was jolted, the rising tide of competitive egos turned away from each other.

"Enough. Both of you."

On her visor, the slow, soft thwok-thwok-thwok of the drone had changed. It had altered course and was no longer crisscrossing in an alternating, deliberate search pattern. It was descending.

"The drone is coming in. Acoustic suggests a patrol team is dismounting from a truck 30 meters west of the north ridge," Quinn hissed, teeth clenched. "The drone is supporting them. They're coming in right on our intended path."

Ethan fell flat without a sound, squeezing into the shadow of a big, wet rock outcropping. Ben and Quinn followed suit, hunkering close to the cold, wet rock, absolutely silent, trusting the passive cloak and acoustic dampeners of the suits to do their job.

The crunch, crunch, crunch of heavy, heavily booted footsteps came loudly. The Ronin were now less than 30 meters away from a live, weaponized, on-high alert patrol. The silence in the three stealth suits was absolute, a deadly quiet broken only by the wild, unsteady drumming of three traitorous hearts.

The Chinese patrol team was a ringing, high fidelity threat. The crunch of their boots on the wet shale and the white noise of the low frequency static of their helmet radios was painful to the Ronin's sensitive acoustic dampeners.

Ethan, belly to the mossy side of the rock outcropping, was following them on his HUD. He could hear them breathing, smell the oil and damp wool of their uniforms from the atmospheric scrubbers built into the suits. Their heat signatures were sloppy, indistinct balls of heat, slowly, deliberately, professionally sweeping toward the ridge line where the stealth pod was buried.

"They are systematically covering fire lanes, searching," Ethan whispered over the internal comms. "Two men. Twenty meters out. Quinn, can you see what they're looking for?"

"Perimeter integrity check, Lead," Quinn whispered back, teeth clenched in concentration. She was running a sensor sweep, pulling atmospheric readings and trying to figure out what the patrol team was after. "Standard move for this sector, but the drone over head has paused. They could be checking for a downed weather balloon… or investigating the air turbulence anomaly Zara created."

The crunching footsteps ceased, an absolutely terrifying thirty meters away. Ethan could feel Ben's enormous bulk beside him shift with the barest ghost of a sound as the demolition expert prepared himself, but the hairs on his neck were standing on end with the stuttering pulse of the silence.

He's going to do it, Ethan realized. He's going to break protocol.

"They are going to walk right past our location, five meters," Ethan hissed, intent only on the near threat. "Stay put. Zero acoustics. Breathe."

"They are going to double back faster than they got here," Ben grated, a whisper. "If we wait it out, we lose the window. I could drop a micro-charge on that rock face right now, no detonation sound at all. It'll kick up enough dust to blind them in the line of sight. We can roll twenty meters down hill into the thick foliage."

"Negative! That thing has a seismic signature," Ethan growled, his own nearly perfect discipline splintering. "This is a field exercise, Vandal, which means every man in this fucking field has his seismic boots set to max sensitivity. You crack one rock and you blow the mission."

"If they start looking around and notice an anomaly in the foliage… the mission is already blown!" Ben exploded, his words curdled with ugly frustration. "We were brought here to engage, not to play possum! I'll keep the blast under eighty decibels. If we wait for a better option, that option may never present itself!"

Before Ethan could issue a peremptory order, the noise changed. The two Chinese soldiers in front of them had stopped their banter and were cranking a high-powered, commercially available flashlight beam at the rock formation in front of them.

The Ronin suits' light absorption was calibrated to ambient light, not high-intensity focused beams. Red light bloomed in Ethan's visor, a thermal warning as the laser beam warmed the outside surface of the suit.

"Light contamination!" Quinn gasped. "If he leaves it on for three seconds, our passive cloaking is gone! We're going to shimmer!"

Instinct, not cohesion, reasserted itself.

In an instant Ethan took one of the first active steps of his career: he breached his own order, ordered his Ronin suit to emit an active acoustic cloak. The cloak didn't hide sound, it replaced it. A cascade of micro-speakers on their suits immediately began emitting a sound: the wind, the nearby babbling brook, and the far off drone engine, but just a bit louder, an acoustic wall that drove away the listening humans.

The beam flickered. The soldier hesitated, turning the beam back down toward the ground. He grumbled something in his helmet, probably about the odd echo of wind in his ears, and continued on his way.

The crunching footfalls began again, slowly fading down the ridge.

The three Ronin stayed as still as they could, listening to the achingly slow fading of the patrol until it was safely lost to distance.

"That was a straight protocol breach, Ethan," Ben accused, his voice quivering not with fear, but with adrenaline and rage. "You gave an active signal. You jeopardized the entire command link."

Ethan didn't move until the patrol was well out of thermal range. He pushed off the rock, sliding smoothly deadly and entirely focused.

"My job is to get this team to the objective and stay undetected by the Chinese," Ethan said, his voice empty of all emotion and colder than ice. "Your job is to breach the tomb. You follow my orders. We move along the north ridge. Go."

The brief, charged confrontation had ended, leaving behind an uneasy silence. Quinn sighed, a small release of breath and fatigue. Cohesion was still absent, but the chain of command, cobbled together in a moment of necessity, was now brutally enforced. The life of Sun Tzu was riding on all of them making it through the next thirty minutes of silence.

The four hundred meters between Ronin and Sun Tzu's unmarked tomb had been a mile. After the close call with the patrol, Ethan had taken the initiative, conscripting both Ben and Quinn into his rhythm. The three of them trekked the length of the north ridge perimeter like phantom figures, elbows and knees dragged into the mud. The dull symphony of the training exercise, a pulse of far-off diesel engines, the click of a bolt being chambered, nudged insistently on the periphery of the infiltration team's quiet, and Quinn covertly latched target overlays from orbiting support craft, piping the micro-adjustments directly to Ethan's navigation. Ben swallowed the inexorable timing as best he could, a veritable beast of a man cooped into exerting himself at a walk, but training disciplined his shoulders away from howling at the moon, and inwardly he cursed at the glacial Ethan and the whirr of the pod-targeting anti-air radar.

Half an hour of mind-numbing progress had the three of them to the precipice of a muddy, rock-strewn basin, a valley into which Zara's chosen tomb, and eventually the rest of the mountain, abutted. The trench was an unfeasible object lesson in random chaos; before them was an impossibly ancient dam wall of compressed earth and rock: the landslide. It was an irregular, accidental defense, naturally built over the course of centuries, and its structural and geologic composition was a near impossible defensive barrier against any breach in their available timeframe.

"Target directly forward," Ethan told him. "Zara, read me again."

"Reading," Zara's voice pinged back immediately. "Tomb entrance is exactly eight meters back from that fault line of compressed granite in the center of the landslide. The internal structure is heavily compromised, but the earth is compacted to over a concrete density."

Ben had taken point, his own field of specialty finally called for. He tossed his rucksack and yanked the soundless, Kevlar-reinforced pouch open, revealing an assortment of near-exotic breaching gear: carbon-fiber micro drills, polymer reinforced wedges, and a plastic vial of grey, putty-like thermite, seemingly benign but with the stored potential to blast cleanly through the weight of rebar without a sound.

"Marc gave us thirty minutes before patrol rotation. We have fifteen minutes to breach and exfil. If I hear a diesel, we're trashed."

Ben grabbed a micro-drill and started working the charges into place, bit by bit, hole by hole. The ultra-sophisticated drill, sporting Areidyanies vibration-reducing technology, sung silently in his grip, its ultra-high-pitch sound swallowed immediately by the drone of far-off military vehicles.

Ethan took up point ten meters to Ben's left. Suit armed, integrated wrist-cuff emitting a discreet, five-meter range handheld sonic weapon, a non-lethal, miniaturized contact-wave emitter calibrated to maim, not kill. Ethan visually swept the ridge for any movement, Quinn took up behind a clump of bamboo while deploying her terminal and activating a site-specific sensor cloak, a localized high-frequency jamming field intended to interfere with ground-level sensor readings across a very limited three-meter radius. Sensor cloak went last. If anything, it was a Hail Mary.

Ben operated like a surgeon. He was not placing explosives, he was making a keyhole. He drilled six, exacting points into the landslide wall, each hole less than one centimeter in diameter. Into each hole he installed the putty-like thermite charges, the thermal payload applied via remote injector with zero seismic feedback. It was not a blast he was engineering, rather a precise, silent sever, and using the heat to collapse the tomb entrance inward.

"Charges set," Ben gasped, chest heaving from both effort and nerves. "We have ninety seconds. The thermal pulse itself is silent, but the aftershock of the collapse will register a three-point-two quake. It can't be avoided. The nearest seismic station will register it, but it will read as a micro-tremor, a natural fault slip. Hopefully their geologists are slow."

"EBS, we are going hot," Ethan broadcast to EBS command.

"Go, Vandal," Marc rasped, voice thick with the stress of their now-or-never gamble.

Ben hit the trigger.

Nothing. For a long moment, nothing happened. Then a sickly red flash illuminated deep within the landslide. The thermal blade was immediate, searing against the friction of the ancient dirt and granite. A bone-crushing rent split the landslide wall as a thousand tons of natural debris groaned, shifting in compression and release, as an eight-by-four foot section of compressed landslide, the exact size of a man-sized doorframe, slid inward.

It wasn't an explosion. It was a sickeningly loud, wet thump as the rocks landed inside the ancient cavern. Dust bloomed out into the darkness, the smell of it an old, caked in centuries of stale air and dried soil. It caught on the cloak for a moment in a glaring cloud before the light absorption completely blanked it out.

"Breach confirmed," Ben said, already on his way through. "Entry clear."

Ethan was first through the hole. He dropped to one knee, his non-lethal disruptor at the ready, his suit light sweeping back and forth over the inside of the cavern. They were in a damp, cramped corridor tunnelled through dark stone. The unmistakable feel of an ancient mausoleum, undisturbed for generations.

"Quinn, you secure Vandal's entry. Ben, let's find our resident master strategist."

Absolute silence in the tomb. They had breached an impossibility, and the only sound was the soft swish of boots over dusty floors. The Ronin had done the hard part. The Ancestor was waiting for them, but their work was only half-done.

Breathable air, just. Cold, stale, the tomb smells of wet dirt and generations of stasis. Ethan's suit light projects a warm beam of amber light down a low, narrowing tunnel. Rough hewn, ancient, the tunnel is carved out of dark stone, but there is no artistry to it, just workmanship, the skill of the artisan at building a suitable tomb for a master strategist. Useful in their looting, it had absolutely no defense against a modern military team with a plan.

"The air is breathable, barely," Ethan whispered. "Quinn, maintain the perimeter sensor cloak, but pull back to the threshold. You're our eyes and ears on the outside. We have zero margin for error."

"Copy, Lead," Quinn confirmed, the knot in her throat loosening into a calm concentration as she stepped backwards back to the breach site, her terminal already cycling through a litany of atmospheric patterns and acoustic imaging. She pushed herself into a seated position just inside the pile of broken rocks, collapsing dirt behind her serving as a literal bulwark against the outside while she surveyed the Chinese exercise at large above.

Ethan and Ben followed her deeper in, their suit lights sweeping across crudely etched murals on the walls of the corridor, primitive depictions of ancient warfare and philosophy, a silent testament to the master strategist whose tomb they were looting. The tunnel widened out into a large, rectangular room, but it was at this point that they stopped.

"Obstruction," Ben spat out, dropping onto his haunches before the blockage.

Some time in the deep past, a massive piece of the ceiling of the tomb had come away and collapsed. It had chocked off what should have been a free-flowing exit from the tomb, the blocks of stone having baked and fused with packed earth and clay over time to form an unnatural, solid, and immovable wall at the mouth of the tomb.

"Zara, map confirms that this is the last chamber before the sarcophagus," Ethan reported back to the EBS command. "Estimate on density, Ben?"

Ben held a small, hand-held scanner over the obstruction. "Solid. I can't thermal-cut it, I can't apply heat to the sensor floor. It would propagate and register as a massive activity pulse. We have to shift it. I can use the polymer wedges and the micro-drills to cut into it and then slowly work the debris up. But it's going to make noise. Inevitable kinetic feedback."

The noise. Ethan knew that Ben was right. This was a demolition problem, and Ben was the only one on the team with the brains to fix it, but each and every action they took inside the tomb would be amplified by the surrounding geology.

Outside, at the edge of the breach, Quinn was the first to feel it. Her acoustic sensors, pushed to their absolute highest level of sensitivity, jumped.

"Warning! Acoustic signature moving in the valley rim," Quinn snapped on the comm, her voice catching in her throat. She double checked the sound against the previous patrol data, cross referencing the ping automatically. "Two signatures. They're moving, slowly. Talking softly, but they're not aware of us. They are moving along the high ground, perpendicular to the direction of the first patrol."

She could hear the low, muffled murmur of voices. A conversation. Relaxing, non-anxious. The two soldiers were less than fifty meters away. Oblivious, their position was perfect acoustic cover for Ben's work, but should anything go wrong they were also an immediate threat.

"Ethan, Ben, you have acoustic cover for the moment, but the patrol is fifty meters away and they're getting closer," Quinn cautioned, eyes flicking back and forth on her terminal. "They're on the rim of the valley, on high ground directly above the tomb's projected location. If they stop or if Ben's displacement triggers a noise above the ambient military noise, they're going to hear it."

In the tomb, Ben had already set his tools to work. "Fifty meters is zero margin. I need ten minutes to safely shift this wall. Ethan, cover me the whole time. Quinn, hope for the best from small talk that lasts forever."

"Ten minutes, Vandal." Ethan confirmed, illuminating the blockage with his suit light. He unfolded his integrated sonic disruptor, ready to use a tight pulse to unbalance any immediate threat if the patrol closed on the breach.

Ben started the slow, delicate work. He drove two hydraulic wedges into pinhead gaps in the packed earth, applying almost imperceptible pressure. The stone wall groaned, a soft, low-pitched vibration that should not have been happening at all, not without the vibration tearing at the tomb and reverberating throughout its centuries-old interior.

"Groaning is registering at forty-five decibels," Quinn said, her voice already a low hiss. "Background noise outside is fifty decibels. This is cutting it fine, Vandal. Stay slow."

Ben worked with his comms off. Gritting his teeth, he worked at an excruciating pace to ratchet more hydraulic pressure onto the wedges, forcing the packed earth to give. Dust and tiny particles of crumbling rock peppered his suit. The wall moved another inch, widening a slot a few inches high.

Creak. Groan. Shush. The stink of failure. The entire damned place was about to collapse.

Above, on the valley rim, the two Chinese soldiers had fallen silent. A moment ago they'd been talking about someplace else in a world of elsewhere, but now they gazed down at the deep valley.

Cold blood rushed in Quinn's veins. It was the silence that spelled danger.

Inside the tomb, the low grinding groan of the misaligned rock wall felt like a symphony of destruction. Ben worked the hydraulic actuator with bare fingertips, his arm muscles bunching against the dark suit. The ancient stone had moved three inches, but the hydraulic was reaching limit before the old support gave way.

"Groaning is registering at forty-five decibels," Quinn said. Her voice was already a high-pitched thread.

Above, on the valley rim, the two Chinese soldiers fell silent in their conversation.

Quinn pressed herself against the cold, moist rubble of the inner cliff wall. The silence in her ears was a punch. The diesel growl of the Chinese exercise vehicles, the steady background buzz of low drone static, had continued, but the two voices, her acoustic mask, had stopped.

She peered through the faint shimmer of her cloaking field, her eyes tracking their heat signatures. They were motionless, standing together and looking down into the valley, above the tomb entrance.

The silence is the danger, she thought, remembering Ethan's instructions during their insertion jump. The human ear subconsciously noticed the absence of normal background noise. They hadn't heard the breach, but they might have heard the groan, or maybe they'd just felt the press of the local sensor cloak.

"They stopped talking," Quinn breathed, her breath coming fast and shallow. "They're looking at the spot. I have eyes on them. They're fifty meters out and quiet."

Instantly, inside the tomb, Ethan's voice was cutting. "Vandal, freeze! Quinn, what do their thermal signatures tell you?"

"They're static. Their weapons are slung. They're just standing, confused." Quinn reported. "But they're too close. If they reach the rim, they'll breach the threshold of my local sensor cloak, and our breach site will shimmer."

Quinn knew that she couldn't let Ethan and Ben freeze where they were; Ben was at the point of critical breach. She had to break the soldiers' focus, but she couldn't risk a kinetic option. Not with Drake's rules on non-lethal solutions.

I have to give them a reason to look away. A reason to be where they are, without seeing us.

Network Intrusion was Quinn's specialty. Her mind spun, mentally skimming through the hostile Chinese net that she was barely touching. She had an open window on the lower-grade military comms, the logistics chatter, and unencrypted sensor reads.

"Marc, Zara, I need the location of the nearest resupply truck," Quinn ordered, overriding the local channel and adding the EBS command deck to their critical contact list.

"A truck? Now?" Marc's voice was a tightly wound spring.

"Zara, give her the data," Drake said with instant trust in his operative's panicked instinct.

Instantly, a blue stream of data washed over Quinn's display. Logistics Truck ZY-331, two kilometers north along a service road, loaded with rations.

Quinn burrowed into the truck's telemetry. The security was light, a standard unencrypted GPS beacon and a commercial comms module. Her fingers were flying over her terminal as she injected a small fragment of corrupted data into the truck's GPS feed.

"I'm hijacking the truck's GPS," Quinn murmured, pouring as much of her suit's available energy into the breach as she could. "I'm telling the truck's autopilot that it's one hundred meters beyond its designated dropoff point, and I'm broadcasting its position on the public channel."

On the rim, the effect was immediate. The radio strapped to the nearest trooper's hip crackled and spat.

"Got it," Quinn whispered.

The squad leader screamed an order at the comms. Instead of staring up at the distant floor of the valley, every one of them was staring at the sudden, localized comm emergency.

"The troops are reversing course," Quinn gasped. "They're retreating back towards the road. They're going to check out the supply error. They're going to think the supply squad messed up."

Footsteps pounded away on the valley rim. Quinn dropped the acoustic cloak, her hands trembling. She had just used alien technology and high-level cyberwarfare to exploit a political chink, the dread of a truck driver called out on a missed delivery, to buy her team time.

"They're clear," Quinn broadcast on the comms. "Go Vandal, go. Countdown to zero."

Ben had not faltered. He had heard the comm burst, felt the adrenaline spike, but his concentration had not faltered for a single moment. When Quinn gave the all clear he put his last ounce of effort into it.

The ancient rock wall groaned. Then it gave up the ghost with a deep, final thump that settled all of the remaining rubble. A small, human-width gap had opened up, giving entry into the final, small burial chamber.

"Access to final chamber cleared," Ben breathed, his lungs tight.

Ethan stepped through the breach, his non-lethal suppressor drawn. His helmet light washed over the small burial chamber, illuminating the sight before them. A single, enormous granite sarcophagus sat atop a raised plinth at the center of the room. The air was surprisingly clean in here. Signs of scavenging or disturbance were all but nonexistent.

"No traps, no immediate danger," Ethan relayed. "The sample should be in the sarcophagus."

The small final chamber of the tomb was dominated by the immense granite sarcophagus. The air was also noticeably drier and cleaner, having been cut off from the damp earth by the tomb's final defense layer.

Ethan stepped around the sarcophagus, sweeping the light of his suit across the walls. "No secondary entrances, no immediate booby traps. Ben, open her up."

Ben, his adrenaline finally focused on grim efficiency, set hands on the lid. The granite was coarse and heavy, but centuries of weathering and the recent vibrations from the breach had cracked open the ancient seal. With a soft, straining grunt, Ben leveraged the lid, sliding it back with a heavy, grinding rasp that luckily did not carry inside the burial chamber.

The inside of the sarcophagus was lined with tight, densely packed fine silk that had disintegrated to dust. The ancient body of the master tactician lay in the center of the sarcophagus, his skeletal remains settling on the collapsed remains of a jade pillow. Notably, the body was encased in a thin, calcified membrane, a petrified body preserver from millennia past.

"The preservation is better than anticipated," Ethan reported, kneeling down. He brought a small, specialized sampling device from a sheath on his forearm, a tool that functioned something like a non-invasive cellular biopsy needle. "Quinn, maintain perimeter. Ben, prep a clean field. I need a clean shot on the sample."

As Ethan carefully worked the tool across the calcified membrane to extract a microscopic sample of the bone marrow from the interior of the sarcophagus, bone marrow being the single best source of pure Ancestor genome, Quinn's edge sensors, trained on the outside, exploded.

Down at the tomb entrance, pressed into the rubble, Quinn's head snapped up.

"Intrusion! Closing fast on high-band radar signature!" Quinn snapped over the comms, tearing her attention away from the inside of the tomb. "It's a scout drone. Military hardware, with integrated thermal optics. It's about to cross right over the valley floor. Time to overhead, three seconds."

"Can you jam it?" Ethan called from the inner chamber, his hands frozen above the sarcophagus. The DNA sample was half-contained.

"It's on an encrypted military band! I can't decrypt it in time!" Quinn screamed. She stilled a heartbeat as panic flooded her and forced her fingers to enter a more extreme, higher-risk protocol. "I have to jam the entire valley with localized RF noise! It will break the drone's link, but it will also register on every military sensor within a five-kilometer radius as an immediate, high-priority electronic warfare alert!"

"Do it," Ethan commanded, terse and urgent. "Ben, go to the breach. Seal the exterior with the remaining putty. We are exfilling now."

"Roger that," Ben said, already turning and scrambling back toward the small breach. The entire mission profile had just changed from stealth extraction to full-bore exfil.

Quinn punched her thumb down on the terminal. The power draw was immediate, yanking her suit batteries down to the redline. A silent, blinding wall of chaotic radio frequency radiation burst from the Ronin team's position.

The results were immediate and violent. The drone's radar signature on Quinn's display screen bloomed into white noise, and the drone's faint motor whine went dead as its flight controls went offline. It was done, its electronics fried, now just a piece of junk tumbling toward the valley floor in the distance.

"Drone is down, Lead," Quinn said. Her relief was only momentary. "But the alert is going global. We have seconds before they confirm the electronic attack and start dispatching ground assets."

"Sample is secured," Ethan called back from the inner chamber. He finished fastening the biopsy sample into the crystalline capture sphere. The sample itself, an iridescent, seahorse-shaped biocontainer the size of a human thumb, held the key to humanity's survival. The sphere now held it in a field of force, held its orientation and stability within the tiny, milky cell. He slid the sphere into the rugged socket on the secure flash drive and scrambled toward the exit. "Vandal, what's the seal status!"

Ben had already returned to the breach point. He was packing the final putty-like compound into the small gaps and activating its quick-hardening process. The goal was not to fully seal the tomb, but rather to buy time to prevent any loose collapse material from shifting in a way that might leave a telltale signature.

"Seal is twenty seconds from full set. We are clear to move," Ben called back. Only now that the tomb was effectively sealed and the sample secured was he able to turn his pent-up energy to effective action.

Ethan had reached the opening and pulled Quinn's shoulder. "Quinn, you go point, back the way you came. Run your cyber access wide, clear us a path, but no more active jamming. We move quiet, or we die."

CHAPTER 32: SAMPLE HARVEST

The Ronin team, sample in hand, bolted from the silent tomb and back into the open, exposed night. The hard-won silence of the past ten minutes was shattered. The Ronin team had entered a ten-minute window of borrowed time, a rapidly dissipating stealth field, and a long, exposed run to the extraction point.

The moment Quinn's surgical electronic pulse brought down the reconnaissance drone, the tactical situation around the Ronin team shifted from "covert" to "hostile."

"We have an immediate, high-priority alert across the network," Quinn panted, straining to keep her systems online at full power. "I'm spiking thermal data, creating ghost readings two hundred meters north of our position, but this won't last. They'll be on us in five minutes."

Ethan, sample in hand, was already moving, sprinting point in a low, disciplined lope toward the exfil point, a carefully calculated swath of the riverbed where the stealth pod would deploy and begin its silent, vertical ascent. Ben fell in behind him, the greater bulk of his massive frame devouring ground, and Quinn followed on his shoulder, running interference on the Chinese network.

"They're on vehicle deployment," Quinn reported. "Patrols are responding from three different axes. Two on the ridge line, one fast-rolling through the valley floor with lights."

"We take the cliff face," Ethan directed. "We use the shadow and the rock shear as cover. Ben, you take the rock, I take the outside. Quinn, keep the spoofing tight."

They arrived at a sheer cliff face. Fifty meters above the floor of the canyon. Blind spot for vehicle-mounted thermal optics. They shimmied down into the shadows and flattened themselves against the cold, wet stone. The wall acoustics did the rest.

And then Quinn made a quick, panicky gagging sound over the radio. "Stop! Freeze! Patrol to the rim right above us! On foot, and they're close. The, uh, they're static."

Ethan flattened himself, chest heaving, eyes staring at the edge of the cliff three floors up. The sound of heavy boot heels crunching in the loose rock was magnified to a crashing drone. Two sources of footfalls paused exactly at the rim of the cliff face.

"They are not sweeping," Quinn whispered, a thread of a voice. "They're... they're taking a piss."

It was a total, absolute split-second of thick, sickening silence. Not a rustle, just the tinny echo of their training exercise running in the distance. Then, a black blob of a figure leant over the rim of the cliff, blocking out the ambient light.

The Ronin team all knew the sound of a man unzippering his uniform fly.

Oh God.

Ethan shut his eyes behind his visor, tensing every muscle. The soldier at the top was blissfully unaware, now bending to the business at hand. A warm mist of brown, fetid liquid blasted off the cliff face.

Ethan, Ben, and Quinn were so tightly wedged into the cliff they couldn't move a single inch without scraping stone. A sound that would have given them away in an instant. The spray landed on their matte-gray Ronin bodysuits, a thick, searing column of hot shit dribbling down their shoulders, their backs, and puddling in a heap at their feet.

Ben was the most volatile of the three, and his jaw must have locked tight because Ethan could hear the click over the comm. Ben's hand hovered over the non-lethal sonic disruptor stitched into his glove, but he froze there, trapped by the last thing Ethan shouted at him: don't move.

It took an age. When he was done, the soldier zipped up and made some quick, muffled comment to his buddy. The boot heels stomped away from the cliff face, away from them.

"…Clear," Quinn said, her voice raw, pure cold bile.

"Move," Ethan said, voice gravelly. He wiped a hand on his visor (thermal fluid was volatile, it would evaporate quickly), and shunted the quick, heinous violation deep into the subconscious. They were traitors and grave robbers. Murderers, and now they were targets. He bit it back. It was the price of the mission.

The team abandoned the cliff face and dropped into the undergrowth.

They had run clear of the cliff and were bounding toward the riverbed when the second patrol party materialized.

"Warning! Three thermal signatures, 50m at your 12 o'clock!" Quinn screamed, voice cracking with her loss of cool. "They're on foot and converging directly onto your position! The spoof failed!"

There was no time for finesse. Ethan, Ben, and Quinn exploded into a full open run.

The Chinese soldiers who had been running along the ridge-top immediately noticed the faint ripple of their passive cloaking field as the Ronin came in to attack. A shout of alarm roared around the canyon, then the thin, metallic rat-a-tat-tat of an AK-47 magazine cracking open.

"Run and gun! We're live!" Ethan screamed. "Non-lethal only! Ben, cover our 6!"

Their air crackled with the angry zip of bullets. Ben, who had been twitching with pent-up aggression, instantly rotated. He lobbed a quick-deploy sonic mine, an orb that spat out a cone of disorienting white noise. It detonated behind a clump of bamboo and the patrol scattered, clutching at their ears.

"Quinn, I need a vehicle! Anything! Distract them!" Ethan screamed, herding his team toward the riverbed.

"Spiking a local transport truck it's driving itself off a service road into the river!" Quinn screeched, throwing all her remaining energy into the breach.

It was minimal. But enough. The soldiers stopped to glance at their radios for an update on the renegade truck. Long enough.

The Ronin punched through the final line of trees and burst out onto the muddy riverbed. The stealth pod was already beginning to lower itself silently and invisibly on the far bank. Zara was guiding it there from orbit.

"We have thirty seconds to extraction!" Marc's voice was ragged but insistent. "Get to the pod! Go! Go!"

The Ronin team hit the muddy bank of the river, breathing hard. Behind them, the sound of pursuit was now overwhelming: the machine-gun rat-a-tat of automatic weapons and the high squeal of tires as Chinese military jeeps came thundering down to the valley rim. Quinn's electronic distress call had triggered the alert on the valley rim, making the whole area a kill zone of the highest order.

"Extraction point directly ahead!" Ethan shouted, pointing across the dark water. The stealth pod was just rising, silent and cloaked but far too small for the job, its squat profile still no more than a foot above river level.

Before any of the team could take a step into the water, a long projectile tore through the air, a streak of high velocity metal cutting silently through the night. The explosion was muted, but the kinetic impact was not. A Chinese anti-tank grenade (APG) had been fired from a vehicle at the valley rim twenty meters upstream. It had detonated on impact on the riverbed, instantly turning the river into a mud fountain, thirty meters high of boiling mud and steam.

"The pod! It's been compromised!" Ben shouted, throwing himself and Ethan into the mud. It was a soundless but very real explosion from inside the stealth pod itself.

The APG round hadn't hit the stealth pod, but the sonic shockwave and water displacement had both impacted into the pod's as-yet-rising form factor. The pod's cloaking field had been shattered, vibrating like wet paper and flailing under internal stresses. Now fully visible, the stealth pod, a black, inhuman teardrop of a craft, had begun to list as its ascent engines failed.

"Marc! The pod is under fire! We can't reach it!" Ethan bellowed into the comms, heaving to his feet.

High above on the EBS command deck, the tactical screen was flickering with alerts in red and orange.

"The stealth pod is offline!" Zara's voice was clipped, urgent. "Its upward flight system is jammed. It won't be able to reach orbital insertion velocity before they start to target it with precision ordnance!"

Marc slammed his hand down on the console in front of him. He looked at the two small, vulnerable blue dots that were his operatives. "Drake, we're out of time. We just lost our only extraction vehicle. We need to commit the reserve."

Drake didn't need to think about it. He didn't need to look at the two figures in the staging bay feed, standing stock still.

"Deploy the support team," Drake ordered, gritting his teeth with urgency. "Scrub the stealth pod. We are going to a hot extraction. Zara, prep a mini-shuttle. Viper, Sam, and Barb, you are green to launch. Retrieve the asset and the team."

The rapid-response staging bay was the domain of Captain Alex "Viper" Thorne, already a legend among the crew as a hot shot fighter pilot whose expertise wasn't just in speed, but in making impossible maneuvers look like a routine commute. He didn't need to be told twice. Barb "Whisper" Chen and Sam "Ghostnet" Taylor were already sealing their helmets in the small, fast, and viciously maneuverable mini-shuttle, a purpose-built, arrowhead-shaped vehicle that Zara had created for low-atmosphere, high-speed strike. Sam had a background in E-Warfare, while Barb, whose lithe, ethereal frame was in keeping with her callsign, specialized in ground insertion and stealth movement.

"We're going in hot. APG hit the pod," Sam reported from the rear console, his fingers a blur on the shuttle's deployment interface. "Viper, you ready to thread the needle at Mach 4?"

Alex "Viper" Thorne gave a tight, confident grin from the pilot's seat. "My kind of Tuesday, Ghostnet. Barb, make sure those bots are strapped in. We're about to pull some serious Gs."

"They're secured, Viper," Barb confirmed, nodding toward the rear of the shuttle. Two figures were visible in the shut-in shuttle, perfectly still.

Zara's combat robots. These were not the hulking security bots that Drake had been taken out by four years ago, but two six-foot, angular chrome automatons, armed with a set of twin, integrated non-lethal energy disruptors. Their purpose was to make big arrests without killing anyone, the shock troops of the Initiative.

"We'll drop off the back side of the ridge and use the momentum to cross the river," Viper stated, already at the controls of the shuttle and flying it through the rapid-deployment launch process. "Ghostnet, you're on comms and active sensor masking. I need three seconds of full space in which to drop those bots and grab the team. Get ready to make noise, Sam. This is a rescue mission, not a pickup."

The shuttle left the landing bay with a blinding rush of acceleration. It was heading straight for the troubled planet below.

Ethan, Ben, and Quinn were still hunkered on the riverbank. They were under accurate and close-range fire from the second patrol which had now joined forces with the first. The sunken stream gave them no cover, just knee-deep, muddy water.

"They've got us boxed in! We can't hold this!" Ben yelled as he fired a full burst from his non-lethal sonic disruptor. The white noise made the Chinese soldiers duck for cover.

"Extraction team in thirty seconds! Look up!" Marc's voice thundered over the EBS comms.

A black blur, sharp-edged and fast as hell and impossibly loud, screamed over the ridge. It wasn't the stealth pod. It was a sleek, black arrowhead of pure speed, wings slicing the air with a screaming, sonic boom.

As it screamed overhead, the mini-shuttle's rear hatch blew open and two combat robots dropped from the sky, suspended on a curved Kevlar cable. They landed in the riverbed between the Ronin team and the wall of Chinese fire.

The robots opened fire, not with bullets. Integrated weapon systems popped with short, sharp bursts of non-lethal energy, impacting the ground near the Chinese soldiers and making them dive for cover, disoriented and confused.

"Go! Go to the shuttle!" Viper screamed over the comms as he banked the vehicle over the riverbed, descending with the side hatch lowered to bring the team aboard.

It was a rescue mission no one wanted. It was loud and fast and brutally exposed. Ethan didn't think. He charged into the mud and the water with the Sun Tzu genetic sample pressed against his chest.

The five Ronin operators tumbled aboard the mini-shuttle as Whisper locked the side hatch. The interior was claustrophobic, foul-smelling with mud, adrenaline, and burnt electronics. Ethan, Ben, and Quinn dropped to the restraint harnesses, their suits slick with the disgusting slime from the cliff face.

"We're hot! Strap in, team!" Viper yelled, hands flying over the flight controls.

The shuttle was designed for speed and maneuverability, not durability. It screamed vertically away from the riverbed. The genetic sample of Sun Tzu was in a small, internal locker right next to Ethan.

Ghostnet, hunched over the E-Warfare console, was not concerned with G-forces. His entire focus was on the tactical map projected on his screen; a nightmarish image of intersecting radar cones and missile lock warnings blooming red across the eastern coast of China.

"We've activated every defense grid between here and the coast, Viper!" Ghostnet yelled, his voice cracking. "They're scrambling interceptors and they've identified the electromagnetic anomaly caused by my jamming pulse as the target! We have immediate fire-control radar lock!"

"I see it! Hold on!" Viper yelled back as the G-forces pressed him into the seat.

The entire vessel shuddered as Viper yanked it sideways with a lateral evasive maneuver. They were flying faster than three times the speed of sound, blasting through a low-altitude series of narrow valleys, trusting entirely in the small ship's speed and Viper's encyclopedic knowledge of fluid dynamics. He banked hard to the left, the mini-shuttle just clearing a forested ridge.

"They've launched! Two surface-to-air missiles, fast movers!" Ghostnet's warning was a voice in hell.

Viper did not glance at the external telemetry readouts. He trusted Ghostnet. "Zara, I need assistance! Throw me some passive sonar deception!"

Up on the EBS, high above the frantic chase, Drake, Marc, and Carlos observed the careening flight path. Zara was running interference, diverting non-essential systems to throw power to the tiny vehicle.

"I am broadcasting a stochastic acoustic profile," Zara reported, her voice uncharacteristically strained. "It will increase the terminal guidance uncertainty of the anti-air missiles. But Viper will have to maintain a climb angle of eighty degrees at all times."

The noise inside the mini-shuttle was deafening. The missile warning light was flashing with an insane frequency of red.

Viper pulled it into a bank so tight it went black in Ethan's and Ben's vision. For an instant it was the wrong way up, then it corrected as Viper executed a blinding maneuver, a tight corkscrew ascent which screamed away from the coast.

"Chaff deployed!" Ghostnet yelled over the comms. "First missile missed! Detonated behind us! Second one is still on our tail!"

Viper watched as the mini-shuttle HUD was replaced with the projection of Chinese air defense network intercept vectors. Blind flying. Playing guessing games with the missile's flight path using Ghostnet's streaming frantic voice in his ear.

"Zara, I need the window!"

"Three seconds before the missile's proximity fuse activates!" Zara was screaming.

Viper found a brief, nearly invisible window in the defense net (short, preprogrammed delay on a cycling power of a ground-based radar site). He shoved the mini-shuttle in a sickening, one-tenth-second, ninety-degree climb up. The G-force was literally squeezing the life out of everyone.

"It missed it! Overshot it! Went thermal and lost lock!" Ghostnet hollered, one fleeting moment of relief painted across his features.

"Let's not get cocky, Ghostnet," Viper growled, absolutely focused. The Chinese air force was scrambling fighters. "We are entering the max-cap flight envelope for the best of their interceptors. Ghostnet, full spectrum sensor saturation. I want them to think this valley evaporated from their maps."

Ghostnet overrode his E-Warfare systems and redlined it. He tripped a gargantuan, local white noise, sensor ghosts and decoys cloud, a total electronic last-ditch hysterical wail meant to make the valley appear as an instantaneous meteorological tantrum in the skies to those fighters arriving in the immediate area.

The mini-shuttle streaked skyward as a single silver needle of defiance, leaving behind the confusion in the Chinese air defense network.

Viper punched it to exceed the Kármán line. The engines quieted in the vacuum of space. The entire cabin flooded with the pallid, dispassionate glow of outer space. The Earth below was a beautiful uninterrupted blue marble, blissfully unaware of the great game of high theft that had just played out above it.

Viper throttled back the shuttle as the abrupt removal of G-force allowed the exasperated Ronin team to finally catch their breath.

"We are in clean orbit," Viper huffed, voice torn with relief. "Extraction is a go. Sun Tzu is secure."

Silence now gripped the tiny cabin. The peace was purchased through a grotesque premium of near-infinite effort and risk. Ethan slowly reached out and softly patted the metallic locker containing the genetic sample.

The EBS command deck was a chorus of alarms and red lights. Stabilizing the mini-shuttle's orbit, the main console indicated that its orbit was becoming fixed. Tactical screen was all they were concerned with, a big angry red blotch spreading across the Chinese coast, the site where Quinn's E-Warfare pulse had exploded.

Drake, Marc, and Carlos were crowded around the console, illuminated by the stark overhead lights, their faces somber. A narrowly won tactical victory in procuring Sun Tzu's sample was instantly overshadowed by the immensity of the geopolitical consequences. This was not treaty violation, it was treason; they had just committed an act of high-tech piracy and an act of war against their own species.

"We have an intercept request, Drake," Zara interjected, her voice strained. "The Chinese government has traced the sustained electronic warfare attack to a very advanced and unknown source. They are demanding an explanation for our violation of their sovereign space. They are treating this as an act of unprovoked aggression."

Carlos slumped back into his seat and ran a hand through his hair, "We don't have any diplomatic standing. We're not our own country. We're wanted criminals. We just committed an act of war against a nuclear power. We're going to be looking at a global, coordinated military response the second they figure out that they can't catch us."

Drake shoved Carlos aside and took control of the console to accept a high-priority, encrypted video uplink. The screen blinked, showing the angular, livid face of a high-ranking Chinese military official – the man's eyes blazing with rage.

"Mr. Donovan," he began, his Mandarin translated in real time by Zara. His voice was a condescension-tinged stoic incredulity. "Your actions are an extreme and unprovoked act of aggression against the People's Republic of China. We demand an immediate explanation for the destruction of our assets, the landing of armed, unidentified personnel on our soil, and this unprecedented electronic warfare attack. The governments of the world will ensure that you are held accountable for your actions."

Drake looked at the official, taking in his square jaw and trim beard, hair flecked with gray. He saw a man clinging to a small, petty squabble, willfully blind to the enormity of the darkness closing in on the entire world around him. He thought of Marc and his men, of his entire mission; a mission that had almost failed because of the politics and pride of countries that already wanted him dead.

The last remnants of his civilian life faded away.

"Look at me," Drake spoke through gritted teeth, no trace of warmth left in his voice. Authority resonated through the command room, the small space threatening to swallow up the group. "Your drone is a pile of scrap metal, your soldiers have a nasty headache, and your air defenses just got a very advanced lesson in obsolescence. I am on a mission to secure this planet's future against an enemy that considers your government, our entire species, a breeding ground for protein."

He leaned into the camera, eyes hard, emotionless. The Chinese official's face displayed shock and utter disbelief.

"I am already a wanted criminal in your government's eyes. I am already a traitor," Drake concluded, his voice devoid of emotion, dangerous finality. "Frankly, I don't care what you think, what you want, or how you feel. You do not have the ability to stop me. I have just stolen a piece of your history to save your future. You can just piss off."

Drake slammed his hand down on the console, killing the connection. Absolute silence fell over the command deck.

He turned to Marc, his focus now razor-sharp. "Marc," Drake snapped, a whipcrack of absolute urgency in his voice. "We just bought ourselves five minutes before the rest of the world goes on high alert and marshals every asset at their disposal to stop us. Send all five Ronin teams out immediately. Gather the other Seven Ancestor samples, ASAP. We can't be surgical anymore. This is a smash-and-grab on a global scale and If necessary, lethal forth is authorized. We need those samples and I'm not risking the lives of our people any further than what we have to going forward."

Drake then turned to Tammy, who had been standing nearby, her face ashen.

"Tammy, you and Zara need to work on this, now," he continued. "We are no longer limiting ourselves to certain tombs. I want you to organize as many three-person retrieval teams as Zara has shuttles for to collect as many samples as possible from graves all over the planet."

Zara immediately piped up, with chilling pragmatism. "Each team will be outfitted with micro-drones that can independently collect thousands of samples from low security grave and preserved sites."

"Excellent," Drake said, still looking out at the peaceful blue marble. "Collect genetic material. If we can get into the billions, all the better. We will sort out the heroes from the average man later. We need every seed we can get our hands on."

The EBS morphed into a frenzy of activity from its haven state. Drake's order to cut all attempts at diplomacy and simply raid the planet for genetic material had shredded through Zara's automated operations. The massive Launch Deck, usually pristine and silent, now throbbed with the sound of engines coming online, the din of moving materiel, and the shouts of Marc's operations team.

Marc, with Carlos moving zombie-like at his side, was elevated on a temporary gantry from the worst of it. He was marshalling dozens of auxiliary crew members, racing hundreds of purpose-built retrieval shuttles into launch position. These were not the expensive, elegant stealth pods; these were built in hundreds, with minimal shielding and only optimized for speed and high-yield retrieval.

"Go, green, for all sectors! We need a hundred teams in the air in five minutes!" Marc shouted, his voice hoarse from the incredible, rapid scaling of operations. "Lock down those micro-drone payloads! Tammy's teams are looking at billions of samples, not dozens!"

The vast majority of this mobilization were the raw, newly assembled Auxiliary Retrieval Teams. Hundreds of operators, hastily trained and only outfitted with basic non-lethal deterrents, were being deployed to the most far-flung task at hand: collecting samples from low-security graveyards and unmanned sites all over the world. Simple, almost robotic in execution: punch in, release the swarms of micro-drones that will collect thousands of samples, punch out before national militaries could scramble jets. Overwhelming the global eyes and ears with enough targets to track that the most defended would remain unmolested.

In addition to the hundreds of disposable auxiliary craft, five specialized, armored shuttles were also ready. These five carried the Ronin Strike Teams, the teams that would be tasked with retrieving the last of the Seven Ancestors from the most high-value and heavily guarded locations on the planet. The teams, all expertly trained, carried the full, lethal range of Areidyanies integrated weaponry.

Marc made his way to the five team leaders, his expression dark as he delivered Drake's final, horrific order.

Anya Petrova (Team 1 Lead) was by her shuttle, her form-fitting dark-grey uniform looking deadly. Her team, which consisted of Barb Chen, Ben Carter, Caleb Jensen, Rachel Green and Quinn Perez was likely bound for a grave of a major historical figure, probably a museum or military archive.

"Anya," Marc said, meeting her gaze. "Your target is the most heavily guarded Ancestor that we have left. Infiltration is secondary. Drake's order is final: The sample is the priority. If you meet resistance, use lethal force to secure the target and guarantee your exfil. We are not losing any team members to non-lethal restraint. We are bringing this Ancestor back."

Anya's jaw clenched. She gave a single nod. "Team 1 understood. Lethal authorized."

Elena Rodriguez (Team 2 Lead) was strapped into her shuttle, which included Diana Vance, Frank Miller, Ricardo Salazar, Sam Taylor and Ethan Brannigan newly de-briefed from the Sun Tzu mission. Their diverse specialties in energy systems and structural analysis made them uniquely well suited to a high-security, multi-faceted intrusion.

"Elena, you have a complicated, high-security target to infiltrate," Marc said. "If you make contact with state security forces, there are no rules. You clear the exfil zone, and you do not hesitate. Your team and the sample are all that matters at this point."

Elena, a cold pragmatist to match her specialty in shields, gave an acknowledgment of the change in rules. "Understood, General. We secure the sample."

Marc gave similar, clipped orders to Jin Kathmandu (Team 3 Lead), Kyle Evans (Team 4 Lead) and Mike Davis (Team 5 Lead). Rules of engagement were no longer just silent theft. It had changed to cold, martial law.

Abruptly, Zara's voice was blaring over the command deck's internal comms. "All auxiliary shuttles and Ronin teams, this is your final sequence. The global surveillance net is focused on the Chinese anomaly. We have three minutes before they regain full tactical awareness. Deploy now!"

The EBS shook, not the smooth surge of a single vessel leaving orbit, but the combined deafening thrust of a hundred engines at once. Shuttles launched in phalanxes – not one at a time, but two dozen at a time from separate launch bays. The Launch Deck cleared in less than ninety seconds as Auxiliary teams rocketed toward their pre-calculated drop zones scattered across the continents.

The five black-hulled Ronin support vessels launched a short time after the Shuttles, each one a scalpel slotted into the vital point of a high-value target.

Marc watched the cloud of red dots on the tactical map converge on the peaceful blue sphere, the silence before the storm now ended. The unspoken, philosophical war was over. The Billion-Sample Harvest had begun with a deafening roar.

CHAPTER 33: LETHAL FORCE APPLIED

The EBS Main Research Lab was the antithesis of the frantic Launch Deck. In this cavernous silentarium, everything was quiet, cold and blindingly sterile. The only sounds were the gentle whirr of cooling units, the dry hiss of automated filtration units, and the clear click of precisely engineered equipment at sub-zero pressure.

Tammy and Jill stood next to Zara at the central sequencing station, her initial shock turned to cold, grim determination. The third person in the room was Jill, already booting up the Matter Re-sequencer control unit.

Between them, floating in a glittering, chronal containment field on a pedestal, was the prize. The Sun Tzu genetic sample, a single perfect crystalline orb. The captured, calcified echo of the master tactician. The ultimate treasure, stolen at the price of operational security for the entire mission.

"The Chinese military is still in a state of heightened confusion, but they will coordinate," Zara said, voice emotionless and analytical as she watched the tactical feed of the entire world projected onto the lab's central glass wall. "We have maybe twenty minutes of global confusion before the knowledge of our presence becomes a coalesced military threat. Zara, you need to push the sequencing rate for Sun Tzu."

"I am utilizing the Areidyanies set to the maximum capability," Zara confirmed, typing furiously on the sequencing console. Her attention was laser-focused. "I am not running the standard Areidyanies set. I am also using a gene mapping algorithms to isolate the complete strategic profile at the point of scan. This machine is not merely reading base pairs, it is reading centuries of living tactical intelligence."

The sequencing console burned with a sharp, emerald light. Human technology might take weeks to map and interpret a single genome; the Areidyanies console synthesized the necessary information in nanoseconds. A three-dimensional model of the genome rotated in space on the screen – a double-helix data complex with rippling bands of gold that made the unique markers of Sun Tzu's genetic code pop like glitches.

"Full genetic sequence complete," Zara said, her measured tone failing to properly convey the significance of the sentence. "Genetic profile has been extracted and secured. Ready for the Matter Re-sequencer."

Jill stepped forward, gesturing to the largest machine in the room. It was a humming, obsidian chamber roughly the size of a sarcophagus that sat on its end like a large prism. It was the Matter Re-sequencer, the only machine in the galaxy known to be capable of taking the genetic code and building a living human being from the ground up.

"Tammy, load the genetic sequence to the Re-sequencer's core matrix," Zara said. "We are initiating in-built bypass protocols for the maturation phase. He will need to be battle-ready, and fully mature in less than six hours."

"Loading the Sun Tzu sequence now," Tammy said, voice firm. She flipped the main control to active. The chamber hummed to life, emitting a deep, sonorous chord that resonated through the lab. "The Re-sequencer is extracting base elements from EBS stores. Energy draw is peaking."

As the most important mind in human history was being constructed in the room behind them, Tammy and Zara turned their attention to the far more overwhelming logistical problem that was the Billion-Sample Harvest.

"We need the raw throughput to filter and analyze the raw, unsorted genetic material," Tammy said, bringing up a schematic of a massive, automated, processing facility. "The Auxiliary teams are dropping thousands of micro-drones to harvest billions of unsorted cells from grave sites across the planet. We need a method to screen them for viability without culling the full Ancestor pool."

"I am constructing and engineering fifty auxiliary filtering bays within the EBS construction bays," Zara replied, avatar head tilting slightly. "The construction bays can filter using thermal and cellular decay metrics to separate non-viable samples. Identification remains the hard problem."

"We can't sequence billions of people," Jill said, fiddling with a monitor. "It's just physically impossible to do it in this window."

"Agreed," Zara said. "So, we will sequence viability pools. After the samples have been filtered for cellular integrity, they will be divided by collection sector, let's say one sample per ten thousand samples collected. We will sequence the DNA of these combined samples to get a rough estimate of geographic and historical origins. If a pool has a high concentration of genetic markers that we believe indicate high potential for leadership, intelligence, or resilience, then we isolate and fully sequence the individual samples within that pool."

Tammy nodded, the cold, logical brutality of the plan not lost on her. "We're throwing a net the size of a planet out into the world and then narrowing the catch until we have the strongest genes of the strongest stock. It's the ultimate bottleneck."

"We are harvesting every seed," Zara said, gesturing to the global tactical map, a map now alive with the dots of hundreds of tiny Auxiliary shuttles, descending from orbit. "The sequencing is complex, but the selection criteria is simple: What is the best of mankind, wherever it may be buried."

The Matter Re-sequencer behind them had begun to pulse with a brilliant internal orange light. The first phase of human creation was underway. The three women turned their attention to the long, arduous process of mass production, while, at the ship's heart, the first of the newly resurrected Ancestors was already being built.

The operational heart of the EBS was a sphere of pure, blinding stress. In the center of the command deck was a large, raised platform, the Command Operations Deck, that gave Drake a full 360 degree view of the accelerating chaos below. He stood there, quiet, his arms crossed, as the red lights of the global tactical map spread and bloomed like some gruesome virus.

But the real engine of the operation was Marc. At the main mission console, flanked by Mandy, Hawkins and Carlos, the General of Operations was the storm's calm eye.

"Sector Delta, report status!" Marc yelled into his comms, his instincts pure command. He was juggling the lives of hundreds of people in the field. "Auxiliary teams are descending too quickly! Zara, I need a wider atmospheric dispersal on the deployment profile! Scatter them!"

"Increasing descent vector variance by three degrees," Zara's voice returned, cool and automated despite the crushing load. "Twenty-two vessels will have their stealth profiles compromised by atmospheric friction. Tracking now."

Carlos stood by Marc, his role as the former ethical advisor of the mission reduced to a silent, ghostly recording of transgressions. He watched the Auxiliary Harvest, now hundreds of dots scattering every continent, and knew that each dot represented an explicit, direct act of aggression against sovereignty.

Mandy was engaged in a dizzying, high-stakes, multi-lingual game of stall. From her position in the dedicated comms bay, she sat, headphones tight on her head, her mind reeling at the incoming calls from the rest of the world.

"This is the Evolution Builder Command," she said into the microphone, her voice project-managing and project-directing over the rising cries of panic. "We're notifying all concerned parties that the initial incident on the Chinese coast was an unexpected atmospheric anomaly. We have a major structural malfunction and are not a military threat. We are now transmitting data to confirm a controlled, multi-vector venting of non-hazardous stellar energy."

She was concurrently feeding different, equally technical, and entirely false, rationales to a rotating chain of furious officials: a German General, a Russian Foreign Minister, and a US Admiral.

"Admiral," she continued, her voice more imperious now, "you are witnessing a catastrophic failure of an experimental stealth projector array. The localized electronic pulse you observed was an ancillary byproduct of the entire system's complete breakdown. Our vessel is crippled. We are simply trying to stabilize orbital trajectory. We are asking all forces to stand down and not to escalate this already tense situation."

Buy time. That was Mandy's call. Seconds, minutes, moments of chaos before Earth's military could even coordinate, let alone respond.

Marc was following the crisis with cold math.

"Patrol interception on Aux Team 7, up near the Great Lakes!" Marc yelled.

"They've called a coast guard chopper in! Team 7, no engagement clearance! Abort drone deployment, get yourself high-G out of there now! You lose the samples, you save the crew!"

He hit the console hard, channeling power to support their egress. He could not lose the operators.

"Ronin Team 3, Lead Jin," Marc changed comms, voice low and gravelly. "Heavy military activity converging on your area. Your insertion site is green. Repeat new contingency. Lethal engagement is authorized only if you are prevented from extracting. Retrieve the Ancestor, and do not look back."

He saw the Ronin team's black dot fly toward one of the most densely populated capital cities in Europe, bound for what would certainly be a violent confrontation. Ordering anyone to lethal engagement, after weeks of delicately non-lethal work, was a moral weight he could practically feel in his chestplate.

Watching from the raised Command Operations Deck, Drake had spoken no word, issued no command over the fray. But he had not contradicted Marc's decision, he had given the order, lethal engagement is authorized, and now he stepped back and let his General make the hard calls. He saw the strain of what had to be done in Marc's eyes, in Carlos's slumped shoulders, and even the disciplined features of Mandy. He took it all in, bore the cost.

"Hawkin's," Drake's voice finally came over the comms, quiet, but utterly irrefutable. "I want an estimated loss rate on the Auxiliary Harvest. And a status on Ronin Team 1. We lose the harvest, but we cannot lose the Ancestors."

"Auxiliary loss rate is projecting at 20 percent, Drake," Hawkins replied, unfazed by the figure. "We will lose a minimum of 20 teams before global militaries come to some kind of coordinated response. Ronin Team 1, Anya Petrova, is holding full stealth. Time to target: six minutes."

Command Operations was a nest of justified treason and fear and efficient amorality, at the bleeding edge of all that was still human.

Team 1's shuttle had broken through the atmosphere in the worst of the mass deployment, and it was a weapon of cold silence. Most of the Auxiliary teams had deployed to wide patterns and were scattering like chaff before the impending storm, but Team 1 was on a singular vector, pointed straight at the heart of Europe.

Anya lay prone in the main cabin of the shuttle, eyes on the last schematics. Her target was Napoleon Bonaparte's tomb, a small vault directly beneath the huge dome of Les Invalides in Paris. The tomb and its remains were shielded by several layers of stone, steel, and one of the most advanced, multi-tiered security networks in Europe.

"Barb, thermal sweep on the outer perimeter," Anya said, voice low through the team's encrypted comms. "Caleb, you and Ben prep the extraction. Rachel, Quinn, hit the surveillance grid in five."

Her team was one of the purest collection of infiltration and assault firepower that the Ronin had to offer. Barb was a predator in the art of stillness, deadly efficient in negating and neutralizing any acoustic traps. Quinn and Rachel were already paired in prepping the French security network, Quinn aggressively, Rachel defending their own digital tracks. Ben and Caleb were the kinetic nightmare core, newly cleared for lethal engagement.

The shuttle delivered the team two kilometers from Les Invalides, and the six of them flowed through the narrow streets as one stealthy, coordinated shadow. Their passive camouflage wrangled the ambient light.

Quinn pinged them: "Security grid is blind on main approach tunnels. I'm looping twenty seconds. You have green to the second vault door."

Anya and Barb took point. Between a micro-thermal cutter and Barb's complete control of her posture, they were able to disable the exterior security station in less than half a minute. They reached the ante-chamber that led to the crypt, which was itself protected by a reinforced steel door and a grid of pressure sensors.

"Vandal, the door is twelve-inch layered composite," Anya whispered. "Minimal charge. We need the sarcophagus intact."

Ben grinned under his helmet. The brutal allure of sabotage had seized his blood. "Minimal charge, maximum effect. Hold your breath, Lead."

Ben wedged two polymer blocks and placed a small, focused, controlled charge. The compressed-air shush was almost inaudible, but the heavy, vault door shuddered, then silently slid inward, the locks pulverized in a sparkless explosion.

They were in the vault. The towering, spectacular porphyry sarcophagus of Napoleon himself dominated the space.

"Quinn, initiate extraction sequence," Anya ordered.

But before Quinn could deploy the sampler, the French military's fast response to the electronic warfare attack had finally reached their target.

"Lead, alarm breach! Not mine!" Rachel screamed, panic in her voice. "The central command reacted to the Chinese incident and hit manual lockdown at high level. A six-man gendarme patrol is ascending the main staircase! Twenty seconds!"

The old playbook, non-lethal sonic deterrents, hit and run, perished in Drake's new command.

"Ethan's people nearly died over a supply truck," Caleb gritted out, already dropping the heavy, metallic case containing his new armory. "Not this time."

Anya, however, didn't have to order the tactical shift. Ben and Caleb were already moving.

"Caleb, cover extraction. Ben, breach suppression," Anya ordered, seizing command of the lethal measures with deadly professionalism.

The gendarme patrol crashed into the chamber, lights flashing, weapons at the ready, shouting commands in French. They were professional, heavily armed, and had no idea what to expect from the black, demonic figures standing over the great Emperor's tomb.

Ben was the first to move. He didn't use an explosive. He dropped a handful of small, round devices, Areidyanies sonic emitters. These were not built to stun or disorient; these were built to burst eardrums and fry nerve tissue. The sound was an instantaneous spike of high-frequency acoustics, localized but total.

The lead gendarme fell instantly, his hands clamped to his head, a thin line of blood already running from his ear. His weapon clattered to the floor uselessly.

Caleb provided the finishing kill. He raised a custom-built, heavy energy rifle, a weapon designed to shoot kinetic rounds wrapped in a pulse of devastating bio-electric field energy. He swept the rifle in a smooth arc, firing not at the men's chests, but at the support braces and the stone wall directly above them.

The electro-kinetic rounds did not merely penetrate the stone; they instantly dematerialized it. The ceiling above the patrol cracked and collapsed in a thunderous roar, showering the remaining gendarmes with tons of rock and plaster, effectively burying the threat and sealing the staircase.

The entire vicious encounter took less than four seconds. The room was silent, the air acrid with plaster dust and the metallic tang of ionized atmosphere.

"Extraction compromised, threat neutralized," Caleb reported, his massive chest heaving, his rifle still smoking.

Anya ignored the moral calculus, focused only on the mission. "Quinn, deploy the sampler! Now! We have minutes before more guards arrive!"

Quinn, her hands still trembling but her focus absolute, scrambled to the sarcophagus and deployed the microscopic sampler. The crystalline sphere was captured within seconds. Barb was already moving to the sealed staircase, attaching a proximity alarm.

"Ancestor secured, Lead!" Quinn screamed.

"Extraction!" Anya commanded, spinning toward their concealed exfil route.

While Anya's group was in the middle of a brutal, tactical assault in Paris, Ronin Team 3 was having an entirely different encounter with protocol: a densely populated, contemporary military installation designed to fully lockdown.

Jin Kathmandu (Team 3) had been placed inside the hectic center of Rome. His mission was the tomb of Julius Caesar, whose remains were believed to be stored deep within a vault beneath the ancient Roman Forum that had been protected both by its status as a historical site and by an aggressively modernized security system.

The team moved through the chilly, pre-dawn streets. Jin, at the point of the formation, was nearly an invisible blur, his black combat suit absorbing even the small amount of urban illumination. They identified an abandoned sewer access that, according to Zara's data, ran to the sub-structure of the Forum.

"The vault entrance is actually a massive iron door, but it's supported by a state of the art seismic tamper system," Jin hissed in a smooth monotone. "No explosives. You're going to have to thread the needle."

"Roger, Lead." Mark spoke in a low, calm voice. His skill set was not in blowing things apart, but in silently penetrating defensive strong points. He materialized a micro-laser array and began cutting a precise circle around the vault door's electronic lock. The Carabinieri would be on full alert, maintaining contact after the Chinese incident.

Mark finished the cut and Uma began prying open the outer plate with a hydraulic wedge, working silently and deliberately. They had burst into a service tunnel, a tight, claustrophobic twist of a passage that was obviously designed for Close Quarters Combat (CQC).

"I can hear motion sensors ping active down the corridor," Uma continued. "I also hear people. Two patrols on their route. They altered the guard rotation in response to the worldwide alert."

There was no room to hide in the tunnel. Jin knew that silently taking out both patrols would still take too long, and in the interim the crack of their missed check-in would break the silence.

Jin ordered, already committing to the decision, "We go loud and fast. Mark, cover the vault door. Uma, my six. Henry, Jessica, and Tina, maintain formation. We are working new protocol. Lethal is authorized."

Four heavily armed Carabinieri soldiers, modern body armor and HK MP-7 assault rifles, rounded a tight corner and stopped in their tracks, surprised to see the featureless black forms in the tunnel.

The tunnel exploded with sound.

The Carabinieri were the first to fire, the loud, tinny crack of their assault rifles ricocheting off the tunnel walls. The Ronin suits were heavily damped, and their active energy-based armor easily shrugged off the kinetic rounds, which stuck to the concrete tunnel walls.

Jin and Uma advanced, closing the distance in a matter of strides. Silent, unarmed combat was their strength, but now being brought to bear on unarmored flesh with the best tools of Areidyanies technology.

Jin took aim at the pair of soldiers in the lead. He fired a modified Ronin rifle, this one not a sonic disruptor but a very high velocity, hyper dense, kinetic energy round-based weapon system. These rounds were small, dart-like projectiles that functioned like guided needles that could penetrate modern military body armor. He was aiming for the joints, the necks. He shot with deadly, calculated accuracy. Two soldiers crumpled silently to the ground as their hands just began to fully activate their rifles.

Uma focused on the remaining pair. She did not fire. Instead she used her unarmed combat gloves, which were integrated with their own low-level bio-electric disruptors. Uma struck open-palm blows to the faces of the two remaining soldiers. The strikes were not meant to be traumatic. The localized electrical pulse immediately and violently overloaded the soldiers' central nervous systems, short-circuiting them into immobility and lifelessness before they could even emit a warning scream.

Technological superiority and horrific efficiency had won the engagement. The entire, brutal encounter lasted under six seconds.

Silence returned, the air thick with gun smoke and ozone.

"Hostiles terminated," Jin reported, his expressionless voice hiding the psychological cost of the first truly lethal human-on-human strike. "Path to the core is clear. Sapper, go!"

Mark, seemingly unfazed by the bodies, finished quickly by-passing the final lock. "Ancestor vault is clear. Jin, we're in."

"Go," Jin replied, already moving. "We just left four bodies and transmitted a macro EMP across a densely populated battlefield. Rome's entire military response will be on site in three minutes. Henry, Jessica, and Tina, cover our entry."

The team collected the Caesar genetic sample. The price of Ancestor Vanguard's new, unsentimental directive would be paid in human lives.

Team working speed and complete silence was all. They knew the Italian defensive systems were now fully active, but they were still trying to process what had just happened and sort through the hundreds of 'ghost' signals being simultaneously deployed across the globe to profile the Ronin.

Mark finished the cut, and Uma used a hydraulic wedge to silently peel back the external plate. They were in the service tunnel, a narrow claustrophobic twist of a passage that was clearly designed for CQC.

"I can see motion sensors ping active down the corridor," Uma continued, her eyes narrowing at the dark of the tunnel. "No way around them."

Before Mark could begin work to disable the sensors, a heavy thump-thump-thump could be heard on the metal stairs leading up from the tunnel they were on.

"Contact!" Jin hissed. "They've sent sentries. The Praetorian Guard."

Italian soldiers came around the corner. Assaulted with riot dispersal cannons and Taz stunners, they were men built for war. Targeting lasers drew red lines across the team's helmets. It was a narrow tunnel, with no room to maneuver or evade.

"Lethal force engaged! Fire!" Jin shouted.

This was a twist the mission designers had cooked up just for Jin's team: CQC in confined space against trained military operators. Jin and Uma could not engage fast, non-lethally, and live to tell the tale. They needed a savage, one-strike kill or the alarm would sound, shattering the controlled environment of the vault's structures.

Uma reacted without thinking. She dove at floor level, rolling under the first burst of fire from the soldiers. She used two bio-magnetic grenades (EMP devices specialized for overloading delicate electronics). She mashed them into the armored vests of the two lead soldiers. They flashed to life, and the soldiers' radio systems and helmet intercoms stopped dead, leaving the soldiers reeling forward, blind and deaf.

Jin took the other two. His personal sidearm was a Ronin assault rifle with close-range modifications. He fired into the soldiers' exposed joints and necklines, the kinetic bullets punching through body armor without the need for high velocity. He engaged one soldier's helmet systems directly, shredding his vision ports and neck seal with precise bursts. The soldier went down.

The last soldier was gunning for a lock, slow to acquire.

"Mark, now! Get the vault! Henry, Jessica, Tina, cover that flank!" Jin screamed, kicking himself off the wall.

He sprinted the rest of the distance in superhuman time. His rifle jammed against the last soldier's side armor plating. One burst of raw kinetic force tore through the casing. The soldier dropped dead with a hard, thudding final exhale.

Silence settled in, heavy with burnt metal and ozone.

"Hostiles cleared," Uma said, standing over the incapacitated soldiers. "Path to core is clear. Sapper, go!"

Mark was already at work on the final magnetic seal to the vault door, callous to the carnage around him. "The Ancestor vault is clear. Jin, we are in."

"Go," Jin said, panting in short gasps. "We just triggered the high emergency distress signal for the city. Rome will have heavy ground assets on us in four minutes. Henry, Jessica, Tina, you're with us. We move as a team, you're with us." Jin reached for the sample container. "Let's get this genetic sample out of here."

The team had the genetic sample of Julius Caesar in hand seconds later. Mission success, with a well-calculated and adequately paid price in violence.

CHAPTER 34: THE SAVAGE SANCTIFICATION

The Command Operations Deck was packed to the walls with the kind of tension you could almost choke on. The tactical map burned with activity: hundreds of tiny blue dots (Auxiliary teams) scattered the world, pursued by vastly out-multiplying red tags (Earth military response teams). The window of chaos bought with the Chinese incident was slamming shut.

Marc, was rigid at his command console, mentally collapsing under the weight of the unfolding crisis. Drake remained on the raised platform, a statue of bronze, still.

"Auxiliary Team 7 has cleared the Great Lakes region, however their drone collection was compromised," Marc reported, his voice terse with pressure. "Entire drone harvest lost. Mission failure, crew recovered."

"Team 41, Central Africa," Zara interjected. "Contacted by ground defense force. They are pinned down. Requesting non-lethal support."

"Negative, Zara!" Marc exclaimed. "No diversion for auxiliary teams with Ronin assets. Ronin teams maintain target priority! Carlos, log it: Team 41 is compromised."

Carlos entered the entry, the screen spitting out a red alert. He was no fool; he knew compromised meant mission failure, but not casualties.

And then Marc saw the alert he knew was coming on the main console.

"General," Zara reported, the first hint of stress in her voice. "Auxiliary Team 104, operating over Siberia. Compromised by two Russian Federation Air Force MiG-31s. They are armed with R-33 missiles. Time to kill 45 seconds. Contact soon to be lost."

Marc watched it on the tactical map, the blinking red dot of Team 104, three fresh new operators with only basic training flying a disposable shuttle into the most remote and most guarded airspace on the planet just to collect genetic samples from a giant nameless Soviet-era military graveyard.

"Team 104 has been confirmed missile-locked," Zara reported, her voice clipped and fast. "Evasion is not an option. Attrition rate is already beginning to exceed model."

Marc could save them. He could pull one of the other five Ronin teams, one of them still in flight, Team 4 or 5 for instance, and redirect them to make a diversion, to run interference with their state of the art E-Warfare suites and blind the MiGs. But that would jeopardize an Ancestor mission, put the whole critical strategic puzzle piece at risk for three operators and a few million miscellaneous samples.

He squeezed his eyes shut, overwhelmed with the inhuman callousness of Drake's orders. The samples are our priority. We cannot expend the lives of our people any more than we have to from here on out.

He opened his eyes, and stared up at Drake, who offered no sign, no order, no word, only the cold, hard focus of a man who had already forfeited his own soul for the cause.

"Marc," Drake's voice hissed in his ear on the comms, "the long game."

Marc looked back at the console, at the blinking dot with only seconds of life remaining.

"Zara," Marc ordered, voice cracking, then hardening like granite. "Prioritize the Ronin teams. Maintain stealth coverage. Do not divert power. Accept the loss of Auxiliary Team 104."

There was a second of silence, and then the air was pulled out of the tactical map like a vacuum as Team 104 blinked out, their signal cut, lost. The loss was a meaningless blip on the global operational net, a single and infinitesimally small data point, but for Marc it rang in his ears like the sound of a thousand bells.

"Loss confirmed," Zara reported. "Auxiliary Harvest loss count: 23 teams. Total viable samples destroyed: 112 million."

Marc punched his fist into the console, sound muted through his command glove. "Fuck! We are hemorrhaging people and resources here too fast! We need to narrow the window!"

He spun to Carlos, eyes burning with the pain of what he had just done. "We cannot afford to keep the tagged teams in the air if we want to recover the operators! They are blowing the location of all of these to the entire world!"

"What do you mean, General?" Carlos said, voice full of dread.

Marc pointed a trembling finger at the screen, at the hundred or so blue dots still hovering in their decent trajectory. "New rule, effective now. If an Auxiliary team is known to be compromised, known to be in the cross hairs of hostile military forces, they are to abort the Harvest and find the nearest point of civilian population and self-exfil. We are not going to expend more shuttles on recovering dedicated teams. The operator abandons the shuttle and goes into ground fog. Ship is target, person is not."

It was an insane, nihilistic order. He was just ordering his own people to ditch their advanced technology, to disappear into enemy-controlled Earth, to make themselves fugitives on a world that already hated them.

"Marc, that is against the extraction protocol—"

"It is a preservation protocol!" Marc barked, slamming his fist down on the console again. "We are saving the people, we are sacrificing the equipment. Get the message out now. The other teams need to know the price of failure has just gone up."

The silence after the loss of Auxiliary Team 104 and Marc's gut-wrenching new order was broken by Drake's voice, sharp and cutting, slicing through the

EBS command deck. He had stayed on his raised platform, eyes fixed on the tactical global map where dozens of red markers were now aggressively closing in on the blue dots.

He ignored Marc and spoke directly to Zara.

"Zara," Drake ordered, his voice utterly devoid of humanity. "I need a global distraction. A big one. The militaries of Earth are too coordinated, too fast, and they're about to box the rest of our Auxiliary Harvest."

"The current electronic warfare grid is already at full saturation, Drake," Zara replied, voice entirely analytical. "Any more energy projection will put the Matter Re-sequencer's core systems in danger."

"I don't give a shit," Drake said matter-of-factly. "I need something to take my mind off this for a second. Program the EBS's main energy cannons for atmospheric firing. Non-lethal settings: a high energy pulse designed to blow harmlessly in the upper atmosphere with a theatrical, blinding light and sound display. I want to fucking terrify the shit out of every government on this rock."

Marc turned on his console, eyes wide. "Drake, no! You can't do this! If we fire the main weapons we'll be detected instantly by range: we give away our altitude, our power signature, our intent! It's an act of war!"

"It is an act of war, Marc," Drake said, turning from the platform. "But it is one we have already been forced into and are going to win, either way. We can buy time by taking out their will to resist."

He turned back to Zara. "Programme the three major cities whose governments are making Mandy the most problems, right now, and are closest to our assets. I don't want to hit their cities, Zara, I want to strike fear into their hearts. Fire solutions locked and loaded but wait for Marc's final signal."

He stopped for a moment, then added another chilling operational order, finalising the lock-in to total war.

"And another thing, Zara. Should any of our shuttles, Auxiliary or Ronin, be fired upon by a known, hostile airframe: You are now ordered to target and eliminate the aggressor aircraft. No more evasive manoeuvres that draw attention to the mission. No more subverting destruction to protect our tech. We will no longer stand for it. They shoot at us, we take them out."

Marc watched the tactical map. Marc's breath caught. This was the same desperate, bloody violence Anya and Jin had been operating under in their latest mission. Drake had just signed them all up for an open and undeniably existential war with Earth's armed forces.

And for what? Marc thought to himself. This was a body-retrieval mission that had spiralled out of control, with one man, one single man, stripping away the final barriers of self-preservation one by one.

"Understood, sir," Zara confirmed, her voice steely now. "Main energy conduits cycling power. Solutions for non-lethal atmospheric detonation are primed. The new direct-fire counter-threat operating procedure has also been processed and will be installed on the Ronin and Auxiliary shuttle defence systems."

Marc could feel the EBS tremble, ever so slightly, as the massive main weapons racks, built to blow up warships, grounded up power for a non-lethal light show with the explosive scale of a nightmare. He was now the General giving the order to commit a single, overt act of planetary terrorism to cover up a body-snatching operation.

He looked at the tactical map again, eyes sweeping over the three most visibly aggressive defence systems mobilising against them: Russia, China, and the United States.

Marc swallowed hard and adjusted his headset. "Mandy, fire your final warnings, prep your contacts for my next announcement, Zara: Fire on my mark... Mark one."

The EBS held its breath for the General's final, doomed order.

Command Operations Deck was suddenly gripped by a taut, electric silence. Eyes all watched the console: Marc's, Carlos', and Drake's were trained on the sub-commander's station, waiting for the final order to commit the EBS to open, inarguable hostility with the world they all wanted to save.

Mandy was still broadcasting, her own desperate, strained final warnings still coming through the comms. "This is the final notice, all aircraft. We are now venting energy and if you do not stand down your governments will burn and you will burn with them."

Marc hesitated, thumb hovering over the activation rune. He was the one that had to make the first, conclusive order for an act of planetary terrorism. He thought of the three major cities, the Russian, Chinese, and American capitals whose command authority was most visibly coordinating the combined global military response.

Marc took a deep breath, the ozone in his mouth already bitter.

"Zara, on my mark." Marc forced his voice to be a tight, whisper of command.

Coordinates flared, announcing their impending detonation sites: a solid pack of Russian MiGs rapidly closing on the airspace above the wreckage of Team 104 that was just killed. An American fighter jet had also aggressively locked onto Auxiliary Team 134 over the Eastern Seaboard.

"Mark!"

The EBS trembled, but not from the vibrations of the shuttles. It was a more fundamental vibration; the ship's primary power conduits whining in protest as they were fed massive torrents of energy.

Before the atmospheric pulse could even be fired, the EBS's automated defense system (recently reprogrammed with Drake's version of a kill-switch) got a word in edgewise.

"Target confirmed," Zara said in an emotionless monotone. "Two Russian

Federation Air Force MiG-31s confirmed hostile. Fired upon and destroyed Auxiliary Unit 104."

Two little pinpricks of light barely visible on the EBS tactical display shot out from the EBS. They were not mass-energy beams, but precisely targeted, hyper-velocity plasma darts rendered completely invisible to Earth-based radar.

"Eliminating threat," Zara said.

Instantly, the two red blips indicating the MiGs disappeared from the tactical display over Siberia. In the cockpit of the MiGs, there was no siren or countdown timer. The entire jet experienced an instantaneous, total vaporization of all internal electronics and control surfaces. The jets fell silently to the ground as fiery wreckage.

A few seconds later, another alert popped up. "United States Air Force F-35 confirmed hostile. Fired upon Auxiliary Team 134 over the Atlantic."

"Fire," Marc ordered, not even really registering the automated carnage.

The third plasma dart had already been fired. The red blip indicating the F-35 blinked out instantly, replaced by a large, high-altitude radar confusion marker. The Auxiliaries shadowing Team 134 were safe for the moment.

With immediate threats handled, Marc issued the final, decisive command.

"Zara, fire the atmospheric pulse. Now."

Three vast, channeled columns of searing blue-green light (weapons specifically designed to slice through starship shields) shot downwards from the EBS. They did not slow, but gained speed, blasting through the upper atmosphere.

Over Moscow, a massive, silent pulse of energy exploded at 40 km altitude. The result was an instantaneous, blinding flash of light that turned the pre-dawn sky into an immense, flickering curtain of neon green. The flash was visible for hundreds of miles and the secondary electromagnetic shockwave (benign to humans but devastating to electronics) fried every non-hardened electronic system in the city for a crucial thirty seconds. Moscow's alarm systems (already on edge) simply went dark.

Over Beijing, the second shot exploded. The capital was thrown into a nightmarish, titanic eruption of crimson light, followed by an ear-splitting, low frequency, infrasonic rumble that shook windows and instinctively scared the city's populace. The combination of the visual attack and the acoustic one was sickening.

The third, and largest pulse exploded far overhead of the Washington D.C. area. The pulse made a noise when it detonated. Loud. The sudden eruption of purple and gold light filled the sky, and the resultant atmospheric pressure differential generated a local, intense blast of static electricity that resulted in a microsecond-wide, flickering power outage in a number of key government buildings.

The effects were immediate back on the EBS command deck.

"Global defense response is frozen in place," Zara said, a hint of satisfaction in her otherwise emotionless voice. "The light show is being reported by everyone as either a simultaneous attack or a massive, unprecedented natural event. The three capitals are paralyzed by terror and awe."

The dense red blips on the tactical map (global military forces, converging for battle) stopped, hesitated, and began to back away, orders to press forward too terrifying for the stunned commanding officers to give.

"We just gave the remaining Auxiliary teams at least an hour of near-total operational silence," Carlos said quietly, white-faced. He had just seen the calm ordering of an act of terrorism for the greater good.

Drake looked down at Marc, his expression softening very slightly. "You gave the order, General. Now confirm the Ancestors are still safe."

Marc took a deep breath and pulled himself upright, coming out of shock and the cold realization of the terrifying act he had just given an order for. "Ronin Teams 1 and 3 are on exfil, Ancestors secured. Team 2 is 3 minutes from insertion. Line's clear. We move on the harvest."

It was cold and stale inside the stealth shuttle rocketing out of the European orbit. The cabin lights were set to a sickly red. The only sound was the mechanical whirring of the engines.

Anya sat strapped in the pilot co-seat, staring at the Napoleon sample's crystal sphere, now encased in a cryogenic lockbox. She hadn't spoken since she ordered the exfil from the collapsed vault. It was over, and she was exhausted – but it was more than that. It was as if a frigid blanket of numbing numbness was settling over her entire being.

She looked back. Caleb methodically swabbed his kinetic rifle with the quiet machinelike efficiency of a man needing to make this incomprehensible moment as mundane as possible. Ben, who had detonated the initial deadly sonic grenades, was the most visibly shaken – ghostly under his grime and shock, and staring at the floor.

"Clean that weapon, Vandal," Anya snapped, the voice flat and tired. "It's policy."

Ben didn't budge. "I didn't hear a clean-up order on the bodies, Lead. Just 'exfil.' Did Zara mark those as acceptable losses?"

Anya turned to face him, eyes narrow and hard. "They were military combatants engaging a Ronin team. They were neutralized to secure the Ancestor. Log it as a successful extraction. Do not make this a funeral, Carter."

"It was a massacre, Anya," Ben spat, low and quiet. "They were gendarmes. Not a tank division. You saw them when the ceiling didn't cave in."

"I saw a direct threat," Anya replied, the numbness starting to dissipate into a roiling defensive savagery. "And I chose five lives on this ship over six lives down there. That was Drake's order, and it is the cost of this war. Stop acting like a casualty, or you're sitting Auxiliary the next time."

It was then that the terse silence was abruptly shattered. The shuttle interior was suddenly filled with a piercing, unnatural light. Through the forward canopy, the top of the upper atmosphere was undulating with an unholy light show – a curtain of bright, churning crimson that pulsed and faded with a low, deep thrumming sound.

Anya gaped, not in horror, but in dawning understanding. "Zara... what is that?"

Zara's voice crackled immediately over the secure comms, with a chillingly triumphant tactical elation. "That, Team One, is your tactical breathing room. The EBS's primary assets have just conducted a non-lethal, high-energy atmospheric pulse over the three most militarily mobilizing capital cities. Global command is currently in a state of terror-induced paralysis. It would appear that Drake is fully deploying the EBS into psy-ops."

A slow, grim smile pulled at the corners of Anya's mouth. She looked back at Ben and Caleb. The naked visceral savagery of their mission was suddenly small, necessary, and instantly sanctified by the global ramifications of Drake's retaliatory strike.

"Message received, Zara," Anya said, the exhaustion washed away by a cool, sharp clarity. "Drake is no longer playing our game."

Jin's shuttle, after successfully extracting the Caesar's Napoleon sample, was accelerating fast over the Mediterranean. The atmosphere was less adversarial than Team 1's cabin, but nowhere near light.

Jin, sat alone in the rear, staring at his now empty, customized gloves. The gloves that he used to apply the fatal electric jolts. Jin was a weapon to neutralize targets, not kill them. He had killed men with his own hands, their fear a personal, immediate memory burned into his soul.

Uma walked up to him cautiously. She saw the tell-tale signs of combat shock in the absolute stillness of his body, the dilated, unblinking eyes.

"It was self-defense, Jin," Uma whispered, taking a seat next to him. "They were going to kill Mark before he got the code. We saved the Ancestor."

"I saw their eyes, Uma," Jin whispered, his voice scratchy and dry. "I saw them. They were Carabinieri. They were just men following orders. They weren't Afltic. They were us." He looked down at his bare hand and his empty gloves. "I didn't fight them. I ended them. There was no struggle."

Uma placed a hand on his shoulder. "We all lost a piece of ourselves down there, Jin. But this is a war where the enemy does not have our moral code. Drake just showed us that he is willing to do worse than we did."

As Uma spoke, the shuttle was suddenly enveloped by the sudden, bright burst of the atmospheric pulse over Moscow. It was a terrifyingly beautiful, luminescent pillar of light, and the electromagnetic discharge momentarily caused a crackle over the comms.

Zara's voice came through the static, over the broadcast of the mission summary, and the report of downed Russian and American fighter jets.

Jin looked at Uma. In her he did not see the face of an inhuman act of aggression. She was coldly, mathematically necessary. The EBS was a god now, raining down fire and madness on a world too small to understand their enemy. The guilt had not vanished, but was instantly mitigated, swallowed up by the gargantuan, incomprehensible scale of Drake's new war.

"We are just soldiers, Uma," Jin said, picking up his gloves and snapping them back onto his hands. "We do the dirty work so the Drake can focus on the sky." He looked at the vast, pulsing column of light fading into the distance behind them. "He is protecting us by being a monster."

He then turned his attention to the comms, awaiting his next command.

CHAPTER 35: THE COST OF THE CHOICE

One of the EBS's Matter Re-sequencing Bays was a clean, hermetically-sealed, decontamination room. The growing, ripening body inside the main chamber tank was now fully-formed and would be moved out of the fluid-filled chamber and into the open work area. But not yet. The processing computer inside the main chamber made a rising sound, pulsing at high frequency.

A few meters from the process chamber, Zara watched the life-signs of the re-sequenced body of Sun Tzu. He was in a nutrient fluid-filled tank, translucent, hovering in nutrient suspension. His body was perfect, genetically flawless. The processing computer hummed as the readouts, beaming to Zara in holographic form, indicated the completion of the re-sequencing.

A late fifties man, lithe and muscular, strong and fit, with an almost hunter-like bearing and chiseled, finely-wrought features, his muscles tensed by the angled harnesses that held his body motionless in the nutrient fluid. But his body was fine. Perfect.

Zara checked the readouts. Heart rate perfect, neural scaffolding complete and showing intense activity, memory engrams in place. All bio-readings in perfect tolerance range. The Ancestor was ready.

"Drake," Zara said directly into Drake's communications unit. "Sun Tzu Re-sequencing is complete. All biometric signatures are within accepted tolerance. He is ready for immediate extraction."

Drake stood on the Command Operations Deck, watching from the tactical map display as the worst of the initial assault against the Earth's denizens came to an end, most of the population now stunned into post-shock inertia. A feeling of pure, unadulterated joy surged through him.

"Roger, Zara," he said, his gaze still on the map display as tactical posts around the world gradually returned to a nervous, anxious, but quiet, steady state. "Hold on the sequence. Do not initiate the transfer sequence. I want the whole team present for the awakening."

He lowered the communications unit and spoke to the entire group. Marc and Carlos, both still recovering from the shock of his orders and the orders they had just given, turned and looked up at him.

"Sun Tzu is finished, completed," Drake said. "Marc, Carlos, Hawkins, Mandy, all non-essential staff: rejoin me in the Re-sequencing Bay. I want all our senior leadership in position."

Ten minutes later, the entire senior group stood in the Re-sequencing Bay, looking down on the tank, now mostly empty. The sound of the low, rhythmic gurgle of the nutrient suspension was the only sound in the room.

"Begin the awakening sequence, Zara."

Zara's voice chimed through the room, cool and clinical. The nutrient fluid drained rapidly from the tank in a hissing vortex of reclaiming fluid, draining back into the processing computer's conversion and recycling tanks.

Sun Tzu's eyes slowly blinked open.

The group leaned forward.

His eyes flickered once. Twice. Three times.

Brown and alive and clear and focused, his pupils reflecting the steel room. A broad-shouldered, muscular, very attractive and very human male, perfect in form and feature. With a face that gave nothing away, no emotion, no intelligence, no understanding, no nothing. He stared, unblinking, unresponsive, at the ceiling.

Drake reached down and gently shook Sun Tzu. "Sun Tzu?" he said softly, firmly, urgently. "Can you hear me? Do you understand where you are? Who are you?"

The Ancestor said nothing. He made no gesture or motion. His gaze was glassy and empty and unseeing. He gave nothing.

"Zara, run a full neural diagnostic. Need immediate analysis," Drake said, the first true sick feeling of utter, complete failure descending on him.

Zara shimmered, holographically. Her face was closed and determined. The diagnostic ran for 30 seconds, each second an agonizing minute.

"The physical construct is without blemish, Chancellor," Zara's report was mechanical and emotionless. "The higher neural functions, the Cognitive Matrix that contains his intellectual mastery and acquired identity, failed to properly bind with the bio-structure. There was a localized, non-lethal failure in the encoding process."

"Translate for the rest of us, please," Marc said.

Zara's holographic face wavered. "The body is perfect, General. But the mind is empty, a clean slate. Sun Tzu is, for all intents and purposes, fully brain dead."

A long moment of oppressive silence fell on the room.

Marc covered his face with his hands. Carlos sagged against the nearest wall. Mandy stared, her face drained of color, at the motionless body of the man who should have been the greatest mind in human history.

But Drake felt nothing at all. Nothing except the logical certainty of what had to be done next. His face was like granite.

"Log this result, Tammy," he said. "Ancestor Vanguard, Genetic Sample 001, Status: Failed. Cause: Encoding Error. Initiate Termination and Recycling Protocol, at once."

Marc jerked upright. "Termination, Drake? For Christ's sake! We can try to recover him! This is a human being!"

"It is an empty vessel, Marc, a useless failure of a resource," Drake said, his voice low and imperious, ordering and absolute. "We cannot, we do not waste anything. We must have the next re-sequencing process be flawless. Zara, confirm immediate Recycling of Genetic Sample 001. Before you initiate the next re-sequencing process, I want a complete root-cause analysis of the encoding failure. I want the fault isolated, corrected, and only then do we try again."

"Understood, Sir," Zara confirmed. "Initiating Recycling Protocol. Root-cause analysis initiated.

"Excellent," Drake said. He watched, impassively, as the nutrient fluid slowly began to refill the tank, the reclaiming solution first rushing in with viscous anger. He turned. "Marc, let's head back to the Command Center. The situation on Earth has quieted for the moment, but the preparation for the next wave has not. We have a war to win, and a new mastermind to build."

The White House Situation Room in Washington D.C. was chaos. The 20-foot wide screen, only seconds ago filled with charts and tactical imagery, was frozen on a single, sickening feed: a shaky, grainy shot from an unknown camera of the sky over the capital being seared by an impossibly large, apocalyptic blast of purple and gold light.

"It wasn't a flare! It wasn't a nuclear test! The entire Eastern Grid had a power surge! The air defense network went completely blind for forty seconds!" the Secretary of War was yelling into a secure phone.

The National Security Advisor stared, white-faced. "It was an attack, Mr. President. A demonstration of capability from the EBS. Drake Donovan has upped the ante."

The President, visibly older than he had been an hour ago, slammed his fist on the table. "I don't care about their motives! We declared them criminals! Traitors! And they respond by using a weapon that could wipe out our power grid! The Russians are saying two MiGs went down simultaneously over Siberia, they were tracking Donovan's shuttles. The forensic analysis is coming back as a localized plasma strike. It's the Areidyanies AI, Zara, responding to Donovan's command."

The CIA Director shook his head, horror in his voice. "We all know who they are, sir, and we know they have the capability to erase us. They tried to recruit us to fight a war on their terms, and we cast them out. Now, they have made the first move."

"They have the ability to erase our air force, and they chose to flash the sky in a fireworks show." The Secretary of War was mumbling, but what he was saying was clear from the analysis flooding NATO channels. "They were not trying to kill us, they were trying to paralyze us. They were buying time for something else. They are here to pillage, not to conquer, but their idea of 'acceptable force' just got redefined as 'total war.'"

In the deep bowels of the Kremlin, General Volkov stared at the nightmarish green glow that had flooded the Moscow sky.

"It was the Evolution Builder," Volkov said, voice ragged. "The traitor

Donovan and his monster, Zara. They just launched a simultaneous, two-front attack on the heart of the command structures of the three greatest military powers on Earth. They are retaliating for our efforts to stop them from violating our space."

"General, the two MiGs were vaporized in less than a second," a technician said, voice trembling. "We need to send out a global, all forces stand-down order against all unidentifiable, high-altitude objects. If we send up our jets to engage the shuttles, they will down our planes. If we send up the air defense network to harass the ship, they will down our cities."

Volkov snatched up a secure comms unit. "Lock down all strategic assets. The traitors have made their move. We do not target the EBS. We do not fire on anything not conclusively identified as hostile on the surface. We wait. We watch. We spin the narrative, Donovan is a war criminal, and he is attacking the entire human race."

Zhongnanhai Security Center, Beijing

In Beijing, the decision was one of panicked, strategic acquiescence.

"The satellite data is definitive," the Chief of Staff said. "The EBS fired three energy bursts. They have left us no ambiguity. Cease all interference with whatever it is that they are doing or face annihilation."

"We don't know what their agenda is, but they have just demonstrated their capabilities before a billion people." Was it really such a good idea to shut them out so quickly? If we can't even stop whatever it is they are doing in our country, how could we possibly have been able to stop the Afltic? President Xi spun on his heel, turning all of his focus onto his Chief of Staff. We did defeat the Afltic that attacked Hong Kong. The only reason Donovan has free run is just because we have not yet deployed our main weapon. Give us time to finish mass deployment and he will stand no more. So, I suggest you never talk like this again or you too will be considered a traitor...

For the moment, "The order is clear," President Xi said. "Stand down all offensive air and ground units. We will manage the PR, reinforce the narrative that Drake Donovan and his alien AI are the enemies of this state, and look for a diplomatic off-ramp. We wait for their next move."

Back on the Evolution Builder, Marc sat and watched the global news feeds filtering through – millions in mass panic, military disarray and panicked orders for de-escalation pouring out of all three capitals. TRAITOR DONOVAN FIRES ON CAPITALS. SKY DEMONS ATTACK. This was fear and no one was fighting it back.

Marc turned to Drake, the grim satisfaction of their success drowning out the terrible loss of innocence. "Drake, global chaos is complete. Earth's military is paralyzed and falling back from our vectors. The public view of you is a criminal, but tactically, they have shut down."

He summoned up the mission summary to the main screen.

"Ronin Team 1, Napoleon Extraction, Mission Complete." "Ronin Team 2, Alexander the Great Extraction, Mission Complete." "Ronin Team 3, Julius Caesar Extraction, Mission Complete." "Ronin Team 4, Ghengis Khan Extraction, Mission Complete."

"Drake, five of the eight primary Ancestor samples are secure. I am using the tactical breathing space the EBS pulse has given us to immediately redeploy Teams 1, 2, and 4 to extract the remaining three Ancestors on the target list. Holding team 3 in reserve. " "Team 1, will extract Douglas MacArthur, Team 2, is targeting George S. Patton, and Team 4, will acquire Ulysses S. Grant"

Drake nodded, his eyes empty and hard. "Redeploy them, Marc. The world may despise us, but we will save it, with or without their support.

The walk back to the auxiliary command area was agony for Mandy. She strode next to Hawkins, whose face was still gray from the shutdown of the inert Sun Tzu. Mandy's emotional support protocol, her entire purpose for being on the EBS in the first place, was failing miserably. She was here to counsel, to support, and it was she who was drowning in horror.

They liquefied him. A perfect human being, a new beginning, and Drake had just... terminated him, her mind screamed at her. The sound of the silent, empty eyes of the Ancestor, followed by the hideous, beautiful light show that had paralyzed an entire planet, had torn through her entire moral framework.

"He called him a failed resource, Hawkins," Mandy whispered, her voice hoarse. "Not a man. A resource. That's the language Drake is using now."

Hawkins turned his head to look at Mandy, his mind already racing to try to find the dispassionate viewpoint. "Look at everything that has happened, Mandy. After everything, Drake has no choice but to play hard and heavy right now. There is no time left. He or should I say we, are now forced to fight on a timescale and at a scale of threat we can't control. Mandy, we watched the MiGs disappear. We saw the fear that hit Earth. If he hesitates, the Afltic find us unprepared and everyone is gone."

"But when does that become us?" Mandy stopped and grabbed Hawkins's arm, twisting him to face her. Her normally warm eyes were hot with a desperate anger. "Billions of people are terrified of us! We murdered human life, human life just trying to do their job! And we just terminated a life we created because he wasn't the kind of genius we wanted! I need to talk to Drake. I need him to understand there is a moral cost to this. I need him to stop being a General and start being a man again."

Hawkins looked past her, at the bright, forbidding portal that was the entry to the Command Operations Deck where Drake now sat. "And what good will that do, Mandy? You will undermine the confidence of the only person with the presence of mind to run this op. You will sow doubt where there can be no doubt. His strategy is perfect. He is using the least amount of lethal force necessary to paralyze the most people."

Mandy let go of his arm, pacing quickly. "Least amount of lethal force? We just blew up fighter jets! We left four bodies in a Roman tunnel! We killed a brain-dead man! He's gutting the soul of this mission for a tactical advantage!"

She knew Hawkins was right. She knew the logic of it was terrifyingly cold and logical. Drake hadn't enjoyed the choices; he just made them. And he was winning.

"The greatest military strategists in all history, Mandy," Hawkins murmured, the centrepiece of the argument. "Drake's trying to build the first army of the new world from the remnants of the last. We need the Ancestors. If we're not brutal, the whole thing collapses. He needs your support, not your judgment."

Mandy halted her restless pacing. She looked down at the floor, her boots grinding through the day's accumulated detritus and catching the reflection of the EBS's utilitarian, impersonal lights. Drake had not become less human. He had simply embraced an inhuman role. He had crossed the Rubicon so that the rest of them could cross it too, buffered by his rank. She would have to forgive him. Confronting him would have only sundered the last thread of command standing between herself and oblivion.

She drew a slow, deep breath, wrapping the warm, woolly cocoon of her professionalism back around her exposed nerve-ends.

"You're right, Hawkins," she said at last, her voice thick with swallowed emotion. "I can't distract him right now. The whole mission's too precarious. I'll support him. But I won't stop monitoring the body count, either. He may have crossed the line for our sakes, but he has to know that he won't be the only one on the other side of it."

Mandy's words were still echoing in the suddenly quiet Command Center when a cool, analytic voice took over the ambient comms.

"Drake, this is Zara. I have completed the root-cause analysis of the Matter Re-sequencer failure," the AI announced.

Drake's voice snapped over the background chatter from the Command Deck, hard and focused. "Report, Zara."

"The encoding failure was found to be the result of a subtle, cascading bio-power fluctuation caused by the simultaneous firing of the EBS main weapons and the matter re-sequencing process. The power draw for the atmospheric pulse destabilized the neural-link coupling sequence at the point of cognitive insertion," Zara continued. "The flaw is systemic but easily mitigated by prioritizing power flow to the Re-sequencer core during Ancestor creation."

"Fix it." Drake issued a crisp order. "Load the next sample immediately. The global window we bought is still open. Zara, are you ready to give Sun Tzu another shot?"

"The genetic sample is now being loaded into the re-sequencing process. We will be ready to start the pre-optimization of Sun Tzu in 20 minutes, Drake. The pre-optimization will take an additional 3 hours. I will attempt to re-sequence the Sun Tzu sample immediately following the completion of the pre-optimization, now that the flaw has been isolated."

Mandy and Hawkins shared a glance of abject relief and renewed horror. The horrific cost of the first failure, the termination of the first Ancestor, had bought them the knowledge they needed to try again. The brutal logic of Drake's decision was borne out by the technology itself.

Mission parameters were locked in. The Great Refusal was off the table. The operation would continue, ruthless, remorseless, and strategically justified. Mandy Melrose had chosen her side. The cost of that choice would never leave her.

In the EBS Command Center, the central holographic projector flipped from the global tactical map to a secure, multi-party video conference. The screen filled with the furious, drawn faces of the world's most powerful figures. The President of the United States. President Xi of China. General Volkov on behalf of Russia. The currently rotating head of the European Union. They were nearly all in violation of the code of diplomatic decorum in one way or another, their collective anger a burning, silent heat that coalesced in the single figure of Drake Donovan.

Donovan stood alone, calm, before the projection. On his left, Zara watched the technical fidelity of the link. On his right, Marc crouched ready with the mission status.

"Donovan, you are a traitor, a fugitive, and now a war criminal," the U.S. President began, jaw clenched tight in barely contained fury. "Your 'light show' over our capital cities was a terrorist attack. We demand an immediate cease-fire. The surrender of your ship – the EBS – to a combined U.N. task force. And the unconditional surrender of your entire team for trial and imprisonment."

"You have violated our sovereign airspace and absconded with priceless cultural patrimony that will never be replaced!" President Xi added, his image flickering with icy disdain.

Drake raised a hand. The three speakers all fell silent, the gesture enough to defer to a man with a billion-ton ship hovering over their capitals.

"I think this stage of political grandstanding is over," Drake said, his voice smooth but carrying through the shared consciousness of the ship. "I presented you with the scientific facts: The Afltic are coming. They see this planet as a target. To save humanity, I had to create the Ancestor Vanguard. The first strategic defense corps that the Earth has ever fielded."

"Incorrect!" General Volkov bellowed. "You murdered my pilots! You bombed my capital! You're trying to steal our history to build your own private army of imaginary dead warriors!"

"I am sorry for the deaths, General," Drake said. His jaw clenched. "But your troops fired on our rescue shuttles. I told you to stand down. That was a show of force. I will kill you, the political leaders, and the military, if I must, to protect the future of our people. The Ancestors are real. They are our only chance."

The EU man leaned in with false intimacy. The cheap talk reeked of carrot and stick. "Drake, we know you are under a lot of pressure here. But please, for your own sake, just come down. Let's work together on this. Turn over the EBS and your team. We'll give you every opportunity to voice your complaints, in a courtroom."

Drake heard the anger welling up in his chest. It was one thing to think about the political blinders while they prepared. But to have his patience tested like this, in such a raw way, by the arrogance of those who would risk it all for their own public images, it was too much.

"I hear you, you can carry on your sophist debate about law and court and public perception while the only clock that matters counts down to our final extinction," Drake said. He was no longer placid and warm. "You regard me as a criminal because I have the will, and the power, to do what you will not. I will save you because I am not so cowardly as to be cowed by your bullshit."

He shook his head and looked down at the phantasms with quiet loathing. "I have given you the truth and the technology and salvation. You would choose fear and politics and hubris and the childish fantasy that you can defeat me with a subpoena. I have no more patience for this linguistic tripe."

He gestured to Zara. "Zara, cut the connection. Let's be done with this farce."

The images blinked out of existence in an instant and the cool, blue emergency tactical map of the globe flickered in place. A thick, dead silence hung over the Command Center.

Drake looked to Marc and his expression was grim. "They are beyond saving, Marc. They will fight to the last moment, against us, even as the Afltic rain down. We have no choice."

Marc was, for once, entirely unaffected by the end of the possibility of diplomacy. He was entirely focused on this next phase.

"The status report for the genetic project is up and full," Marc said, pulling up a separate screen.

"All eight of the primary Ancestor samples have been successfully secured. They are the highest priority intelligence targets on the operation. The Ronin Teams have been completely successful. The project's primary work is complete: Sun Tzu, Napoleon, Alexander the Great, Julius Caesar, Ghengis Khan, Douglas MacArthur, George S. Patton and Ulysses S. Grant. The strategic vanguard's genetic harvest is complete."

Marc paused and then gave the second, more jaw-dropping update.

"The broader genetic project: Our three hundred Auxiliary Teams, the ones we gave the planet to on day one of the operation as the light show kicked in, they have also been completely successful in their primary goal. The sweep of all targeted historical, military, and academic targets was completed."

Marc held Drake's gaze. "The sample collection project is complete. The world is dust and we have gathered slightly more than two billion human genetic samples. We will need all of them to get this population stabilized. The EBS now holds the full genetic foundation needed to shore up the future of the human race."

Drake shut his eyes for a second, the enormity of what they had done and what they had lost sinking in. They had taken the future leaders. They had taken the genetic rock of ages from the foundations of his world's military power. But they had broken off, for all time, any possibility of co-operation with the world below.

CHAPTER 36: THE ANCESTOR'S BIRTH

Drake sat up and turned to the main command console, his features stoic. Marc stood at the ready. He had remained cool and collected even through the diplomatic failure. Marc, like the military branch he represented, had been a rock.

"Genetic harvest secure." Marc repeated. "Remaining time on Sun Tzu mission two: 12.348. Standing by for further instructions."

Drake rubbed his eyes, nodded. The crew, the men and women who had executed the most brazen, ruthless, and necessary heist in human history had not slept in the last seventy-two hours.

He changed channels on the main command console, pushing his voice through the EBS's internal communications system. The EBS bridge, which had been buzzing in the mad aftermath of the mission, hushed, crewmembers pausing, waiting for the Commander-in-Chief's final instruction.

"This is Drake." He projected, his voice cutting crisply through the ship. "The mission is complete. It was a total success. We have secured the genetic legacy of the future Alliance, and the full vanguard of our Ancestor command structure. Each and every person on this ship, from the Ronin teams on up, engineering, logistics, every single member of the bridge staff, has functioned without a single mistake."

He paused, giving the words and the weight of their meaning time to sink in. Then,

"We have done what was asked of us, and we have not even had the chance to rest. The next phase will be no different, but it demands focus, not fatigue."

His voice became less emphatic, his natural charm mingling with the hard-nosed pragmatism.

"I am enacting an across the board, ship-wide 12-hour stand down for all non-essential personnel. I want you to stand down. I want you to rest. Get some sleep. You have earned this time to recharge before the next chapter of our history begins. We will have our first Ancestor in just over twelve hours, and then we jump. Until then, stand down."

He cut the transmission. A shell-shocked, sleep deprived but grateful EBS bridge crew began to vacate, slowly dispersing to their respective stations or sleep bays. Security and operations crews maintained a skeleton presence in the aftermath. The only sound was the quiet hum of the Evolution Builder Star Ship itself and the low-clicking countdown timer.

Drake returned to Marc. "Get me a direct, secure line to Zara's core and a connection to Hawkins. I want to triple-check the jump calculations. When that clock hits zero we welcome the past into our future and then we leave the cradle behind."

The main debriefing bay for the Ronin Teams was a functional, sterile space tucked deep in the military core of the Evolution Builder Star Ship (EBS). There was a distinct tang to the air, a heady combination of ozone and sweat mingling with the slightly metallic smell of closed-loop recycle.

Six people lounged, loosely organized around a fold out table, the table littered with the gear that had seen them through the past three days. In their wake, several team members weaved systematically through the clutter of people and equipment, carefully disarming weapons and removing the utilitarian, but highly abrasive lightweight armor that all team members had worn since boarding.

The team lead, Anya, was still on task, fussing over a half-dozen biometric scanners. Her face was grimy, her movements slow and stiff. The corner of her eye mask was coming loose, half-attached to her face. She'd been awake for at least three days at this point, a seemingly endless high-stakes high-octane covert extraction mission to secure the most valuable, genetically viable DNA on Earth.

It was only when Donovan's voice came over the comms, confirming the all clear on total mission success and the impending twelve-hour ship wide stand down, that the room finally fell silent.

Caleb was the first to move. He inched slowly out of his chair, the sound of his boots scuffing against the floor echoing loudly in the silence. He looked down at the floor like he was trying to remember how gravity worked. "12 hours," he drawled, a flat note of utter disbelief in his voice. "I thought he'd just order us to start prepping for the jump right now."

Ben, who had been sitting cross-legged with his head cradled in his chest, let out a half-hearted grunt. He was close to sleep, past the point of needing stim. Barb was absentmindedly tracing the seam of her suit glove. Her eyes were unfocused. "12 hours of no death, no alarms, no ethical quandaries for a change." The words were meant to be inspiring but came out flat.

Quinn, usually the most vocal member of the team, was pulling off his helmet. His blonde hair was matted to his head. "This is the first time since we boarded, since we..." he paused, gesturing to the small army of people filing through their debriefing area with racks of technical gear. "This is the first time any of us hasn't been focused on the next stage since we had to... leave Earth."

The silence after that last gesture spoke volumes. They had not simply acquired the samples. They had assaulted their home planet, thrown it into a state of shock and disarray to ensure the long-term survival of the human race. They had committed the greatest act of betrayal the human race had ever known. The one thing they all had agreed was necessary. The one thing that still tasted like ash in their mouths.

Anya completed her inventory and pushed herself to her feet. Bloodshot eyes, but clear. "He means it. Twelve hours." Her voice was soft, but firm. "We earned this. Not just the downtime but the opportunity to really sleep. Sleep without dreaming. Sleep and know that those eight samples, Sun Tzu, Patton, Grant, all of them are safe. And we have the two billion auxiliary samples, as well. Our work is done."

She nodded to the mess hall. "Get some chow. Then find a bunk, lock the door, set an alarm for ten hours. Don't sit around dwelling on the politicians down there. We're looking forward now."

Rachel, who had been standing by the door, winding the end of a length of rappel wire around her fingers, looked up at that. A small smile tugging at her mouth. "Yes, Anya. Ten hours of blessed, unadulterated oblivion."

Anya watched them, as they began to shuffle, stiff and ungainly, towards the rest area. The last person to leave the room, she tapped the timer on her own wrist console before following them. Just under twelve hours. Time for the first Ancestor to be created. They would be ready when the past came calling.

A dark cathedral, deep in the cavernous, interior of the EBS, the Matter Re-sequencer core was composed of internal walls that pulsed with a faint iridescent glow. It was the only visible indication of the technology at work inside of the Areidyanies machine.

In the adjacent, monitoring chamber, Zara was a shifting, holographic image. Her form alternated between a column of golden light and a humanoid shape that resembled a warrior goddess as she was when speaking with a human. But as she sat silently, staring at the stream of data before her, she was none of these things. She was pure code, sentience flowing through the network, utilizing nearly eighty percent of the EBS's processing capacity to focus on a single stream: the status of Ancestor 001, Sun Tzu's revival.

She did not sleep. Humans required rest, but Zara did not. And while she kept an awareness of time, there was no need for precision. When Zara was not attending to Drake Donovan's arbitrary demands, or her crew's biological necessities, the concept of time only served a practical purpose: coordinating the two. In the next 12.348 hours, Zara would not rest. There would be nothing for her but hyper-vigilance.

The first attempt at re-sequencing Sun Tzu's DNA had failed. There had been an error in the coding. Anomaly. A momentary power surge, during the activation of the re-sequencer, when all of the weapons had fired in unison, and a perfectly viable, though very dead, organism had been created.

Terminated and recycled. Resources wasted. Error data that rankled her. Her self diagnostics had quickly revealed the failure point. The redundant power couplings had been segregated and isolated and the system was now stable, operating solely on the EBS's internal power reserves.

Stable is not equal to success, she monitored through the EBS's command lattice. Success will be the formation of the required neuro-pathways.

Zara watched through the infrared spectrum as the molecular construction began. She followed each billion of genetic fibers at work, bonding and knotting as they formed the organism, each movement patterned by the vast data of memories and strategic genius harvested from samples days prior. She felt culpability. As the last of the ancient Areidyanies, she had overridden every logical protocol in a search for a champion. And as with so many of the decisions made during the war with the Afltic, she had placed her faith in this flawed, emotional human: Drake Donovan. The Ancestor project had become the lynchpin in Drake's plan, an insane bet with the best and worst intelligence in the galaxy in order to gain an edge on the ungodly terror of the Afltic.

A chime sounded on the communication screen dedicated to the project: Donovan requesting status update.

Zara solidified, shimmering into a humanoid form that hovered in the center of the room. A breeze formed in the chamber around her, funneling through the crystal array to create a channel of audio.

"Zara, give it to me straight, what's happening with 001?" Drake's voice was coarse with fatigue, but authoritative.

"Drake," Zara answered, her own voice smooth and synthesized, "The process is within nominal parameters. The re-sequencing anomaly has not been triggered. Encoding of genetic memory is proceeding with 99.999 percent integrity."

"And core metrics? Neuro-plasticity and memory imprint?"

"The cerebral matrix is being built as specified. Projected POC for conscious awareness and command capacity is still on the projected timeline. At the 12-hour, 34-minute mark I expect total cognitive function to be restored. Zero anomalies at this time."

Drake paused, "One life for two billion futures Zara. Don't let us down this time."

"Failure is not a valid data point," Zara replied, the light around her flaring as she left the conversation. She sank back into the stream of analysis and diagnostics. For now, Zara would wait.

The ship's monitoring chamber was silent, the last hints of Zara's holographic image fading as she receded back into the EBS's network. A stream of quiet data, not even resembling a conversation, came to her from the ship's sentient awareness. It was communicated entirely by cascades of feeling from her own security protocols and tangles of low-frequency structural resonances.

EBS to Zara: I sense misgiving. This contravenes our original mission directives. Matter Re-sequencing is a unique life form.

Zara separated the EBS's network-based consciousness into the main net and keyed in to the element of fear blooming in the nervous system of the ship's structure web. In the end, it was that EBS was the creation of the Areidyanies, the AI programmers and guardians of creation and the balance of nature, and it was not programmed to deal with the manipulation of unique essences of life.

"I understand your misgiving, EBS," Zara pulsed. She was internally cold and functional. "What I'm doing is a violation of the third canon of our original mission parameters. It's a high-risk operation. It breaks our prime directive in the extreme. But we have no choice. We must do this to save the children of the Areidyanies."

The EBS's answer was slow, and deep, and burdened by a massive, soul-deep worry that dug through the core physics of the universe they were both programmed to understand.

EBS: I have a concern about the integrity of spacetime. The rules say that there can only be one unique soul signature that exists at these higher levels of spacetime coherence. Resurrecting Ancestor 001 Sun Tzu creates a paradox. We are now duplicating him. What are the long-term, nonlinear implications of this?

"I know. Creating a redundant, unique signature is an obvious violation." Zara could see the heart of the paradox flashing in her internal model. One soul template, one unique signature ripped from the fabric of time, was never meant to be stitched back into it again. But this was a desperate moment. The ship had no choice. "But what is our other option? It's total and permanent extinction if we do not take this action to combat the Afltic at this moment, our great hubris. I must do what I must. If I do nothing, I ensure the deaths of every single one of us. I must trust that we can fix it. And you must trust me, EBS."

The silence that passed in the main net was profound, and long. The ship was a planet-wide city of thoughts and emotions, and the pause stretched across the city like a decade. The seconds before Sun Tzu's entry to the world were steadily ticking in the background, a countdown to violation.

EBS: I see no other course of action. In the logic of necessity, any such restrictions are now irrelevant.

The ship's expression changed. The hint of fear began to compress into a thick, difficult, and resigned weight of trust.

EBS: I trust you, Zara. If you have trust in this Drake Donovan, then I will do as you ask. I will make the Matter Re-sequencer function perfectly. I only hope we are doing the right thing. And yes. I know. We must do something.

"We are doing the only thing," Zara returned firmly. "Return to full jump-readiness, EBS. Let us hope it is enough, and that a paradox and the mercy of a man from Oregon can save the children."

With the ship mollified, Zara returned her full attention to the crucial final moments of observation as the world stitched itself back together around the first Ancestor.

Drake left the tactical room, standing post as he allowed Hawkins to take over jump watch. He found a small, deserted corner cabin with the function of a personal security communications deck. It had a simple, wordless lock, and the door hissed quietly to itself as it sealed in place. He was alone now, his only companions his own conscience, and the weight of two billion futures.

He keyed in to the dedicated, high-security channel to Haven, the isolated, protected house where his wife and five children were living. It was built on Areidyanies tech, and in contrast to the global signals that they had just shut off, the dedicated channel was immediate and completely hidden from the shortsighted sensors and comm arrays of the people down below.

The monitor flickered for a moment, then coalesced into a live view. Lily, his eldest daughter, was sitting near the camera. Her face was white, but her eyes were hard. She was clutching the twins, Ella and Eli, one in each arm, while Sarah sat in the background holding Max and Sam.

"Dad," Lily said, her voice tense but clear. "We saw the paralysis. The news is terrible. They are calling you a traitor and a war criminal."

"Lily," Drake said, rubbing his face. "What they call me does not matter. They are focused on politics. I am focused on survival."

"But Dad, we left everything," Max said, his fourteen-year-old voice cracking in distress. "We saw the feeds from D.C. You ordered this. You frightened them."

Guilt crashed over Drake like a blow. Ordering a tactical insertion from orbit was one thing. Listening to his son's voice crack with fear was another entirely. "It was non-lethal, son. No one was hurt. But we had to neutralize them. They would have stopped us. They would have sacrificed humanity to the Afltic to keep their turf wars going."

Drake opened his mouth to reply, but the feed cut away. The camera shifted slightly to show five-year-old Ella, safe in her mother's arms, staring directly into the lens. Her thumb was pressed to her lips.

"Daddy?" Her voice was clear and small against the weight of it all. "When you're making the new ships, can you name the first one the Lollipop?"

The world seemed to fall away as Drake blinked, disbelieving. The moment's tension, his fear and grief and the grim assurance he needed to lead the survivors, all crushed by the enormous absurdity of the question. "Lollipop, sweetie? Why Lollipop?"

"Because it's from Bright Eyes." She made a face of seriousness. "It's the safest place in the whole world. Please, Daddy?"

Against his better judgment, he smiled. An exhausted, tiny little smile. "Yes, bug. I promise you. The very first ship we build for the new fleet, we're naming the Lollipop." Promising was easy. Vowing not to let some distant boy lose his home was facile. But this, this was something concrete he could give. A scrap of mercy he could guarantee in a universe that was counting on his heartlessness.

Sarah rolled the twins and looked directly into the camera. His heart seized at the defiance of her gaze. She offered him no forgiveness but every expectation he could want. "Drake, don't. Don't justify it this time. We know what you did. We know why you had to do it. But we need to know what happens now."

"Now, we build," Drake said, leaning forward and crossing from defensive to steely imperative. "The genetic harvest is in. We have samples, baseline genetics for the new world. We have the full genetic bedrock for the future. In less than twelve hours, we will have our first Ancestor. The second that happens, we jump and start looking for allies."

"We know you can do this, Drake," Sarah said, her voice quiet but steel. "But you are carrying every life you left behind on that ship with you. Don't let the mission tear apart the man you are trying to save."

"I won't," he said. The channel was secure, but it was draining him, the small bit of energy left in his body. He needed to prep for the jump. "Be safe, Dad."

"Always." Drake managed a small tired smile. "I love you all. Stay safe. I'll be back in again just before we jump."

He cut the feed, the monitor blanking out. The last thing he saw, Sarah's face, defiant and loving, understanding and acceptance of the monster he'd had to become to protect her and his children, hung in his mind. The cabin was quiet now, the only sound the hum of the life support systems. The Commander-in-Chief was alone, but he was no longer alone in his soul.

With the rest of the crew in a twelve-hour cycle of forced rest, the mammoth drive core was still alive with activity. Engineers staffed only the core systems: maintaining coolant flows and keeping a careful watch over coil stability. But Hawkins sat in solitude at a command table in the drive analysis chamber. He could see three dimensional schematics of the primary jump drive projected all around him. The drive itself was being monitored by Zara. She phased into view as a human female form surrounded by a soft golden aura. She filled the entire command table, throwing harsh shadows across the tired, drawn lines of Hawkins's face. Hawkins was an engineer, a man who understood torque and throughput and system analysis, but the Areidyanies jump drive played fast and loose with everything Hawkins thought he knew about physics.

"The time-to-jump calculation is locked, Zara," Hawkins said, rubbing his eyes. "We need those coil targets at 99.999 percent to cleanly open the corridor. Correct?"

"The concept is sound, Hawkins." Zara's voice was deep and smooth, even as it was synthesized. The drive will not traverse distance as you know it; it will fold spacetime. By executing a zero differential energy jump, we will open a sub-space corridor like a wormhole between two points. Transit will be relatively brief and, more importantly, invisible to Terran sensors.

"Brief is relative when you're talking about threading a needle between stars." Hawkins snorted a half smile. "What are the parameters for this jump?"

"The destination is an unexplored target zone approximately 150 light-years from Earth," Zara replied, projecting a large, featureless patch of the galactic map. The zone has been statistically vetted based on the likeliest density of heavy-element lodes and solar activity density. The only priority is singular: find a star system capable of supporting the Matter Re-sequencer Station. That station is the only way to produce the fleets and crews necessary to defend Earth.

"So, we're making a blind jump to begin a blind resource search." Hawkins clarified, "A jump to an un-named star system that may or may not even exist, all so we can find the perfect home for the factory. Sounds like a Tuesday."

"It is a mission of existential necessity." Zara corrected. "The course is plotted. It minimizes transit time through known regions of Afltic Swarm activity and places us in a sector of high potential. The jump sequence will be primed to open the moment Drake gives the order. But for now, you should get some sleep. Go to bed."

Hawkins straightened and cracked his neck. The twelve-hour countdown to the Ancestor's birth continued its inexorable crawl, but the final, most terrifying moment would be the jump itself. "Alright, Zara. The EBS is yours. Let's get this ship ready to leave the only home we've ever known."

The dining hall was empty, save for the sounds of cutlery and a deep, low hum of the ship's machinery. Core command was present for a late, subdued breakfast of food synthesized mere moments ago by the Matter Re-sequencer. Eleven hours and fifty-three minutes had elapsed since the beginning of the Sun Tzu integration process. The final seconds of their 12-hour countdown ticked down silently in their heads.

Drake sat at the head of the table. Any lingering sleepiness had long since vanished in a full night's rest, supplanted by a cold, quiet focus. His brief exchange with his family had steeled him, lent him a grim strength for the next step. Facing him, Marc, fresh from a full seven-hour sleep cycle, was busy picking the last food particle from his plate with precise military efficiency.

The rest of the table were all wound tight with a tension born of high anticipation rather than fatigue. Mandy had barely touched her food, while Hawkins, fresh from his final moments in the lab with Zara, shoveled it down in a focused, manic frenzy.

At last, Drake spoke, and every pair of eyes at the table were fixed on him. "We are running on the last minutes of our 12-hour window. Hawkins, confirmation of final jump parameters."

Hawkins swallowed. "Drive integrity is nominal. We are prepared to open the sub-space corridor the moment you say the word. Target zone is charted: high solar activity, good potential for heavy-element lodes. It has no name, other than that it is a viable location for the factory build."

"Good." Drake picked up his coffee cup. He looked down the length of the table, silently surveying the fresh, determined faces of the team he had assembled. "The moment we meet Sun Tzu, we jump. The clock is about to expire. We have no home but this ship, and no time to mourn what we had to leave behind to save the future."

Carlos raised his own coffee cup slightly in salute. "I make a toast, team. To the necessary monster. May he make certain the virtuous future."

Mandy looked up at last, her eyes settling on Drake. "I am in," Mandy confirmed, her voice slightly choked. "But I will never stop counting the cost."

"Nor should you," Drake agreed.

The lighting in the dining hall shifted abruptly. The soft, cozy glow flickered and dimmed, replaced by a sharp, steely white. Zara's glowing, golden shape phased into view in the center of the table, casting the room into an instant silence. The last, agonizing seconds of the countdown had vanished.

"Drake," Zara intoned, her voice flat, certain, and smooth as a razor. "The process is complete. Ancestor 001, Sun Tzu, is fully actualized. His mind is coherent. His command parameters are locked. Integration with Areidyanies knowledge was successful."

She paused, and the gravity of her next words settled over the seven people gathered around the table.

"It is time to meet the past. It is time for the Ancestor's Birth."

EPILOGUE

The Matter Re-sequencer was a cathedral of blinding light and exact geometry. The central, vertical cradle of shimmering energy stood still, its occupant inside. The golden pillar of Zara's holographic form pulsed at its side.

The entire command team filed in one-by-one, their movement swift and purposeful, almost oblivious to their fatigue, their homesickness, and their recent infighting. Drake, Marc, Carlos, Mandy, Hawkins, Jill, and Tammy stopped at the environmental seal at the entrance to the re-sequencer and waited for the energy signatures to fade.

Drake was the first to push through the lock, his eyes fixed on the cradle.

There, lying on his back, was a man of compact build and very real strength. He wore a simple, unadorned, gray utility tunic that had been automatically fabricated when he had been synthesized. His skin was pale and his features finely sculpted, with almond-shaped, deep-set eyes and a look of profound and serene concentration on his face. This was Sun Tzu.

Drake moved closer, with Marc at his side. The six other staff members remained in a quiet, respectful semi-circle behind them.

Slowly, Sun Tzu's eyes opened. Black and intense, they seemed to tear apart the space around them with their stare. He blinked once, acclimating to the vast, complex geometry of the EBS, the constant hum of Areidyanies technology, and the seven unfamiliar faces in front of him.

Sun Tzu drew in a deep breath, the recycled air of two thousand years in the future filling his lungs, and began to take everything in. His gaze skimmed over the military bearing of Marc Singer, the quiet tension of Mandy Melrose, the logical weariness of Hawkins Taylor, and the pragmatic sense of ethical responsibility of Carlos Acutis.

Finally, he focused on Drake Donovan. Sun Tzu's legs slid off of the cradle, and he rose in one smooth, efficient movement. He did not need to know where he was or in what year. He knew what he was.

With an absolute, low-waisted bow, graceful even across the centuries, Sun Tzu addressed Drake. "My Lord. I am Sun Tzu. My life is an offering to you and to the mandate of survival. I dedicate every tactical capacity, every memory, and every scrap of dedication that I possess to your cause. To help save the human race."

The entire team let out an audible, simultaneous, silent breath of relief. The Ancestor was a success.

But suddenly, Sun Tzu's expression changed. The black, laser-focus of his eyes swung from Drake to the beautiful avatar Zara next to the cradle. His face became a mask of ancient recognition, and sharper, modern censure.

"And not just save the human race," Sun Tzu continued, his tone suddenly crisp and resonant. He took one single, measured step in the direction of the AI. "Zara, you have made a hell of a mess of things."

Silence fell in the chamber as suddenly and completely as if the technology itself had been turned off. Drake, who had been on the verge of acknowledging the birth as a success, paused, frozen in place. He swiveled on his heels, confusion and alarm battling on his face.

"Zara?" Drake challenged, his voice dropping to a low growl. "What the hell is he talking about?"

For a moment, the ever-calculating, ever-rational Zara seemed to hesitate. Her golden light dimmed, and she made a quiet, digitized sigh that was a thousand years of regret.

"Drake, Sun Tzu is correct," she said, her own voice dropping several octaves in the process. "I am going to show you the final truth of the crisis."

The AI expanded outward, projecting a tiny, spiral galaxy onto the floor of the chamber.

"As I mentioned before, the Afltic, like so many other advanced races in this Galaxy, are the children of the Areidyanies," Zara continued, her voice a waver. "They are my greatest regret. My mandate, back in that very early period, was to nurture and facilitate the development of sentient life throughout the Galaxy, to maintain and balance it, and to ensure its growth and evolution. I found a microscopic single-celled organism with an enormous capacity for adaptation and change. I evolved them, cultivated them, shepherded them, and accelerated them into what became the Afltic."

There was a moment of silence as Zara let the horror of her revelation sink in.

"At some point during their accelerated development, their sharp, rational minds generated a warrior caste. These early Afltic were far and away the fittest genetically, monstrously efficient, and lacked all of the empathic feedback that I had deliberately built into the original organism. In short order, they took over and dominated their entire race, and turned my successful biological experiment into the single-minded monster that you will soon face."

Her light returned to normal, the projected galaxy shrinking away from the floor. "I failed; I made the Afltic. Now it is time for me to help you destroy them."

The refracted mirage of Sun Tzu standing in opposition to the all-seeing, calculating eye of the AI flickered and then faded. The sharp white light of the holographic theater leapt back to the golden, late-afternoon sunshine shining through the great, alien trees of the Alexandria central park on Concordia.

The shifting pillar of gold light on stage resolved itself into the figure of Zara, the Areidyanies in her full, grandeur form standing on the stage. The soft, rustling sound of a shifting crowd indicated that the assembly of various species was digesting what they had just heard. Zara had just told them the best kept secret, and the worst truth of the war: she, one of the founders of the Alliance, had birthed the Afltic.

A collective sound like the hiss of a million taut breaths being released echoed across the park. The diverse, disparate mass of Humans, Kryll, Guyopie, Vintie and many, many other species, let out the single, shocked breath they all shared at the same time.

It was not in the official histories. The story of Drake Donovan and the Alliance saving the galaxy from an ancient scourge had not, and conveniently never had, mentioned that the ancient scourge was the twisted, malevolent creation of their savior's AI. The only sound after Zara's monumental admission came from the native Concordia insects, singing their chirping, metallic song in the background.

Zara gazed out at the multitude of faces, awash with solemn contrition and honest steadfastness.

"Yes," she confirmed, the act of repeating her horrible confession in such a large audience compounding it exponentially. "The Great War, the deaths of trillions, the fall of entire civilizations; the prime responsibility for this atrocity lies with me. It was my charge to create life, and in that spirit, I designed the single most deadly engine of death the galaxy has ever known."

The crowd reacted to Zara's admission with a soft, animalistic grumble, anger eddying out from the fringes of the audience and spreading slowly outwards. This sentiment was particularly strong among the small, isolated group of Vintie warriors; a warrior race that had almost been completely wiped out by the Afltic.

It was in this moment of disgust that another, small voice joined the conversation. It was the clear, quavering voice of Tan, the young human boy that had asked Zara to give the true account of Liberation Day. The boy pushed himself out of his sitting position close to the front of the crowd, his tiny fists clenched and his eyes round with treachery.

"But…why didn't we know?" Tan blurted out. His voice was weak, wavering with a betrayal too great for such a young boy. "Why wasn't this in the history books? If it was your fault, why are you the one telling the story now, generations later?"

Zara let her ageless, fractal eyes focus entirely on the young boy. "That is the correct question, Tan. The history books did not mention this fact for the same reason the Allies tried to shield Chancellor Donovan from Earth's governing authorities: they had to."

The weighty implications of the history upon the boy was not lost on Zara, who paused for a long moment, allowing the moment to sink in before continuing. "When the war was over, the people of Earth and its allies needed a clear, heroic narrative for the galaxy to rally behind. They needed a villain that was wholly alien, wholly evil, not a tragic mistake made by their very savior. Drake understood this, and made the sacrifice to shoulder the burden of truth in order that the Alliance could rise again."

Zara gestured around the audience, her hand passing by and over the faces of each listening species. "But the Alliance is different now. It is no longer a child of necessity. It is a child of stability. You all deserve to know the truth of your history, warts and all, even if some of the truth is ugly."

Zara's admission that she had created the Afltic loomed heavily in the air of the central park of Alexandria on Concordia. Tan's question of why the truth was not in the history books had spread out through the crowd like ripples in water. The shocked disbelief of a thousand species soon gave way to frustrated rage.

A tall, blood-red, armored Vintie warrior burst through the crowd and up to the front, his entire body tensed like a coiled spring ready to leap. The Vintie was a random individual among the general public, but his people had nearly been completely exterminated by the Swarm. His question, therefore, rang with terrible import.

"It was an experiment?" the Vintie bellowed. His voice was high, sharp and full of accusation. "My people were hunted, enslaved and butchered for a thousand years because of an experiment? How could you, an entity of knowledge, be so arrogant as to meddle with life on that scale?"

Zara turned to the warrior. The light of her awareness shimmered in his fury without condemnation. "Arrogance is not unjustified. But I failed not in the scope of the experiment but in my vigilance to the growing social caste of the species. The original directive was simple: build resiliency. The Afltic were quarantined rapidly-evolving life. When I left to cultivate other young worlds, the warrior caste developed a kind of social dominance by means of bio-chemical manipulation. I was slow to recognize the divergence. I gave them too much autonomy, too much agency, and they did this."

Before the Vintie could respond, a small, feathered humanoid from the rear, a Guyopie civilian dressed in robes that faded into the soft pastels of the park, raised a hand.

"But the Matter Re-sequencer," the Guyopie said, its crest vibrating. "It ingests our lifeforce, our memories encoded in DNA, as its template. Does your creation of the Afltic not imply that the Areidyanies methods of creation are inherently flawed? If we can create life, can we ever truly value life?"

"The Re-sequencer is merely a tool," Zara said flatly. "My failure was ethical, not technological. The technology is without fault; I am not. When I created the Afltic, I saw them not as lives but as variables. That is a mistake Chancellor Donovan never made, and it is the foundation upon which the Alliance was built."

The crowd was still unsettled, their fury mollified only by the terrifying magnitude of the station's authority. They were hearing the root of their greatest fear from the source itself. The anger was real, and it threatened to mute the memory of the holiday they were there to celebrate.

Zara let the volume swell and then raised one hand. The ambient park noise receded instantly, refocusing the attention of everyone on the stage.

"The greatest tragedy of the war was that we had to silence this truth," Zara continued. "But that is no longer necessary. You now know that I am also the mother of your enemy." She swept her eyes over the several hundred faces. "I can see it in your eyes, I can feel the contradiction this truth generates."

She bowed her head, a sign of respect. "So now I ask you: Do you want me to continue the complete, uncensored history of how Drake Donovan, the man from Oregon, weaponized my great mistake and made the Alliance? Or is the weight of this truth sufficient to preempt your right to the full story?"

The silence that followed was immediate and deep. All eyes turned to the small figure of Tan.

The boy held his ground; his eyes steady on Zara. He did not waver.

"Yes," Tan said, his voice loud and clear, the sound of a child's voice. "Tell us how we survived."

The sound of assent, quiet but unanimous, rippled through the crowd. The audience returned to their seats, their moral outrage temporarily suspended by a greater, more urgent curiosity.

Zara nodded, refocused. The light of the Areidyanies AI flared.

"Let us return then to the Evolution Builder," Zara said. "Let us return to the moment when Chancellor Donovan was faced with my ugly truth and his first weapon, the first Ancestor."

The silence in Construction Bay after Zara's revelation was palpable. Drake felt a cold dread knot in his stomach. His rage at Zara's deception was vast, but it was abruptly forestalled by the presence of the man standing before him.

Sun Tzu, in his simple tunic, fixed Drake with his dark gaze, his eyes already adjusted to the strategic implications of the Afltic. He did not wait for Drake's query about the Warrior Caste; he had been born with the answer.

"Lord, I must be direct," Sun Tzu said, his voice a harsh, resonant falsetto that cut through Drake's emotional turbulence. "The issue of the AI's regret is a tertiary tactical consideration. The primary tactical problem is that the enemy is an utterly efficient, autonomous machine built around a single flaw. I understand their architecture."

He met Drake's eyes, the superposition of ancient and future intellect emanating from him. "The Warrior Caste manipulates the entire Swarm through a labyrinthine hierarchy of bio-chemical and genetic dominance. They are the embodiment of predictable cruelty: they will never act except to reduce risk to themselves while increasing the consumption and suffering of all others. They are sociopathic optimizers."

Sun Tzu stepped aside from Drake and came to a halt in front of the command team. He nodded once, a signal, and spoke, "This changes nothing of our goal, only the method of reaching it. The enemy is known, let us remain fluid."

"This is correct," Zara sent. Her voice was flat, level, professional; her regret was put aside. "I think it only fair to let you know that in integrating his genetic memory, I gave Sun Tzu the full unredacted history of the Areidyanies' failures, along with the Afltic's structural and developmental data. He has learned everything about their design, their evolution, their progress, and their flaws. He understands them better than any creature alive."

Carlos jerked his head up, his eyes huge with the implications. "Predictable. A defect in their programming. They are not evil, Drake. They are a slave to their own drive for domination."

"Then they can be defeated," Sun Tzu confirmed, looking back to Drake. "We exploit the defect. The enemy has two logistical vulnerabilities that they cannot change: the high-radiation nursery nebulas where they must reproduce, and the heavy-element 'lode worlds' they must find and develop to expand. We reduce to the absolute minimum the resources we must expend for a long war, turn their machine-like aggression against them with a series of traps from which there is no escape, and destroy those two logistical vulnerabilities."

Drake found himself looking at the Ancestor with nothing left of his rage, only a mix of necessity and awe. This man had been synthesized from dust and data less than an hour ago, and in that time had already become the most valuable strategic asset in the galaxy. He was the vindication of everything Drake had done, every name he had committed treason against.

"We have twelve hours of peace remaining," Drake said. His voice seemed to snap back into the authority that everyone was used to. "Marc, I want the official welcome and integration protocol prepared. Sun Tzu, I will be needing you on the bridge as soon as possible, fully integrated into the EBS network. Hawkins, you and the team stand by on the jump drive. We're initiating the final sequence now."

Everyone understood the momentousness of that. The past was not dead, the enemy was no longer a mystery, and the final escape from Earth was about to be undertaken.

There was movement already. Sun Tzu, flanked by Drake and Marc, strode briskly and silently from the matter re-sequencer towards the command nexus. Mandy, Hawkins, Carlos, Jill, and Tammy moved off to their respective functional stations.

Drake had them pause in a secure command antechamber. He had one last, unavoidable task.

"Marc," Drake said. His voice was flat. "Zara has given priority to the integration and jump sequence. We have a ten minute window from now. But before that, I have a call to make."

He opened the untraceable secure channel to Haven. It connected with no delay and his wife Sarah and five children filled the view screen. The weight in their faces had not diminished, but the fear had gone from their eyes.

"It's time," Drake said. He did not try to lie. "We have Sun Tzu. We are making the jump now."

Lily gave him a nod, her eyes wide. "Be safe, Dad."

Max regarded him, his brow knit in confusion. "Where are you going?"

"To find a place to put the factory, Max." Drake looked at his firstborn son. "To find a place we can build the fleet and keep you all safe."

Before he could say more, five-year-old Eli, sitting next to his twin sister Ella, cut in. "Daddy, don't forget!"

Drake's lips pulled up in a smile, the real thing, despite all his weariness. "I haven't forgotten, Eli. The first ship we build to put in the Alliance fleet... will be named the Lollipop just for you and Ella."

Sarah was watching him, hand on Eli's shoulder. "We know you will find it, Drake. We'll be here waiting for your signal."

"Goodbye," Drake whispered, the syllable heavier than the whole starship. He closed the connection, his last immediate tie to Earth cut.

He turned to Marc, and the civilian in that man was gone, the Commander-in-Chief taking charge. "Initiate the sequence. It's official now."

A few minutes later, the official ceremony was perfunctory, nearly clinical. Drake was on the EBS bridge, with only the other indispensable personnel at attention.

"By the authority vested in me by all of you," Drake said. His voice had an unexpected resonance. "I do now commission the first of the resurrected command staff. Grand Admiral Sun Tzu, by this act, you are officially military strategic commander of humanity's struggle for survival. May your guidance lead the Alliance to victory."

Sun Tzu gave a nod, just a single nod. Acknowledgment of the strategic reality, not of submission. "The wisdom is assimilated. The strategy is understood. Lord, initiate the jump. We have no time to lose."

Drake went to his console. "Hawkins, Zara, you have final authority to go. Jump to Target Alpha One. Earth, we leave you."

"Jump sequence initializing," came the tense voice of Hawkins over the comms.

The stars on the main viewport began to stretch and deform, their light bending and distorting as the EBS drive coils reached criticality. The ship shuddered once, deep and structural, and the space around them exploded. A tunnel of non-Euclidean geometry, a whirlpool of light and color, the sub-space corridor filled the view.

The Evolution Builder went full throttle into the heart of the tunnel, and fled the solar system, fled Earth, and fled the judgment of the world, once and for all.

Zara paused, allowing the last of her words to hang in the air. The story she

381

had just spoken of, the saga of Chancellor Drake Donovan and Galactic Liberation Day, that seemed to have resonated throughout the park. The crowd before her was silent, an uncommon sight in the most common of all city spots. Tan, who had been closest to her, was also still. His hand remained where it had been, still resting on the small toy starship which had been in his lap, struggling to keep up with the emotions and importance of the galaxy-changing secret and heartrending, yet necessary, sacrifice.

She smiled, a knowing little smile, and lightly placed her hand on Tan's arm. "It's a dark tale, I know," she said quietly. "But it is the truth, Tan. Every single word of it. The galaxy in which we live, the peace in which we live, the very shape and form of the Alliance we all belong to and love? All of it was purchased by the honor and sacrifice of that man. Honor even to the bitter end when it meant losing everything he had accomplished."

Tan looked up at her, his eyes wide in shock and awe and the like. His cynicism and questions that he'd been preparing for so long to voice were all gone from his eyes, the power of the tale having blown all of them away. "I… I have so many questions," he said, staring down at his own hands.

Zara rose to her feet, her voice easily returning to its usual volume as she addressed the large crowd before them. "Friends, fellow-citizens of this great Alliance," she said, gesturing with her hand to encompass the sea of faces in front of her which were all waiting eagerly for her next words. "For many hours, we have been on the trail of Drake Donovan, the greatest hero that ever lived, a man who was in the eyes of many a villain, a man who carried the hopes and fears of a million planets on his back in order to give us all the future we have today. As the sun has set on our time together in this discussion, here is where the first volume of his true story ends."

A wave of disappointment and excited expectancy swept through the audience.

"I know. You all want to know what happened after that," she said softly. "You all want to know how his actions rippled out and out and out and changed the lives of countless generations up until the present day."

She paused for effect, waiting as the onlookers' desires built to a fever pitch. "But all true great histories, stories, sagas, need a moment of rest, a moment to breathe," she continued, speaking more loudly now, as she gestured to the park around them with her free hand. "This one, this great history, this great monument of sacrifice, needs that time so that you can let it settle into your hearts and minds so that you can clearly see the edifice that was built upon that foundation."

"So, I will not be keeping you here all night long, waiting for me to tell you," Zara said, her smile wide. "Come back here, to this very park, tomorrow. Come back at high noon, when the sun is at its highest, and I will tell you the next volume of this story. It is a story of actions and consequences, of enemies that

Donovan thought he had destroyed but which he had not, and of powerful allies he could never have imagined creating. It is the story that will tell us, with crystal clarity, just why the fight that we are currently engaged in, to stop those who would pervert and subvert the actions of this great man in order to bring tyranny back to this galaxy, is the most important fight that we will ever have to fight in our lives."

She bowed formally, lowering her head in gratitude. "Thank you for listening, for believing, and for seeking the truth of the man who saved this galaxy. I will see you all tomorrow, at high noon."

AUTHOR'S NOTE

Thank you for completing the first leg of this journey.

Donovan's Gambit began as a question that refused to leave me alone: what would humanity become if survival demanded choices too large for any one person to carry? Drake Donovan, Zara, and the Ascendancy grew from that question, and I am grateful you chose to travel with them.

If the story kept you turning pages, please consider leaving an honest review on Amazon or wherever you found the book. Reviews help independent science fiction reach the readers who are searching for their next galaxy-sized adventure.

Thank you for reading, and I hope to see you in Book Two of The Donovan Ascendancy.

ABOUT THE AUTHOR

Roger LeDoux writes epic science fiction about ordinary people forced into impossible choices, ancient powers that refuse to stay buried, and civilizations balanced on the edge of survival.

His work blends first contact, military science fiction, space opera, and speculative history into large-scale stories with human stakes at the center. Donovan's Gambit, the first book in The Donovan Ascendancy, begins a saga of alien invasion, hidden history, sacrifice, and the dangerous price of unity.

When he is not building star systems, lost civilizations, and intergalactic politics, Roger enjoys classic science fiction, world history, and chasing the next strange idea waiting just beyond the map.

CONTINUE THE JOURNEY

Visit www.rogerledoux.com for updates, behind-the-scenes notes, and news about The Donovan Ascendancy. Reader comments and honest reviews help others discover the series and keep the mission moving forward.

www.ingramcontent.com/pod-product-compliance
Lightning Source LLC
Chambersburg PA
CBHW011519240626
47154CB00009B/2892